And So—Victoria

And So—Victoria

Vaughan Wilkins

———

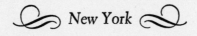

Lenoir Rhyne College
LIBRARY

New York

THE MACMILLAN COMPANY

1937

PRINTED IN THE UNITED STATES OF AMERICA
BY THE STRATFORD PRESS, INC., NEW YORK

To My Mother
and her kin in Texas
and Louisiana

... *My little girl (Victoria) is, I am delighted to say, strong and healthy; too healthy, I fear, in the opinion of some members of my family, by whom she is regarded as an intruder.*

Edward
Duke of Kent
IN A LETTER TO A FRIEND

Table of Contents

And So—Victoria

Prologue

MR. WILLIAM ROSS AND GEORGE HIGGINS CALLED ON Monsieur de Boucher so early that he was still breakfasting with his wife on coffee and rolls in a sunny sitting-room overlooking the Thames.

The long windows were wide open: a sailing-barge swung easily at her mooring-post on which a gull was perched: two or three children hung over the river wall of the narrow terrace immediately under the wrought-iron balconies: a small breeze rustled the leaves of the plane tree that stooped above the water by York Stairs: the river was grey and shining, and dotted with flotsam like steel spotted with rust.

Monsieur de Boucher, a beautiful discontented Apollo in a morning gown of Chinese silk, leaned back upon his elbows against the mantelpiece, and spoke his mind bitterly to his wife upon the subject of coffee-making in England.

She sat at a small round table, on which the materials of their breakfast were assembled about a china bowl full of crystallized strawberries. She was wrapped in a loose *négligé* of green and silver, with a scarf of lace as fine as sea-foam hiding her graceful shoulders. There was no powder upon the piled masses of her dark red hair. She had a throat as long and lovely as the throat of a Madonna by Baldovinetti: her skin was the flushed warm white of a moonstone, and her eyes green. Around a bared arm shone a bracelet of enormous opals like shining bubbles.

'Coffee! Bah! Filth!' said Monsieur de Boucher. 'This is sheer muck out of a Marseilles sewer!'

'It is, dearest,' assented Madame de Boucher, leaning back, and stretching in voluptuous luxury. Her white arms tensed over the sides of her chair; she hollowed her shoulders so that the curves of

1

her throat and bosom were emphasized: she smiled and yawned—
or yawned and smiled—and her teeth showed against the red of
her lips as white as those of a puppy.

'It is execrable muck! It tastes of mud. It smells of mud. It looks
like mud. Who made it?'

'One of the maids of the house, I suppose. There is nobody else.
You hurried Louis to meet the courier with the diamonds from
Amsterdam. Grégoire has gone with your letter to Papa. And I
have sent Suzanne to fetch the boy.'

'Seigneur Dieu!' said Monsieur de Boucher, tasted his coffee
again with a despairing gesture, looked wryly at his wife, and shot
the contents out of his mouth on to the small fire. 'Pah! They are
not Christian folk in this filthy country!'

'I'd rather drink undrinkable coffee than lose my head,' remarked
his wife, and filled her empty cup with warm milk. 'In fact there
are a lot of things I would do, rather than stay in France, and regard the world as a bodiless head on top of a pike carried by some
filthy porter from the Halles!'

'Sweetheart!' exclaimed Monsieur de Boucher, in polite horror.
He knew what was expected of him: he took two long steps to her
side and clasped her in his arms in neat deprecation of the terrors
she had conjured up. His wife gave her embraces to him with none
of the mildly permissive complaisance of marital affection. She
responded to his caress with a sort of furious abandon that con-
trasted with his rather mannered elegance. He removed himself
eventually from her clinging lips a little abruptly, and took up his
stand again by the fireplace, with somewhat of the air of a cat that
is tired of being stroked.

'Nevertheless, they are a dirty, perfidious lot, these English!' said
he continuing and expanding the scope of his complaint. 'Their
coffee is as bad as their manners—or their code of honour! It's
symbolic!'

'Those bonds?' asked Madame de Boucher.

'Those bonds!' assented he. He took a folded document from
the mantelpiece, and tossed it on to the table by her. It was of stiff
expensive paper, and fell with a light tap like a discreet finger rap-
ping gently on a door.

'My precious!' said Madame de Boucher, making no attempt to

unfold it, 'you know that I shall understand but one word in ten. Read it to me!'

He retrieved the paper, chose the largest strawberry in the bowl, dipped it into the cream jug, popped it into his mouth in the most delicate way imaginable, and wiped his lips with a lace-fringed handkerchief of pale blue silk.

He translated fluently, and with a concentration on the document in his hand which showed that there was another side to his character as well as that of elegant amorist. His wife watched the powdered romantic head bent over the paper, with the fierce intensity of one who beholds a vision, listened with the devotion of an inquirer to whom the Oracle speaks.

Perhaps some inner awareness had told her subconscious self that already Mr. William Ross and Mr. George Higgins had turned out of Downing Street and were pursuing their unhurried course along Whitehall towards Charing Cross. Mr. Ross—who should have known that it was impossible to wear anything with a plum-coloured coat except various shades of canary, and almond green or a jetty black—was wearing a waistcoat of an almshouse red, and eating a very young carrot with avidity. Mr. Higgins would have looked horsy in his yellow cords and riding-boots, if the cords had been rubbed about the leathers, and if the boots had not been trodden over at the heels in a manner which showed that they were more habituated to pavements than to stirrups.

Stooped over the document M. de Boucher lost something of the look of an exquisite Apollo. There was a peering intentness in his eyes that ill became a god: his face seemed narrower than a god's should be. In some subtle way those sheets of thick bluish paper transformed him from aristocrat into business man, revealed the descent from an old scoundrel of an army contractor whose fortune had been builded upon shoddy and short measure.

The letter that he read to his wife ran:

43, Chancery Lane,
London.

October 20th, 1793.
Dear Sir,

In accordance with your esteemed instructions we have taken Counsel's opinion on the question of the nonpayment of interest on the bonds in your possession, representing twenty shares in the loan negotiated on the Continent on behalf of their Royal Highnesses George Prince of Wales, Frederick Duke of York, and William Duke of Clarence.

Mr. S. Shepherd, the Solicitor-General, before whom we have laid the case, states that in his opinion your claim upon their Royal Highnesses is just and legal, and that there is nothing to prevent your suing their Royal Highnesses as a creditor.

During your absence from Town a copy of Mr. Shepherd's opinion was sent to the Prince of Wales with a letter expressing the hope that His Royal Highness would render all legal measures unnecessary, by ordering the interest to be paid. No reply having been received to this application, on the 14th instant we wrote again to His Royal Highness stating that if immediate satisfaction was not forthcoming it would be our painful duty to take such legal steps as were necessary to compel him to pay.

This morning an agent of the Home Department called at this office and made a number of inquiries regarding yourself, and from remarks let fall by this person we are under the impression that their Royal Highnesses contemplate repudiating the loan *in toto*, although we are at a loss to imagine upon what ground they can do so.

We accordingly informed the agent that we proposed to recommend that you should forthwith take legal action. Our Mr. Swan will, therefore, wait upon you at any time convenient to yourself, to take your instructions in the matter.

We are, dear Sir,
Your obedient servants,
Swan, Hunter and Swan.

The mere reading of the letter reawakened the anger that had been simmering within him. He flung it on the floor, with a theatrical gesture that he had inherited, with his slim romantic beauty, from the Marseilles actress who had trapped the contractor into matrimony in his senility.

'They are just common bankrupts—pitiful frauds! Dirty dishonoured sots!'

'How much of the loan did you take up, dearest?' asked his wife. 'Surely it isn't a serious matter?'

'Money loss is always serious. And this is sheer robbery! Sheer robbery—by Princes of the Blood! The three blackguards floated a personal loan in Paris, with the revenues of the Duchy of Cornwall and the Bishopric of Osnaburgh as security. A lot of people invested. With revolution and God-knows-what threatening, it seemed a good sort of thing to put one's money into, against the time one cleared out of the country.'

'Did Papa take any?'

'Your papa wasn't a banker for nothing. He had every franc he'd got invested abroad long before—in English Government stock; in industrial undertakings; in land. He'd been shifting his capital out of France very quietly for years. Why, he bought that house with the unpronounceable name in Wales nearly ten years ago. Trust him! No, he's not been bitten. I have!'

'But for how much, dearest?'

'Fifty thousand francs!'

'Henri, sweetest! I thought you'd lost half a million from your manner! What's fifty thousand francs? I shouldn't make a fuss about it, if I were you. If you start pressing George, he'll get unpleasant—he hates people he has borrowed money from. He likes to forget his debts and his creditors.'

'He won't forget me in a hurry,' said Monsieur de Boucher, snapping his teeth together, and looking like a Greek god with a slightly Semitic strain in his ancestry. 'He owes me six thousand francs in interest, alone. The money doesn't matter'—nevertheless he looked as if it did—'but I don't see why he should be able to borrow and then fail to implement his undertakings. Dirty bastard! In our case, except for the principle of the thing, it doesn't matter; but there must be dozens of others—émigrés like ourselves—who put all they could scrape together into the Princes' Loan and then bolted to England to live peacefully on the interest. Out of the shadow of the guillotine.'

'The shadow of the guillotine!' said Madame de Boucher. Her green eyes dwelt for a moment on the grey river, and the clutter of flat barges tied up against the wharves on the Surrey side, and the white insolent gull perched upon the mooring-post hard by the terrace wall. An old man in a long red coat and three-cornered hat had come out of the lodge at the Villiers Street entrance to the river walk—a queer little lodge more like an ornamental casket than a dwelling. The old man was trailing along the paved terrace, casting handfuls of breadcrumbs, from a yellow dish he carried, to a following cloud of sparrows. The small dingy birds drifted to the ground, like leaves, from all quarters: they followed hopping in his footsteps, just as leaves travel briskly and jerkily before a puff of wind. Madame de Boucher shut her eyes for a moment: the break-fast-time conversation of the sparrows was as insistent upon the ear as the subdued hum of the city, and the distant echoing call of a street-seller peddling shrimps—

> 'Live or boiled,
> Limping alive—O
> Penny a pint!'

The shadow of the guillotine was very far away—she thought—from the drab prosperity of the great city. The twitter of sparrows and the bourdon of movement and life in the miles of streets seemed to have no relationship with the uproar and the cries of that appalling night when they had left Paris—when the world they knew came to an end in clanging bells, in gunfire, in bloodshed, in flaming torches casting strange lights on the black torrent of the mob which surged between shuttered houses that hid stark terror.

'Henri!' she exclaimed, 'for the love of Jesus, don't talk of that accursed thing! I can't bear to think of it. You and I—and Papa too, of course—are here, away, safe. Don't let's think about it. I shall scream if you say another word!'

'My lovely,' said Monsieur de Boucher, 'you are overwrought. Command yourself.'

He helped himself to another strawberry—the largest; dipped it into the cream jug again, and ate it with delicate appreciation.

His wife sat silent, her regard lost on the grey oily waters in which the thin sunshine drowned itself. She found herself hating the sluggish tide. In a little it would be sucked away, between those flat misty mast-studded banks, past London Pool, the drab dullness of Tilbury and Gravesend, out into the narrow seas; and some of those molecules that made its mass would be specks in the foam that broke against the French coast, or be absorbed into the flood of the Seine and swim under the bridges of Paris and receive the blood that ran daily from the sewers.

'Henri,' she said, 'let us go away for a little while. I can't bear it here! . . . Anywhere! . . . Even Papa's! Somewhere where France is much farther off!'

She rose as she spoke. In the split second that she took to come to him, and put her pleading arms about his neck, and press her hungry lips to his, Monsieur de Boucher permitted himself to admit a weariness of wifely passion, and to recall the hard, firm body of a young lady he had recently met—a young lady who responded more than adequately to desire, but did not herself initiate any demand for affection. Women, he felt, should be responsive, but not initiatory. He was, however, courteous enough to respond with a show of enthusiasm; but was unfeignedly thankful for the reprieve afforded by a tap on the door.

A plump pale maid, all mob-cap and bosom, appeared on the threshold. She sketched a curtsy with the easy leisureliness of a cow. Monsieur de Boucher found himself admiring her slow-moving comeliness: it was restful. He smiled approvingly.

'Two gentlemen to see you, Mounseer!' she announced.

'But who are they?' asked Madame de Boucher sharply. She swung round, and looked at the white panels of the door as if they were a barricade that was breaking—a defence she suspected of imminent collapse.

Her husband frowned.

'What is the matter with you this morning, Mathilde?' he inquired, speaking in French. 'Sit down and compose yourself. It will be, without doubt, persons from Swan and Hunter . . . Show them in, my dear!'

He helped himself to a last strawberry. His wife sank back into her chair, and sat silently watching the door over her shoulder, as if she expected something monstrous to come in. But it was only the plum-coated Mr. William Ross who entered, in a deprecating manner, twiddling a bright young carrot in his left hand, his black dusty hat in the other. Mr. Higgins, who followed him, shut the door in a quietly secretive way, breathing very loudly as he did so;

and remained propping himself against the panels, sucking his teeth, and revolving his wide hat slowly in his hands, as if he could not satisfy himself that its brim was round.

'Mounseer Henry de Boosher?' asked Mr. Ross, with inquiring affability, showing a mouthful of yellow teeth. He collected up the assent in Monsieur de Boucher's expression, even before it was uttered. 'And so Mounseer Henry de Boosher it is! Mounseer Henry de Boosher, a French subject, twenty-four years of age! And the little lady will be Madame de Boosher—Matildy de Boosher. Likewise a French subject, I do suppose!'

The protruding eyes under the sandy eyebrows travelled round the room. They were dead, expressionless eyes, the whites a shiny blue like peeled hard-boiled eggs. He set down his hat upon a chair, accommodated the carrot temporarily, like a cheroot, between his teeth; and sought for something within his coat—a matter of difficulty owing to the very tattered state of the lining.

'But my business,' he remarked during the operation, 'is only with Mounseer Henry de Boosher. I have . . .' Something had got involved in a rent in the Italian cloth . . . 'here . . .' But it was not 'here' yet, and he spaced his speech out to meet the emergency.

'Nom de Dieu!' interjected Monsieur de Boucher. 'If you've come from Swan and Hunter you can tell me what it is all about without producing any more documents. They suffer from a documentary diarrhoea.'

'Ha! Very good! Very good, indeed! Very good, Higgins, ain't it?' His shiny red face, the colour of underdone beef, split in a smile in which his eyes did not join. Higgins dropped his long jaw and groaned assent.

Madame de Boucher's eyes had not left Mr. Ross since he entered the room. She watched his struggles with his coat as if she were a child expectant and horrified before a conjuror; as if he might produce a snake of fabulous girth from amid the tatters that disclosed the canvas stiffening of his garment.

He found whatever he was looking for, and extracted to their view a large folded paper with a great blot of red sealing wax on it. With its discovery his manner changed. He placed the gaudy carrot with its feathery plume on the fine white cloth of the breakfast table, and his hat back upon his head. He unfolded the document with the momentous solemnity of a herald about to read a proclamation.

'Henry de Boosher,' said Mr. Ross in measured tones, 'I have 'ere—here—a warrant addressed to Myself and George Higgins under the seal of 'Is Grace the Duke of Portland, Secretary of State for the Home Department. Di-recting Us to take you into Custody. Until such Time as arrangements can be made for you to be Sent back to your own Country.'

Monsieur de Boucher slipped from the marble curb of the hearth upon which he had been negligently balancing. His mouth opened as if to say something. Then suddenly he became as cold as death, as grey as death. His romantically dishevelled head drooped to his chest with the abrupt movement of a marionette— as if he had received a mortal wound, as if he would hide his twitching face.

His wife had rollowed the slow speech of the Government agent, comprehending but a tithe of the words he had used, but knowing—even as she had foreknown at the heralding tap upon the door—their import. Her lips parted, but no speech came: her eyes fell to the table—to the convoluted dragon twisting about the china, the golden truncheon of Mr. Ross's carrot, the bowl full of scarlet strawberries. A bowl full of scarlet strawberries, like the basket before the guillotine full of bloody heads!

Monsieur de Boucher raised his ravaged face. He stuttered 'W-w-what is t-the charge?'

Mr. Ross holding the warrant against his hip, like a marshal's baton, explained with the somewhat grudging air of one not legally called on to give explanations.

'There ain't no charge. No charge whatsomedoever! No charge h'is—is—necessary. I speak by book, ain't it, Higgins? A beautiful, neat little h'instrument, h'as ever I did see. No one is called on to commit 'imself in no ways to reprobium. All above-board and as square as a trivet! Beautiful—beautiful! This 'ere—here—warrant is the consekence, the nateral sekel as you might say, to h'an Order of H'expulsion issued by the Home Department—by 'Is Grace of Portland. It makes no bones about it. It says "John Henry Jones", or "Henry de Boosher", as the case may be, "as an Alien we should be glad to see the back of you. H'under the Aliens Act we are within our rights in shipping you off 'ome, to your native state. H'and *that*, John Henry Jones, or Henry de Boosher, is just percisely what we are going to do!"'

The speech that had been dammed up within Madame de Boucher's breast burst out in a torrent of rapid French. She rose to her feet and stood by the breakfast table, drumming her fingers upon it while she strove to reach her husband's numbed brain.

But he did not even seem aware of her presence, standing with sunken head, chin dropped on to the gold and green of his morning gown; it was as though he had been turned to stone by the Medusa's head that Mr. Ross had carried within the tattered recesses of his plum-coloured coat.

'Henri!' cried his wife, and her voice rose to a scream. The tapping fingers suddenly plucked at a fold of the white linen upon the table, drew it upward into a hillock . . . into a hill . . . into a volcano, hurled it with all the apparatus of breakfast upon it to the floor. The china broke with an appalling crash, and the sugared strawberries, like freshly severed heads, rolled about the polished boards. Mr. Ross's young carrot lay in a mud-coloured pool of coffee.

'Highstrikes, poor lady!' said Mr. Ross looking regretfully at his ruined vegetable. 'Highstrikes, that's what it is, Higgins. It offen takes them that way! . . . Come, ma'am, that won't do you any good. Keep calm and collected! On'y a little journey for Mounseer here! On'y a little journey! We'll look after him something wonderful. Don't you take on so!'

Her violence, however, served its purpose. Monsieur came to life. He unloosed his gown, revealing a waistcoat of pale green sprigged with roses beneath. Two of his fingers fumbled with something in one of the pockets that crackled and rustled as he withdrew it—a Bank of England ten-pound note.

Mr. Ross and Mr. Higgins watched the emergence of the note; Mr. Higgins with the devout attention of one who speculates arithmetically on the quantity of liquor that can be bought for a given sum; Mr. Ross with the glare of a butcher wheedling an unruly ox into the slaughter-house.

'There is no charge!' said Monsieur de Boucher. 'Would this make it worth your while to tell me what then the reason is for this order for expulsion? It . . .' he paused, and as he faltered, Higgins, who was an imaginative man, saw in his grey unbeautiful features the face of a dead man, the blood-drained face of a bodiless head . . . 'it . . . is . . . a sentence . . . of death!'

Mr. Ross took the note as if his right hand were acting entirely independently of his consciousness. Without looking at the oblong of paper he thrust it into a fob pocket. He took his hat off.

'What I should say,' said he, ignoring the transaction in words, 'is that you've been a-asking 'Is—His—Royal Highness the Prince of Whales for money. That's what I should say if I were asked as man to man. Private. Confidential. Without prejudice. That's what Higgins would say. Wouldn't you, Higgins? I can't say fairer nor that . . . I did 'ear—hear—and I'm not saying how true it may be . . .' He stooped to his carrot, and wiped its coffee-drenched curves with a dirty red handkerchief and a tender care—'I did 'ear as the Prince had got very annoyed with a lot of furriners—Frenchies, with no disrespect—what was wanting their money back and the like. What a one, to be sure, 'Is—His—Royal Highness! What a one for the spondulicks! What a one to make the goldenboys fly! What a one to put it over the ladies! . . .' He laughed lightly and tolerantly . . . 'I did hear . . .'

'Stop!' said Madame de Boucher. 'Do I understan' you say, sir, that this Prince évite—ev-vade paying his Franch creditorrrs in sending them back to France? An' he knows, knows they nevaire come back to ask again?'

'Now, ma'am,' said Mr. Ross deprecatorily, ' 'Is Royal 'Ighness is a very 'igh-spirited—high-spirited—young genelman. 'Ere's this-y-ere h'Aliens Act, and there's his creditors. "H'Aliens Act . . ." says 'Is Royal 'Ighness, as might be—"H'Aliens Act . . . H'Act of God!" Down goes word from Carlton House—"Mounseer Pingo or Mounseer Pongo, as the case may be, is a bloomin' newsance! H'Aliens Act him, my dear Portland. Yours affeckly, George." H'and Aliens h'Acted they are, accordingly!'

'Oh, God,' said Madame de Boucher in French. 'Fifty thousand francs! For fifty thousand francs this prince would play Judas Iscariot . . . Write to him, Henri, and say you don't want your fifty thousand francs. Papa shall make him a loan—a big loan—a million francs. Papa could do it easily! Give these men money—

much money to let you have a few days to make arrangements. Mother of God, Henri, something can be done! Must be done! Henri, promise them a hundred pounds—five hundred pounds, for a day or two. I will go to the Prince. I will remind him of 'Toinette. I will tell him that I am 'Toinette's sister. That her child—his child—is my nephew. I will appeal to him for the sake of the love he bore her to spare us. Henri, offer them money, quickly—much money!'

On the grey river, with the turn of the tide, a barge with a large red sail slid slowly across the window. The sail was the colour of a napkin stained with dried blood. That smooth oily stream was pouring out into the sea—into the narrow seas where it would be dashed in foam against the flat dull coasts of France, where its molecules would swim into the mouth of the Seine and mingle with the freshets of blood pouring from every Paris sewer.

Monsieur de Boucher's hand went once again to the beautiful waistcoat with its gay rose-sprigs.

Mr. Ross shook a regretful head. He knew what was coming without being told. He knew the limits set by safety.

'Nothing doing, Mounseer!' said he, fondling his carrot. 'Very sorry, Higgins and I, to appear disobliging to a proper genelman. But you must come along of us. One of us will help you pack what you want. For the journey, ha-ha!'

Mathilde de Boucher knew the meaning of that head-shake. She crossed from the tall window where she stood, past the bare round table amid the litter of broken china, and came close to Mr. Ross, so close that if he had ventured to look at her with those eyes of his—so like hard-boiled eggs!—he would have seen the utter flawlessness of her complexion, and seen the strange secret lights in her green eyes. But with head half averted he stared in an embarrassed manner at a singularly unlovely engraving by Hogarth upon the wall. She put her slim fingers upon the shoulder of his plum-coloured coat. The circle of opals about the white arm blazed with all the fire that she held suppressed within her.

'Listun!' said Madame de Boucher. 'Listun! You—and your fren'—shall have so much money, so so much money! Just a few days! The Prince cannot know! Myself, I will go to him. My sis-terr was Anglish—the wife of one of your noblesse, one of the

Prince's fren's. She too was fren', a great, great fren', a so-great fren' of the Prince.'

Her fingers were caressing the greasy collar of Mr. Ross's coat, stroking it as if they were soothing an enraged cat. Out of the corner of his eye Mr. Ross watched the great opals burn with their furious inward fire.

'Listun! My sisterr is dead, but he worshipped her. Like a *déesse* —like a goddess! He would not have so great a . . . a . . . a . . . *malheur* arrive to those she loved. You shall not lose by it!'

What did she care about telling that far-away story of her sister's dishonour—of the light love of the Prince who had betrayed his best friend and seduced his best friend's wife—to this clumsy man with a carrot in his clumsy hand, and scurf upon the collar of his incredible coat? Anything that would gain enough time to stop that appalling journey for Henri; that journey from the twitter of sparrows at their breakfast, and the peaceful hum of an orderly city going about its business, and the cry of the street-vendor—she could hear him, now, outside the lodge at the river-terrace gate: the journey from this drab peace, to the murk of streets where the lamps bore swaying forms with sagging heads; where crowds rushed to and fro with no set purpose but blood-shed; where old women sat knitting under the shadow of an obscene instrument of death, with the same preoccupation that they would sit by their stalls under the shadow of a market-cross.

Yet all the while she knew it was useless—that Mr. Ross's name was Death; that Mr. Higgins's name was Death; that Henri de Boucher's name was Death.

'Oh God!' she cried, and flung away from Mr. Ross so that he staggered; flung herself to her husband, that figure of death, and took him to her, as if she would have taken his very body within her own, instead of merely into the shelter of her arms.

'Come, ma'am,' said Mr. Ross after a while. 'Cheer up! While there's life there's 'ope—hope. Never say Die! There's lots on 'em done this little journey, to my own certain knowledge. And maybe . . .' His voice tailed off for a moment. There had been no 'maybe'. The fate of those other French creditors of the Prince of Wales had never been uncertain. He spoke as to a stone.

'Twenty-five on 'em there's been,' said Mr. Higgins, gently

scratching his thigh. 'Twenty-five on 'em. This y-ere makes it twenty-six! An' none on 'em 'ave ever come back to worrit 'Is Royal 'Ighness no more.'

With the suggestion that there should be consolation in the thought that at any rate His Royal Highness George Prince of Wales had not been troubled any more, Mr. Higgins came to the end of his resources as comforter. He fell into a remote silence in which he reflected on the varying public houses that should help him spend his share of the crackly note that Willie Ross had pouched: on the gift he would give the amiable Fanny in the kitchen of the George in George Court as thanks for value received.

'Ma'am,' said Mr. Ross, bringing back his hard-boiled-egg eyes from their long study of Hogarth's grim portrayal of *Mariage à la Mode*, 'I think we had better be running along, if Mounseer will get ready what he needs. I've got to get 'im—him—to Dover tonight. Take plenty of money, Mounseer! Allus useful: wonderful how it greases the wheels: wonderful 'ow it softens the hardest heart!—Not as it would ever h'affect Higgins and me,' he added quickly, in order to show that the limits of concession as far as he was concerned had been already reached.

'Now, ma'am! Now, Mounseer!'

He stepped forward on to broken fragments of china that crackled underfoot, with outstretched hand. With a jerk of his head he motioned his colleague to hold himself to be in readiness should any trouble arise. He placed his hand, with the broken nails and the mist of dark hair along the back, upon the filmy lace that covered Madame de Boucher's shoulders—a little warily, tentatively, but ominously.

She had held her husband's head—that romantically tousled head so soon to be nursed in the basket in the shadow of the guillotine—against her bosom, buried in the scented folds of silk and lace. She turned like a tigress at the touch. There was that in her marble face, in her green eyes, in the lines that knitted her white brow, before which Mr. Ross for a moment quailed. She was the incarnation of anguish and hate, a shell so full of despair and love and pain that her humanity was transcended by it, a body inhabited by a spirit that was cursing God.

'Phew!' said Mr. Ross's Consciousness to Mr. Ross, 'I wouldn't care to come up agin her. I wouldn't care . . .'

At that moment Mathilde de Boucher fell to the floor without a word, and lay silent among the broken china and the fallen strawberries, with her red hair spread like a halo of fire about her pale face. Only the great bracelet of opals shone on an outstretched arm, as if animated by the hate and despair that were shut within her motionless body.

'Come, Mounseer! The good lady's only fainted. Best go afore she comes to and makes trouble.'

Mr. Ross's grip suddenly tightened on the arm beneath the elegant Chinese silk sleeve. De Boucher, no longer an Apollo, no longer even a man, but a thing without will or thought, responded to the touch with the automatic obedience of a puppet to the strings of the puppet-master. He suffered himself to be led away, without even a glance at loveliness prostrate on the floor.

He was gone from the house, was rattling over the cobbles in a post-chaise, with Mr. Ross and Mr. Higgins for company, on the first stage of that journey which must inevitably end in death, when the united efforts of the women of the house at last succeeded in bringing back his wife to a semblance of life.

Mathilde de Boucher had carried with her another life—its burgeoning hidden beneath the loose green and silver folds of her wrapper. Within a few days it was born in the great bed—hung with curtains embroidered with flame-coloured phoenixes—from which she stared unceasingly at the river, at the stippling of a plane tree's leaves against the pale sky, at the huddle of barges and buildings upon the farther bank. She did not think as she lay there: the time was not yet ripe for thought and planning. She lay unmurmuring through her pangs, unnoticed the soothing babble of her attendants, drawing within herself—into body, soul and brain—overwhelming hate. A hate that ran in her veins and arteries and heart with the blood—so hot, so scalding that she thought her frame would burst with its pressure!

Someone pressed against her lips a soft silver spoon full of pap sopped in wine. But she shook her head and remained unheeding, with her half-shut eyes fixed on the red sail of a barge sliding down river.

One great tremor shook her: pain tore her as if her body were being rent asunder. She thought her hate had burst through the fleshly bonds and was faring out into the world, disembodied, to do its work of vengeance. She was glad. She laughed. With that her baby was born. . . .

The little creature was being washed in warm water, powdered with fine fuller's earth, by a fat woman with a red shiny face, while its father jolted in a cart across the streets of Paris, his body shaking to every movement as if it were a doll from which the sawdust were running out.

'Luckums, Duckums,
Have a Suckums!'

recited the fat woman in a fat sing-song, and presented the tangle of feebly-struggling limbs to the mother.

Mathilde de Boucher did not look. She shook her head, and raised a hand in a feeble gesture of waving it away. Just as she had rejected the wine-pap. She would give suck to no living thing; she would but suckle demons and cursing spirits that should drink in hate from her swollen breasts, and thus refreshed fly thence to do her bidding. She put up her arm so that it lay as a physical barrier across her bosom.

The fat woman, thus rejected, walked up and down the carpet, treading with her even pace from pattern to repetition, her large face bent down to the flannel bundle in her arms, talking to herself, to it, and to the second fat woman who sat with vast spread lap in the window.

'Sally,' she said, 'it's 'ardly breathin'! I like a h'infant to holler. I like a h'infant wot kicks and squawks. I like a h'infant wot takes 'is food like a young calf. I like . . . Sally, my girl, water—hot—very hot: h'and at oncet . . . For Gawd's sake, Sally! Quick!'

But no water, however hot, however quickly brought, would bring back the faint spark of life to that small scrap of flesh and blood. The fat woman, nursing basin and child upon her knees, looked up to her companion, and shook her head.

'Pore little critter!' she began—in Paris, at that moment, they were bundling a great basket sodden with blood into a cart: for

His Royal Highness George Prince of Wales had added death to the debt he owed to yet another creditor—'Pore little innercent! . . . Sairey, my dear, see that the pore thing don't take on! Give 'er 'er drops! Quick!'

Madame de Boucher was sitting up in bed. Her green eyes were open very wide—were staring through the long picture-frame of the window, out on to the grey river and the red-sailed barge . . . and beyond. The locks of her red hair twisted and writhed about her head as if they were the deadly locks of Medusa: her face was set and stony as if it had gazed upon the deadly face of Medusa: the fine linen of her shift had fallen back from her swollen breasts.

'Henri!' she cried, 'Henri! Je te vengerai! Je te jure!' and burst into a babble of promises to that poor head with the matted hair that even then rolled like a ball into the pit behind the Picpus buildings.

'Henri!' she cried, as if her voice could reach beyond the grave —such as it was—into infinite space. 'Henri!—je—te—vengerai. Je—te—jure!'

'Don't take on so, there's a ducky!' said the fat soothing voice of Sairey. 'Don't take on so! Take yer nice, nice drops, there's a love!'

But Mathilde de Boucher's spirit was far away in space, communing with the dead, promising vengeance to the dead, comforting the dead, blasting the very ear-drums of the Most High with the urgency of its hate for the House of Hanover, and with the insistence of its demands for unutterable revenge upon all the line.

More than half an hour passed before she quietened, and suffered the ministrations of the women.

The years go by. The guillotine no longer demands victims; but War demands them a hundred-fold. Liberty, Equality, Fraternity have given place to the imperious autocracy of Napoleon which crumbles with the Old Guard before the British squares at Waterloo. Pantaloons are becoming trousers; top-hats are evolving, and waist-lines have travelled upwards as far as they physically can.

The old King of England goes mad—and mad a second time. His sons quarrel among themselves, and hate among themselves; they pile up vast debts—those lusty fine gentlemen!—for their country to pay; they dishonour themselves with shameful intrigues and corruption. The world whispers of strange violence and murder, of incest and unmentionable crime. Strange things, too, are said of those six unfortunate daughters, whom the genealogical tables show as sterile as mules.

The old King of England is near his death—he has been as good as dead these many years. George Prince of Wales is Regent: his heiress, conceived in disgust and born in hate, has died suddenly and strangely in child-bed: a trifle late the Royal brothers are deserting their concubines to wed in panic and produce heirs to that tarnished throne. The years are gone, stripped like leaves from the Tree of Life . . . It is the year of Our Lord 1819.

Chapter 1

Groundwork . . . for Murder

THE GREAT WINDOW-BAY OVER THE PORCH BECAME A very private place after the waiter had drawn the curtains before its recess. The small boy, crouched on the seat that ran round three sides of it, was not sorry to be shut out, with the fading daylight, from the cognizance of the two gentlemen sitting at wine over the fire in the room beyond.

The porch-bay, like a square watch-tower, was projected from the face of the inn across the wet cobbled pavement, so that the two squat columns supporting it impinged on the very roadway. It commanded, accordingly, the steep main street. The left-hand window showed the line of jutting house fronts and peaked gables as far as the grey bridge and almshouses at the foot of the hill; that on the right showed the market-hall set on arches at the crown.

Dusk was earlier than usual, for there had been rain, and heavy clouds still overhung the town. The apprentice at the apothecary's opposite appeared at the windows, one after the other, hanging dangerously over the sills—his bony wrists shooting far out of his tight cuffs—as he lit the lines of fairy lamps across the house front. The flags and bunting that fluttered everywhere had lost their gay colour: even the scarlet uniforms of the town band, clustered about an unlit lantern on a pole before the market-house, were saddened into a dull mulberry by distance, twilight, and drizzle.

The thin expectant line along the curb thickened into a hedge of bonnets and bell-crowned hats, frieze coats, surtouts, cloaks and pelisses. Chatter swelled and deepened into the humming of a crowd which served as a background for a sudden cackle of laughter or the shrill cry of a small boy.

By slow degrees the calico transparency which covered the front of the baker's shop across the way awoke to a faint glow. The daughter of the house, in a large mob-cap with a wide ribbon in it and a little frilled apron, came out at intervals and studied the effect. Each of her disappearances through the dark oblong of the doorway marked a slight increase in the illumination.

In the half-light, of course, it was impossible to see details, but Christopher, on his morning walk under escort of Captain Heywood's servant, had viewed the decoration by broad daylight. It had promised to be extremely imposing. It bore at the top the words, 'Vivant Dux et Duchessa et Leur Enfant Royal'. Underneath the loyal inscription there were life-size portraits of a large lady—principally bust—with ostrich plumes in her hair, and of a brown-complexioned gentleman in a white bag-wig and the top half of a Windsor uniform. It had been pointed out, as a matter of fact, that the Duke of Kent wore his own hair and that what there was of it was dyed an incredible black. The argument, however, had proved irrefutable, that a wig added to the dignity of the representation—and was much easier to delineate.

At the bottom there were pictures of Kensington Palace and Windsor Castle, each with a crescent moon sitting over its chimneys, and a multitude of rectangular windows through which the light would stream in the most realistic manner once it was dark.

There were other transparencies as well as this—at the saddler's, at the library, and particularly at Mr. Bastable's, the grocer, for he had already received an overwhelming order in advance for his commodities from the royal visitors. Every window from which heads were now poked out would burn at least one candle by way of illumination and rejoicing, and two cressets were to be lighted, when night fell, before the market-hall. Under the colonnade, there awaited the august arrival, in all the panoply of office, mayor, aldermen and councillors (faintly redolent of real black-strap port), mace-bearer (gin-flavoured), beadle (reeking of beer) and a mass of the more important citizens of the ancient borough, with flanking parties of hungry-looking children from the charity school under the orders and discipline of ushers who looked almost as hungry as their charges.

To Christopher Harnish, with nose pressed against the side

window of the bay, there came the clatter of hoofs from far down the street.

A gentleman with a drab top-hat and flying coat tails cantered by in an important manner. He shouted, 'They're coming!' as he passed, and a moment later the bells of the parish church surged into a clangour of welcome.

A mob of the local militia on clumsy horses jogged up the street to the loud creak of leather and jingle of accoutrements. Their high black shakos rode uneasily at every sort of angle on their unaccustomed heads.

Scattered cheering greeted the open carriage drawn by four weary horses with postillions, that followed them.

It was a large conveyance, but it appeared inconveniently crowded. A large man sat in it, with a large lady in an enormous bonnet, and a large nurse holding in her arms a large baby. Besides these there was a thin little girl to whom nobody paid much attention, and two large footmen in red plush livery and cocked hats who just—and only just—fitted into the rumble.

The large gentleman bowed and raised his curly-brimmed hat to the cheers; the large lady bowed right, and then left; and the large nurse raised the large baby in her arms a fraction at short intervals as if to indicate that it would have bowed, too, in a properly royal manner if it had been a few months older.

The royal entourage filled two more open carriages with bonnets and cocked hats; and the interiors of the four closed vehicles that brought up the rear were presumably packed as tightly with domestic staff as their roofs were piled with imperials, uniform cases, trunks and hat boxes.

Christopher's regard appeared to rest upon this very matter-of-fact cavalcade. The direction of his serious eyes, indeed, was toward the travel-stained landau with the jaded horses and the jolting cavalry; but he did not see them.

The coming of that poor parade had been but the knock behind the curtain of the theatre of his imagination. He was gone ten worlds away . . . He looked down from mullioned window upon another throng—in some fairy city where roofs were peaked into the sapphire sky, and the street was a river of purple and cloth-of-silver and steel, and a princess on a white palfrey went by amid her guard of pikemen in strange helmets with spade-cut beards.

He did not see the poor pomp of this world at all, for it was transformed—before the retinas of his eyes had sent the physical message to his brain—into something fantastic and far more rich. Already his busy mind was weaving it into the vivid pattern of that other life to which none but he had entrance. It was another incident for the living tapestry of day-dreams with which he clothed the secret galleries of his mind—galleries into which he withdrew from the world about him: tapestries he wove and coloured by the aid of the magic in the books upon which he had secretly browsed since first he had learned to read.

It was the affair of the pantaloons that brought him back to earth. For as the last carriage passed by with its rearguard of bumping cavalry, the topmost bandbox toppled from its perch, fell past the window and burst—a bombshell of millinery—on the wet road.

A cry of anguish from within halted the postillion. An agitated bonnet peered out of the window. The carriage stopped, and the escort reined up—but not before one of the horses in the leading rank had trampled the fragile wreckage into the thin slime. A torrent of excited French avalanched from the vehicle; a hand in a black mitten wrestled in vain with the handle of the door.

A red-faced young cornet slid from the saddle, plumed shako lurching over snub nose as he did so. With his naked sword still held at the 'carry' he clanked the few paces to the scene of disaster.

Willing hands collected up the fallen garments and piled them over his free left arm. He advanced towards the carriage. As he did so the infernal shako slid completely forward on to his nose. His sword-hand went up to save it: his left hand went up to save it: the topmost garment immediately fell off the pile, unfolded its width, and spread itself upon the ground revealing to the world its generous lines and character.

A roar of laughter burst from the crowd. . . .

'Vod is id? Vod is id?' demanded a guttural voice from behind the curtain.

One of the two gentlemen had come from the room beyond into the window-bay unseen and unheard, and was watching the scene over Christopher's small figure. His movements were always silent and his speech gentle; not as if he were too tired for violence, but as if he were conserving his energy for it. He slightly turned his head as Christopher looked up, and replied to the other, his unseen interrogator, through the curtains.

'My good Ompteda,' said he with a dry chuckle—and his voice was only raised to the exact pitch needed to carry it beyond the thick folds. 'The crowd are admiring Her Royal Highness the Duchess of Kent's pantaloons. Admirable pantaloons! Generous pantaloons! A trifle muddy at the moment—but still quite admirable! . . . Is it treason, do you suppose, Ompteda, to admire the Royal pantaloons? A delicate question, Ompteda! Is there anything in the Royal Marriage Act about it, do you imagine?'

The man behind the curtain had no comment to make. The soft-voiced man turned back to the room. Between white, plump finger and thumb of his left hand he took the boy by the ear. The action was not rough, but neither was it gentle.

'So here they are at last!' he said. 'Come, brat, it is not suitable that you should look on Royal pantaloons. You are too young. It is well to learn early that danger lurks in female pantaloons. Doubly so in pantaloons that are Royal as well as female.'

He conducted Christopher back into the long room, which was lighted at the far end by a fire and two candles on the high mantelpiece. The curtains before all the windows had been drawn. On either side of the hearth was a tall-backed chair with a small round table and a bottle of wine at its elbow. In one sat a long uneasy man, with an enormous nose, projecting teeth, and a long melancholy face made all the longer by the faint black whisker that curved from ear to cheekbone.

'Sit there!' said the soft-voiced man, and guided Christopher by the ear to the other chair.

The child sat down in it, very upright, his yellow hair all ruffled, rubbing his ear. His small legs in their white pantaloons just reached the floor. There was a narrow frill to the collar of his shirt, and he wore a short green double-breasted jacket with red buttons.

The soft-voiced man took up a commanding position facing fire and audience. One black lock of hair lay across his sallow forehead. He clasped his hands behind him, under the tails of his coat. His chin was sunk into the white folds of his neckcloth. Two buttons of his striped satin waistcoat were undone—for he was becoming a trifle fat, although he could not yet be thirty years old.

He looked straight at the fire when he spoke, and appeared to soliloquize rather than address his companions—a disconcerting method of conversation, Christopher felt.

'And what are we going to do now with our Master Harnish?' asked he with cold geniality. 'What shall we do with him?'

He seemed to demand no answer. There was none.

'Well,' he repeated, 'what *shall* we do with him?'

He did not look at Christopher as he spoke or turn his head. Only an increased emphasis in the colourless voice suggested the need for a reply.

There was a pause. Christopher licked his lips.

'I do not know, sir,' he ventured.

'We do not know? We do not know what is to be done with Master Harnish! This is lamentable. It is obvious that he cannot continue as he is—that we must take some steps for the education and enlightenment of Master Harnish. It would not have been good for him to continue under the care of his excellent aunt and his cousins any longer . . . Would it?'

His voice sharpened. He repeated, 'Would it?'

'I don't know, sir,' said Christopher. Tears rose to his eyes as he thought of the pleasant house—now far away—in a valley of the Cornish moors; of Aunt Howell and the young ladies; of his low-ceilinged bedroom with the apple tree against the window; of the cabinets that stood one upon the other in the drawing-room; of kind Jane, and of Tib the cat. Perhaps Baron Ompteda had never come riding up the valley. He was just dreaming! . . . He was in reality back there now, sitting quietly by himself in the little chair in the out-of-the-way corner behind the sofa; and Hannah was lighting the candles with a taper from the fire, and moving one in a sort of square silver dish to the ledge of the bookcase behind him, saying as she always did, 'Young gentlemen must not strain their eyes reading'.

The voice went on. . . .

'I am afraid that Master Harnish's education has been sadly neglected. That while Mr. What-d'you-call-him, the curate, may have taught him some ciphering and Latin, he has learned none of the many things that a gentleman must learn—and learn early. Women and parsons—both petticoats—are no use to teach men. . . . Is not that so, Master Harnish?'

A pause.

'I do not know, sir.'

A tear slid down his cheek. He remembered the unappreciated half-hours with Cousin Jennifer in the sunny morning room—the very squeak of the slate pencil as it wrote down totals that were to be wiped away, a moment afterwards, with the fragment of damp sponge kept in an old willow-pattern saucer.

'You perceive, my dear baron,' the voice continued, 'that Master Harnish does not even know that a feminine education for the young male is highly unsatisfactory. As his guardian you must take him in hand yourself.' The voice paused, and purred on. 'I shall be glad to help. As you know!'

The baron shifted uneasily in his chair. He crossed his legs at the ankles. He uncrossed them. He poured himself out a glass of wine, and raised it to his lips with an uncertain hand. Christopher could not see his eyes, but felt that he was looking at him all the while.

'Master Harnish may, indeed, be able to cipher and do his Caesar, and conjugate "aimer", but . . .' the voice was suddenly raised, and the white face turned on Christopher with a quick regard from narrowed eyes under the heavy lids '. . . but, can he use his fists? . . . Can you box, Master Harnish?'

Christopher stammered his inability.

'No? An important accomplishment for a gentleman. Master Harnish must learn . . . But perhaps he is a horseman? He goes hunting on a fat pony? . . . You can ride, of course? . . .

'No! That is a very serious omission. Baron Ompteda shall teach Master Harnish himself. He is a perfect horse-master, and there are, I am told, some excellent livery stables here . . . Come, you must have some manly accomplishment. Let us see . . .'

Here an interruption occurred; for Ompteda, who had been looking fixedly across the hearth at the small boy, raised his hand

and smote the arm of his chair twice with a sudden and surprising violence.

'I do not like id,' he said with his thick German accent. 'I do nod like id, Captain . . .' and hesitated, 'Captain . . . Heywood.'

Captain Heywood turned his gaze slowly toward him. He made no remark. The coals in the grate fell with a crash, and the fire became but a red glow. The only light was from the two candles on the mantelpiece. The small boy and the thin man in their chairs on either side of the wide hearth were shielded from one another's regard by the shadows cast by the high chimney shelf.

Such light as there was seemed to be concentrated on the figure between, with the pale face, the pointed chin, the straight nose with curving nostrils. The great room beyond him was a wild pattern of heavy shadows.

'Do you swim, Master Harnish? . . . Cht—cht . . . Too bad. That I will endeavour to teach you myself. A pleasant pastime as well as a useful one.

'Well, you don't box; you don't ride; you don't swim. A serious list of deficiencies for a young gentleman bred up in the country . . . Perhaps, now, you can—shoot?'

He said the last word as if he himself had shot it from a gun, and as he spoke he looked, not at Christopher, but at Ompteda.

The baron had pulled himself upright. A jet of gas burst from a lump of coal, and by its momentary flare his forehead glistened with beads of sweat. He opened his lips.

'I don't like . . .' he started, and subsided before the glance.

'Do I understand you to say that you cannot even shoot? . . . You have never bowled over a rabbit, or brought down a fat rook! . . . A very Utopian, humanitarian, old-maidish sort of life you have led, Master Harnish!'

He let his eyes wander round the room for a moment, appeared to recognize—even in the dark—some distant object with a little start, as of surprise.

'Now here is a happy chance!' said he. 'The baron and I can actually take the preliminary steps towards rectifying one of these omissions in the short half-hour before dinner . . . I had forgotten my pistols were down here, my dear Ompteda . . . Very fortunate . . . Bring me the mahogany case from the sideboard, Christopher.'

While Christopher fetched the brass-bound box, Soft-Voice seated himself in the vacated chair, leaned forward, lighted with a taper a candle at his elbow, and swept clear a space on the table top.

Within the case, upon a bed of green baize, lay two long-barrelled pistols. They were very plain, with stocks of dark walnut, but beautifully kept. They lifted out on a tray, and underneath in separate compartments were two small brass boxes, a flat, leather-covered flask with a curious metal cap, a huddle of oily rags, and a wash-leather bag.

Captain Heywood picked out one of the pistols. He balanced it for a moment with approval on his forefinger; cocked it, and held it under the candle to close, grave scrutiny, before easing the hammer home with his thumb.

'It is a very pretty weapon, with a really beautiful balance,' he remarked, and laid it down.

Ompteda said nothing, but poured himself out wine, slopped some on the table, and raised the glass to his lips with a hand that shook.

'Watch me, Christopher,' said the other. 'See how I hold this in my hand—my second finger round the trigger, my forefinger pointing along the barrel, my thumb holding the hammer eased between half-cock and full. I should fire so a fraction of a second sooner than if I pulled the trigger—even though it is a hair-trigger.'

He raised the pistol with a long, straight arm, pointing across the fire-place. Ompteda, bolt upright, stared at the muzzle.

'I should fire—so . . .' And the hammer fell with a snap at which the long man flinched, as if in his mind it were magnified to the crash of an exploding weapon. 'So! And I should be a fraction of a second quicker than the other man, and a fraction of a second can spell life—and death.'

He handed the deadly thing to the small boy standing at his elbow.

'Let us see what you make of it!'

Christopher's wrist was not strong enough to hold the heavy

weapon level, nor were his fingers long enough to press upon the trigger. He steadied his right hand with his left, but the long barrel still wavered down toward the table, up toward the clock; first to Baron Ompteda, then to Captain Heywood.

'Id is too heavy for de child,' said the former with—it seemed—a sigh of relief. 'Id is absurd to think he can hold a bistol of that size. Even if he could hold id, he could nod fire id.'

'Fortunately when it comes to firing practice,' replied the other, 'we have your pocket pistols. Pretty little things—as deadly as asps, with the additional merit that a child could use them . . . Even these, however, will do for the preliminaries. Hold your arm out straight, Christopher. Support your right wrist with your left. Now pull the trigger.'

But the trigger was not to be pulled.

Christopher laid the weapon on the table. He looked apologetically at Captain Heywood.

'I am afraid I am not quite strong enough to do it yet, sir! I have really tried very hard.'

Heywood cocked it, and pushed the butt towards the child.

'Leave it lying on the table. Hold it steady with your left hand . . . So! . . . That is right! . . . Now see if you can press the trigger with your thumb.'

It could be done. The hammer clicked to its place, jerking the pistol on the polished surface.

Ompteda leaned forward. His face twitched. He moistened his lips. His eyes only left the pistol to glance swiftly, furtively, at the small, puzzled boy, to cast an almost pleading look at the sallow face of his companion.

Heywood cocked the pistol once again and restored it to its place on the table.

'You saw what happened, boy, when you pulled the trigger? The hammer fell upon the little nipple in the breech of the pistol . . .' A white hand took out one of the small boxes in the mahogany case: opened it, produced a small metal object hollowed like a tiny thimble, revolved it to gaze for a moment between plump thumb and forefinger, and placed it in position on the nipple. . . .

'When the hammer falls,' the indifferent voice went on, 'the

blow fires the speck of explosive in this cap . . .' He took it off the
nipple and pushed the weapon nearer Christopher. 'Look at the
nipple for a moment. There is a little hole in it—a mere thread.
The flame rushes down that tiny passage and fires the charge within the barrel.'

Heywood took up the flat leather flask. It was like a very large
peardrop. There was a spring catch at the base of the neck. He
pulled it back, and held the powder horn upside-down for a moment, and then released the catch again. The cap twisted off and
he tilted the contents into his palm—a little heap of shining black
grains like coarse seed. It was seed—a seed that germinated not
life, but death; that came not to flower, but to flame.

'Here is the powder. The top of the flask holds the exact measure. It is poured down the muzzle of your weapon and kept close
up to the breech by a wad . . .' From the other box came a small
disk of thick wadding.

Heywood made the small boy take it in his hand and examine
it. He demonstrated how it should be pushed tightly home down
the barrel by the ramrod. He produced a round leaden bullet
about the size of a marble from the chamois bag, and told how it
should be dropped into the pistol next and kept in position by
another and slightly thinner wad.

Not once as he spoke in his cold, even voice did he look up.
There was something inhuman in the indifference with which he
gave this unsought instruction, in the languid movements of the
plump hands that demonstrated the ritual of death-dealing.

'Do you think you could charge a pistol now?' he asked at last.

Christopher thought he could.

Captain Heywood rose. He picked up a footstool from before
the fire and walked down the room carrying it, followed by Ompteda's regard. At the far end, in the wide space between massive
dining-table and yet more massive sideboard, opposite the door,
he placed it on the floor.

'Then you shall show us how well you can do it, Master Harnish,' said he. 'Bring the case with you. Sit on this footstool, and
load that pistol. Imagine that your life depends on it! . . . Here,
you shall have a candle on the sideboard to see by.'

He paused a moment to watch the earnest start of the operation, and then went back to his chair by the fire, chuckling so faintly that none could hear him but himself.

Ompteda was staring across the room as if he were hypnotized, although he could see nothing except the top of a yellow head beyond the long table in the candle-light. He wiped his face with a large handkerchief. He cleared his throat:

'I don't like id,' he began without turning his head.

Heywood ignored the remark.

'I think a brandy and hot water on a chilly evening would not disagree with our wine, or spoil our dinner, my dear Ompteda,' he observed. 'It would keep your—our spirits up.'

He reached out to the tasselled bell-rope hanging on the wall—paused, his hand in air. . . .

'How are you getting on, Christopher?'

'I am putting the powder in, sir.'

Heywood rang the bell.

So it was that when the waiter opened the door, the first thing to meet his gaze was the small boy sitting on the floor in a circle of candle-light, gravely pushing the ramrod down the barrel of a long pistol.

Neither of the gentlemen over the fire, at the other end of the room, appeared to be aware of what was going on. For Heywood was talking in a low voice at his companion, who had unwillingly torn his gaze away.

The fat waiter did not like firearms. His slow mind debated whether he should draw attention to the dangerous game in progress. Firearms meant violence, noise, death, buckets of blood, horror. It revolted him to see the flushed and earnest face bent over the gleaming thing held awkwardly against the footstool. The muzzle, with the ramrod projecting from it, was pointed towards him. He hurriedly moved out of the line of fire.

Before he could decide what comment to formulate, if any, he found the pale face and invisible eyes of Captain Heywood turned towards him.

'Waiter!'

'Yessir?'

'Bring some brandy for Baron Ompteda and myself.'

'Yes, my lord!'

'No. "*His* Lordship".'

'Yessir—my lord!'

'Whatever you like! . . . My Honour and *His* Lordship want brandy—if you have any drinkable. Large glasses. Some hot water—mind it is really hot!—loaf sugar, and two silver teaspoons. None of your filthy taproom spoons . . . And more lights—many more lights! The room is damned dark! It is dark and cold!'

To the waiter, his mind astray, watching the child on the floor loading the pistol, the room seemed very dark—and very cold. He turned unhappily, and went to execute the order.

Ompteda's gaze swung back across the room to the shining locks that barely showed above the table edge.

Heywood chuckled again.

'What a tale the man will have to tell to the taproom!' said he. 'Child playing with a pistol on the floor! Anything might happen! My groundwork is exceedingly good, my dear Baron. I have always devoted great attention to preliminaries. It pays in the end—always! Does it not, Ompteda? . . . Is the pistol loaded, Christopher?'

'Yes, sir!'

In a few cat-like strides Heywood crossed the room. He held up the pistol and surveyed it in the candle-light; tested the packing of the charge with the ramrod, examined the little shining copper cap sitting on the nipple.

There was a heavy footfall on the stairs.

Ompteda half rose to his feet. He supported himself with one hand on the arm of the chair. His face was ghastly, and his mouth opened into a black round as if he were about to scream.

Heywood swung the pistol to and fro negligently. The small boy, sitting on his heels, watched the shining curve of the weapon.

'You will see, Christopher, that the force of the explosion, when this is fired, throws the muzzle up. You must always aim low at your target.'

The footsteps on the stairs were nearer now: they were accompanied by the musical jingle of glasses.

The pistol swung forward in its arc towards the wall by the window-bay.

As it did so it exploded with a horrifying crash and dart of flame. Its muzzle, with a stream of acrid smoke pouring from it, jerked up; and the ball struck the wall with a thud. Plaster trickled into a little patch of white powder on the polished floor.

There was a moment's deathly silence, broken by a strangled cry from Ompteda, and the smash of fallen glass and a woman's scream without.

The pistol, with a wisp of vapour still drifting from it, was flung on the footstool before the fascinated gaze of the child.

With incredible swiftness Heywood was back by the fireside before the door was burst open.

The waiter with gaping mouth and slanting tray stood on the threshold, behind him a goggling maid with a heavy candelabrum. He took in the smoking pistol—the petrified small boy.

'My God!' he ejaculated. 'What 'as 'appened!'

Heywood came down the room. He ignored the waiter. He looked at the pistol, at the white scar in the wall, and then at Christopher.

'How often have you been told not to play with firearms?' he said in cold, even tones.

He raised a fine white hand, and struck the child upon the cheek, without angry violence but as if in deliberate punishment.

Other hurried steps were on the stairs. A babble of voices broke out below.

'Come in, and close the door,' said Captain Heywood. He turned his back on the group and walked towards the fire, casting one slow sneering look at his companion.

'The young gentleman has been playing with my pistols without my knowledge. He has been warned before . . . Put the case upon the table, and go to bed, sir! . . . Bring some more brandy and set the light down. No harm has been done.'

'The young gentleman might of a-killed hisself!' said the waiter severely.

'He might have indeed. But he has not. Set the lights down, and explain to your master.'

'The bullet might of gone through the door. It might of killed me,' said the waiter.

'So it might!' said Heywood in a tone which showed that he was unconcerned by the possibility.

'The young gentleman might of killed you, your Honour,' said the waiter.

'I think not,' replied Heywood. 'Bring some more brandy. Set the lights down, girl, instead of goggling there! . . .'

'I saw the young gentleman a-playing with that there pistol on the floor by hisself, and I thought to myself . . .' said the waiter.

'If you had told me, instead of thinking so much, it would have been even more useful,' said Heywood.

When they had gone he turned his narrowed regard on his companion, who appeared incapable of speech, trembling, his face glistening with sweat.

'Come here, Christopher,' said he at length.

The child came towards him with hanging head, the heavy case of pistols still in his hands, his tear-stained face crimson from the blow, his mind singing with misery and puzzlement. A sob broke from him.

Heywood looked down on him a moment with unchanged expression.

'This is all very odd, Christopher, is it not?' said the cold soft voice. 'Very odd, indeed! It is what we call groundwork; do we not, Ompteda? I have always been very insistent on good groundwork.'

'Groundwork! . . . Groundwork! . . .' said Ompteda. His voice rose until it broke—'Groundwork . . . for . . . murder!'

Chapter 2

Reckless Intrusion on a Lady

WHEN MISS MATILDA HAD ONCE ENTERED THE COM-
partment of wood and glass that was known as her count-
ing-house, there was no human force on earth that could have
extracted her, except her own. She fitted it as snugly as a tortoise
fits his shell; and from the square-paned sash window that overlooked the wide hall of the Seven Stars she would peer from time
to time, just as a tortoise might occasionally dart out his head from
the shelter of his carapace.

The hutch was so small, Miss Matilda so large, and the exertion
required for entrance and exit so great, that the lady breakfasted,
dined, teaed, and supped in it; and would have unquestionably
slept in it, if there had been a sufficiency of space within for her
to make the conventional adjustment of attire. Her post of duty
clothed her, as it were, in an outer garment of wood and glass
which she assumed immediately she had risen, and put off on
going to bed.

The life of the inn did not begin officially—was informal, so to
speak—until that moment when (after a pause to recover from
the strain of entry which had brought fine beads of perspiration to
her broad pink forehead and made visible a slight dampness at the
armpits of her pink muslin gown) Miss Matilda bent her elbows
on her writing ledge, pressed her fat fingers against the frame of
the sash-window before her, and shot it up with one forceful
shove. The crash and rattle of the operation signified that the
day's work had begun; that the shining black eyes, and shining
black ringlets, and the admirable and large bust of Miss Matilda
were now on view to the world in their yard-square frame.

34

The walls touched her knees, her back; the narrow shelves caressed her shoulders; her enormous bosom wriggled like a couple of fat kittens upon the desk before her; her elbows, as she squared up to her ledger, rubbed the sides of her sentry-box.

The eyrie had, however, been built for head-turning, if not for body-turning. Around it the life of the inn flowed, perceptible through the window at which she sat, and the narrow panes that flanked her right and left.

She saw who entered at the great inn-door, and registered their importance by the vehemence with which she pulled bell-handles that summoned severally boots or ostler, waiter, chamber-maid and host. She gauged their social position from the way strange ladies climbed the stairs to bed; judged to a nicety when the impertinence of a spark to a barmaid should become of suffi-cient interest to repay the effort of a peep into the parlour-bar through the flawed glass panes on her right; watched the progress of dishes, under vast covers like the dome of St. Paul's, from the dim passage beyond the stairs to the coffee-room door; learned through the narrow slit on her left who sat in the privileged sanc-tum of the landlord's snuggery, and caught stray fragments of their gossip.

There was never a flicker of an eyelid, or a whisper, however low, within her range, that was missed by her dark eyes or her sharp ears hidden behind the bunches of ringlets. She watched, and she listened: she always watched and listened. It was, indeed, com-monly believed that when she went to bed she left the door of her chamber ajar so that no rustle, no creaking board, no word of muted speech should escape her.

At any rate Miss Matilda, at the task of keeping her brother's books, saw everything that was to be seen; heard everything that was to be heard. What she did not see or hear, she was told—by the fat head-waiter with a puffed shirt-frill like a pouter pigeon, standing with his back to her and whispering over his shoulder with barely twitching lips; by the small head-chambermaid in flowered gown and mob-cap, who stood on tip-toe to hiss her in-formation into the valley between Miss Matilda's recumbent bosoms; by the ostlers; by her sister-in-law, the landlady; by any and every visiting servant, townsman emerging from bar-parlour or snuggery, and tradesman.

Captain Heywood, descending the stairs with soft tread on the morning after the royal arrival, saw such a conclave terminating. Even across the width of the shadowy hall he recognized the sallow face which was silhouetted for a moment against the pink amplitude of Miss Matilda's muslin-covered bosom—for the yet pinker amplitude of Miss Matilda's face was not visible except from the ground level. He paused a moment in the angle of the stairs out of view, until the man departed with a quick gliding walk and obsequiously bent head; and then loitered elegantly across the flagged floor, as if awaiting a companion; and so drifted to the square opening of Miss Matilda's sentry-box.

'Well, Miss Matilda!' said he, leaning his shoulder against the ledge, and turning his pale sleepy-lidded face towards large pink bosom and large pink face. 'Well, Miss Matilda, so you've found another victim!'

'No, Captain!' said a fat and bronchial chuckle. 'Quite an old friend, Captain!' . . . Wheeze . . . 'One of my regulars—lately. A very pleasant and gentlemanly person!'

Heywood, turning his head over his shoulder just a little, unveiled his sleepy eyes for an instant. Miss Matilda felt his regard rest upon her large smooth face with its unlined forehead, big black eyes, moist red mouth; travel down her jolly double chin and lose itself in her bosom, like a slumbrous caress. Her soul shivered with horrific pleasure.

'I seem,' drawled the Captain, having thus made the lady aware of his appreciation, 'to have seen the person before.'

Miss Matilda lowered her voice.

'He does not like it to be known, sir! But it is Mr. Sheldon— Gentleman to His Royal Highness the Duke of Kent . . . Own' . . . Wheeze . . . 'Gentleman!'

How Miss Matilda rolled out that sonorous title! Trumpets sounded; drums rolled; plumed shakos quivered; spurs jingled; velvet backs bent till they were almost broken, in the murmurous rhythm of that respectful whisper.

'He came down in advance of their Royal Highnesses,' she went on. 'To see that all was properly prepared. The Duke greatly relies on him—very greatly, Captain!'

'He arranged their accommodation at the Grange, I presume?' asked Heywood, as if he were indifferent to the subject, but anxious to keep a conversation going.

Miss Matilda understood so. Mr. Sheldon had discussed it at length with her during one of his regular twice-a-day visits, she having known the Grange since a girl.

Captain Heywood, with a white hand resting on the ledge— 'Such a nobleman's hand!' thought Miss Matilda—and his face half-turned from her, gathered a great deal of information—interspersed with wheezing and coughs—about the private life and daily routine of the Royal Pair and the infant Princess. He rejected what he did not need, absorbed the rest, arranged it and catalogued it. All the while his calm, pale face was expressive of nothing but a remote interest in the subject, as if it served only as an excuse for the gratification of his desire for Miss Matilda's company.

'A strange household!' said he, when her fund of knowledge was obviously running low. 'I should like to know more about it; but now that they have arrived I do not suppose Sheldon . . .'

'Mr. Sheldon's time is very much as he chooses to make it . . . Although His Royal Highness has a daily inspection of his staff, like a barracks, every morning! Mr. Sheldon said he should be coming in every evening as before . . . Very dull household, sir! Very dull. Everything done at the same time every day—like clockwork. No more doing in the housekeeper's room than above-stairs, nowadays! . . . He always stands here, and drinks a dock-glass of port with a measure of brandy, while he talks to me.'

'Without so much as offering you a little refreshment, yourself?' said Captain Heywood in high astonishment.

'Well . . .' said Miss Matilda coyly. 'It has been known . . .'

'The moment is just ripe. Now I insist . . .' and Captain Heywood enveloped such of her person as could be seen in a warm, secretive regard. 'I insist that you join me. If only for the sake of that very troublesome cough of yours.'

Miss Matilda reddened with pleasure.

'Well, just a thimbleful of port wine, if you really make a point of it—to please you, sir . . .' Wheeze . . . 'A glass of port wine has indeed been known to give the most immediate relief. I have been bronchious ever since I forsook the boards . . . Astley's . . . Not to

put too fine a point on it, perspiring too freely and wearing garments that exposed the kidneys to every draught wore me to a
shadow. To speak frankly, Captain, tights, though decent enough,
are no protection to a delicate female. And only five years ago . . . !'

She shook her head as if overcome by memories, wheezed
loudly, and jogged with her right elbow against the partition that
divided her from the parlour-bar. A moment later the little door
at the back was set ajar and one of the young ladies demanded
her pleasure.

They discussed very amiably the large glasses of tawny wine,
royal eccentricities and the weather.

Eventually Captain Heywood set his glass down on the ledge.
He drew himself together, as if regretfully.

'I had better see that my friend's young ward is not trying to
shoot himself again—or breaking his neck hanging out of the
window.'

'The young gentleman,' said Miss Matilda, 'does not look too
well.'

Heywood paused on his journey to the stair-foot . . . How she
admired the cut of his wonderful coat, the high arch of the collar, the moulding of the grey pantaloons to his well-shaped legs,
the single lock of black hair that lay curved upon his forehead!
. . . He paused, and then in his soft voice said:

'The child has been ill—very ill. Once before he nearly killed
himself playing with firearms. He cannot be kept away from them.
The baron thought a little sea air would be a tonic before they
go to the Continent.'

He smiled at her slowly and curiously—almost promisingly,
Miss Matilda told herself as she watched him go upstairs. Almost
promisingly—Miss Matilda told herself speculatively; for she was
by no means a virgin. Like many an outside Juno, she was filled
with the desire to be the petted plaything of a man.

The smile did not leave Heywood's face, even when he opened
the door of his great sitting-room on the first floor. . . .

'Where have I been, my dear Ompteda?' he replied to a question. 'Just a little more attention to groundwork. Rather a specialty
of mine, you know! You ought to realize that by now!'

The Weekly Intelligencer and Courant had expressed in its current issue the fervent and loyal hope

'. . . that the salubrious climate, the delicate attentions of our inhabitants, and the picturesque beauties of our town and countryside—so far more refreshing and restoring than the artificial pleasures of continental resorts—will form an unparalleled inducement for the Royal Parents to prolong their sojourn amongst us with the infant Princess Alexandrina Victoria, whose tender age cannot fail to be benefited by the mildness and purity of the air of Devonshire.'

The climate may have been salubrious, but it was also extremely wet. The only Royal nose that poked outside the lodge gates of the house on the hill outside the town was that of the Duke of Kent. Accompanied by one, sometimes two, of his gentlemen, wrapped in a large dark cloak or frogged surtout, the rain streaming from the brim of his hat, he would descend on the town, walk beyond energetically and dutifully on a 'constitutional' of a mile or so, reappear, nod with a meaningless good humour in reply to respectful salutes, and vanish again beyond the thatched and white-washed lodge.

Neither did evil weather deter Heywood from his expeditions. No one knew when he went out, or why, or where, or when he came back. It simply came about that at times he was no longer in the inn; and then he would be suddenly standing in the window-bay, looking thoughtfully at the dripping roofs and rain-stained house fronts, with only the mud-sparks on his riding boots to show that he had been without doors. Or he would appear, propped elegantly, indifferently, like any idle man of fashion, against the edge of Miss Matilda's lamp-lit window frame.

He encouraged her to talk, especially after Mr. Sheldon, the Duke's gentleman, had paid his evening visit; and, if she showed any inclination to diverge, brought her gently back again to the one subject he had interest in—the household at the Grange.

Miss Matilda exerted her utmost to please: she preened; she plumed; she shaped her mouth into genteel shapes. She leaned forward; she ventured a story that had been a success but a few years ago in the Green Room at Astley's when she was a slim—no, slimmish—coryphée. Her bosom heaved with jollity, and was convulsed individually and collectively upon its resting-place.

Heywood appeared to appreciate the story, and even more—which was personally gratifying—the struggling bosom; insisted on purchasing a glass of rum-shrub to soothe the paroxysms brought on by his comments—and led her gently back to the matter in hand.

Ompteda and Christopher were thrown very much upon their own resources during these days. Ompteda, indeed, avoided as much as possible being alone with either Heywood or the child. He forsook the great sitting-room on the first floor, and sat much in the small snuggery beyond the bar, with a roaring fire, a bottle of gin and the brandy-faced landlord, or the landlord's plump and comely wife.

He drank a great deal from the time when he arrived downstairs on a morning until late at night, when the waiter and one of the potmen guided him up to bed and blew his candle out, for fear he should set the bed-curtains alight.

Heywood never failed to appear as onlooker of the nightly procession. He seemed to know when it was due and would stand at the stair-head watching, with a slight smile and remote air. He never commented; he never offered to help. But one night Christopher, lying sleepless in his little room that was without window or fireplace, heard a soft voice he knew in low, emphatic monologue next door. Twice there seemed to be protests: but each time these protests were not so much beaten down as surged over, and obliterated by the even tones.

Then there was silence: there was no sound of opening or of shutting door—none from the creaking stairs. The only thing which told that Heywood had gone was the passing of a flash of candle-light across the wide crack at the bottom of his door.

There was utter quiet. Ompteda's fitful groans and disjointed babblings were stilled. The bed that had creaked to his tossing responded no longer.

Christopher lay in bed and trembled.

The silence was far more terrifying than an infinitude of small unexplained noises. His imagination ran riot with him . . . He only was left alive in the dark silence! Outside his door there was nothing living except intangible horror! Ompteda was dead! Heywood had killed him—as silently as he did everything!

Christopher in his imagination saw the baron, his head pressed back against the pillow, tasselled nightcap pulled down to the start of his faint curved whisker, mouth with the misshapen teeth fallen open to an O. Perhaps the blood was trickling on to the bedclothes pulled up against his throat!

Christopher sat up in his truckle bed. His small frame shuddered with the thoughts of horror that tumbled through his mind. His nightdress was drenched with sweat, was so wringing wet that it clung to his body.

The terror was such that it was impossible to be borne alone—and in darkness, for, though he had a candle, he had no means of lighting it. It was in a blind search for human support that he set bare foot to bare floor, and ventured out into that black waste of creaking board, and creeping shadow, which was the landing.

Except for the faint noise of his own tread there was no sound, no movement in the passage—none, indeed, it seemed in the whole of the great house. It was as if he alone were alive in a vast mausoleum, that was full of ghosts.

He crept along the passage, passed Ompteda's door with quickening breath, came to the stair-head. The moon riding high sent a faint down-slanting light through the long panes of a window on the half-landing below.

Christopher paused. Downstairs was Captain Heywood; behind him that suddenly silent room. He could not go down; he could not go back—past a door that might swing open, by no natural means, and reveal unknown horrors within. He went on.

At the end of the chill passage a line of light showed under a door. Now that he was immediately outside he could hear faint sounds of movement within.

He pressed his left ear to a panel, and was immediately brought into contact with the warm flow of human life for which he ached.

Someone within was humming, opened drawers, trod quickly with light foot about the room, came near, went farther off, sang a snatch below breath, put something down with a little click upon a bare table.

Christopher was happy for the first time. He was prepared to stay outside that pleasant door all night. It was better to be there with a shivering body but comforted heart, than to be full of panic under the blankets.

With cheek pressed hard against the wood and with eyes shut, he tried to visualize the scene within with its warmth and unafraidness.

As the minutes went by, however, he became increasingly conscious of the cold. His damp night robe clung to him like a clammy shroud, and he could not keep his teeth from chattering.

At last, very warily, he shifted his weight from one numb foot to another. As he did so, the floor-board beneath him gave a furious creak.

The room beyond fell into silence. Then a voice said quickly, but without alarm:

'Who's there?'

Christopher was too frightened to attempt to fly. He remained huddled against the door, motionless, with held breath, as if he would even persuade himself—much more so anyone else—that he was not there at all.

'Who's there?' said the voice again, this time more imperatively. There was, too, sound of movement, as if someone were about to investigate the noise without.

'It's me!' said Christopher, and raised the latch and entered, pausing on the threshold, the door still in his hand.

The room was softly lighted. Half-way down a four-poster bed, with curtains at its head and its foot, confronted a small bright fire in a basket grate. It threw enormous shadows on to the low ceiling. There were candles on the mantelpiece, on a round baize-topped table beside the bed, on a serpentine-fronted chest of drawers, before a mirror between the curtained windows.

On the far side of the fire, facing him, newly risen—so it seemed —from a large arm-chair, was a young and lovely lady with a light wrap thrown over her bedgown. There was lace at her wrists: her feet were thrust into slippers trimmed with swansdown: her long dark hair fell into two great plaits upon her breast.

For a moment she said nothing, but took in, with wide grey eyes, the woebegone figure with bare feet and tousled head.

'What do you want, sir?' she asked, and raised her arched eyebrows in question.

Christopher said nothing, but continued to stare at her.

She read an appeal in his gaze, although she could not sense its purport. He was very small and very unhappy. A faint suspicion of a smile curved her lips.

'You men!' said she. 'You are all the same whether you are . . .' she paused to gauge his age . . . 'nine or ninety! . . . You begin your adventures very young, sir!'

'Yes, ma'am,' said Christopher still holding the door, and thinking it best to agree.

'I wonder whether I really ought to encourage you?'

'Yes, ma'am,' said Christopher.

The lady looked past him, through the black opening of the door, and made pretence of a slight shiver.

'I think,' she said, and now even her eyes were smiling, 'that it would be as well if you were to close the door very, very gently . . . You may stay this side, for a moment. The world is very censorious. We poor women . . . ! You men are so rash, so careless of us . . . Shut it gently—ge-e-ently! My reputation is in your hands!'

There was laughter in every curve and line, in every shadow and brightness of her face, as she watched the small boy close the door, with exaggerated care let the latch slip noiselessly into place, and then turn and look anxiously at her.

She took a step or two nearer to him.

'Are you a gay deceiver?' said she, and, 'Am I safe with you?' and 'Are you safe with me?'

'Yes, ma'am,' answered Christopher, pleating his nightdress into folds.

'Hardly flattering, are you?' she commented, and cocked an eyebrow. 'In that case I wonder what you really wanted?'

No answer was possible to that. Christopher stood and shook with cold in silence. His eyes were full of tears, but they were tears of relief, and gratitude for the gay, soft voice and the light and the fire.

'I wonder what you want! I wonder what you really want!' the voice said. 'Come and sit on this footstool by me while I sit in the chair. Sit there and tell me about yourself. A gentleman's visit to a lady's bedroom at midnight needs some explanation, especially if your intentions are honourable. And you say they are!'

He came across at that invitation, and sat down on the low foot-stool before the fire, sharing it with her slim feet.

He did not speak, but just watched her face, attendant on her pleasure.

She returned his gaze, looking down on him with chin cupped between two hands, elbows propped on knees; her dark tresses swung forward till they almost reached the floor.

'What is your name, visitor?' asked she.

'Christopher, ma'am.'

'Christopher what?'

'Christopher Harnish, ma'am.'

'And how old, Mr. Harnish?'

'Nine years and seven months, ma'am,' replied Mr. Harnish, feeling more at his ease when confronted with questions that demanded facts in reply, and not metaphysical or psychological research.

'Where is your mother?'

Christopher shook his head. His mouth rather shaped than uttered the words:

'She is dead. She died when I was little. Soon after I was born.'

'Poor Christopher,' the lady meditated. 'And your father?'

'My father, ma'am, is a colonel. He is in India. It is a long way off, you know. Aunt Howell says he has never seen me.'

So they sat over the fire in long converse.

The strange lady learned how Christopher had been brought up in the quiet white house in the moors: of Aunt Howell, and Cousin Jennifer and Cousin Sarah, her daughters; of William Jenkins, the Welsh groom-gardener, with a face like an old white goat, who had been a soldier under Clive, and helped capture the French when they landed at Pembroke. She learned that Christopher had bread and milk for breakfast in a blue-patterned bowl: that he had read *Evelina*, *Robinson Crusoe*, *The Fool of Quality*, the *Moral Tales* of Miss Edgeworth, the plays of Richard Cumberland, the works of Monsieur Perrault and Madame d'Aulnoy, and that the main source of his education gushed from the pages of *Mangnall's Questions*; but that the Reverend Mr. Charles had walked over three times a week to instruct him in Latin and mathematics.

He also told how Baron Ompteda had come riding up the long

valley toward dusk attended by a thin foreign servant; how he had talked in private with Aunt Howell; and then the next day Christopher had been told he was to go away—abroad, to some cousins of his father (he thought) to be educated; and the day after that the baron had returned again, and they had driven down the by-road, along the valley stream, in a post-chaise with red wheels, out into the great world.

This narration came out in no continuous story, but was drawn from him in a rapid fire of questions.

'Where are you going now, Christopher?' the young lady asked at last.

But Christopher could not reply; for he did not know—any more than he knew why they had halted so long at the little resort on their way to the Continent.

'So you are alone with these two gentlemen and their servants?' said the lady, half to herself. 'I think I have seen them. The tall one spends his time getting drunk. The pale one creeps about the inn—ugh! You got rather . . . rather—tired of them, I suppose, and so came here?'

She leaned a little farther forward.

One of her plaits brushed against Christopher's shoulder. He edged closer, against her knees. Goddesses, he felt, must have been such as she—kind and beautiful, and protecting.

'Poor Christopher—no, I think I shall call you Tops . . . It's more friendly, isn't it?' she said, and patted his small arm, and forthwith started back.

'Heaven help the child, he is wringing wet!' And two swift hands explored his body.

'How did you get into a state like this?' . . . Stayed for no answer . . . 'Get up, and stand before the fire.'

She was kneeling now upon the footstool, holding him by the shoulders. He stood before her, with hanging head.

'Tops,' she asked, 'were you very, very frightened, poor lamb, by something?'

He could not bring himself to confess his fear in words; so mutely nodded.

'You are soaked through, and still cold.'

The busy hands went up to his neck, deftly undid buttons, and, with two swift jerks, sent his nightgown to the floor about his feet.

He stood naked before her.

His face and neck turned crimson: he made little modest gestures. He did not dare look up and meet the gaze that enveloped his nudity.

'Fie, Charlotte!' said the lady. 'You embarrass your visitor!'

She took his hands in hers, and rose to her feet.

'Now, Mr. Harnish, you shall see how truly depraved a female can be! You perceive this bed?—In fact you could hardly fail to! It is mine, but it is warm! I suggest that you scuttle into it.'

He scuttled into it—up the high side, down into the depths of the billowy feather-bed, sheets and blankets up to the chin. He was no longer frightened, or alone, or naked.

For the first time he smiled a little, as he lay there watching Charlotte about the room.

There was the door to be locked, his night shift to be spread upon the footstool close to the fire, the candles to be extinguished —all but that which burned upon the bedside table with the baize top beside the little pile of books and the glass of water and the bottle of toilet water.

Then Charlotte sat on the bed beside him.

'Comfortable, Tops?' she asked.

'Yes, ma'am.'

' "Yes, Charlotte",' she corrected. 'It is bed etiquette to call your companion by his or her Christian name. There are exceptions, of course. Did you know that?'

'No, ma'am!'

' "No, Charlotte!" '

'No, Charlotte!' And they both smiled at one another, and found it all perfectly enchanting.

'Well, Tops, this is the first time I have ever been to bed with a man! . . . I don't suppose it will be the last! . . . And here goes!'

With that she slid under the sheets, down the slope of the billowy feather-bed, and into the very valley that Christopher had pressed out into its depths. Her warm body touched his. He turned a little towards her, smiled confidingly into her smiling eyes, was taken into her arms, and went to sleep held tight in security and warmth, pillowed against the curve of a soft shoulder.

Chapter 3

Morning Exercise . . . with Pistols

BARON OMPTEDA APPEARED LATE THE NEXT MORNING, more sallow than ever, more silent. He ate no breakfast, drank nothing except light table ale, and replied with grunts to the barbed witticisms of Heywood. Obviously the lecture of the previous night was remembered, and still rankled. He sat sulkily at table, picking his teeth with German thoroughness, his eyes fixed on the white splash of plaster scored by the pistol bullet on the wall.

During the night the London mail had arrived, and with it the newspapers. One or two had been bespoken, and Heywood rose from the table when he had finished his meal, and took up his stand in the window, with a small sheet in his hands.

Everything about him was neat and dapper past belief. His high-collared green coat fitted without a wrinkle: his stock looked as if no human hand had ever touched it; the black satin fob ribbons that depended from the pockets right and left were of an exact length: the polish of his Hessian boots was only equalled by the whiteness of the small-clothes into which he seemed to have been poured. He wore no vestige of whisker, and his servant had shaved him to such a nicety that one could have sworn no hair ever grew on the marble white cheek.

The sun shone over his shoulder into the room, winked on the silver urn, revealed the dark stubble on Ompteda's chin, and winked, after that revelation, on the usual inn huddle of plate on the side-board—salvers, toast-racks, urns, jugs, coffee-pots, tea-pots, muffin-dishes—under the picture of the celebrated encounter between Richard Humphreys and Daniel Mendoza at Odiham on January 9, 1788.

Heywood looked up from the newspaper.

'A paragraph, my dear baron,' he remarked at last, 'about our kind . . . patron! Very sad! Very upsetting!'

A sudden, swift flash lightened Ompteda's long face—as if he had hoped to learn that his kind patron was dead. It faded as swiftly as it came—such a hope was asking too much of God!—but a trace of interest remained. He raised his eyes from the tablecloth.

Thus encouraged Heywood read aloud:

'*A Royal Duke:*—We hear on unimpeachable authority that a Royal Duke, now residing on the Continent, contemplates a speedy return to England with his consort and infant son. We would remind him of the words used by Mr. Bennet during a recent debate in the House of Commons upon the subject of his marriage—"I have no hesitation in saying that the union is an improper one, however much the parties may be suited to each other from their habits and morals." We would remind him that by their vote the House of Commons, the elected representatives of the nation, concurred in that view. We would remind him that his Revered Mother, the late Queen, declined to receive his bride. We would remind him of the names Sellis and Garth, and ask if they mean anything to him? We would ask whether he still cares to see the P——s S——? The respect the British Public feels for the good old King, his Father, for the Prince Regent, his brother, and for the rest of the Royal Family, does not extend to this Royal Duke. We suggest that he should stay in Hanover, and not bring his unfortunate proclivities for scandal and intrigue to these shores.

'The ostensible reason for His Royal Highness's visit is the precarious health of the young prince, and the need to consult certain eminent London surgeons.'

Ompteda smacked his lips.

'Dey say all dat?' he inquired in a satisfied tone. 'Dere's no newsbaber in Germany dat would dare say as mooch!'

'*The Times*', said Heywood, meditating upon the liberty of the Press, 'has had no hesitation in imputing murder to our patron! Regardless of the decencies it has even told the Regent that his unfortunate wife is the "greatest and perhaps best" woman of the day. Very free we are in dear old England! Reptiles, imbeciles, traitors, assassins—those sort of words are the small change of journalistic chit-chat nowadays!'

'Id is good—very good,' commented Ompteda. 'And de baby die, *vielleicht*? Sins of de fader visited on de child!'

'The sins of the mother, as well,' replied Heywood. 'She is, probably, every whit as pox-ridden as he is. You must ask after that too attractive Pole of hers, Eugène de Bréza, when you reach Hanover. The Duchess will have discovered, I fear, that he is a young man with venereal disease and no principles.'

The misfortunes of the Duke and Duchess of Cumberland had a tonic effect on Baron Ompteda. He brightened up, rang the bell loudly for the waiter, ordered his favourite breakfast dish of grilled sausages with apple sauce, and relapsed into pleasant day-dreams. As an appetizer he snuffed up violently a small sort of sand-dune of pale snuff that he had poured on to his wrist.

'Id vill make a difference if de liddle brince dies—a so great difference!' he remarked when his breakfast had arrived; and Heywood, having finished the news, was studying the advertisements for toilet preparations, macassar oil, 'Mineral Magnets', and the herbal fumigation cure for toothache. The captain looked over the top of his paper with a coldly speculative eye.

'Why should it?' he retorted in even tones. 'Our august patron's ambitions are for himself, and not for any son.'

Ompteda lestered a roll with his fork, and with such violence that he all but broke the dish. He spread butter on the bread with a lavish hand, bit a deep crescent into it, and chewed the mouthful, his entire face working vigorously with the slow act of mastication. The bristles of his long upper lip retained a good deal of the snuff he had taken; he had a sort of dirty yellow moustache stained upon him.

When at length he spoke, his mouth was so full that his naturally thick speech became almost incomprehensible.

'You don't mean,' Heywood understood him to say, 'that we— still—go on?'

'I mean precisely that,' replied Heywood.

'Herr Gott!' moaned Ompteda. He put down the roll, and surveyed his breakfast with distaste. 'I do nod like id! I do nod like id!'

'Must we go over all that ground again?' asked Heywood, with
a trifle of weariness in his voice, rather than impatience. 'Nothing
at all is altered in our plans. The circumstances are unchanged.
We—I am going ahead as originally arranged.'

'Id is *schrecklich*—horrible,' said Ompteda, pushing back his
chair. 'I do nod like id!'

'Strangely enough, my dear Ompteda, your personal feelings have
not been consulted. You play a very minor part in the affair . . .
And, to tell you the truth, I am becoming tired of your objections.'

Heywood's low voice became still lower. He spoke so slowly that
every word stood with a separate menace in his sentences. 'If you
think that your squeaks of protest are going to make any difference,
you are sadly mistaken! You don't appear to realize that, if you are
paid for treason, you've got to do treason.

'You are paid to do the Regent's dirty work. Good! You do it!
You are also paid to tell Cumberland all about that dirty work.
Fine! You do it, too! You are not asked to associate yourself in any
way with what use is made of the information. Neither are you paid
to squall because you don't like the use to which we turn the information. Is that clear?'

Ompteda remained silent, staring at the congealing sausages.

'You tell us that the Regent has found out about this boy after
all these years. That he is going to send him in your charge out of
harm's way—where there is less likelihood of any more scandals
or blackmail being arranged. The Duke of Cumberland is interested. He is always interested in little things of that sort, which
may turn out usefully.

'What is the consequence?—I hurry to meet you here on your
journey from Cornwall. Nobody knows me: nobody certainly has
ever heard the name I go under at the moment. I suggest the boy is
run down. The local doctor agrees—very open to suggestion! Very
open! The boy stays here on his advice. Whatever happens now is
nothing to do with you. It's all very pretty and straightforward!'

'Very britty!' said Ompteda.

Heywood looked at the melancholy face and the sagging shoulders, his pale lips curved in a sneer.

'If you continue to complain I shall think that you are weary of
serving our—patron. He is not quite like the Regent. A strange,

furious, unforgiving fellow! A remorseless, violent fellow, for all that he's half blind. Not the sort to put up with any obstacles when a crown's the prize. Not any obstacle at all!—Baron or . . . !'

'Ssh! Ssh!' said Ompteda, and clapped his hands over his ears. 'Somevun vill hear! Somevun vill hear!'

'Pull yourself together, you damned fool!' said Heywood with extraordinary violence, although his voice was not raised and the expression on his face was unchanged. 'If suspicions ever are aroused, it will be you who arouse them. Remember what I told you last night—that with wine in, wits go out. To avoid people even thinking that you might babble in your cups, it might be as well to indulge yourself less in liquor! An unfavourable report from me might have strange repercussions!'

As he spoke he again raised his heavy head, and gave a quick darting look at Ompteda, who shrank before it.

'No! No!' he muttered quickly. 'You misunderstood me. Vod I do nod like—is dat you mix two businesses up together. I do nod like id either dat we should be so near—so very near to vod is to happen. Vod you say our patron (as you call him) desires, dat shall be. I do nod like your way of doing id. Dat is all!'

The long man stirred uneasily and rammed another great load of snuff into his hairy nostrils.

'I am suitable, berhaps, for a knave,' he continued apologetically, 'but nod for a scoundrel! Liddle things—nod big! Zo small adventures—nod . . . !'

'History,' said Captain Heywood acknowledging the heroic implication in the word 'scoundrel', 'is made by scoundrels, but not by knaves.'

He dropped the matter, and rang the bell for his servant. The man—a lean, small Gascon—arrived at once, and was given the orders for the day in quick and fluent French.

Heywood paused. Something had occurred to him: he swept the room with a swift glance.

'Where is the child this morning, Fonblanque?' he asked. 'I have not seen him to-day.'

'He was dressed very early, monsieur—already before I came to call him. I gave him his breakfast, and now he is in the inn garden.'

'By himself?'

'With a lady, monsieur.'

'What lady?'

'I do not know, monsieur.'

'I will not have him walk with ladies, or with anyone except myself or you, in the garden or anywhere else; or talk with anyone except when you are there, or I say he may. Is that clear? He is to be kept from all contact with the outside world. It is you who are responsible in future. . . .' Then, after the man had gone, 'There will be enough of questions afterwards. We want no suspicions before.

'You see, my dear Ompteda, our groundwork demands another little comedy—an airy trifle—un morceau—just like that . . .' He raised his shoulders, spread out his hands in mockery of the traditional French gesture of depreciation, but his smile was very chill, and the eyes that caught Ompteda's eyes and held them mesmerized were as cold as any snake's.

The baron rose from table, stammered an excuse, and made an awkward exit from the room.

He sought a refuge from the sneering face in the cosy snuggery where red short curtains shielded the inmates from view through the passage windows; sought a refuge from fear and thought in innumerable glasses of gin and hot water—in overhearing half-comprehended discussion between the landlord and his cronies on the price of cattle and corn, the health of the King, the Duke of York's dropsy, and the inevitable story of rick burning and farm outrage and equally inevitable hanging.

Although it was market day few of the farmers had yet finished their business, and not all were welcome to the landlord's inner room. So it was that but three or four had assembled there, and they were clustered at a round table a little away from the fire beside which the foreigner sat, with his long thin legs—in tightly strapped blue trousers—stretched straight before him.

First one, and then another would listen to their comrades' babble with big red face turned speculatively towards the dishevelled elegance, or would peer over the top of raised tankard.

The landlord's obsequious 'Yes, my lord', as he brought further spirituous provender, added to the interest.

Even Red-Face sitting with his back to the fire did serious damage to his neckcloth and his rheumatics, by the frequency with which he craned over his shoulder. The lowered voices told that a new subject of prime interest for conversation had been found.

To this expectant audience came Heywood—at first looking in through half-opened door as if in search of someone; finding that someone with a smile of recognition; and then stepping gracefully into the centre of the room.

Ompteda was the last to be aware of him. Heywood was, indeed, at his elbow and addressing him before he realized his presence.

'Ah, there you are, my dear baron! I have been looking for you everywhere,' he said in his cold, clear tones.

As he spoke a hush fell on the group near by, and it prepared to listen and be interested. The tapster, hearing a new voice, appeared in the doorway to the bar.

'Is this yours?' continued Captain Heywood, suddenly producing, like a conjuror, a pistol from some recess in his garments. 'For it certainly is not mine.'

He put the weapon into the nerveless hands of Ompteda, who turned it over several times, before he could control his twitching lips sufficiently to admit the ownership.

It was one of a pair of pocket pistols, barely as long as a man's hand, and very plain. The silver shield on the wooden butt bore neither crest nor initial. Although short-barrelled it carried a large ball, and had a hair-trigger that folded flat and was without a guard. As Heywood had said once before, it was a weapon as deadly as an asp—and a child could use it.

' 'Tes a pistol!' said Red-Face to Red-Face; and the farthest of them half rose, and craned across the table in gaping inquisitiveness.

Heywood recovered the weapon from the shaking hand, and examined it as if he had not properly studied it before. He held it up a little towards an outer window so that he could see it the better, for the room looked on to the courtyard of the inn and was low-ceilinged and not too light.

'A ve-ery nice weapon, Ompteda,' he remarked. 'But I would ask you to lock it in the case and put it where the prying hands of your small ward will not meddle.'

The white-aproned tapster caught the implication and forwarded the drama, glad to be able to take an intelligent speaking part with such distinguished players.

'The young gentleman, again, if I may ask your lordships?' he questioned.

Heywood deigned, by a glance, to include him in the explanation he offered the wretched Ompteda.

'How the lad discovered it, I do not know—or where. I noticed a bulge in his coat as he was going out walking with Fonblanque . . .' —'The capt'n's man,' interjected the tapster by way of clarification to the Red-Faces.—'I found it in his pocket—loaded. The young master told me, glib as you please, that he might shoot a rabbit on his walk. I thought it better to correct the idea—and him—on the spot. You will not think I have unduly infringed on your prerogatives, my dear fellow, I hope!'

Heywood smiled slightly, the nicely graduated smile of an indulgent parent who has been forced by convention to reprove precocity.

Red-Faces guffawed: Ompteda did not; his long countenance had grown sallow, and his uneasy eyes roamed restlessly about the room. He ran hairy fingers between neckband and throat.

'I vill tell my man to lock de bistols avay,' he grunted at last, hurriedly pulling himself together to meet the emergency.

The tapster, venturing into the company, gave Red-Faces a full and inaccurate account of the narrow escape of Fred, the fat waiter, but a few days back.

Red-Face number one expressed the view that the young master would end by a-shooting of hisself. Number two thought it extremely probable, and hazarded the theory that boys would be boys, that it might not be a bad thing if the young gentleman were to hurt himself—just a little—with a pistol, for it would learn him, and burned children feared the fire.

Heywood courteously encouraged the interesting discussion, by asking the gentlemen if they would not drink with him; and, thus fortified, Red-Face number three became reminiscent of sudden death. He was something of a connoisseur of bloody crime.

Ompteda did not understand it all. The broad West Country speech was beyond him. He caught a constant repetition of the word 'blood', of 'gore', of 'brains'; and the goggling eyes of the circle, avid for every horrid detail, enabled him to guess that a dish of horror was spread before them.

Of a sudden he felt extremely sick—physically, mentally, spiritually sick. He rose like a man smitten with illness, and made for the door.

He went to his room: he was sick.

Then he sat on his bed, shuddering as with cold, his hands deep in his pockets, and meditated flight—knowing well that it would be futile.

There was a flask of brandy in his dressing case; and he tossed down a great draught.

Then he burst into tears, and, with drops coursing down his huge nose, his chest gulping with unrestrained sobs like those of a child, he went rummaging in his trunks.

But his case of pistols was nowhere to be found. It had utterly vanished.

It was the next morning—after being cheered by an over-night vision of Charlotte escorted on the stairs by an enormous man with badger-grey hair, who was dressed in an extremely tight-waisted mulberry-coloured surtout—that Christopher was made aware of a change in his daily programme.

It was barely light when he was aroused by Heywood who was fully dressed. He awoke to find the captain, enveloped in a black cloak of military pattern, at his bedside, and to encounter for one brief moment an anxious searching gaze, that would appear to have been attempting to wrest the secret of the child's future from his unconscious sleeping face.

'I am getting fat, and you are not obtaining sufficient exercise,' Heywood said. It was a statement of policy, not an explanation. 'Therefore you and I will go out walking before breakfast. We will start to-day. You will be ready in five minutes.'

The child's coat with the two-tiered cape was in the sitting-room, over a chair-back, before the newly lit fire. Heywood held it for him to slip his arms into—the only recognition he gave of the child's presence either then or throughout their entire walk.

The coat seemed to weigh most uncommonly heavy. Christopher put his hands into the side pockets. There was something large, and weighty, and cold as death in each. His fingers closed on those things, recognized their shape, and were about to withdraw them; questions were rising to his lips; and then he found Heywood looking at him with so peculiar a regard that a chill of fear froze in his heart, and he dropped the pistols back and was silent.

They walked, then—as they were to do on many days afterwards —through the town, and towards the sea, till they came to a white lodge set in a high wall and line of bare beech trees. There they turned up a lane which looped the grounds of a low house, running at one point so close to the side of the dwelling, that you could have tossed a biscuit, without effort, across the evergreen hedge and narrow strip of grass, into the French windows. In the sunshine you could see people moving inside.

After making the circuit they went home.

Still later Christopher was made to take that walk by himself, unaccompanied except by the deadly things within his pockets. He started from the inn at eight o'clock each morning; he never diverged from the allotted path by so much as a yard, nor dallied unnecessarily, in the manner of small boys, by the way.

Up the hill; past the market-house on its squat arches; across the market-place with the Waterloo obelisk, like a sugar loaf, in the middle; through the churchyard passage into sight of the sea; back on your tracks a bit, skirting the elm-set green until you saw the whitewashed lodge and the stained stone wall.

There were small cypresses, shaped like giant silk cocoons on stalks, along the hedge in the lane against the house; and, on the other side of the track, a little dark copse of pine and yew and larch and holly, behind a high wall. There you waited at a gate, according to instructions, until the church clock struck the three-quarter hour—in case Captain Heywood should come.

But he never did.

Still, it was quite interesting. There seemed to be many people in the house.

Once a gentleman stood at the corner window on the top floor. His face was covered with white stuff—lather perhaps.

And at another time a lady came to the French windows, carrying a baby in her arms. She was there but an instant, and Christopher did not see her go, for something crackled in that sinister little wood behind him, and he turned his head to see that no monsters lurked in its recesses.

The rest of the day he had much to himself. There were silent meals in the sitting-room, at which Ompteda, if he had not over-drunk, guzzled greedily and noisily, while Heywood delicately picked lean from fat, and the whiter parts from over-ripe cheese. The dinner hour was never certain: it depended when Heywood should suddenly appear after a mysterious absence, unruffled, immaculate and economical of word.

Otherwise Christopher was left to amuse himself as best he could, although Fonblanque was never far away.

In the mornings he would like to sit on a small stool before the harness-room fire, while Fonblanque, in broken English, exchanged salacious jests with the stable helpers, as they polished saddles or rubbed dubbin into cracking traces on the big wooden stands. The dark walls glinted with burnished bits and curbs and pole chains, and long reins hung snakily from a dozen pegs. Sometimes they would give him to clean a tarnished silver snaffle, delicate and strong, with perhaps a thread of chewed bright grass still clinging to the joint. And with it a broken saucer and a bit of rag. At other times they would fill a little sack with sand and powdered brick and chains that needed burnishing; and he would sit there shaking the jingling, jangling, clinking bundle until each arm was tired.

In their way everyone was kind to the lonely child. The fat barmaid in the four-ale bar let him sit on a high stool in the ill-lit cubby-hole from which she kept watch, while she washed glasses in a lead-lined sink.

Once she gave him a tiny glass of something very sweet and strong and hot, that tasted of nuts.

Fonblanque, missing him, had caught sight of the yellow locks through the little window which opened on to the sanded bar with its settle and open hearth. He had come in, although there was barely room for all three within, and there had been an amorous horse-play, which ended in the girl squeaking when he pinched her plump behind, and the arrival of the landlady who had said, 'For shame! And the child there, too! Now do a' done, do!'

So they had both been turned out.

The head waiter, who looked as though he exuded from his fat face and body and clothing all the grease of all the meals he ever served—bar that which was left on the dirty plates—went to some trouble on his behalf. He brought him all the literature of the inn, and piled it for him on the seat of his secret lair—the bay-window that jutted out like a watch-tower into the main street of the town.

There were two tattered volumes of *Tom Jones* out of an edition of four; Smollett's *Adventures of an Atom*, with neither beginning nor end; a work on Land Drainage, and a complete *Innocent Adultery*.

'Quite a scholard!' said he. 'Better scholard nor shot!' and smiled showing a mouthful of rotten teeth like broken palings.

With these books Christopher would remain coiled up—now dipping into a quarter-comprehended page; now pressing a nose against a window pane and dipping into the more comprehensible life of the little town, as it flowed up and down the street; now lost in the fairy world that his imagination conjured up. Until dusk.

Then, if Fonblanque remained aloof, and Ompteda were still immersed in the task of submerging his woes in drink, he would come out, and stand at the corner of the gallery that ran about the inner courtyard of the inn. From there he could watch the constant comings and goings below—smocked carters greasing the axles of wagons piled with goods first-floor-high, booted farmers crossing to the bar with snuffling dogs, the passage of a stray elegant with tas-selled boots and dainty cane, the washing of a high curricle with yellow wheels, the weary crawl of jaded post-horses with the traces across their backs towards stable and oats.

It was an even better vantage point than that, for, in the angle of the house behind him, the stairs wound down to the coffee room and offices of the inn, and upwards to the bedrooms. In that half-hour at dusk the place awoke from its afternoon doze: there was a constant passing up and down of servants and of guests.

Twice he saw Charlotte: once she saw him and came to him, and kissed him, and stood beside him silently looking down on the scene below.

'Things better, Tops?' she asked, holding his hand.

'Yes, ma'am—Charlotte!' he had answered.

'If you want to see me again, Tops,' she said, 'you know where to find me . . .'

And at that moment Ompteda had come up the stairs, and she had stooped and kissed him again, and gone, disdainfully passing the tall man without a flicker of a glance.

Christopher had come to know many other people by sight. There was a big red-faced man, bandy-legged by reason of the worn sides to the heels of his rusty wellingtons. His tread shook the gallery, and his voice was never less than a bellow. Sometimes a woman in lilac with puffed sleeves and a great bonnet was with him—every whit as blowzy as himself. . . . The whole inn would know his needs—'Fred! The grummet and I want noyeau and buttered toast! . . . Bill! The grummet and I want moy chay! . . . Fred! Moy little lady and I want some shrub—rum-shrub!' Now and again he threw a word at Christopher as he passed, like a man throwing a kind word to a dog.

Most often, however, he saw the gentleman he had seen with Charlotte—the vast man in the incredibly tight-fitting mulberry-coloured suit.

At first he had just said, 'Ha! boy! Good-day, boy!' whenever he saw Christopher.

Then one twilight he had stopped beside the small figure. Christopher was conscious of something very big and friendly, that smelled of tobacco and snuff and horses and leather. He looked up at a big red face and a big red nose and green eyes that twinkled under bushy eyebrows, and beneath a thatch of tousled iron-grey hair.

'Ha, boy!' said Charlotte's friend. 'Good-day, boy! You're the boy, are you, that's seduced my ward, are you?'

'Yes, sir,' said Christopher, and smiled timidly up at the human tower.

The big man laughed: he roared: he shook with titanic laughter. The incredibly tight coat strained at each button across his enormous chest. The last button of his long hunting waistcoat flew from the restraint of his pinched waist. Two great globes of tears trickled down his cheeks.

'You've succeeded, have you, my jim-along-jam, where a hundred have failed, have you?'

He slapped a great thigh; from some recess of his person a thin jangle answered the blow.

In the flash of a moment a preternatural solemnity swept over his face. He thrust a great hand into his right fob-pocket, and produced a watch, from which was pendent on black ribbon a cluster of seals; regarded it anxiously, and laid it on the broad flat balustrade under Christopher's nose. From the left pocket he extracted another, regarded that, too, and laid it beside its mate.

There were little figures on the black and silver dials. On one, two plumed negro warriors stood, guarding the time-face with lifted axes under a golden bell. On the other, two goats were salient across the hours, horns butting at a silver gong.

Charlotte's friend pressed a knob on each; and as they lay there each time-piece struck the hour; the figures were charmed to a sudden life, warriors clanging with rhythmic strokes upon the bell, goats stooping their horns against the disk above them.

It was obvious that all was well with the striking trains. His face cleared like that of a large child, then clouded again. There was a variation of a minute between the two!

'Ha, boy!' said he. 'What's the use of two watches if you can never tell the time? Tell me!'

Christopher could oblige him with no information.

'Set one this morning a minute on by the other, but I don't know which! Do I put one on, boy? Or do I put one back, boy?'

Christopher again was unable to advise him. He had been mesmerized by the volcanic activity into which the little machines had burst, and followed regretfully their disappearance into the fob-pockets, where they lay bulging the outline of Charlotte's friend's dark grey pantaloons.

'Must find out, boy, if you don't know!' said the large man. 'Golden rule, boy, always know the time—know the time!' And vanished down the creaking stairs.

Chapter 4

Meditations of a Father of Thirteen

A TALL AND PORTLY GENTLEMAN IN THE EARLY FIFTIES, wearing nothing but his nightcap, stepped to the flat sponge-bath set on a fleecy white rug before his dressing-room fire.

He had a high complexion and a rather foolish face, despite its aquiline nose. As he tested the temperature with his foot, he hummed beneath his breath in a dignified manner, as if he did honour to the tune in remembering it and the action in performing it.

The water was quite adequately warm, and the substantial glass screen about the bath conserved the glow of the well-made fire, and shielded him from stray draughts in a most efficient manner.

All was well with the world! The early sunshine flooded in on the cream walls through the square panes of the high windows, showed up the richness of long purple curtain and thick-piled grey carpet, the sleek sheen of mahogany tall-boy and high chest, and made a silver lake of the tilted cheval-glass in the centre of the room.

Beyond one door of wine-coloured wood his comfortable lady lay, sunk in her billowy, snowy bed—rather high-coloured perhaps, and not in her very first youth, but on the whole satisfactory in many ways, and properly grateful for Olympian condescension. Beyond the other door, there waited call a valet whose gravity, responsiveness, and discretion were past belief.

And downstairs, too, a large plump baby should be making a large meal in a few minutes—he glanced at the clock, for Our household ran to a time schedule like a military establishment . . . yes, in eleven minutes—against the large breasts of a large, plump nurse! His baby! Heiress after him, perhaps, to the throne of Great

61

Britain, to a score of realms beyond the seas, to Upper and Lower Canada, to vast tracts in India and Africa, to islands like green and gold gems in distant oceans, to a whole continent half the world away!

That fat baby, guzzling and nuzzling against her fat nurse in the print dress downstairs, after him would be heiress to all that had been wrested from Frenchman and Dutchman, Spaniard, Indian and Mogul, and feathered, fuzzed or naked native, by generations of adventurers and by a million lives! *Perhaps* . . . and perhaps not!

Edward Duke of Kent got into his bath, and, squatting on his hunkers, took up his turkey sponge. He remembered his nightcap in time and tore it off, revealing his shiny bald crown with a fringe of even shinier jet-black hair.

The nightcap was sooty-stained inside—he had newly dyed his scanty locks last night—and he flung it on the floor behind him, where he should not see it. For it reminded him of things best left forgotten—of fading hair, of falling hair, and thus of spent youth, of the insidious passage of years. It was better, though, than the elaborate boyish toupee of his brother, the Regent, or the fussy flaxen wig of his brother Adolphus of Cambridge—who was seven years younger.

The warm water from his vigorous sponging cascaded down his broad chest into the bath. It left a narrow wet line across his person, where the drops gathered in the guttering wrinkled by the protuberance of his stomach.

He patted the protuberance in order to assure himself that it was no larger than its wont. He even slapped it: but it gave out a firm and dignified note, for it was not just a flabby mass. Not like the Regent's great stomach, which swung about and dropped before him like the sail of a full-rigged ship, now that he had given up stays! He was little more than a grown-up lad, it seemed to him, although his brothers were elderly men while yet their aged father's addle-head bore the crown.

The Regent could not last for long. Cherry brandy and his fat women would see to that! The Conyngham would make sure that he did not marry again—if he ever freed himself from Caroline.

York had dropsy and his wife was dying.

Clarence, the half-wit!—Well, poor William was as bad a life.

William, in fact, ought to be in a strait-jacket. William was definitely eccentric to the point of imbecility. And William's kindly duchess could never again successfully undertake motherhood! Baillie had told him so—and Baillie ought to know! . . . Drip, splash of sponge water. . . . Ve-e-ery satisfactory! . . . More drips and splashes. . . . Ve-e-ery satisfactory!

He rose erect, shining wet in the firelight and sunlight. He looked appreciatively at his hairy chest and forearms, avoided the unfortunate curving contretemps of his belly, and admired his muscular thighs and well-shaped calves.

A fine figure of a man, his consciousness told him. He would out-live the three: he was younger, more vigorous! He might even have another child, a man-child—quite soon. His wife was a buxom creature, made for child-bearing.

He stepped out on to the bath-rug, and vigorously towelled himself before the fire.

Little Victoria—Vicky—was a fine child, too! Plump as butter. Healthy as they made 'em. No doubt about it. His . . . and he paused to tot the total up—and then to count again, and even to check once more . . . thirteenth child! The other twelve, of course, had been born the wrong side of the blanket.

Thirteen children! He was a very hearty fellow. No question about it. . . . Thirteenth! . . . Thirteenth child! A shadow crossed his mind. Thirteen was notoriously an unlucky number!

The towelling slowed down while he brooded on the figure, and cast about for consolation. . . . Thirteenth! . . . Then there came back to him from long ago the prophecy of a gipsy woman. He was to die in happiness. His only child was to be a great Queen. That meant his only legitimate child, of course! Well, Vicky was his only legitimate child, and she was indubitably a female. Her ways, apart from her anatomy, already told that—a very determined young female too!

How could the crone—he remembered now that it was at Gibraltar, oh so long ago!—know that he would have a legal child and that one female? He was living with the St. Laurent then. No talk of marriage there!

To be a great Queen! Odd—very odd!

He wrapped himself in his towels, and rang the little silver handbell which waited as unobtrusively on the mantelpiece as Sheldon waited for its summons without.

With the quiet opening of the door and the appearance of that smooth-moving black figure, the demeanour of the towel-clad gentleman changed.

A moment before, he had been the human being, Edward of Kent, chatting very frankly and confidentially with himself. Now he became ducal, dignified, royal—a Royal Highness, potential occupant of the greatest throne in the world, progenitor of a Queen-to-be. It was nonsense to say that no man was a hero to his valet: he was—not perhaps a hero, but—a god, a royal god. Sheldon utterly believed in him: that was essential in your subordinates—that they should thoroughly believe in you. His manner, and that of Sheldon, showed the position was understood quite clearly between them.

He was inducted, with the grave ceremonial with which a priest is robed for mass, into a vest, an elaborately pleated shirt, his drawers; even the insertion of his lower limbs into the pale grey small-clothes that revealed their royal contours was a worshipful ritual. He was robed in a dressing-gown of dark red silk. It was a parade. Life, indeed, except in bed and bath, was made up of parades. He liked parades. They called him 'The Corporal'—Creevy once had told him. Hardly dignified, perhaps; but then, Buonaparte had been called the Little Corporal, even when he was Emperor. The bestowal of a nickname, Creevy had explained, was a sign of popularity. He was amazingly popular, of course—not like the rest of them, particularly Cumberland! Cumberland, with his face like an angry eagle—the thought of him gave him the shudders.

He twitched his portentous eyebrows.

'Ha, Sheldon!' said he, in abrupt barrack-square manner. 'No dispatches this morning for me?'

'I am instructed that there is nothing that calls for Your Royal Highness's immediate attention.' Sheldon's attitude neatly conveyed the suggestion of extreme relief that His Royal Highness should not have further claims on his royal and valuable time, and surprise that wagon loads of urgent dispatches should not be awaiting so important—and royal—a personage. The duke rarely had

any correspondence of moment, but he kept up a voluminous let-
ter-writing, about anything or nothing, and a secretary and two
clerks to deal with it.

'Odd, Sheldon! Odd!'

That His Royal Highness should condescend to make a comment for the benefit of so humble a servant was acknowledged by
Sheldon's deep bow. He bowed so frequently: he was so often in
the position of being about to bow, or of recovering from a bow,
that no man above-stairs had ever seen him quite erect.

'The London newspapers are here, Your Royal Highness. I ventured to think that Your Royal Highness might care to inspect
the *Morning Chronicle.*'

From a side table Sheldon produced that newspaper. It was two
days old, but it had been ironed so that no crease or fold should
mar the ease with which royal eyes might glance over contents, or
royal hands spread it out to view.

It had also been a little dampened, so that it seemed as though
straight from the press. His Royal Highness always liked his newspapers so when away from town. The synthetic newness livened up
news items that were two or more days stale.

'Any news this morning, Sheldon?' he barked.

'I had not ventured to look at Your Royal Highness's newspaper,
Your Royal Highness,' said Sheldon, presenting the paper to him
on a silver tray.

Quite right! Respectful, too! Royal Highnesses should hear the
news first and then pass it on, if they saw fit.

In a condescending manner he ran his eye along the columns,
standing before the side window which looked out on to the narrow lane at the side of the house.

Suddenly he paused; peered more closely at the small-type head-
line, read the paragraph beneath with pursed-up mouth and eyebrows raised in an expression conveying just so much shocked surprise as a Royal personage should permit himself.

We were informed on the best authority last night that the condition of our aged and revered Monarch, King George the Third,
has taken a turn for the worse, and is causing the most extreme
anxiety. His Royal Highness the Prince Regent is hourly in expec-

tation of receiving a summons to the bedside of his beloved Sire at
Windsor.

Why had he not been told? Why had no one written to inform
him? Why should he learn news such as this through the columns
of the Press? It was a conspiracy to ignore him—a conspiracy to
keep him out in the cold by the Regent, by York, by Clarence!
They were all jealous of him because he had an heiress, and they
had none!

He would write to George about it! He would not be ignored—
he, who would outlive them all, and was to reign one day in their
stead; whose daughter, his thirteenth child, was to be Queen! . . .

There was a crack, as of a giant whip, from without: a sound that
was followed, quicker than speech or thought, by the crash of
shivered glass and then by an appalling smash. There was a heavy
fall in the room below. A woman began to scream and a child to
wail.

Oh, God! What was that?

He was no longer royal and splendid, foreseeing and youthful.
He was an elderly, frightened man.

His mouth was working as he turned to Sheldon.

'Thirteenth! Oh, Christ!' said he, and staggered against the wall.

Downstairs the woman went on screaming. Beyond his doors
there were a flutter of voices and a scurry of hurried feet.

Sheldon did not permit himself to view his royal master stripped
of his royalty and his masterfulness.

One quick glance through the side window had showed the
empty grass plat without, a small frozen figure in the lane beyond.
In the sunny windlessness the faintest wisp of grey smoke was
drifting over the small figure's head into the darkness of the copse
behind.

With consolatory murmurs masking the swiftness of his ef-
ficiency, Sheldon glided from the room, flowed down the stairs,
threw an instruction to two powdered plush giants at the nursery
door, and entered, locking the door after him.

There was a great star radiating from a hole in the French windows, and underfoot crackled the glass of a large mirror that had
been shivered into atoms on the wall behind him.

In a low nursing chair, before the window, was slumped a fat and screaming woman. The bodice of her print dress was wide open, and heavy breasts hung nearly to the waist. Her eyes were shut; her great red hands were clenched on the vast spread lap, and on the shoulder of her gown was a little streak of blood.

Face downward on the rug at her side was an apoplectic baby wriggling convulsively in the entanglement of its long-clothes.

Another and young woman, her face chalk-white, stood as if paralysed beside a mahogany swinging cot, one hand clenched on the curtains of rose-coloured silk.

'Shut your noise, you screeching cow!' said Sheldon suavely to the screaming woman, and scooped up the baby from the floor.

Its face was scarlet and crumpled from yelling. Its tiny fat arms in ridiculous pleated sleeves beat frantically. A small smear of blood on the lace-fringed linen of its shift caught the valet's eye.

'Shut up, cow! bitch! sow!' said Sheldon with low-pitched insistence, inserted a hand under the baby's wrapping and shot the mass in one quick movement over its head. For a second he surveyed the royal nudity in front; turned the fat wriggling creature over between his capable hands, surveyed its back, and then veiled it again, satisfied that it had come to no harm. He brought the younger woman to her senses with two obscene and bitter words, and handed her the child.

Then he bent over the wet-nurse.

'Pull yourself together, you incestuous cow!' he said, and kicked her fat calves with a pointed shoe, so that in amazed indignation her screams died down and she sat up.

'Put your cap straight! You look like a drab after a street fight! . . . Do your dress up, you great lump of . . .' he sought a moment for the right word, '. . . of sour milk! You are only grazed, the worse luck!'

Already there were urgent knockings, questionings, rustlings at the door. Through the shattered glass of the French window he saw two large figures crossing the grass, each gripping firmly a small boy by the arm.

With sleek dignity he slid through the door, swept away inquiries, surged up the stairs, and presented himself, curved as ever, before the stricken man with the trembling hands in the grey and wine-red room.

'A slight accident, Your Royal Highness. Nothing to concern Your Royal Highness at all. Her Royal Highness is entirely unhurt, Your Royal Highness, but is objecting very strongly to the contre-temps. . . . No one is hurt—at all. I would suggest to Your Royal Highness . . .'

He was at a mahogany cupboard by the wall: he was back: from somewhere there had appeared in his hand a cut crystal tumbler on massive salver, winking with yellow fluid.

'. . . a small restorative!'

The elderly face became a little more royal, shook off one fraction of its look of poor worried humanity. Bushy eyebrows settled into lines of authority over eyes in which fear still lurked.

'Ha, Sheldon! Good! You are right, Sheldon! I was *almost* unmanned. Tell me what happened!'

Christopher had waited very dutifully by the gate into the wood, for obedience was a matter of instinct with him.

He did not like doing so, for he was always frightened when he reached the gate. Something told him that there was some unimaginable but intimate connection between the dark small wood with its small strange noises, the low white house, and the cold things that slept in his pockets. But if he were not to wait on that spot for so long as he was told, somehow Captain Heywood would know.

The fat woman had come to the window; she seemed to be undoing her dress; she turned and took a baby from someone behind her. At that moment the church clock began to strike. Christopher stooped to pick up the absurd six-sided hat of grey felt that he had set down on the grass. As he rose he saw a hand come round the gate-post, just above his head—a white plump hand gripping a long pistol, one finger along the barrel, thumb holding the hammer from falling.

He did not want to see the face behind it, veiled in the shadow of the wall; he did not need to see it. All the blood seemed to have drained from his body, and his heart beat against his ribs as if it would shatter them in effort to escape. He was rigid with horror.

And then it happened—while he was still staring over his shoulder upward: a jet of flame from the muzzle, a violent shattering of the silence followed by appalling crashes in the house.

He opened his mouth to cry out, but no sound came, only the snapping of dry twigs, and a rustling within the wood.

Thus, speechless and paralysed with sheer terror, he was seized a few moments afterwards by two large panting men.

'Got the little bastard!' said one of the giants, as triumphantly as if a colossal task had been accomplished; and struck him on the head a heavy blow that dazed him. The other—to intimidate so bloody a scoundrel, without doubt—seized an arm and twisted it until he would have screamed with agony if he had been able.

'Where's the barker?' the man demanded.

He and his companion surveyed the spot, but there was no sign of a weapon. One of them ran a white cotton-gloved hand over Christopher's coat, plunged it into a pocket, and produced the small pistol that nestled like a snake within.

The hammer was down on an exploded cap. From the other pocket he retrieved the companion weapon with the hammer at half-cock.

There was a duet of 'O-o-hs!' and 'A-a-hs!'

'There's a bloody-minded little vagabone!' said the man who had struck him.

'Ripe for the gallows or the hulks!' said the other.

Together they dragged him with threats and curses to the house —by his arms, by his collar, by the top-knot of his ruffled yellow hair.

From sundry doors in the back premises faces peered curiously at him. Two buxom maids, breathing heavily, hung over the balusters of the back stairs, up which he was taken to a small room on the first floor.

A tremendous mahogany wardrobe entirely filled one wall. Facing it, on the window side, and running the length of the room was a row of shoes—dress shoes, court shoes, Hessian boots, wellington boots, hunting boots, lacquered walking boots with tassels in front, high-lows, and even a square-toed comfortable-looking aged pair of mahogany tops. The only other adornments of the room were a little table by the door at the far end, and a black-dressed gentleman with a pale face and plain ruffled shirt.

'A trifle diminutive, our captive!' said Sheldon advancing to meet them, his secretive face permitting itself the ghost of a smile.

Then he saw the angry mark on Christopher's cheek and temple.

'Was it necessary to strike the child!' he said in his low voice, with a violence that was all the more urgent for being subdued. 'Which of you great hulking brutes laid your ugly ham-hand on him?'

'Like an eel to lay hands on, Mr. Sheldon!' protested one of them.

'Don't lie!' said Sheldon icily. 'You couldn't catch a tortoise unless it was tied by one leg!'

He put a hand out for the pistols, which he placed indifferently on the table.

'Leave him with me. Wait downstairs until you are called, and keep the cottonwool out of your cauliflower ears, or you will be given something to stuff them with as soft as iron filings.'

His narrowed gaze was bent on the small boy when they were alone.

'What a desperate small villain!' said he. 'What a violent assassin to disturb the equanimity of a royal duke—royal bullfrog—royal gas-bag! What were you doing, child? Shooting sparrows? And why not? And what's the harm in gingering up that mass of cowmeat downstairs—or raising the wind up old jelly-belly upstairs?'

His questions were not meant to be answered, and he punctuated the soliloquy by consolatory pats.

Not one word, however, conveyed its meaning to the child, who stared at the floor with an ashen face scarred by a crimson bruise.

Sheldon took Christopher's overcoat off, folded it very neatly and placed it away; produced gold-mounted brushes and gently reduced the tousled hair to order; set the little green jacket with the red buttons to rights; dusted the red shoes, and straightened as best he could the creases in the frilled collar of the white lawn blouse.

The child stood as still as a statue under these attentions.

The valet picked up the pistols, looked at them closely, put his nose to muzzle and breech of that which seemed to have been fired. A puzzled expression printed itself on his features.

'Funny that the powder smells so faintly!' he said. 'Very funny! Hardly noticeable at all!' And turned the pistol over in a discontented manner.

Above the door a little bell, at the end of a 'C' spring, rang furiously.

Sheldon took the child's hand in his own, smiled down on him, and led him to the door.

'Don't be frightened of old jelly-belly!' said he in a whisper. 'Don't be frightened of the fat fool! He's only an ordinary idiot. He can't eat you. . . . Now, sir!'

Down a long passage panelled in green they went; down wide shallow stairs hung with enormous oil paintings, to knock deferentially at a high door of mahogany. A voice said, 'Come in'. They entered.

An ineffably royal gentleman stood at a carved and gilded table between two tall windows. A yellow-faced man with a thin red nose warmed himself at the log fire, with one arm against the florid mantelpiece of white marble.

The table was strewn with a hotch-potch of papers, and several thousand books, standardized to dullness by uniform bindings, lurked behind the glass fronts of high wall-cases.

Sheldon, clasping the small hand in his own, advanced to the middle of the polished floor.

'The young person, Your Royal Highness.'

Royalty became terrific in a grandeur that was frozen except for the twitching of portentous eyebrows.

'Has he anything—h'm—to say for himself?'

'I rather gathered, Your Royal Highness,' lied Sheldon smoothly, 'that the young person had been shooting at sparrows.'

'Sparrows! Sparrows!' cried Royalty in a bellow. 'He shoots at my daughter in mistake for a sparrow!'

'It seems to me more likely a case of indifferent marksmanship,' said the man by the fire.

'I gathered that the young person, Your Royal Highness, is anxious to express his regrets for the incident.'

'I do not "gather", myself, that the "young person" is at the present capable of expressing his regrets. Or even capable of speech,' remarked the man by the fire, who had been watching Christopher closely with a professional look.

The small boy's staring eyes were riveted on Royalty: his breath came very fast; his nostrils were pinched.

The duke ignored the interruption.

He turned a baleful glare on to the prisoner before him.

'You shoot sparrows, sir! You shoot at sparrows and you nearly assassinate a Princess of Great Britain! Is the Royal Blood of Britain to be spilled because you go shooting at sparrows—a Throne to be lost and a Royal Line lopped off, for a sparrow?'

We were royally angry—with a small boy who might have wasted the fruits of the marriage which had entailed so much sacrifice; with Ourself for having imagined worse calamities, and for having lost for one minute, even to Ourself, that impeccable majesty which kinship to the throne must bring; with reaction from overwhelming relief.

'Are you aware, sir'—he addressed the swaying child—'that your hands are all but imbrued with blood—with royal blood? That you are within an ace of having been guilty of murder, of high treason? Do you know what the penalty is? Do you know what the gallows means? And beheading—and disembowelling—and quartering? Quartering—being chopped to bits? . . . Do you know that even now you could, and may, be sent to prison? Are you aware that . . . What is your name?'

The child—battered by a torment of thundering words, by the angry glare of the pompous gentleman who addressed him as if he were a public meeting, by a vision of the red joints in a butcher's shop, by the memory of the white plump hand and the wisp of smoke from a pistol gullet—opened his mouth. No words came, only a little whispered groan.

Sheldon felt a sudden clutching at his heart. He cleared his throat, and looked appealingly at the man by the fire.

The latter responded.

'I rather fancy, sir,' said Dr. Stockmar, 'that the young person is about to faint.'

'Faint!' said Majesty-to-be sitting down. 'I won't have him

faint. I never faint. Why should he faint? He might have changed
the history of England. I won't have him change the history of
England. Do you realize, sir, that the little bastard nearly killed
my daughter, sir! My daughter—the Princess Alexandrina Victoria!
Who may be Queen some day. And then you object to me making
him faint. I am conscious, Stockmar, of my duty in showing
him . . .'

'Pfui!' said a fat, comfortable voice. 'Wherefore does Your
Royal Highness all this pother make?'

A plump, youngish woman in a capacious négligé of dark blue
velvet had entered. She had a high colour, a bad-tempered mouth,
and small dark eyes that glistened in a rather watery manner, as
though a thin film of tears were always present.

The duke rose to his feet; Stockmar at the fireplace straightened
himself and bowed.

'Vot one pretty lee-dle boy,' said the duchess in slow halting
English, turning her eyes on 'Christopher. 'But 'e is one ve-ery
badt boy,' she added severely. ''E must vipped be. 'E 'as nearly
my lee-dle Viki killed.'

She looked more narrowly at him, and a mother-instinct countered that of retaliation. She relapsed into German.

'Your Royal Highness has frightened him enough. He need not
be whipped. It was an accident. He meant nothing. You are fierce
because you are more frightened than I.' A majestic gesture of
dissent. Kings-to-be were not frightened. They were concerned.
'Boys will be boys.' Pity Red-Face was never to know that Royalty
was at one with him!—'A peasant boy nearly blinded me with a
catapult in the old days at Rosenau. . . . Ach, the poor little fellow!'

For the child was sagging to the floor, and was only saved from
complete collapse by the quick tightening of Sheldon's clasp upon
his hand.

The valet stooped, scooped up the small body, and stood facing
the duke respectfully, with it lying limply in his arms.

'Pfui, Edward!' exploded the duchess. 'Thou art a brute. He
shall go. . . . Take heem avay! Poor lee-dle von!'

Near-to-Majesty was for a second time that morning discon-
certed. A wife's outburst, a panic-stricken child's collapse were not

on any routine order. Royalty for a moment (aware of the quizzical gaze of the man by the fire; fearing that the quality of Godlikeness to a valet might be lost) became almost as limp as the little body—then recovered itself.

'The boy may withdraw for the time being,' he said; and with that, losing no vestige of his admirable poise, Sheldon retired with his burden.

The Duke was conscious of a considerable irritation. He felt that a dignified reproof would be needed later for a lady who forgot that one did not deal so summarily with matters affecting the well-being of the Ruling House of Great Britain. The affairs of His Royal Line were on a different plane from such as she was accustomed to—the trivialities in the unimportant existence of the Houses of Leiningen or Saxe-Coburg-Saalfeld.

The duchess, however, was unaware of this. She clapped her hands delightedly.

'Poor little love!' said she sentimentally. 'He was more frightened than any of us. So well-born, unquestionably!'

Sheldon had placed the pistols on the marble top of a rococo gilded chiffonier, the glass doors of which displayed an orgy of ornate china. Stockmar now crossed the room and examined the weapons, casually at first, and then with deeper attention. Finally he put his long red nose to the barrel of one of them and smelled at it rather loudly; smelled again; peered down the barrel, scratched his head regardless of royalty, and then brought the pistol to the table and laid it amid the papers.

'Take it away—the ugly thing!' said the duchess in German, with an affected shudder.

'But, madam,' protested Stockmar in his precise voice, 'there are certain points of interest about it.'

Standing at the table between the duke and duchess, he unscrewed with his long fingers the little barrel from the breech of the pistol. He held it at a slight angle over his thumbnail, so that the sunlight was reflected up into the iron tube.

'See,' he said, passing it to the duke, 'how little fouled the barrel is! Fouled—yes; but not so much as one would think, if it had been fired so very recently. Moreover, if you smell it, sir, as I did, you will find that the smell of powder is so faint as to be barely noticeable.'

'Indeed!' said the duke ironically, 'you will be telling me next, Herr Doktor, that the pistol has not been fired at all: in fact that no bullet has ever been fired; that the window downstairs has no hole in it, and the mirror remains unshattered!'

Stockmar remained imperturbable.

'If Your Royal Highness will meditate for a moment on the extent of the damage to that mirror, you will find it curious that so much destruction could be done by so small a ball.'

The duke looked at the barrel, into the barrel; raised it to the royal nose which he always held as if there were a bad smell beneath; sniffed at it; paused a moment to estimate the calibration.

'Well, Stockmar?' he asked, a trifle uncertainly.

'You men!' interrupted the duchess. 'Why will you make mysteries out of nothing? A small boy goes sparrow-shooting. He nearly ends by royalty-shooting. It is our good fortune he does not succeed. What does the calibre of the pistol matter? Na! Na! No amount of theorizing on ballistics can alter facts.'

'The point, madam,' said Stockmar turning to her, and pronouncing his sentence very slowly. 'The point, madam, is whether the small boy ever went sparrow-shooting, or shooting at all!'

The duchess shrugged her plump shoulders. Her reddish face, her large moist mouth curved in an incredulous smile.

The duke, however, did not smile. He strummed his fingers on the table, and turned a puzzled face on Stockmar.

'You mean . . . ?' he asked.

'I only ask Your Royal Highness to do a small sum,' said Stockmar drily, reverting to his precise English. 'Please to note these points I raise: the very faint smell of powder; and the singularly slight fouling—the smell and the fouling of a pistol that has not been fired for an hour at least—to my mind.

'Then I continue my sum. This pistol has a very short barrel. Yet the shot carried the length of the nursery and entered the wall the other end, at approximately the same level as the hole it made in the French window. That is no line of trajectory for a weapon of this sort. That is my sum, sir! Add it up!'

'The good Stockmar will have us believe . . .' began the duchess, who had followed his English with difficulty. She spoke in German, and fell silent at a gesture from her husband. His nostrils had become nipped with white. He plucked at the bottom button of his green satin waistcoat.

'That is a strange sum you set me, Stockmar!' he said harshly.

'I have become a little used to strange sums in the last few years,' replied the other. 'Two years ago I stood by the deathbed of the heiress of the throne. I saw the life of the Princess Charlotte fribbled away—a life lost that should not have been. To-day have I seen that happen which might have cost the life of another heiress to that same throne. I have heard and seen strange things between.'

The three stood about the table, but, while Stockmar confronted the other two, he would not raise his head, for fear they should read in his eyes all the dark thoughts and suspicions that surged through his mind.

He added, 'You need not believe my sum, sir—or what it adds up to. It is all easy of disbelief and hopeless of proof. Every moment the smell in this pistol gets fainter, and a fleck of the fouling loosens and will vanish. No experts will ever be able to say in an hour's time if it was fired to-day, or yesterday—or if it was loaded and fired at all. "Loaded", sir! For do not forget that a pistol can be fouled without a shot being discharged! I know, too, that no two experts will ever agree what may be done for the trajectory by the amount of charge, or the angle of fire. If the child were to maintain that he did not discharge the pistol, I greatly doubt whether we should be ever able to prove his story.

'But I still say to you, sir, that one does not necessarily disbelieve what one cannot prove . . . Children are singularly prone to cause trouble when they play with firearms. Shooting accidents sometimes are another name for murder. I only suggest—I cannot assert—that a small boy with a pistol might well be used as a stalking-horse by another hand . . . and another pistol. I only suggest it!'

'Another pistol! . . . Another hand! . . . My God! man, you are mad!'

'Or,' said Stockmar very slowly, 'someone else is mad!'

And he cast one quick bright look upwards—a look so full of knowledge and certainty that the other flinched as if he had been struck, flinched from the acceptance of a monstrous thought. He fumbled with his stock with the feeble fingering of an old man. His lips moved but uttered nothing.

The duchess had gone to the fire, shrugging her plump shoulders petulantly as she went. She stood tapping a satin-shod toe against the marble curb.

The sky had become overcast: the room darkened, and against the long windows came the insistent pattering of rain.

'Stockmar,' said the duke rather brokenly at last, and touched the other's hand as it rested on the table, as if to attract from him another look—one in which there should be support and inspiration. 'Stockmar, why should they aim pistols at me and mine? I am a Whig—even a Radical. They know I favour Reform. I have done no one harm—not even any woman. I have been honest. Even the Jacobins can have nothing against me of all my House. And, oh, my God! Why hit me through my child? Of what use to the cause of a revolution to strike down a few-months-old child? Answer me, Stockmar! I cannot bear it. Is there to be no security—not for me; I do not matter—but, for her?'

But Stockmar would not look up. He pressed his fingertips together before him. The nails whitened under the pressure.

'Jacobins? . . . Revolutionaries? . . .' said he, with so little emphasis in his voice that he might merely be repeating a statement by the other: and raising his brows so slightly that the action might almost have been the beating of a heavy pulse.

'It is not for me, sir, to speculate as to who might have raised that hand against your child. But a hand that has been raised once may be raised again. The pistol that is fired once may be replaced by another and deadlier weapon.'

The duke flung himself into his chair, chin sunk on breast, hands stretched wide on the paper-littered table, beads of sweat standing on the shining dome of his head.

'Who, Stockmar?' he asked in a voice that was almost a groan.

Stockmar remained silent, and motionless.

Beside the fire the duchess had turned, and was gazing gravely down the darkening room. Her foot no longer tapped the curb and her plump ringed hands flashed as they clasped and unclasped before her.

'Who, Stockmar?'

Stockmar remained wordless.

'Herr Stockmar, I too insist.'

He turned a little towards her, and bowed:

'There can be no answer to that question, madam; only sur-mise. His Royal Highness has as much basis for speculation as myself—more!'

Barely had he spoken when the older man, raising his heavy head, shot one word at him, below his breath, so that even the listening woman should not hear it:

'Ernest!'

Their eyes met and held for an instant.

It was as if the utterance of that name were the pronouncement of a forbidden spell, evoking a dark and secret power. In the minds of both men there was called up the sinister figure of him who symbolized to them, and to half England, hatred, conspiracy and rumour. They saw the half-blind face, famished with ambi-tion, and the great body in which violence was implicit. For a mo-ment he seemed to be hiding in the shadows of the room, an ogre possessed by tempestuous lusts. Even to his brother it seemed that here could be no merely gross-sinning Hanoverian prince, but a changeling whose tremendous frame was tormented by the pas-sions of Borgia and Medici.

These things doctor and duke told one another in interchanged glance.

Then Stockmar spoke, and in speech ignored what had been said wordlessly between them.

'I think, sir, it will be fruitless to make this matter public, or to raise any hue and cry. We may be wrong. I will talk to the boy in a little while when he is recovered, and ascertain what I can. I fear it will be little or nothing.'

The prince rose to his feet and moved about the room.

'The Regent must know.'

'How can he be told, sir, what even we do not know ourselves?'

'But . . .'

Stockmar explained patiently.

'But, sir, what charge can you make, and against whom? If my theory should be correct this has been too well-planned for us to have any evidence. And even if a charge could be made, would you make it? The only thing you can do is to hint to the Prince your desire for greater protection. His Royal Highness should sympathize. He has been attacked frequently enough. It might even be well to suggest that the duchess has been gravely concerned. She feels that this strange accident is a warning how easily a wilful tragedy may be brought about.'

The woman by the fireplace tightened her interlaced hands until the knuckles whitened and the blood rushed to the fingertips.

'I shall nefer haf peace again,' she said, and shook with the vehemence of her speech. 'The child shall nefer leaf my side till she is old—fery old! She shall always haf some great responsible person wit her! She shall nefer look out of a vindow—nefer! She shall . . .' And so went on piling up precaution on precaution.

At each clause the prince nodded his head in approval. General routine orders were being issued. That was all very understandable and straightforward. He would certainly countersign them.

The ludicrous bird-like vehemence of the duchess brought him back from the plane of sinister imaginings. There was nothing like being on the safe side; although, of course, it might have been an accident after all. Stockmar was imaginative—too imaginative.

He suddenly caught Stockmar's comprehending eye upon him. He read something of contempt in it and looked quickly away.

He had come to a pause beside one of the great book-cases, with the monotonous rows of calf and russia volumes blurred behind the glass. Two books were rather larger than the rest, and their titles in bigger lettering.

'History of England: Hume,' he read. The history of England! And into his mind a subconscious train of thought brought the story of the Princes in the Tower—the hideous betrayal of the Fifth Edward and his little brother by their uncle, Richard Crookback. He stood there pallid, ferreting back into half-forgotten things. The blinded Arthur and his uncle, John Lackland. The Duke of Rothesay, heir to Scotland, starved to death by his uncle, Albany. There were others: many others. Always the uncle—the wicked uncle! Uncle Cumberland! Ernest, Duke of Cumberland, the wicked uncle!

In that moment he was sure.

He turned to Stockmar. The majestic personage, the concerned prince had gone. For once in his life he spoke as man to man.

'Stockmar,' he said, 'I may die . . .' and paused. 'I may die, whether king or no, before my daughter comes of age. The guardianship of the child must be in sure hands. There must be no question of . . . of . . .' He paused once more. '. . . of my brothers. My will shall be made at once. The guardianship, of course, must go to the duchess. It must all be arranged so that it cannot possibly be upset.'

It was as if the shadow of what was to be in so few days' time had touched him for an instant; as if a glimpse of the candle-lit drama about his curtained bed had been vouchsafed him—of dark shuffling figures that should drain him of blood with their cuppings and their leeches and their bleedings, until he should pass on, and the tattered mantle of his protection be lost to his child.

The duchess cried out. Like all women, talk of wills seemed to her the prophecy of death.

Stockmar approved. Standing at the table, he jotted down a line or two on the back of a crackling document with a silver pencil—watched, as if he were an artist at work by the others. He read out what he had written:

'I, Prince Edward, Duke of Kent, being of sound mind, do nominate, constitute, and appoint my beloved wife, Victoire, Duchess of Kent, to be sole guardian to our dear child, the Princess Alexandrina Victoria, to all intents and for all purposes whatever.'

'Good, very good!' said the prince. 'Concise. No verbiage.'

Here was something written: something concrete: something that looked like an Army order: something to discuss without thought of what had given rise to it.

Later that day when he sat down at his writing table, amid a mass of fatuous correspondence—there were six letters about the engagement of a groom amongst it—he wrote voluminously about the incident. Afterwards he re-read the sheets; realized how little he really knew, and how much too much he had said. He tore the letter up, again, again—and yet again. He handed the fragments to a florid man at his side.

'Conroy,' he said. 'Burn it! Now!'

And watched Conroy until he saw the pieces drop amid the glowing mass.

He drew another sheet towards him, and began again:

'My little girl,' he wrote, 'thrives under the influence of a sea-side climate, and is, I am delighted to say, strong and healthy; too healthy, I fear, in the opinion of some members of my family, by whom she is regarded as an intruder.'

While the duke thus cautiously unburdened himself, Stockmar talked with Ompteda at the inn, in the large sitting-room, mournful with the massive furniture of a past age and mildewed engravings of ancient steeplechases and forgotten pugilists.

Ompteda had entered the room in the early dusk of the winter evening to find a precise jaundiced man in black coat and pantaloons awaiting him by the fire. Mud sparks spattered the sleek polish of the baron's riding-boots; long hours in the saddle had apparently made dense dark circles about his eyes; but carefully spaced doses of brandy had cured the frantic nerve-storm which had followed a discursus by Heywood in his bitter, quiet voice that morning.

'Dey tell me dat you have been vaiting my return,' he said thickly. 'I am Baron Ompteda.'

The other bowed, and, since he spoke to a compatriot, gave his style in German, and would have gone on, but that Ompteda afforded him no opportunity.

The sound of his own language bestowed on him a sudden feeling of confidence. In his mother-tongue he could explain, suggest, convince as never in English; he could be glib, confidential, important. He suffered in England from the consciousness that he was probably spoken of behind his back as a 'bloody foreigner', and was looked upon as socially and intelligently an inferior to the native-born. But this man was a German, too, a nobody—not even noble, but a mere upstart regimental surgeon!

The stimulus of brandy, the removal of his inferiority complex.

and the knowledge that he was thoroughly rehearsed, gave him faith in his ability to play a leading rôle brilliantly—if perhaps with a shade of over-emphasis to the ears of an acute and sceptical critic.

He propped himself up against the mantelpiece negligently, sucked his teeth.

'They tell me,' he said in a condescending manner, 'that my ward has caused a serious incident in His Royal Highness's household. For that I am sorry. You have detained him, I suppose? My friend, Captain Heywood, and I have sought for him since breakfast when we first found him—and my pistols—missing. My friend is still searching for him, in fact. We thought he must have been stolen by gipsies! I heard nothing of this affair until my return a moment ago! . . . I will myself wait upon His Royal Highness, whenever convenient to him, to present my apologies. I can assure him that this prank of my ward's will never be repeated. . . . It is the second fright he has given us in the past few days.'

'So I am told!' said Stockmar. He did not like the glib, rather hurried speech of Ompteda, the aroma of brandy that clung to him, or the careless way in which was greeted an emissary from Blood-Royal. 'You are aware that what you term a "prank" nearly cost the life of the Princess Victoria?'

'I gathered that,' remarked Ompteda, recognizing the other's antagonism, and injecting a trifle more concern into his voice. 'I am extremely sorry. Very sorry indeed! I will do myself the honour of returning with you to the residence, and there, if so desired, chastise the boy in your presence . . .' He paused a little, as if doubtfully '. . . I suppose my brief carries me as far as that!'

Stockmar's eyebrows were raised. He read some secret pleasure in the other's clumsy face, some faint surface ripple of a malicious amusement that stirred within.

'Your authority over your ward would appear extremely limited, if you must ask yourself if it extends to beating him for such a serious offence,' he said sarcastically.

'The authority of a guardian, sir, depends upon the quality of the ward,' replied Ompteda sententiously. He assumed a look of meditation on far-off things, produced as though unconsciously a gold snuff-box, helped himself to a liberal pinch and sniffed it up—like a rooting pig, thought Stockmar.

He dusted his fingers and then closed the box with a snap that appeared to bring his manners to mind.

With apologies he tendered the golden thing to Stockmar who refused, but imagined—and correctly—that the gesture had been made for him to see the Royal Arms of England engraved deeply on its flat top, and wondered why.

'We have not got your ward,' he said, revolted by the yellow snuff stain on the other man's upper lip and the bitten nails of the hand that had been extended to him. 'We caught him, it is true, but he escaped before we could find out anything about him.'

Ompteda was palpably staggered.

'Gone?' he ejaculated. 'Gone again?' and pulled violently at the bell-rope.

It was one thing to put up a mock hunt for a truant—loitering as long as he dared over comfortable inn fires—when you knew all the time that he was under lock and key; and another to chase after a sort of will-o'-the-wisp through a wet cold and muddy night. To say nothing of the fact that if he lost the child there would be serious trouble with the Regent.

'Bolted through a window on the first floor and got away. Why the child did not break his neck, I cannot think.'

'My God!' said Ompteda, and pealed the bell once more.

Stockmar, with unchanged expression, gazed at the fading print of Escape winning the Two Thousand Guineas at Newmarket in 1791, which adorned the wall over the fire-place. The man's obvious concern for the child did not seem to fit into the pattern that his suspicions had built.

The ostler came: the horses were ordered—fresh horses for the baron, for manservant; word to be left for Captain Heywood; a decanter of brandy.

Stockmar, the prim emissary of correct dukedom, found his errand and himself ignored in the stream of orders and preparation.

'You will forgive me, sir,' said Ompteda at length, 'but the search for this child is just now of more moment than the appeasement of the Duke of Kent! I am far more worried about the child than the duke—who, after all, has not been hurt in any way.'

There was that in his voice so derogatory of the royal dignity which Stockmar represented, that his yellow cheeks flushed. He refused curtly to take any brandy. Ompteda helped himself lavishly, tossed it off, poured out another tot.

'As a friend,' said Ompteda with swaggering confidence, 'I should strongly advise the duke to treat the incident at its true valuation—to forget it!'

He snapped his fingers as if dismissing the affair as an airy trifle of no account; and staggered slightly as he did so.

'Even should the worst have happened, my advice would have been the same—and not my advice alone!' said Ompteda still remembering his lesson, although his utterance was a little clouded. He was doing very well—couldn't be better. He wondered if Heywood were listening behind the curtains of the porch window. That dark man with the secret eyes was somewhere about, but he certainly would not want to be seen and possibly recognized by Stockmar.

'When your advice is required by His Royal Highness he will . . .'

'. . . Find it is the advice of one greater than I . . . greater, indeed, than himself!' Ompteda completed the sentence as if it were a stage one. He was rising to sublime heights in dealing with this nasty little surgeon person! Surgeons were only a degree better than barbers! He hiccoughed and did not trouble to raise his hand to his mouth—Stockmar noted.

The horses even now waited. The baron shrugged himself into his riding coat. He took up the hat and crop that lay upon the table. By his manner Stockmar was made to feel himself to be no longer the friend and confidant of princes, but the unfledged physician from an unknown German town, whose evil digestion made him show anger in a burning red nose. Ompteda overdid it, and Stockmar's annoyance began to evaporate before the amusement that he felt at the man's assumption of aristocratic arrogance.

'I am, like you, sir, the servant of a prince,' Stockmar was told.

'. . . In fact I have the honour to be a very confidential agent of His Royal Highness the Prince Regent.'

Stockmar's jaw dropped.

They were in the galleried courtyard of the inn: horses and men waited by the archway that gave upon the street. By a lamp set above a low-browed door Ompteda halted, drew from his pocket a wallet holding three documents, which he extracted and held to the flickering light for a moment. It was long enough for Stockmar to recognize the signature to each—that scrawled 'George P.R.' with the incredibly long-tailed 'G' and the flourish at the end. There could be no question about the credentials. He suddenly felt that he was on the fringe of some very strange mystery. His preconceived ideas were shattered: no theory seemed wide enough to embrace the factors that he had imagined as well as this new one.

With a foot in a stirrup and reins gathered about the withers of the horse as he prepared to mount, Ompteda threw him a last few words in a patronizing manner, and in a tone so conspiratorially low that to hear them Stockmar had to trust himself far nearer uneasy hoofs than he cared.

'There have been many . . . shall I say? . . . scandals in the Royal Family. There are undoubtedly more to come. By to-day's contretemps the Duke of Kent's household has been brought within the orbit of one of the greatest of those scandals.'—Oh, well done, Fritz! You ought to have been an actor! He rounded off the drama—'And one of the most tragic.'

Perfect! And still more perfect if the horse had not at that moment swung about, and sent Stockmar scuttling for safety!

Ompteda threw a leg across the saddle and eased himself into it. He leaned low over the pommel, and finished what he had to say. He spoke with such dramatic pauses, hesitations, lowerings and raisings of the voice, that Stockmar felt as if he were listening to the Young Roscius.

'Whitewashing the Regent is no concern of mine,' said Ompteda frankly. 'But this, I may say, is no immediate affair of his, except that he acts for the King as head of his House.'—Confidentially.

'As for my interest, I have shown you my credentials.' More frankness!

'No one, of course, can possibly think that our young sportsman is homicidal.' The appeal to reason.

'So I implore the duke to let things be. There are things that— I assure you—have no relation whatever to this unfortunate accident which must not come to light.' Intense drama!

'The dangers before the House of Hanover are sufficient as they are'—the appeal to loyalty—'without putting her enemies in the way of ferreting out fresh weapons.'

He waited for no reply. It was the moment for a dramatic exit. He raised his voice to a curt 'Your servant, sir!' set spurs to his horse and crashed out under the arch into the road at a canter.

Stockmar stood for some little while looking into the dark gap after the vanished figure, with a puzzled expression, fiercely scratching his head in a rather vulgar manner.

From the dark shadows of the gallery round the yard, Heywood watched him walk slowly away, with a smile on his thin lips. Ompteda had managed the matter far better than he would have imagined! Clever fellow, Ompteda, if you frightened him sufficiently and allowed him just enough to drink, and no more!

Chapter 5

The Odyssey of a Young Gentleman Begins

A THIN AND BITTER RAIN HAD BEGUN TO FALL WHEN Christopher escaped. He had dropped from the window of the room in which he was confined—into a dripping rhododendron bush that crunched and crackled beneath him, seared his forehead and his hands with rent branches, and rolled him into a wet and empty flower-bed of red earth.

He rose, clotted with mud and stained with blood. It meant nothing to him; he had been beyond thought, as well as speech or cry, for a long while. He was possessed by but one driving force, the instinct of flight—anywhere away from the crash of exploding pistols, from the silken movements of his pale mentor, and from the man who conjured up pictures of the red joints in a butcher's shop.

So he ran, blindly and fast, across the path and a long lawn strewn with beech twigs, through an open door in the ivied wall at the end, into an orchard of old apple trees.

He ran without hesitation, as if some objective were clear before him, although he had no purpose but to leave house and town far behind him.

Twice again he fell before he came into the open, once over a twisted root, and then in scrambling down a slippery ditch, beyond the high hedge that was the orchard boundary. It was a loathsome, stinking ditch into which a house drain emptied itself, and from which a scavenging magpie rose with a flutter of white tail. He did not pause on rising, however, to assess the damage, but ran on with small hands clenched, panting, dripping with liquid mud, his yellow hair damp with sweat and straggling over his white panic-stricken face.

87

For long he ran like that, unseeing, blundering, under the lee of high woody hedges in hillside fields. Once, struggling through a gap on hands and knees, his face brushed against the body of a fat rabbit hanging limply from the loop of a snare. He did not know it. A wall-eyed farm dog, poaching along a plantation edge, saw him, and circled barking about him for half a mile. He barely realized it.

From the hilltops now he might have seen the rain shiver dense along the valleys like a shaken muslin veil. The grey sheet of the sky tented a wet world that was silent but for the hiss of rain and the roar of a swollen stream.

Even when the first urgency of his panic had gone and he no longer ran, there was no connected thought in the chaos of his mind. Swift pictures succeeded one another in the broken kaleidoscope: hacked joints on a stained butcher's block: a white hand holding a pistol: a line of light passing across the darkness of the crack under a bedroom door: the goggling eyes and dropped jaw of the fat waiter: long plump fingers with shining nails tilting a shiny powder flask within which rustled dimly the little gunpowder seeds of death. On!—On!—Away from the place where evil dreams lurked and became true! On!—Away from the echoes of a soft fierce voice or a loud fierce voice, or the crashing voice of the pistol—and the strange mad smell of smoke.

He came to a little wood of larch and ash on the crest of a hill, and plunged within. The ground was thick with the giant trailers of bramble. At each step a long tentacle rose from the ground, and seized him and tore his clothing and his flesh. His hands bled in a dozen places from the wounds sustained in his efforts to release himself.

For a moment he stopped amid the grey straight shafts, under the thin low roof of interlacing boughs. As he did so there was a rustle amid the tangle at his feet, and something rose behind him and clashed its shark teeth with a jangle and a crash.

With the loud gasping sob of a creature that meets a death too sudden for outcry, he ran . . . and fell . . . and ran again.

Behind him reared, knee-high, the half-hoop of a man-trap, its serrated iron jaws sprung by some trailer in his passing.

It was long after, towards the end of the short day, when the rain had stopped, that he came to a shallow valley enclosed by low wooded hills. Narrow green meadows ran its length under a bluff fringed with oak and beech and evergreen, and bounded on the other side from the climbing woods by a swift stream.

He came down a gentle slope to it, following the course of a rivulet across whose glassy surface thin dark lines were drawn from the tips of floating weed. It streamed over shining red and grey and black and green stones bubbling over gentle declines, chattering over a sudden fall, spouting indignantly over an obstruction.

He slackened pace when he reached the level ground and halted for a moment, shivering with cold and fear, by a ford where the two streams joined. His clothing hung in tatters about him: his frilled collar had gone: his shoes were lumps of filth: his face was a mask of mud smeared with blood. He became conscious, for the first time, of hunger and the desire for warmth. For the first time he knowingly followed a set route, along the alder-lined bank of the larger brook.

It was a swift sherry-coloured stream. Here, there were wavelets that broke and seemed to crawl in a line of foam against the tide. There, it surged quickly onward, its surface moulded by movement into a swift succession of ever-repeated patterns.

The rains had swollen its rush, and the hungry waters had gnawed at the banks, so that, between the pairs of guardian trees stooping over it, a shallow arc of earth and grass had slid down towards the devouring current.

At one such spot he climbed down, and tried to wash the dirt from off his hands, and drank, kneeling upon a flat wet stone.

Into this little recess, between a holly and an old willow that leaned over the water straining at the anchorage of its roots, cut brushwood had been thrown. Just above water level there was a hollow in the pile, where some larger sapling had fallen and bore the burden of a tangled roof of twig and bramble and brush, as high as the bank top.

It was secret and snug, and offered some protection from the cold and wet.

He crept into the spiky bed, and lay within, hidden from sight.

Across the stream a young oak tree bowed five dull silver shafts over the current. Brown leaves lingered on it, and tiny bright ivy climbed it.

Its neighbour was undermined by water, and had become the prey of life more vigorous than its own. There was a vivid moss about its base: ivy climbed upward to the hole from which sprouted the ribbons of hart's tongue fern—upward to the boughs and twigs clothed in the sad green of lichen.

A dipper flew up the stream, its wings almost touching the water.

Christopher lay curled in his secret place. Although his eyes were open he saw nothing, only the gashes in a hand that did not seem to belong to him, a finger that had lost half its nail. Only those—and a stick which projected from the floor of his nest beside that hand and finger; a stick from which a square of silver bark had been torn and rolled back showing its orange lining and the black rotted wood below . . . His mind went back. He was in the hay-loft at home over the pony's loose-box. He could almost hear old Jess whinny as she came in from the shafts, and nuzzle amid the fodder in the manger . . . It was real . . . He could hear her . . . None of this had happened . . . He was playing by himself—a Cavalier hiding from the Roundheads in the stable-loft . . . He was playing . . . He was playing till Jane came to call him in . . . He was King Alfred hiding from the Danes . . . He was a Prince of Fairyland whose enemies had seized his princedom . . . He was . . . asleep.

Darkness had fallen when he was awakened by a creature that scrabbled and dug in the brushwood pile above him—a creature that whined the while softly and urgently, as if talking to itself.

A man spoke to the beast in a low voice, and the scrabbling became yet more vigorous, and the whining yet softer although its quality did not change.

Frozen with a new terror he lay motionless, staring at the dark tangle that lay over him, like a rabbit crouched in its burrow while the terriers dig.

There was a sudden fierce crackling of twigs, and a splashing of feet in water. A light shone into his hiding place and a hand irresistibly plucked him out, and set him on his feet in the shallow edge of the stream.

Whoever had seized him now held him by one shoulder, and, with his other hand, flashed a dark lantern in his face. He did not try to escape the rough grip, but stood wearily blinking in the glare, framing with trembling lips protests and excuses that would not come.

At first he could see nothing of his captor but that he appeared to be a shapeless mass, with high sloping shoulders that bore no head. Then as the shutter of the lantern was closed, he saw that he was a short man, nearly as broad as he was tall, in a long dark coat having his head hidden in a sort of sack which fell about his shoulders and on to his breast.

' "Rejoice with me, for I have found my Sheep which was lost." —Luke fifteen,' said a low voice from the middle of the sack. 'A very wandering sheep! . . . I am the Good Shepherd! I will lead you back to the pastures, Sheep! What are you doing here, Sheep?'

The voice was educated and not unkind, but there was an accent to it that Christopher had never heard before, something more nasal than the burr of the West Country. It was an ugly metallic intonation that had none of the softness of the South.

The speaker did not wait for Christopher to explain. He had propelled him up the bank, and set off swiftly and silently along the streamside, with a firm clutch on the child's collar. The dog fell in behind, and trailed them nose to heel.

They marched through the darkness, in a silence broken only by the dog's snufflings and the rush of water on their right.

As they proceeded the valley narrowed; its dark wooded slopes became steeper, and the path left the verge of the stream and climbed gently upwards towards the thickets. They passed above a long reflectionless mill-pond with a water-mill's unlighted bulk between it and the rushing brook, and so up a dim bank, through a gap between a grey stone wall and dark hedge, on to a causeway that crossed the valley.

The square man heaved a great sigh as they emerged on to the road which was slippery with frost. He released his hold on Christopher and loosed himself from his hood.

' "No longer will I hide my face from thee"—Psalm eighty-eight, more or less,' said he; but in the obscurity Christopher could see little except an inordinately long thin nose and a wide straight mouth.

The other secreted the hood in some inner pocket of his capacious coat, and flashed his dark lantern once again over the child, as if to satisfy himself that he had not been metamorphosed in the last few minutes. He made the beam to travel slowly upwards from the torn shoes, pausing as if to absorb every detail of the tattered small clothes, the rent and muddied jacket, the smeared white face with the frightened eyes. He even turned the little figure about and ran a strangely gentle finger amid the damp yellow hair where a matting of blood told of a scalp wound.

' "I stick fast in the deep mire, where no ground is: I am come into deep waters, so that the floods run over me. I am weary of crying; my throat is dry: my sight faileth me for waiting so long upon my God"—Psalm sixty-nine.'

He declaimed the sonorous phrases so that the night was shattered, and the dog whimpered at his heels.

'If you care to step along the road with me, Comrade,' he went on, 'I may be able to help you a little on your journey through the world—though God knows where you are bound, or indeed any of us! Runaway parish child, I'll swear, but *I* shan't give you up. Don't tell me. I don't want to know. Step out, Comrade, for there'll be meat for supper. Meat! Meat! Meat!! Meat!!!'

His voice rose triumphantly on the word, a trifle higher each time so that at last it became a shriek.

They had crossed a small bridge; at the forked way beyond there was a huddle of low buildings dim against the mass of the hill, with here and there a faint light in a window.

They entered under a creaking sign by a door between two bow windows.

A dark flagged passage led into a large room with benches along the wall, lighted by a single candle on the central table. Settles were ranged on either side of the chimney-breast, and the fire-light flickered on the implements set ready for the use of travellers, upon the ledges of the big open grate—kettle, gridiron, frying-pan, iron pot and conical beer warmer.

A labourer in a long patched smock sat by the fire, nursing a mug of ale upon his knee. The hand that held the tankard was knotted and twisted into the semblance of a root. His woollen stockings hung in folds about his calfless legs. The lower half of his face was hidden by a tangled mass of iron-grey beard. His head hung forward upon his chest. He saluted the newcomers with a knuckle to the forehead.

'Good evening, Comrade!' said the square man, stamping to the fire. 'Good evening, Comrade!'

He signalled to Christopher to take the seat on the settle nearest the fire; undid his heavy frieze overcoat; produced a small sack from an inner pocket and threw it upon the floor, and then flung the garment over the shivering child.

He wore high leathern gaiters and a full-skirted coat of green with a spotted scarf about his neck. His face was as square as his body: his bright red hair was cut flat along the top: his mouth was a straight slit across his face under his long thin nose.

He drummed with his heels until a slatternly woman appeared in the doorway. Her eyes rested indifferently for a moment on the small boy under the coat, and the sack upon the floor. The green man ordered ale for the labourer as well as for Christopher and himself.

When the liquor had come he poured a mugful for the child into the beer warmer, and stuck the sharp end of the vessel among the red-hot coals.

Then he picked up the sack, undid its neck and tilted the contents on to the floor. There were three fat rabbits.

'Not bad for a townsman!' said he. 'One for the house'—and handed it to the woman who took it, and went, without a word—'and two for me and the boy. Oh, praise the Lord, for he "hath given meat unto them that fear him"—Psalm one hundred and eleven! "Meat unto them that fear him." Ha, meat!'

A sudden thought seemed to enter his mind, for he looked up sharply across the hearth at the labourer who sat staring in silence at the clump of fur upon the stones.

'How often, Comrade,' he asked in a changed voice, 'do you eat meat?'

The other gazed at him stupidly.

'Meat, Ma-äster?'

'Aye, meat, Comrade!'

'Meat? . . . Aye! . . . We doän't get meat in these paärts!'

The square man had opened a jack knife. With extraordinary rapidity and neatness he cleaned the rabbits, skinned them, and flung the bloody entrails to the dog under the settle. As he worked he shot questions at the labourer.

'Wages too low?'

'Wages, Ma-äster?'

'Aye, wages, Comrade!'

'Wages! . . . Eight shilluns a week. Vive on us to keep, and bread be sixteen pence the gallon!' He spat on the floor. 'Aye, bread be sixteen pence the gallon!' He took a sup of his beer. . . . 'Aye, sixteen pence the gallon!'

The square man poured some of the warm ale into a mug and held it to Christopher's lips. The smell of the beer mingled with that of the fresh blood that stained his hands. The child opened his eyes, obediently swallowed a few sips, and drowsed off into the sleep of complete exhaustion.

The square man split the rabbits and placed them on the grid. A strip or two of bacon rind emerged from one of his capacious pockets, and served as lardoon.

Sitting on a stool over the fire, moving the sizzling meat about the bars with his knife, he extracted the labourer's story, at first word by word, and then in a rush in a broad West Country accent.

It was more than a year since he had eaten meat except bacon scraps. The last time was Christmas twelvemonth when Squire had thrown mutton chops at the villagers from the windows of his coach as he drove from Church. It was always bread and 'taters, bread and 'taters: occasionally some skim milk when Farmer could spare it from the pigs: the chillun would now and again come back with a turmut dropped from a farm cart in the road, or berries, or hedgerow roots and leaves that could be boiled into a mess that filled the stomach. For tea a handful of rye roasted and ground, or young and tender leaves dried, or burned crusts. Sugar —butter—jam—tobacco! He smiled wryly, and spat.

How could he afford to drink beer, even if it cost but five half-pence a pint? Why, mistress gave him a pint three times a week for doing odd jobs. She was a widder woman.

The square man nodded at the roasting meat.

'Rabbits?' he asked with a lift of the eyebrow.

The other steadied his mug on his agued knees. His sunken

eyes gazed wistfully at the grid: his wide hairy nostrils snuffed up the aroma. He shook his head.

Squire (said he) had sworn next poacher he caught should be put away proper—should get a sentence of transportation. The Bench—and pa'son sat on it—had sent Janie Matthews and Prudence Truscott to six months' imprisonment for walking, accidentally, on a partridge's nest. Henry Halliday, up by the mill, had gone to jail for twelve months for cutting a switch from a hedge. They said no one could want a switch but a poacher. Many of them about here went poaching all the same, and pilfering in the orchards and fields by night. He was afeared to.

'The earth is the Lord's and the fullness thereof the Squire's,' said the square man jabbing a rabbit viciously with his knife.

He raised his long nose to the smoke-stained ceiling, and cried out loud:

'Meat! Meat!! Meat!!! Meat for the snufflers in the hedgerows, for the sharers in the pig troughs! Meat for those who fill their bellies with burdock leaves and sodden 'taters! Meat for the eaters of mouldy crusts and apple parings! Rich man's meat for the poor man who earns it! Meat for skeleton children and shrivelled workers, for the paupers living on bone dust—and for you and for me.'

He cried out at first as a butcher might cry his wares; and then as his voice rose it seemed as if he were crying other wares—other and strange and unmentioned wares for which his song was a mounting dithyramb.

The woman of the house reappeared in the doorway. Her impersonal gaze took heed of the man and the sleeping boy.

'You will wake the child!' she remarked, and turned away.

'We will burn and burn, and break and break, so that there shall be meat for all!' said the square man in a loud voice, paying no attention. 'We will have roast white meat, and roast red meat, and roast brown meat. And we shall stuff our mouths with both hands. Aye, Comrade Furry-Face! The day shall come when you will emerge from your pig-sty and I from my slum, and eat the forbidden meat, all the denied meats! . . . And that day comes soon!'

He suddenly tilted his head back to its normal position, grinned widely at the labourer, and prodded the cooking rabbits.

'With my own hands I trapped these, although no countryman. I risked transportation in catching 'em: will you risk indigestion in eating 'em, Comrade Furry-Face? Join me in the "fat burnt sacrifice with the incense of rams"—Psalm sixty-six—Comrade Furry-Face! I have sworn a great oath—among many—to eat only meat I catch and kill myself. Since I have neither land nor cattle, it stands to reason that someone else must provide the wherewithal.'

He took a whole rabbit off the gridiron and laid it on the smocked knee of the working-man. He tore the hind legs off the other and laid them on the settle beside the sleeping child.

With a sigh of satisfaction he raised the carcass to his mouth, and gnawed the sweet meat along the spine, as if it were a cob of maize.

For a little Comrade Furry-Face sat staring at the rabbit on his knee as if mesmerized by it. Then he set down his mug and touched it, as if to assure himself of its reality.

As though the touch had conveyed some new impression to his brain and released the spring of action, he suddenly seized the body in his hands, tore it in half, and crammed his mouth savagely with meat. He ate no less savagely, crunching the bones with his teeth, and swallowing them like a dog. The thigh bone protruded from the corner of his mouth as he gnawed it. Saliva streamed on to his beard.

'Good, Comrade Famine?' asked the square man, looking up from his meal.

Comrade Famine emitted some incomprehensible sound, and nodded a rusty-jointed head. Speech was obviously impossible for him.

There was silence thereafter for a time but for the munching jaws.

The square man was finished before his fellow banqueter. He wiped his lips and fingers on a red cotton handkerchief, after he had thrown the remains of his feast to the dog.

'Comrade Hunger!' said he, and there was something so urgent and compelling in his tone that the other stopped chewing, and raised leaden eyes to his face.

'Comrade Hunger,' said he with rising inflection. 'You shall soon eat not roast rabbit, but roast beef! And we will roast our meat at blazing ricks and burning stacks. "He hath filled the hungry with good things: and the rich He hath sent empty away"—Luke one. You eat boiled nettles and dried crusts; your bones stick out of your brittle skin; your teeth are rotted in their gums from thin gruel; your wife's dry breasts hold no milk for her babe; her bed is a tattered rag spread over leaves; her children like living skeletons fight in the gutters for apple-parings and bits of grease!'

He had risen to his feet. His voice was raised. He paced to and fro addressing his meeting of a sleeping child and a shrivelled giant. He thrust his hands out: he clenched his fists: he stamped with his feet. He had used the words and phrases and sentences before; they streamed easily from his accustomed lips—but with sincerity. They were as a sword kept bright and sharp and well-used.

'And they pay you eight shillings a week, so that the fat farmer shall get fatter, and the fat gentry get fatter, and the fat Princes get fattest of all!

'You are starving in the midst of plenty so that Fat George may build more palaces and drink more lush; so that Fat Frederick and Fat William and Fat Edward may keep their bastards in luxury and toy with new mistresses; and Fat Ernest may plot like a spider in the web.

'They turn the dragoons on us when we ask the right to live: they turn the hussars on us when we ask the right to vote!

'But the day is near, Brother Hunger! We will have great fires to warm our hands and roast our meat! We will tear down the mighty from their seat, we will . . .'

'Master, you must go! . . .'

The woman of the house had reappeared in the doorway. Her face was entirely expressionless, but her hands were clenched fiercely at the edges of her apron.

'. . . You must go!'

The square man came back to earth. For a moment he looked a little foolish. He protested, but in vain. She neither added to nor explained her order.

'You must go!'

'Don't you like my politics, ma'am? God help you! Or is it just the noise?' he asked, confronting her.

She remained immobile.

'Or are you just frightened? See yourself taken for a walk off the cart-end one fine morning for being privy to treason?'

He gathered up his coat off the sleeping boy without disturbing him.

'You're a silly old bitch,' he added without heat. 'You will know one day which side your bread is buttered on.'

'You must go!'

'You can take a penny or two if you like when next the bloody dragoons or hussars come round. Tell them that Oliver Drysdale is in the county—preaching rebellion. Oliver Drysdale who was at Peterloo! Turn me out now; and sell me to-morrow!'

Every muscle in her face tightened in resentment of the insult, but she said nothing.

Drysdale saw it. A flush crept over his face.

'I was wrong. You are just frightened. God help us all!'

He felt in his pockets and extracted a silver groat which he put on the settle by the mug of ale and the rabbit legs at Christopher's side.

'Will you let the child be till morning?' he asked. 'He will do no harm.'

'He can stay,' said the woman.

Drysdale walked to the door and then he turned.

'Good-bye, Brother Hunger,' he said. 'One of these days we'll dance round a bonfire with Squire on top of it—you and I. Good-bye! . . . Good-bye, ma'am.'

Daring and impudent he leaned a little as he passed the woman, and bussed her loudly on the cheek.

She did not move. She might have been made of stone. She remained motionless, looking into the room, as his footsteps echoed down the stone passage, and out into the night. The dog poked its nose out from under one of the high-backed seats, and pattered after him.

'The wagon is late to-night,' said the woman at length to the labourer, when the footfalls had died away. 'He will probably want help to-night and to-morrow morning. It will mean a penny or two for you, Richard!'

'Aye, mistress!' said Richard.

When she was gone he rose rheumatically from his corner and crossed to Christopher. His frame was enormous, but his tattered and patched smock did not hide the fleshlessness of the man. He walked with bent knees as if they were not strong enough to support his body, shrunken though it might be.

He looked down on the child, gauging the depth of his sleep; then stooped and seized one of the pieces of meat at his side. He stuffed it whole into his mouth, as though to put every scrap of it beyond possibility of restoration.

His claw-like distorted hand was outstretched for the other fragment, when from out of the night came the muffled strokes of a church clock, and with them the distant rumble of something on the road, the click of hoofs, and the faint jangle of little bells.

The boy stirred slightly in his sleep: his hands clenched themselves and unclenched: tremors shook his body, and from his parted lips came a little whimpering noise.

Brother Hunger, with one last wistful look at the envied tit-bit, turned away and hobbled to the door.

The rumbling of slow wheels, the music of small bells, the creaking of a heavy vehicle—like that of a ship at sea—came nearer and nearer; reached the inn and ceased.

Christopher awoke as the first light of day crept in through a small deep-set window.

The fire had died down to red embers, but the room was very warm. His mug of ale was still beside him, but groat and rabbit tit-bit had gone.

In the dim grey of the early morning he realized that there was a newcomer in the room, stretched full-length on the opposite settle. He had presumably just awakened, for he stirred and presently sat up yawning prodigiously, shook out the long cloak with which he had covered himself, and pulled the shabby green overcoat (in which he had slept) into normal folds and lines.

He was a man of about fifty, fat and pale, with a shiny face, protruding stomach, two protruding front teeth, and one protruding green eye—the other being hidden behind a lowered sunken lid, if indeed it existed at all. There was a large inflamed spot on the side of his nose, and he scratched it delicately with the bright steel hook that replaced his left hand. His hair was cut short and, even at a distance, looked as if it must be full of scurf. His whole person, indeed, from soiled neckcloth to lustreless boots, was the apotheosis of dust and shabbiness.

From without came the jingling of harness, an impatient stamping of heavy hooves, and the juicy sound of horses sucking water at a trough.

Brother Hunger appeared in the doorway.

'Ma-äster,' he announced in his almost incomprehensible West Country dialect, 'Ma-äster, Wagoner du zay how 'e'll be ready vor ter start in three-fower minutes.'

The one-armed man consulted a great turnip watch.

'It iss nearly eight o'clock,' he said. His light intonation, careful division of the syllables of each word, and insistence on the phonetic dentals and sibilants marked him for a Welshman.

He threw a glance at the boy who had drifted back into a drowse, took in the stained and tattered clothing, the muddy feet. His prominent eye travelled over the small frame, assessing it, as though he were a farmer examining stock in the market.

What he saw apparently interested him, for he even got up and approached the child quietly the better to see him. He seemed to make some calculation in his mind, and grunted his satisfaction.

'He iss small, fery small!' he said approvingly. 'Fery small!'

He licked his lips, and then closed them in a straight thin line as if he would recall the gesture. He shot a quick look at the other man, who was watching stupidly.

'He hass no trade whateffer—he iss too young?' he asked.

This was beyond Richard, who opened and shut his mouth without saying anything.

'What a chance, inteet, that poy is missing—what money he could earn—what a life he might haf before him! Yess, yess, inteet!' said the Welshman, shaking his head as though in regret for lost opportunities and disregarded genius.

'Aye, aye, ma-äster?' Richard did his best to show interest, although his attention was concentrated on the nearly full mug of ale that wasted beside the boy.

'He earns sixpence a week, perhaps, bird-scaring and helping on the farm, yess? . . . He should, inteet, be in a trade. . . . Just the figure for it! . . . Lovely bones, inteet! . . . Made for it, cer-tain-ly! A few years' work and he would be a master himself with a beaver hat and an ofer-coat—like mine!'

The thought of this wasted life was too much for Mr. David Lewis. He took a short agitated stroll up and down the room, coming at last to a pause before Richard.

'Iff you wass a good father, an honest father, iff you wass me,' said he, 'you would say, inteet, "I must not stand in the way off my poy. It is for hiss good. He musst go with Mr. Lewis!" '

It gradually dawned on the slow mind of Richard that Mr. Lewis for some obscure reason had jumped to the conclusion that the sleeping child was his. For a moment he sought for words of denial, but Mr. Lewis's compelling eye was on him, and the waving steel hook was punctuating another burst of speech.

Efery house in the land had a chimney—two chimneys—three chimneys—perhaps four chimneys. Efery chimney had to be swept at least once a year. There were, inteet, nowhere near enough chimney-sweeps to deal with the business. It was—yess, yess—a fery healthy trade. Soot was good for the lungs. It was an evil slander that the climbing boys got cancer: why, the moment they learned their business they got three shillings a week, and when they had grown and could no longer climb chimneys, there was nothing to stop them becoming master-sweeps themselves. Pot of ale before a job: pot of ale after a job—why cer-tain-lie! Nothing to do at all, then, but to collect the money. Mr. Lewis knew all about it. Wass not hiss own brother the most-thought-of master-sweep in Swansea?

Mr. Lewis paused to gather the impression he had made.

The cold winter sun was filtering through the window; a beam lit the face of the sleeping boy, the pale clear skin stained with weariness, with mud smears, and with dried blood on the temple.

From without pole chains jingled, and clumping beasts were told to 'Whoa!' to 'Steady! Steady!!' and to 'Back a bit!' There was also a curious human twittering, sibilant, and very low.

Mr. Lewis came to the crux of his argument. He tid not mind saying that the poy wass small, yess, remarkably small. That wass fery useful, especially for some of these chimneys that were all curved and bent and carried across ceilings to get to the stack!

That being so, he felt justified in saying that hiss prother, Mr. Lewis of Swansea, would pe fery glad to take the lad as apprentice. 'Twould pe like home for the little fellow: plenty of food—meat twice a week, pread, pacon, cheese, ale. And the work—nothing to speak of. And such good training, inteet.

Richard, standing regarding the gnarled hand that held the settle-back, seemed a figure of indecision to the philanthropical Mr. Lewis. Actually he sought for words to explain that he knew nought about the child, who was probably a runaway bastard from the poor-house.

Lewis spurred consent as he had done a dozen times before. He undid his overcoat, and thrust a hand into the depths of a pocket in his breeches. It emerged with a fat red silk purse that sang of crown pieces and double florins. He swung the purse gently to and fro by the metal ring that girt its middle. Richard's heavy eyes followed its travels, and its passage to the table.

Lewis plunged into another pocket. He produced a packet of dog's-eared papers, and flicked them over as a bank cashier checks notes.

'There are twenty children I have here,' said he, 'who would sadly envy, inteet, your little son. Look you, my little family!' He flicked over again the papers, which were indentures binding the persons named thereon to labour in a cotton mill and live in the adjoining prentice house until they reached the age of twenty-one, if they ever did!—'Twenty little tickets to Forr-tune!

'Now, master, my prother would not forgive me iff I offerlooked a lad so made py nature for the art and profession of a chimney-sweep. Inteet, he would not. You think off your child: I think off my prother. I think, too, he would—tell me—that, perhaps—he would—even—pay—a little, a fery little—for the pleasure of teaching his craft—to one sso likely!'

There was a crown piece on the table: it was followed by a second, by a third, by a fourth—and by a fifth that fell, and span as it fell, with a clear ringing note.

Richard licked his lips. The five crown pieces—twenty-five shillings—represented an incalculable fortune. If a gallon loaf were sixteen pence! . . . if a gallon loaf were sixteen pence! . . . He raised his bowed head with its matted iron-grey beard, its bald dome grey with dirt. He slowly glanced toward the little figure sleeping uneasily upon the settle.

Thoughts for which he could find no vehicle of expression crossed his mind: but against the formless clouds in his brain there shone, where the sun reached them, those five great disks of solid silver—solid reality against vague ideas. Five great silver disks that spelled bacon, beer, tea, flour, and gallon loaves—a vast store of eating to a man with food, lodging, clothes and firing to find for five people out of eight shillings a week!

His bony hand went out uncertainly towards the money, and closed slowly on the coins.

Outside a cock crew shrilly.

'Taäke 'un, if 'ee will,' said he. 'But doän't 'ee tell she!'—He nodded his shaggy head toward the door.

Lewis had dealt with women-folk in these matters before. They either drove a harder bargain than the men, or else became sentimental.

He saw a minimum profit of seven guineas on his bargain. Climbing children fetched high prices when they were very small, and no questions were ever asked. He did not propose that anyone should interfere between him and that profit. He was a little surprised at the warning against the woman of the inn, but imagined that she might be some more prosperous connection of the gaunt man's wife.

He walked to the door, and looked along the passage.

'I will go and speak with the woman off the house,' he said. 'Do you take the child out to the wagon while I am gone.'

He disappeared down the dark passage immediately he had spoken, and his voice could be heard somewhere within the dark recesses of the inn.

Richard shook the child by the shoulder.

'Coom, coom! 'Tes time 'ee went,' he mumbled, as Christopher's eyes opened wide upon him. He avoided the innocent gaze, and fell into an incomprehensible burble of broad vowels and blurred consonants.

Christopher gathered that he must go somewhere he did not know, for some reason he did not understand. Obediently he slid off the seat and followed the other out.

A little later Richard stood in the dark, low room alone.

He had left the five crowns on the table, for he could not think of two things at once. His mind had been occupied with the departure of the boy.

They were still there—five broad and shining pieces of silver. He looked at them dazedly. They spelled food—and feasting.

The woman of the house peered in.

'The child's gone, Richard?'

'Aye, the child be gone, mistress,' he said, and his great knotted hand covered the coins.

Outside there was the musical jingle of little bells, the crunch of ponderous wheels, the creaking of a heavy vehicle, and with it an undercurrent of the strange low twittering. It grew faint. It died away.

He picked up his billhook and a bundle wrapped in sacking. He stumped out, his head sunk on his chest, his eyes unseeing.

Chapter 6

Setoun Remembers ... a Kiss

HENRY URBLINGTON SETOUN BY UPBRINGING WAS AN adherent of lost causes and forlorn hopes; by nature an eager student of the new and unknown; by reason a republican and believer in the equality of man; and by instinct an apostle of the Divine Right of Kings. He was probably the last practising Jacobite in Great Britain, and belonged to every Stuart Club in the country, from the Oyster and Parched Pea to the Cycle of the White Rose —livery, blue coat and primrose waistcoat. Since he declined to acknowledge the Hanoverian tenancy of the throne, it goes without saying that he had taken no steps for the removal of the attainder placed on the peerage he should have held, after the collapse of the rebellion of 1745.

But if he made no effort toward the recovery of barony forfeited over seventy years before by his grandfather, he found malicious delight in insisting upon his style of third Viscount Setoun. His aforesaid grandfather had received that title at St. Germain-en-Laye in 1747 from the exiled King James the Third, as some measure of consolation for the loss of his birthright: for vanished estates that nobleman had more than compensated himself by wedding an astonishingly rich Dutch lady with plantations in the Netherlands East Indies, factories in Guiana, a share in a dozen enterprises in New England, a third part in a banking business in Amsterdam, and a fleet of ships in the China trade.

Setoun was by no means purse-proud or ostentatious—his vast wealth meant little to him; but he took a childish pleasure in flaunting his coronet in places and circumstances where it was most likely to cause embarrassment. He flatly declined to be presented to the Regent on the score that 'the fellow was no gentleman'; he had served with the Prussian forces during the last phases of the Napoleonic War, because he refused to take the oath of allegiance; he caused pin-prick annoyance to the Duke of York by constant reference to him as 'His Reverence' in allusion to his title of Prince Bishop of Osnaburgh. He maintained that Charles the Second was the greatest and most lovable king England had ever had, and that no books ever had been—or would be—written to equal *Robinson Crusoe*, *The Pilgrim's Progress* or *Tristram Shandy*.

Which all goes to explain why he sat at the round table in his sitting-room at the inn, with a large map of the border counties stretched before him, planning a theoretical invasion of England by the Scottish clans on behalf of the House of Stuart.

It is true that with the death of Henry Stuart, Prince and Cardinal, he had become more than a little uncertain who the legitimate King was. That, however, was a mere side-issue. The essential point was that his invasion would be proof of a new technique in military mobility. He would have no cavalry at all, and no infantry—in the accepted sense of the word. His soldiery would be mounted infantry; mounted, be it understood, on hobby-horses—two-wheeled concerns which the rider propelled as he sat astride the frame, by pushing himself forward with alternate foot to earth. By this means he calculated he could make his whole army move along the roads at between five and six miles an hour—a speed double that of the normal rate of march. Lightning raids of his hobby-horse army should paralyse the nerve centres of the Hanoverian enemy.

Hobby-horses—velocipedes—whichever you liked! That was the kernel, the *alpha* and *omega* of the scheme! No water; no forage; no sickness; no upkeep; no stampeding horse-lines; no waste of man-power on horse-pickets! Mobility, without the disadvantages of cavalry!

With his dividers he pored over his map, planning an attack that should spread fanwise over England from York.

In his mind's eye he visualized the flying columns astraddle their hobby-horses, wheeling down the Great North Road, on to the flat fertility of central England. . . . He saw his lines pushing forward where there was no resistance, withdrawing easily in the face of superior forces—mobile, fluid, as uncatchable as water. It might

even be that there should be advance parties on velocimanipedes—
three men to each machine, one to steer, one to pedal at the geared
wheels, and one as passenger.

He worked out the distances along the roads with his dividers,
made laborious calculations on a tablet beside him.

Of course, the business of propelling yourself forward on your
mount—first a toe to earth on one side, and then on the other—
meant unusual wear on the tips of the boots. That would have to
be got over—iron tips, a special pattern of hobnails, something of
that sort.

Lost in contemplation of the problem he looked out of the window, to the leafless woods that rose steeply beyond the little curving river; and at last became conscious of the passage of time. He
drew his repeater watches out of his fobs, set negro and goat at
their japes, and compared them anxiously. They coincided within
a few seconds, and with a sigh of relief he returned to his map and
imaginary campaign.

As he did so there was a light step without; the door opened, and
Charlotte appeared. She wore a cherry-coloured bonnet with a high
crown of silver-grey, and a long close-fitting pelisse of grey velvet
with a little shoulder cape all edged with smoke-blue fur.

He rose ceremoniously at her entrance.

'Well, Hurbles,' said she coming into the room, and peeling off
her long gloves. 'Still playing! Playing when you ought to be de-
fending the honour of your ward!'

'Ainh?'

'You see me ferocious, Hurbles darling! You see me breathing
fire and fury, blood and frenzy! Frenzy with a p-h . . . Phrenzy! I
shall swoon—swound, I mean, on the sofa with a p-h . . . Sopha!'
She accented the letters. 'A young girl's honour has been assailed
while you day-dream.'

He smiled at her, the laughter-wrinkles creasing about his bright
blue eyes.

'Another adventure with your very young paramour?' he inquired. 'More improper conduct with babies, Carlotta?'

'A fat baby this time, Hurbles,' said she, tracing the thin line of
a road along his map with a slim finger. 'A fat baby, Hurbles! In
fact—now, I won't have you get angry—the Duke of Kent!'

'Duke of Kent!' said Setoun. 'Duke of Kent!' The angry flush that rose to his face deepened its weathered redness to the dull red that lies in the depth of a storm cloud. 'I'll wring his filthy Hanoverian neck for him! . . . I'll stuff his pompous mouth with his nasty coat-tails, and make him eat 'em! I'll tie his liver in knots round his neck!'

'Not a bit of it,' said Charlotte briskly. 'Not a bit of it. You'll enjoy the fun as much as I did. And not do anything foolish—as I did.'

'Anything foolish—as you did?' repeated Setoun, a look of almost comical anxiety exploring his face. 'What have you been up to, Carlotta?'

'Nothing that a wicked old man can straighten for me,' said Charlotte affectionately. She put a hand on his tight mulberry-coloured sleeve, and regarded his dividers, map and tablet of calculations with a wise, tender and parental discernment. She picked up a document from among the litter:

' "Specification of Velocimanipede to be built to the order of the Right Honourable Viscount Setoun, Prince of the Holy Roman Empire, etc. etc." '

she read aloud with a quizzical expression.

'In the name of all that is merciful, what is the ridiculous person throwing away his money upon now?" she inquired.

'Very little! Very little!' said Setoun in some confusion. 'The invention of the century! Do away with horses. Do away with chaises. Carry three people. Propelled by man power. You see, Carlotta . . .' He paused, suddenly conscious that he was being sidetracked. . . .

'But what's this about your disreputable duke, hey, girl? Hey, girl?'

'It's an odd story,' said Charlotte, dropping into a chair in the window and twisting the bracelet on her wrist. 'I have got to tell it you, Hurbles. But there is no good in getting angry with me or the duke.'

'With you? . . . With you?' said Setoun reproachfully. 'Am I likely to? Have I ever?'

'Don't interrupt me, Hurbles! Let me tell you what happened. Some is important, and some just silly.'

Setoun sat himself upon the edge of the table which creaked beneath him, swinging a long leg.

'Well, I curtsied to the duchess prettily. She was most affable . . .'

'So she should be! So she should be. What's a tin-pot Coburg to a Harringay or Setoun?'

'. . . Showed me the royal baby. So very royal, too, Hurbles! She kept on saying in her appalling English, "Zhe is ze image of her great-fader—ze image eggsact". Then she would dandle the fat little creature up and down. 'Pon my soul, Hurbles, the child *is* exactly like King George! There's something about the upper lip and forehead. It may sound absurd, but I will swear that when she is old and fat she'll be the image of George the Third as I remember him at Weymouth when I was a child.'

Setoun grunted in depreciatory comment of the Royal Family in all its branches.

'Then the duchess walked me down to the far end of the saloon. Away from the nurse and her ladies. She looked at me with eyes swimming in tears and said, "Zhe vill be like ze good old King in zoul, too, *if zey let her live!*" Hurbles, I swear she said that to me—in a hushed whisper as if she were afraid of being overheard! She was as pale as death. There were little beads of perspiration on her forehead. Her dark ringlets were damp. She kept on looking from side to side as if the long curtains hid someone. As if the heavy furniture concealed assassins. Her fingers twitched. She was in an absolute panic.'

'What the devil'd she mean?' inquired Setoun, taking up one of Charlotte's gloves from her lap, and smoothing out the fingers of it as gently as if he were caressing the hand whose faint warmth lingered within.

'You remember that lonely child . . .'

'. . . Your bedfellow?'

'My bedfellow!' assented Charlotte with half a smile. 'It seems that yesterday he went shooting sparrows—with a pistol, with two pistols! One of the bullets missed the baby by the breadth of an eyelash. It grazed the fat nurse; smashed a mirror to smithereens.'

'Gentleman ought to be walloped,' commented Setoun. 'But what's there to make a song about? Woman's an old hen!'

'The point is—don't wreck my glove, Hurbles—that none of them think the child fired the shot at all!'

'A-umph! Well, who did?'

'She drew me to a corner and sat me on a sofa overlooking the dark dripping garden. The perspiration made little wet patches on her florid cheeks. She held me by my arm. Even her hand was wet, Hurbles! . . . She just had to talk. . . . She said, "He is mad! Zo many of zem are mad!" And then she moaned and rocked herself to and fro. I have never heard anyone moan before. It seemed to come from somewhere deep within her. It wasn't a human sound at all.

'I said briskly, "Mad, ma'am? Who's mad?" She looked about the room as if he might be grinning at her in the shadows. She lowered her voice to a whisper I could barely hear. She leaned over to me till her moist face almost touched my ear. "Cumberlandt: ze Duke of Cumberlandt!" she said.'

'Cumberland!' said Setoun, and whistled. He thrust his hands into the tight pockets of his pantaloons and looked out, lost in meditation, to the dimming river and the hills. 'Should think he is quite capable of it. Murderous, ill-conditioned fellow, if ever there was one. Mad? . . . I should think so . . . But . . .'

'In that dark room and with that frightened woman, Hurbles, I'll swear I felt the presence of some sinister power. It seemed to brood in all the shadows. It lay in the dampness no fire could dispel. Something evil and ungovernable and mad! I got frightened too. I felt as if I might see a face pressed against the rain-misted windows for a moment, or hear a soft, heavy footfall on the gravel without, and know that no one physical was there.

'Then she poured out her story. You could not stop her or comfort her. She went on, and on. Her lips almost against my ear. And she panted as she spoke, as if she were running for her life.

'She made him a monster, a murderous creature who would stop at nothing in his lusts. He grew before me. I seemed to see his blind-eyed gaze and twisted smile and dark face.

' "Four big strong brudders between him and ze trone of Eng-

landt," she said. "He vill not touch zem. But after zem, one zo
small babe alone!" '

She copied the duchess's accents.

' "Four big strong men! And but one childt among zem! George
—vot happened to his only childt, Charlotte? Vy did she die? Vy
did ze only man who knew cut his t'roat? Did Sir Richard Crofts
cut his t'roat . . . or . . . ? Vy did ze nurse vanish from ze face of
ze earth? Frederick—no childt! . . . William—no childt! . . . My
'usband—a leedle girl. . . . He tries to shoot her!

' "Vot happened to Sellis? Vot happened to Princess Sophia?
Verever he is, zere is death or disaster or zomething 'orrible!" '

Setoun twisted a great gold ring on his little finger, so that the
bezel which he habitually kept on the palm side came uppermost.
He looked at it reflectively before speaking.

'Still, Carlotta, you can't accuse a Royal Duke—even if he's a
Hanoverian, and Cumberland at that—of conspiracy to murder,
on the word of a small boy.'

'The small boy does not come into it, Hurbles, in that way. He
accused no one. They say—Stockmar says—he never fired a shot
at all. That the bullet was fired from another pistol. They can't
prove it. Never will be able to. They think he was a sort of stalking
horse.

'And I believe they are right. I will tell you why in a moment.
. . . It is a horrible story—a wicked story, a damnable story. . . . I
don't mind so much about the little princess. They can look after
her. But the poor child. Hurbles, there's more real evil about this
family than any other in the world. They are hateful . . . and mad
. . . and bad. . . .

'The theory is that the child was to take the blame. He had a
pistol that had been fired: somebody else fired the shot. Whether
the baby was killed or not the thing would have to be hushed up.
You could not bring the ostensible culprit himself, and the hideous
scandal about him, into the open. . . . It was very clever, and
damnable!'

'What do you mean?' asked Setoun. 'What in the name . . . ?'

'He could not be accused of shooting his cousin.'

' "Shooting his cousin!" '

'He is a nephew of the duke. He is a son of Princess Amelia.'

'Amelia!'

Setoun's red face paled: he shot a glance at Charlotte who sat regarding the long hands in her lap. He rose and walked stiffly to the window, and stood with squared shoulders looking out at a landscape of which he saw nothing.

Once again, after ten years, he saw the pale face with the forget-me-not blue eyes, and the curved pale lips. He felt the light touch of that quick kiss bestowed so long ago by a princess. He saw her, as he had first seen her, at a distance, amid her sisters and their ladies on the terrace at Windsor, with the flags streaming in the breeze against a blue sky, band playing and eager crowd. He saw her as he had seen her at Weymouth, slim and pale, blown laughing before the seashore wind. He saw her again, as on that night when he had stood bowed over her bed in a softly illumined room, her transparent hand swallowed up in his. He heard again the canary flutter within its covered cage upon her table—flutter with that same whisper of sound with which she spoke to him.

'Amelia's son,' repeated Charlotte very low. . . . 'She made a secret . . . marriage!'

'I know,' said Setoun. 'She told me when she . . . was dying.'

'She had a son.'

'I did not know! . . . They let me stay but one moment with her . . . one moment!'

'She did not know that the man she married . . . was her brother George's . . . natural son . . . until too late.'

'She did not,' said Setoun, as if he bit each word off.

He found that at the memory of that agony for her and him the tears had trickled on to his weather-beaten cheeks. He forced himself to speak:

'Few people knew he was George's son. And few, again, of them that knew ever heard of her marriage to him.'

'He . . .' began Charlotte.

'Don't speak of him, Carlotta. Name sullies your lips. Swine son of a swine father! I should have killed him. Long ago. . . . But I promised her. . . .'

Charlotte looked up at the broad back in the window-bay—the broad flat back with the great shoulders, and the straight, strong neck. The tight sleeves strained under the tensing of his muscles as he folded his arms. She had a sudden fancy that in his mind he held gripped in deadly embrace the body of the man he hated, heard the bones crack against his own beneath the pressure of his enormous strength.

'Only thing that isn't clear to me at all,' said Setoun at length, 'is how the child came into the business.'

'It was horrible, Hurbles. The duchess seemed to forget her fears a little while she gloated over scandal. I felt as if she were licking her lips while she rummaged amongst dead love . . . and tragedy . . . and sorrow. I hated her then.

'The princess had hidden Christopher's existence very well. . . . No one knew about him. . . . The Regent only discovered by acci- dent the other day. He knew of the "marriage", of course. When he learned about Christopher he nearly went out of his mind. He saw the appalling scandal that might be spread. Heard the word "incest" whispered until it rose like thunder. She was his favourite sister: the man, his secret son. He knew the thing, if it were ever spread abroad, would cast yet more dishonour upon him and his family. . . .'

'There was none to warn her!' said Setoun, and groaned. 'So how should she know?'

'My dear,' said Charlotte, and rose and stood beside him, her face averted so that he should know she was not looking at his contorted features. 'Who is there can blame her? She was innocent and young. A prey of evil men and unhappiness and restraint, like the women in every generation of her House. Who can ever say a word against her!'

Setoun stammered. He was no longer a middle-aged gentleman with a whimsical mind, but as fiercely eager and young and dan- gerous as long ago when he had stood outside a darkened house at Weymouth, and stared at the blank windows and thought who slept behind them, and watched through all a summer night like any knight-errant.

'I-if anyone d-did, I'd k-kill him,' he said. 'I-I'd kill him.'

Charlotte pressed her hand within his folded arm, patting his sleeve rhythmically.

'Anyhow, it seems the Regent was not content to let things be.

Was afraid the boy might get to know. Or his guardian might make use of him as a sort of blackmail. Thought the best thing was to whisk the child out of England, and plant him in Hanover somewhere with a careful synthetic pedigree. To lose him, in fact, to those few who knew of his existence and history. So he sent Baron Ompteda to take him to the Continent. The man's been his agent and spy for years. On their way up from Cornwall the child fell ill—at least that's the story—and the doctor insisted on his staying here. Then a mysterious friend of Ompteda, a Captain Heywood, turns up, and goes away again—no one knows where! Stockmar thinks that Ompteda is also Cumberland's man, and has been double-crossing the Regent. It may be so. Anyhow I am sure that Heywood is Cumberland's spy—and assassin, if you like!'

'Cumberland?'

'Cumberland. . . . You've got the structure of the story there.'

Charlotte's hand touched his left hand where it clasped his right arm at the elbow. She shot one quick glance down at the four strong fingers that showed gripping his sleeve—the branched veins that ran into the valleys between the knuckles, the faint reddish hair upon the joints, the crystal bezel of the great ring with the pale twist of a lock of hair enshrined beneath it.

'I know more than they do,' she said at length. 'Before ever this happened there was an incident. Heywood was responsible. The child told me . . . that night. I thought it best to keep my mouth shut. Couldn't do any good by talking!'

She told Christopher's tale of the loading of the pistol, and that quick shot which brought the plaster trickling from the wall and a goggle-eyed waiter stampeding to the door.

'And,' she finished, 'now the boy is missing. He was very frightened. He ran away, and now they cannot find him.'

Setoun pictured the child he remembered—the bright eager face hypnotized by the wonder of his watches—son of a princess, son of a girl he had loved, stray in an unfriendly world.

'He must be found. At once. I will look for him myself.'

There was no sign of emotion left when at last he turned his head, and looked down into Charlotte's face.

'Carlotta dear,' he said. 'Your business here with the old manor must go. The decorators must look after themselves. We must find the child. *Her* boy can't be stray in the world . . . or in the hands of his filthy grandfather—uncle—whichever you may call him.'

They had a large-scale map on the table before them, plotting out a search when, suddenly, he remembered:

'What did Kent say to you?'

Charlotte raised wide eyes from the chart. There was a hint of laughter in their depths.

'He was very polite, Hurbles dear. Very polite. He walked me in their wet garden afterwards in a perfect caricature of a coat . . . and was very polite indeed!'

'Yes?'

There was no answering laughter in Setoun's regard.

'He explained the duchess had taken a great fancy to me and would like me to be in waiting upon her. He felt that I would have her confidence. . . . He hinted, very obliquely—now, Hurbles, I will not allow you to be naughty—that there might be another position open to me! Spoke of a long-standing *tendresse!*'

Setoun exploded.

When he had roared about the room, Charlotte hushed him.

'I thanked him—very obliquely, too, of course—for the favour. I explained, most indirectly, that his elder brother, Clarence, had once offered to make me his duchess. I left him to infer from that statement that I was unlikely to accept any equivocal position which might be tendered.

'He hurriedly covered up his tracks. Swung his wide face with the absurd chin over his high stock, and looked at me as if he were hurt that I could think naughty things about him. Hoped I would fall in with his wife's suggestion.

'How I loathed the man—all of them, hypocritical, Sabbatarian debauchees. They are not rakes, Hurbles, they are debauchees, and dull ones at that. I was so angry that I said in my most prunes and prisms manner: "You will forgive me, sir, if I am unable to obey Her Royal Highness's command. I am shortly to proceed, sir, to the Continent to offer my services to Her Royal Highness, the Princess of Wales." I didn't add—"the woman you and your family loathe and abominate and torture and despise; whose husband does his best to drive her mad." I swept him my best curtsy and took myself off, my bonnet nodding with indignation!'

Setoun had stopped his pacing. He stood in the middle of the room as if turned to stone.

'Caroline of Wales!' he said. 'That bedizened harridan! Carlotta, you are mad!'

'That wretched harassed woman! That poor creature they harry when they can! . . . Hurbles, that was my revenge! That I preferred to serve the least-considered outcast of their House to mixing with their psalm-singing, whoring, snuffling Royal Hypocrisies! . . . Our family, Hurbles, is twice as old as theirs, and much more respectable—and they know it! It makes them as sick as dogs to know we despise 'em. . . . Caroline, they say, can get no ladies. They are afraid of social ostracism. I am not. I . . . and you . . . stand above it. Are you sorry I am going? . . . Shall you be as sorry as . . . ?"

Setoun stood at the table before her. His fingers beat a tattoo upon the polished surface. He looked a little old and stooping.

She suddenly felt that she was abandoning him to his ghosts; was removing life from his orbit, and leaving him alone with whimsies—and hobby-horses.

'I . . .' she said.

'When I have found the child,' interrupted Setoun, looking up, 'I—I shall come, too.'

A little later, as she stood at the door, poised to depart, she said—as if she meditated out loud, 'I supposed you loved her, Hurbles . . . very much!'

Chapter 7

Begins with Bread ... and Ends with Rum

THE HOODED WAGON LURCHED ALONG THE RUTTY ROAD behind a team of eight horses, like a Dutch galliot riding a choppy sea.

As she pitched and rolled, her body groaned and creaked; and all the oddments pendent from hooks along her giant sides—drags, lengths of rusty chain, iron kettle, and saucepan—set up a loud clattering and banging on the battered timber and stout ribs. Against the background of this uproar the little bells jingled sweetly.

She was a mountain of a thing to pass along the ill-made highway. It was at least twelve feet from the ground to the rounded top of the hoops supporting the patched and stained canvas that covered her from end to end. The rear four of the six great wheels were nearly six feet tall, and their rims so broad that five widths of iron tire formed the tread over the wooden felloes. If there was any paint on spokes and naves and body it was hidden under a crust of the dense red mud that caked the folds of the wagon cover where it was corded below the raves.

Forward on the starboard side of this land-ship, was a brass lantern, proportionately vast, with windows of horn.

There was a wide platform behind the shafts, under the high, blunt front of the body. On it lay Mr. Lewis at length, resting upon a huddle of old sacks over straw, refreshing himself at intervals from a black bottle, and contemplating the exertions of the wagoner who conducted his operations mounted on a small pony with the aid of a long whip and two Welsh sheep-dogs.

A third dog, as if on patrol, trotted to the rear of the vehicle and never left its place.

117

It had snowed a little during the night, and, in the early sunshine, flakes lay like crystallized sugar on the green banks of the road. Ice crunched in the ruts beneath the wheels. A frozen pond, away from the sun, lay grey among the alders. On the northern slopes, which they now climbed, the snow had not melted, as in the valley, and lay densely white on the fields, and grey on hedge and tree.

On a bare bough beside the road, entirely unafraid, sat a magpie, his chest so white it might have been thought that his companion had been snowballing him.

'One for sorrow!' said Mr. Lewis, blowing on his five remaining fingers to keep them warm. He ran over the jingle in his mind: but, do what he would, it was impossible to make out the sight of a single magpie as other than a bad omen.

'One for sorrow!' said Mr. Lewis reflectively, preparing to get to the ground. Little as he liked the exercise, walking seemed to be the only sure method of restoring circulation after rum, mufflers, overcoats and cloaks had failed.

His head had been pillowed on an old nosebag. This he deftly skewered with his hook before struggling clumsily to the ground.

The road was very narrow and he had to stand back, pressed against the hedge, until the wagon had rolled by. Then he fell in at the rear, with the dog.

The wagon cover came into a great bunch at the back, but it had been corded very firmly to rings and hooks in the tail-board. He unlaced a corner with considerable difficulty, and shook the contents of the nosebag through the gap.

The top of the tailboard was so high that he had to hold the nosebag well above his head. A sideways lurch of the vehicle caused him to miss his aim, and two large hunks of greyish bread fell to the ground, into a mass of fresh horse droppings.

Mr. Lewis picked them up with a curse, and, with considerable accuracy shot them one after the other through the hole.

The twittering within the wagon was stilled while this went on, and even after he had laced the tarpaulin up again, and, falling a little behind, had burst into discordant nasal song.

For a long distance the uttermost pace of the wagon was barely two miles an hour. Mr. Lewis was, therefore, enabled to amble

peacefully along, now talking to the surly dog at his heels, now taking a pull at the black bottle that bulged his coat-tails, now singing
items from his choice repertoire of Methody hymns.

> 'Make us fit Tripe for
> Thy heavenly Table:
> Make us Meat ripe for
> The Banquet of God!'

sang Mr. Lewis.

> 'Oh Let our Blood be
> A Wine of good Flavour:
> God's goblets filling with
> Sweetest of Savour!'

This was a high favourite, and he intoned it several times
through his nose, finding on each occasion fresh beauties in it, before he launched out into secular ditties of which he had a large
command—all gross, and mostly obscene.

So singing he clumped along with his knock-kneed gait, his steel
hook and projecting front teeth glinting in the pale sunshine—at
peace with himself, the world, and God.

There were six children huddled together in the tail of the
wagon, on what floor space was left free from the roof-high mass
of crates and cases.

There was not room for them all to lie at once on the stinking
urine-soaked straw. Four of them sat crouched against the sides or
tailboard, while one was stretched at their feet. Christopher stood,
wedged against the jolts, in a corner beside a crate, higher than
himself, that occupied the entire width of the wagon.

In the half-light which filtered through the hood, his companions' faces—hollow-cheeked and bony—took on the greyness of
death. They tore at the lumps of mildewed bread like famished
dogs, exchanging no word. Christopher had rejected all but the
centre part of his portion, and dropped the filthy crust into the
straw. There had been an immediate snarling struggle for it, in
which the bony creature on the floor had won. He had thrust the

morsel into the straw beneath him, and laughed once, on a high note. His eyes were meaningless, his skin leaden, and as he ate saliva trickled from the corners of his mouth.

Christopher watched his companions silently, for they had not addressed him since he was hoisted up, without a word, by Richard, and pushed over the tailboard into their midst, an hour before. He had landed head first on the idiot boy, who had cried out feebly and struck aimlessly towards him.

The others had huddled together and stared at the newcomer, like cornered sheep facing a dog. Until the bread had come they had remained staring at him with wide eyes, whispering and twittering together in a tongue that was incomprehensible.

There were two girls, a boy of his own age, and a child who could not have been more than six, whose only garment appeared to consist of an old sack with holes for his head and arms.

The elder girl was, perhaps, twelve years old. She had what might have been a lovely face, broad at the brow and pointed at the chin. Her grey tragic eyes were fringed with long lashes, and her nose delicately shaped with fluttering nostrils curved like a dove's wing. Her black hair was incredibly matted with dirt and grease, and her arms so withered that the flesh seemed to have dried up into a thin wrapping for the bones.

The younger girl, who clung to the smallest child, snivelled all the time, and dripped from nose and eyes. Her mouth was ringed with sores, and her face and neck and arms were covered with the bites of vermin.

The elder boy's face was that of a skeleton. His eyes were sunk deep into their sockets: his cheeks were mere hollows between cheekbone and jaw: the hands that held a filthy crust to his mouth were raw and bleeding from innumerable chilblains. Ringworm had made him nearly bald. . . .

The wagon rumbled on: the bells jingled: smoke rose from every cottage chimney straight up into the clear cold sky: a thaw and then a frost had set the hedges glittering with beads of ice like crystal berries: and Mr. David Lewis shuffled along in the pleasant morning hymning his praises of a beneficent Creator. . . .

The idiot twittered meaninglessly to himself as he played on the floor with a piece of string. He made water over himself as he lay, and whimpered a little in complaint at the discomfort. Christopher watching him, mesmerized, saw a grey small creature crawl from his shirt, over his ear and into the tangle of his hair.

Herded as they were together, there was still no warmth; and yet the chill draughts that trickled in through every crack and every hole in the canvas roof could not sweep clean the stale foul odours of their prison.

'Where are we going, please?' said Christopher at last to the elder girl, who was nearest him.

She turned a face like that of a lost fairy towards him, but made no answer.

The others ceased their whispering and stared.

In the silence Christopher repeated his question.

'Dunno,' said the girl in a low voice of incredible hoarseness, shaking her matted hair.

'Are we going to Cornwall?'

He squatted down beside her.

'Cornwall?' she said. 'What's Cornwall?'

'Cornwall—the country?'

'Dunno!'

'I want to go to Cornwall,' said Christopher, formulating for the first time consciously the idea behind his flight.

The beautifully shaped lips—so cracked they were!—parted in something that was nearly a smile.

'You'll 'ave to go where you're took,' she said.

'But where are we being taken!' he insisted. 'I couldn't understand the man who put me in here. . . . I don't think he knew I wanted to go to Cornwall—unless I talked in my sleep!'

She could not follow him, and watched his lips forming the sentences with a puzzled expression.

'Dunno!'

'You must know where you are going,' he assured her.

Again she shook her tangled head.

'Dunno! Been bound to someone—all on us.'

This was equally incomprehensible to Christopher. He fell silent.

After a little the child leaned across him. She tapped the imbecile on the shoulder.

'Simmie,' she said, 'give 'un 'is bread!'

Simmie screwed up his face, threatening tears, his cunning eyes watching her to see the effect. It had none.

'Simmie,' she repeated remorselessly. 'Give 'un 'is bread!'

Simmie rolled over, extracted the crust from the damp filth beneath him, and gave it into her hand.

She pressed it on Christopher. The smell of it was sufficient. He pushed her hand off.

'Take the filthy thing away!' he said—and was sorry for the discourtesy. 'Thank you very much. Have it yourself, or give it back to Simmie.'

She still had hold of it, uncertain, when the boy with the ringworm stretched forward and suddenly snatched it from out her hand. He crammed a great piece of it into his mouth.

Like a flash she was up and on top of him, tearing at what was left of his hair, and scratching at his face. They struggled together for a moment, rolling against the others in the confined space. Flying limbs struck the six-year-old on the jaw. He uttered no cry of pain, but for a moment his wizened face—like that of a very old man or a monkey—took on a devilish expression. He beat twice with puny blows at them, cursing with the oaths of a grown man in a piping treble.

Simmie made no effort to get out of the way. Indeed he could not if he would. But he lay seemingly insensible to kicks and jostling, avidly regarding the struggle. Once even the pair rolled on to his head, but when they broke clear he had not stirred at all: only his dull eyes moved as he watched.

The battle ended in the girl recovering the greater part of the crust, which she returned to Simmie, who accepted it without thanks and restored it to safe-keeping beneath his person. . . .

The wagon came to a standstill. There was shouting from the front, and, after a little while, someone came to the rear and undid the lashings, swearing as he did so. The tailboard fell with a crash, and the sunlight and fresh air streamed in.

'Come on out off it, ye peggars,' said Mr. Lewis. 'Come on, plast ye!'

He carried a thick leather thong in his hand, and was escorted by the wagoner's boy, a husky lad of fifteen in a smock, with a red face so fat that his small grey eyes were nearly hidden.

With cramped limbs the children got stiffly down from the high tail. All except Simmie, who was dragged out—by the wagoner's boy—since he would not move, and rolled over the edge, a three-foot drop to the road. He fell, making no effort to save himself, and was kicked to his feet by the lad.

They were halted outside an ale-house at the foot of a long steep hill. The frosted road narrowed after it left the low, whitewashed building, and ran upwards between high banks crowned with hedges in which brown-leaved beech alternated with the dark tangle of blackthorn.

Mr. Lewis joined the burly wagoner in a tankard of ale before the door in the pleasant sunshine, while the horses steamed in the cold air. The wagoner's boy climbed into the vehicle and kicked the sodden straw into the roadway. After he had done that and thrown two armfuls of clean bedding on the floor, he jumped to the ground and leaped straight upon the poor imbecile, beating him about the head and shoulders with the short stock of his whip.

'Ton't tamage the goodss too much!' cried Mr. Lewis, lowering the tankard from his lips to take breath, and thoroughly appreciating the fun.

The idiot made no effort to protect himself, but ran moaning hither and thither from the shower of blows.

'I'll larn ya, ya dirty swine!' . . . Crack . . . 'I'll larn ya, ya bloody loony' . . . Crack . . . 'I'll larn ya.' . . . And this time the blow missed and came down with such force on the hub of the great rear wheel that it jarred the wrist of the striker, and he dropped the whip.

Simmie ran stooping under the wagon. He peered out, presently, gibbering at his assailant, from between two wheels.

The other children had clustered together, watching as dispassionately as hinds will watch the cavalcade of a hunt in full cry after a stag, another's agony being their own security.

There was a wooden horse-trough outside the inn.

'Coom,' said the girl, taking hold of Christopher's hand and leading him to it. In some way she had sensed his utter ignorance of the manner of their wayfaring life, and was taking it upon herself to induct him.

'Coom!'

She released him, and, kneeling on the frozen cobbles, bent her head over the green-stained side of the trough and dipped her mouth into the scummy water.

After a little pause Christopher followed suit. The water tasted of mud. It was as cold as charity, and broken ice bobbed up and down against his chin and nose.

When he had drunk he felt in a pocket of his tattered pantaloons. A handkerchief was crumpled in it, above the little knitted purse with four of the silver shillings Aunt Howell had given him —years and years ago, it seemed.

He dipped the handkerchief into the brown cold water, and to the interest and surprise of his companion, scrubbed at his face and neck with it. He ran his fingers again and again through the disarray of his hair, and with the sopping rag washed off some of the clotted blood that matted it together.

Mr. Lewis, returning the wagoner's hospitality, had a hearty laugh at this comedy.

'Inteet, these poor-house prats are pecoming as partickler ass dukes,' said he.

'Aye, aye, maäster,' answered the wagoner. 'They'll be wanting 'ee to toock 'em in their bed o' night and hear 'em say their praäyers!'

He was a big man with a big thirst. He emptied his mug, and called loudly for more. Mr. Lewis had rum this time.

Christopher, having finished his toilet, came towards him.

'Please, sir . . .' he began.

'Yess?' said Mr. Lewis, lowering his mug and shutting his mouth tightly so that his two projecting upper teeth lay on his lower lip.

'Please, sir, are we going to Cornwall?'

' "Please, are we going to Cornwall?" ' imitated Mr. Lewis in his lilting sing-song. 'Yess, we are going to Cornwall—or is it, No! And what iss it to you, you little pastard, iff we dto go to Cornwall —or iff we dton't?'

There was such a hidden menace in the high Welsh voice that Christopher flinched. He had not questioned until so short a time ago that in this strange company he was leaving the horrors of yesterday behind, and was going back to the peaceful valley from which the rounded hills of the friendly moors could be seen, away from pistols and silent men and blustering men, back to the quiet life he knew—the world where silver tinkled against old china in rooms that smelled of lavender.

'I w-want to go home,' he stammered, and tears reddened his eyes.

'Want to go home?' cried Mr. Lewis setting his mug down on a bench at the door in shocked surprise. 'Want to go home! Do you hear that? Diw! Diw! Here am I taking this little scum at great, fery great expense, inteet, to make hiss fortune, and he tells me he wants to go home!'

'Want must be his maäster,' said the wagoner, wiping his lips on the back of an enormous hand.

'It musst, inteet,' said Lewis, fastening Christopher with his goggling eye. 'Here I haf arranged with this scorpion's Da' to start him in life at great expense and he wants to go home! Tid I give your Da' twenty-fife silver shullun to take you for a trive in a coach and eight? Tid I give your Da' twenty-fife silver shullun for nothin'?' . . . As he spoke he swung—idly, it seemed—the great strap behind his back. . . . 'Tid I give your Da' twenty-fife silver shillun for to pe told that you want to go home? . . . Home? . . . You ain't got a home!'

His voice rose to a high pitch of passion on the last words, and as he spoke he brought the doubled thong down across the child's shoulders.

With a scream of pain and terror Christopher fell on his knees. The lash fell again . . . again . . . and again.

The spectacle was so entrancing to the imbecile that he came out from his refuge and capered with glee. . . .

In a little while they moved on, the children trudging in the rear of the wagon, guarded by the dog and the wagoner's boy, who lurched after them whistling and flicking at the hindmost with his whip.

For miles they stumbled on in the bitter cold, shivering under their thin rags, their hands mottled blue and red, their faces growing more and more pinched and dark with fatigue. The child with the sores rubbed and scratched until a bleeding ring surrounded her mouth, which looked like a great wound covering the lower half of her face.

By and by the youngest fell. He staggered to his feet, to fall again half a mile farther on. The wagoner's lad was loitering well behind; and before he came up with his lash, Deb, the elder girl, had pulled the child to his feet, and with the help of the boy with ringworm, was half-pulling, half-supporting him along the road.

They held him up under the armpits so that his large head and wizened goblin face appeared to rest on the narrow shoulders without the intervention of a neck. His feet in clumsy shoes bound about with rags dragged at each step, and his small bruised knees so often gave under him that for nearly a mile he was virtually carried by the other two.

He did not whimper; nor did he speak. From time to time he peered up at the faces of his supporters, as if he would assess their ability to go on. The idiot walked with them, blubbering with fatigue and cold. His face was distorted with his weeping, and he thrust his bony fists, with chilblains on every joint, into his eyes as though to stop the stream of tears.

Christopher, trailing a little in the rear, aching with cold, with hunger, with pain, with weariness and fear, was beyond thought. He neither recollected the past, nor speculated on the future. He lived in an inexplicable present. The sheltered life of the past in a quiet valley, and its terrific unsettlement caused by the arrival of Baron Ompteda, had not fitted him to cope with a present which was only just a little more mad than the present of yesterday—the yesterday of a bursting pistol, of blows without reason, of angry men, and the silent-footed Heywood who came and went like a reasonless ghost.

The sun vanished. The clouds grew more leaden, and a shrill small wind whispered in the high hedges. A flake of snow blew into the open back of the wagon as if on a journey of investigation. One struck Christopher gently on the nose. Almost at once the air was full of them—thick white whirling feathers that reduced the world of spacious sky, and wide prospect of chequered valleys, into an orbit of wagon tailboard and trailing children: all else was wiped out.

Mr. Lewis had had one successful break-away by a prentice-to-be on the first day of his journey. Word also had been left for him of an attempt that failed in just such a storm, from the cargo he had sent on ahead of twenty children from the poor-house at Plymouth. He did not propose to run any risks of a similar happening.

The vehicle was accordingly halted, while the captives struggled aboard. Before they were laced up securely once more they were given their midday meal, a broken kettle full of water and six slices of bread—if bread it could be called, which was made of bean meal, adulterated with plaster of Paris and ground bones.

Knee to knee, shoulder to shoulder, they squatted on their hams amid the clean straw, eating in silence, except for the whimpering of Simmie, for whom no room had been left to lie down. Once, indeed, he tentatively stretched out a shrunken leg, but Deb, who sat between him and Christopher, struck it sharply.

'Simmie!' she said warningly, and he withdrew it with a foolish giggle.

The wagon rumbled on. Sometimes it jolted so much that its passengers were thrown upon one another, and the kettle slopped water over them. Once, in turning a bend, the near-side wheels slithered off the road into a shallow ditch, and for a moment the vehicle took on such a list it would seem that she must capsize.

A small jute bag, from somewhere amongst the corded cases that towered above them, broke loose from its moorings, and fell to the floor suddenly in their midst.

They all stared at it stupidly, until, as the wagon shook back to the vertical, the sack slid over till it touched Deb's legs and rested against them. She felt it tentatively with her hands, lifted it—it was the bigness of a man's head—and smelled it. She looked round the huddled group, as if to gather from their famished gaze some approbation for what she was about to do.

Spreading her knees as widely as she could, with the sack resting on her abdomen, she fumbled with the string that bound its neck. The finger-nails on her chapped and roughened hands were beautifully shaped, although broken and edged with ebony dirt.

Four small cotton bags of corn samples were inside, each one tied tight with tape. She undid them and tilted the contents into her lap—fat brown grains of wheat.

A sort of sigh went up from the watching children, and the boy darted a hand out. Deb was quicker still. She closed her knees, and in a flash had picked up the hems of her dress and petticoat and brought them up and over the prize in her lap, baring her narrow thighs as she did so.

'No, Gibbie! No!' she said hoarsely. 'Play fair, will ya.'

Still clutching the protecting folds with one hand, she pushed the empty bags and string towards him.

'Put 'em out!' she commanded.

Gibbie obediently scrabbled in the straw beside him. There was a large knot-hole in one of the planks, through which with difficulty he crammed the evidence of guilt so that it fell into the road.

After that in turn they took handfuls of the raw grain, and ate greedily with stuffed mouths.

Deb doled out the spoil with the strictest justice. If anyone's ration fell short it was her own, and the few grains left after division were given to the smallest.

So they journeyed on in the dim half-light that the thick dirty sail-cloth of the tilt admitted from the dark winter afternoon. Through a rent in the roof snow drifted in, and a sudden lurch sent the kettle on its side drenching their feet and the straw.

Vergil—for so some humorist of a poor-house chaplain had named the child—was sick. He brought up half-digested crusts and grain and even strings of green grass. After a little he ate the bread in his vomit.

Christopher crouched as closely to Deb as he could. He was bitterly cold; his head ached; his back was raw from the lashes and sudden fits of shivering seized him. Some vital warmth seemed to come from her: she was, perhaps, stronger than the rest physically because of her few more years, and, from some unknown strain in her blood, stronger spiritually and mentally. Because of this she seemed aloof from the others, and paid little heed to the weary occasional speech they squeezed out.

Christopher leaned closer against her. He sought for one of the rough small hands that lay in her lap, and closed his own over it. For a moment she seemed disposed to resent this intimacy; then she appeared to decide to bear with it.

Later—much later—she was shaken against him by a jolt as the wagon ground its way out of a rut. They tilted together in a corner, his head against her shoulder, and remained so until at length, slowly, as if ashamed, she brought her arm up and curved it round his neck.

So in the end they slept while their moving prison rumbled, rattled, lurched, and groaned, up hill, down hill, out of the snows into upland sunshine, never at a greater pace than three miles an hour, and sometimes barely covering the mile.

It was just after five o'clock in the evening when they halted for the night, outside a large lonely inn on a high plateau. The house looked across a strip of common dropping abruptly to a valley, beyond which the moors mounted to a high ridge, black against a fading sky. The heath-covered hills between glowed like hot coals where the dipping sun caught their rounded sides, and the hollows were filled with luminous shadows.

The wagon was drawn up, close under the lee of the high wall that continued the frontage of the inn along the bay in which it was set back from the road.

Lewis loosed the children while the wagoner and his boy led the jingling team through a wide arch into the stable yard, to water and full mangers and piled straw. The Welshman was sodden by then with drink, and stared into the gloom within, checking the tally with a glazed eye.

'One—two—tree—four,' he counted, and staggered, and saved himself from falling by catching his steel hook at the side.

'Tree—four—fife . . . fife.' It could not be right. He tried again —and to disengage himself simultaneously from the ring in which his hook had caught. He accomplished both feats with an effort.

'Shix!' he announced triumphantly. 'Shix! And, look you it ish shix when I come again! . . . Shix!' He memorized the figure, and staggered off to the inn.

The cessation of the interminable rumble had waked Christopher, but he and Deb had stayed motionless, clasped to one another, until the white flat face of Lewis had peered in on them.

Then they had slowly eased their cramped limbs before crawling to the ground with the others.

There was no idea of privacy. All of them together relieved nature, with the unconsciousness of small animals, in the narrow passage between wall and wagon. Afterwards they clustered about the frozen horse-trough which was set before a gaily-curtained window of the inn.

The water was frozen too hard for any of them to break the crust and drink.

A gaitered, good-natured ostler in a sleeved red waistcoat watched them from the door. Twisting a straw between his lips, he came over with lazy strides.

'Poor little beggars,' said he, 'it's a bad drink! It'll rot your innards, if so be it you've got any.' He took up a stone and cracked the ice and pressed the black, broken surface down, so that the water oozed up over it.

He stood awhile watching Christopher scoop up the water in his hollowed hands, and the others kneel and suck up the liquid with eager lips, like drinking beasts.

'Aye, rot your innards!' said the ostler reflectively chewing the straw.

'You're an odd looking lot o' cattle, aren't you?' said he, addressing Christopher.

'Yes, sir,' said Christopher.

'I wonder where it'll be you're going with One-Hand-Pretty-Face?'

'He won't tell us,' answered Christopher, plucking up courage and coming nearer to the man.

'Oh, he's got a little surprise for you, has he?' returned the ostler rather grimly. 'Where do you come from?'

Christopher, remembering pistols, and fierce men and words, and joints in a butcher's shop, hung his head.

'I don't know,' he stammered.

'If you don't know where you come from, it looks to me,' said the ostler biting his straw, 'that it don't matter where you are going to.'

Christopher edged a little nearer to the protection of Deb. Together they stared at the man. He found something so disconcerting in their gaze that his eyes dropped, and he spat out the straw and swung round on his heel.

He took up his stand again, against the lintel of the wide door, pretending to gaze into space, but in reality watching the little group from the corner of his eyes.

As the sun sank a chill wind arose and whistled dusk up the valley. The children, gathered aimlessly together, neither talking nor playing, shivered in their rags.

'I am so cold,' said Christopher at last.

'So'm I,' said Deb, beating her hands together. ' 'Twor cold last night in wagon. 'Twill be much colder to-night.'

'In the wagon?' asked Christopher in amazement. 'Do we sleep in the wagon?'

'In course we do, stoopid! Where do 'ee think? Under quilts in the best parlour?'

Christopher was taken aback.

'But there are no pillows . . . o-or sheets!'

Deb looked at him for a moment as if he were as mad as Simmie. Then she burst into laughter, rocked with hoarse laughter— 'Sheets! Pillers!'

At that moment there was a clatter of hoofs along the highway. A couple of livery servants in cockaded hats and dark blue coats tittuped by on grey horses.

A claret-coloured chaise with an enormous coat-of-arms on its door followed, the postilion steadying the off-side animal with his short whip-stock pressed upon its withers. Last of all, riding behind, came a large middle-aged gentleman in a mulberry-coloured overcoat incredibly tight at the waist and puffed at the sleeves. He passed, an orgulous, high-nosed figure on a seventeen-hand bay mare with a bone-shaking trot.

It was Charlotte's friend.

A wild cry rose in Christopher's throat—but passed his lips only as a strangled sob. Charlotte—oh, Charlotte! He remembered that warm bed, and the warm arms that had held him very close. He suddenly burst into a passion of tears.

Deb had witnessed unmoved the tears of the others: there had always been tears—tears, and lashes, and hunger, and cold—in her life. They meant little to her in the ordinary way. But this sudden outburst by the stranger boy was something different. An instinct told her, without knowing it, that he wept not as a denizen of earth might weep for immediate anguish, but as an angel lamenting forbidden heaven.

She took his hand awkwardly.

'Don't 'ee! Don't 'ee!' she said, and the quick comfort of her clasp checked the violence of his tears. . . .

Twilight was passing into night: the inn windows glowed yellow, and from within came a gust of laughter and wavering song. There was no sign of Lewis or yet of the wagoner and his boy. The ostler still stood in the doorway.

The cold became more intense, and in the quick flurries of the wind there was promise of more snow. Simmie blubbered as he shivered, and the younger girl kept up a perpetual whine from the pain of her sores. The child Vergil had watched Christopher's breakdown with a fixed stare, his eyes deep in their sockets alive with some strange intelligence as if he saw—though could not tell —the past and the future. He very rarely spoke, and now, although in the light from one of the windows his face was blue with cold and his teeth chattered, he made no demonstration of distress.

'I'll ask him,' said Christopher, nodding toward the ostler, 'if we can get back into the wagon. It'll be warmer.'

The others followed him on his errand, and paused a yard or so from the door.

'Please, sir,' asked Christopher, 'may we go back into the wagon?'

The man withdrew his gaze from the distance and looked down on the small figure.

'And for why,' said he, 'should you want to go back into that dirty wagon?'

'It's so cold, sir, outside,' said Christopher.

'Cold is it you are in your pretty clothes on this fine evening? And I'm not surprised! You tell old Filthy-Face to buy you a tot of rum to warm your bones! Faith, I'll tell him myself!'

'Rum?' said Christopher.

'Rum,' said the ostler. 'r—u—m. M—Melts frozen kidneys, and M for Makes the dead walk.'

'What's rum?' asked Christopher, intrigued by the capabilities of this magic.

'Rum, my boyo, is just rum. You drink it on nights like this, when you're rich like Filthy-Face, but not when you're poor like you and me.'

'Could I buy any rum?' inquired Christopher, deciding on the spur of the moment to break into his precious store.

'Could—you—buy—any—rum?' said the ostler slowly and thoughtfully. 'You could buy rum if you had the money. You couldn't buy rum if you hadn't.'

'Can I buy a shillingsworth?' asked Christopher. 'Would that be enough for us all?'

'If you had a shilling,' returned the other, 'you could buy a shillingsworth. And it would be enough for all.'

He hesitated a second, swung round and vanished up the bright wide passage.

Christopher, standing in the doorway alone, fumbled in his pocket, found his purse, opened it, extracted one of his shillings, and was putting the remaining treasure back, when he found Deb beside him.

'Where did 'ee pinch that?' she said excitedly. 'How much have 'ee got?'

He did not understand her first question and was about to answer her second when the ostler returned accompanied by a rosy landlady with white hair.

'What's all this about? What's all this about?' said she. The ostler, lounging negligently behind her, smiled knowingly to himself as if things were going according to plan.

'Please, ma'am,' asked Christopher, 'can I buy some rum?'

'Rum, child?' said the good lady. 'What in the name of fortune do you want with rum?'

'We're very cold, ma'am, and I've got a shilling!'

The shilling was a matter for great suspicion which was allayed as soon as the ostler suggested that it had been stolen.

'Don't be so uncharitable, Tim. The little boy says it was given him, and I'm sure he looks honest. . . . But rum?'

'They've been out in the cold for well-nigh an hour, ma'am,' said the ostler. 'You see what fine fur coats and thick clothes it is that they have to lounge out-o'-doors and smoke their seygars! I shouldn't let 'em have it, ma'am, meself!'

'For shame, Tim,' said the old lady. 'Why should we not serve them? Their money is as good as anyone else's. . . . Poor little creatures, they look frozen. With plenty of hot water it'll do them good.'

'A lot of good, ma'am, indeed on empty bellies! I'll be bound they've had no suppers.'

Yes, it was true they had had no supper. They had had some bread midday, and for breakfast.

'I heard their gentleman friend, ma'am, tell the carter's boy an hour agone to take 'em out a ravishing feast.'

'Ravishing feast, Tim?'

'Aye, ma'am. Six pounds of cold boiled potatoes in a bit of sacking it was to be. They've got to keep their figures jimp, especially the young leddies.'

'We must see what we can do, Tim, for a treat, once in a way. I'm sure Ellen can find something.'

'Well, ma'am, it may be a good thing. They'll need a hearty meal to-night when they sleep out in that wagon with no covering and wet straw. That meal'll just put them right. Otherwise the parish 'ud have the berryin' of the lot, for sure!'

'I think, Tim,' said the old lady, 'that you get more brutal every day! Now you go at once and find some more straw and plenty of empty sacks to keep them warm. And let me have no more nonsense from you! . . . Bless the child, what's that for?'

She stared at the shilling Christopher proffered her.

The ostler grinned.

'Faith, "Their money is as good as anyone else's",' he quoted. 'You just keep that for a day when you really need it. . . . I'll go and see what I can do.' And the old lady, with jingling keys at her waist, bustled off, followed by her man.

A moment later the latter reappeared. He held the wagoner's boy by the ear and marched him, protesting, out of the door. He kicked his fat buttocks with dispassionate vigour every few yards.

'An hour ago you were told, for I heard it meself,' said the ostler, 'an hour'—kick—'ago'—kick—'you were told. . . .' The procession faded through the archway into the stable yard.

'Wish 'is bottom bleeds!' said Deb viciously. 'Wish 'e gets bleedin' piles, that Dai!'

The procession returned. The wagoner's boy staggered under a large truss of straw, the ostler following with a pile of old sacks thrown over his shoulder, and a lantern in his hand.

'Clean that place out, young guzzle-guts,' he commanded, 'and put thisy'ere lantern inside out of harm's way. . . . All aboard, my lords and ladies. . . . I'll be back in a bit with the banq'et. . . .'

They timidly approached the wagon tail. The lad, having put the lantern on the high crate which was the inner wall of their banqueting hall, stood in the archway formed by the draped tilt. There was such menace in his attitude, such a glint in his small eyes, that none of them dare get in.

The ostler had vanished within the hostelry.

'C'm on, ya little bastards,' said the boy half-crying. 'I'll larn ya to peach on me. See if I don't!'

He leaped to the ground and darted among them like a killer dog attacking sheep. His elbow sent Christopher flying. With one hand he struck the younger girl on her bleeding mouth; the other fist he smashed into Simmie's frightened face. He kicked out with his heavily shod foot and brought Gibbie to the ground with a moan of pain.

'Get in, blast ya!' he cried like one demented, and caught Vergil and hurled the little bag of bones into the wagon on his face. With piteous hurry the others scrambled to obey, while he assailed them with blows behind. Christopher, clawing his way frantically in, was kicked twice with an iron-studded shoe so that he screamed with agony.

The elder girl was the last. She confronted the raving lad, as if daring him to strike her. He drew back his fist, dropped it. He approached his face to hers in the struggling light of the lantern. For a moment he seemed shaken by something that he saw in her eyes—something that was more than patience and restraint, though it partook of the quality of both; something that was infinitely long-suffering but infinitely dangerous.

He shook off the momentary chill. He caught her by the hair with one hand, forcing her head far back and her body against his, fumbling about her with violent indecency. She uttered no word, her wide eyes in the strained-back head staring into his with a passive contempt.

'Get in, get in,' he said thickly, and flung her against the wagon, thrusting her, pushing her in with violating hands.

'Now,' said the ostler appearing silently from the darkness, 'this is where I'll deal with you! This, my bonny boy, is where I'll larn 'ee! This is where I'll make 'ee sorry yer ma ever bore 'ee! This is where . . .'

He set down what he was carrying in the shadow. A whipcord arm shot out and seized the paralysed lad by the scruff of his neck. With slow deliberation, regardless of frenzied struggle, he stripped him of his smock, tore in one rending wrench his breeches off him, and forced him to the ground.

He set a foot on the writhing body, and drew from his gaitered leg a whip with a short lash. With an unflurried ease he cracked it once, and then sent the thong curling about the lad's bare buttocks. With the regular throb of a metronome he flicked it down so that the knotted end drew blood at every stroke.

The choking cries were unheeded. He did not stop until the boy's back was a raw, bleeding jelly. Then he turned the body indifferently over with his foot.

'Get out!' he said, and looked inside the wagon.

'Well, lords and ladies'—and his eyes twinkled—'there's nobbut better sauce to one's sorrow than someone else's. . . . See here!'

He lifted from the ground a great pitcher full of steaming liquid with aromatic smell.

"See here, here's your rum. If that don't make 'ee sleep and forget, God A'mighty himself couldn't. . . . And here's summat that'll fill your bellies without just blowin' 'em out. . . . The dish isn't too good. What's in it is.'

He pushed within a handless chamber-pot full to the brim with broken meats and white bread crusts and green vegetables.

'When you've got round that,' said the ostler, 'you can wash your faces and say your prayers and crawl between the silk sheets.'

The rum was mixed with hot stewed tea, but very strong—so strong that they were all more than a little drunken from it when they had finished.

And so, drunken and warm, they quickly fell asleep, their small verminous bodies huddled closely together, cloaked with old sacks.

Chapter 8

'Then Shall Appear the Wrath of God in the Day of Vengeance'

❧

D AY AFTER DAY THE WAGON ROLLED NORTHWARD AND eastward into the heart of England. Shortly after dawn each morning it would set out, and only halt for the night when dusk began to draw in.

For several hours each day the goblin procession of children trailed after it along the deeply rutted roads. As the journey progressed so they became more haggard, more famished, and more lamentable.

Christopher's shoes had fallen to pieces. He shuffled on as best he might, his swollen feet bound round with strips of old sacking to twice their natural size.

Vergil, the child, could barely walk at all: at the end of an hour his strength gave out, and, since he was not allowed to get back into the wagon, he had to be supported, or even carried for the remainder of the way. To the imbecile, strongest and biggest of them all, this task mostly fell. He performed it with perfect good nature, and for mile after mile would stumble at the tailboard with the child riding on his shoulders, chattering and gibbering as he went.

The other boy scavenged all the way. There was not a ditch that he did not watch, nor a cottage threshold that he did not inspect. A turnip fallen from a farm cart he shared with the rest, as he did a tallow candle that was jolted out of the wagon lanthorn: potato parings that he grubbed out of an open drain he kept, however, to himself. He would, indeed, have essayed to eat raw a blackbird he found frozen in a hedge, if the wagoner's lad had

137

not arrived as he was about to feast, and lashed him till he sullenly dropped his prize.

Upon Dai had developed in great part the business of superintending the routine of the passengers, for Lewis left them very much alone. The man's ceaseless potations had begun to take effect. He became increasingly morose, and spent most of his time dozing and tippling alternately, in the front of the wagon where a sort of canopy had been rigged over his reclining place.

This gave Dai full scope for his malice. He became to the wretched children a rosy-faced ogre, a monster with iron-shod feet and whistling lash always at their heels. His little eyes encased in fat were ever on the watch for an opportunity to harry. Their rations of water, and of stale bread or potatoes—once there was a stinking lump of bullock's head—were always short. Sometimes at night, too, he would crawl in among them, and worry the girls with little but insistent indecencies. The younger, Grizel, moaned: once she screamed, and he vanished as quietly as he had come. But Deborah lay still: she submitted to his inquisitiveness, rigid, wordless—as if she knew that some relief was near at hand. Only she clutched Christopher the tighter when at last he went.

For the most part they trudged in silence, their eyes on their broken shoes, all their energy of mind and body absorbed in dragging their blistered feet to journey's end. They saw nothing of the country through which they passed—for they were too weary to take note; and when they approached a township they were always shut up as soon as the outskirts were reached, and not released until the last cluster of houses was well behind.

Once, outside Wells, in Somerset, they halted at midday on a high hill whence they could look back on the city and the great square towers and roof of the cathedral shining in the sunlight. There was a faint blue haze of smoke over the jagged housetops: the bells sang sweetly in the still air: the sacred hill of Glastonbury lay, a strayed pyramid, beyond.

A little farther up the road there was a grassy bay at the side, and set in it a high gibbet. From its arm hung a sort of iron cage, which held something that had once been a man and was tarred to an utter blackness save for three white teeth in the unrecognizable dark mask of the face.

They stared at the hideous thing without speaking, chewing their midday ration of grey bread. The wagoner's boy with his whip could just reach one of the dangling feet. He struck it, and the whole contrivance with its burden swung gently round like a great meat-jack, creaking as it went.

'My da' was 'ung!' said Gibbie at last, rather proudly, his eyes glued to the blackened mummy in its corselet and headgear and trousering of iron bands and chains.

His fellow passengers were definitely impressed. Even Dai cocked an ear.

'Your da'. . . . Whaffor?' asked Grizel, turning her ravaged face to him.

' 'E was 'ung, like thissen, in chains,' said Gibbie, savouring to the full the sensational value of this announcement.

'Whaffor, Gibbie? Whaffor?'

' 'Ung fer murder, 'e was. 'E cut my ma's froat. A seed 'un do it. . . . Like that. . . .' He drew his hand, with fingers as bony as a grasshopper's leg, across his throat with violence, from ear to ear.

On another day they were halted by the roadside and were turned out into the teeming rain. A little wicket in an unkempt hedge gave on a narrow path that led through leaning tombstones to a dark church porch. Lewis and the others had betaken themselves to a tumble-down tavern opposite, and the horses steamed and dripped and nuzzled into their nosebags unattended.

The tailboard, when in place, was too high for any of the children to climb, so they sought refuge at first from the bitter downpour, with their bread, under the wagon where stalactites of mud thickly encrusted axle-trees and planking. A thick paste of mud covered the roadway, and their clothing became so plastered that they resembled small clay figures built up on a foundation of rags.

Then one—it was Deb—more daring than the rest investigated the merits of the porch. So in the end they all flocked there, and sat eating on the slate-topped seats on either side.

One half of the nail-studded door was shut and decked with stained and blotched notices: the other half was ajar, and through the gap came the mumble of a service, said quickly in a dusty monotone.

Christopher peered within.

Three or four heads only showed over the shining waste of pews which stretched to the desolation of the choir. At his desk a bald-headed clergyman in a voluminous surplice grumbled his way toward the last 'Amen'. The window over the altar and the cross was broken in one corner and stuffed with rags. The tessellated floor was gritty with fallen plaster and spotted with bird-droppings. Everywhere on the walls were greenish patches of damp, and over all was the dreary colour of decay. It was the sort of church that in itself is the funeral service for Christianity.

Stray words bumbled down under the echoing roof on which the rain pattered.

'. . . shall appear the wrath of God . . . mumble—mumble . . . Then shall they call upon Me (saith the Lord) but I will not hear . . . gabble—gabble . . . too late to knock, when the door shall be shut.'

At that moment the priest lifted his head and glanced down the church. He had a little red face under an enormous shining dome of a head, and hot angry eyes. He paused for a second when his gaze reached the small face peeping in, as though he were about to bark out an instruction. Then he looked back at his book, lost his place, and, eventually finding it, snarled his way on.

In five minutes' time the congregation clattered out, and the priest, coming cat-footed down the nave, suddenly flung open the leaf of the west door and confronted the humble party in the porch. He stood, looming over them, his bald head and cassock-covered shoulders blotting out the cross upon the shabby altar. A stale smell of brandy and tobacco invested him.

'What are you doing here? What are you doing here? What are you doing here? Why are you here? Who told you to come here?'

He spoke with as intense a ferocity as if he had found them banqueting within the sanctuary. There had been trouble about the tithes; the Lord of the Manor had been obtuse over a hint that a dinner invitation would be acceptable; and he had had too much port the night before. Bad port—he couldn't afford good! He had taken it out of his flock by unexpectedly adding the Commination Service to Matins, and was pleased to find a further vent for his alcoholic spleen.

'I will not have you lousy beggars leaving your vermin over my church,' he said. 'Be off with you! Be off, or I will turn the beadle on you!'

They looked up, not stirring from the stone seats, gaping with surprise and fear.

'We are only eating our bread out of the rain,' said Christopher, humbly apologetic that such as they should have contaminated the Holy Threshold.

The parson looked at the sodden lumps of bread at which they gnawed—lumps of bread that looked as if maggots might breed in them. He hiccuped. He retched. His eyes became still more hot in the small red face under the shining dome, and the lines from nose to mouth yet more bitterly incised.

'Bread!' he cried, striking with his stick on the stones. 'Bread! You eat your filthy repast in my porch, fouling my church! Fouling my church! Fouling my church! Take yourselves and your bread off! D'you think this place is meant to be a tavern and an eating-house? Take your stinks away!'

He flicked his stick in a drunken gesture of dismissal, and the ferrule struck the bread out of Gibbie's hand to the floor. The boy flung himself on the fallen bread with a scream of rage, and clutched it to him, scowling on his knees up at the angry man.

Christopher remembered his manners.

'I beg your pardon, sir,' he said. 'We didn't know that we were doing anything wrong. I'm sure we're very sorry.'

'Lice on the altar! Lice in the pulpit! "Nothing wrong"! Blast you! Come in here dripping with vermin, and think you are doing nothing wrong!'

His fury was so insanely outrageous that they slipped from their seats and ran from the church, and from him, as if from something obscenely wicked. He watched them go, mumbling in rage, beating his stick upon the stone seat as if to hurry them.

'I'd a-kilt 'un,' boasted Gibbie, as they crouched once more under the wagon. 'I'd a-kilt 'un, I would, if . . .' He cast a conspiratorial look round, fumbled within his dirty shirt, and produced the stump of a table knife found in his scavengings. There was a bare three inches of blade left to the long haft, but he fingered its edge lovingly; and, when he had finished eating, set to stropping it on a flat white stone.

'I'd a-kilt 'un,' he repeated again and again, half to himself, each syllable coinciding with a backward or forward movement of the blade upon its grindstone. The rust wore off, and bit by bit the steel began to wear a grey icy sheen.

'I'd a-kilt 'un,' he said, testing the edge again. 'The old bastard. And for why? . . . My da' kilt my ma. I saw 'un do it. . . . I know how to kill a man.'

They all watched him without a word, and Simmie's eyes followed each movement of the blade, travelling with it to and fro.

It was a little after this that Simmie fell on a loose stone, as he followed the wagon down hill. He rose blubbering, and hobbled on awhile as best he might; but twice again his ankle gave beneath him, and at last he halted and awaited the coming of Dai and his attendant dog, with frightened resignation.

The other came up to him with lifted lash.

'Git on wi' it, looney,' he said, and flicked the thong across his shoulders.

With burbling words and gesticulation Simmie tried to show that something was very wrong. The tears streamed down his foolish face.

'Get on!'—lash—said Dai.

Simmie hobbled a pace or two, and stopped again.

Lashing and cursing were repeated. The dog watched inquisitively, leaping a little sideways to keep clear each time the whip was raised.

Simmie sank in a huddle on the ground. He was kicked to his feet. He staggered afresh, blood streaming from his nose.

Dai changed his tactics. From behind he suddenly propelled the blubbering victim to the wagon-tail, and lashed his wrists to it by a dangling rope.

There was no escape. At first Simmie stumbled on as the wagon moved; then he fell and was dragged after it by his stretched arms, his useless feet trailing along the stony road, his limp body jolting like a half-full sack.

Gibbie set him on his feet again, and walked beside him, half-supporting him, until the tormentor with an oath and a blow forbade interference.

Gibbie fell back scowling and fumbled in his tattered shirt.

He opened his mouth, but saw the fierce small eyes in the fat red face glaring at him, and cowered as if from a blow.

Simmie fell once more.

This time he could not rise and was drawn along, his battered shoes scrambling up earth and stones. He sagged still farther so that his knees touched the ground, and in a few instants the thin cloth of his breeches was worn away into round holes, and his flesh showed through covered with a mess of blood and mud.

His screams brought Lewis back from his perch in front. The Welshman aimed a blow with his stick at Dai.

'What iss it you do, you limb?' he shouted. 'I will not haf you sspoil my goodss, inteet! Undo him.'

' 'E won't walk,' said the lad surlily.

'Ton't answer me pack! Undo him. . . . Get into the wagon, ye prats.'

Once, at late dusk while they waited at a roadside ditch for a broken trace to be repaired, the skirts of history brushed them by.

Out of the mist and twilight came a crowd of men, walking swiftly with some urgent purpose. They passed in silence, some carrying unlighted lanterns, some hay forks or scythes, and one a bundle of splinters of tarred pine. One or two looked hungrily and curiously at the heavy-laden wagon as if assessing its cargo, and Lewis shrank low on his couch of straw as he saw them. But they went their way, unmolesting, and the gathering darkness swallowed them up.

The wagoner, driving a hole in tough leather with his knife against the wagon-side, nodded after them:

'By golls! Vine doings there'll be to-night,' he said, with his mouth full of twine. 'When poor volk walk like that, quiet and quick, with torches in their hands!'

Lewis grunted in reply: 'There'll pe ssome fine hangings!'

'Blast this y'ere trace,' mumbled the other, making a fierce knot. 'A want tew git away from trouble—an' there's trouble brewing y'ereabout.'

That night they came late to an anchorage, under the lee of the Cotswolds, which lay over them like a dark coastline brooding over a vanished sea. Above them the main road mounted straight and steep into a wood of whispering pines, and below them far away shimmered the spread lights of Gloucester. The wagon was drawn up on a grass patch in a by-road beside a sheltering copse; the horses' bits were slipped, and the beasts tethered by their bridles to the pole and wheels.

The passengers fed, and sat huddled in the wagon-tail.

The cover had not yet been pulled down on them, but was draped back on either side like the gathered curtain of a stage. As they crouched there, they saw through the gap a faint bright-ness appear against the sky, on a headland of the dark hills, like the premonition of the rise of a full moon.

A fierce wind got up and tore about the wagon, so that the tilt strained at its cordage. As the wind grew so the light on the horizon increased, till it became a blot of dusky gold in the sky with bright patches travelling to and fro along its base. It was fanned to a fierce intensity, and flared high and luridly against the night.

Rags of white blaze were torn from the mass, and travelled through the darkness, and lit fresh fires that rose up swiftly with flames as yellow as marigolds.

The wind increased in fury. The air was full of the noise of its passing, of the roaring with which it shattered itself against the hills. The trees creaked and groaned: boughs and hedges whis-pered and chattered: the folds of the tilt flapped wildly, and through a knot-hole in the floor a gust came whistling in. To everything a tongue was given with which to sing the might of the great wind or moan its frenzy.

In the midst of that vast uproar, the sound of hoofs and the jingle of their garniture swallowed in the clamour of the storm, a troop of cavalry went by unheard, their dark cloaks streaming behind them, so that they seemed no mortal soldiery but familiars hastening to a witches' Sabbath.

All night the fire burned on the hill; nor was it extinguished when dawn came to a world that was still gale-swept.

For three days and nights afterwards the wind kept up, as the wagon crossed the border counties and lumbered into Wales. The fields and orchards on the way were strewn with shattered trees, their roots torn from the earth and revealed twisted like serpents in agony. In the copses along the roadside, where the saplings were bent before the gale like strung bows, broken firs leaned heavily against their mates. The streets of the villages they passed through were white with flakes of lime-wash blown from house walls, and strewn with fallen tiles and chimney pots.

So violent was the wind that the thin bodies of the small way-farers could not make headway against it. They clung to one an-other, staggered a step or two, halted and leaned against the gale as if it were something solid; went on again, halted—until Lewis, taking pity on them, shut them in their moving prison.

There they remained, penned in a perpetual half-light. Icy draughts blew in on them through the raves, through the joint of the ill-fitting tailboard, through every rent in the straining cover, every crack and knot-hole in the timber. Huddled close together on the sodden straw, they spoke but little, for there was nothing of which to speak except misery. They ate their rations when they were given them, automatically, without desire; and for the rest dozed by fits and starts, waked by a more violent battering of the wind, or the restless movement of one of them seeking ease for cramped and numbed limbs.

To Christopher it seemed as if the end of the world were at hand, and the mighty voice of the wind were the great tuba of the archangels sounding the last trump. He squatted close to Deb, trembling in his soul for the blast that should be greater than the rest and dissolve a reeling world into dust before the hurricane of God. His misery was such that he could not even withdraw into the fairyland of his own: the portals were shut by which he en-tered among the day-dreams of make-believe.

As night fell he crouched still closer, for she alone seemed real against the chaos of darkness and wind that was too dark and too windy to be real.

Once he essayed to say something of what he felt.

'God's angry!' he ventured in a low voice.

'God! . . . God?' said Deb, and chuckled hoarsely. God had not manifested Himself in the Plymouth brothel where her twelve years had been spent until the creature she called mother had drunk herself to death, and she had been flung into the poor-house.

'Doan't 'ee laugh at God,' reproved Gibbie, whetting his knife-edge on a stone. 'Or else 'E'll strike 'ee dead!'

'Don't care if 'E do,' said Deb.

As she spoke the folds of the hood above the tailboard blew violently back revealing a triangle of sky and thin clouds that streamed swiftly across the moon. Six faces were turned fearfully towards the gap. They saw a head and shoulders rise above the tailboard. The younger girl screamed—a shriek that was torn from her lips, and dissipated into nothingness by the wind that leaped into the wagon, like a sea breaking through a breach in a wreck.

'Shut yer face,' said Dai, and struggled over the edge and dropped in among them, trampling on their crowded limbs.

He thrust Christopher to one side and crouched on the floor beside Deb, seizing her to him like a clumsy satyr. She said nothing to the brutality of his advances, but sank under the weight of him, her legs doubled beneath her. In the intermittent moonlight the others waited, watched in hideous expectation, shuddering with some fear that was more than physical.

Suddenly she writhed a little, and beat at his face with her hands, shaking her head from side to side to escape his hot breath. He set an arm about her neck and ground her face into the pleats of his rough smock. His other hand travelled up her body, until it felt through the stuff of her dress the thin curve of a childish breast. There it halted, clung, clutched, and gripped until it seemed as if his finger bones would meet through the violated flesh.

Even then she did not cry out, but only sighed a long-drawn moan.

It was too much for Christopher. He flung himself sideways upon the lad's back, battering at him with angry and ineffective fists. The other, taken by surprise, let go his hold. He turned a distorted face on Christopher, shook himself free, and struck him one blow on the temple that sent his head crashing against the side of the vehicle.

Dai rose. He stood erect in the moonlight, in that confined space with the crouching bodies at his feet. He mouthed oaths and threats.

Then he stooped like a vulture to his prey, and seized Deb by the hair, dragging her to her feet. He caught her in his arms, and raising her light body endeavoured to thrust her on top of the deep shoulder-high case that filled the width of the wagon.

'No! No!' she cried, and beat at him, and clung to his neck and the shoulder of his smock. They struggled to and fro amidst the huddled children for a minute, until the girl became suddenly unresistant and submitted passively so that he was able to push her limp body on to the high ledge.

He paused a moment out of breath, and glared arrogantly down. 'That'll learn 'ee!' he snarled, and trod on someone's fingers, and in answer to the cry kicked viciously at Gibbie's arm.

He turned, and setting his hands on the high case, bent his legs to spring up beside the silent girl.

Even as he did so Gibbie got to his knees, raised a thin arm and brought the short blade of his knife down into Dai's buttocks—and again.

With a scream of surprised pain the lad let go his hold and fell on all fours to the floor.

For a moment Gibbie was frozen into immobility by the fear of what he had done: but in that moment Simmie flashed into action. With incomprehensible babble he flung himself on top of Dai so that he was spread-eagled on the floor. Gibbie joined in, and for a while they rolled in a furious struggle, their cries swallowed up in the ceaseless greater crying of the gale.

Dai rose to his knees, and then to his feet, his assailants hanging to him like dogs at the throat of a deer. Shrieking with fear, he tried to reach the refuge of the case top. His hands and arms were already on the ledge; he heaved himself upward. As he did so Deborah struck him in the face. He hit out at her and lost his leverage, and hung for a moment gripping only with one hand. As she lay she set her teeth to that hand and bit it to the bone, so that he let go and fell once more to the floor.

The other two were on top of him again. Vergil flung himself on a thrashing foot, and was drawn into the floundering heap. Strong as he was, Dai could not tear himself free from the clutching hands, nor strike a telling blow against the closely pressed bodies.

Once more he struggled to his feet with Simmie gripping him about the neck and biting at his face like a dog; with Gibbie clinging with all his weight to his free arm, and Vergil hanging to one knee, and Christopher to another.

For the last time he stood erect in the moonlight, swaying under the hate-given strength of his opponents. He swung them about with him as he took one step—one step towards the opening in the tilt and the outer air.

Then his foot slipped in the wet straw and he fell backwards under his enemies. His head struck the side of the great case and he lay senseless.

For a moment they knelt panting over him, wondering at his vacant face, with the dishevelled hair and the little trickle of blood —black in the moonlight--that ran down the side of his face from a nostril.

Gibbie gave an exultant laugh. He fumbled in the straw and brought up his fallen knife.

'Oh, no! Oh, no! Please, no!' cried Christopher, and hid his eyes.

Gibbie delicately pressed the blunt tip of the weapon against the neck of the fallen boy. He put both hands to the haft and drove the blade in deep. He dragged the steel towards him from one ear to the other, a great bubbling wound opening in its wake. The body quivered, was shaken by a great spasm, and was still.

Simmie watched with puzzled eyes the stream of blood that soaked into the straw. He dipped a finger into it, and put it to his mouth, and giggled; and dipped again, and sucked the finger thoughtfully. He burst into a loud and cheerful babble.

Amid all the clamour of the wind there came a screaming blast through the narrow valley, more savage than any that had gone before. It tore the wagon cover off the hoops as if it were but a rag in its path, and swirled it away into the darkness; and left the wagon naked to the night and to the troubled moon.

Chapter 9

Two Aspects of a Judge

THE SHADOW OF CIVIL WAR LAY OVER THE LAND. MEN argued, conspired, starved, drilled, rioted and were hanged. Men asked for votes, for bread, for ease: they were charged by cavalry and lodged in jails; they were ground down by new measures of repression; they were incited to open violence, and then informed against by spies enrolled in Whitehall.

' In London the Law Officers of the Crown formulated charges of high treason against conspirators who had plotted crack-brained revolution and mass murder in a stable loft off the Edgware Road. In York a dozen men lay awaiting the coming of the Spring Assizes and inevitable conviction for assembling a multitude to demand reform—a multitude that had been ridden down by troopers on the field of Peterloo. In Scotland general insurrection was planned. Ricks burned; machinery was destroyed; cabinet councils dithered and oligarchy armed itself at all points to resist democracy.

At Carmarthen Assizes four prisoners were on trial for the murder of one David Evans, a wagoner's boy, on the night of January the thirtieth in the year of our Lord 1820, being the first day of the first year of the reign of King George the Fourth.

It had been a strange journey from the naked wagon to the spike-guarded dock. It had been an unhurried but nightmare process that eventually brought them into a sort of pew, over the chin-high wall of which Christopher peered at the man set high above them, as if it were on a throne—a man whose long face, like a blanched almond, was skirted by a silvery wig.

149

That process had begun when Grizel had flung herself to the ground and run screaming, as one demented, across a narrow bridge to the near-by inn. Gibbie then had waked from a frozen dream: he had leaped out, too, and run, the knife still in his hand, and vanished into the night.

'Quick, quick!' said Deb urgently.

With frantic haste she lowered Vergil to the ground. Simmie and Christopher had tumbled out with her, and run drearily, pressing against the shrieking wind—into the arms of men who flocked from out the inn door. A wide beam of yellow radiance gushed out across the roadway. By it the inn company could see that their hands and dress were dabbled in blood.

'Tes trew, then!' said the wagoner slowly. With Lewis, dangling a lantern from his steel hook, and two other men he went to the wagon and looked within.

Somebody dropped the tailboard and dragged the limp body out.

'Murder!' said one of the men who held them. 'Murder!' echoed the woman in the doorway.

'Murter, inteet!' said Lewis. He walked alongside, as the body was carried by its arms and legs towards the inn, swinging his lantern so that the moving shadows on the dead face made it seem alive again.

The wagoner looked at the captives.

'Tew on 'em be missin',' he said. 'A boy and a child. . . . Shut these y'ere up in a loft while us look for 'un.'

All night voices rumbled, a low bourdon to the wind. All night from some adjoining room came the screams and moans of Grizel. Only with dawn did there come silence—and a recaptured Gibbie; Gibbie with the face of an old man, and his smock stiff with his victim's blood.

Vergil alone escaped. He escaped everything. For they found him, many days after, lying face down in the stream, where it bent away from the narrow road and leaped downwards to the gully bottom through steeply climbing woods.

The days that followed were full of the grumble of men's voices—blows, pushings, questions, crowds, journeyings; with a brief respite when they stood in a low-ceilinged room, before four or five grim men sitting behind a wooden barrier on a sort of dais. And always the word 'murder' humming and echoing through whatever else was said!

Then more journeyings followed, until at last they came to a town upon a hill, to a place of echoing stone corridors, and to a small room on an upper floor, with a heavy door and a window crossed by iron bars set in the thickness of the wall.

For some weeks that small room was a home for Christopher and the imbecile, for Gibbie and the girl Deborah. There were four pallets, each covered with a dusty brown blanket, set length-wise along the wall; a bench under the window and an earthen pitcher of water on it; and, in one corner, a leaking wooden tub for ordure.

Standing on the bench they could look down on a silver strip of river curving through flat green pastures, and on the wooded slopes that narrowed in toward the bridge below the jail. Starlings grazed in the meadows: a pair of crows lumbered to and fro, and sometimes the gulls swept up on long wings from the distant sea.

While Gibbie sat on the floor staring into space and Simmie lay mouthing and moaning on his pallet, Christopher and the girl passed all day, every day, peering down between the bars of the unglazed window on to a fairy-tale world.

A knight might ride from out the woodlands to tilt beside the river (thought Christopher), or a goose-girl that was a princess in disguise might drive her cackling flock over the pointed arches of the bridge, or a fairy galley with a cinnamon-coloured sail might slip down the white flood towards the great waters. In the shad-ows of Death and in the strait place of prison his old faculty came back to him. He suddenly found that he could withdraw once more to the Land of Dreams. He pictured a sort of gateway in his mind—a mysterious portal of a magic wood with valves of some shining metal through which his real self could pass into such a tale as he chose to create, beyond the reach, and even conscious-ness, of earthly circumstances.

Sometimes the mere words 'And so', whispered to himself, were enough to send him back amid the pageantry he evoked. Some-times he had to retell consciously, anxiously, to his soul that which had gone before in the adventure whereon he was engaged, ere he could find that ghostly entry and pass on, to sit entranced before the wizard tapestry it would spin for him.

He told Deb something of this strange enchantment, and she would listen eagerly and lead him on, until he began to spin stories for her about the strange people who waited but one magic word to surge out of the concealing woods in gallantry of fluttering silks and silver.

For all his fancies, though, it was she who found that the thin gruel they were given in wooden bowls was really a rich porridge, made with milk, and having fat raisins in its depths and laced golden with treacle.

She even invented a history for the clumsy vessels. The wedge-shaped chip out of a rim had been made when He (she did not specify who He was) had been drunk and thrown it on to the stone floor! And she had kept her money in another, in a corner of the cupboard by the chimbley!

The greasy meat they had three times a week—a vast luxury, to be wolfed greedily—came from a warm great kitchen, where the kettle was always on the boil, and twiddly bits of pastry with jam on them lay on the table all day, and a fat cook perpetually basted enormous joints hanging on a mechanical jack before the fire! Even to the dull mind of Simmie she built a picture of that kitchen, complete in every rich detail—based without a doubt on the memory of a peep through a half-open door into the kitchen of some inn during their wanderings.

Her imagination would not soar with Christopher's right off the earth, but she could carve out of a reality a wonderful picture circumscribed only by the narrow limits of her knowledge.

They were not, however, unvisited. People came and asked questions, and went; and returned and asked more—one in particular, a man in black, with cold knuckly hands and a long shaven upper lip.

There were various little matters that Mr. Lewis had thought it would be better not to raise at the trial. For that reason he had instructed his old acquaintance, Mr. Price, to brief counsel for the defence—a counsel who might be advised to steer clear of dangerous waters, 'but not, inteet, too dear; not one of your high-fliers, Mr. Price!'

But Mr. Price, somewhat handicapped by this, found it difficult enough to build up any sort of case: he met with a dreary resignation, an utter lack of comprehension.

He stood by the door, a violently scented handkerchief in his hand—for the reek from the tub was heavy and insistent—and addressed them.

'You don't appear to understand,' he complained. 'You are charged with murder—M U R D E R. You may be hanged—quite likely will. Hanged, you know!' And he put his hand up to his throat and jerked his head back significantly.

'Do you—ah!—want to be hanged, Master Lee?' He looked at Christopher who did not answer.

'Don't you understand, boy?' said he, waving his handkerchief to and fro, and thrusting out a bony forefinger.

'My name's not Lee,' said Christopher.

'God bless my soul. Then whatever is it?'

'I'm Christopher Harnish,' said Christopher, putting his hands behind his back as though reciting a lesson. 'I want to go home.'

'Christopher Harnish? There isn't a Christopher Harnish. What are you talking about?'

He picked up a blue canvas bag from a little stool that had been brought in for him, and extracted a mass of documents. He wetted a thumb, and turned them over deliberately, one by one.

' "Deborah Hunt",' he read out. 'That's you!'—nodding toward the girl. ' "Simeon Corday"!' He looked for a moment with distaste at the soiled muddled face of Simmie. ' "Gilbert Smith". You, my friend! And . . . and'—triumphantly—' "George Lee"! Here are your indentures as they were given to me. Your indentures are to David Lewis, mill-owner in the parish of . . . h'm. . . . Do you still say you are not George Lee?'

'I am Christopher Harnish, please, sir!'

'Do you deny that you were with this party at the time of the . . . er . . . incident—that you knew the deceased—that you were there at all? You plead an alibi, my little friend! It is not good enough. It won't do indeed.'

'I was there, sir,' said Christopher in a great state of confusion. 'But I'm Christopher Harnish!'

'Christ Almighty!' ejaculated Mr. Price, cracking his fingers.

'If you admit you were there, and these papers say that you are George Lee, then you are George Lee. Whether you call yourself Christopher Harnish or the Duke of Caerphilly does not make any difference to the Law. The Law—ah—is interested in you as a suspected murderer, and not as a suspected Christopher Hardface. Let us have no more of this time-wasting! When I say George Lee, I mean you, whether you're Christopher Hardfist or Christopher Hardfast. If you're not very careful, sir, very careful, you'll be Christopher Hangedfast. Aha!'

An errant breeze strayed in through the embrasure, and wafted a peculiarly repellent gust from the tub to Mr. Price. He extracted a phial from the tail of his coat, liberally besprinkled his handkerchief from it, and rubbed the stopper to and fro on the long upper lip.

'It is true,' he conceded, 'that Mr. Lewis may have been in error. But what—ah!—is in a name? The evidence refers to you, my young friend, as George Lee; the indictment refers to you as George Lee; Mr. Lewis refers to you as George Lee.'

In point of fact, Mr. Lewis, having utterly omitted to inform himself of Christopher's name, had concluded that it would make for easy regularization of an informal arrangement if he bestowed on Christopher the patronymic and papers of the runaway whose place he had taken.

Even a less welcome visitor than Mr. Price was one first introduced by a Methodistical turnkey, who, amid other and more solid kindnesses, evinced some concern in their moral welfare.

He opened the iron-studded door one afternoon and ushered in a lumpish man with a pasty face and short coarse, black hair, who wore extremely brief trousers showing an expanse of white sock.

'This is the Reverend Jones, Pant-y-felin,' announced the turnkey, adding the pastor's address to his name in accepted Welsh custom. 'He has had the kindness to come to lead you to Grace.'

'Grace through the Plood! Grace through Fire! Grace through Torment,' snuffled the Reverend Jones, preparing to intoxicate himself with words. 'Peace o-pon ye, sinners! Peace o-pon ye!'

'Amen!' said the turnkey.

For some moments the Reverend Jones regarded them in excited silence—as if he were intoxicated with the Word and with the sadistic pleasure of looking on murderers ripe for the gallows. He stood biting the flat nails of his dirty hands with little snappings of his teeth, and spitting fragments upon the floor, while his small black eyes devoured the children as if he would make them re-enact for him the bloody drama of that windy night.

'Lit-tel heathen, I fear, Mr. Rees,' said he to the turnkey. 'Fery —fery far from Grace.' And he groaned, and the turnkey groaned.

Christopher wanted to protest that he was not a heathen, that he was lawfully baptized and used to go to church.

'Ravagin' lit-tel heathen,' said the turnkey. 'Murderin' lit-tel heathen, as I fear!'

The Reverend Jones eased himself down upon his knees; sat back on his heels so that his trouser-ends rode up over his sagging socks and showed dirty hairy legs; screwed his eyes up tight; lifted beseeching hands to heaven.

'Let us pray!' said he.

'O Lord, look favourably, inteet, o-pon Thy servant! Give him strength of Soul and Pody to support Thy battle. Pestow on him Thy Grace that he may show Thy Light to these ignorant little heathen. That he may guide their feet away from the eternal fire and the torments of Damnation.

'And if it be Thy Will that they should die o-pon the gallows, grant Thy servant eloquence to persuade them to submit to Thy Verdict, acknowledging the justness of the sentence and the heinousness of their offence.'

'Amen!' said the turnkey, and left him to his task.

The Reverend Jones's method of saving souls had the merit of extreme simplicity. It was his principle to frighten sinners to the path of Salvation: and on each successive visit he painted for them a more lurid picture of the horrors of hell, the tortures of the devil, the gnawing of the worm, unless they repented and took a mysterious path of salvation—whatever that might mean. After he had orated himself hoarse he would stand staring at them with unwinking gaze as if his soul took pleasure in meditating on the earthly and supernatural terrors and tortures in store for them—as if it liked visualizing their small hands red with the blood of murder, their earthly bodies corrupting in shallow graves, and their simulacra roasting and crackling and scorching on beds of red-hot coal in hell.

During his visits the girl Deborah kept her back turned, staring out of the window; while Gibbie never altered his position—Mr. Jones might not have been there for him. Simmie, however, revelled in the horrifying details of hell-fire and torment, with complete personal detachment. Christopher himself paid the man the courtesy of apparent attention; but that was all. After he had gone Deb would mimic his whining sing-song, kneel on the floor and wrestle blasphemously with heaven much as he had done, and wring her hands over Simmie's head. Simmie's delighted laughter and the glimmer of amusement in Gibbie's sullen eyes spurred her on. She imitated Lewis's light-toned Welsh, and walked about the narrow cell with her little flat stomach thrust out before her, and scratched an imaginary pimple on her nose with a hand and wrist as stiff as any hook of steel. She became Mr. Price waving a dirty rag that was a handkerchief before her nose, carrying a corner of her tattered dress as if it were his blue bag tied up with tape.

'"Christopher Harnish? Christopher Harnish! There ain't no Christopher Harnish!"' she declared, and Simmie crowed with delight.

One morning the Reverend Jones came earlier than usual. The cold cell was lit by pale slanting sunshine; a thin wind blew the evil odours out into the passage.

He bent over one of the figures wrapped in a blanket on the floor, and shook it awake.

'Wake up,' he said. 'Wake up! It iss no time to sleep. The Day of Judging iss at hand, when the souls of men shall pe weighed. The wages of sin iss death! Come with me.'

Christopher woke to see the dark face bowed over his own. There was a cluster of small red spots with yellow tips amid the bluish stubble on the chin. He started up with a cry.

The others were aroused, and, under a guard of turnkeys, led along echoing passages to a lofty room with a flagged floor. The walls were hung with fetters, like giant watch-chains, with leg-irons, and with manacles; and in the centre of the floor there was an anvil with a blacksmith's hammer beside it.

Mr. Jones waved a hand toward the three tall windows.

'Behold the Wages of Sin!' cried he. 'The Wages that iss Death!' They were taken to the windows.

Below was a small square market-place, dark with heads except at the far side, where, in a clear space, a farm cart stood under a black gallows.

Three men stood in the cart: a parson in gown and white bands, whispering into the ear of a pale lad, whose arms were bound at his back, whose ankles were tightly corded, whose neck was in the noose of a rope that hung from the gallows beam above him. The third man stepped forward. He placed a white cotton nightcap on the prisoner's head, and pulled it down over his face with a quick jerk.

He climbed from the open tail of the cart. The clergyman placed his hand on the condemned man's head in blessing and farewell. Then he too descended, awkwardly enough.

Christopher could not turn his eyes away: he felt the rough hairiness of the rope about his own throat—the coarse stuff of the cap on his own nose and cheek—the springy floor of the cart beneath his own feet.

There was silence. And then the axle of the cart gave a creak. It moved slightly, and a turnip like a baby's head rolled out of a corner into the centre. For a moment the bound figure pawed frantically with its roped feet at the edge—still touched with its toes; then, as the cart moved farther away, swung clear with a sort of shudder, the head hanging to one side, low over a shoulder.

'The Wages of Sin! The Wages of Sin!' said Mr. Jones very loudly, breathing very heavily through dilated nostrils. 'The bodily wages of sin! Take warning! Repent! . . .'

He came again that night, by candle-light.

He stood in the window-place, with two candles guttering on the bench beside him, and preached of the spiritual death that followed earthly death, of the penalties exacted by God after man had done his worst.

He ranted of hell-fire; he railed of damnation; he roared of roastings and fryings and boilings.

Three of them sat listening on their pallets as if in a nightmare, while Deb stood by him staring with a sort of quizzical smile twisting her lips.

'You,' he cried, turning on her. 'You! Do you think earthly anguish can compare with the pains of hell? Repent! Repent!

Away with thee, Sa-tan! Avaunt, Beelzebub! Back, Apollyon! Shall I not save thee?'

A thin scum was at the corner of his mouth; he took the child by her hand; his voice became very low.

'Shall I not show you,' said he, 'from what pains your souls and podies must be delivered by prayer, and fasting, and wailing, and gnashing of teeth?'

Suddenly he forced her bare arm over the candle and held it down so that the flame licked at it.

She screamed; she writhed. She endeavoured to pull away, but he held her by the other arm firmly and there was no escape from the agony.

'Lo, these pains are ass naught to the pains of hell-fire! Ass naught.'

Mingled with the foul odours of the cell was a smell of flesh that bubbled into blisters, and cracked and charred.

The child's screams became a torture.

There was the sound of feet in the passage, and a loud, rough voice.

He dropped her arm.

'So,' he said resonantly, 'shall ye know what pangs the damned shall suffer! Repent before it iss too late. On your knees, sinners, and repent!'

So now 'George Lee' stood with the other three in that high wooden pew, watching the long face, like a blanched almond, and the silvery wig fade with the fading daylight. A large and incongruous posy of flowers lay on the desk before the face—a humble offering, as it were, to some coldly furious god.

Between them and the still figure in red enthroned high up against dark panelling was a wide space filled with paper-littered tables, about which men in little grey wigs and men without wigs sat whispering and conferring or staring about them.

Only heavy breathing and coughing and the shuffling of feet told of the crowded public gallery behind them, under the vaulting of the roof.

It was so nearly dark that candles were brought and starred the gloom with little yellow flames.

Suddenly there was silence. From under the oaken wall that was the sanctuary rail between the figure on the throne and lesser humanity, a man in a wig rose. He read something from a paper quickly, and paused expectantly.

Mr. Price bobbed up in a most surprising way from below the spike-set ledge. He guided them through the preliminaries without a hitch; except that when the treble voice of Christopher said, 'Not Guilty', a woman above cried, 'My God!' and was hushed to silence.

Then a sonorous and beautiful voice had begun, 'My Lord'—as if it addressed God!—and gone on to tell the story of their journey. Almost it seemed as if the voyage had been a pleasure jaunt, with Youth at the prow and Lewis at the helm—a gentle amble through a smiling countryside towards a goal of employment that would be half recreation.

The voice went on—'Deeply laid plot to escape. . . . Premeditated murder. . . . For what purpose should the wretched boy procure a knife and grind it, as he did, to a razor sharpness? For what purpose, but murder? . . . The dead lad . . . long stretches their only guard. . . . Surprised them in the act. . . . The question of age does not enter—only awareness of the deed. . . .'

Men came and went in a little pulpit set to one side of the space before them. Then by and by Grizel appeared. Delicately she was led through her story, bit by bit, till it all fitted into a picture that showed a desperate band plotting escape in the dark cavern under the wagon tilt, and surprised as they were about to make their breakaway.

She was neater and cleaner than she had ever been, but her mind was a chaos, in which memories of bleak horror jostled her imaginings and alien ideas implanted by long hours of subtle questioning.

'Her hit 'un in faäce . . . 'Ess! 'E tuck 'un by leg, and draäged 'un down!'

Yes, they had talked of escape. . . . The prisoner, Smith, had spent long hours sharpening his knife. . . . There had been threats against Dai.

Someone else rose, mumbled questions of the child, and received mumbled answers.

An ice-cold voice came from God on the Altar.

The someone hastened to reply.

'Yes, m'lud! No, m'lud! . . . I raise the question of provocation, m'lud.'

After that Lewis appeared. His one protruding eye, his protruding teeth, the hook by which he anchored himself to the ledge of the witness-box, caught little glints of light from the candles placed on the ledge before him. His protruding belly pushed the buttons of his waistcoat against the wall of the box, so that they made little clicking noises in the silence as his breath came and went.

He was allowed to explain his position. Shortage of child labour in the north. Had gone himself to arrange with the Plymouth poor-house to take their children. Always plenty of pauper children at Plymouth—especially after a good nut year.

'Nut year?' asked the icy voice of God.

Mr. Lewis deferentially explained that there were always more bastards than usual in Devonshire after a good nut harvest. Bastards went to the poor-house, of course.

'Go on!'

Mr. Lewis sent a batch of twenty to a cotton-spinning friend in Lancashire, who was in sad straits for labour. He also procured a few for himself for a small cloth factory he was starting on water-power in the Amman valley. Very difficult to get children there. Yess, yess—so many were employed in the mines from the age of seven onwards.

Illegal, was it, to take child 'prentices more than fifty miles from their domicile? Coot cracious! Since when? Two years! Inteet he did not know it! Inteet not! He was a fery law-abiding man. Yess. Yess.

The boy Dai was a good boy. A good-natured boy. Perhaps a little prankish, but what would you?

Christopher was very tired. He rested his chin on the ledge, and changed his weight from one weary leg to another. The spikes in front of him were as long as the palm of his hand, he calculated. He reached out timidly and touched the point to see if it were sharp. He looked at Gibbie who stood beside him. Gibbie was just looking at the floor and licking his lips with the sound like the turning of a bookleaf. His smock had been washed but there were still tell-tale yellow stains all over it. Deb in some curious way seemed to be enjoying the performance: there was a sort of bright radiance in the way she looked about the crowded court from face to face, and ever back again at the long, pale face above the gown of red. She held to him very tightly, notwithstanding. Her other hand rested on the ledge of the dock against a bunch of withered herbs. He saw against the whiteness of her under-arm, above the wrist, the angry crimson of the burn.

He was too tired now to take an interest in things. He knew it was a trial for murder, that he was on trial; but there was none of the reality of the damp straw and sodden bread of the wagon, of the pistol that had burst into fury just above his head, of the body of Dai with a second red mouth opened below his chin.

It had grown quite dark. The faces of the men who succeeded one another in the little pulpit were barely visible by candle-light.

Questions were being asked him. . . . 'Yes, sir! . . .' 'No, sir! . . .' 'I didn't, sir. . . .' Asked Gibbie, who remained mute despite threats. Asked Simmie, who gibbered, who mouthed, who burst into frantic blubbering. . . . Asked Deb. . . .

'Hated 'un, zur.'

'Why?'

' 'E 'urt me.'

'Why did he hurt you?'

She did not know why Dai had hurt her, except . . .

' 'E laiked a-doin' of it.'

'Is it true you said you would like to kill him?'

'No, zur.'

'You did not do anything to hurt him?'

'No, zur.'

Another voice: 'If you did nothing to hurt him, why did you bite his hand?'

'Did'unt, zur.'

'The witness Grizel Coombe says you did. . . . If you did nothing, why did you run away afterwards?'

'Was a-feared.'

'Afraid of what?'

And so it went on—questioning, talking; one wigged man bobbing up and another bobbing down.

Silence.

The ice-cold voice spoke. Few words it said in short sentences;

and a clatter of feet followed. Some of the men at the foot of the high altar filed out. The red figure vanished. The scarlet face of the turnkey showed over the entrance to the dock.

'You can sit down,' he said.

Christopher found himself sitting down beside Deborah. He leaned against her. His head slanted on to her shoulder. He fell asleep.

They were on their feet again. The red figure was back. Someone was talking.

A man rose. He said one word, and with that one word something between a great sigh and a moan rose into the dark vaulting of the lofty roof. The hall was full of eyes that stared wide open at the dock.

A voice came from the throne, from the long face in the silver wig. It spoke without emotion, with an icy clarity, as if a statue had spoken. It spoke so slowly that the official note-taker wrote at ease, turning his head at intervals and looking through silver-rimmed spectacles at the four faces above the dock ledge.

His Lordship described the provocation to the accused as a 'teasing that was no justification for murder'.

He spoke of the need for rigid disciplining at a time when disorder and violence and sedition were rampant.

The note-taker saw a distinct resemblance to his youngest son in the smaller of the three boys: tried to wipe out from his mind the odious comparison, and concentrated on his task. His swiftly moving pen wrote, as the words fell from the cold lips.

'All the circumstances attending this dreadful deed manifest the precocious tendency to crime and violence of its perpetrators.

'The need that such a charge as this should be investigated in this court, and that these proceedings, however painful, should run their normal course, is obvious. Otherwise there would be infinite danger of its going abroad into the world that children may commit so gross a crime with impunity when it is clear that they well knew what they were doing.

'On this ground—of their awareness—I cannot comply with the application of their counsel to respite the judgment because of their tender years. But I would remind the prisoners that it is still in the power of the Crown to interpose in every case that is open to clemency.

'You, prisoners at the bar, have been found guilty of the wilful murder of David Evans, and by the Twenty-fifth Statute of King George the Second, I am bounden to pass on you the sentence imposed by law, and that is:

'That you, Deborah Hunt, Gilbert Smith, Simeon Corday, and George Lee be taken from this place to a lawful prison and thence on Monday next, the twenty-seventh day of February instant, to the place of execution, and that you be there hanged by the neck until you be dead; and that your bodies be afterwards delivered to the surgeons of the hospital of this place, to be dissected and anatomized pursuant to the Statute. And may the Lord have mercy on your souls.'

There was another silence.

Then a woman screamed, very dreadfully, as if her cries should mount through the arched roof and press right to the Throne of Mercy.

Deb turned a starry face to Christopher. She was smiling as if with excitement.

'They'm a-goin' to hang we, Tops!' she said.

Gibbic leaned forward till his forehead struck the ledge. He retched. He was violently sick.

Christopher knew he was going to be hanged, but he knew with a far greater realization that Gibbie was vomiting.

They were shepherded away with rough kindness by sour-smelling men, between banks of staring eyes in a blur of faces. Except for the scuffle of their feet upon the boards, there was no sound until they came to a door with a lantern above, and a man who stood in the throng about it stepped a little forward.

The pale light shone on his red head, his long thin nose, the green of his coat. He was somebody real in a world of unreality.

Although he did not speak, Christopher heard his voice as it had declaimed in the dark road outside an inn, on the first night of his flight: it beat on his ear-drums and sent a message to his brain as all the sonorous, ice-cold, or mumbling voices of the past days had never done.

Christopher's mind was incapable of co-ordinating a sentence of its own. It relayed from his lips Deb's phrase, word for word, inflection for inflection:

'They'm a-goin' to hang we!'

Oliver Drysdale said very softly:

'Why, little Comrade Sheep! . . . You've strayed a long way this time, little Comrade Sheep!'

And then his voice rose so that even the pale head on the distant throne heard it and moved its eyes.

'They cannot do it!' he cried. 'They dare not do it. . . . They shall not do it! I swear they shall not! The Lord shall "defend thee under His wings, and thou shalt be safe under His feathers".'

'Hush, master,' said one of the turnkeys. 'Let us pass.'

Drysdale fell back. His hat was in his hand, and he suddenly sent it spinning—as if he were a boxer throwing down a challenge —into the very midst of the hall, so that it dropped upon the table before the clerk of the assize.

'I challenge you to hang them!' he cried out in a great voice, and struck himself on the breast with an histrionic gesture.

The cold voice from the bench said:

'Detain that man!'

But Drysdale had turned on his heel as he spoke, pressed ahead of the prisoners out of the door, and disappeared into the street. Ushers and constables sought for him in vain. . . .

Two hours later they would have found him, if they had continued their search, drinking brandy and water rapidly at the Ivy-bush Inn. He stood in the square flagged hall before a window which framed a rosy and smiling face, and gave glimpses of a firelit snuggery twinkling with unnumbered bottles.

Rosy-Face was helpful to the point of indiscretion about the distinguished guest who lay above stairs, with a guardian constable sitting without his door. She knew what he had said to the High Sheriff when his Marshal had discovered bedbugs in the Judge's Lodging; how he had declined staying with any of the local poten-tates—'Welsh half-wits,' he had called them—and insisted on rooms at the Inn: she knew what he ate and drank, what he wore, had even investigated his bed-chamber and knew the colour of his nightcap and the quality of his toilet articles.

The account was interrupted without a by-your-leave by a large man, who thrust his bullet head through the window-opening:

' 'Is lordship wants a bottle o' brandy, three lemons, a basin o' sugar, and a kettle o' really 'ot water. "Really 'ot", them's 'is words. And I 'ope the old buffer won't a-keep me up till three in the morning like what 'e did yesterday.'

As the man spoke Drysdale slipped into the gloom of the far end of the hall and, cat-footed, mounted the shallow stairs to the first floor.

A chair outside a door at the head of the stairs showed where the judge's sentry had been keeping vigil.

He turned the handle quietly and entered without knocking.

A heavy old man with hooded eyes, who sat by the fire in the large well-lighted room, looked over the top of the document he was studying.

'You appear to have mistaken the room, my friend,' he observed, and returned to his reading.

Drysdale advanced toward the round table in the centre of the bright green carpet.

'I do not think so, my lord!' he answered.

The judge set his paper down on the wine table beside his elbow-chair. He raised his heavy lids, flashed one quick look at Drysdale, and let them fall again as though a continuance of the effort were too wearisome for him.

'If you are thinking of taking it, I may assure you that this apartment will be free to-morrow, that it is comfortable, warm, and airy. I am a little occupied at the moment, or I should be glad to point to the quality of the upholstery, the pile of the carpet, the neat studies of some of our more eminent actors upon the walls, or to answer any question with regard to it you might put. As it is I am somewhat engaged and must beg you to excuse me. Good evening, sir!'

'You were a little more anxious to see me earlier this evening, my lord,' said Drysdale.

'That anxiety—of which I have no recollection—has not persisted, my good sir. In fact, although I hesitate to say it, my anxiety at present is not to see you. . . .' He cast another quick look. . . .

'Ah, I perceive it is our red-headed friend—our red-headed knight errant! Well! Well!'

Drysdale bowed acknowledgment of the recognition.

'It would have gone ill with you if I had seen you when I wanted to, my friend,' observed the judge drily.

'I felt at the time,' remarked Drysdale, 'that a discussion between us as between Bench and Dock, White-wig-and-red-robe and dusty prisoner, might be a trifle one-sided. That it might be of more value if we were to have an amicable conversation over your lordship's fire.'

'You prefer to criticize my awards in the safety of privacy?'

Drysdale rubbed his long nose.

'Your awards! Your awards, Brother Judge? I don't criticize you. Why should I? The awards and judgments and sentences are not yours, but those laid down by the Law whose mere servant you are.'

'Exactly, my friend! And in that case I do not see what we have to discuss!'

'A good deal, my lord. . . . You permit?'

Drysdale sank down into the chair opposite the judge, who eyed him in silence for a moment. Outside, the jingle of glasses told of the return of the sentinel with the materials for punch. The judge appeared to be considering what course he should take upon the arrival of his guardian. Then he leaned back and folded his hands precisely before him on his black silk knees.

'You, as a puppet of the Law, do not interest me,' declared Drysdale in a loud voice, pulling his green coat-tails from underneath him and laying them over his thighs. 'Neither does the guilt or otherwise of your prisoners interest me. What does interest me, what does horrify me, is the ethical system that compels you to try and to sentence with all abomination these children. These children, Brother, in happier circumstances would be in their bibs and pinafores in a nursery, nursery, NURSERY!' said he in crescendo.

'I really cannot ramble with you into a discussion of the ethical aspects of the case,' said the judge.

'I am not going to ask you to do so,' asserted Mr. Drysdale, witnessing with approval the appearance of the materials for a most substantial punch.

'If you do not discuss my position, or the guilt of the prisoners, or the ethics of trial and sentence, I cannot find that we have anything left to discuss. If, however, you would care to talk of other matters with an old man for half an hour before bed-time, I should be glad to offer you some refreshment. . . . Randall, bring another tumbler!'

' "Lord, what love have I unto thy law: all the day long is my study in it"—Psalm one hundred and nineteen,' quoted Mr. Drysdale ironically. ' "What love have I unto the law!" What love! . . . You may not be interested in the ethics of our penology. I am. But I don't propose to discuss them. To gain my ends I propose raising another matter altogether. A matter which should intrigue your lordship! Normally I despise those who pull strings and use influence due to rank—rank, what is't?—and wealth?—the fruit of years of money-grubbing! But anything will do so long as it helps me to prevent a crying, screaming, bloody scandal—to save the victims of our festering legal system. Festering, Brother Judge! Festering!'

'A moralist!' commented the old man, a thin smile creasing his long face. He poured hot water on to three pieces of sugar and then tilted the brandy on top. 'A Jesuitical moralist, I fancy! A Jacobinical moralist, I fear!'

'I hate and despise all these idle and gluttonous vampires that suck the blood of the poor and the riches of the land! I loathe and abominate the rich, and the proud, and the princely. I call on God, "Arise, thou Judge of the World: and reward the proud after their deserving. How long shall the ungodly triumph? They smite down thy people, O Lord: and trouble thine heritage"— Psalm ninety-four. The God of Vengeance shall trample down those who have trampled down justice and mercy and set up a judgment of blood.'

'Hear, hear!' said the judge sarcastically, clinking his spoon against the tumbler. 'That is a good anathema. Drink to its health!'

By a gesture he invited Drysdale to help himself to a glass of steaming liquor.

Drysdale, a trifle shamefacedly, dropped into a lower key. He also took up a tumbler of punch, and set it down hurriedly, shaking his burned fingers.

'. . . But I will call on the ungodly, the princely and the rich if it will prevent injustice and the perpetration of bloody crime in the name of bloody law.'

'So far,' commented the judge quizzically, 'you have dismissed me in one sentence or so, but you have taken a good many to describe your own position in the matter. Interesting analysis, of course, but I imagine, my good sir, that you did not burst in on me for that.'

The young man stood for a little moodily by the mantelpiece, his freakish nose sniffing up the inviting odours from the contents of his tumbler.

'I have come, Brother Judge, to "let the sorrowful sighing of the prisoners come before thee". In the words of the seventy-ninth psalm to appeal to you "according to the greatness of thy power, preserve thou those that are appointed to die"!

'I have come to ask for a respite of sentence on these children, so that they shall not hang, as otherwise they must, in three days' time.

'I don't know much, but enough to be certain—as certain as I am that you and I, Judge and Jacobin, are hobnobbing over the fire—that I can save them. Given time I can obtain not merely a reprieve: not a commutation, but a free pardon!'

'You become interesting, my friend,' said the judge, raising the tumbler to his lips and sipping the hot beverage with satisfaction. He stretched his legs out before him, as he set the glass down, and contemplated his black well-fitting pantaloons, and neat ankles set off by black silk stockings. 'Perhaps you had better explain.'

'Some little while ago I met a man upon my travels. I knew him of old to be confidential agent of the fat man who is now King. My lord, he was searching like a man demented for a boy—for the smallest of those children you have sentenced to death . . .' he glanced at the clock on the mantelshelf '. . . barely three hours ago!'

'How do you know this is the boy he seeks?' asked the judge.

'I saw the child by chance upon the day he was lost. Despite the changes due to the loving tenderness of the nursemaids of His Majesty's jails, I still can recognize him. Well, this spy of the King became very excited when I said that I'd seen the child·

examined me: cross-examined me: sent his servants clattering off east and west. Money was there to flow like water in the search. I said I supposed that the Regent had lost one of his bastards, but that surely one more or less made little odds! The fellow looked at me strangely at that, said it was a far more serious matter than a Royal by-blow—and then looked as if he bitterly regretted the remark. He offered me a hundred pounds if I could produce the child. Curious, Brother Judge?'

'Ve-e-e-ery curious! Ve-e-e-ery curious, indeed!'

'There is more curious to come,' said Drysdale, lighting a stained clay pipe at one of the candles and puffing out a cloud of rank tobacco smoke. The judge eyed him askance.

'Barely had the fellow gone—a glib, dark foreigner—when a lady came into the room. It was at an inn. Without a prelude she said, "I heard a little of what you were talking. You know something about the boy. Tell me!" So I told her too. She then asked me if I should ever come across the child to let her know *before* I told the Fat Man's agent. She gave me her name, Brother Ermine, and ten pounds as earnest of more to come! She was a great lady, Brother. A very great lady, and, I think, a very good lady!

'That lady is one of the women-in-waiting to the wretched woman who is now Queen of England. . . . Still more curious, Brother White-wig?'

'And still more curious! Very, very, very curious.'

The judge rose to his feet and stood with his back to the fire, his head bent in thought, the chin of his long face resting among the frills of his shirt.

'King's man . . . and Queen's lady . . . both searching for a child —a little felon! . . . Shall you do as the lady asked if I grant you a respite?'

'The Queen is not in the country. She would have no power if she were. I must go to the King's agent.'

The judge took up some papers. He selected two and handed them to Drysdale.

'These,' he remarked, 'may interest you.'

Drysdale glanced at the top document. It contained a printed list of names in alphabetical order. Against each one were set the particulars of a crime, and after these a spidery scrawl recorded the verdict and the sentence. There was no case of murder amongst them, but many of riot. Puzzled, Drysdale turned to the second sheet. Four names were on it, bracketed to the word 'Murder', and in the margin 'Let them be hanged'. An illegible signature was appended, and beneath that again 'The sentence to be respited until His Majesty's pleasure shall be known'.

'You perceive, sir,' observed the judge, coughing amid a cloud of tobacco smoke, 'that I, the "puppet of the law", having fulfilled the Law's requirements, give rein to my own humane instincts. What do you propose now?'

Drysdale looked at the old man for a moment. He set his hands on his hips, his thin mouth widened across his face in an appreciatory smile.

'Almost, I believe, Brother Wig, that you are a Christian as well as a judge; that your bowels of compassion have not become atrophied with age. . . . I will write forthwith to the royal sycophant. Allowing for the post he should be here within the week with instructions from the royal sty.'

'Why not go yourself—to London, is it?'

'Easier said than done.'

The old man's eyebrows rose up into his forehead.

'You cannot spare the time from sedition-mongering, er—Brother —er—Jacobin? You see I know something of your reputation, Mr. Drysdale! I heard you at your polemics once in a little Norfolk market town.'

'I can spare the time,' said Drysdale nonchalantly. 'The sedition will keep. But I cannot spare the money.'

On a table in the bow window there stood a large crimson leather-covered box. The judge unlocked it. He stood fumbling amid the contents, and then glanced up impishly.

'Well, Brother—er—Sedition,' said he, 'I fancy your ideas are correct. In the words of your favourite psalmist, "out of the heaven will the Lord behold the earth; that he may hear the mournings of such as are in captivity: and deliver the children appointed unto death". Though I am damned if I know what psalm it is. . . .'

'One hundred and two—"Domine, exaudi! Hear my prayer, O Lord!"' obliged Mr. Drysdale.

'That being so,' said his lordship, taking out of the box a handful of crackling notes, 'I had better curry what favour I can with the Most High by forwarding his deliverance of the "children appointed unto death". To say nothing of doing His Most Gracious Majesty . . .'

'. . . Most Gracious Majesty,' concurred Mr. Drysdale with emphasis.

'. . . a good turn. Earning a little credit both ways! . . . Take these for your expenses. You had better travel post, and repay me when you have recovered your outlay from the King's agent.' He added with a wry smile, 'If you are ever able to! . . .

'. . . Now go, and go quickly, for there are strange things here of which it is unlikely that you and I will ever know the truth. Meanwhile, I myself will see that no harm comes to your important small friend—or, for that matter, to any of his fellow-felons. . . . No thanks! . . . Be off with you. . . . Good journey. . . . I shall probably—ethics or no ethics—have to hang you one of these days —er—Brother Sedition. . . . You shall be sentenced with the most distinguished courtesy!'

The old man sat listening, with a half-smile, to the sudden uproar that broke out in the inn-yard, to the sound of hoofs and wheels clattering over the cobbles and rattling away into the night.

He rose and spread upon the table the printed calendar. He ran his eye down the long list of names and sentences: paused a moment, dipped a quill into the inkpot, and signed it with a sigh.

Chapter 10

The Odyssey of a Young Gentleman Ends

CHRISTOPHER WAS RELEASED UNDER THE TERMS OF A free pardon.

A scrawled signature at the bottom of a stiffish sheet of paper cancelled a verdict, nullified a judgment, unbarred doors, and threw gates wide open: a signature written by a fat elderly gentleman with his romantically dishevelled wig more romantically dishevelled than usual in token of his dreadful state of mind; supporting his troubles with cherry brandy.

'No scandal, dear boy! No scandal, by Christ!' had said the fat elderly gentleman, his mottled cheeks quivering with emotion. 'Think of *Me!* I rely on you to see we get this all hushed up. To suppress this dreadful Drysdale fellow. To get the child out of the country before the man Setoun finds out about him.'

He gave a final loop under the 'George R.' which he had inscribed, and sat looking at the signature before he sanded it. He flicked a puffy finger, and a man stepped out of the background, filled up the glass at his elbow, and retired into the shadows. The liquor glowed on the tortoise-shell inlaid top of his desk with the deep ruby light of a sanctuary lamp in the darkness of a church.

'Sins of youth! Ah, sins of youth!' said the fat elderly gentleman, smacking his large lips. 'I little thought, my boy, that one of the first things I should do as King—KING—would be to sign a pardon for my . . .'

He paused as though undecided what relationship to assert. He decided on:

'. . . Nephew.'

At the same moment Ompteda filled in the gap:

'. . . Grandson!'

They fell silent.

'I am an unhappy man!' said the elderly gentleman, and clenched his teeth and squared his jaw, to demonstrate how dramatically tight-lipped and grim he could be in tribulation. 'There is a curse on me, my boy, I fear. I have always been of an affectionate nature, giving friendship, giving love—and asking so little in return. Did I get affection? Did I get friendship? Did I get love? . . . My dear Ompteda, how well you know! . . . Hated by my mother, by my father, by my wife . . . by my daughter!'

He dabbed at the corner of an eye with a scented silk handkerchief. It was a histrionic gesture symbolizing grief, rather than a necessity.

Ompteda waggled his long, dark face sympathetically. . . .

And so, one fine morning Christopher was summoned to the office of the Keeper of the jail. He walked out of his cell, never to return to it. There were, even, no farewells.

In a dingy room looking on to a dingy courtyard Baron Ompteda, wrapped in a fur-lined travelling cloak, was talking to an obsequious official with a stubbly chin. A paper with a great red seal lay on the table between them. The seal was the only vivid thing in a room as grey and dusty as a cobweb.

Ompteda swung round at the sound of the small feet: relief and consternation mingled in his expression.

'Herr Je!' he exclaimed. 'I should not have known you, Christopher! . . . Poor liddle devil!'

Christopher shrank back; already he seemed to hear the soft voice of Heywood again, to feel the dark, cold eyes bent expressionlessly upon him, to see the plump dangerous hand negligently hanging by a thumb from the pocket of the grey satin waistcoat—like a white bat.

A comical look of disgust twisted the baron's face.

'Faugh!' said he, 'the child stinks! Ve must vash him, and bath him, and clothe him. Sofort! He is incredible!'

'Must I go?' asked Christopher, tightening his grip on the turnkey's hand.

The man, in his rough way, had been kind to him, and to them all. The draughty cell with its strange smells and its view of enchanted river and woodlands had come to be—not home, but a sort of fort wherein he was secure against goblin memories. One had forgotten about the possibility of being hanged. One played at games of 'Let's Pretend' with Deb; one walked twice a day, under the casual friendly eye of the turnkey, in the courtyard, and was even allowed to peer through the iron gates out on to a hilly street. An old man with a long white face had come one morning, and sat on the stool and asked questions in a very clear, gentle voice. And a man who stood respectfully in the doorway, had made notes, and said, 'Yes, my lord! . . . No, my lord!' Simmie and Gibbie had been sent away: Deb would have gone too, were it not for the distress which Christopher had displayed when the old man had added, 'And the girl!' The old man had heard all the story of the wagon; the small boy standing, with his hands behind his back, against the bony black-covered knees. 'I think, Mr. Sheriff,' said the old man at the end of the recital, 'that it would not necessarily be improper for a prisoner—for two prisoners . . .' he took in the girl with his hooded eyes, '. . . to receive certain extra comforts and even luxuries at the charge of their judge. There would even be a luxurious irony if the sheriff who would have been responsible for their'—he lowered his voice until the word was barely audible —'extinction, were to contribute to their entertainment.' His heavy lids were raised for a flashing impish glance. 'There might be no cash return, but a certain amount of gratitude might be expressed in . . . high quarters.'

So—

'Must I go?' asked Christopher, tightening his grip on the turnkey's hand.

'A reg'lar little curio, sir!' said the turnkey. 'Old-fashioned-like! . . ."Dan," 'e says sometimes to me, "Dan, it's very conformable 'ere now! They won't take us away, will they?" I come in one day, and that there gal and he hadn't got a stitch on more'n a handkercher roun' their waists. A-prancin' about like mad, they was. Actin', they was. Anthony and Koolpater—whatever that means—they said.'

'I don't want to go,' said Christopher, seeing those secure grey walls vanish before Ompteda's wizardry like the walls of Jericho before the trumpet blasts of Joshua—seeing an outer world full of ferocity and menace beyond them.

'Finds it an 'ome from 'ome,' said the jail-keeper, highly gratified by the tribute to his establishment.

'De boy's mad,' said Ompteda crossly. 'Make out his discharge!'

'Is . . . Captain Heywood . . . ?' asked Christopher, with his eyes on the floor, on the clumsy shoes and the grey woollen stockings of the turnkey, the rusted grate full of half-burned paper—anywhere but the long face with the dark whiskers that curved to. points high on the cheek-bones.

'He vill be glad to see you,' said Ompteda, thinking it was what was expected of him.

The jail-keeper, regarding the little prisoner for the first time, saw that his face was as white as if he were about to faint, and that large tears were rolling slowly down his cheeks. Even to his slow mind there was something very strange about the child's unwillingness to depart. He took up the document that lay upon the table. But it was in order, and phrased more urgently than he had ever seen the like before. He turned it over, as if he expected to find some clue, perhaps, upon the back.

'I don't want to go,' said Christopher, clutching the rough serge of the turnkey's jacket. 'I don't want to go. Can't I stay here with Deb? Can't I go home? . . . I didn't shoot the pistol. . . . He said I should be cut up like a butcher's shop. . . . I didn't shoot. It was Captain . . .'

'Hush!' interjected Ompteda hurriedly. 'Id is all right. You shan't see Captain Heywood unless you vant to! Come along, and don't be seely!'

When the door had closed on the pair of them—fur-cloaked baron and unwilling child—the two men exchanged glances.

'That's a rum go, Dan,' remarked the jail-keeper.

'Werry rum go, sir!' said Dan, scratching his head. 'You'd almost think that there child was afeared they were a-goin' to put him away!'

The landlady at a largish inn where the baron halted towards late afternoon, also thought it a 'rum go', when she saw that the fashionable was accompanied on his journey by a small boy wrapped in a coat many sizes too large for him, and wearing the most deplorable shoes.

'Liddle accident. . . . My nephew. . . . New clothes. . . . You vill buy? Please!' said the baron, offering no explanation, showing his large horse-teeth in a winning smile, and producing a purse that clinked prettily. 'Vimmen know about these things, is id nod?'

He played the complete foreigner with such success that he got Christopher bathed, and reclothed without anybody understanding what it was all about.

The child, himself, submitted as if he were in a dream. His eyes never left Ompteda who supervised the various operations. His lips shaped 'Yes' and 'No' to questions, but he vouchsafed no comment of his own. Once only he spoke:

'I *shall* see Deb again, shan't I?' and waited breathless for the reply.

'In a liddle. . . . In a liddle—if you are a good boy.'

With that he had to be satisfied.

Later that evening, while the baron was at dinner, the landlady panted upstairs. With hand to heaving bosom she peered into the child's room. He lay on his back, very still, staring at the ceiling, the bedclothes tossed off him. The glimmer of a shaded night-light showed the shining tracks of tears down his cheeks.

'What is it, love?' she asked, and came into the room. With big red face bent anxiously over him, she pulled sheet and blanket and quilt back into place.

'What is it, my little love?'

But he just sighed, and pushed feebly at the coverings.

His cheeks were very flushed, and stricken by a new notion she put a large moist hand upon his forehead. It was burning hot. Suddenly he began to babble—of Deb, of pistols, and hangings, and butchers' shops, and again of Deb.

She pulled the bell-cord twice. An old bony chambermaid, wizened as a jockey, appeared.

'Stay with the child,' she said, 'till I come back, Mari. He is ill.'

She went downstairs to her best sitting-room, where Ompteda sat in state at a round table on a bright green carpet, eating walnuts, his servant waiting on him.

'My lord,' she said, speaking very loudly and slowly—because he was a foreigner—after she had sketched a curtsy. 'My lord, the child—the boy is ill. He has a fever. He must have the doctor.'

'How?' said Ompteda, cracking a nut so casually that the shell littered her carpet. 'Id is *unmöglich*. Ill? . . . Please?'

'Very ill,' she asseverated, watching him sweep fragments of nut and shell on to the floor. 'He is out of his mind. . . . He must have the doctor—apothecary—surgeon.'

'Ill! . . . Vod nonsense! 'E is—'ow you say?—tired. . . . Id is nodings.'

Ompteda wrapped himself in his defensive cloak of foreignness.

'Begging your pardon, my lord,' said Mrs. Hart, bridling, 'it is not nonsense. The—child—is—ill."

'I vill go to see. . . . 'E cannot be ill. . . . Ve must go to-morrow. . . . Id is nodings—nodings at all. Yes. I am sure.'

'Begging your pardon, I've had six of my own. I know when a child's ill, my lord. He—is—ill. You should have a doctor.'

'To-morrow, *vielleicht*,' said Ompteda.

'To-morrow!' . . . said Mrs. Hart and stopped.

The foreigner was strewing nutshells on her new carpet. He was drinking gin mixed with cream. His manservant had a little red claw of a nose. He himself was picking at his nose like a carter. These foreigners! Gentleman, he called himself! Real gentlemen didn't pick their noses in public. She lost her respect for him: she just felt disgust.

Indeed, if Ompteda had not picked his nose, Christopher might have died: at least he might never have met Charlotte again: everything might have gone according to plan. Victoria, even, might never have reigned.

But because Ompteda pulled and picked at his long melancholy nose, she spoke tartly, without due reverence—

'To-morrow? To-morrow the child may be dead!'

In the sudden sideways glance he gave her at that, she saw something that her mind read as a hope. That silent unwashed child with the strange tattered clothes: these horrible foreigners! She read strange dramas behind the travels of the queer companionship. She became angry and frightened.

'I don't know what the child is to you,' she said, and her voice was shrill. 'But as God's my help, he will die if you travel to-

morrow. He is ill. . . . This is a respectable house. . . . He may
have the fever. . . . Where shall I be? . . . We may all get it. . . .'

'I vill take him away—at vunce!' said Ompteda, rising to his feet.

'You will not!'

'You are mad, woman!'

'It would be—murder!'

Murder!

He threw his clenched fists into the air and spun round on her.

' 'Ow dare you say dat, you bad woman! . . . Murder. . . . I vill
not be spoken to, zo! . . . Idiot! . . . You are mad!'

Murder!

But in her fright, as she shrank back to the door, she saw that he
was frightened, too.

'I shall send for the doctor,' she said.

And this time he said nothing.

So for days and nights Christopher lay raving in a darkened
room about which a fat nurse moved soft-footed. In which he
would awake from nightmare to see strange but kind faces bent
over sewing in the candle-light beside his bed. In which he could
see through the shadowy walls, as if they were but veils, and across
the intervening miles so that his vision was once again focused
through a cell window on the curve of a river and the slope of a
woodland—could hear the lilting voice of Deb making mock of
Lewis, of Price, of Death.

For days more he lay exhausted and silent, watching the fire-
light flicker on the bedposts, the dust motes dance in the sunlight;
listening to the subdued noises of the inn-yard and the occasional
clamour of the gulls.

June was upon them before he was ready to take the road again,
was wrapped up and kissed by Mrs. Hart, and put into the post-
chaise in which Ompteda reappeared. . . .

They crossed a Channel that shimmered in the sun, and dis-
embarked from the packet amid a gabbling crowd of fisherfolk and
porters and curious on the quayside at Calais.

With their baggage trundling after, they traversed the small
place, and made for the shady gardens and yellow-washed walls of

Dessein's Hotel. There they had dinner, and then walked abroad about the melancholy town in the cool of the evening.

Once or twice the baron was hailed by an acquaintance, but he responded shortly to their overtures.

'Yes. My small nephew,' he explained concisely to an inquisitive little man in a white top hat. 'I take him home vid me—to Hanover.'

He encouraged no further inquiries, and with a bow moved on.

'Too many peoples, Christopher,' he said with a scowl. 'Many too many people. Ve go back to de hotel.'

They passed the Silver Lion on their return. A knot of English servants were gathered at the door, watching the strapping of valises to a travelling carriage. As they approached, a well-dressed man emerged from the inn, and paused with a foot on the carriage step. His whimsical face was like a Cruikshank drawing of a London cockney—intelligent, perky, bright-eyed.

'How do, Baron!' said he, and chuckled, and went on without waiting for reply. 'Come to meet the Queen—too?'

'The Queen?' said Ompteda in puzzlement, coming to a halt as he replied to the salute.

'The Queen, my dear fellow!'

'The Queen! How you mean, Mr. Brougham?'

'There's a coincidence!' remarked Mr. Brougham in high glee. 'Queen travelling to Calais. Baron Ompteda—her husband's favourite emissary—in Calais! Is it a coincidence? More than meets the eye perhaps! Well! Well!' He took in Ompteda's disconcertment, and sniggered. 'You didn't know? . . . Well, I'd hurry away if I were you. I can promise you that she's on her way here. By to-morrow. You were never one of her favourites. She'll probably want to eat you with mint sauce!'

'I haf been very busy—very busy, indeed,' said Ompteda importantly. 'His Majesty's business. Oder business. Very urgent business! I saw him a few days ago. He said nuzzing about her.'

'He did not know—a few days ago.'

Ompteda started to go on: paused . . .

'Vot she vant?' he asked.

'Her Majesty,' said Mr. Brougham, 'is on her way to England. She's the lawful wedded wife of Gracious Majesty. If not beloved.

Loathed, not loved'—he chuckled drily again. 'On her way to England, therefore, to claim her connubial rights. Rights, Baron—not nights. To claim her share of the Throne and Royal perks! After six years' wandering on the Continent, coming home like—like the Prodigal in the Scripture for the fatted calf. . . . Your boy?'

But Ompteda ignored the question. He had set off at a fast pace, almost dragging Christopher with him, muttering as he went. . . .

The next morning saw them on the road again, a dusty poplar-fringed road, with lush meadows and small red farms along it.

Shortly before midday they stopped at a gaunt green-washed tavern, and Ompteda drank a jorum of Armagnac.

Christopher sat back while they waited, and admired the post-chaise. It had been an Englishman's travelling carriage and picked up as a bargain by the posting master. The shiny green leather of the upholstery was studded with shinier green buttons; the window-lifts were of yellowing ivory. There were shallow lockers under the seats, and a ledge in front that served as a table or a writing-slope. In the back of the head there was a sort of porthole with a shutter which could be raised so that the lamp behind it illumined the interior at night.

He ran his hand over the warm leather; picked at the shiny buttons; caressed the window-lifts; rapped gently with his knuckles on the spread of glass before him. It was all real, material, solid. That windy cavern in the rear of the wagon was something, perhaps, that he had dreamed. He had gone to sleep and had been ill, and dreamed it all. He could hardly visualize the faces of his companions in the long journey—only, perhaps, that of Deb.

When he shut his eyes very tight he could just catch a glimpse of her—not in his eyes, but somewhere in his mind, in a sort of dark mirror that seemed to lie at the back of his eyes. Perhaps, he thought, there was really a mirror there that reflected what the eyes saw in the world. Perhaps, too, it reflected those bright things his mind perceived in that secret world to which he alone had the entry.

For a fraction of a second he succeeded in focusing that mirror at the right angle; he thought he saw the wide grey eyes and arching brows, the little hollows in the cheeks and the pale lips. Then the picture flickered and was gone. It would not return.

'Deb! Oh, Deb!' he cried, and burst into tears.

Ompteda, plumping himself on to the well-padded seat, looked down with surprise and embarrassment. He patted his charge clumsily on the knee.

'Vot's the matter? Vot's the matter?' he inquired.

'Deb!' said Christopher, sniffing.

'Deb? Vot's Deb?' asked the baron, who had forgotten.

Christopher explained.

'But vy cry about her? Vot is dere to cry about?'

'Did . . .' Christopher paused, for the question seemed one that —once formulated into words and spoken out loud—should unlock the door of memories which he tried hard to keep shut. . . . 'Did . . .' said Christopher again. '. . . Did they . . . hang . . . her?'

'They hanged nobody, nod nobody at all,' said Ompteda. 'The girl vas free in so short a time,' he added magnanimously. 'You may write to her, if you like. I vill send the letter to England vid my dispatches.'

'Not even Gibbie?'

'Nod nobody,' said Ompteda emphatically. 'You shall write to her this night from St. Omer. I vill frank the letter myself. There!'

'She won't be able to read it. She can't read or write. None of them can.'

'Pish,' remarked the baron testily, settling himself into his corner to drowse. 'She shall get somvone to read id her. . . . I go to sleep.'

They rolled on: changed horses: paused for more Armagnac: halted to buy some cherries at a dark *épicerie* in a narrow street that was cluttered with fowls and children; and once, in a little village square surrounded by plane trees, for Christopher to drink from the cord of water trickling from the fountain jaws of a mildewed lion's head. There the children clustered about the carriage, mindful of the generosity of the soldiery that had tramped the country after the war five short years before. There was a chorus: 'I say, you give me one sou!' 'Johnny, one sou!' Ompteda scattered a handful of small coins among them.

In the early evening they stopped to dine in the garden of an inn. They sat at a table spread with a chequered cloth under the cherry trees. The fruit above them glowed in the ruddy sunshine, and the trees cast long shadows on the grass. The road lay but a little way off behind a low hedge, against which grew a few tall honey-coloured lupins. Bees played hide-and-seek in the secret places of the flowers.

Ompteda ate and drank enormously. He finished two bottles of thin red wine, except for the little mixed with water that Christopher was given. Afterwards he soused himself luxuriously in his chair, and dozed, legs stretched out before him, and head bent back till the tips of the curved whiskers on his cheekbones pointed straight upward.

Christopher, left to himself, explored the garden, exchanged smiles with a one-legged scullion in a faded soldier's tunic of scarlet; peered in at the kitchen windows, investigated timidly the thatched bee-skeps, and returned to survey the road over the low hedge.

A white goat, tethered by a rusty chain, browsed on the grassy verge of the wide highway. He amused himself for a considerable time in throwing cherry-stones very gently toward the animal, which ever and again looked up and regarded him malevolently. The irises of its amber eyes, he noticed, were not round but oblong. In some way—due to its whiteness, or its malevolence, or the intentness of its straight gaze—it reminded him of Captain Heywood, whom he had not seen again, of whom he had not spoken, and whose memory he tried to shut behind a still faster door even than that which locked out Lewis and the wagon and the dead boy.

As he stood watching the goat, there was a distant clatter; looking across the level fields, he could see a long dust cloud rise amid the poplars where the road curved back on itself to a tree-girt village. A minute later a horseman rounded the bend and trotted rapidly by. The steed was poor, but the man magnificent in a short red jacket slashed with gold, with a velvet cap upon his white wig.

He was followed by a calash with two men in it, and then by a yellow English travelling chariot, which had an enormous coat of arms upon the door-panels and the initials 'C.P.W.'

Someone within leaned forward, and looked out of the window over the blazonry.

They were driving into the eye of the declining sun, and in the radiance the lovely face at the open window was entirely visible, and glowed as if with a pearly-warm transparency.

Christopher flung up a smoke-blue arm.

'Charlotte! Charlotte!' he called shrilly; and then his heart stood still for fear she would not hear.

The carriage slowed. It came to a standstill outside the door of the inn. And with it halted the following train.

Regardless of the goat or of brambles, Christopher flung himself into the hedge, forced his way through and ran towards the high yellow chariot.

Its door opened. A lady stepped down. Her adorable face smiled under her grey bonnet with the little white flowers set within its wide brim. She wore a grey spencer trimmed with fur, and she ran towards Christopher.

'Christopher! My little Tops!' said the lovely lady, and went down on her knees in the dusty road and held him to her, and kissed him very tenderly.

'Charlotte,' said Christopher, stammering with the urgency of his request, 'you must take me with you. You must never let me go. I want to be with you—always.'

'My lamb,' said Charlotte. 'You shall! You shall! You shall! And I don't care who says you shan't, even if it's the King himself.'

'Eh, ma dragonne! So you, too, have a lover, such a pretty little lover! I wish he were mine.'

A mocking, kindly voice broke in on their love-making—a voice with a foreign accent, that would obviously become marked in moments of stress.

A fat woman, with the ruins of a handsome face and eyes set deep in her head, had come up, and stood beside them smiling. Her long red velvet pelisse was trimmed with ermine, and held together by an enormous jewel. A ruff of Mechlin lace rose about her throat; a preposterous hat surmounted by four ostrich feathers crowned her too-dark hair. She made a brave and rather shattering show. In fact, she reminded Christopher a little of Mrs. Hart as he had seen her once on a Sunday morning.

'A better lover, Ma'am, than many I could name,' said Charlotte, rising to her feet. 'Let me present him to you, Ma'am—Mr. Christopher Harnish, a very modest gentleman . . .' she paused, and laughed, 'although he has slept with me!'

Christopher made a small formal bow.

The elderly lady smiled a little more: and with the smile something girlish and sweet came back to the lined and sagging face, raddled even as it was with paint and powder. She put her hand out to the child.

'Christopher,' said Charlotte gravely. 'This is the Queen—the Queen of England! You may kiss her hand.'

So Christopher kissed the swollen fingers that were heavy with great rings and not over-clean.

'I am going to ask a great favour of you, Ma'am,' said Charlotte, when the ceremony was over.

'Dere are very few that I can do for anyone,' replied the Queen. 'I suppose it has something to do wid de boy?'

'Your Majesty is travelling with adopted sons—and an adopted daughter. May I not follow your example and adopt a son, too?'

'Are you mad, girl?' said the Queen, eyeing Charlotte with the profoundest astonishment.

'Madder than you think, Ma'am. I should be kidnapping an involuntary ward of the King!'

A broad smile illumined the royal countenance.

'He will be very angry?'

'Very, very angry!'

'I wish your adopted son were triplets, den, my dear Charlotte. I wish he were quadruplets—quintuplets! I wish you would adopt six sons or daughters, if it would make the King six times angrier . . . But why?'

Charlotte glanced meaningly at the boy, who was looking from face to face as if to gauge what his fate should be.

'That, Ma'am, it would be better if I were to tell you later.'

'But the Monster will only get him back again.'

'I do not think the King has any right to him at all. The King is not legal guardian of all his family. I know a good deal. I can guess more. The Duchess of Kent was . . . indiscreet, Ma'am. Setoun has filled in some gaps. This child has been with entirely unworthy persons, Ma'am. There were some very strange incidents when I first met him. I will tell you more later. I swore then to Setoun that the King had stolen the boy, and that I would steal him in my turn.'

'And what did my lord say?'

'Setoun said he thought he could deal with the Regent—the King—very nicely. "Very prettily", were his words. He sounded as if he would enjoy doing it. Setoun will back me up, Ma'am!'

'Setoun—Setoun—Setoun. Always Setoun!' declared the Queen. 'I believe you are in love with that ugly old man!'

Charlotte coloured brightly.

'Aha! Aha! *Dragonne!* You like them young and tender, Charlotte. And den by contrast old and stringy!' She shook a roguish head. 'Well, sweetheart, we'll adopt the boy, and damn de consequences, and damn de King! It will all add to the bill he will make me pay—if he can!'

Ompteda, waking slowly to the clatter and to the drift of dust across the orchard, and to the noise of voices that followed, opened his eyes; found himself staring at a coach which towered above the hedge. There was something familiar about it, and yet so out-of-place that he rose, yawning like a large cat, to investigate. Standing by the hedge he saw, then, that painted on its travel-worn sides were the words LONDON AND DOVER, and the British arms were set in an elaborate star upon a shabby panel. A couple of hairy-heeled farm horses steamed in the traces, and the postboys looked as if they had come straight from the plough.

For a moment he thought he dreamed—to see in mid-France a coach that should be posting with English mails through the orchards of Kent. It was palpably in use as a baggage wagon, for it was piled high with trunks. He realized that atop the mass upon the roof was a long black case, on which fat white letters announced the owner—HER ROYAL HIGHNESS, THE PRINCESS OF WALES. TO BE ALWAYS WITH HER.

Opposite the inn door a yellow travelling carriage was halted, and beside it were two ladies, one of them with her hand resting upon Christopher's shoulder. Even although he could not see the face of the other there was something about the flamboyancy of her attire which told Ompteda who the shorter figure was.

They had told him in Calais that the Queen was at St. Omer awaiting messengers from London; he cursed himself below his breath for not having found another route; and still more so when the taller figure raised her eyes to his and beckoned him to approach. He was by no means anxious to see the Queen; her memory was long, and some of the gentlemen of her suite violent—as he had good reason to remember.

He stepped over the hedge, and slowly walked toward the little group beside the high carriage.

He bowed very low to the Queen.

'I trust my liddle boy has not detained Your Majesty!' he hoped.

'The Queen,' said she, 'is more likely to do the detaining, Baron!' A rather bitter smile straightened her lips, and she added, 'I wonder what brings my husband's spy along this road this very day! A strange coincidence, I tink!'

Ompteda ignored the insult.

'I take the child to his home,' he said.

'Home,' inquired Charlotte. 'What home?'

'His home in Hanover, Madam.'

Ompteda recognized her as the girl he had seen at the Seven Stars, and again at a moorland inn when he had been seeking frantically and in vain for Christopher. A vague new anxiety surged up within him.

'Is your home in Hanover, Tops?' asked Charlotte.

The implication that his statement was not to be relied on sent the blood rushing to Ompteda's sallow cheeks.

'His home vill be in Hanover, gnädige Fräulein,' he said. 'By Lauterberg, in the Harz Mountains. Vid his people.'

'His people? . . . And who are they, if I may ask, sir?'

'Dey are cousins of mine,' he lied glibly.

'And living on your estate?' It was more an assertion than a question.

'On my estate, Madam,' agreed Ompteda.

'Or is he, perhaps,' interjected the Queen, 'one of your own early mistakes, Herr Ompteda? You take him back to his native land now tings have blown over?'

There was so malicious a glint in her eye as she spoke, that he contented himself with a low bow for a reply.

Charlotte looked coldly at him. She did not release her hold of Christopher's shoulder.

'I think you are under an illusion, Baron,' said she. 'You may, in fact, be ignorant of the child's antecedents; I, however, know who his family really are—and who his mother was, Herr Ompteda! ... Who his mother was, Herr Ompteda!'

There was such a peculiar emphasis in her voice that Ompteda lifted his deferentially bent head to study her expression: that the Queen turned her deep-set eyes from the dark drooping man before her to the small figure of the boy. She passed over the smoke-blue jacket with silver buttons, the frilled shirt collar, and short yellow trousers, as if she did not see them. But she studied the pale oval face, the arching brows, the slightly aquiline nose, the grey eyes, the fair hair ruffled over the high forehead, as if they formed a sketch of some picture she would recall.

She stared for so long that at last Christopher grew uneasy under her gaze. He shifted his feet, and smiled uncertainly, as if he would apologize for his appearance, and even for his existence.

'Come here!' said the Queen.

She tilted his chin upwards with a fat soft finger, and sought for something in his face with her weary eyes—for something that was not only the repetition in physical structure of another face, but a shadow across the years of a remembered expression.

'So you are one of . . . us!' she said—and corrected herself— 'So you are one of . . . them!'

She paused, drew the child to her, held him pressed against the ruby richness of her pelisse, patting his arm in slow rhythm as she spoke.

'But my master or his brudders—no! If you had come from them I should have known—to tell you God's truth—by the . . . smell! You are not one of them . . . Charlotte! His mother was . . .'

She saw the quick freezing of Charlotte's body, and stopped.

'. . . Your mother was, I tink, a very nice—a very unhappy woman. . . . Like me!'

She bent down, extinguishing him with her enormous hat. Her large face suddenly approached his. . . . The Queen had kissed him —a kiss that smelled of rouge, and powder, and strong scent, and— faintly—of wine!

Ompteda, watching the scene, regained his poise.

'After that, Ma'am,' said he, 'have I Your Majesty's permission to withdraw? Ve have some considerable distance to go.'

'I tink,' answered the Queen slowly, 'that your "ward" remains with me.' She made to turn, Christopher's hand in hers.

'But, Ma'am,' expostulated Ompteda stepping forward. 'But . . .'

'I do not tink you or your master are fit guardians for this boy. His mother would not have desired it. I shall take him with me.'

'Forgive me, Ma'am, but I really cannot permit this.' Ompteda threw out his hands in a beseeching gesture. He had grown very pale.

'You cannot permit *me?*' said the Queen, and laughed.

'Captain Hownham!' Charlotte raised her voice. 'Please to come here.'

A man detached himself from the nearest of the groups that had descended and stood waiting by their carriage doors. He was a little lean man, the colour of mahogany, with high polished cheekbones and a fierce grey eye, which he cocked at Ompteda as he approached.

'I think, Captain Hownham,' said the girl in grey deliberately, 'that you have met Baron Ompteda before?'

'I have, your ladyship,' replied Captain Hownham, putting his hands in his pockets as if to make certain that the baron should not seize one and shake it. 'It gave me no pleasure. Could have done without seeing him again.'

'Perhaps, then, you would be so good as to reason with him. . . .'

'Doesn't want reasoning, my dear! Wants a dog whip!'

'He objects to Her Majesty taking with her a small boy who, he maintains, is in his charge.'

'Charge!' said the peppery Captain Hownham, eyeing the tall Hanoverian up and down. 'Isn't fit to have charge of half an old hen's egg in a bum-boat woman's store!'

'Exactly! If the baron had any sort of paper to prove his right to the child—to show his authority, it might be a different matter. . . . *Might* be!'

The Queen turned toward the carriage door, holding Christopher fast; as if completely indifferent to the scene; as if everything had been most satisfactorily arranged.

Ompteda, confronted by the tall grey girl and the mahogany-coloured man, shuffled his feet uncomfortably. He had no documents to prove his guardianship. He had had verbal orders only, that the child should be taken out of the way to Hanover, placed with a complaisant farmer on his own small estate, and provided with a new name and all the necessary papers. Such things could be done in Hanover very pleasantly and quietly.

'If Her Majesty wants to adopt or kidnap anyone, she can! Anyone!' said Captain Hownham. 'Or I'll know the reason why! She adopted me, bless her heart. She's a mania for adoption. She can adopt one of these furry-faced postilions—if she wants to! . . . Draw the line at a nasty piece of work like you, though!' he added reflectively.

'This is a jest,' said Ompteda thickly. 'My duty to the King . . .'

'Your duty to the King, sir!' Hownham turned on him with swift ferocity. 'It was your duty to the King that set your dirty fingers a-grubbing in Her Majesty's desk when you thought no one was looking, not so many years ago! Your duty to the King made you eat her bread and spy on her, you dirty sea-cook! Your duty to the King made you refuse to fight me when I called you out, you lily-livered scum! Your duty to the King made you howl like a dog when I laid my whip about you, you herring-gutted baboon!'

He advanced with doubled fists on the baron, who retreated, backing along the grass verge before his approach.

There was a clanking of chain behind Ompteda, and a cry of warning that came too late. The goat had watched his withdrawal with deep suspicion. It lowered its curved horns, and leaped, like something projected from a catapult, at the tails of his coat. He received a sudden and terrific blow behind, that sent him on his back on top of the struggling demented animal.

The Queen had paused, and turned with one foot on her chariot step. She burst into a roar of laughter at his downfall. Her face reddened; tears streamed from her eyes; she shook like a jelly.

Ompteda, lying on his back, bemused, stared up into the bearded face of the goat as it butted frantically at him again. He rolled clear of the threatening horns, and then sat up. The sound of laughter was borne back to him, mingled with the jingle of harness as the horses took the strain.

He was still sitting there when the last of the cavalcade passed by in a cloud of dust.

Looking back in later life, Christopher realized that the whole of one epoch in his career was bounded by two similar processions.

It had started with a convoy clattering over wet cobbles toward twilight, and a fat nurse bouncing a fat baby in her arms as if she would make it acknowledge the scattered greeting of the crowd. It had started with solemn Royalty trailing into a town, with escort of bumping militia and jangle of church-bells. It closed with the preposterous cavalcade of a dispossessed Queen—a cavalcade marshalled by a rather vulgar hop-merchant, with farm-hand postilions astride plough horses; yellow chariot, curricle, stage coach and travelling carriages; mustachioed servants, turbaned servants, yapping lap-dogs, twittering cage-birds, two adopted sons—one the offspring of a dock labourer, the other the bastard of a court official—as well as an adopted daughter aged three: all the tawdry pomp and noisy circumstance of an ill-regulated circus.

Christopher was taken into the yellow carriage—it had a pale blue lining—with the Queen and Charlotte, thereby dispossessing a very small girl, stiff with satin and crumpled with weariness, who was sent back to the charge of a maid.

There was ample room to sit between them, and even for the thin cushions which served for arm-rests for him on either side.

A hinged ledge on the door made a little table before the Queen. On it was a small box in which three hot-house peaches were packed in wool. The Queen spread a folded linen napkin over her knees, and proceeded to peel and cut up one of the fruit with a pearl-handled knife. The juice ran over her fingers.

'Shut your eyes, my sweet,' she commanded. 'Open your mouth, and see what love will send you!' And she popped a segment of melting sunshine into a mouth that obediently became an O.

'Poor Willikin,' she said across the yellow head to Charlotte. 'I am sorry he is growing big. I am determined to have another little boy. I must always have a boy child wid me.'

'Would you rob me of my lover, Ma'am, by appealing to his

greed and my pity?' said Charlotte smiling. 'I thought you still are
very fond of Willikin.'

'To be sure. To be sure. I love him very dearly, but I must have
a little child. He is growing too big—too much of a man!'

'Would you desert me, Tops,' asked Charlotte, 'for the Queen?'

He looked up into her face; he sought for her hand and clung to
it: then he glanced apologetically at the Queen who sat back in
her corner, and shook his head.

'I have my answer,' she said. 'But what shall you do wid him, ma
belle dragonne? You can't adopt him—you, an unmarried girl!
What happened when I adopted Willikin fifteen years ago? Was
dat not proof enough of the dangers dat confront those of us who
have had to suppress our natural mothering instincts!'

Charlotte nibbled her gloved finger-tip, and meditated.

'My answer to the problem is a very easy one,' she said at last.
'It should have come straight from my lips, Ma'am. . . . Setoun
shall adopt him, of course!'

The Queen laughed uproariously.

'Setoun will be a trifle surprised, I tink, at his unexpected pa-
ternity. But while you are with me, the child shall stay under my
protection: is it not so?'

The journey became a fantastic thing—a series of turbulent pictures linked by the curious caravan procession. . . . They were back
in Calais with a surging crowd about the carriages. . . . Once more
they were on the shimmering Channel, only this time the white
cliffs drew near, instead of gradually vanishing in a grey warm haze.
. . . They approached Dover, and cannon from the Castle thun-
dered a salute: smoke drifted upward from the embrasures and the
seagulls wheeled uncertainly, screaming protests, over the packet.
The shores and the quay were black with people; the thin sound
of their shouting echoed over the still water.

The tide was out, and the vessel could not enter the harbour.
So they took boat and were rowed to land, the Queen's great hat
straining perilously at its moorings with every puff of wind.

They stepped ashore and went on foot through a roaring, ac-
claiming crowd. It was a hurricane of cries; a kaleidoscope of waving hats and arms and handkerchiefs. From it the Queen drew an
electrical strength into herself: her deep-set eyes shone in a trans-

formed face; her weary shoulders straightened, and her head was lifted high on her short neck. She was no longer a flamboyant woman who might be the hostess of the Cawdor Arms in church-going attire. She even invested her monstrous hat, her over-sump-tuous pelisse with a dignity that made them seem to be royal robes —part of the regalia of queenhood.

They left the town to the sound of the National Anthem, be-fore nightfall, in a carriage drawn by a shouting mob, and were received at Canterbury with addresses of welcome with frenzied cheers, by a torchlight procession.

The carriage was open and the occupants illumined by the red and yellow flare. The hop-merchant, Mr. Alderman Wood, was with them now, and Christopher sat on the thick fleecy rug on the floor among their feet, watching the sparks and smoke blow in the wind from the streaming torches, assessing the faces which, livid in the strange light, peered over the carriage side and called blessings down upon the Queen.

In such disorderly fashion did the King of England's Consort pass to lodging through the scrambling streets of the Cathedral city, with the rag-tag following of duke's daughter, hop-merchant, adopted children, and waif; with her hugger-mugger of baggage battered by six years of travel.

Set within the flickering succession of scenes of uproar that marked that strange triumphal progress to London, there was one picture that Christopher was to remember more vividly than all the rest.

That night at Canterbury he slept on a truckle bed in Charlotte's room, adjoining the bed-chamber of the Queen. The sound of voices awakened him, and he sat up in the half-darkness, to look through wide-open folding doors as if on to a lighted stage.

The Queen stood perhaps thirty feet away, at a marqueterie table against the white panelled wall. She wore a loose claret-coloured robe: and as she bent intently over something that lay on the table, a diamond earring swung forward from amid the studied mass of ringlets, and flashed like a drop of falling water in the candle-lit radiance of the room.

Her hands were very busy—with what he could not see.

She looked up and said something to which an unseen Charlotte made reply. Then with finger and thumb she delicately robbed each of the burning candles, in the six-branched candelabrum before her, of a little of its warm wax, and rolled it in her hand.

Suddenly she straightened.

'Here is my Monster!' she said in a high voice, and turned toward the open door, holding up something before her as if she were a priest revealing a relic to the faithful.

'Here he is!'

And Christopher saw that she held in her fingers a little grey-white image of candle-grease with out-thrust legs and arms, like a child's drawing of a man.

She gabbled something in a foreign tongue. Her eyes flashed; her body trembled with excitement. The invisible Charlotte murmured words that Christopher could not hear, but sensed their soothing.

The Queen set down the image on the table. With a slow curving movement she brought her hands up to her head, and felt with delicate pressure among the ordered array of puffed ringlets.

She drew out a long jewelled pin, and, grasping it as if it were a dagger, brought it down with such sudden ferocity upon the thing lying on the table, that Christopher could hear it stab into the wood.

'So!' said the Queen. 'So, I torment him! As he tormented me, so I torment him. . . . I torture him in his heart. . . .'

She drew the weapon out of the table with an effort, and stabbed it in again with even greater violence.

'. . . I torture him in his belly . . . in his head . . . in his genitals . . . in his arm. God torture him for me! Oh, God wound him— strike him! . . . God smite him in his liver . . . in his leg!'

The flashing jewel rose, and fell again and again; her voice rose in shrill urgency. Finally she raised her hand above her head, and brought the long pin down with the tigerishness of a novice witch making her first blood offering at a Sabbath. The steel shaft shivered into pieces as it struck, and Christopher heard the jewelled head rattle on the surface of the table.

A moment's silence: the Queen gave a cry.

'Charlotte!' she said. 'See the Monster, he's steeped in blood! . . . God answers my prayer! . . . See how he bleeds! Every drop shall burn him. As if it were fire.'

She stood a moment with one hand raised, blood running from a long wound torn in the palm by the broken pin.

She laughed shortly, and then spoke in a changed voice.

'I am a foolish woman. I do not mean it! I do not mean it!'

Charlotte hurried to her side; and the Queen stood silent, facing the darkness beyond the open doors, as any actress might confront her audience, passively submitting to the deft attentions to her wounded hand.

'I don't mean it,' she said very slowly. 'I don't . . .' She paused, so that Charlotte lifted her bent head from her bandaging and looked up expectantly. Christopher saw the pale exquisite contours of her rose-pearl face against the haggard rouged sallowness of the Queen. '. . . I don't mean it!' And then violently—'But I do! O God, I do!'

Christopher mentioned the matter a week or two after.

'So you saw it all!' said Charlotte thoughtfully. 'Well, now you know the depth of hate a bad man can create. A good lesson for you, Mr. Harnish, being who you are, with the record that lies behind you—with the record you must break!'

'What do you mean, Charlotte?' he asked; and because he looked at her with eyes so innocent of comprehension, she caught his face between her hands and kissed him.

The mad confusion of the first day in England was, however, as nothing compared with the chaos of that which followed. They travelled with an ever-growing train of horsemen; with an incredible tail of crowded carts and shabby carriages. They were halted to be presented with addresses, to be shaken by the hand; by the sheer density of the crowds that pressed cheering about them; by the wheeling into the line of the procession of vehicles that were used as moving grandstands, and from which perpetual uproar arose.

They entered a London in which the streets were almost impassable and handkerchiefs fluttered from every window. They crossed Westminster Bridge to a roar that echoed in the House of Commons and the fat King's home in Carlton House. London greeted the injured Queen with a frenzy and hysteria of enthusiasm, with the smashing of Cabinet Ministers' windows, and with illuminations at nightfall.

Christopher travelled in a coach with the hop-merchant's son and young 'Willikin', a gentle, melancholy youth, who shook his head repeatedly, sighing, 'It's too good to last. It's too good to last.'

He stood beside them in the crowded drawing-room of the house they reached eventually.

Through the heavy curtains shrouding four long windows came a noise like the murmuring of the sea, and mingled with it little shriller cries and sharp whistling.

Two great doors at the end of the room were suddenly folded back. Someone announced in a loud voice:

'Her Majesty the Queen!'

She came slowly up the room, followed by her ladies. Twenty years had rolled away from her: she walked with grace and dignity: her eyes were wet with tears, and the smile of a happy girl curved on her lips.

Christopher could not think that it was she who last night had made a little figure out of candle-grease and stabbed it with a pin.

Two footmen in crimson flung wide the curtains from a window.

The Queen stepped on to the balcony, and a great shout rose from without like the crash of a breaker on a stony shore. Its thunder rose and fell, and rose again, broke for a moment into a foam of calls—'Burn Carlton House!' 'God Save the Queen!' 'Down with the Tyrant!'—and surged up anew into a roar that beat at the heart. The voice of an angry people!

Chapter 11

Dreams and Prayers

CHRISTOPHER'S ATTIC WINDOWS LOOKED OUT FROM under the gables of Brandenburgh House, the one on to the grey and silver river, and the other on to the rook-haunted elms at the side of the building.

He was less interested in the Thames, with its Sunday throngs of sightseers rowing to and fro before the lawns in the hope that the Queen might show herself, than in the doings of the birds. Their monstrous nests were black knots amid the foliage of every tree. One elm in particular being so favoured by them that he called it the 'Slum'. They were busied on mysterious errands; they gossiped all the day, held parliaments, and went forth in their armies on inexplicable expeditions. Their activities reminded him of the strange romance of 'Peter Wilkins' and the Flying Men; and to his magic world of day-dream he added bird-people whose homes swayed in long galleries on the lips of cloud-piercing precipices, or in gigantic nests above an endless sea of dark pine forests.

He would sit for hours at the small casement—ignoring top-hatted oarsmen and their bonneted companions—lost in reverie and the fairy tales that the magic of his mind caused to rise like a tapestry of mist before the shining foliage and the dark trunks and the glimpsed red roofs.

In the dream life that overlapped the real, the avenue of elms no longer led to the King's Road in the village of Hammersmith, but to an embattled gateway with high peaked towers, and a highway that ran past impenetrable forests, through dark gorges cleft in purple mountains, to a white harbour with marble houses set by a rolling sea the colour of dark lavender. Along the avenue a guard marched to and fro; they saluted as they tramped by his window. And the princess looked up when she passed amid her ladies: sometimes she wore a cloak of scarlet and dark blue that blew behind her in a magic wind; sometimes a dress of cloth-of-silver with sleeves of green as pale as the sea where it curves from under the keel.

In an old memorandum book he drew a map of these fairylands where his other life was spent, showing the cities and the seas and the enchanted forests, and the distant islands of which he was prince—islands where great castles and abbeys and woods rose sheer and sudden out of an ever-summer ocean. He painted his map, and the plans of his cities, with his water-colours in the most accepted manner. He compiled, too, a grammar of the language which they spoke in these happy lands—a simple mixture of Latin and French and the better-sounding English words. There was, as well, a manual of military organization by which—for now he was the captive of his deadliest foe—he should rebuild his shattered armies and, marching across the high bright moors, fall on his walled towns one by one and drive the enemy back to a last desperate battle; a battle fought in a shallow valley where meadows were yellow with daffodils and a river ran steel-coloured under a windy sky.

These documents were very precious: the crackling of the dog's-eared leaves—the marbled cover of the volume that contained them—were in themselves a spell sufficient to send his soul out adventuring on a never-ending tale. None else might see them—not even Charlotte.

He kept the magic book under lock and key in a polished mahogany box inlaid with brass, with a little hidden drawer you opened by pushing at a knot in the satinwood lining. Flat acanthus leaves of metal were let into the wine-red wood at each corner, and the shield of the key-plate thrust out at its angles into wavy golden ribbons.

It was a fit repository. It stood locked upon the small chest-of-drawers that held his wardrobe; next to the glass case in which there sailed for ever the model ship Setoun had given him. A ship it was that pressed on across an unchanging sea to a port she would never reach, her white sails cracking to an undying wind. A magic ship! A craft in which enchantment was instinct! Such a craft as that in which he sailed over the rim of the world to the islands of his princedom.

This secret life and the orderly routine of childhood were led amid the chaos of Queen Caroline's affairs and the disorder of the court she held at Brandenburgh House.

Each morning he set off for school towards Earl's Court, under the escort of a powdered footman carrying a vast umbrella—a small boy in frilled collar with giant attendant in crimson plush. . . . Behind the blank windows of the house secretaries were already sorting out the vast mass of correspondence that poured in.

At midday he and his 'guardian came back together, talking at random on strange lands and the seven seas—for the man had been a sailor—until they reached the long elm avenue, and the rooks, and the gabled roof above the Palladian walls, when his companion fell silent and dropped a respectful pace behind. . . . Within, as he crossed the black-and-white marble squares of the great hall, the hum of voices would come through the opening door of a conference room where the advisers of the Queen sat at interminable debate.

After his dinner, which he took in some state in the small parlour with Willikin and Captain Hownham, he would be summoned to the Queen. . . . Across a mile—it seemed—of shining parquet to kiss a beringed plump hand; to bow (and smile gravely) to Charlotte; to greet, perhaps, with an inward rapture, the large tightly dressed figure of Setoun.

'He cannot go yet, Setoun,' said the Queen. 'Not till I beat dem. He is my talisman. You must let me keep him till I triumph.'

He had supplanted Willikin and the girl in the royal favour. Each afternoon he drove abroad with the Queen, usually in a huge landau behind a pair of glittering greys, stiffly facing Majesty. The carriage party would talk, unsuitably for childish ears, of the coming trial of the Queen, of probable perjury, of the House of Lords' procedure, and the morals of her king husband—'my old Heliogabalus'. But it made no odds, for Christopher was far away —in another and brighter coach, behind other and speedier steeds, along other and more romantic roads than those which ran through the market-gardens of Hammersmith or wound about the cot-

tages ornées of Turnham Green or the moss-grown walls of old Chiswick.

Sometimes the two of them would drive out alone—small boy and elderly woman crowned with a hat of enormous plumes, sitting side by side, communing together in silence. It was as if he drew from her store of memories of pomp the pageantry for his dreams, and in return gave back to her for a brief space the faint rapturous visions that possessed him.

People at the street corners would cry out after them as they passed: 'God bless you, Ma'am!' The knots without the tavern doors would bellow cheers, and even quite genteel females would delicately flutter loyal handkerchiefs.

On one occasion when they drove together unattended, a fat old woman with a grey moustache and a red face paused at a corner to let them pass, and called as they went by: 'God bless you, Ma'am, and your little boy!'

Christopher looked up to find the Queen's quizzical regard upon him.

'She thought I was your little boy,' he said, appreciative of the joke.

The Queen smiled and nodded.

'If I were,' he reflected aloud. 'I should be really a prince, shouldn't I?'

'Would you like to be,' she countered gravely, 'a prince, and my little boy?'

On meditation he was a trifle embarrassed.

'My mother . . . perhaps . . . wouldn't have liked me to . . . be someone else's.' He paused. 'Of course she didn't know me—very well. . . .' He added politely: 'So if I wasn't hers, I should like to be, Ma'am'.

'I wish you were, Tops,' said the Queen. 'I should like a t'ousand little boys. They would all be very dear—very dear!'

She sat silent, thinking of the dead daughter who had been reft from her by the father, and of the unborn sons she would have loved—the unborn sons who might have walled her in with their love against the ceaseless enmity that surrounded her. Christopher wriggled in discomfort: it was an infallible sign of an onset of

royal emotion when Majesty encountered difficulty in the pro-
nunciation of her th's.

'I want a great tall son, Tops, to be with me now—a tall son to
fight my enemies. I get old . . . and tired.'

A tear rolled down her hot and powdered cheek.

There was a little silence as the carriage rolled down a dusty
lane past a gaunt Academy for Young Gentlemen, and so into the
road that curved through fields and market gardens towards Brandenburgh Place and the long avenue to Brandenburgh House.

'You know, Tops,' said the Queen at length, 'that in a few days'
time I am going to stand my trial?'

'Trial, Ma'am!' said Christopher amazed, and visualized Majesty
standing in just such another spiked box as that in which he had
once stood, and facing across a sea of wigs and sallow faces a scarlet figure high up as on an altar or throne.

'Dey say I, de Queen, have done wrong. Dat I have done what
he, de King, only can do. And so dev do not want me to be Queen
—and try me.'

'Like King Charles?' asked Christopher, seeking information as
to the mode of trial.

'Like King Charles,' agreed the Queen.

'Do they want . . .' Christopher paused to make the question
sound more delicate, '. . . do they want, Ma'am, to . . . cut your
head off?'

'Dey would like to,' answered the Queen vigorously, but patting
his knee in a reassuring manner. 'Dey would like to very much.
But dey won't. Dey are afraid to. Dey are cowards, like all bad
men. De people love me. . . . All people love me. . . . How dey
love me!

'De King will not even give me sentinels to stand before my
house. But I don't need them. There is none to do me harm—
except him and his friends. . . . Everybody else love—love—love
me. So much!'

'When I grow up I'll be sentinel, Ma'am,' Christopher promised in a stammer of embarrassment and loyalty, and was glad as
they turned into the avenue, swung round, and drew up before the
great entrance of the house. He noted what he had never missed

before, that there were no tall soldiers in scarlet and gold with gleaming bayonets before the portico.

Within was the usual confusion: flurried servants, a worried chamberlain, a more worried secretary with inky fingers; an uneasy deputation was clustered about a pillar in the hall; a couple of stray sympathizers waited on the extreme edges of hard chairs; Mr. Brougham was demanding an immediate audience; the Lord Mayor, Recorder and Sheriffs of the City of London were kicking their heels in the long reception room that looked upon the river; a Nonconformist divine and his elders from a Denmark-Hill Bethel crowded the small anteroom; a mean little man in black with tight shiny pantaloons clutched determinedly a most sinister blue bag from an attorney's office; a smell of hot humanity mingled with the faint camphor odour from little used Sunday-go-to-meeting clothes.

All day long it went on—the constant stream to the wide fan-lighted door. The porter no longer withdrew into the recesses of his hooded chair which was set by one of the tall windows beside the door. He stood the greater part of the day with his hand upon the latch. His fellow drooped wearily over the visitors' book on a table before the other window, guiding inexperienced scribes, sanding their signatures, bowing before a washerwoman as to a duchess.

The chequered floor of black-and-white marble was stained with much trampling, and echoed to the unceasing clatter of feet.

At the foot of the wide shallow staircase, with a vast battlepiece lowering over its crimson treads, one of her gentlemen halted the Queen. He spoke to her in a whisper, and her face lighted up.

'Here?' she asked. 'Now? . . . Where is he? Tops, you shall come, too.'

In one of the lesser rooms—its walls populous with miniatures and indifferent portraits—they found a tall gentleman who had drawn up an elbow chair to the open window, and so sat with his back to them, facing the river. He was greatly at his ease in velvet skullcap, and with curling meerschaum pipe which emitted clouds of smoke that looked like tobacco smoke but smelled like a bonfire of dried leaves. He did not hear their entry and rose in a flurry when the Queen addressed him.

'Augustus! Dis is a pleasant surprise!'

'Pipe, my dear Caroline,' said he in some confusion. 'I apologize. Never expected to be received in this room. Pipe—very awkward! Most awkward! Don't go out much! Honoria doesn't mind. Says marriage has accustomed her to tobacco and Bibles!'

'Bibles!' said the Queen in surprise, extending her hand over which he bowed.

'Bibles,' he repeated a little hurt. 'My dear Caroline, my collection of Bibles—remarkable! Superb! You must have heard of it. Common knowledge! Anything about Bibles—"Why," say they, "you must ask poor old Sussex!" Quite a reputation, I assure you. When I have a clerical soirée in my library I always have to have a couple of attendants to make certain the reverends don't make away with any of the volumes.'

'It is a pity that George doesn't share your taste!'

'Ah, now, Caroline,' said he shaking a finger at her. 'You must not be too prejudiced. At heart George is a religious man—deeply religious!'

'I have heard him called many things, but never that,' said the Queen. She paused reflectively. 'It is true I once heard one of your sisters—Elizabeth, I think it was—speak of him as a "dear angel". Speaking as his wife now I should say . . .'

She sat down stiffly in a high-backed chair with her back to the light, without finishing the sentence. She drew Christopher to her side; her hand, clasping his, lay on the rose-brocade chair-arm.

'A little refreshment, Augustus?' she asked. 'A glass of Madeira? . . . Christopher, pull the bell!'

'And who have we here?' said the gentleman, turning mild, bulging eyes on the child, and rubbing the folds of his chin from side to side against the stiff frill of his shirt.

'This is Master Harnish,' said the Queen. 'Tops, this is your— the Duke of Sussex! Bow nicely to him. He is better than most of his family.'

Christopher, heels together, bowed to the tall figure from the hips—as Charlotte had taught him—a little jerkily, perhaps.

The gentleman smiled at him.

'So this is the boy,' he said. 'This is—h'm. Marked resemblance. Very marked. You must come and see me some time, my child,

and see my Bibles! Very fine Bibles. You know your Bible? . . . I
. . . h'm . . . was very fond of your mother.'

'Did you know my mother, sir?' asked Christopher in astonishment. Nobody in this new phase of his life had ever mentioned
her, except Setoun who had shown him the faintly yellow lock in
the little crystal shrine within his ring.

'Very well, indeed,' said the duke, resting his elbow on the high
mantelpiece, and looking from him to Caroline. 'Come here!'

Christopher approached the tall man, who tilted his chin upwards with a pair of smoke-smelling fingers and studied his face.

Burning crumbs of his strange smoking mixture had fallen on
his green velvet waistcoat and marked it with brown singeings.
There was a little snuff speckling the white of his ruffled shirt. He
had a shiny pink face and fat curving lips. He resembled a slightly
intoxicated cupid. Christopher thought he looked rather a silly
old man.

The duke lifted his regard back to the Queen.

'You don't . . . h'm . . . propose to make use of the boy, Caroline?' he asked more than a trifle awkwardly.

Her crimson face whitened suddenly with blotches of anger.

'Dat is an infamous idea,' she said. 'I at any rate wish for no
more public scandals. I do not cast mud.'

Sussex gave her a sideways look—a quick flashing look in which
cunning was blended with his native simplicity. In the half-turn
of his stooped head something a little mean showed in his expression; something a trifle querulous in the line etched from the
centre of his well-shaven cheek down to the jawbone; something
stupidly secretive in the veiling of his eyes by sandy lashes. He was
no longer just a garrulous elderly person, but such a one capable
of petty meanness and unimportant plottings.

The Queen noted it.

'So your visit was not just a friendly one, Augustus,' she said
reflectively. 'There was a purpose behind it. I might have guessed
it. . . . Another glass of Madeira, Augustus?'

'Even if my visit was not "just a friendly one",' replied the duke,
'I still—h'm—can come, and do come, as a friend. . . . Thank you,
I will have another.'

His mild eyes traversed the bright lawns, and fixed themselves upon the small craft that manœuvred on the steel-coloured river beyond—small craft crowded with sympathizers of the Queen on pilgrimage to her shrine.

'You won't see dat at Buckingham House,' said she, following his gaze. 'The loyal subjects of my husband are more likely to throw stones at him than wait for hours on the chance of seeing him.'

'It's for that I have come. . . .'

'As his emissary?'

'Not his emissary, Caroline. Without his knowledge. As—h'm— I trust to your discretion . . . as the emissary of his family. We realize, Caroline, as George and the Government do not appear to, that the country is dry tinder to which only a match need be set . . .'

'I don't hold the match!'

'You can restrain the hand that does. . . .'

The Queen said nothing, but signalled to Christopher to refill her empty wine-glass.

The elderlyish gentleman, in a most absent-minded way, curled his fingers about the bowl of his large pipe. It was still warm. He caressed it in an abstracted manner, rubbed it against his nose equally forgetfully, found the amber mouth-piece close to his lips, inserted it in his mouth, gave it a tentative puff, found it was still alight, pulled very heartily, and then seemed to withdraw for protection behind the vast billows of smoke he ejected.

'You are aware that there has been a mutiny in the Guards, Caroline?' he inquired. 'Good God, Ma'am! A mutiny in His Majesty's Guards!' He blew a volley of smoke out before him as if he were a firing-party dealing with the rascals.

Caroline shook her head. She coughed. Christopher coughed. Anyone within range of the duke's portable bonfire would have coughed.

He took his pipe from his mouth, and looked at the flushed lady concernedly.

'Bronchial! Very bronchial, my dear girl,' he said. 'River damp. Now this helps me a great deal. A herbal mixture—very soothing to the chest. Highly recommended. I am very asthmatic myself— have been so from a child when dear Mamma used to have me whipped when I had an attack. Some funny idea in her old head that I had the fits just to be aggravating. . . . Honoria herself will take a puff in the morning, if her chest is not clear. In the privacy of our bedchamber, of course, you understand. Before our morning chocolate.'

'Miss Matilda always used to smoke, too, when she went to bed,' said Christopher, anxious to be of assistance. 'I could smell it under her door. She said it eased her chest, when I asked her. She said there was nothing like brandy and water, hot, for the chest. Shall I order some, Ma'am?'

The Queen brought the duke back to the subject on hand.

'The Guards have mutinied!' she repeated, taking a hearty sip of Madeira as a linctus.

'The Guards; yes, Ma'am. They've been very concerned at the Horse Guards. . . . You were made the excuse for it, Ma'am. You are being made the excuse for a lot of trouble. I'm a good Radical. I'm for Reform—all the world knows it. But these Jacobins are making use of the mob-sympathy you arouse to start the most damnable Republican plots. Republicans, Ma'am! . . . And others —no names, no pack-drill—are making use of *them*, in turn. These others are employing spies and *agents provocateurs*. They urge on the wilder elements to disorder and conspiracy for their own profit. They'll foment rebellion to frighten respectable people, to put 'em in a panic, to make 'em think the only way for safe Government is to establish autocracy. Tear down old liberties, suppress constitutional freedom—set reaction and dictatorship on the throne!'

'For reaction, read Cumberland, I suppose,' interjected the Queen. 'I hate Cumberland, but I hate George worse. The one is a great violent lustful monster; but de odder is a fat cowardly more cruel monster. One is a tiger—the odder is a hyena.'

'Heaven forgive me for saying it of my own brother,' said the gentleman, puffing away most vigorously. 'But if ever there was a man without conscience or without honour or heart—who would set brother against brother, or husband against wife, it is Ernest! And now you know.'

'If I accept George's terms dey will drop proceedings against me, and the danger will go?'

'I think I can assure you of that.'

'Then,' said the Queen vehemently, tapping her toes on her foot-stool, 'I shall do nudding of the sort. It is for the King to save his Country, not me. I vill go away—abroad—for ever, as they vant. I 'ave said so before. I vill take his allowance. I 'ave said so before. But I must be recognized as Queen. If dere is no King of England, I do not mind not being the Queen. If dere is anudder King, I do not mind not being the Queen. But if George is King, and as long as George is King, I vill be Queen.'

She suddenly turned on Christopher.

'Have you been told to pray for your enemies, child?' she asked.

'Yes, Ma'am,' said Christopher.

'Well, child, the King will not let the people pray for me. Dey have been ordered to take my name out of the Prayer-Book. It is forbidden for me to be prayed for.' She grew more and more excited. Her black shoe-tips tapped up and down; her knees rose with the movement like the cranks of an engine; her face grew redder and redder. 'I, de Queen, must not be prayed for in de same breath with de Monster.' Her voice rose to cry—'Nor with all de rest of his Brood. I, Caroline of Brunswick, am not fit to be mentioned with all dose dirty, adulterous, lousy Hanoverians! I . . .'

She seemed to be in some sort of fit. Her face had become purple with congested blood, her eyes bloodshot, and she struggled for breath in convulsive heaves. Her black ringletted wig slid down towards her nose, and her wine-glass fell to the floor, and the dregs soaked into the bright green pile of the carpet.

All this was to the great alarm of Christopher, who pulled gently at her sleeve as if to draw her attention to the fact that her conduct was unusual.

The incident remained in his mind for long afterwards: purple face beneath plumed hat, distorted and mouthing against the rose-red back of the high chair; green lawn and river shining through the tall window that lighted the white walls crowded with little fussy pictures; pervading everything, the bonfire smell of the duke's smoking mixture.

It fixed in his mind a horror of the King which he was never to lose. He associated that seizure with the fact that the King had ordained no prayers were to be made for the Queen: that, in some way past his imagining, she had become thus excommunicated, and liable and vulnerable to the physical assaults of evil powers; that, deprived of the shelter of prayer, her soul had been delivered defenceless to the presence of the devil. To imprison, to torture, to execute seemed to him to lie within the bounds of normal justice; but to forbid prayer seemed to transcend those bounds. He visualized the King no longer as a wicked man with kingly powers, but as an evil spirit with powers of damnation as well as life and death.

When he had had his supper that night, and played a game of chess with Charlotte, and drunk his cup of arrowroot, and climbed the stair to his small snug room, and gone to bed in the fading light under the respectful care and attention of Williams, the exsailor, he lay between sheets a long time struggling with God.

He might damn his soul for ever by praying for the Queen: he might be committing the sin against the Holy Ghost by so doing. What was the sin against the Holy Ghost? Praying for the Damned—for those for whom no prayer should be uttered?

He took a sudden decision. Lying on his back, staring through the dimness at the little ship in its glass case sailing to the Port of No-Man-Knows, he said out loud, and very deliberately, "O God, bless the poor Queen!"

Then, as the darkness pressed through the windows to the sighing of the trees, and the room lost shape about him, he became very frightened and solitary. He alone in the world had prayed for the Queen!

He leaped out of bed, and knelt stiffly upright on the blackand-red rag rug, and prayed aloud for all those for whom no decent Christian was supposed to pray.

He prayed for the Queen. He prayed for Judas Iscariot. For Pontius Pilate. For Satan and all the fallen angels. And then—because he was very afraid—for himself, for forgiveness for praying for them.

Charlotte, tip-toeing to his door long after, found him on his knees, his face buried in his hands upon the coverlet, fast asleep.

Chapter 12

Setoun Breaks His Watch

'TWO VISITS IN A WEEK, MY DEAR HURBLES!' SAID CHARlotte with uplifted eyebrows. 'That is a sort of suffocating pleasure! I have really no business to see you. The world will say you are *amouraché* of me. We are most frightfully rushed, too. Caroline is going to Town next week?'

Setoun appeared to fill the small boudoir, already full of armchairs and roses, to overflowing. He stood square and large, in blue riding-coat and buckskin breeches, amid the pink-and-white fripperies.

She came to him on tip-toe, and kissed the crow's-foot by his left eye. He gratefully patted her silken shoulder, and smiled at her from under shaggy brows. He waited until she was seated, and then lowered himself carefully into a fragile chair.

'If you did that often enough, Carlotta, I'd lose my wrinkles,' he said. 'Be like the Beast whom Beauty kissed into a handsome Prince.'

For all that he smiled at her again, there was anxiety in his regard, and a hesitation in his manner. For a minute he fiddled with the tails of his coat, stooped down to adjust a spur, and looked up again, redder in the face than ever from the effort.

Charlotte, her hands folded on her grey silk lap, nodded a smooth dark head.

'You'd better tell me what it is, Hurbles,' she said. 'I know by now when you've been up to mischief.'

'Mischief!'

'Is it women, Hurbles? I've always thought you might be a bad old man.' And she laughed as she spoke at the mere thought of her Hurbles, her romantic fantastical old bachelor Hurbles, being tangled in such a way.

'Well,' said Hurbles slowly, looking beyond the proud smiling face at the rain and the dark trees of the avenue. 'Well, in a sense it is!'

She was a little shaken. She looked sharply at him for reassurance—and did not see it. He would not meet her eyes.

'Hurbles, what do you mean?'

She spoke almost sharply, and her candid eyes clouded over. She suddenly grew very still.

'Oh, not in that way!' said Hurbles, hurriedly. 'The Queen, I mean!'

She was angry that she should have thought any ill of him, and angrier that she should have shown dismay.

'What are you maundering about?' she asked. 'What do you mean—the Queen?'

Setoun looked at the mud sparks on his boots.

'We went to Church on Sunday—Christopher and I,' he said. 'Boy burst into tears during prayers for the Royal Family. Had to take him out. Went off in floods of tears. Entire congregation watched. Most embarrassing!'

'Williams told me about it when he got back. But what, in Fortune's name, has it to do with Caroline?'

'She has this to do with it. She sings her sorrows to him . . . Told him that she mayn't be prayed for. That her name's struck out of the liturgy. That she's not treated as a Queen should be. That she's to be tried like a felon. That her only child was taken from her. . . . Even that she's no sentries at her door!'

'And it is all true!'

'All very true, Carlotta,' he agreed, 'but not necessarily told to a highly strung child of ten or eleven.'

'Not necessarily—but where is the harm?'

'The harm? Is it good that he should have for ever the sordid side of life presented to him? The squabbles, the violence, the injustice?'

'Caroline . . .' began Charlotte in her most stately manner.

'Wish you wouldn't call her Caroline,' he interrupted almost with violence. 'It—it seems to stress an intimacy which I should hate to think existed between such a woman and yourself.'

'Six months ago, like a little snob, I went to her, condescending to do her a favour, as I thought. She was just a fat, funny Queen. Then I found how good and kind she was! How damnably used! What a fund of humour and good nature she had! So now I stand by her as one woman stands by another who is misused. I serve a friend—not a Queen . . . Caroline! . . . Caroline! . . . Caroline! . . . There!'

She shot the name out at him, nodding her head each time with the vehemence of the challenge, so that her long pearl earrings shook madly to and fro.

' "Six months ago"!' he repeated, and rose to his feet, and stared out of the window. 'Six months ago, you were a child . . . almost! Now . . . !' His mind moved on. 'Damn the Queen! Because of you—but what can I do about *that*?'

She would have interrupted, but he drove on.

'She has no right to talk before Tops as she does—to talk to him as she does! It's damnable! And . . . and I can do something about that. And I will!'

'Do you mind turning round!' said Charlotte plucking at a cameo bracelet. 'I would like to get this clear. You think . . .'

'She may be good, she may be kind, she may be ill-used, but she's a disgusting woman all the same. She isn't even a—lady. . . . Won't let him have anything to do with her. . . .'

Charlotte rose to her feet. She was very angry with Setoun, for the first time in her life.

'I presume this means you wish to take Christopher away,' she said, and let each word fall from her lips as if it had been freshly chilled. 'And *that* you shall not do.'

Then suddenly she relaxed; and came to him where he stood gloomily in the window, and stroked that tight blue sleeve, and put a slim hand on the great shoulder, and leaned against him, so that he felt the soft pressure of her body against his arm.

'Don't be unkind, Hurbles,' she pleaded. 'Caroline is very fond of Tops. He is her mascot. She loves young things. She has so much to make her sad. It would hurt her very much if she thought you wanted to take him away. When everything has come right, then you—then we can take him away . . . Besides'—a clinching argument in the after-thought—'what excuse could you possibly make?'

He turned to confront her face to face. She stood almost within his arms. He hesitated, and then:

'No excuse will be needed.' He flinched before Charlotte's uplifted brows, and went on hurriedly, as if to get the matter over. 'Have already arranged it. Williams will take him back to the Place from school this morning. His things can be sent over any time.'

Charlotte started back. Indignation reigned in her eyes, in the uplift of her chin, in her clenched hands.

'You can't do it! You shan't do it! Christopher's mine!' she stammered.

'Have done it,' said Setoun meekly. 'The boy will be at the Place any minute.'

'He will stay with me.'

'He will not!' still meekly.

Charlotte stamped her foot. Her hands clenched on the folds of her wide skirt. Tears rose to her eyes.

'He will!'

'He—will—not!' Meekly—yes, meekly, but very firmly!

'This is ridiculous, Setoun. We cannot go on saying "Will", "Won't" to one another, like a pair of cross-talk comedians! You can't leave me to explain and apologize to Caroline!'

Setoun fiddled with a roll of papers. Charlotte noticed for the first time that the high-bridged nose was not just a well-designed anatomical feature; that the crumple-lidded eyes with the crow's-feet at the corners were not merely whimsical; that a dozen little things portrayed a hitherto unrealized firmness in his expression.

She appealed to him again.

'Hurbles,' she pleaded, 'don't make things worse for her! If you take Tops away now, you are humiliating her! She's had enough humiliation! She's only a poor battered woman. She's very sensitive; it would be such a reflection upon her! Be kind; remember what she has been through—what she is going through! Make it easy for her just now. Even if you don't like doing it! . . . Please—please!'

'Have to think of the boy,' said Setoun, and looked at her with level eyes.

'Think of her pride, poor thing! Don't let her feel you think she's not fit to have him under her roof! And I . . . I love him just as much as you!'

'Would not have her feel it,' said Setoun gravely, '—if it can be helped. But facts remain the same.'

She appealed to him once more by gentle touch, without a word. He looked down into the bright grey eyes and at the smooth dark tresses and level brows—and sighed.

'The child is in an atmosphere of hate and violence. And for how long? You know it, Carlotta! You told me yourself how he saw the Queen making a tallow image of George, and behaving herself like a maniac with it! Is that the right atmosphere for a child of his unfortunate birth and history—after all that he has been through?'

She took her hands from off his sleeve, and half turned away.

'I do not want Christopher,' said Setoun steadily, 'to see any of his family again. The curse of hate that has lain on them shall not come to him through contact. It is a contagion—a contamination. I will keep him out of the infected place . . . He has a right to keep what dreams and fantasies he still may have. To have ideas of chivalry and honour—and fairyland, if you like. How can he keep them here where the ugliness of his family encompasses him? . . . What chance will he have, brought up amid unnatural conspiracies and family loathing? . . .' He talked rapidly, and half to himself, while Charlotte with averted head said nothing . . . 'Just think of this last century! Think of the hatred and malice this family have shown amongst themselves . . . Father hating son . . . Son hating father . . . Mother hating son . . . Husband hating wife . . . Brother hating brother . . . Dishonour—shame everywhere.'

He took an unwilling hand in his large one. In the pressure Charlotte could feel the bezel of his great ring against her flesh. . . .

'He might have been—mine. I would not have a son of mine caught in this mire. Would not have her son caught in it. He shall have a chance to see life as a pleasant wholesome thing.'

' "Might have been a son of mine",' repeated Charlotte, and

flung away his hand. She hated him at that moment. Never before had she failed to get her way.

' "Might"!' she said again, and there was so faint a note of interrogation in her voice that the word became an insult.

He looked at her in such a way that her heart failed her: looked at her, his ruddy face a little paled; protest, deprecation, apology, forgiveness trembling on his lips. She fled toward the door before tears overcame her, and paused, hand on handle to strike again.

'All this talk of contamination! Judging from your early romance you did not fear it once . . . You have not worried about me being "contaminated"! . . . Well, I'm going to remain "contaminated" ' —with a fine accent of scorn upon the word!—'If you have the boy, you shall not have me . . . I am of age . . . You are no longer my guardian . . . I can do as I please . . . You won't expect me to come back! I—I shall make other arrangements.'

'Charlotte!' he appealed, and was answered by a slamming door.

In such inauspicious circumstances did Christopher become an inmate of Kensington Park Place, the rambling villa which Setoun owned on the very summit of Campden Hill.

It was a strange dim house of bow-windows and many slanting lawns. All the lower rooms were obscured by the shrubberies that pressed close against the windows, so that they swam in a greeny haze, as if they were a succession of caverns beneath the sea. White statues gleamed, like mermaids in the depths, in the corners of corridors tapestried in green and grey, or at a dark stair-foot. The polished fronts of ebony chests and vast furniture of dark mahogany, the fading surfaces of ancient mirrors—all gave back faint reflections of a light drenched in the greenness of the dense verdure without.

But when you reached the drawing-room floor the old house emerged triumphant above the tide that encompassed it. The many windows, each with its balcony, rode clear of obstruction, and looked out over steeply sloping lawns, winked at the carefully tended cedars that were permitted on their velvet surface, and smiled on the elms and beeches and walnut trees which encircled them and hid the outer world with their shivering, rustling barrier of leaves.

Christopher liked best the study on the ground floor. It was there Setoun sat—in a green morocco chair that shot out leg-rests and book-rests and candlesticks at command—and evolved such plans as to cross the world by air balloon, to invade France on hobby-horses, to perfect steam-driven phaetons, or make rain- and wear-resistant garments from material woven from small fish-bones.

The room fascinated Christopher more than any other. The high box hedges never let broad daylight flood within; and in its green dimness and the shadows cast by heavy curtains and cases and cabinets, he always felt that he should find something further new and strange. On one wall a green blind would roll up with a snap and reveal faded maps of curious lands with the words *Terra Incognita* writ across them; or incomprehensible charts with numbers only on the central blankness, and a fat face in one corner blowing with puffed cheeks, and in the other a full-rigged ship steering towards a leviathan.

The ceiling-high cases were full of model ships rising shelf on shelf—till they were almost out of view—with spread sails and weighed anchors, for all that they rested on their stocks. Model coaches and wagons and curricles stood on the ledges of the cup-boards beneath, as though waiting for the sea-borne passengers who never came.

On a sort of dais in the big bow-window rested an astonishing contraption, something between a bath-chair and a treadmill, with too many wheels and a precarious dickey aft, and a still more precarious perch for'ard. Setoun called it a velocimanipede, and once, under his instructions, it had been taken out to the lawn and Christopher had had a nightmare drive with one footman panting at the pedals and another balancing himself for grim death upon the saddle in front and utterly failing to master the steers-man's art. With the result that they overturned down a gentle bank in a flurry of fat silk calves and hair-powder and wheels.

After dinner—and sometimes before—Christopher would sit stiffly in an arm-chair, with a book upon his knee facing Setoun. He did not read much: his gaze wandered from the ships lost in the shadows on the topmost shelves to the green blind that hid what little knowledge there was of unknown lands; to the brass odds and ends of unfathomable instruments twinkling in the lamplight; to what he could see of Setoun's face behind his book.

He would lose himself in reverie, in speculation, in his land of dreams: but ever his gaze would return to the large figure lounging opposite, with the tight grey trousers moulded to the large limbs and strapped under shining lacquered boots, tight mulberry-coloured coat strained back from the primrose satin waistcoat, roll collar, and frilled shirt.

When Setoun started a book he would hold it first at arm's length from his eyes, as if he were uncertain whether he desired to make its acquaintance. As he progressed the volume would be allowed to approach more nearly, until in the end he read with his high-beaked nose thrust almost within its pages.

At last he would become conscious of the steady regard. He would drop the book upon his knee.

'Ha, boy! Well, boy!' he would say, as if discovering Christopher all over afresh.

'Is it an interesting book that you are reading, sir?' would ask Christopher making the second move of his opening game.

'Interesting? Tomfoolery! Man doesn't know what he is talking about. Dash my wig—I know more than he does. Trying to prove that animal power is superior to mechanical power for transport on roads! Says it is more economical! Be damned to him! He's a fool! . . . Quotes from Tredgold. Tredgold was a fool! . . . Quotes Desaguliers and Smeaton. Everybody knows they were fools! . . . Says the average force of traction of a horse is two hundred and sixteen pounds! If that's an average power I will eat my hat, and my boots, and cravat as well! Man's mad—as well as a fool!

'Horse is a wonderful animal, Tops, but you won't see one in England except as a curiosity in a hundred years' time.'

Christopher does sums in his head.

'Can't a horse even pull two hundredweight?' he asked in astonishment at length. 'There were six horses in—in—in the wagon' (he rather boggled at a reference to that journey so long ago). 'Six times two is twelve! That's only little more than half a ton, sir; but yesterday when we saw the West Country mail-coach leaving the Gloucester you said that it weighed much more than a ton—and there were only four horses pulling it!'

'Ha, boy! That's where you're wrong!'

Out with a big gold pencil: down with one of the knobs of the magical chair: up with a writing slope of polished mahogany as if from space!

'Come here, boy!'

They bend together, grizzled head and fair head, over the slab and a sheet of paper on which figures are scored, crossed out, and entered afresh.

'Traction power is the force a horse exerts. But all being equal the load he can draw is fifteen times greater. Do I make myself clear?' says the senior conjurer. 'Say—to make it easy—that he's got a comfortable collar power of two hundred pounds, then he can pull thirty hundred pounds without distress . . . You follow? If he's got traction power of two hundred and sixteen pounds, as this fool says, then he will—h'm—h'm—h'm—he will draw'—pencil is very busy—'h'm, a load of three thousand two hundred pounds.

'That leaves, mark you, speed out of consideration. There's traction power gone in that—lots! Some of his two hundred and sixteen pounds goes there. If he travels at four miles an hour, for instance, he will only have—God bless my soul, can't I get a single figure right?—he will only have—h'm—ninety-six pounds to pull with.

'But now, supposing . . .'

'But now, supposing . . .' The spell has been pronounced: the magical words said.

And so away at a hand gallop into the realms of fantasy! Whip up the steeds, shovel sea-coal under the boilers, for the coach that is the mind of the Right Honourable Henry Setoun, third Viscount Setoun, Knight of the Golden Fleece, Prince of the Holy Roman Empire, is off into space, is flying on wings between the planets, is careering like the chariot of Neptune across uncharted seas, is steaming fit to burst itself over mountains and valleys. It has a passenger on its journey, one little happy puzzled passenger, about whom heaven and earth whirl confusedly; who catches a glimpse of wheels and wings and widespread prospects amid a vast disorder; who knows now there is another magic world beside his own, and that he has been made a citizen of it.

The establishment was presided over, theoretically, by Setoun's aunt, an old lady with a nut-cracker face topped by the most enormous frilled cap, who never spoke unless she was first addressed, and—owing to the absence of all her teeth—was perfectly incomprehensible when she did so. Christopher always associated her with the large wooden spice-box which stood on the high red-frilled shelf over the fire-place in the housekeeper's room, between a brass candlestick and a big pepper-mill in which, once a week, the housekeeper herself ground the little dried pellets to the exact consistency that his lordship fancied.

A snug wet afternoon, in Setoun's absence, with Mrs. Synge on one side of the hearth, himself the other, a plate of hot buttered toast on one hob and a singing kettle on the other, was sure to be interrupted by the appearance of the old lady's very trim Abigail:
'She . . .'

A sort of storm would sweep over Mrs. Synge's forehead, which from a placid sea would suddenly become corrugated with deep billows that even set the top of her wax-smooth hair twitching.

' "She" is the cat, I would have you know, Smith!'

'Her ladyship,' says Smith sulkily, 'presents her compliments, and would be glad if Mrs. Synge could let her have a few more cloves, her ladyship having eaten the last.'

'Her ladyship is very heavy on cloves,' sighs Synge. 'Now if it were nutmegs . . .'

She rises, and takes stock of the supply in that section of the spice-box devoted to the commodity, doles out a dozen.

'Not in your hand, girl! Not in your hand! One of the Belleek saucers on a salver. A coffee saucer. They'll look more.'

For the Lady Jane Grayson was devoted to spices. According to common report nutmegs were sewn into pockets in her most intimate undergarments as a specific against rheumatism. She was for ever making pomanders which she carried about very withered and dry in her capacious reticule, or sent to her numerous friends and acquaintances; or pulling out the cloves and eating them dipped in a little honey as a specific against chills, hoarseness, or aching gums. A small silk bag full of caraway seeds was also her constant companion; from which, as secretly as possible, she would sprinkle the dishes set before her.

The whole of the old lady's public life was passed in the Rose

Drawing-Room, for she breakfasted in bed, and lunched from a little tray on mulled claret and a chicken wing in the chintz-covered chair beside her bedroom fire.

In the early afternoon she would appear in the great saloon, covered with a fine white shawl, sitting in an easy-chair set slightly toward the wide hearth, a diamond-shaped tapestry fire-shield on a thin mahogany rod protecting her from the glow; so small and shrunken and silent that you might almost overlook her in a chamber where everything else was so big as to be almost overwhelming.

Amid its vastness Lady Jane was so still and motionless and so pale, despite the rose-coloured curtains, that Christopher often felt that she was dead.

Then—if dinner had been over for half an hour—there would come a faint tinkle, a tiny jingle from without the door. The Lady Jane's head would rise a little, would turn a little; her sunken mouth would move a little—into the ghost of a smile: one shrivelled hand would twitch as if it would be up and doing.

The door would open in a stately manner and a solemn procession enter—footman with a silver tray set with the appurtenances of tea-drinking; footman with silver urn; footman with silver teapot, and butler with nothing at all.

The Lady Jane would give the ghost of a chuckle. She would say something—nobody would ever know what.

The table would be put at her side: put a little to this side, shifted a little to that, all according to the semaphoring and pats of the withered hand. The great pedestal tea-caddy would be placed within the easiest reach, and the lids of the four caskets within set open.

The Lady Jane opens the teapot—with such a shaky hand; peers into it. She nods her old head. Her nut-cracker jaws become more nut-cracker than ever. She says something—nobody ever knows what. She nods her old head again. All is correct. All is satisfactory. Everything is ready. Tea-time has really arrived! . . .

Into the smooth life of this quiet house Christopher fitted as if he had always been a participant. He breakfasted with Setoun, off blue china in the small breakfast-room which looked on to a statue of Diana, a very small grass-plot, and an ivied wall; and then set off to his studies with the Reverend Mr. Severn under the escort of Williams, who had been appointed his personal attendant, and aide-de-camp.

He returned shortly after midday to go driving in the Park with his guardian in a slap-up phaeton with cream-coloured wheels and the smallest of tigers; to have his immense discussions swallowed up in the vast arm-chair in the study; to dine very upright with his elders in the long dining-room with the two tall windows —each with its little iron balcony—open on to the gardens, drink exactly half a glass of old Madeira, and listen to a disquisition on the wines of Portugal, Spain, Madeira, and the Cape, with an aside on the 'resinata' of Greece; to be taken once a week to a box at the theatre, and on the other nights to retire early to bed in a sort of panelled dressing-room which connected with the vast warm apartment where Setoun bestowed his bulk on a shabby campaign bedstead.

While Christopher worked and played, led his dream life, or was caught up into fantastical discussions with Setoun, little was seen or heard of Charlotte. She left unanswered Setoun's humble epistles. In all the youthful violence of her loyalty to an ill-used woman she worked herself into a cold fury against one who would not himself subscribe to the same fealty.

The income from the estates that were held in trust for her was hers to do with as she pleased; and she pleased to open the vast town house in Cleveland Row that had lain silent behind closed shutters for a generation; and she pleased to bring up to town as chaperon an elderly aunt with snapping black eyes, snow-white hair, and a weak-eyed husband who perpetually dripped at the nose, although he was of the bluest blood in Scotland.

Once they saw her driving in the Park, with a tall young man in immensely high stock and with very long stirrup leathers trotting beside her carriage on a grey blood horse.

Charlotte had stopped, bowed coldly to Setoun, and beckoned to Christopher.

'Charlotte!' he said, glowing with excitement at the meeting as he brought his pony alongside. 'Why do you never come and see us? Uncle and I miss you very much. We are always talking about you! . . . Oh, Charlotte, and Uncle is giving me another pony—

a chestnut. We are going to Scotland in September with Sir John Wake. We shall see Culloden and where *Guy Mannering* was written . . . Aren't you coming too?'

Setoun had exchanged a word or two with Charlotte's cavalier. He sat upright on a great bay as if awaiting a greeting; but Charlotte never once raised her eyes from the small figure at her side.

'Can't I come and see you soon?' babbled Christopher. 'Mrs. Synge read me a bit from the *Observer* about your new house the other day.'

'Of course you shall come,' promised Charlotte. She lifted her voice but not her eyes. 'But just now if I ask you, your Uncle will think I am going—to steal you from him, for the Queen.'

She spoke with icy malice that was lost on Christopher, but not on Setoun who would have broken into speech, but that, obedient to a word, the chariot rolled on into the great slow tide of carriages that curved about the Achilles statue.

They saw her again one night at the play, smiling and bowing from her box at half a hundred acquaintances in the house. Beside her sat the dowager with feathers nodding on top of her white hair; and over her bent deferentially the classical features and romantical locks of the tall exquisite.

Setoun sent Christopher round to pay his respects.

Charlotte was glad to see him; she gave him a long white hand and held him against her while they stared together over the red plush edge of the box and the mosaic of heads and faces in the pit below, at all sorts of interesting people whom she knew.

'Good gracious!' said she amidst their gossip, 'I declare you have not been presented to a very particular friend of mine . . . Lord Dunscore—this is Master Christopher Harnish, of whom you have often heard me speak . . . I want you to be great friends.'

The young man shook Christopher by the hand, was 'vewy pleased to meet Master Harnish', swept back the lock that had crept too far down his white forehead, settled the fold of an excessively tight cravat, examined a large ring on his finger, and appeared to forget all about him.

Christopher commented on this to Setoun when he returned.

'A pup!' said Setoun. 'An ill-bred pup at that!' He stared across the auditorium with so hostile a gaze that the youg lord looked up—as if he had become conscious of it—and flinched before it, and bending down said something to Charlotte at which she laughed and tapped him with her fan.

It was on the road back from their Northern tour that they next heard of her. They had come slowly from Carlisle into Nottinghamshire, where Setoun had an old small house of red brick in the minster town of Southwell. The shadow of a grey tower fell across the high-walled lawn, and the rooms were full of the clangour of bells at noon and eventide—so full that they seemed to hum with the deep music long afterwards, as conch-shells echo with the sea.

Setoun was in the stable-yard one morning, conning the horses against the morrow's journey, when a groom rode in, threw his leg over the saddle and dropped wearily to the ground.

'An urgent packet for your Lordship,' he said, and added, pride getting the better of his weariness, 'Thirteen hours from Lunnon, my Lord! Beat the night mail to Newark!—Post horses, too, my Lord!' And he threw a glance of disparagement at the foundered sweating beast which stood shuddering on the cobbles. Then proffered his piece of news.

' 'Er Majesty's acquitted, my Lord!'

'Good! Very good!' said Setoun absently, his eyes fixed on the flowing writing and the great seal on the packet. 'Get yourself a meal. Warren will see to the horse. See me before you go.'

He turned toward the house, cutting round the seal with his penknife, and casting a searching look at the jaded horse.

'Give the brute a bran mash, Warren. It's all in. . . . Put some malt mash with it. . . . Only a post horse? . . . To hell with that! . . . Mind you don't mix the malt with boiling water, my fine fellow! You're too fond of doing it. Boiling with bran—medium with malt! And don't you forget it!'

He passed through the house on to the lawn, and unfolded the sheet in the thin autumn sunshine, as the Minster bells swung out over the murmur of the little town.

For a moment he did not dare look at the paper with its close lines of script. Twenty-four hours had not passed since she had laid down her pen, and folded it, and melted the wax at the silver taper-holder she fancied, and pressed down on it the great signet ring her father had always worn.

The pigeons that had risen in a cloud from pinnacle and louvre as the bells started, swirled back to their roosting-places.

'Dear Cousin Henry,' he read. . . . A man had clattered through the night along the straight miles of the Great North Road, waking the echoes of little towns, bringing pike-keepers and sleepy ostlers from their beds, travelled half a dozen counties, to bear him such news—that 'Hurbles' was still forgotten, and 'Cousin Henry' reigned in his stead!

Charlotte wrote, after that unpropitious beginning, a letter that was a compound of chill hostility and the gossiping strain in which she had written to him in the old days.

'You may be interested, although not glad, to know that the Queen has emerged *Triumphant*. A few hours ago the Government announced that they were dropping the Bill against her. You will still probably refuse to believe that she was not guilty of "a disgraceful, licentious, and adulterous intercourse" with Bergami, or whatever the official phraseology was. *Tant pis!* I know you hate her, and despise me for my loyalty to her!

'If the Government had not given way I am assured there would have been a Revolution. Everybody has gone quite Mad. Every house illuminated. The church bells are ringing, and I can see the glow of bonfires from my windows.

'I have had my share in the Triumph. I wrought so urgently with Dunscore that he and his clan—who would at the most have only abstained from voting—went into the Opposition lobby. I flatter Myself that those Four votes did the trick.

'The Queen thinks so too. She will keep full State and has offered me the post of Mistress of the Robes, after my Marriage.'

There were a few words after: narrow-mindedness' and 'High Tory' caught his eye. They meant nothing to him. . . . 'After my marriage!' After—her—marriage!

His hands fell to his sides: the blood receded from his ruddy face: he stared unseeing at the jewelled glass of a transept window as if it were a magic mirror wherein his vision might overpass fifty leagues and more. His mind, voided of consecutive thought, swam with the clamour of the bells.

A sudden silence fell, and the Minster clock chimed the hour.

Almost automatically his right hand went to his fob pocket, and he withdrew the fat gold watch with negro princes on its dial. He pressed the catch; they raised their hammers to the bell above them, and thin and sweet as the notes of a musical box, their strokes tinkled out.

'Ten o'clock on November the eleventh. Ten—o'clock—November—eleven!' he said out loud; and sent the watch skimming from him till it struck the wall and fell jangling into a bare black bed.

Across the years he saw again the pale long face and mournful eyes of one he had loved as a lady of romance, who had kissed him on the lips in a June rose garden. She had forsaken him for another and more shameful lover.

He saw again, too, Charlotte as first he saw her when he came back, new to his guardianship, from India; a slim thing in a high-waisted dress of white percale, laughing up at him with dark grey eyes from under a bonnet edged—he remembered—with apricot-coloured ribbon. She, also, had now forsaken him. He had promised himself nothing: he had dreamed of nothing: he was too old for promises and dreams of that sort now. He had not thought, though, it would end with 'Dear Cousin Henry. . . . After my marriage.'

All because of the son, the tragic son, of one who had been a lady of promises and dreams and kisses—when promises and dreams and kisses were laudable and desirable and permissible.

He went towards the house, suddenly feeling very old.

'Why with that nincompoop—that brainless fop—that bankrupt parasite of the rich?' he asked himself, and clenched his teeth.

Old Sir John Wake, companion of his tour, came stepping delicately across the grass. He was a precise old man whose white hair came low in a peak like a widow's cap upon his brow; who still wore black satin breeches, silk stockings and lacquered pumps as normal attire, and did not ordinarily stir without doors, even for a garden walk, until he was wrapped and booted.

His quick faded eyes saw the letter in Setoun's hand, assessed the change in his face—and guessed the cause.

'You've heard from Charlotte!' he asserted rather than asked.

Setoun answered with a nod.

'Forgive me asking, but did she . . . did she . . . ?'

'She talked of marriage. If that is what you mean. With that pimp Dunscore,' said Setoun, halted before the old man.

'Hrm'ph!' said Sir John, and scrubbed his chin with a thin dry hand. 'My man has just fetched me some mail from the post-master's. It has followed me about for days. Chased up to Inverness, always a week behind, to judge from the direction.' He paused and suddenly barked like a very old dog.

'Did she say she's sold herself for votes?'

'Sold?' echoed Setoun.

'Sold,' repeated Sir John. 'And for votes that were not needed!'

'This is sheer madness,' said Setoun. 'I must go back to Town—and at once.'

'Madder than you guess,' said Wake, taking him by the arm. 'No, listen to me a moment!' He restrained the other, almost by violence, from turning to the house. 'Listen to me, will you?'

'I beg your pardon, Wake,' said Setoun. 'I am considerably disturbed. Charlotte, I fear, is being rather rash. . . . You were saying?'

'Charlotte *has* been rather rash,' corrected Wake. He looked at his thin shoes and the damp grass, and sighed as he led the younger man out of earshot of the house.

He rustled one of his letters open, and read from it in his dry, precise voice, casting sidelong looks upon his companion.

'This is from Lady Granville. She writes: "There has been so much perjury by the Italian witnesses that I can't believe the Queen guilty of anything except folly. I have been to one or two of the sittings. She actually dozed during proceedings! But not when Mr. Denman compared our Most Gracious King (!) to Nero, and called his brother, the Duke of Clarence, an 'infectious calumniator'!" '

'This hardly bears on the subject of Charlotte,' said Setoun irritably.

'But wait a moment!' retorted Wake. He read on with emphasis:

' "The voting, when it comes to the push, is going to be very narrow. The Queen's party are very anxious about it, and that mad creature, Charlotte Harringay, has made a bargain with the unspeakable Dunscore that she'll marry him if he'll take his vote and lead three other Tory peers into the lobby against the Bill. Dunscore 'ud do anything to get a wife with £50,000 a year, and he's got half a dozen Scottish relatives who are as clannish as all the Scots—especially when money's about." '

'Christ! Sold for votes!' said Setoun, with a face like iron.

'A moment!' said Wake. 'It's worse than that!'

'Worse?'

The old man turned over the sheet. 'Lady Granville goes on: "Granville was told by the Prime Minister in confidence yesterday that the Government are going to drop the Bill whatever the vote may be. They had let the King know they wouldn't be answerable for the consequences to the country if they carried on with it." She underlines the next sentence—"*And Dunscore knew it—he's Liverpool's nephew—when he made his bargain with Charlotte Harringay*"!'

'By God, the little fool! It must be stopped . . . if I have to shoot the dirty swine.'

'There is more in a postscript,' said Sir John, and took a pinch of snuff. 'She ends: "I have just heard that the girl has promised to marry Dunscore, if he keeps his side of the bargain, within four hours of the Queen's acquittal. Get Lord Setoun to . . ." '

But Setoun was already half-way to the house—in the house—in the stable-yard.

'Warren! Watkins! Harness up! . . . The cabriolet. . . . Four horses. . . . I leave in ten minutes. . . . Send a man ahead at once to make certain of post horses. . . . We'll change at Grantham—the Angel. . . . Quick, on your life!'

Behind his quick speech and decisive gestures; behind the red face and arrogant eyes, his mind was saying over and over again:

'Oh, God, why didn't I know in time! Oh, God, why didn't I know in time! Ten o'clock on November eleven! Oh, God, why didn't I know in time!'

Even as the men leaped to the stalls, to the coach-house, a good Whig Chapter set the bells of the Minster a-tossing into fresh song, into a swelling paean of triumph, into a thunder of rejoicing. into a wild *Te Deum* for the victory of a wronged queen.

He knew quite well that he was already many hours too late.

Chapter 13

A Queen Passes

$\mathcal{C}\!\!\infty\!\mathcal{Q}$

CHRISTOPHER ATTENDED THE SAME CLASS AS HE HAD done from Brandenburgh House. Setoun had no belief in tutors; he felt that the boy must mix with his own kind and age every day, in moderation. He remembered Severn at Cambridge— a painstaking man with a great reputation for scholarship. So every morning at eight o'clock, Williams stepping behind him with cocked hat and long staff, Christopher made the two-mile pilgrim- age downhill to Barkston House.

The school stood in the fields, already rapidly being built over, between Kensington and the village of Earl's Court. It had once been a snug and comfortable farmhouse, but the passing years had seen it expand in all sorts of directions; here a wing, there another story; here a new door, there a new window; until it had become such a jumble of old red brick and dingy new brick, and bright new paint and cracked and blistered old, that no one could have sorted out its history by any chance. Its windows were of all shapes and sizes, and not a single one of its multitudinous chimney- pots resembled its mates.

Two large wooden green gates, over which, and through which, it was quite impossible to see, severed the drive from the dusty road; and a line of elms still further secluded the house from vul- gar gaze.

But no unchaperoned male foot pushed open those gates, or trod the smooth gravel, past the monkey-puzzle trees to the shin- ing green door.

The dozen or so small boys who imbibed their knowledge from the Reverend Septimus Severn, went through a narrow wicket, and were restrained from straying by two high walls until they came to a meek and unassuming door in some stray prom-ontory of the building. A flagged, damp-smelling passage led to the class-room, and to a narrow sort of closet with barred window, which might once have been a housemaid's pantry, and now was given up to a row of coat-pegs—all just too high to be comfortably within reach—a washstand with the smallest possible basin and ewer, and an old night-commode with a piece of green carpet tacked on the top.

At the far end of the passage was a baize door studded with brass nails. Bold spirits who had investigated swore that behind it was yet another door; a heavy one, bolted and barred, and—they even added—chained.

The fact was that the Reverend Septimus's tutorial class was but allowed to exist by courtesy in a corner of his sister's much-thought-of and highly successful seminary for young ladies—Miss Severn's Female Academy. No breath of suspicion must ever rest upon that virgin flock—nor could it, with the male element thus bolted, barred, chained and walled away, so that not even a flicker of a square inch of a ten-year-old's trouser leg could be per-ceived by maiden eyes.

Even thus Miss Augusta delicately ignored the existence of her brother's establishment—in much the same way that she would have ignored the existence of the liaison were he to have wed the tart-shopkeeper's daughter at the corner of Wright's Lane. He left to attend his class by the front door, and returned in the same manner; and very wet he would get on the journey sometimes, and stand coughing on the step with his thin grey hair dank with rain, a drip on the end of his long whimsical nose, and his anxious eyes watching for Mary, the pretty parlourmaid, to open to him.

'The poor precious,' said Mary to the cook. 'Streaming like one of them there catacombs! All because that old image will have the door locked. Thinks the young gentlemen will rape the young ladies!'

'More like it the other way round,' replied Cook. 'Them minxes! If they was to get holt of a man! . . .'

As it was, Miss Augusta put up with, and ignored, the dangerous proximity of a dozen young gentlemen of ages varying from nine years to eleven, for the sake of the moral benefits to her establishment accruing from the fact that 'divinity, theology, and moral philosophy are imparted to the young ladies, according to the most accepted principles, by the Resident Chaplain (elderly).'

So the Reverend Septimus presided over the studies of his class, in a half-basement room, with two barred windows, and a mildewed dark red wallpaper, an old sideboard covered with tattered books, and a large globe over which an ink-bottle appeared to have been spilt at some remote period in the past.

The class sat at a very large table, covered with stained green cloth, like a large board of very small directors, each with an ink-pot and copy-book before him.

'To-day, gentlemen,' says the chairman settling himself into his elbow chair at the head of the table, and studying the agenda of the meeting neatly tabulated on a sheet of bluish foolscap before him, 'To-day, gentlemen, we will turn our attention to a science which should help us in our studies of our own and foreign languages, and lend interest to our researches into classical speech. . . . Etymology, gentlemen, I refer to the science of etymology!'

The large board of small directors look grave and shaken. The syndicate has had dealings in Latin, history, theology, French and mathematics: its activities have never, however, spread to etymology.

Mr. Fitzroy, a red-polled gentleman—who sat on the chairman's right, as if he were secretary of the company, and was partly hidden from his view by a pile of books, a water carafe, and a stationery rack—feared the worst. He made frantic efforts to dispose of a lump of sweet-stuff which he had crammed into his mouth immediately prior to the chairman's entrance.

'And what is etymology?' inquired Mr. Severn, rubbing his long nose and looking appealingly up and down the confronting rows of small faces.

'And what is etymology . . . Fitzroy?' said he, suddenly peering round the tower of volumes in a most disconcerting manner.

Fitzroy had that moment succeeded in removing from his mouth the tacky mass of hardbake. For future disposal he had placed it to hand on the tablecloth in the shadow of a lexicon that lay between himself and Christopher. He bobbed up, his freckled face shining with innocence and intelligence.

'Insects,' said he, and bobbed back.

'Next boy,' said the chairman, with a pained expression, and pointing to Christopher with a round ivory ruler.

Christopher rose, setting his hands to the table as he did so.

'Something to do with words, sir!' he opined, and found the fingers of his left hand pressed into the sticky mass beside him. The look of astonished disgust that crossed his face was only fleeting, but it was not lost to the quick eyes of the chairman—nor was the cause.

'Etymology,' said he, cracking the ruler upon the table in order to concentrate upon himself the attention that was being devoted to Christopher's efforts to remove the foreign substance, and to clean his fingers upon the underside of the tablecloth. 'Etymology is a very beautiful science. It deals with the history and origin of words. Often, gentlemen, with the most entertaining results. . . . Fitzroy, stand up! . . . I presume you found your speech sufflaminated by this disgusting lump of sweetmeat; that you ejected it to the manifest discomposure of your neighbour . . . Take it up and eat it, disgusting boy!'

Unwillingly Master Fitzroy picked up the sticky brown mass. His fellow-directors with awful joy watched him return it to his mouth and prepare to sit down. Master Fitzroy had lost his mother a month before, and there was a strong school of thought that sweetmeat-eating in the early days of such a bereavement was hardly the thing. A stifled titter showed lack of sympathy with him in his tribulation and he glanced furiously down the table.

'No, I think you must still stand, Fitzroy. We can better study etymology—and anatomy, gentlemen—with Master Fitzroy's kind assistance. . . . If you will look at Master Fitzroy's face, gentlemen, you will see a small lump at the angle of his jaw on either side. No, Brooks, I do not refer to that made by the great store of sugar-plum or what-not that he is now engaged in masticating. . . .'

Here the chairman pointed to the exact spot on the scarlet face of Master Fitzroy with his ruler. One or two of the more daring spirits half-rose in their places to get a full view of the demonstration.

'That lump is the masseter at work. The masseter, gentlemen, is the muscle that controls the lower jaw—that opens and shuts it, that enables Master Fitzroy to chew his sugar-plum. . . . You have taught us some anatomy, Master Fitzroy. . . . The word "masseter" comes from the Greek word *masasthai,* which means to chew: chewing muscle! . . . We are learning etymology from you, too, Master Fitzroy. Thank you!'

The unhappy Fitzroy, embarrassed beyond any nightmare, the cynosure of every eye, with one frantic gulp swallowed the lump of toffee whole. Tears rose to his eyes. He looked sullenly down at the table.

The chairman crowed with delight.

'Master Fitzroy has, indeed, ingurgitated his sugar-plum. . . . What is "ingurgitate", little Harnish? Next boy. Next?'

But no one knew.

'Ingurgitate, gentlemen, means "to swallow greedily" . . . from two beautiful Latin words, *in*—into, and *gurges*—a whirlpool. *Gurges, gurges*—just the noise made by a whirlpool! That is how words are made! The sweetmeat has been swallowed up as if by a whirlpool—Master Fitzroy's whirlpool! . . . Sit down, boy!'

But as Master Fitzroy sat down, his discomposure and hurried gulping combined to shatter his frame with a most tremendous hiccough.

'Master Fitzroy re-gurgitates,' said the Reverend Mr. Severn, in great fettle amid a general titter. 'Harnish, what does that mean?'

Christopher rose. He avoided the inflamed eye of his companion.

'Re—back; *gurges*—a whirlpool,' said he painstakingly. 'Fitzroy brings back from his whirlpool.'

'Excellent, Harnish, excellent!' said the chairman cordially, and proceeded to amble on amid all sorts of footpaths into the depths of an etymological forest in which he lost himself and mislaid his pupils. He did not stray so far, however, as to fail to perceive it when the shabby clock over the sideboard announced the stroke of eleven. He laid down the ruler, cast a mildly reproachful glance at the persistent rain beating against the barred dark windows, turned up the collar of his threadbare coat, announced, according to custom, 'There will be a ten minutes' break', and shambled out into the passage.

A moment later his figure at a knock-kneed gallop passed the windows on the way to the back door and the kitchen.

There, on a clean check cloth, laid across one end of the scrubbed table, awaited him a vast cup of tea, a crust of new bread, at least a pound of yellow butter, a slab of cheese, and—more often than not—a plate full of all sorts of curlicues of pastry glittering with jam; curlicues that represented the delicious ends and scraps of a morning's cake and pie making. The kitchen felt—Cook felt, Mary felt, the head housemaid felt, the under-house-maid felt, the kitchenmaid would have felt, if she had been believed capable of having any reasonable feelings—that the poor dear was as starved by his sister as he was oppressed by her; that the meals he ate with her in her private sitting-room might be, perhaps, suitable for an acidulated spinster, but not for a man.

It had started with a cup of tea—'Just leave it for me inside the kitchen door, Mary!'—and had by degrees developed into a full-dress if hurried meal, supplied out of the kitchen rations, and eaten in the warmth and sparkle of the big room with a sympathetic audience limited by convention to Cook and Mary.

While he ate he had his only friendly and human intercourse of the day.

'It's terrible wet,' said Mary, pulling his chair out for him, and looking pityingly at the wet patches on his thin coat.

'Very wet, Mary!' said he shivering, and turning his chair a little so that he could get a glimpse of the cheerful blaze behind the bars.

'Let me put your coat before the fire, sir,' she urged. 'It'll be nice and warm for you when you come to put it on again.'

Cook produced a windsor chair, planted it in front of the hearth ready to receive the garment, but Mr. Severn hesitated.

'Now, sir,' said Cook, her fat arms akimbo. 'You take your coat off, there's a duck. . . . It won't be the first time Mary and I've seen a man in his shirt-sleeves—by a long way. Nor the last!'

With that, almost willy-nilly, the two women extracted him

from the garment, and stood over him with shining faces, like a pair of good-natured mothers, while he ate and drank.

This pleasant scene was interrupted by a distant but loud crash, and a sudden hubbub of small voices. Mr. Severn started up in his chair, but was immediately pressed back into it by a'large, red, fat hand upon his shoulder.

'You've got five minutes left, almost. There's no call for you to go fussing and fretting yourself about anything the young gentlemen get up to. . . . Mary, you run along like a dear and see what them limbs are a-doin' of.'

While Mr. Severn was taking his secret meal the board of directors would debate their personal affairs, in fine weather in the walled passage out-of-doors, in foul weather in the musty little closet devoted to their wet hats and overcoats.

As Christopher with the rest had pressed his way on this particular day into this convenient conference-room, the red angry face of Master Fitzroy was thrust into his own.

'Sneak!' hissed Fitzroy.

'I'm not,' expostulated Christopher.

'You are!'

'I'm not!'

'What did you show him it for? You waved your hand on purpose.'

'I didn't. I didn't really. I didn't know it was there. I didn't know what it was,' protested Christopher, keeping his head as far away as possible from the furious visage of the red-headed boy.

'Yes, you did!' said Fitzroy coming closer still. 'And you're a coward. . . . Take that!'

And he drove a bony fist into Christopher's ribs.

'Don't,' said Christopher. 'I'm not a sneak, and not a coward!'

He retreated as far as he could against the wet coats. A ring of faces surrounded Fitzroy and himself—a ring of grinning faces. 'Hit him, Fitzroy!' 'Sock him one in the eye, Harnish!' 'Yes, he is!' 'No, he isn't!' said everybody, talking furiously all together and all at once.

Fitzroy looked round the ring. Although he was perhaps a year younger than Christopher he was easily the largest boy in the class.

His red hair was rumpled, and his face so scarlet with anger that the nearer boys pushed back to be out of range.

'I say he's a sneak,' he announced. 'I say he's a coward. . . . My gov'nor says he's the Queen's barsteward.'

As Fitzroy had not the faintest idea of what a bastard was—only judging it to be something unpleasant from the expression of his father's face when he announced it at breakfast—and as neither Christopher nor his co-directors had any conception either, the peculiar offensiveness of the term was entirely lost upon them. Christopher, however, took it to be some sort of reflection upon the Queen.

'Liar, I'm not!' said he, clenching his fists and standing his ground.

'You are! You are! Barsteward! Yah!' cried Fitzroy prancing round him.

Without warning or word Christopher suddenly flung himself upon the bigger boy, and they fell together to the floor, rolling over and over among the legs of the spectators who hastened to give them room.

Fitzroy, on his back, caught hold of Christopher by an ear, and with his other hand struck repeatedly at his face. Christopher twisted both hands in the long red hair of his antagonist, and bumped his head against the flags violently enough to have addled completely anyone with a less hard skull. They lay kicking and struggling furiously on the floor for some moments, until Christopher's strength gave out and he collapsed on top of his opponent, his hot face an inch from that of the other.

For a few seconds Fitzroy lay still, glaring up into the face above him; then, with a jerk, he heaved himself to his feet. Christopher rose more slowly, and as he rose, Fitzroy with a shrewd blow to the nose sent him reeling into the washstand. In the appalling crash that followed both combatants drew a little apart, breathing heavily and muttering threats at one another.

It was upon this scene that Mary looked, over a crowd of small heads, when she arrived. A flushed and triumphant Fitzroy was brushing his knees, and Christopher, standing amid the ruins of water jug and basin, was endeavouring to staunch the blood that streamed from his nose over his short blue coat, his Byronic collar, and white nankeen trousers.

She pushed through the mob, cuffing right and left.

'What have you been a-doin' to him?' she cried, her sympathies at once enlisted on the side of the smallest; and stood over Christopher like an avenging pink-and-white angel, with the neatest white apron and smallest white cap, and the blackest ringlets imaginable quivering indignantly.

Fitzroy sullenly kept silence, and studied with gloomy intent a long tear in his pantaloons.

'I hit him first,' said Christopher untruthfully in a voice muffled by the large handkerchief he held to his nose. 'He called me a sneak, and I wasn't!'

'You bad, wicked boy,' said Mary to the unhappy Fitzroy, going down on her knees beside Christopher to assist him stem the flow of blood. 'Oh, you little cannibal, I'm sure I don't know what will happen to you!'

'He said I was the Queen's barsteward,' added Christopher very distinctly, while his own gory rag was being exchanged for a very large handkerchief of Mary's. 'And I'm not. And'—to make things quite clear—'and she's not. So I hit him.'

It took Mary a moment or two to assimilate this remark. When she did so, she rose to her feet, holding Christopher by the hand, and looked down upon Master Fitzroy with an expression before which he quailed.

'You 'orrible little licentiate,' said she. 'You foul-mouthed little —crocodile! To speak of a poor young innocent like that, and a poor lady who may be dying this very minute for all you know or care!'

With that she gave him such a hearty box on the right ear that his head sang and he staggered on his feet. She followed it up, before he could protect himself, with another on the left ear, to make certain that he maintained his balance.

The good-natured girl then conducted Christopher from the stricken assembly to the kitchen, by way of a little gate in the walled passage which was always kept locked except for those few moments when Mr. Severn was known to be coming for his 'elevenses'.

'Tut-tut,' said the tutor, struggling into his coat, as they arrived. 'What's all this about?'

'A young gentleman,' answered Mary, 'used very terrible words to Master Harnish. A red-headed young gentleman.'

'Ha, Fitzroy!' said Mr. Severn. 'And what did Fitzroy say?'

Mary flushed very brightly, but made no answer.

Christopher, watching Cook bustle about with a roller towel, a kettle of hot water, and many exclamations, felt called upon to explain.

'I hit him first, sir. He called me the Queen's barsteward.'

Cook paused. Mary flushed even brighter. Mr. Severn looked puzzled.

'Barsteward? Barsteward?' inquired he mildly.

Cook's one glance at Mary had informed her of the rights of the matter. As an older woman she was prepared to elucidate:

'The little dear means "bastard", if you will excuse me mentioning it, sir! No word at all for a young gentleman to know—much less to soil his lips with. A word that would make anyone act a little old-fashioned!'

'Bastard! Oh, bastard!' said Mr. Severn with a relieved air, watching the progress of surgical operation in a meditative manner. 'Tut-tut! Very naughty! . . . An interesting word, little Harnish, while we are talking etymology. . . . Now, I am sure you can't tell me its derivation, Harnish. . . . Nor you, Mary?' . . . But Mary in her embarrassment had turned her face away. . . . 'It comes from the Old French—*Fils de Bast*, son of the pack-saddle. . . . Meaning someone whose birth was a trifle unceremonious. A trifle unceremonious. . . . Very pretty! Very pretty!'

Mary gave a smothered laugh, and hurried with averted head into the outer kitchen where she appeared to laugh herself into and out of an attack of hysterics.

'Lor', sir, you do run on, you do!' said Cook, turning a large red face from the task of holding Christopher's streaming nose over the basin. 'But it's no language to use to a child. "Unceremonious" birth. *He* was a miscarriage, I'll be bound! I'd have given him . . .'

But Mr. Severn was already on the road back.

When Christopher, restored and cleaner, reappeared through the door of the dark class-room, the board of directors had been transformed into a court of inquiry, the president sitting back in his chair at the top of the table with his ivory ruler held upright in his hand like the wand of a High Steward, or the sword in the hands of a playing-card King.

'You are better, now, Harnish?' said this dignitary, interrupting his discourse for a moment. 'Sit down!'

The small faces that had been turned on Christopher swung round once more to the drooping figure standing by the water-carafe and pile of books. The secretary had been transformed, too —into the prisoner at the bar.

'We have studied the etymology of the word "bastard",' continued the president of the court. 'It is unnecessary for me to go deeper into its dictionary meaning than to say that it connotes a person to be the offspring of parents who have performed the facts of matrimony without undertaking the ceremonial. Socially such behaviour is incorrect; but it should have no bearing on the position of their offspring. Historically it is often true that bastards have been more vigorous, more intelligent, better-looking, than their legitimate brothers. William the Conqueror was a bastard— you will remember that his mother was a tanner's daughter. So was the great Dunois, Bastard of Orléans, who helped to drive the English out of France. The great Marshal Saxe was another; his mother came of a family our own Royal Family has good cause to recall. Don John of Austria was the fruit of a ceremony-less marriage. There are interesting physiological causes for this.

'The fact remains . . .' and as he spoke he placed down the ruler, opened a drawer in the table, and produced a neat yellow cane bound against splitting with black waxed thread at each end. . . . 'Despite all this, the fact remains that the term is not one employed in society by one gentleman to another. It is reprehensible, ungenteel, and an insult, according to modern convention, to a gentleman's parents, which he is bound to resent.

'Fitzroy has been a coward, because he struck one much smaller than himself. Fitzroy has been a blackguard because he behaved in a manner ill-becoming a gentleman. If little Harnish were a bastard, what business is it of Fitzroy, or of anyone, except Harnish's parents? Fitzroy has, therefore, also been a busybody. . . . Come here, Fitzroy.'

Mr. Severn rose as Fitzroy unwillingly approached him. He looked a little uncertainly from boy to cane, and back again.

'Face the wall, and bend down,' he commanded.

Every head was craned over the table to catch every detail of the drama about to be enacted. First Mr. Severn removed his chair, because there was not too much room between table and wall. Then he made Master Fitzroy stoop till he touched his toes. Then he made Master Fitzroy straighten himself, and go a little nearer the wall, and bend over again so that his bright red hair brushed the stained wallpaper, and his white shirt showed between the top of his pantaloons and his short jacket, and the seat of his nether garments strained over his small person until it would seem that it must split.

Christopher bobbed up.

'Please, sir, it was I hit him first,' he expostulated.

'Sit down, boy!' said Mr. Severn, flourishing the cane in a most unscientific manner. ' "*Ille crucem sceleris pretium*"—I shall give you three strokes, Fitzroy. One for being a coward; one for being a blackguard, and one for . . .'

At that moment the door slowly opened, and a gaunt lady in a voluminous dark dress, with strongly marked eyebrows, and smooth iron-grey hair under a small lace cap, appeared in the opening. Her cold dark eyes took in the scene without a change of expression. She folded her arms about her gaunt chest in such a way that her mittened hands became invisible.

'Mr. Severn!' said she.

Her brother, manifestly discomposed, lowered the implement of correction.

'My dear?' he inquired apologetically.

'I desire a word with you.'

Obediently he withdrew with her from the room into the passage whence a dozen pairs of small ears—including those of the respited criminal—heard a swift interchange of incomprehensible sentences.

A moment later he came back with a grave air, looked strangely at Christopher for a moment, dropped his gaze to the bluish schedule lying before his place, and said: 'Harnish, you are wanted at home. You may go.'

Outside the green wicket Christopher found Williams waiting for him with a hackney coach; but the man knew nothing. When he got home, Setoun was absent, and no one would, or could, tell him anything, but that he was to be tidied up at once and sent post-haste to Brandenburgh House.

Smith herself presided at the tidying-up process with many ejaculations at his blood-stained linen, and kissed him in a most tearful manner just before he set off in the carriage with Williams.

He had not seen the long avenue for many months. The elms were black and wet, and the rooks' nests were like great blots amid the etching of their branches. There was, too, a forlorn look to the great house, as if it had given up heart. The wet gravel of its sweeping drive was cut up with hooves and wheels; the blinds of some of the windows were down, and curtains left pulled or half-pulled as if the inmates had other and more pressing things to do than worry over such trifles as night or day.

He was taken again into that little room with the crowded wall, and left to himself. There was the dark stain on the carpet where the Queen had spilled her wine! There the small miniature by the head of the chair in which she sat—a miniature of a young gentleman with long dark hair tied back at the nape with a black ribbon, and a green coat with many buttons which had begun to fade! The two tall windows showed the Thames, across the lawn, reflecting the high, white sky. And on the river, as on that last day, an infinitude of small boats rowed to and fro, the faces of the oarsmen turned toward the high front of the palace.

He noticed that the mantel was dusty, and on the round table in the middle a number of glasses with dregs of wine in them had become sticky with long standing.

It grew dark, but nobody remembered to bring a light; so he seated himself on a little stool in the window and listened to the rising wind, and, gazing unseeing across the water, slipped away into his magic lands.

Night had fallen when the door opened, and turning sharply he saw against the lighted corridor the slim form of Charlotte, and the oval of her pale face with a half-smile on her lips, and her white shoulders rising from the wide folds of her pearl-grey dress. As he ran gladly to her he saw that her eyes were wet with tears.

'Charlotte, darling Charlotte!' he cried, and flung himself into her arms, and knew that he loved her better than Setoun, or Cousin Jennifer, or any of those people of long ago.

He knew that she was the fairy princess who passed with proud head down the corridors of his dreams; who watched, amid her ladies and scarlet pikemen, epic battles waged across grassy garths and terraces that overhung valleys full of opal mist.

He might hold her now and press his face against the satin of her dress, and in so doing know that his dreams were real—just as real as the floorboard on which he slipped a little as he strained upwards; as real as the trickle of wax that dripped over the edge of the candle in the silver sconce on the wall behind her—that dripped the colour of crystal, clouded, and then solidified as a bead of yellow-white. They were real, only with a different sort of reality.

He knew now that she was in his dreams: and since she was real, then were his dreams real—more real perhaps than this other sort of reality in which one hated and was hit; in which one was made to fire pistols and heard a scarlet figure very far away intone sentence of death; or saw a frightened schoolboy bend double awaiting the cane; or note the frayed linen of an usher's cuffs, and the glassy shine upon his coat where he bent forward over his desk all day.

'Charlotte, I do love you!' he said. 'I do. I do. Indeed, I do!'

She smoothed his hair, and held him very tight, and kissed him. They sat together a long time in the darkness whispering just a word to one another now and then, and listening to the rising wind and the sound of distant singing on the river.

Presently the door opened and a man's head peered in. He said nothing audible, although against the yellow light without they could see that his lips were moving. Charlotte, however, understood. She rose and told Christopher to follow.

They crossed the hall, which was half lit, and full of shadows and silent people; and went upstairs along a soft-carpeted corridor where more silent people pressed themselves against the wall to let them pass.

Toward the end of the passage two lackeys—large silent men in crimson and gold—stood barring the way, but moved aside unbidden for them, so that they came to a high mahogany door with a man in black bending low over the handle, his ear almost pressed against the panel.

A little puzzled, Christopher took hold of Charlotte's hand.

'You must be very good, Tops,' she said in a whisper. 'The Queen is very ill. She wants to see you.'

They entered a bright lofty room, hot from an enormous fire that roared up the chimney at the far end. Everywhere there were lights, and mirrors that reflected a dozen times the vast canopied bed—which faced the long curtains before the windows—and the dark weary face that was so small amid the billowing pillows.

There were many people there, waiting with bowed heads about the room; two stood beside the looped crimson hangings at the bedhead looking down upon that face which was so familiar and yet so strange to Christopher.

On the other side from them a man crouched on a low chair, holding within a gentle clasp a hand of which only the lace ruffle could be seen. A globular gold watch was on his knee, and ever his gaze would go from watch to face, from face to watch. Once he got up and bent down gently over the form which barely ridged the stupendous quilt of flowered silk. He listened intently for a moment, his eyes fixed on the pale lips. Then he sank back again, and resumed his vigil.

They waited in silence.

The wind rose. Through the thick curtains they could hear above its rustle and sigh the faint burden of hymns sung by the crowds who waited on the river.

Then someone took Christopher to the bedside, and for a moment the man in black surrendered to him the thin hand he remembered to have been so plump. There was no stir or movement in it. It lay in his, motionless—incapable of motion.

As he kissed the cold fingers two great tears rolled from his eyes and splashed down on to them. Horrified, he looked up at the face upon the pillows; but there was no change, only that the shadows about the sunken eyes seemed to be darker, and the white lips had parted a trifle so that the troubled breath came whistling through.

The man in black took back the chill hand from him, and, smiling a little at him, motioned him back with a touch.

A clock somewhere struck ten silvery chimes. The wind at that instant rose to a roar. In one great wave it hurled itself against the house. It bent down the fastenings of the windows and flung them open to the night; it overthrew a lamp and silver candlesticks; it tore the door out of the usher's nerveless grasp. It filled the room with motion and night and noise and torn staves of old hymns from the choirs without.

At that moment the Queen of England died.

He for ever after remembered driving home bolt-upright and dry-eyed in the dark green depths of the closed carriage, facing Setoun and Charlotte.

He said no word; nor did Setoun speak, and Charlotte, her loose cloak slipped from off her shoulders, lay in the protection of Setoun's arm, her dark head hidden against his chest.

In the pale, scant flicker of the cabriolet lamps he watched Setoun sitting with his great chin sunk into the tight folds of his high white cravat, and his head bent over the dark tresses beneath. As the big hand rose in its rhythmic task of patting consolation the glint of his great gold ring showed for a moment, vanished, and appeared again like a clockwork thing.

The Queen was dead (he thought) and would never know that he had prayed for her! Even when she was dying she had no sentinels! There should have been heralds about the bed—he felt—to sound her entry into another world, to announce her earthly style and dignities as she put them off; and trumpeters to sound a call, and halberdiers to bring their arms clashing in salute.

Instead a great wind had blown her windows open and blown her candles out, and taken her with it out into the night, to the slamming of doors and rattle of casements.

He wanted to cry again, but resolutely stopped himself, by thinking of Fitzroy. Only that day Fitzroy had said she was a barsteward or had a barsteward! Now she was dead, and unavenged of the insult, and Fitzroy was in some way to blame for it all!

He was to have been her tall son, her sentinel. He would show Fitzroy you could not insult a queen with impunity! He watched the infrequent lights flit past, swayed to the rocking of the great C-springs, and heard the quick trot of the horses slow down as they climbed the slope of the windy bastion from which their house

looked down on London. But all his thoughts were on Fitzroy—
Fitzroy who had slandered the Queen—the Queen who had been
so kind to him, who had no sentinels, no prayers, who had been
put on trial like King Charles, and died in a gust of wind.

He choked back a sob.

Chapter 14

The Wonderful Arabella

CHRISTOPHER WAS NOT, HOWEVER, DESTINED TO WREAK full vengeance upon Fitzroy immediately, for Setoun kept him at home to 'cheer up Charlotte', he said. The Charlotte who had burst into tears as she entered the house that night and cried 'Fool! What a fool I was!' and run upstairs and been no more seen. It was not, indeed, until the Queen had been dead a week that he passed as usual out of the little door in the high garden wall and set off with Williams down Church Lane for Kensington and school.

It was a grey and rainy day: the drenched trees that overhung the wet iron-coloured walls on either side dripped tearfully on to the footpath. The foot-passengers—and there seemed to be more than usual—hurried with heads bent and collars upturned against the drizzle. From a distance came a deep, low murmur. The noise grew louder as they rounded a bend with a clutter of small prim houses, and looked down the slope to the junction of the lane with the High Street at the grassy churchyard of St. Mary's.

A little nearer than the graveyard, between the low buildings with their thronged windows, a tight tangle of vehicles was crammed athwart the road—a towering hay-wain, an empty brewer's dray, two or three market carts, a gig, and nearest of all, a private carriage overturned against the barricade, with its coachman in furious controversy with a knot of threatening men.

Horses that had been taken out of shafts, whickered and stamped upon the roadway, or nuzzled over the pavement in the care of small boys, while hatless men, leaping from cart to cart, lashed the wheels together and to scaffold poles and ladders reft from an adjoining builder's yard.

From beyond the barricade came the sound of a great crowd surging: the High Street—such portion as could be seen of it—was black with heads, and the grass and gravestones of the churchyard invisible beneath the throng. It was a crowd in which there was no shouting, and no crying; a whispering, murmuring, muttering crowd.

Williams pulled up at the bend, by the doorway of a small shop that looked squarely down the street. A little man, with a white apron and a fluff of silver hair on either side of his bald crown, stood at the top of the three-four steps.

'What's to do?' asked Williams, jerking his gold-laced hat in the direction of crowd and barricade. 'What's to do?'

'Queen's berryin'!' said the shopman laconically.

'But what's all them carts got to do with it?'

The shopman hesitated, stropping upon a leathery hand a short knife which he held in the other.

'It's all right,' said Williams, glancing down at Christopher. 'We are Queen's people all right. The little 'un's all right. He's —her god-child.'

The sharp eyes of the shopman took in the crest and coronet upon the silver buttons down the long front of Williams's livery topcoat; and turned with fresh interest to the small figure gazing down the lane from under the tent-like shelter of the lackey's green umbrella.

'What I say, is a queen should have a queen's berryin',' he said. 'A fine berryin' don't make up for the dear departed, but it's a linctus to the soul, a balm for those left behind. For those who loved the deceased. A fine berryin' heals wounds; it ass-uages grief. . . . Yes, ass-uages grief.'

'But . . .'

'That bein' so; that bein' taken for granted: 'ow can the wounds be 'ealed, the grief be ass-uaged of the 'undreds of thousands as loved 'er, if this 'ere bloody Guv'ment tuck 'er away as privit as they dare?

'This 'ere Guv'ment says: "Let's take the relicts round side streets and back ways and along lanes and footpaths by the common sewer, and then nobody will remember about 'er, and nobody will pipe the eye, and George will say to us—'Good boys, werry good boys! Another bottle of laudanum, another bottle of cherry brandy, boys, and we'll make a —— night of it'!" '

The lane was filling up with people. It was almost impassable now, and many of the bystanders turned to listen to the old man's harangue.

'We'll best 'em yet,' said the shopman raising his voice. 'We've planned it, and we've plotted it, and we'll see that there's no 'ole an' corner about it. We've put up barricades, an' we've locked gates, an' we've torn up roadways. . . . I tell you, as true as I stand 'ere, that this 'ere berryin' will be remembered in Lunnon when you and I are dead and berried too, an' longer'n that! I tell you this 'ere berryin' is goin' through Lunnon, Guv'ment or no Guv'ment and through the City of Lunnon, with My Lord Mayor, and the Aldermen, and the Sheriffs. Whether they bring in the Horse Guards, and the Foot Guards, and the Bloody Blackguards, or not!'

' 'Ear! 'Ear!' said the crowd.

Christopher, who had listened with deep attention, stepped back a pace from the ring at the foot of the steps, closer into the protection of Williams.

'We'll never get down to the college, Master Christopher! . . . Not in a hundred years!' said the man, gauging the density of the throng that now packed the lane from side to side, swaying a little where those nearest the waiting horses pressed away from the danger of trampling hoofs.

'Step in for a little!' urged the shopman. 'Out of harm's way!' And led them up narrow stairs into a small front room smelling of leather, with hides of all sorts hanging like disused garments from the walls, and a half-made saddle sitting on a stand, rather like some strange joint in the process of being carved.

'Can't I go to school, to-day, Williams?' pleaded Christopher, slowly crossing to the windows. He saw his revenge delayed by yet another day, and regretted it.

'What an unnateral little gentleman it is!' chuckled the shopman, stopping to regard Christopher as if he were something altogether outside nature, and scratching his bald pate in an alarming manner with the fine point of the knife he carried.

He winked in the most knowing way, and led the child to an open window.

'You can't go through that mob, little master!' said he. 'And you don't want to. There'll be many a broken head to-day—and worse!'

The crowd had fallen very silent. In the downpour their wet hats looked from above like a channel of wet pebbles where a brook runs into the sea at low tide.

Across the silence suddenly came a hoarse shout of command. Into view over the barricade there swayed a line of red plumes— a line of plumes, and nothing more, against the crowded tall windows of the High Street. And then another line of plumes. They halted.

The silent crowd broke into a babble: the babble became a rumble. The first line of plumes swung round. There were eight red plumes now, just visible over the top of the barricade, like geranium heads over the edge of a distant window box. Then eight more came up behind them. They halted again. Back in the main street there was a mass of red plumes, a perfect flower-bed of them.

No word of command could be heard, but presently the red plumes advanced a little toward the barricade. The stream of men below the windows pressed forward as if to support from the rear the fortifications that were defended by their fellows before it.

From somewhere a black object was lobbed into the air and fell among the plumes; and then another—this time from the churchyard—described a slow parabola and fell dead upon a plume which immediately disappeared. Its fellows bobbed down and up as if a gale had struck the geraniums in the box; and then wavered and gave ground.

The thunder of the crowd had become a cataract of noise, a stupendous, deafening, crashing Niagara of sound.

Christopher, looking about him in the interlude of action, saw against the railings of the steps next door but one the red head of

Fitzroy and caught his freckled face straining to see over the hats before him.

The rain had suddenly stopped, and a watery sun shone through the banks of cloud.

Without a word he slipped from the room, and was gone downstairs, and was in the street before he was missed.

He was not quite certain what he would do to Fitzroy, he told himself as he wormed his way through the crowd. He tried to picture a duel, but as a practicable idea it did not seem to work. . . . Horsewhipping? But then he had no horsewhip. . . . And when it came to stark facts, he had no Fitzroy; for the boy was no longer on the well-worn steps with rusted holes at the edges where the iron supports of the handrail had broken away.

The house to which these steps led up was the last on the curve wherefrom any view could be had of the disturbance; beyond it, hence, the crowd thinned out. He pressed delicately through a thicket of wet coats, and stood clear. Fitzroy was not to be seen.

A little farther up, the narrow road was deserted and ran between walls fringed with trees and studded at intervals with gates.

Someone had entered the nearest wicket, for a booted groom in canary-yellow breeches and claret-coloured coat had been standing sentinel upon the entry and was himself about to turn in. The man was hatless and dishevelled, and Christopher realized that he wore the same livery as the coachman of the wrecked britzka; he realized, too, that the livery was that worn by the servant who escorted Fitzroy to school every morning.

He ran, and arrived breathless before the man had let the latch fall after him.

'It's only me!' he said, and on that excuse—and, probably, his appearance—was allowed to pass through the portal into a long dark tunnel under an arch of trees, running between high ivied wall and high dreary hedge of evergreen.

The pathway was grey—the deathly grey of ancient gravel that the soil is swallowing up—and there were little shallow hollows in it with green scum on them. At the end of the alley glistened the wet pale stucco of a large house.

From somewhere out of sight came voices. The fading tread of feet behind him told that the groom was not following him, and had taken some other path. Visible ahead, alone, was Fitzroy whistling as he dawdled along, jaunty in a dark blue jacket and short white trousers that showed his bright red socks.

'Ssst!' he called. 'Fitzroy! Fitz-roy!'

He did not know what he would say.

The Queen was being buried and someone was sending her funeral up back streets! He felt that Fitzroy symbolized all the past offendings—and this new one.

Fitzroy stopped; looked over his shoulder, and then turned round with open mouth.

Christopher ran up to him, halted, breathing heavily, panted: 'You said she was a barsteward!'

Then hit the freckled nose with all his strength.

The boy was so taken aback that for a moment his hand hung motionless by his side. In that space of time Christopher struck him yet again; and the blood streamed from his nostrils.

'You're mad!' said Fitzroy, and flung himself upon the other, endeavouring to close with him and overthrow him by superior weight. For the space of two minutes they fought upon the hard-beaten path; but Fitzroy, frightened and taken by surprise, battled on the defensive, and gave ground repeatedly before the furious onrush of his small enemy.

Once he gripped Christopher round the arms so that he could not strike, and held him thus for a moment, dripping blood from wounded nose on to upturned face. But it was only for a moment, and then Christopher wrenched himself free and hailed whirling blows upon him, like a very small windmill in a gale that stormed from every quarter of the compass at once.

Fitzroy broke away, turned to fly, tripped over his own feet, and fell to the ground, shielding his face as best he might and shrilly calling 'Pax!' and, when he found 'Pax' was of no avail, screaming for help at the top of his lungs.

Christopher, kneeling against the cowering figure and raining blows upon it, was too occupied to pay heed to the crunch of heels on the gravel. Unexpectedly he was seized by the collar, and torn protesting from his victim by someone who said, 'Blast the little bantam! He hangs on as if he were a game-cock! . . . Now, let him be, will you!'

He was released, set down, and immediately turned at bay.

A big man with a curled white hat and huge fawn coat with a cape about the shoulders, stood over him. He had a plum-coloured face and a great beak of a nose, and his dry mauve lips were parted in a mirthless smile in which his teeth shone as yellow as old ivory. In his one quick look at him Christopher found something horrifying in the deep-set eyes which were shining and stony.

A tall still woman in a long cloak stood at the alley's mouth a few yards away. She looked from the wailing boy upon the ground to the small defiant figure above him without a flicker of expression. She raised her gaze slowly as if she sought within the damp gloom of the path some object that would deserve her interest, and knew it would be vain.

'Well, Tom Bruiser,' said the big man with a sort of ferocious joviality. 'And what are you beating up our Charles for? Hey?' He seemed to speak with clenched teeth, and the thin wide smile remained on his face after he had done.

The fact that Charles had been beaten, and was still moaning on the gravel, appeared to concern him not at all. It gave Christopher courage to explain the situation.

'Fitzroy,' said he in his clear treble, 'called the Queen a bar-steward . . . sir!'

'And was she not?' asked the big gentlemen, as if with a show of polite interest in a subject to which he was indifferent.

'No, sir!'

'Well,' remarked the big gentleman still smiling, 'to-day alone she's given Charles a black eye and a bloody nose, and smashed to firewood three hundred pounds' worth of britzka!'

The still lady at the alley's mouth put a slow hand up to the hood that covered her head, as if to adjust the unseen tresses. A bracelet of great opals shone like ice slivers against the pale stillness of her face—as though they had absorbed all the hidden fires of her nature.

'Charles seems to have got his deserts, my dear Ernest,' she said with a slightly foreign accent. 'Charles curses the Queen, and is beaten. You curse a mob for obstructing your path, and wreck a new britzka. It is just as well that no one recognized you. You might have come off rather worse than Charles. One would almost gather that the King and his brothers are not too popular.'

'Mob! Mob!' said the big gentleman, in a towering passion which distorted his face, and dilated his great nostrils so that the wings of them whitened. 'By God, Mathilde, if I had the dealing with them I'd send a squadron of cavalry through them. A knife through butter. By God, there would be the end of treating them like mother's darlings.'

'You'll be able to do that, one day,' said the lady in an ice-cold voice. 'Something to look forward to, Ernest! Until then I should avoid contact. You don't want to make yourself more unpopular than you need. It would not have done your cause any good if someone had recognized the Duke of Cumberland in a brawl with the crowd. And . . . and at his sister-in-law's funeral!'

As she stated her case with the uttermost dispassion, a step sounded behind her, and a third person—dressed from head to foot in black—came into the dark frame of the alley and its background of drab wet stucco glistening in the thin sunshine. She did not even turn on his arrival. He halted beside her, and stood with his pale face and dark chill eyes taking in the scene. He was hatless, and one black lock had fallen over his brow, and a plump pale hand played with a knot of seals that hung from his fob. His head was thrust a little forward, and swung like a snake's a trifle from side to side, so that he should absorb each detail.

'And what have we here, Your Royal Highness?' he asked in slow, soft tones.

At the sound of that even voice Christopher's regard was wrenched from the woman.

'Charles has been fighting one of his friends, I gather,' said the woman, answering for the duke. 'Where does he get that combative instinct from, I wonder? Not from you; it must be from his late lamented mother. . . . He appears to have had the worst of it. I do not know why His Royal Highness must interrupt. If they wish to . . .' She shrugged her shoulders, as though the gesture would save her from the weariness of further speech.

Christopher shot one startled glance of decisive recognition at the man he knew as Captain Heywood. Spattered as was his face with blood and dirt, yet the expression of horrified discovery revealed his identity to the newcomer instantly.

'Why!' said he gently. 'Why, it's my little friend, Master Harnish! It's little Christopher! Doing his best to murder my poor, motherless son.'

In that one instant Christopher knew that flight was the only course before him.

Panic-stricken though he was, yet his limbs answered the message of his brain; he darted past the quick clumsy grasp of the gentleman who had been called Ernest; dodged by the woman—who made no effort to restrain him, nor even turned her head to watch the progress of his flight—and raced along a flagged walk that edged a low house from its sopping lawn.

A whistle shrilled—how often had he seen Heywood take the little silver thing from his vest pocket to summon Fonblanque!

The duke spun about, bellowing servants' names and imprecations. He was, however, restrained from following in the chase by a slim hand that fell on his sleeve.

'You don't want to be mixed up in this in any way, my dear Ernest,' said Madame de Boucher in an indifferent tone. 'If George can catch the child—well and good! Though I very much doubt whether we can make use of him again. He has served his purpose.'

'"Served his purpose!"' quoted the duke, and bent his lowering blind-man's regard upon her. 'By God, Mathilde, you are a cold-blooded serpent.' He paused in meditation, and then said suddenly, 'I wonder what it is has kept me attracted to you for over twenty years.'

'My body when I was young,' said Madame de Boucher. 'My brains now I am old. And my money all the time. I've got better brains than you, or any man you know! And more money!'

He had forgotten the chase that was in full cry across the dripping garden. He looked broodingly at the still figure shrouded in its long cloak and hood.

'By Christ,' he said, 'you've got a tongue like a poisoned dagger, Mathilde! . . . You aren't young any longer, though you're still devilish good-looking; and I've always liked 'em young. But I always come back to you.' Again he stopped to reflect . . . 'I wonder what you find in me?'

'I wonder!' said Madame de Boucher, and stared down the dank green tunnel of the alley, with eyes that saw in the distance—as if she were looking through the wrong end of a telescope—a red-sailed barge sliding along a grey river, a bowl of strawberries, and a figure like a discontented Apollo propped against a marble mantelpiece.

Christopher had run quickly, and, turning at the corner of the flagged walk, came to a wide terrace with urns and statues on its balustrade; and saw a manservant emerge from a door and stand uncertainly in his path.

He swerved aside, and fled down a flight of steps, across a lawn toward a high wall along which gay hollyhocks stood sentinel; and then down the path beside the wall looking wildly for some hiding-place or outlet of escape.

There was an arched door in the wall ahead. He ran to it and shook it, his breath coming in sobs as he did. But it was immovable, and ivy was creeping up its blistered side, and over the rusted hinges. It did not even rattle as he thrust his weight against it; only a little dust filtered down from the interstice between door and lintel.

He looked across his shoulder. His pursuers, certain that he was trapped, were advancing slowly across the lawn, the saturnine Fonblanque in front, and the rest of them spreading fanwise out behind.

A voice suddenly spoke to him from above. He looked up. A laughing face that seemed to be almost a golden brown amid a tangle of golden hair was regarding him from the summit of the wall.

'Boy!' said the voice. 'Are they chasing you?'

Christopher cast an agonized glance across the grass. Fonblanque was, perhaps, eighty feet away, and was beginning to run. Another minute, and it would be too late. He saw that white plump hand again—bursting pistol—felt the calculated harshness of the blow upon his cheek—the cold eyes regarding him with some unknown menace in their look.

'Let me in!' cried Christopher. 'Let me in!'

'Down to the end of the wall,' said the head jerking itself in the direction. 'Quickly! . . . Quickly! . . .' And vanished, still calling 'Quickly', with a rustle and scramble, presumably down a ladder.

In the corner where the hollyhock-guarded wall joined another there was a high bank covered with ground ivy, and a fig tree stooping outwards. He made for it at top speed, scrambled up and stood panting against a breast-high wall, looking on to a trim and ordered garden.

'Quick!' said the head bobbing up like magic before him. 'He's just behind!'

Christopher raised himself by his hands; flung one leg on to the coping; spurred up his energies for the last effort, when he felt his coat seized, and heard Fonblanque cry out, 'I haf 'eem!'

But the head was not without resource. A pair of arms were flung about his neck and gripped him tight. Their owner then appeared to step off whatever she stood on, into space; precipitated herself backward, Christopher's head clutched to her bosom, into a rending, crashing, smashing cucumber frame . . .

He rose, a little shakily, crunching glass beneath his feet, and offered his hand to the owner of the head who appeared entirely undisconcerted, and lay on her back amid the debris shaking with laughter.

She was a child of his own age, enveloped in a dark green cloak with a hood from which a tangle of golden brown curls escaped. (The heavy mantle probably explained why neither of them had come to harm.) She had green eyes that laughed as much as her golden face, the twitching dimple in her chin, and the short upper lip that curved in mirth.

She went on laughing as she sat up.

'Look at him! Do look at him,' she said pointing from amid the wreckage of the glass frame.

Christopher looked round.

Fonblanque was staring down over the wall top, consternation imprinted on his sallow countenance—in dropped jaw and goggling eyes.

There was a heavy tread on the gravel.

'What you doin' thar? We don' wan' none of yo' po' white trash snoopin' into dis yere garden!'

An immensely tall and thin negro in a suit of faded blue cotton had appeared beside the children. He shook a threatening fist at the manservant who discreetly vanished.

He wagged a woolly grey head at the golden lady, scooped her out of the wreckage with arms as long as a monkey's in their very short sleeves, and set her on her feet.

'Thar, Miz' Arabella!' said he reproachfully. 'Why'm yew rumbusticatin' in my punkin bed? Why'm yew layin' down in dis yere glass'us as ef it wuz yo' bed—and laffin' fit ter beat the band?'

Miss Arabella gave herself a shake. She took Christopher's hand in hers as if to sponsor him through anv trouble that might come; and turned away.

'I like sleeping in the pumpkin bed, Uncle Mose,' she said. 'And I like laughing in the pumpkin bed. . . . We both like lying in the pumpkin bed. . . . And we're going on lying in the pumpkin bed, aren't we—what's your name? Mine's Arabella!'

Christopher introduced himself under the disapproving gaze of Uncle Mose, who continually shook his head, and mumbled a hope that he might be doggoned if somethin' or other, and then brightened up and said, 'Thar's Miz' Case. Yew go 'n' talk to dem, 'n' leave a po' ol' nigger to his work!'

The old man looked at his frame, sighed, and, curiosity or idleness getting the better of him, carefully set foot on the top of the ruin, and peered over the wall into the next garden.

'They're only my aunts!' said Arabella. 'They are all right.' And led Christopher along a path between neat little box hedges and a riot of flowers.

Two little old ladies were hurrying toward them on pattens—if such a word as 'hurry' could suitably be used to their pace; two little old ladies in wide, black satin dresses, precisely folded lavender-coloured shawls, and wide straw hats tied under neat, small, pink faces. They were so alike that if one little old lady had not been carrying a pair of gardening scissors and the other a gardening basket, Christopher might almost have felt that he had made a mistake and was seeing double.

A pace behind them was another lady; a very tall woman in a prim bonnet with a red face and a suspicion of grey beard about her chin.

A fat negro, with a full moon face, full moon spectacles and a full moon figure arrayed in a blue swallow-tail coat, formed a panting rearguard.

'Dear me!' said one of the old ladies. 'Why, it's a boy!' And they both came to a standstill.

'This is Christopher,' said Arabella with much directness. 'He was running away. So I helped him over the wall. We fell into the cucumber frame.'

'Facts!' said the other old lady with a smile of approval. 'Most succinct. All facts. Very good, Arabella! Very good, indeed!'

'You will forgive me inquiring,' said the lady in the prim bonnet speaking rapidly over the two straw hats in front of her. 'But why was this—this young person running away?'

Christopher, thus called on for explanation, stepped a pace forward. With his hands behind his back he presented the bones of the affair.

'I made Fitzroy's nose bleed. He said the Queen was a bar-steward. So I hit him. Then . . .' a little lame the explanation here perhaps '. . . then I ran away!'

'Bar-steward?' observed the second small lady in black in great perplexity. 'What does the boy mean, Aaron?'

The fat negro edged his way up to act as interpreter. He bobbed his head until his double chin appeared to impale itself on the sharp points of his incredibly high collar.

'I take it, Miz' Anne,' he said, 'that the young gem'p'n means a bahst'd—a come-by-chanct. Yes, ma-a-am! A come-by-chanct, as one mout say!'

'Good gracious me,' remarked the grenadier severely. 'What a precious little horror! . . . What should the boy know about such things? . . . He probably comes from Pottery Lane—a most dirty, diseased neighbourhood.' And she drew herself together with a small shudder, as if she feared moral and physical contamination from the propinquity.

'Oh, a bastard! A bastard!' said Miz' Anne easily. 'Now, really,

my good Wordsworth! Facts of life, my girl! Facts of life, my
girl! Why shirk them? At my time of day, and Miz' Elizabeth's
time of day, we are fully aware that there are bastards, and'—
ended she triumphantly—'why there are bastards. There's no blinking it!'

The grenadier appeared to remain unconvinced; the other small
lady in black, however, regarded Christopher intently. She dropped
her garden basket, and clasped her mittened hands together in a
perfect ecstasy.

'Oh, you dear child,' she said in a voice that was as tiny as
herself and twittered like a small bird. 'How romantic! Someone
uses bad words about the poor Queen, so you defend her. Just
like a knight errant; isn't it, Anne? Like Sir Launcelot, isn't it,
Wordsworth? In the Morte d'Arthur, you know.'

'Sutt'nly, ma-a-am,' said Aaron; looking at Christopher with a
smile that showed a great mouthful of white teeth and pink
gums. 'The young gem'p'n sutt'nly did defend her. Ah sees de
udder from de ladder as he comes to de wall. 'N' ef he ha'n't got
two of de purtiest black eyes, 'n' a nose a-bleedin' laike a squeeged
orange, Ah'm pore black trash! Yes, ma-a-am!'

The description of this scene of violence caused the grenadier
to shudder more violently than ever; Miz' Elizabeth to clasp her
mittened hands still tighter in her ecstasy at the completeness of
the victory of virtue; and Miz' Anne to nod her grave appreciation
of being thus brought into close contact with more facts of life.

'I still don't see—forgive me, dear Miss Anne; forgive me, dear
Miss Elizabeth!—I don't understand, that is to say, why your
cucumber frame should be broken, so to speak, because of knight
errantry?'

This led to such an involved statement by Christopher, such a
digging into past history—which he really did not understand
himself—that Miss Anne and Miss Elizabeth decided the discussion should be continued within doors.

The golden-haired girl took Christopher's hand as they walked
behind her aunts and the grenadier toward the house.

'I say,' said she excitedly. 'Did you really give him two black eyes
and make his nose bleed?'

'Yes!' replied Christopher without embellishment.

'Oh, good for you!' said she swinging his hand in the most vehement manner. 'I wish I had seen! He must have looked a sight.'

They went under a colonnade, paused for patten removal, and then passed through long windows, into a warm dim room aromatic with strange scents, its bare floors of polished red pine, its walls panelled with cedar, its lofty ceiling quartered by beams of oak. Although it was midsummer a fire of cherry logs burned in the open hearth, and waked to life the gold dragons that writhed on lacquer cabinets, and gave warmth to Chinese jars of pale green and rose, and brought the scent from the spiced leaves in porcelain bowls.

With it all there was, too, a hint of the earthy scent and warmth of far-away savannahs and forest swamps; for beyond wide-open doors there was a large conservatory, and huge fantastic blooms showed waxen against the massed foliage of grotesque plants.

The two little ladies sat down side by side on a damask-covered settee as near to the fire as possible, the grenadier standing on guard behind.

Arabella threw off her cloak. She planted herself firmly beside Christopher on the bearskin in front of the hearth. As if that were not a sufficient declaration of loyalty she put an arm round his neck—a golden-brown arm with a short puffed sleeve of green gauze that got very little farther than her shoulder.

'Arabella!' said the grenadier, shaking a monitory finger at her. 'Is this becoming conduct? Is this decent? The young man may have—mumps. He may have measles!'

'Shucks!' said Arabella curtly.

'I think Arabella may be right!' twittered Miz' Elizabeth, turning to her sister. 'The dear child is giving us a lesson. In her own way, of course. A lesson in loyalty, Anne. Do the Cases ever question their guests? . . . Do the Cases ever deny their protection —to anyone?'

'Even when they come over the garden wall?' inquired Wordsworth.

'Even when they come over the garden wall,' said Miz' Elizabeth gravely. 'Over the wall? . . . Certainly.'

Miz' Anne nodded her agreement to this statement of policy.

'Would dear Papa have hesitated for a minute . . . ?'

Miz' Anne shook her head decidedly. She was convinced that dear Papa would not have hesitated.

'I think, however, we may perhaps ask the young gentleman where he resides, sister? There is no breach of hospitality there?' she said in a slightly lower twitter than usual—in the sleepy tattling of birds at nightfall.

Miz' Elizabeth agreed.

She repeated the question a little louder, as if to show her realization that their guest's good manners would not permit him to reply to any remark not immediately addressed to him.

'I live at Kensington Park Place,' said Christopher. 'The house with the funny sort of tower. I live with my uncle—at least I call him my uncle!'

Both little old ladies looked at one another in a most knowing way, and their little old heads nodded like the heads of nodding china figures. Then they both looked simultaneously and triumphantly over their shoulders up at their gaunt aide-de-camp—a feat of some difficulty owing to the width of their yellow chip hats.

'Viscount Setoun, my dear!' said Miz' Anne.

'The mysterious, ro-man-tic Viscount!' said Miz' Elizabeth in a new ecstasy.

Miz' Anne rose and seated herself before a davenport.

'A note had better be sent to his Lordship at once. Explaining the facts of the case. . . . Aaron had better take it himself. . . . Mr. Christopher'—she paused with a large quill poised in the air—'I suppose "The Right Honourable the Viscount Setoun" is sufficient address? Or should I put anything more—any further titles?'

'He's a prince,' said Christopher doubtfully. 'He's a prince of the Roman Empire, and a count and a baron as well. . . . But I think they only put that on pictures—or tombstones.'

Miz' Anne was still debating with Miz' Elizabeth whether titles used on tombstones should be employed in the superscription of letters, when the door at which Aaron stood on guard was suddenly opened by a negro footman in a green velvet coat resplendent with gold lace.

'De Cap'n Heywood, ma-a-am!' said he at large to the room, bowing his powdered woolly head very low. His great hands encased in white cotton gloves were clapped tight to the sides of his scarlet breeches.

Pale, correct, as if he had stepped newly from the arcana of his dressing-room, Heywood bowed his way in.

'I must apologize for this intrusion, ladies,' he said, bowing again, and more specifically to the romantic Miz' Elizabeth. 'The intrusion of my ward'—and the cold eyes flickered toward Christopher and away again—'must serve as the excuse for my own.'

Miz' Anne and Miz' Elizabeth rose. They both sketched little bobbing curtsies.

'Captain Heywood?' inquired Miz' Anne. 'But I understood that Viscount Setoun was this young gentleman's guardian?'

'A very involved family quarrel, about which I hardly like to speak,' said Heywood easily. 'Especially before these young people. I can assure you that I am the authorized representative of this boy's relatives. . . . Of ve-ery important personages.'

'Personages?' said Miz' Elizabeth, greatly impressed. 'Viscounts —captains—wards—per-son-ages!' said she in a whisper full of exclamation marks, to the grenadier. 'How romantical!'

But Miz' Anne had taken an instinctive dislike to Heywood. He was too assured, too pale, too mysterious for her: she objected to the casual air with which he twirled the seals at his fob. It gave her the fidgets to watch him: no gentleman should cause a lady to suffer from the fidgets.

'I should have nothing to say, sir,' said she, 'but for the fact that the young gentleman gave me to understand that he was living with Viscount Setoun. I take it that that is a fact?'

'Lord Setoun—as he chooses to call himself—took advantage of some very unusual circumstances to abduct him,' replied Heywood.

'In that case would it not be better, sir, if you dealt with his Lordship direct? . . . You will admit the position is one of difficulty for us. My sister and I have to deal with facts as we find them. And those facts are, Captain Heywood, that this child is at present under the guardianship of Lord Setoun. You have admitted that yourself. If we return the boy to his Lordship, then my sister and I have cleared ourselves of our responsibility. And you can deal with his Lordship!'

'I must protest, madam. You fail to understand that this child is under very high—ve-ery high protection. That I am the agent of that protection. That he has been abducted!'

Miz' Anne sketched another small curtsy.

'We—I speak for my sister and myself'—and here Miz' Elizabeth, who had been taking everything in from her post on the settee with the uttermost excitement, nodded in an emphatic manner, 'we wonder, sir, in such case why this mysterious personage you speak of has not taken legal steps to force his Lordship to surrender this young gentleman.'

Heywood thrust his thumbs into his vest pockets. The slightest of flushes rose to his pale full face. He raised his sallow eyelids and stared at Miz' Anne with large dark eyes full of cold insolence. He made her no reply. Without even turning his head he said in his even tones:

'Christopher, come to me!'

Christopher stood frozen on the rug, staring at the short shapely figure, at the smoothly coated shoulders that stooped a little because of the out-thrust head. He was incapable of speech or movement, like a rabbit mesmerized by a snake, and unaware, therefore, of the little becks and nods and gesticulations that set Miz' Elizabeth all of a flutter like a small doll in a high wind.

But Arabella had taken them in. She loosed her clasp about his neck, seized his hand in hers once more.

'Come on!' she whispered against his ear.

'Christopher . . .' began Captain Heywood again, and turned at the clatter of small feet across the polished floor.

He started, as if with thought of pursuit. One hand flew to the black silk cord about his neck, as though to whistle up his henchman. He became immobile: his hand dropped to his side.

'I regret, madam,' he said with a thin smile, 'that you should not see your way to oblige the high personage I represent—or me. . . . I can assure you that you have shown no wisdom in your action. You will have very serious cause to regret it.'

Miz' Elizabeth had received her cue. She rose to her feet, dropping the gardening basket she had clutched throughout the interview. She pulled the long crimson bell-cord hanging against the cedar-panelled wall.

'Do you threaten us in our own house, Captain Heywood?'
What echoes of romance tinkled in her old voice! 'We spurn your
menaces, sir! We . . .' but no further repudiation came to mind.
'. . . We—we'—and then, oh! triumph—'We . . . h'm . . . with
contumely! . . . With contumely!'

'You also . . . h'm . . . with scorn, madam, I suppose? Shall I
add derision, madam?' said Heywood sarcastically.

In this shattering moment Miz' Anne came to the rescue of her
sister.

'A fact that may interest your master! . . . We are no serfs of a
tyrannical aristocracy, sir! We are citizens of the United States of
America. We are the Misses Case of Case, Alabama! Your threats
shall be placed before our Minister. . . .'

'Isaac,' said Miz' Elizabeth, getting the last blow in, 'Isaac, the
door!'

And pointed to the portal in as histrionic a manner as a Dresden
china figure could be expected to do. . . .

Over the door was a musicians' gallery with a bulging balustrade.
Two shoeless figures lay upon its dusty floor watching the drama
below. Arabella craned forward making odd small noises! Her
closed lips were pouted out; her cheeks hollowed.

Captain Heywood crossed the floor to the door held open wide
by the cotton-gloved hand of Isaac.

'Isaac,' said Miz' Anne, 'if this . . . this person should call again,
we do not receive him!'

Heywood turned to bow ironically.

At that moment Arabella leaned more forward: her rosy lips
parted; she let fall unseen the large store of spittle she had collected, in one great juicy balloon.

It landed in a bubbling gob upon Captain Heywood's shoulder,
unknown to him but marked by the negro lackey. It trickled down
the immaculate back like snail-lime.

Heywood turned to go out, to see the rolling astonished eyes of
the manservant fixed on him, and to see the black face broaden
in one enormous grin—hidden but badly by a huge hand in a
white cotton glove. He heard the swift catch of breath that stopped
the outburst of a peal of high laughter.

He almost halted. He reddened. It was a crowning insult to be laughed at by a black slave. He passed into the hall aware of broad grins and a frantic dumb-show passing between the lackey and the fat butler who awaited him. Beneath his set face he seethed with fury.

'Oh!' whispered Christopher, horrified and delighted at the same time. 'What *will* he say?'

'Don't care!' said Arabella, rolling from side to side in a paroxysm of suppressed mirth.

He looked at her with respectful homage. She had spat on Captain Heywood—on his lovely black coat. She had hit the mark although she was a girl—perhaps American girls were better than English at that sort of thing!—and the great blob of spit had fallen straight on to him, with a long wet tail that had spread when it hit.

'Oh, Arabella,' he said again, 'you—are—wonderful!'

'Aren't I!' said Arabella.

Chapter 15

Arabella Continues to Be Wonderful

THE LONG YEARS PASSED. THEY SAID THAT TROUSERS would become still wider at the hips, and dresses yet wider at the shoulders; that laudanum-sodden George suffered from a form of agoraphobia and lay abed all day in a greasy nightcap at Windsor. They said that stays would soon be coming back; and that dark Cumberland was always whispering at his kingly brother's elbow, was spinning webs of strange conspiracy; had turned his command of the Household troops to sinister purpose. They said that muslin *à la giraffe* would be all the rage; and that rioting in town and country was spreading, and that Wellington had given solemn warning to Parliament of 'the unutterable horrors of civil war'.

The long years passed; but the wonder of Arabella remained unchanged. She ruled Christopher; she ruled her great-aunts; she ruled their household with a rod of iron: even Setoun bent to the arrogance of her will.

He had come post-haste to Alabama Lodge in reply to the urgent note on that exciting day.

'Well, young lady,' he said after he had heard the tale. 'So Tops owes a lot to you!'

'Yes,' said Arabella with no pretence at modesty. 'I helped him over the wall. We fell into the cucumber frame. And then I spat on Captain Heywood!'

The old ladies fluttered at the impropriety of which they had not heard, and the grenadier repeated the word 'spat!' three or four times in a crescendo of horror.

Setoun, however, politely disregarded the question of correcti-

264

tude. He asked for details and was given them. He measured the distance from the gallery to the floor with his eye.

'Six-foot drop!' he commented. 'Wonder you did not miss!'

· 'I should have spat again if I had,' said Arabella decidedly.

'My dear,' said Miz' Elizabeth, 'I really think the subject should be changed. His Lordship will think that we Americans are quite barbarian!'

'It is a gesture, ma'am, that many English ladies would often like to imitate. . . . There are some men who want . . . er . . . spitting on!'

Arabella tossed her head. Her wide grey-green eyes lit with an unholy fire. They were—thought Setoun, smiling at her—the eyes of a mermaid; the green of shallow sea-water.

'I could have hit him much farther off than that!' she said, and turned to leave her elders to debate the propriety or impropriety of her act, if they pleased. She knew what she would do, regardless of their decision. She took Christopher by the hand.

'Come and see the puppies!' she said in a tone of command, and dragged him away.

'A strange child,' reflected Miz' Anne. 'But then her father— our nephew—was a strange man, too. He disliked watermelons and gentlemen from the Northern States. The sight of either, he declared, put him in a perfect pet. He said you could smell a gentleman from New York a mile away. . . . I never noticed it, myself. It may have been a fact, all the same.'

'Like Christopher,' said Setoun towering down from the hearthrug on the two old ladies, 'perhaps she does not meet enough children of her own age.'

'She does not like young females,' said Miz' Anne. 'I fear that she is too rough for them. She calls them—milksops, I think. Her father was a little violent, too, I am afraid. . . . A very great duellist, poor fellow! He thought no more about calling another gentleman out than I should of . . . of . . . cracking an egg."

She shook her head in regret not untinged with pride.

'Such a romantic, chivalrous fellow! A little wild, perhaps, but a perfect paladin!' agreed Miz' Elizabeth. 'Always coming home with his arm in a sling. Or on a hurdle. Or with his head bandaged up. He broke his neck hunting a runaway slave. Always so rash. A great loss!'

And both little old ladies shook their heads so that the wide black ribbons of their hats, which they had undone, swung in a perfect paroxysm of grief.

'Christopher must be much like Miss Arabella in some ways, ladies,' Setoun remarked. 'For he doesn't care for boys of his own age. Can't be bothered with them! Spends all his spare time in grown-up company. Bad for him—very. But pleasant for me!'

Miz' Elizabeth looked up with admiration at him. A perfect figure of a great nobleman—she thought—with his arrogant nose and his kindly eyes, and his grizzled hair, and his leather face with the high red cheek-bones. Already she had told herself a tale of romance-to-be that ended in wedding-bells. She nerved herself to speak:

'Arabella appears to have taken a great fancy to your little boy— that is to say your ward—I mean your nephew. And so, I think —don't you?—it would be very pleasant if they could meet sometimes?'

'Very pleasant indeed,' said Setoun. 'Much appreciate the suggestion!'

'So pleasant after this contretemps,' continued Miz' Elizabeth greatly stimulated. 'After all this cucumber-frame breaking, so romantical, I think. Say, once a week! He shall be very well guarded, shall he not be, Anne? There are five men in the house. We could give them muskets—or cutlasses, if you prefer—when he came. They could do regular sentry-go, don't you know. Up and down before the house, and look under the bushes and in the cellars. Like the Beefeaters at your Parliament.'

But the precautions were not required, for the man who called himself Captain Heywood never reappeared, except in the tangle of Christopher's nightmares. Sometimes at night for several years the boy would awake, crying out in an agony of fear; and in the next instant Setoun would appear round the bedroom door, candle in hand, in a white flannel bedgown and nightcap with red tassel, ready to comfort and protect.

Otherwise there was no mention of the past. Even Deb had to be forgotten—because remembering her would have meant recalling everything: but he was conscious of a feeling of guilt when he pressed back the recollection of that heart-shaped face into the limbo of the hateful past. His adventures had become evil dreams—the evil dreams of a young gentleman who had lived in the security of Kensington Park Place ever since he could remember. A young gentleman who grew in time to look on Alabama Lodge as yet another home—to grin in reply to grinning negro lackeys and women servants with their heads tied up in coloured kerchiefs; to win smiles, even, from the grenadier.

He would walk round in the evening sometimes, and play spillikins or dominoes with Arabella in the drawing-room that smelt of spices and rose-leaves and strange woods. And they would drink tea with mint leaves in it quite late at night, and eat thin slices of currant loaf with sugar icing that had powdered cinnamon spread over the butter; and argue whether the Americans had really beaten the British in the late war, or not.

Sometimes he would pay his visit in the afternoon and play in the garden—at first Red Indians and pirates, or other games in which Arabella was infinitely the rougher of the pair. Then they would dine with much ceremony on curious dishes with still more curious names—like 'gumbo' and 'chowder', or 'candied yams' and 'pecan pie'—in a room full of cabinets of old china; and afterwards cross to the drawing-room and tea through a hall lighted by candles set in tall and narrow-waisted jars of glass.

Setoun would often come and advise the old ladies on their affairs, and sample the odd drinks and odd conserves that came to them by almost every ship from across the Atlantic. He would send his carriage round to inquire how they did and when they would be sufficiently recovered to receive after the fatigues of any journey—even if it were only the twenty-eight-mile expedition they made once or twice a year to an old friend beyond High Wycombe.

Lady Jane called in state on the Misses Case, and the Misses Case returned the visit. So sometimes Arabella was fetched with much pomp and taken to the pantomime, or to a 'hippodramatic composition' at Astley's, or to see Mr. Edmund Kean as King Lear, or Charles Kemble in *Falconbridge*.

One summer they made a joint expedition to Brighton, and the children bathed from discreetly hooded bathing-machines, under the charge of old Betsy, the bathing woman, whose mother had been patronized by all the bucks of forty years before.

Another time they had gone, with the Lord-knows-how-many carriages, all the way to Sir John Wake's house in Shropshire. Setoun and the old man had smoked innumerable cigars—in the glasshouses, in deference to the visitors—and fished and shot: the old ladies had sat under a shady cedar most of the day and gossiped to the tinkle of tea-cups—at least the Misses Case had tattled, and the Lady Jane had listened, or appeared to: and the children had looked for birds' nests in ivied walls, waited for squirrels to scamper from trunk to trunk, urged on fat spaniels in hopeless chase of baby rabbits, and plundered strawberries and raspberries from the walled kitchen garden.

At least the children were thus innocently occupied if Arabella could find no more sensational amusement.

It was at Wake House that she made her first acquaintance with a water-closet—even at that late date a considerable rarity. She locked herself and Christopher in one afternoon, with a jar of tadpoles, newts, and small fish. After one or two experiments in which the luckless aquarium most annoyingly disappeared every time a fresh waterfall broke over it, she stuffed the trap with underwear. So they had a fascinating—if damp—time until the contraption overflowed and seeped through the floor into the silver pantry, where the butler was dozing over his afternoon glass of port.

The affair, accordingly, ended in a supperless confinement to their bedrooms—although Setoun was gravely concerned at a possible injustice to Christopher.

Arabella, too, invented a pastime which brought Angus, the Scotch head gardener, to the brink of apoplexy. It consisted of exchanging the terra-cotta labels that were stabbed into the turf before the various rare trees. When Angus discovered the label announcing 'Cryptomeria Japonica 4 ft. 1751' had been replaced by 'Cupressus Lawsonia 3 ft. 1751', he so far forgot himself as to chase the pair into the orchard, where Arabella unwisely pelted him with apples.

Setoun, again, had grave doubts as to the equal guilt of the two

parties, though he imposed an impartial sentence of two days'
bread and water.

Sometimes when Setoun had gone abroad Christopher stayed
at Alabama Lodge. He did not stay at Stornoway House, for Charlotte was never there.

In the tall panelled rooms of the palace in Cleveland Row,
Dunscore rioted as he liked. Trim little ladies from the Italian
Opera ran quickly up the steps, and later showed themselves with
the most tremendous bucks at the windows, while music and
babble and the popping of champagne corks echoed out into the
silence of Green Park.

Charlotte never said much about her married life to Setoun,
except one night when Christopher was not there and she remained at the dinner table with him.

'You know, Hurbles,' said she, tilting her half-empty wine-glass
at a perilous angle. 'You know my wedding was . . . only form . . . !'
She paused, but Setoun's gaze was fixed upon the pattern of the
damask tablecloth. 'It was . . . a candlestick each . . . even on our
wedding night. . . . George goes his way—and an unpleasant way
it is!—and I go mine. Marriage very much à la mode, you know.'

'H'm,' commented Setoun, meaning anything she liked to think,
and held his wine-glass up to the light as if all his interest were
caught in its ruby glow.

'I said I'd marry him. I said nothing more,' said Charlotte. 'I
did exactly what I said, and not an iota more.'

There was silence. And then . . .

'Christopher and I,' said Setoun, 'have been working out the
possibility of a voyage by air balloon across the Atlantic—following the Trade Winds, you know.'

She ignored his crude effort at divergence.

'I was a fool, I suppose . . .' and was angrily conscious of a tear
trickling down her cheek. 'He asked me to marry him a dozen
times. Then the Queen's business looked so desperate, and I knew
his clan would vote with him if he pressed it . . . and so . . . and
so. . . .

'It was a hateful night, and the Queen was quite mad. After the
wedding she danced in a pink dress that began, or ended, practically at the waist. He egged her on! I almost hated her that

night. I loathed *him*. I wanted to bolt. . . . I didn't know where you were . . . or I should have run away to . . . to you.'

Her voice broke, and the tears blinded her eyes.

'I'm sorry, Hurbles,' she stammered, shaking her head in anger at her weakness, and then laughed shakily.

'See, Hurbles, I've splashed tear-drops in my wine!'

He rose and came beside her chair and patted her, as one might caress a child. His big hand took her glass and held it up.

'Tears and wine, Carlotta! . . . Bitter and sweet! . . . We'll make of it a loving-cup, between you and me!'

He raised the glass to his lips and drained it to the dregs.

So Charlotte was here, there, and everywhere: they would hear from her in Paris, in Scotland, in Vienna, at Bath, in Sicily. Then suddenly and without warning her great berline would be at the door, and she would appear smiling amid baggage in the hall, to stay a day, a week, or a month.

'They're growing up,' said she once regretfully, on her arrival at Kensington Park Place, as she watched from the drawing-room windows the two children walk demurely across the lawn.

Arabella was talking eagerly: Christopher shook his yellow head in dissent.

Arabella pressed her point; she seized the spotted scarf tied loosely about his wide shirt collar: Christopher still shook his head, and laughingly retied his neckwear.

Arabella stamped her foot, as if she would shake off the lace-fringed pantaloons that matched her sprigged muslin frock and clung about her ankles: she insisted with a nodding that set her tawny curls a-tossing: she put out a long golden arm and seized Christopher's yellow locks and pulled till he cried for mercy.

'Not so much growing up about that!' said Setoun laughing.

Charlotte looked at him with a motherly eye.

'I don't mind betting that Arabella and Christopher will be grown-up and grand-parents long before my little Hurbles, bless him.'

He stooped to rescue one of Lady Jane's clove oranges as it rolled across the floor, and was so saved the need for reply.

'Seriously,' commented Charlotte, with half an eye to Setoun and half to the comedy without doors, 'you'll have to send him to Oxford or Cambridge pretty soon. And in a year the girl will be mincing about with dressed hair and stays and puffed sleeves!'

'Oxford—Cambridge! Good God, Carlotta! Never!' He was horrified.

"You're very violent about it,' she remarked.

'The universities are loathsome hot-houses. Propagating young slugs—badly dressed, no manners, coarse, smelly, ignorant, undisciplined. Hate 'em. Turn 'em out prigs or parasites.'

'You will have to do something about him, all the same!'

'Thought—when he was nineteen, say—to send him abroad. Give him four years as a cadet or volunteer in the army of one of the German states. Say Saxony. Quiet life in small towns. Much more discipline than at a university. None of the officers will have much money. He won't learn riotously extravagant ways. Not that he would, I think. Von Reichberg would look after him. First-class soldier and a great friend of mine. Will be excellent training for Tops. Shan't like parting with him. Severn has given him a good grounding in history and the classics. I have taught him common sense. . . .'

'Common sense!' interjected Charlotte sotto voce, with a world of scorn.

'What he'll want as a finish will be a spot of army discipline and knowledge of men. Nothing like army life for education. . . . Hate colleges! . . . Then I thought we'd make the Grand Tour together—he and I. Fun for me, seeing the world through young eyes!'

'Heaven protect a pair of innocents let loose,' said Charlotte. 'I had better come, too, to look after you! God knows what mischief you'll be up to otherwise!'

Arabella had had her way. The pair were retracing their steps across the lawn to a summer-house beside the pond which was Christopher's special sanctum. She had linked her arm with his and danced gaily across the grass.

'And the girl?' asked Charlotte, laughing.

'Goes this spring to a finishing school. To Severn's sister, in fact. They say she polishes the young female to a nicety.'

'She's a puss now,' said Charlotte. 'When she's a well-trained female, she'll be a panther.' And with that enigmatical remark, left the subject.

There was, indeed, no doubt that they were growing up.

If Smith no longer hugged a small boy to her thin bosom, yet she would give sidelong looks at a tall lad, and sigh and find little bits of gossip to whisper in dark passages. And Vera-Lou, the dusky lady's maid at Alabama Lodge, tied with a great bow about her impertinent waist as if she were a little black doll, would ogle him with enormous eyes, and wriggle her slender hips as she passed.

But of this Christopher was unaware. Life went on in much the same way as before. He had special French and German tutors, but still sat for a few hours several times each week for instruction in history and classics with the board of directors—although it was now diminished to three or four members, and Fitzroy had never reappeared—under the chairmanship of Mr. Severn, who grew shabbier and more repressed and more anxious-eyed.

Christopher still had his dream life—the life that in some curious way seemed more real than the common round. He still could pass at will through the portal within his mind, and enter a realm of strange adventure and brilliant colour and fantastic happening. He could sit quite happily without a book, through a dull sermon, with a boring companion, and be transported far away—a world away—a planetary system away.

'I sometimes wonder, Hurbles,' said Charlotte abruptly, looking up from a book one winter night, 'when I see you and Tops sitting over the fire, silent, and apparently unoccupied, whether you are really there! . . . I sometimes think the you I know are not there, but gone somewhere out of my reach. And that you have just left bodies behind you that respond automatically to any social or physical requirement. I feel as if I were sitting with the husks.'

'Oh, Charlotte,' said Christopher for both, 'don't you sometimes let yourself dream—you know, just imagine things?'

'I've given it up,' said Charlotte rather bitterly.

A little later when the boy had gone to bed she turned on Setoun.

'I believe, Hurbles,' she declared, 'that you are bad for Tops. At his age no lad should spend his time in day-dreams. He's nearly seventeen! You just encourage him in fantasy. He ought to have friends of his own age, and hobbies. He has neither! He doesn't care for either!'

'No good forcing his tastes,' replied Setoun uncrossing his long legs. 'He has got hobbies, anyhow. There's a cherished collection of alphabets!'

'Alphabets?'

'He's dug up from God knows where no fewer than fifty-seven different alphabets from Hebrew to Cyrillic! And he writes! What, also God alone knows! Have a theory that it's poetry. Know the other day he was immersed in Ossian. Good stuff in that, fake or not! Better for him than *Sandford and Merton* or *Moral Tales*. Know too he's had a Keats phase. He left a sheet or two in imitation of *Endymion* about somewhere. Not bad either!'

'Poetry!' said Charlotte, with such a twitch of the lip, such a wrinkle of the nose that the word might have represented a bad smell. 'He ought to be out rampaging with his young friends and come home dirty, with his pockets full of all sorts of odds and ends. Ought to be a real boy!'

Setoun was up in arms at once.

'He's thoroughly manly! You know it, Carlotta! He'll ride anything, and go into any stall in the stable, what's more. . . . Don't think that by reason of the inbreeding of his birth he'd ever be a rumbustious lad. He's well-informed, too. We read all the news, and all the new books. We have debated Cobbett's *Unnatural Mother* . . .'

'My God!' interjected Charlotte.

'. . . and *Unjust Judges*. We go to the new plays. We sit over our port—half a glass!—discussing them all. We believe in Catholic Emancipation and the Reform Bill! We are more than a trifle Radical!'

'That's exactly it—treating him practically as if he were your contemporary! Making an old man of him at sixteen!'

' "Old man"!' said Setoun, much hurt, and shooting up in his chair and pulling his waistcoat down. ' "Old man"! That's a nasty hit below the belt!'

Carlotta relented.

'No, Hurbles darling! I don't mean a really old man, but just an *old* man. Not a doddery old man; not a toothless old man; but a young old man—a vigorous, bright old man! I don't mean old in years, but old in manners and little ways and modes of thought. Who'd be shocked at things we do and say nowadays—even though he's quite young enough to do them and say them himself.'

As Christopher grew older he was not conscious of any change in the texture of his dream life: of the warmer colours to it; of any transmutation of the secret surging of his blood into strange glamours; or that the wraithlike princesses passing through his fantasies—dreams within a dream—had now become the bright centre of their pattern. Even then, in that world on the other side of his mind, while spears were broken for them, and cities sacked and wide seas ventured on their behalf, they still remained aloof—fairy creatures for all their splendour, who would vanish at a touch, being infinitely desirable (why, he did not know) but eternally unattainable.

Arabella and he no longer tussled when they disagreed. He began to feel in her presence a certain restraint which she endeavoured to break down by saying the most outrageous things to him.

'You are slow!' she said once. But he never understood why.

It was at this time that the urge became overwhelming to put on paper the thoughts that filled his mind.

There was an epic which was begun in a slim album bound in red russia leather, and petered out after the first three hundred lines of blank verse had been completed. There was a hymn to the Blessed Virgin which resulted in the disappearance of many quires of Setoun's best paper. Then followed an Old English fragment in very antique language patterned after the alliterative poesy of Saxon bards. Most notable of all was a version of the fairy story of the 'Seven Dancing Princesses' in the style of *Hyperion* with an Ossianic flavour superimposed.

He spent a ravishing two days when convalescing from the measles in copying them all into the red russia-leather volume, and inscribing the front page of the volume with the words in careful Gothic:

THE COMPLETE WORKS
OF
CHRISTOPHER HARNISH
POETICAL AND MUSICAL
LONDON
1826.

While the book represented his complete literary output, he realized that the items themselves were usually far from complete and most of them had to be labelled—'A Fragment'; 'The Seven Princesses—A Fragment'; 'Iodor—A Fragment'. The musical section consisted of an air in a minor key which he had composed, one finger at a time, on the pianoforte in the big drawing-room to the old poem:

> King Jhesus hung upon the Cross
> 'And hast Thou sinned?' quod he . . .

It was a highly mournful tune which Christopher for at least two days had sung and hummed with much relish—particularly those staves where, by a masterly transposition to a major key, the lines of the refrain:

> 'Sedebis apud angelos
> Quia amavisti'

were made to trumpet the victory over hell.

Chapter 16

Arabella Becomes Too Wonderful

THERE WAS NO DOUBT THAT ARABELLA WAS GROWING up. Her frock developed a waistline; the hated pantaloons vanished; and tawny formal ringlets framed her golden face and sea-green eyes and hid her ears.

She underwent and disliked the finishing process in Miss Severn's Female Academy which was so carefully secluded from the male eye, so carefully walled off and locked away from lustful small boys, so carefully guarded by acidulous shepherdesses, and confined in propriety as in a pair of tight stays.

She aired her views to Christopher one spring evening, on the occasion of her fortnightly visit home. They paced the twilight garden together to the manifest disapproval of Miss Wordsworth, who popped a watchful head out from the various windows of the drawing-room in succession.

'I promised I'd stay two years, Tops,' she said swinging her bonnet by its strings. 'But I'm sorry I gave my word. It's beastly. The mistresses are like jailers. They creep about and listen at the doors. And the girls are young ladies! They are all as pale as things that crawl under the ivy. They have horrid little passions for one another. They can only talk about clothes, and how rich they are, and their beaux, and quarrel with one another, and make it up . . . like dolls. And say dirty little things to one another under their breath, and snigger. . . . Do boys do that, Tops?'

'I suppose so,' replied Christopher, a little embarrassed. 'They tell one another dirty jokes and things.' And added, not from self-righteousness, but as a statement of fact, 'I never listen.'

'They looked shocked to death when I said I like to lie on my

276

bed with no clothes on in the sun. . . . Dirty brats! . . . One of them said something to me last week,' continued Arabella. 'I didn't like it. So I slapped her face. Do you know she screamed like a pig and ran away and cried! Her eyes were like a white mouse's. . . . Augusta shut me up in a cupboard in the dark for punishment. . . . It took four of them to get me in,' she added proudly.

The agitated head of the grenadier attracted her attention. A hand beckoned.

'The woman's a pest,' said Arabella, and shepherded Christopher grimly into the drawing-room.

Her great-aunts, in lavender dresses, were seated by the window knitting by the last of the daylight.

The grenadier stood by the fire with a taper to light them a candle.

'What do you keep waggling your head and your finger at me for, Wordie?' demanded Arabella, halting on the threshold.

The grenadier advanced to the table between the Misses Case. She paused to gather up mutely in one look their support, and then gazed over her shoulder with mingled reproach and reproof, as she lighted the candle.

'Young ladies—and you are a young lady now, dear Arabella; is she not, Miss Anne, Miss Elizabeth?—do not walk in the garden with gentlemen. At twilight! Unchaperoned! . . . And nearly seventeen! . . . Of course, dear Mr. Christopher . . .'

'Why not?' asked Arabella in her most metallic voice.

'It's not—proper!' said the grenadier in the most explanatory way, and looked round for support—but received none—from the ladies in lavender, who never interfered with their great-niece if they could possibly help it, and were terribly busy stitch-counting or dealing with a difficult corner.

'Why not?' asked Arabella, the earnest investigator.

She waited for a reply in an embarrassed silence broken by the low murmur of Miz' Elizabeth, who endeavoured to fill in the awkward pause by continuing her stitch-counting to astronomical figures.

Arabella came a little farther into the room, followed by an abashed Christopher.

'I *will* walk in the garden whenever I like, with anybody I like,' she declared with a stamp of the foot. 'Even if it's pitch-dark. . . . What do you think we should do together in the dark?'

Miz' Elizabeth gave the smallest of squeaks.

'Do you think I should take all my clothes off . . . and . . . and . . . dance with him in the bushes?'

In this threatening tempest the Misses Case forsook their hench-woman. They bent their heads lower over their work; they knitted faster and counted faster than ever, Miz' Elizabeth's face brightly pink.

'You bad, wicked girl!' said the grenadier lighting another candle with a trembling hand. 'How can you talk like that?'

'I *shan't* take my clothes off,' said Arabella, 'but I should if I wanted to. Anyhow, Tops knows what I look like under my clothes.'

'But Arabella . . .' protested Christopher, anxious to clear him-self of any hint at indecorum.

'We are all naked under our clothes. I know what Tops looks like under his clothes. I know what you look like under your clothes, Wordie. So does Tops. Why should we pretend? What does it matter?'

For the first time in her life the grenadier blanched. She stood by the small table shattered at this revelation of her nudity.

Arabella, in a swift change of mood, leaped at her. She seized her by the arms and danced her by force in a ridiculous measure to the centre of the room.

'Look, Tops!' she cried. 'Wordie and I've got nothing on—nothing on—nothing on—and we're dancing with nothing on!'

She stopped by the alabaster figure of a Venus with robes slipping from her knees.

'See, Tops!' she said. 'You know I'm just like that! Just like that! You know it! . . . So's Wordie!'

Said Miz' Anne to Miz' Elizabeth in a very low voice, not daring to look up:

'Well, you know, sister, after all they are facts!'

This did not mean that Arabella was unconscious of the beau-ties and desirability of dress. On her visits home she came in time to discuss the vagaries of fashion with Christopher who knew nothing about it, or the grenadier who knew less: the vagaries of fashion, that is, as observed by the young ladies of Miss Severn's Female Academy.

Charlotte was herself called into consultation when the time arrived for the choice of the first evening dress. The *Miroir des Dames* had been studied, and the *Gazette de la Mode*, and the *Petit Courrier des Dames* and the *Belle Assemblée*. Every kind of material, flounce, pleat, tuck, fold, puff and band had been debated with the greatest seriousness for nearly three months. Then came Charlotte; listened, laughed, objected, tossed the *Maids', Wives' and Widows' Magazine* into a corner, whisked Arabella off to her own dressmaker and whisked herself off to Brighton.

The occasion was the mid-May evening party held by Miss Severn for her young ladies, their relations and respectable connections. It was a soirée distinguished by party manners, weak negus, sandwiches, trifle, romantic songs and firework pianoforte solos by the more accomplished young ladies, and a dance programme featuring quadrilles and stiff little waltzes. All under the benevolent patronage of Miss Augusta herself, with the assistance of the teaching staff, who continually counted noses to make certain that none of the young ladies had disappeared into dark passages or untenanted rooms with partners of the opposite sex.

A three-day mid-term holiday was always arranged, to give the young ladies the uttermost chance of preparing themselves for the function, and of recovering from the attendant fatigues.

This occurred just after Christopher's eighteenth birthday, when Setoun and he had gravely discussed together the problem of his future over their port, had evolved a dozen fantastical but very satisfying schemes, had diverged into a debate on the prevailing winds along the West Coast of Africa and the South Atlantic in their relation to aeronautical navigation, and had finally and utterly lost sight of their original objective.

Setoun had gone to visit an old friend in Rutland a few days afterwards, with the comfortable feeling that everything had been properly dealt with: that arrangements were, so to speak, in train.

Christopher stayed at Alabama Lodge. He was to escort the party to the wild dissipation.

He waited in the wide shining hall in all the new splendour

of high-collared coat, stiff cravat, shirt frill, and trousers marvel-
lously full at the hips and tight at the ankle. Aaron came to admire; Isaac came to admire; Samuel came to admire—large negro
faces split wide with smiling approval.

To him came Arabella, stepping delicately in a wide sea-green
dress from which her golden shoulders rose, her hair parted
smoothly and her face framed by long ringlets, against whose
dark gold there danced long emerald ear-rings.

It was a great shock to Christopher. This was a strange lady
who appeared before him with such self-assurance. He felt as if
someone that he knew was dead; as if he had been abandoned
and left a companionless child in an adult world. He wanted to
go away, to lock himself in his fairyland out of grim reality.

'Well?' asked Arabella, with lifted eyebrows, halting before him.
Her face was shadowed with disappointment at the lack of
ecstatic comment.

'You look very nice,' said Christopher, rather obviously recalled
to the business of approval. 'Oh!' said Arabella in a cold tone, and
'Really!' in a still colder voice.

Christopher rushed into a stammer of praise. It fortunately was
not too late. Arabella opened out like a flower to the sunshine of
admiration. She smiled. She turned round for him to admire the
back view. She tossed her head to show how the ringlets danced.

'And I've got stays on!' she declared. 'Feel them!'

She took his finger and assured him of the fact by prodding it
against the whalebone.

'They are the very newest, too! Made in two halves!'

She ran his finger up the front of her bodice, so that he should
feel the studs of the metal busks.

'They lace, of course, at the back,' she added, and threw him
then her meed of approval.

'You really look splendid. Oh, Tops! What a collar! . . . And
the fob! . . . I love your hat. . . . Put it on!'

She clapped her hands and jumped with delight. 'Fobs and
stays! . . . We're really grown up! I feel so old, Tops! Do you?'

The function was a great success. The weak negus went like
magic: the young ladies forgot neither the words of their songs
nor the twiddly bits of their pianoforte solos: the old ladies and

gentlemen gossiped and admired and were condescended to by Miss Augusta; and the young gentlemen clustered around Christopher and pressed for presentation to Miss Arabella. Mostly, however, Christopher himself partnered her in stiff decorous dances—under the approving eyes of the Misses Case who sat on little gold rout seats and twittered together like a pair of starlings; under the beady eyes of the dancing mistress, who by-and-by stole up to the head of the establishment and whispered and shook her head.

Miss Severn sailed over to them as the violins came to a halt. She smiled as nearly as her sallow forbidding face would permit. 'I think Miss Case is flushed,' she said. 'Too flushed! She had better rest for a little. Will you please conduct her to her great-aunts, Mr. Harnish. Then, if you will come back to me, I will present you to one or two other young ladies!'

A mutinous Arabella was accordingly taken back to her great-aunts; and Christopher was presented to a very young lady with a wide blue sash who said nothing; and, after that, to a fat young lady in pink with split gloves who whispered small talk about the teaching staff all the time that they danced.

Later on Miss Severn was to see that the two gold heads—dark and fair—had come together again amid the throng of dancers, and her narrow lips compressed themselves tightly.

'The old beast!' said Arabella fiercely as they drove home together facing the Misses Case in their old-fashioned carriage. 'She treats me as if I was a child. I shall be eighteen in six weeks, and thank God that'll be the end of her!'

'Sssh!' said Miz' Elizabeth.

'But I do thank God,' declared Arabella. 'And if I thank God, why shouldn't I say so?'

Miz' Elizabeth was a little doubtful about the range of what it was respectable to thank God for; so she held her peace, especially as Anne appeared to agree to the premise.

'I thank God when I say grace at the end of a meal,' continued Arabella logically. 'So why shouldn't I thank God for the end of old Fish-Eyes!'

'Fish-Eyes?' murmured Miz' Anne.

'Well, that's what we do call her. It's a fact—one of your facts,

Aunt Anne. Some of us call her the Snake because she creeps about and hisses! One of the girls called her the Virgin Viper last term. She got to hear about it!'

'Whatever happened?' asked Christopher.

'Two of the governesses held her over a desk, and Fish-Eyes beat her with a birch—before all the school. . . . She was as old as me!'

'But, Arabella . . .' protested Miz' Elizabeth.

'It's true,' she declared. 'They took her clothes off and put her in a sort of long blouse—and beat her. . . . I should have killed them first. . . . Fish-Eyes liked doing it! All the servants were there. *She* never minds what she says or does in front of them—while we . . .' She ended the sentence with a shrug.

The carriage rolled into the drive.

'Ough! My stays hurt! My inside's all squeezed up. Can I thank God for letting me take them off, Great-Aunt?'

She skipped out of the carriage and pirouetted into the shadowy hall with candle-light reflections on its cedar panels.

'It was great fun all the same, Tops. . . . You dance quite well' —condescendingly—'it's much nicer dancing with a man than Miss Walrond . . . her breath smells. . . .'

Christopher had forgotten his earlier reactions. He took her hand as she dropped him a deep curtsy, and bowed over it in his best dancing-class manner.

'You looked far the nicest, Arabella—honestly,' he said. 'I liked dancing with you so much best.'

'Oh, Tops!' she cried springing up. 'Do you really mean it? Nicer than Miss Campbell? . . . Isn't her brother a pet?'

She clapped her hands and, suddenly bending forward on tiptoe, kissed him on the lips.

'There!'

Christopher had half drawn back before the fleeting pressure of the soft lips. He blushed furiously.

'Great-Aunt Anne! Great-Aunt Elizabeth!' cried Arabella in high fettle. 'I've kissed Tops—and he blushed!'

Miz' Anne was unshaken, as a woman who knew the facts of life: Miz' Elizabeth's china-blue eyes sparkled from the reflection of romance: the grenadier shook her head in foreboding: Arabella ran up to bed triumphant. . . .

Christopher retired to the room that had come by convention to be called his. He took off his very beautiful coat, and put on a silk dressing-gown that Setoun had brought him from Lyons. He soused himself down in the comfortable chair at his bedside, and meditated profoundly.

In just one day everything had been altered. He hadn't changed, of course. It was Arabella; who wasn't Arabella any longer, but was a disturbing and puzzling somebody else. In some ways she was like Charlotte; but then, there was no out-of-the-ordinary sensation in being kissed by Charlotte. While Charlotte, too, somehow came into one's dreams, you couldn't have Arabella in them when only a year ago she pulled your hair, and but a short time before you were tumbling like puppies together on the lawn.

He sighed at the problem, and became aware of a gentle scratching on the door-panels.

He walked across the room, opened the door and looked out into the lofty gallery chequered with moonlight and dense shadows. No one was there; he paused irresolutely, and then heard a voice that, raised no higher than a sigh, whispered 'Tops!'

On his right the gallery bent sharply into darkness, and then bent back again to end past Arabella's door. He crept to the corner and looked round. The curtains before the great bay window that faced the door were partly closed. A moonbeam slanting through the narrow gap gave radiance to the dull gold of one of the two squat Eastern gods that sat on scarlet lacquer chests on either side the portal.

No one seemed there. He drew his thin gown about him and hesitated.

'Tops!' said the voice, and the farther of the long curtains before the alcove quivered.

He tiptoed down and peeped between the folds. Arabella was there, in white, sitting on her heels upon a wide ottoman, and looking sideways over her shoulder into the moonlit garden.

'Look!' said Arabella in a whisper. 'Pull the curtains to, behind you!'

He knelt on the seat, and followed her pointing finger. A spreading cedar stood in the middle of the tree-shielded lawn which was black and silver under the moon. In the depths of its shadows something played, scampered into the borderline of dark and light, whisked into the moonshine for the blink of an eyelash, and flickered back again.

'What's that?' whispered Arabella.

'I think it's the black kitten,' he whispered back prosaically.

'It might be a little goblin or elf!' said she almost reproachfully, as if she would chide him for lack of romance.

So they remained for some time looking out at moonlight and black kitten and dim shadows, until Christopher moved uneasily as if he were about to take flight. He was conscious that Arabella's regard had shifted to himself.

'Don't look so stiff and uncomfortable, Tops,' she said. 'Why don't you sit like I'm doing? . . . Don't you *like* looking at the moonlight with me?'

She put her hand on to his shoulder, and he sank obediently on to his heels.

'Don't you like looking at the moonlight with me?' she repeated.

'Somebody may hear!' he protested, casting a glance behind him at the heavy folds of velvet.

'Silly!' she said. 'Of course they can't. Why shouldn't we sit in the moonlight and talk? Unless you don't want to.'

'Of course I do!' although oppressed by some dim consciousness of wrong.

'You don't look like it!'

He protested again.

'You've changed—in some way, Tops. You know you have. We haven't done things like we used to. . . . We don't . . .'

How untrue it was! It was not he who had changed. It was she who had become like Charlotte, and disturbingly unlike her.

'And then you didn't like me kissing you this evening. . . . I wonder why!'

'I did,' said Christopher.

'You didn't!'

'I did. I did,' he urged.

There was the slightest of pauses.

'Then you kiss me this time.'

He had been staring in confused fashion into the garden. At this he looked quickly at her to find her eyes on his, and on her lips a smile the purport of which he could not read. Once more he was angrily conscious of the colour that flooded to his face.

'You are blushing again!' said Arabella; and there was a hint of mockery in the low gurgle of her laughter. 'You daren't! You daren't!'

'I do!'

'You don't!'

'For two pins I would!' declared Christopher with a stammer. 'Owe you two pins!'

He leaned over, desperately wrought to the adventure; but she would not advance her face to his, and he was forced to rest a hand upon the window ledge to keep his balance. So supported he put his lips blindly to her cheek and withdrew, a deeper crimson than ever. He was very unhappy.

Said Arabella a trifle curtly:

'It doesn't seem to me that you enjoyed it. . . . In books they always do!'

'I *did*,' asseverated Christopher.

'Do you mean it, really?" she whispered in a kinder tone.

'Of course I do.'

Then she said an astounding thing, without preface.

'You don't do it . . . very well.'

' "Don't do it very well!" ' he echoed, stupefied—not from hurt vanity, but at her revelation as an expert in kisses.

'Well—not very exciting! . . . When young Mr. Campbell kissed me . . .'

'Campbell!' he repeated. Once again he looked into her wide eyes. There was a light in them that was beyond his comprehension. He stiffened, and averted his gaze.

'When Mr. Campbell kissed me—it was terribly thrilling. I pretended I didn't like it, of course, but . . .'

'Arabella!' he said in shocked tones. Naturally she was joking, but—'How can you?'

She moved along the ottoman closer to him as he sat back on

his heels staring out of the window. He wanted to get away, for he felt that a crisis accompanied her approach.

She came closer till she was actually at his side. The crisis was upon him.

'Tops,' she said in a very small voice. 'Supposing *I* like being kissed.'

'Well?' he asked cautiously, not turning.

'Just supposing I did. Is it very wrong? Look how Great-Aunt Elizabeth smiled when I kissed you. And Great-Aunt Anne! You are the only person who doesn't like it.'

'But I do!'

'No, you don't.'

He gave another sideways look. He was a little taller as they sat side by side with their feet under them; and in the pale moonshine he caught the curve of a golden cheek, and the curves of her bosom pressing out her gown and visible like faint silvery shadows within its thin veil. He suddenly became aware that her form was not hidden by her dress at all, but made mysterious by it; and that it was only mantled by it as a pool is mantled by a summer mist. He found a little pulse beating furiously in his temples. He could hardly speak when he said at length:

'I do!'

He had a mind to shake her as he often had, so that this strange spell should be dissipated. He reached out his arm to do it, grew frightened as it touched her farther shoulder, and let it fall—let it fall so that it rested nerveless against her side.

Arabella said nothing: she swayed closer to him. He felt cool fingers seize his hand and bring it round, until it was pressed so hardly against her body that he could feel the warm flesh through the fine texture of her gown, and the curve of her form as it was within the curve of his arm.

He shut his eyes. Panic and something else ran through his veins. She swayed a little closer yet, half-turning so that now he felt the pressure of her breast against him; and felt a sliding arm travel up slowly to his neck until it circled it, and the hand caressed his cheek and chin.

'Tops!' said Arabella. 'This . . . *is* . . . exciting! . . . I wonder when you'll have to shave . . . I don't think you shall—kiss me when you do. . . . It would be rough, I should think . . . like brick dust. . . . Tops, give me your other hand. . . ."

He found his hand under hers pressed to the roundness of a breast.

'Tops. . . . Now! . . . Now! . . . Kiss me!'

Her clasp tightened. She leaned to him so that her warmness was on him, so that her lips met his, so that her breath was as the breath he drew, and the fire within her was communicated to him and roared through his veins.

For a moment they remained so, held in that first wild kiss, forgetting, trembling, with eyes closed to the world and the moonlight and reason.

Just for a moment; and then he leaped from her arms, panic-stricken, shame-stricken. He was on the verge of some knowledge —some profound earthly knoweldge—some strange secret knowledge that would burn through his mind, and enter the portal of his dreams; and the dreams would blaze up in it like arras eaten by fire, and become ashes in a desolation. He was on the brink of some knowledge that part of him hungered for, and part of him shunned. Within his soul he felt the whole fabric of his inner world—its fair remote princesses, and its pageantry, and its spirit —quivering as if on the verge of dissolution at an enchantress's spell.

He tore himself away violently . . . and ran without a word to his room; and sat in his chair all night in chaos of the mind.

Chapter 17

Court-Martial by the Misses Case

M R. SEVERN HAD COUGHED HIS WAY ROUND TO THE kitchen. He sat huddled in the corner under the great chimney-breast, in the cheerful glow of roaring fire, red tiles and copper pans. Dressers full of crockery and racks of metal dish covers sparkled along the walls. His face was the colour of a dying bruise under the ruffled thatch of grey hair, and all the attention of his dark anxious eyes appeared to be concentrated on the thin hands he rubbed as if they would never be warm again.

'There, sir!' said Cook, who had temporarily evicted her assistants. 'Here's a bowl of hot broth that'll put 'eart into you, or my name's not Sarah Leadbetter. Now you eat it all up!'

She put into his hands a large bowl full to the brim with steaming soup, and on the fender by his feet a plate of toast cut into wedges convenient for dipping into the liquid.

'Where's Mary to-day?' asked Mr. Severn, thanking her and cupping his hands about the vessel's hot sides.

Sarah paused on a bustling journey from the fire.

'Mary'll be back in a minute, sir, I do hope and believe. She's got 'arf her silver to do. I can't think why Missus's kep' her. Very awkward this time of the morning!'

He sat, making no motion to eat his broth, listlessly gazing into the fire. She reproved him, hands on hips, and jolly red face puckered into a very mask of determination.

'I don't know wot you've got on your mind, sir,' said she. 'But care killed the cat: and it looks to me as if it would kill you, the way you're goin' on. Now you eat your broth up, there's a good soul!'

288

He took up the spoon, and obediently made pretences of eating.

'Don't you go a-worryin'!' said Cook. 'You'll be better after that soup. All real good stock!'

One of the doors flew open, and through it Mary bounced in; black ringlets, little apron and cap-ribands a-flutter with wrath.

'That old cat's given me my notice!' she exclaimed, before she saw the bowed figure by the hearth. Her bright face reddened; a dull flush crept up Mr. Severn's cadaverous cheeks.

'What in the world for?' said Cook.

'Good gracious, Mary,' said Mr. Severn, 'you don't mean it, really?' He looked from one kind woman to the other, still fumbling with his spoon. 'It won't be the same without you. It won't indeed!'

'What-h'ever for?' asked Cook a second time, arms akimbo, as if she were about to confront Miss Augusta personally with a demand for explanation.

'It's too bad,' said Mr. Severn timidly, giving up all pretence at eating, and feeling in a way responsible for his sister's action. 'I'm sure you can't have done anything very wrong. Shall I speak to Miss Severn for you?'

'What-h'ever for?' demanded Cook again. 'Bless the girl, can't you answer a straightforward question?'

'I suppose I shouldn't have done it,' said Mary.

'Done what?' screamed Cook in exasperation. 'Done what?'

'It's not what I mind going,' said Mary. 'Except for you and Cook, sir! There's as good fish in the sea as ever came out of it!'

'If you don't say what you been up to, my girl,' said Cook slowly, 'I'll smack you.'

Mary propped herself against the vast scrubbed kitchen table. She had somewhat of the air of a heroine who had been triumphant amid persecution.

'One of the young ladies stopped me in the passage. She asked me to give a note to Mr. Harnish. I'd got it right in my 'and, when Miss Augusta pounced out of a door, from nowhere-like. She snatched it away. She was in a taking—an old-fashioned taking! And no mistake!'

She was about to say more when the door opened, and Miss Severn herself appeared, an iron-grey woman in an iron-grey dress, with smooth iron-grey hair, and a face of iron with bitter lines from nose to mouth. From her waist hung a large bunch of keys and two pairs of scissors that tinkled in a subdued fashion with her movements. She looked like an angry abbess, with a rosary at her girdle.

She stood just within the doorway, with iron-grey mittened hands folded before her.

'So this is where you frequent, Mr. Severn!' she said. 'This, then, is the company you keep in your moments of leisure! . . . I have been looking for you in your class-room, as there is a very serious matter for discussion.'

He endeavoured to rise, encumbered with his enormous bowl of soup.

In one sweeping glance she gathered the story in their faces.

'Do not trouble to rise, Mr. Severn,' she said. 'Kitchen manners are good enough for the kitchen. . . . I see your friends here . . .'

'Yes, my *friends*,' he murmured in insistence, sinking back in the chair.

'. . . have informed you of the occurrence. A shocking, incredible, disgusting occurrence! Since one of them herself is implicated, and you have yourself chosen your company, we can deal with it here.'

'But, Miss Severn . . .' he protested.

She turned her cold furious eyes upon Mary.

'This wretched young woman playing the part of a pander, a procuress, was prepared to act the go-between for one of your low, filthy-minded youths and a foolish girl. To carry a note to him of the most sordid character, hinting at what infamy I dare not think! . . . Read this!'

She flung upon the floor a little billet that she had held crushed in her iron-grey hand.

Mary stooped to it, picked it up, smoothed its folds silently, and passed it to Severn.

With the bowl balanced uneasily between his knees he read it aloud to himself:

' "I hate you. I abominate you. Why did you go? I shall hate you more than ever if you don't tell me. Even then I shall lothe you. If you . . ." '

And there it finished at a rent in the edge made, doubtless, by the wresting hand.

'Cacoëthes scribendi! What a dangerous thing it is!' he murmured and turned the missive over. The words 'C. Harnish Esqre.' were written in pencil across the leaf, which was the title-page torn from a Book of Common Prayer.

'A letter to a youth written on a page of a sacred volume! I shudder to think what iniquity has culminated in this blasphemy.'

'If it had been a page of prayers, Miss Severn,' he apologized, 'I could not condone it. But I find little harm in secular writing on what is practically a fly-leaf, after it has been removed from the sacred book!'

'Tscha!' said Miss Severn, and pronounced it exactly as spelled. . . . 'I have dealt with this young woman, as she knows! I shall know how to deal, too, with my delinquent! . . . You will deal with this Harnish! You will flog him within an inch of his life! You will teach him he cannot creep in and corrupt the morals of a young ladies' seminary, like . . . like a freebooter! I insist!'

Mr. Severn, sitting shrunken in his chair, looked most unlikely to be capable of flogging anyone within an inch of his life. He was, perhaps, aware of this, for there was a faint smile on his face as he said:

'I really must ask you to let me deal with the matter in my own way, my dear sister.'

The public mention of their relationship always infuriated her, and she was about to make a bitter reply when a shadow darkened one of the windows. It was Christopher come to warn his tutor of the inquiry made for him.

'Come in, Harnish!' Severn called, and Christopher accordingly entered the kitchen, taking in the scene with some surprise.

'It is rather an awkward moment,' continued Severn looking from his pupil to his sister. 'For a certain offence, which we may consider later, Miss Severn is anxious that I should thrash you "within an inch of your life". The question of the offence apart, what is your view on the subject?'

'Thrash me!' stuttered Christopher in amazement. He cast an appealing look from one to the other, the wildest conjectures in his mind. 'Me?'

'You,' assented Mr. Severn.

Christopher halted to collect his thoughts.

'I say, sir, aren't you joking? Really? . . . Well, you don't mind me saying . . . but . . . I . . . I . . . er . . . don't think . . . it can be done.'

'I don't either, little Harnish,' said Mr. Severn, looking up whimsically at the tall lad. The faintest suggestion of an 'I-told-you-so' lay in the regard he then turned on his sister.

'Do I understand,' she said, dropping each word into the silence syllable by syllable, 'that you decline? That you propose to leave unpunished this young person who has undoubtedly violated the first principle of this establishment?'

Mr. Severn, his eyes fixed on the fire, the broth gently silting over the edge of his bowl on to his knees, nodded his grey head very slowly.

His sister's bony fingers were plucking at the iron-grey mittens: they wrenched a tear in an iron-grey palm.

'If you have so little tenderness for the reputation of my establishment, then . . .'

'Augusta,' he appealed, 'for heaven's sake be reasonable. Let us discuss this matter elsewhere. This is not a suitable place.'

'You chose it yourself,' she retorted, as he rose and set down the bowl upon the table. 'There is nothing to discuss!'

'Harnish,' he ordered, 'return to your class-room!'

'Stay!' said Miss Severn. Her lips, iron resting on iron, had compressed themselves until they had squeezed out an iron-coloured foam at the corners.

Christopher paused uncertainly, one hand on the door that led to the kitchen-yard.

'If that iniquitous boy goes unpunished,' said Miss Severn slowly, 'you realize that I can no longer expect you to remain a member of my household?'

Christopher saw the stooping figure flinch before the threat. He felt the humiliation of that old frightened man as if it were his own. He knew something of the circumstances of his tutor, and his dependence upon his sister, and realized the deadliness of her threat.

'Sir,' said Christopher, 'you may beat me if you want to. But I don't know what for.'

'Harnish,' said Mr. Severn, 'thank you very much. I will not do so—even with your permission.'

'I *should!*' urged Christopher.

Mr. Severn shook his head.

'I appreciate the offer all the same. . . . Augusta, consider for a moment! I implore you. This is a most unreasonable attitude. You cannot blame the recipient of a letter for that letter. Much less an intended recipient. Let us talk over the matter quietly upstairs.'

'I shall not condescend to argue,' said Miss Severn, barely moving her lips, her nostrils so white and so pinched that her uneven breath whistled through them. 'The tone of the missive shows how corrupting an influence has been at work. You have heard my last word.' She was gone on her soft-soled shoes, the keys and scissors jingling their faint complaint at her waist.

'Oh!' cried Mary, bursting into tears. 'It's all my fault! Where shall you go? What will you do, sir?'

'I must find a little room somewhere, and shall get on splendidly,' said Mr. Severn. 'Now, you mustn't cry, my dear. There's nothing to cry about. It's all, doubtless, for the best.'

He patted her arm reassuringly.

'It's all my fault,' repeated Mary in a voice broken by sobs. She sat down in one of the windsor chairs, threw her apron over her head, laid her head upon the table, and gave herself up to the luxury of violent crying.

Mr. Severn stood over her, his anxious face regarding her with much distress. He patted her arm with little anxious pats. He made little anxious noises.

'There! There!' he said. 'There! There!'

'She'll be all right,' said Cook. 'Don't you worry about *her!*'

'But where shall you go, sir?' asked Christopher, as he walked back to the board-room with the chairman.

'To be honest,' said Mr. Severn slowly, 'I haven't any idea. I shall be only able to afford very little. My pupils are falling off. When you go, at the end of the term, my—my resources will be small! Definitely small!'

He smiled deprecatingly, as though apologizing for bringing the hard facts of life to Christopher's attention.

Christopher wondered what the word 'resources' meant when applied to an elderly gentleman whose coat was green with age, whose shabby pantaloons were dappled with vestiges of Scotch broth. Mr. Severn shambled along at his side, his hands behind his back, his head poked forward.

'I shall devote myself to my new translation of Lucian's *Alethes Historia*,' said he. 'Franklin's version is notoriously unsatisfactory. Do you know, Harnish, that Rabelais, Swift, Cyrano de Bergerac, and Voltaire all drew on the *Historia*? A lively translation should appeal to the modern mind, I think. To come to earth, I imagine there should be money in it, shouldn't you, Harnish! . . . Money! "*Pecunia regimen est rerum omnium!*".'

'Resources!' thought Christopher—a substantial word to apply to an unwritten translation of the airy fancies of the late Mr. Lucian!

'There has been no complete translation,' said Mr. Severn thoughtfully. 'Franklin left much of value out. A clumsy fellow! A botcher! Not a scholar! Harnish, my dear fellow, I'm afraid we shall have to postpone the renewal of our studies while I find a little home—a *domus amica!*'

'Resources!' thought Christopher. He coughed.

'Very little!' said Mr. Severn, his mind still voyaging with Lucian to the Country of the Moon, and the Island of Cheese. 'My income—h'rmph—will not exceed, not exceed fifteen pounds a year. I shall have to be economical—at first!'

He discovered with mild surprise that Christopher was no longer with him.

Christopher was back at the kitchen door. The room appeared full of the flutter of cap-ribbons and shrill female voices saying: 'It's a shame, that it is!'

'Mary! Oh, Mary!' he said, poking his head round the door.

'Sir?' said Mary—once again a very triumphant though victimized Mary!—and came to the doorway.

He drew her without.

'What's going to happen to Mr. Severn?' he asked.

'She's sent down word that his things are to be put together at once—the old cat!' said Mary.

'But where's he going? He—he hasn't very much money, you know, Mary!'

The tears came to her eyes.

'I don't know, sir, that I don't. I wish I did. He's like a perfect babby.' She paused, and looked at him a little doubtfully. 'Mother . . .' and stopped.

Christopher drew from his pocket a red silk knitted purse. He drew the ring in the middle, and tilted into his hand the remainder of his quarter's allowance. There were three sovereigns.

'Mother,' said Mary paying no attention to the action, 'would take him in. But it is no place for a real gentleman. I daren't arst him.'

'Why?'

'Mother keeps a little public—very respectable, of course.' She brightened up. 'We've a lovely room he could have. Not what he's used to, but . . .'

'Nonsense!' said Christopher. 'He won't know where it is or why, and wouldn't mind if he did. If it is your mother, Mary, it must be very nice—very nice, indeed! You send his things there. Somebody's got to arrange things for him. And this money! It will help. And if more's wanted, I'll let you have it.'

'Lucian,' Mr. Severn was saying to the diminished board of directors, when Christopher returned, 'was one of the few authors in history who became really rich men. . . .'

After he had got home, Christopher sat in Setoun's empty study and meditated; and sat opposite Lady Jane at a long silent dinner and meditated; and sat opposite the old lady in the fading light of the drawing-room afterwards, while she pressed cloves into small oranges—and made herself very sticky doing it—and meditated.

Meditated on cause and effect. Arabella and he had kissed, looking out on a moonlit garden. So Mary had got dismissed. So Mr. Severn was cast out on those resources of his which were 'definitely small'. So a new edition of Lucian would be offered to the world: might become a classic! might be read in a century's time. All because Arabella and he had kissed two nights ago.

He wondered if the ripples set up by any action, however

small, went on and on through time for ever. He was not to know that if Baron Ompteda had not picked his nose in front of the landlady of the inn on the Carmarthen road, he would never have seen Charlotte again, never have met Arabella . . . and Victoria might never have reigned.

Sitting back in his chair, he watched Lady Jane's old crooked fingers tremble and strain as they pressed the cloves, like tin-tacks, through the golden rind; and succeed with much effort, and then quiver against the lawn handkerchief in which the fruit was held in endeavour to wipe off the minute particles of oil. As he watched he wondered whether she had withdrawn, but for such little movements, from the outer world into those inner galleries of the mind with their furious imaginings, and found it better so. Or whether she just remembered and fed on memories.

For one flash it came to him too, that all the nightmare weeks of that sinister journey with the goblin children of long ago had not pressed against the veil of his inner self as had the two min-utes—the three minutes, in the shadowed gallery with Arabella.

The tea-things tinkled at the door.

Lady Jane looked up. Her toothless jaws mumbled the un-known words. A faint, comprehending light came to her eye. She laid the mutilated orange carefully on a little saucer at her side.

The procession entered: this time, however, the butler was not empty-handed. He bore a salver, as the server at the altar carries an alms-dish.

'A letter, my lady! Very urgent!' he said.

Christopher, watching the shaking fingers fumble at the folds, was aware of the large form of Hughes bent ceremoniously before him, proffering the great silver platter.

'A letter, sir! Very urgent!' He dropped his voice. 'From Miss Case. Very urgent, so Aaron informed me, sir!'

Had Arabella said something? Otherwise he could not imagine why Miss Case should write to him so urgently.

He opened the missive, which was addressed very formally and correctly, 'Christopher Harnish, Esquire, etc. etc.' with the grim-mest forebodings.

'ALABAMA LODGE,
'Wednesday Night.

'Dear Christopher'—it ran in Miz' Anne's angular script—'I should not have troubled you if dear Lord Setoun had not been away. But such *terrible* things have happened that my sister and I both feel that we must have a gentleman's *Support and Advice*. We have known you *so long* that you are quite one of the family, and there is no one but you and dear Lord Setoun to whom we can look for help—or should want to. The matter is too *horrifying* to be committed to paper. My sister has written to dear Lady Jane asking if she can *possibly* come, too. It would be such a comfort to have her advice. She is always such a calm, good soul.

'Your distracted and sincere Friend,
'Anne Case.

'P.S. Would it be too inconvenient if we said at 10 o'clock in the forenoon to-morrow?

'A. C.'

Lady Jane, stirring her tea, snuffing up its delicate aroma, raised her head for a moment. The faintest of smiles set twitching the muscles of her sunken face. She moved her lips, and, supporting the tea-cup on a tremulous knee, produced her missive from the side of the chair and the folds of her shawl, and held it out with a shaking hand.

He read the letter. It was in much the same terms. As he handed it back the old lady lifted her eyes to him: somewhere far back in them he saw tiny lights as if her soul had peeped through the veil of her inner mind and laughed at the follies of humanity.

Her thin eyebrows twitched.

'I suppose we had better go!' she enunciated quite clearly, but with a faltering tongue as if it were unused to speech and were driven unwillingly to utterance.

They arrived at Alabama Lodge in time, and were conducted by a solemn Aaron to the drawing-room across the rosy cedar hall. The great saloon, shadowed by the colonnade without, was grey and cold. There was no fire upon the hearth. Across the long expanse of polished floor the Misses Case were sitting side by side upon a settee drawn before the closed doors of the conservatory. The grenadier stood behind them like a black sentinel.

They rose and fluttered toward the door, twittering, protesting, and apologizing as they came. The old lady submitted to their kisses, and Christopher gladly welcomed the guiltlessness implied in the fluttering embraces they gave him.

They led Lady Jane to a high wing chair set close to their settee. Christopher ranged himself beside her. A single empty chair faced them.

What outline of events Miz' Anne was about to present was never known, for barely had they settled themselves when steps sounded outside the door.

'Early!' observed Miz' Anne. 'Perhaps it is better. You will be able to judge for yourselves, dear Lady Jane, dear Christopher. Without prejudice. Which is so very important!'

The door opened; Aaron mumbled something; and Miss Severn entered, and moved across the polished boards toward them like a grey iceberg sliding through the sea.

The Misses Case did not rise, but acknowledged her salute with little formal bows; and Christopher was so paralysed by her appearance that the grenadier must stalk round and conduct her to the chair set facing her hostesses.

'I was glad,' said Miss Severn, seating herself composedly, and regarding the mittened hands in her lap, 'to get your letter, Miss Case; and glad to come and see you. The matter is one which deserves consideration. Very serious consideration.'

'Undoubtedly,' remarked Miz' Anne.

'I am glad that you should have summoned the young man who is so gravely concerned. I presume you have done so that we may explain the reprobation his conduct must incur.'

'We thought it best he should be summoned,' said Miz' Anne.

'Of course, what I say must be very painful to you in your position as guardians. . . . But you realize, that if this unfortunate young lady had not taken the law into her own hands and made her escape to her home, I should very seriously have had to consider the question of her public expulsion?'

'Yes?' said Miz' Anne, very gently.

'I have always endeavoured,' said Miss Severn, 'to keep the moral tone and the purity of my establishment consistently beyond reproach. What can I think, or say, or do, in the case of a young woman who bribes a mere servant—notoriously an immoral person—to take a passionate letter, implying I know not what degradation, to a young man—temporarily under the same roof? . . . What?'

As she spoke she looked to Christopher. In the greyness of the room, and beneath the shadow of the deep brim of her iron-grey bonnet, her eyes had the cold fire of a light reflected in a window that looks out on to a pitch-black night.

'I gathered; that is to say, we gathered—my sister and I—that you *had* thought, *and* said, *and* done!'

Something peculiar in Miz' Anne's tone attracted Miss Severn's attention. She appeared to draw within herself.

'I deduce—I may be wrong—from your expression that perhaps you do not altogether approve of my action,' she said. 'You have to remember, however, that I must think of your great-niece's companions—young ladies whose characters are not yet formed, whose minds are still ductile. . . . But this Mr. Harnish . . .'

'Forgive me a moment, Miss Severn. I wonder if I may ask you for facts. Apart from the question whether an offence was committed or not—or of its gravity. Just facts. Such important things!'

Christopher had never heard Miz' Anne speak in such a voice. It was small. It was cold. It did not twitter. She sat with one hand resting lightly on her sister's. There was a large and very old-fashioned ring on one finger. He could have sworn it had never been there before—to his knowledge. Miz' Anne frequently regarded it as if gathering inspiration from it.

Miss Severn bowed.

Miz' Anne continued.

'My great-niece arrived home. She ran upstairs without a word. She bolted herself in her room. For four hours no one could get in, and she would not utter a word. She is locked in again, now.'

Miss Severn looked her indifference to this idiosyncrasy.

'I gather. We gather—my sister and I. We were enabled to gather from her in a brief interview that she was publicly birched.'

Miz' Anne appeared to have some difficulty with enunciation. She spoke more quickly. 'In the midst of the school . . . before servants. . . . That she was held down over a form by four—by four of your satellites.'

Miss Severn composedly bowed her agreement with this version. 'That—that—that her undergarments were removed. That she was beaten in a thin blouse. Am I—are we, my sister and I—correct in our understanding?'

Old Lady Jane was nodding, nodding.

Christopher, a yellow lock fallen over his brow, stood stiffly above her chair. He shut his eyes. He remembered once more the window in the moonlight, and the warm body pressed against his, visible through its raiment like a thin shadow upon water. He remembered the quick pulsation under the curving breast. . . . Now he saw in imagination this outrage—this violation. He opened his eyes. He saw Miss Severn's iron-grey figure bent a little forward as if to catch each word—as if to gloat over it; he saw her iron lips compress—as if with satisfaction. He felt as if she had murdered something dangerous, pagan, but very beautiful—as if she had been a frenzied iconoclast, who had smashed a lovely idol that one might not worship but still would leave within its temple. He was aware of a deadly rage.

'You have omitted to state that she defied her punishment. That she resisted it with violence. With a furious violence.'

Miss Severn slowly raised her head and moved it along the line of old ladies, as if to emphasize the delinquency; but Christopher saw that also she would wordlessly demonstrate a spreading bruise upon her cheekbone. He saw it with pleasure.

'I understood,' said Miz' Anne, 'that there were ten strokes extra. I, that is to say, we, gathered they were on that account.'

'I am sorry if you take my efforts to correct a very dangerous tendency so much amiss,' said Miss Severn, barely stirring her lips.

She half rose in her seat as if about to take her departure.

'Please!' said Miz' Anne staying her. 'My sister and I would still like to understand a little more. Should we not, Elizabeth?'

Miz' Elizabeth, whose eyes of larkspur blue had never once

quitted Augusta Severn's face, nodded assent without removing her regard.

'The letter you were . . . good enough to enclose in yours, was the missive in question?' went on Miz' Anne in her high, thin voice.

'It was.'

'You are not aware, perhaps, that it was written to a young gentleman she has known for seven years? Her daily playmate for many of them? A young gentleman in whose conduct I—my sister and I—have the greatest confidence. . . . In fact . . .'

Miz' Anne came to a halt.

Miss Severn struck in.

'It does not alter the position. The letter shows a precocity which gives me the gravest fears for the young person who wrote it. In your retired life you are not aware of the great moral dangers attending indiscriminate correspondence between the sexes.'

'My sister and I, although old maids as yourself, are sufficiently acquainted with sex to be fully aware of it. We are fully aware that—er—the increase in population is not due to schizogenesis. We are aware of sex. Sex is a fact. We are aware of facts. We face facts. We make allowance for them.'

'Such broadmindedness!' said Miss Severn with the sketch of a sneer.

'Leaving that matter to one side. Are you informed of the fact that our great-niece is nearly eighteen years of age—practically an adult?'

'Her age is, I believe, entered in the Academy's register.'

'At what age, may I ask, do you think a lady should be no longer publicly birched?'

'It depends, I opine, upon the young person. I do not think that any definite period can be set.'

'She said "No definite period", Elizabeth,' said Miz' Anne, turning once more to her sister. ' "No definite period"!'

Miz' Elizabeth nodded assent.

' "No definite period"!' she echoed, and the two old ladies sat in silence for a moment, looking at one another with their heads faintly nid-nodding.

Miz' Elizabeth took up the thread of discourse, and the strange thin voice was so like her sister's that Christopher was unaware for a few seconds that the words came from another mouth.

'You probably do not know, Miss Severn, but in the Southern States we have a very high standard of family honour. A stain on the fame of one member is resented by all. . . . And avenged by all.'

Miss Severn summoned up another small bow.

'My dear father shot several gentlemen who were foolish . . . foolish enough to impugn our good name. My dear nephew. . . . A most romantic person! . . . Most romantic . . .'

Miz' Anne called her back by a slight tap of the hand.

'My dear nephew, I was about to say, avenged any insult—with death. We—ourselves—left the United States because . . .'

'I think, sister,' interrupted Miz' Anne, idly playing with the gold signet ring upon her finger, 'that it will do if we say that we are the Misses Case of Case. That our family honour is safe in our hands.' Here her voice changed again—so utterly that it was as if a third Case had come into the room, and was speaking with the voice that in some dim room five thousand miles away, and a generation ago, had snarled threats at an insolent. 'That we will deal as we have always dealt with those who endeavour to put disgrace upon us. That we still can avenge a wrong, if we cannot right it.'

Miss Severn, bold upright, stirred uneasily.

The voice went on.

'Because we are little and old, we have called on our friends to advise us lest we go wrong. We shall tell them what we propose.'

Said Miss Severn harshly:

'You will forgive me if I withdraw before this madness becomes intolerable!' She looked to Lady Jane, who sat sunken in what seemed to be a lightly smiling meditation. She rose.

'The door,' said Miz' Anne, 'is locked.'

Miss Severn stopped in her tracks as if struck.

'We propose,' said Miz' Anne. 'We . . . You remember, dear Lady Jane, dear Christopher, that this . . . creature said that there was no definite age-limit which could be set for the chastisement of a lady. . . . We propose, if you agree—dear Christopher, would you give a pull to the bell rope, one only!—to treat her as she treated the youngest Miss Case.

'We propose to birch her—if you think right. We propose to have her held over a chair, and birched with the same number of strokes she inflicted herself. We propose—do we not, Elizabeth?— to have her undergarments removed. And a little blouse put on her. The same sort of little blouse. We thought, dear Lady Jane, that perhaps you would see the punishment inflicted. If you please? It is wrong, very wrong to let coloured people witness the disgrace of a white person, still more to inflict it. But it may be forgiven in this case, I think.' How still Miss Severn was! Not iron now! Not granite! But the stillness of a rabbit surprised by a snake. 'We are little and old, but our coloured maids are strong and young. Very strong. So we thought three of them should deal with this . . . person. And the rest should watch. You see, the birching was public, was it not, Miss Severn?'

Miss Severn turned to the line of long grey windows. She had the face of a woman who is only half conscious.

'Dear Christopher,' said Miz' Anne affectionately. 'We feel a little guilty at drawing you into this. You are so very young. But we have called on you in this case because you are so much one of our little family. . . . At a court-martial the youngest officer always gives his verdict first. . . . Forgive the apparent rudeness, dear Lady Jane! . . . So, what do you say, Mr. Christopher, to our plan?'

The eyes of the woman in the centre, confronting her self-imposed judges, were turned on him. They were desperate eyes. But he did not even have to harden his heart to say thickly:

'Yes,' and no more.

'And you, Lady Jane?' asked Miz' Anne, bending toward the old lady and casting a quick glance of approval on the lad.

Lady Jane was nodding, and nodding. Her old lips were mouthing words that never issued, and shaping themselves for a smile that never came. But she looked upwards, almost slyly, from under her brown drooping eyelids, with a split second of flashing intelligence at the gaunt figure. She might almost have been said to leer.

Miz' Anne nodded in a satisfied manner.

'I am so glad you agree. . . . Dear Christopher, will you pull the bell cord *twice*, please? . . . They are ready. . . . You, I know, would not care to be present—nor should be, in decency. Supposing you wait in the anteroom with the doctor. . . . We summoned him in the case of necessity. . . . Or try to persuade dear Arabella to come out and talk to you, though I am afraid . . .'

He turned at the door amid a throng of hushed negro maids with rolling eyes. Across the waste of polished floor gleaming dully in the cold light and tenuous shadows, he saw that iron-grey figure standing before the three little old ladies, against the glimmer of the high glass folding doors. She was silent: she made no protest, even as two great negro women took her by the arms.

Chapter 18

A Gentleman on His Travels

CHARLOTTE HAD PERMITTED SETOUN TO DIVERGE FROM the subject under discussion into some fascinating by-way without displaying undue impatience.

'Supposing,' she said at length, 'you save up this fantasy for your after-dinner meditations. Let's get on with the business in hand.'

She sat upright amid the folds of the fur-edged pelisse, which she had shrugged off her shoulders upon her arrival, half an hour before, from Bath.

A large and distracted Setoun sat opposite her in his study, which was dense with cigar smoke as if with the fume of battle. A drum of cheroots was at his elbow upon a small glass-topped display table, and, as he had been endeavouring to pack the ash down the slot of the empty scabbard of a sabre held between his knees, his person was lavishly strewn with greyish powder.

'You've told me everything, I suppose, Hurbles?' she continued, and underlined the word 'everything'.

'Everything I know myself, Carlotta. All I could get from Tops; from Old Anne and Elizabeth—and even from Aunt Jane!'

'Anne, Elizabeth, Aunt Jane and Tops!' said Charlotte, and she lay back within her sumptuous mantle and laughed. "I can't help laughing, Hurbles, whenever I think of that ridiculous tribunal. It would be funny past words, if it didn't threaten to have such drastic consequences.'

Setoun grinned, although his brow was still corrugated.

'Laughed till I was sick,' he assured her. 'Serve the old hag right, I thought! Laughed like a dog indeed, until two days after

I got back. Then the flood of attorneys' letters began. Letters for everybody. Threats against everybody. For everything. Assault and battery. Civil action for damages. Conspiracy. Incitement to murder. Tops an abettor! An accessory before the fact! Tops!'

'She'd never bring an action. It would ruin her and the school. . . . Unless she's mad.'

'She *is* mad. And she's made all the money she wants. Only wants revenge.'

He continued.

'So I shot the Case ladies off on the spot. Out of reach for the time. Out of the country, of course. While we try to compose the affair. Poor Tops I've planted with Wake! But it'll be safer to get him abroad. Till it's blown over. There'll be talk enough, anyhow.'

'It's not the Severn I'm afraid of,' said Charlotte, after a short reflection, and smiled at his puzzled expression. 'I know my own sex and few women will stand for ridicule, mad or not. Think of the inextinguishable laughter if the case came to court. The Severn won't make trouble . . . It's Arabella I'm afraid of.'

'Arabella!'

'I said long ago that she was panther, not puss. . . . I was once birched when I was her age—no,' she corrected herself, 'I was sixteen! It's not unusual, dear Hurbles, despite everybody's vast indignation. I'm not at all sure that I shouldn't have been inclined to agree to a walloping—a reasonable one!"

'My God, Carlotta, you're a Gorgon! . . . It was a foul thing to do for such a trifle!'

'I was thinking of Tops,' explained Charlotte. 'It was so very good for him!'

'Arabella's punishment was so very good for him? Don't follow you.'

'Darling Hurbles!' she said, and patted his ash-covered knee to emphasize her point. 'The funny old man understands so very little! We want Tops to have a run for his money—you and I; and I have had my suspicions of that minx for nearly a year. She's grown up too fast. I watched her at Lady Charlotte Campbell's garden party last summer, and I saw more than she thought! She's a nice enough child, but we don't want our Tops—our dear romantical Tops—to grow up quite so fast . . . and in the same way. *He* has been innocent enough, let's keep him so for a bit!'

'But that doesn't explain why Arabella's beating is good for Tops. You women! All with minds like corkscrews!'

'Yes! But we open the bottle. . . . Pop! Like that! . . . See what Carlotta will pour out for her Hurbles! . . . Our romantical Tops can't have much romance left when he thinks of his lady spread-eagled over a desk—the part of her that's meant to be slapped presented most prominently to a roomful of people.'

Setoun chewed the end of his cigar in silence.

'Don't know it would make any difference to *me*,' he grumbled.

'Meaning that *I* could be so spanked . . . and you'd still . . . find romance in me?'

'You could be . . .' he began vehemently.

'Dear, dear Hurbles! You'd better not invent any embarrassing degradations for me. But the difference is that you are fantastical, you see; and Tops is romantical! . . . A vast of difference! We've got to get him out of harm's way before romance resurrects.'

'Do what?'

'Do what you said you would. Give him some military service. Let him go while the going is good. Your old plan. Which you seem to have forgotten, and I remembered.'

Setoun rose from his chair, put the scabbard on the floor, dusted himself; and leaned a great shoulder against a stand of pikes by the wall, clasping the shaft of one of the weapons below the crimson tassels which hung near the steel point.

Charlotte examined the red face, with high-bridged nose and jutting chin, and wrinkles about its wise eyes. Against the line of spears it seemed more than ever the face of a knight who was both counsellor and paladin.

She took a letter from the muff upon her knee.

'When I first heard your plan of giving him three or four years in the Saxon Army, Hurbles, I didn't fancy it. You can't plant Tops straight from such a life as he has had here and as he makes for himself, into a town like Dresden—knowing no one, among a hundred youngsters more sophisticated than himself. I know my Dresden—and you don't! Or have forgotten it! With one busy

man, who will have little time to look after him—however great
a friend of yours he may be.'

Setoun acknowledged the justice of her objections with a nod.

'I thought that you were right in turning him loose by himself
to learn discipline—and things, with lads of his own age. But I
thought I could make better arrangements on the same lines. I
wrote to someone I knew; had a reply at once; wrote for further
details a month ago, and had my answer, as luck would have it,
just before I rushed up from Bath.'

'Who's the someone, Carlotta?'

'The Great Duchess of Hesse-Neipperg.'

'One of the Hanoverian brood!'

'Yes. But she doesn't love her family! She is a dear old thing,
and as English as you please.'

'English!' He accented the word scornfully.

'Well, the old lady knows who Tops is. She's sworn to protect
him herself, and after all she is a Great Duchess of a Sovereign
State. It's your plan—only a little town instead of a big one; a
little army instead of a large one; a little old-fashioned Court
instead of a great one.'

He grunted a qualified approval.

'Well, listen to this. I'll just read you the necessary bits:

' "I have spoken, my dearest Charlotte, to Frederick, and it is
with great pleasure that I can now tell you he will be happy to
permit the dear lad to join the Garde du Corps as a cadette. This
means that he will have the equipment and status of an officer
without the rank.

' "I sent for Colonel Baron Michaeloff, the Commander, immediately the Great Duke had given his consent. He is a Charming man and, Frederick says, an excellent soldier. The Regiment's
quarters adjoin the Palace, and the Colonel's residence is within
the Grounds. He would be glad to take into his Household your
young friend, and I can Assure you that a happier, more Christian
and delightful instructor you would not wish to meet.

' "I think £60 or £70 a year would more than cover this Ex-
pence. I know that money does not matter to you Mogulesses, but
I become such an old Stinge that I count every groschen myself.
For the Cost of Living has been horrible since the War. Another

thing we must thank the Monster, Buonaparte, for! Equipment and Uniform—which he must get here—should not exceed 480 florins.

' "Frederick has just come into the room. He has been suffering from a sort of confined gout which has attacked the nerves, but he is better, and I hope shortly to see him well. He says to tell you that our young friend will get a thorough Military Training as well as Ceremonial Duty with the Garde.

' "It will be pleasant to see a dear English face here, and I shall try to play some part of an elderly Relation towards him, knowing what I do. We lead a Very quiet life, and you need have no fear that we shall make a Roué of him.

' "Usually a Cadette must provide attestations of having learnt what will be useful for his advancement, papers to show that he belongs to no Secret Society and has the Permission of his Sovereign to enter the Service, and Baptismal Certificate. In this Exceptional case Frederick will himself nominate him, and they will not be necessary."

'It's only tattle after that, and she signs it, "your Affectionate old Frump!" '

Christopher was accompanied by Setoun as far as Paris on the way to Neipperg, the capital of the Grand Duchy. Thence he had travelled for a week by himself with all the deference due to a claret-coloured carriage with coroneted panels and the discreet livery of Williams in the rumble—to say nothing of a semi-military frogged coat, yellowish white tall hat worn at an angle, and a voluminous black cravat which took at least a quarter of an hour to arrange.

Setoun's parting gift, for which he had demanded one sou in exchange, had been a case of ivory-handled razors—one for each day of the week.

He stood by the carriage door to say good-bye, twiddling an absurd child's toy bought from a street vendor—a paper windmill on a stick. In the chill early morning wind that blew down the street, the little vanes revolved.

'Well, young feller-me-lad,' he said. 'You'd better go. On your own now! I've given you your liberty—and your razors. Don't cut yourself with either! . . .'

He watched absently the frantic movement of the paper sails. 'Wonder if one couldn't make a revolving razor on that principle. Work it on a ratchet. Four little blades. Save a lot of time. . . . Good-bye, Tops, and God bless you! If you don't write every week, I'll . . . !'

Christopher kept his head thrust out of the window until they swung into the Rue Laffitte. Setoun still stood at the entrance to the hotel courtyard, the pink windmill whirling away in his hand.

The journey from Paris gave Christopher adequate time to gather all that there was to know about the ancient principality from the time of its foundation by Ludwig of the Silver Leg. He learned that its area was four thousand three hundred square miles, its population a trifle over three hundred and ninety thousand; that the royal household included seventy-five servants; and that the army amounted to five thousand four hundred and seventy-three men, of which the Garde du Corps accounted for two hundred and sixty-four. The artillery consisted of one battery of six-pounders, and there were three two-battalion regiments of infantry.

The Grand Duchy lay in the last dark rolling folds of forest that the mountains of central Germany thrust out northwards to the great European plain. A handful of grey towns, with steep red roofs and towers like candles topped by extinguishers were scattered along the wider valleys and the larger streams. Like green lakes in the hollows of the wooded hills, orchards and meadows slept around scattered hamlets and solitary castles.

Here and there, it is true, within the forest tracts, workings for iron and copper seared the mantle of the trees; and in one of the winding valleys a line of new white villas glimmered among the pines as if they were pebbles among moss—forerunner of a Spa that was to be. In Neipperg and in Sontheim they manufactured porcelain, fire-arms, musical instruments and linen cloth. Among the workers there may have been subversive elements—radicals demanding other government than a benevolent autocracy; for the most part, however, they were a fat, contented people, liking beer and tobacco and cherries and fairy-tales.

When at last the travelling carriage swung round a foxglove bank, and he saw the city lying as a jumble of roofs and spires and gardens in the plain below, he could have answered any question on the Great Duke's descent, and gone into the matter of his connection with the vanished Lords of Limpurg-Sontheim and Nassau-Ottweiler, or his relationship with the ruling House of England.

Viewing the tangle of high gables tilted over twisted alleys, the battlemented walls of the castle fretted with innumerable turrets, the top-heavy gatehouse built athwart the bridge over a rushing river, it appeared to him, however, that hard facts were out of place. It was more fitting to recall the legend that the Lord of this fantastic city, by walking round a burning house, could immediately extinguish the flames, than that his wife was an English princess, own sister to that fat slug, King George the Fourth, and to the pineapple-headed William of Clarence, his heir and successor.

Chapter 19

He Meets Royalty, a Soldier and an Amorist

THEY DROVE ALONG AN AVENUE OF POPLARS TO THE bridge, were halted by the guard on duty at the gatehouse, and rattled at last over the cobbles into the town. They travelled slowly through narrow streets of high overhanging houses that lay in shadow throughout the day—except at noon—like mountain fissures. They crossed a busy market-place where fat old women sat gossiping by chicken and vegetables and cream cheese; past a grim Calvinistical cathedral whose spire had a queer knob on it—a sort of onion on a skewer; so to the Ludwigplatz where Ludwig himself in bronze sat eternally, with undisturbed peruke, reining in a rearing steed before the grey façade of his palace.

There, on the direction of a man smoking a tasselled china pipe, they swung into a promenade that ran between the battlemented wall of the palace grounds and a row of lime trees, along a hustling shallow river flecked with foam like beer. So round a corner into a small and shady square where cavalry horses were sucking water or lifting dripping lips from stone troughs about a fountain; and a sentry in uniform of white and red stood on duty before a gate in a high blank wall.

A sergeant escorted the carriage through the palace grounds, along a formal alley between a lofty clipped hedge of yew and a loftier wall with marble nymphs, cupids and satyrs posturing in niches.

At one point through a gap in the green rampart, Christopher saw a wide stately garden—statuary dimly white against trees and hedges that were distorted into strange shapes; lawns smooth as moss; fountains with tritons; terraces set with orange trees and

312

urns; and, over all, the many shining windows, towers and chaotic gables of the palace.

A hundred yards or so from the entrance gate a long narrow house stood against the outer wall, built over a cloister of stone columns. The sergeant stopped the carriage and pointed to a flight of steps in a dark corner.

A man who was about to ascend turned at the sound of wheels, hesitated, and then came slowly toward Christopher as he dismounted at the edge of the colonnade.

'It is His Excellency himself, Your Excellency,' said the sergeant, saluting.

His Excellency was tall and thin and stooping. He wore a white uniform with huge gold epaulettes and his lined face peered over so high a scarlet collar that it was as if his chin were resting crumpled upon a fence. His grey hair was swept forward at the sides toward his mild blue eyes. He carried an immense cocked hat under his arm.

'Baron Michaeloff?' said Christopher with a bow. He had recited his introductory speech all the way from the town gate. 'May I present myself, Chris . . .'

'Ah, it is our newcomer! The new member for our little family— Meester Harnish! Excellent! Splendid! You are welcome!—Very welcome!'

He shook Christopher by the hand, and patted him on the arm in a reassuring manner as if to say, 'Yes, you are really here, and I am real, and the palace is real, and the fairy-tale town is real— although you might not think it!'

He hurried a string of instructions to a manservant who had appeared; then seized Christopher by the arm, and, without further prelude, led him across the alley through an arch in the hedge, talking rapidly the while. They emerged in a Dutch water garden; they crossed a rose garden; skirted a labyrinth and dived into a sophisticated thicket with winding paths.

'There are not many young people of your age at Court,' said the baron to the anxiously attentive Christopher. 'All of us are getting a little old. Though, thanks be to the good God, a green old age! Very green! So you will have the less distraction from your military studies. Above all you must get to know the men and horses. All the men and all the horses! That was Buonaparte's secret. His officers knew their men. Ours didn't.'

They crossed a rustic bridge, at the foot of a waterfall, into a decorous glade. There in a little marble temple with a green copper dome sat three elderly ladies having tea: at least two were having tea, and the third and fattest was reading aloud to her companions. Her head was wrapped about in a black silk scarf, which was surmounted by the largest lace cap with the widest frill that Christopher had ever seen.

She laid down the book as they approached, and looked up smiling all over her bland red face.

'So you are—Charlotte's young friend!' said she as Christopher stood bowing before her; and gave him a plump hand to kiss. He remembered bending over just such another hand; so long ago—it seemed—that it must have been other than he.

'Because you are,' she continued, 'I told Baron Michaeloff that you must be presented to me immediately you came. To show you that you have already a friend here! . . . Now sit down and have some tea. You must be tired after your so long journey. . . . You sit by me, Mr. Harnish! . . . Real English tea! . . . Tell me about England, and that dear Charlotte and the queer Setoun!'

He was conscious of a close regard as he sat beside the Great Duchess; and once or twice she patted his hand. It might have been a gesture of approval, but Christopher felt that, like the baron, she meant to reassure him that everything was real, that here he was in a real palace in a real city—fantastic though they might be—in familiar conversation with a very real old lady who was cheerful, talkative and shrewd.

The tea was too hot. She poured it into her saucer and blew on it.

'Don't you write home and tell Charlotte that I am like an old English washerwoman,' she said.

'Charlotte told me to tell you, ma'am, that though you signed your letter to her as her "Affectionate old Frump", her opinion was that you were really a grig.'

' "Grig"!' said the Great Duchess in immense delight. 'Charlotte thinks I am a grig, does she? Bless my wig, she calls me a grig!'

She retailed the story to her ladies in rapid German, but as there was no obvious translation for 'grig' their smiles were merely dutiful.

'Well?' the old lady remarked at length, 'it is time we took our exercise, Ottilie. A little weed-pulling for the figure, eh, Augusta?'

Augusta, who was fat, sighed.

Ottilie, who was fatter, drooped.

'Ach, Highness,' said Augusta piteously, 'I sometimes dream that I am weeding an interminable plain. I could weed in the dark now, I know the feeling of a groundsel's ribs so well. I dream of their hundred little yellow eyes.'

'It is the only weed you do know,' said the Great Duchess. 'I have noticed it. It is pulled up, perhaps, more easily than the rest.'

'The stooping—the stooping, Highness!' protested Ottilie. 'It so discommodes the digestion. And the stays!'

The Great Duchess clapped her hands to her own fat stomach. She drummed upon it, and rose relentlessly, but laughing.

'If you stooped often enough, Ottilie, you'd need no stays. . . . Think of your figure! . . . You shall come and help us weed one of these days, young man! . . . Baron, take him off and give him an early supper and dispatch him to bed. . . . You don't read in bed at night, I hope, Mr. Harnish! A most dangerous habit. The candle, you know! You fall asleep; the flame catches the curtains; and there you are—burned to a cinder!'

As they withdrew from the presence, the old lady summoned the baron to her side, and spoke to him in a low tone. Christopher, seeing the direction of their gaze, knew that they spoke of him.

The house of Baron Michaeloff, reared over its shadowy cloister, seemed at first to consist of a very long dark tunnel lighted by windows at either end. There were many doors on the side toward the garden front, and the blank wall was hung thickly with old armour whose shape was lost in gloom.

The baron, however, led Christopher up a narrow stair to the floor above—to a gallery bright with sunshine and portraits. There he opened a door and showed him into a pleasant room with windows that looked from under low eaves down on the lime trees of the promenade, the rushing river, and the gardens and white houses on the slopes beyond.

'Your man has put your things in order, I see,' he said, and cast a glance around the elaborate outfit on chest and dressing-table and chairs. 'Nowadays it seems to take a vast equipment to be a soldier—in peace time! When I was a lad! . . .

He shook his head. and Christopher looked as apologetic as he could.

'Well, I daresay things change! . . . We usually eat at half-past nine, for I play cards with the Great Duke before he goes to supper. To-night, however, we will sup at eight . . . then you must go to bed! . . . To-morrow we will deal with the question of uniform and duties, if you have sufficiently recovered from your fatigue.'

Christopher's protestations that he was not at all tired were brushed to one side.

'It will be no trouble,' said the baron. 'We are a small family— my widowed niece, Frau von Osterode and her stepdaughter, Luise. Your fellow cadet,' and a faint smile curved on his long face, 'is undergoing discipline—a very gentle discipline!'

They supped at a long narrow table in a long narrow room into which the westering sun filtered through a multiplicity of curtains.

He sat by Frau von Osterode, daughter of the old man's dead sister. She was a young slow-moving woman with moist lips, who held the conversation to herself, and ate and drank very heartily, and wriggled her plump shoulder and her hips as if to draw attention to the luscious desirability of her body. She was but little older than her stepdaughter, who barely spoke or even raised her pale eyes during the meal.

A young officer with a small nose and greedy face and long black hair made up the party. He was Luise von Osterode's betrothed, but Christopher would not have known it had he not been told; for the youth sat with his hungry eyes fixed on the luscious curves of the stepmother, and it was mainly to him that her remarks and glances were addressed.

Frau von Osterode, however, by no means ignored the newcomer. She complimented him on the perfection of his German, and held his hand a fraction of a second longer than seemed necessary when he said 'good night'.

Christopher was more tired than he had thought. He was glad

to retire after the meal to his room, which was dominated by an enormous feather bed with a down quilt shaped like a bolster, under a canopy of red hangings.

He was leaning, half-undressed, out of a window, looking into the darkness of tree and river, when a low voice—speaking at his elbow, it appeared—said in German:

'I say, will you lend me a razor?'

He turned round quickly, but no one was in the room; and he realized that he had been addressed by somebody from the next window. He looked out again to see the blur of a head a few feet away.

'Ah,' said the head, with a sigh of relief. 'I was afraid you had gone! I say, give me the loan of a razor!'

'Razor?'

'Shall only be a few minutes with it. I'll let you have it back, honour bright—but you'll have to fetch it yourself. . . . You're the new fellow, I suppose? . . . My door is next yours. Only I can't come out.'

'I'll bring it,' said Christopher, choosing a razor from the set in the new case. The day was Saturday, so he took the seventh from the slot in its bed of blue velvet.

The occupant of the next room welcomed him at his door. He held a candlestick in his hand, revealing a shock of bright red hair, a snub nose, and large mouth full of large white teeth.

'Von Eckstein,' said he bowing.

'Harnish!' said Christopher.

'I'm most infernally obliged to you, Herr Harnish,' said Herr von Eckstein. 'I've blunted my own past use.'

Indeed it lay in the middle of the floor amid a mass of pasteboard fragments.

'It's most awkward,' he rattled on. 'Here's old Father Michael-off confined me to quarters, and I was to meet Anna to-night—the girl from the pastry-cook, you know!—No, of course you don't! Anyhow, I was. She'll be outside in ten minutes, and I've only got as far as P. Look out and see if she's under the tree by the bench, there's a good fellow, while I get on with it!'

Herr von Eckstein sat down on his bed and began slicing away with Christopher's razor at a fresh sheet of pasteboard.

'There's no one there yet,' said Christopher drawing in his head, and regarding the other's operations with some misgivings.

'She *is* a one, and no mistake!' said von Eckstein. 'She's just plummy! I am mad about her. . . . I'll introduce you if you like—one day. . . . No dirty work, of course!'

'I should like to,' assented Christopher.

'Not like the daughter of the old fellow at the Golden Lion. She was hot stuff! But I always felt—well, I don't know! . . . It was a shame the old man saw me with Anna last night. He's given me three days' confinement. He doesn't know who she is, or, Lord God! there would be a row.'

'What are you doing now?' asked Christopher surveying the mysterious work in progress with increasing dismay.

'Cutting out an alphabet,' said von Eckstein. 'You see I've got all the candles on the table in the window. I shall draw the muslin curtains to, and then I'll hold the letters up against the light like this, so that they show up on the white. She'll be able to read them from the road. . . . I can send her all sorts of messages. It'll be a bit slow—but still! . . . Lord God! She'll be here in five minutes, and I must have a Z!'

'Why a Z particularly?'

'Can't make HERZ-GELIEBTE without a Z, you chump,' said Herr von Eckstein in a friendly way. 'Keep an eye on the window like a good chap.'

Christopher stationed himself in the window, and von Eckstein rambled on.

'Have you met Luise yet, and that hungry-looking chap of hers, von Metzsch? Luise had better look out, or Sophie will be up to her tricks with him.'

'Sophie?'

'The old man's niece. Between you and me a bit rapid, I think. She used to put her foot on mine under the table and press it—at least I think so. It's pretty dull here, but some of the girls! . . .' He left the sentence unfinished and shook his head. 'You keep clear of them. They're the devil! . . . Seen the Great Duke?'

'No, but I was presented to the Great Duchess.'

'She's a nice old thing although she's English—sorry, you know! And *he's* all right. He gets pretty tight at times. Then the old lady goes round saying the poor dear's suffering from "confined gout", or influenza of the nerves.'

'There's a girl in a white shawl under the trees now,' said Christopher. 'She's looking up to the window.'

'It's Anna,' said von Eckstein, bounding to the floor. 'Isn't she a darling? And I've got a Z ready at last. Thanks so much! . . . Good night!'

Chapter 20

'Christopher P.'

SO CHRISTOPHER WAS FITTED BY AN OBSEQUIOUS COURT tailor with a tight uniform of cream-coloured cloth, learned to accommodate his chin to the high collar of scarlet and gold, and his wrists to the flapping braided cuffs. He had caught his spurs in the winding stairway of the Wall House, and admiringly drawn his new sword half out of the scabbard fifty times a day.

He attended early morning stables, superintended the evening watering, drilled on one or other of the grey horses Setoun had sent from England, went the rounds with the officer of the day, and twice—in the absence of a subaltern—acted as Lieutenant of the Palace Guard. He dined frequently with Highnesses, played cards in the evening at one of the four tables always spread in the lesser drawing-room, and escorted into supper on occasion one or other of the fat ladies-in-waiting or less important guests.

He sat in an embayed window of a bare office in the barracks on a winter afternoon, meditating out loud for the benefit of von Eckstein who was inditing with much labour a letter to his newest lady love.

'There's something odd about a Court, Eckie,' he declared. 'Here we've got a romantic castle all towers and turrets. A bodyguard. Sentries. Chamberlain. Master of the Household. Master of the Horse. Treasurer. A.D.C.s. Gentlemen-in-Waiting. Ladies-in-Waiting. Gentlemen ushers—with white rods, with batons. White uniforms. Red uniforms. Gold uniforms.'

Von Eckstein looked up from his letter. He beat time to the recital with his pen.

'We've got stars and orders and medals. A watchman who trum-

320

pets the hour at night. Running footmen. Link men. Coaches like Cinderella's, and white-wigged coachmen and white horses,' continued Christopher. 'We've got all sorts of pomp and panoply and ceremony. With it we encrust—what? . . . A few funny, dull old people! We're like the big elaborate gold setting you see round the sort of . . . of lustreless stones old ladies wear—like cairngorms and things.'

'Look at it the other way, Tops,' said von Eckstein. 'It all exists for us. The dull stone for the setting. It's so that the world shall have a pageant, all for nothing. For you and me to wear pretty uniforms. For me to walk down the Ludwigstrasse and get smiled at by the girls. Where would I be without it all?'

'We're a pageant without a purpose,' insisted Christopher.

'We're a pageant for our own purpose,' said von Eckstein. 'Lisbeth always says she would never have noticed me but for the uniform.'

'We're a pageant without a central incident. You can't call a few nice old people, who dress how they like and doze half the day, a purpose for a pageant. . . . I want the trumpets to blow a call to arms: princesses in balconies; adventures, romances and plots. Something to justify us.'

'Princes are never fond of plots,' said the husky voice of the Great Duke, who had stood silently for some moments in the doorway behind, his square hands holding to the jambs. He wore a great diamond star upon his coat, and sucked his heavy grizzled moustache. His solitary attendant was the stable cat which wound round his strapped white trouserings with arched back and waving tail. He smiled affably at Christopher as the two young men sprang to embarrassed attention.

'Princes hate plots, Mr. Harnish,' he repeated. 'There are no wars. One princess only in a thousand is beautiful. Romance went out with the last century—and there is only one kind of adventure left to a prince. And that is usually too facile.'

Christopher stammered some reply.

'Usually too facile!' said the Great Duke, obviously pleased with the phrase. 'As princes often know! And princesses! And near-princes, too! . . . Your family . . .'

He pulled himself up and looked at Christopher meditatively.

'Near-princes!' he said thoughtfully; stumbled a trifle over the phrase; squared his shoulders; bent down to caress the cat; addressing her as 'naughty puss' as if she were responsible for any lapse he might have made; and then rambled out as though unaware of impaired dignity.

'He'll be having an attack of "confined gout" shortly!' said von Eckstein meaningly, when the sound of the uneven footsteps had died away down the stone corridor.

'Why did he say "your family", and look at me like that?' wondered Christopher. 'What did he mean by a "near-prince"?'

'You are not a royal love-child, are you, Tops?' asked von Eckstein with such interest, and in so serious and simple a manner, that obviously no offence was meant. In fact, it was apparent that he was prepared to be impressed if such were the case.

'Oh, nothing so romantic,' said Christopher swinging his booted legs. 'My mother died when I was born, and my father was serving in India. He died without ever seeing me. I was brought up by my aunt in Cornwall, and then by my guardian, Viscount Setoun.'

'An English milord!' said von Eckstein, much impressed.

'I was a sort of page to the Queen of England,' added Christopher proudly.

It was, perhaps, the sight of the humble shaking of Eckie's head before this glory that made him think of other dim adventures in his record—of the boy whose torn throat had gaped like a second mouth in the lamplight in a country road; of the bellowing man with a shining bald head in a book-lined study; of Simmie dragging in the dust behind the wagon; of the long white face hunched into scarlet robes above a sea of staring eyes—of Deb! He suddenly saw her pouring out the grain from little canvas bags into the hollow of her lap; saw the chipped chamber-pot full of a swill-tub mixture of broken bread and meat and vegetables; saw the bright thrust of flame from a pistol mouth, and watched the plaster trickle from the gash in the inn wall.

Of this Eckie knew nothing: he gazed respectfully at the ward of an English milord, the attendant of a queen, and went back with a sigh to the task of writing a love letter to an inn-keeper's daughter. . . .

Sometimes, on the other hand, Christopher felt that the dull, quiet circle, which was enveloped by so much parade and glamour, represented security in a dark uncertain sea.

The fat old ladies, the grizzled high officials went placidly to and fro upon an eventless routine; their only anxiety to cover up the Great Duke's occasional and amiable lapses into 'gout'; their only anticipation the coming of the candles for the nightly game of cards, some new delicacy for supper, or the weekly budget from Berlin or Vienna. They paced so easily down long galleries to dinner, carrying their napkins tied with coloured ribbons; sat tattling in vàst saloons. As if about them did not surge a strange unquiet life.

He wondered, as he stood stiffly while they passed in babbling procession to the dining-room, if they knew that the Captain-in-Waiting, von Brahe, who stalked behind them with a black patch on his eye, had caught a foul disease in town; that someone slipped into the Wall House at night and out again before the dawn; that von Hompesch, the Court Chamberlain's son, was far too well-favoured by fortune at cards—and far too quick on the trigger for anyone to raise an eyebrow; that the head footman had got a girl into trouble; that there were sinister whispers about the silent-footed librarian who always seemed to be listening for something or someone as he bent over his catalogues; that in the town they drank good health to the Paris Revolution of July; that Eckie could not pay his bills and had wept when he had been lent five hundred florins.

The Great Duke was a square tobacco-smelling old fellow, with a light froth of grey whisker about his face, and a magnificent moustache, which—instead of being pleached, as it were, across his features—curved down on his long upper lip like ivy that has climbed a wall and hangs over the other side.

Christopher was enormously puzzled by him. He would find the rather washed-out blue eyes of Highness fixed thoughtfully on him at supper sometimes, or during flurried inconsequential visits to the stables, when the old man would indulge in reminiscence of his campaign with Suvarov and the Archduke John. Christopher often thought that 'Old Humbug'—as Eckie called him—had something in his mind to say, and could not bring himself to do it.

Beyond the range of these shadows and surmises there was a pleasant social life of hearty feeding and simple amusement.

Plump young ladies, with a most satisfactory number of quarterings, laid themselves out to charm: the rich Englishman was popular in a dozen houses; there were picnics in the forest and skating on the frozen Neipper. There was, too, a dusty bookshop in a dim alley where he browsed and discovered Hoffmann and Hauff and Adalbert von Chamisso and Goethe, while Eckie ogled his latest girl; and he would sit reading by the hour in his room under the eaves.

He and Eckie made expeditions together. Once they went to the shabby castle in the woods of Hanover, where Eckie's widowed mother kept up a threadbare state, amid halls of bare stone and smoky chimneys and hard-breathing maids. She was a thin woman with a drip on the end of her thin nose, which Eckie never succeeded in dodging when he kissed her. Christopher wondered if there was no way of avoiding it; he thought he had escaped it himself when she embraced him affectionately on their departure, but as he rode away he found a drip mark on the chest of his white tunic.

In the spring and summer the pair of them would often ride out and dine at an outdoor restaurant on the banks of the Neipper, listen to the orchestra and dance afterwards in a rustic pavilion. Sometimes they would spend an evening over beer or wine at a little green table under the trees of the Luitpoldgarten where the town band in crimson and lilac played till long after dusk.

Once they had gone in plain clothes to a tavern outside the walls, dingily gay with lewd mural paintings; and so noisy that conversation was impossible.

A couple of young ladies, very much made up, had approached them forthwith: one of them sat herself upon Christopher's knee, flung an arm round his neck and kissed him extremely moistly. Christopher, to Eckie's disappointment, had recalled an engagement, and they had left very quickly.

'That was a pretty girl,' grumbled Eckie for the hundredth time, as Christopher opened his bedroom door. 'A very pretty girl! I don't see why you wanted to drag me away!'

Christopher rushed to the wash basin. He soaped his mouth, and scrubbed at his lips with his nail-brush.

'Lord God!' said Eckie. 'What in the name of fortune is the matter with you?'

'Beer! Very sticky!' lied Christopher, and produced his tooth-brush and cleaned his teeth with enormous vigour.

'Beer?' said Eckie. 'I didn't notice anything wrong with it. Better gargle with salt and water!'

Then there was the affair of Lieschen, the exquisite little brunette who sold flowers and made wreaths at the florist's shop in the Marktplatz. It was a tiny booth in which there was just room for Lieschen, her brilliant ephemeral wares, several pails full of water, and one customer.

Christopher for a period bought a posy there every day, and spun out the process until it spread over three-quarters of an hour. Lieschen, with busy fingers twisting wire about the stems of tortured blooms, would cast shy little glances up at him and make hesitating replies in a small sweet voice to his awkward attempts at conversation. He envied Eckie who could rattle away to a girl he barely knew, until in ten minutes they were on the basis of old friends. He himself never succeeded in achieving the personal touch.

He dreamed, however, of Lieschen, and wrote a sonnet or two to her in which happy play was made on the fact that, a perfect flower herself, she spent her life among flowers.

'We've all got such old-fashioned ideas on marriage,' said Christopher to Eckie as they walked along the river front one afternoon, discussing subjectively the important question of Woman.

'I've got no ideas of marriage,' remonstrated Eckie, turning to look after an exceptionally pretty peasant girl. 'None at all!'

'Supposing you had,' said Christopher, 'and the question of money didn't arise, you would never dream of marrying, say, Christiane!'—Christiane was Eckie's latest. She was the daughter of the host of the Rote Adler.

'Lord God!' interjected Eckie. 'I say! She's perfectly sweet and all that. She's lovely to cuddle—but marry!' And he whistled shocked astonishment.

'There you are, Eckie!' crowed Christopher. 'A great big snob! She's prettier than any well-born girl you know! She's more intelligent; and actually she'll have, I suppose, more money than most of them; and yet the idea of marrying her shocks you!'

'But her accent! What would my mother say? I'd have to leave the army! Anyway, I've never thought about it. I'm sure she hasn't.'

'Snob—and snob again!' said Christopher. 'You just couldn't marry Christiane or Anna—she's a sweet little girl, too—or any of the others because they've got accents and their fathers are innkeepers or something! And they're a cursed sight nicer than most of the girls we meet, with quarterings and all the rest!'

Eckie looked at him unhappily but made no comment.

'You with the particle "von" want fresh blood,' remarked Christopher loftily. 'Want strong new red blood to make the stock more vigorous. . . . Now, I've often thought that really *the* thing to do would be not to mind in the least social distinction. Nice, pretty, good-tempered girl! What does it matter what class she comes from? Marry her! Have her educated first, if you like. Give her a year with some really nice people to train in new ways. Mould her, yourself! How much better than marrying someone with manners and conventions and social knowledge all ready made? Make your wife yourself! . . . In fact, mould her!'—repeated Christopher, rather impressed by the phrase.

' "Mould her!" ' echoed Eckie thoughtfully. 'Still, it would be rather an expensive sort of affair! . . . Where are you off to, Christopher? I thought we were going to the Lustgarten!'

'I wanted to order some flowers,' said Christopher reddening slightly.

Eckie groaned.

'You'll be hours in that case. . . . Must you? . . . I can't see what you can see in Lieschen. She's as pretty as paint—but her hands!'

'Her hands?'

'Well, you know,' explained Eckie, 'her hands are like dead fish, cold and wet—I suppose it's the water. And they are so chapped! Terrible!'

Christopher, watching Lieschen's busy fingers, found Eckie's disparaging criticism ever-present in his mind, although he tried to forget it, since the mere remembrance seemed disloyal. But it was hideously true! It could not be gainsaid that Lieschen's small hands were not her strong point. Although it was summer they were dull and red and rough, and creases in the little joints were cracked and raw, and the nails lustreless and grey.

From thenceforward the intervals between Christopher's visits to the booth became greater and greater—whole days elapsed without him appearing in the doorway. He felt a traitor; and Lieschen sometimes wondered what had become of him, but not overmuch —for she had no idea of the great things Fate might have held in store for her.

Perhaps, too, the Great Duchess had something to do with the matter. Driving through the town on a shopping expedition in an open carriage the previous day, she had spotted Christopher entering the little shop. She recollected having seen him come out of it only a day or two before, and then to smile sentimentally and shyly upon someone within.

'Ottilie!' she said without prelude to her plump companion. 'Where's that pretty niece of yours?'

'I have at least seven nieces, Highness,' said Ottilie, returning from a reverie on the subject of thoroughly well-planned dinners. 'All pretty, and all poor!'

'I mean—what was her name? . . . Sab . . . Sab . . . something.'

'They are all Sab-something, poor girls!' said Ottilie apologetically. 'My brother-in-law was a great admirer of the theologist Sabillius. His only son is called after him, and all the girls have names beginning with Sab. There's Sabama, Sabarini, Sabatacha . . .' she thought a minute '. . . and Sabina and Sabania . . .'

'Sabania! That's it!'

'Why does Your Highness ask?'

'Truth to tell, Ottilie, I think we want some new young faces about us at home. We are getting fat and old and dull!'

Ottilie looked sulky.

The fact that the Great Duchess all the time was bowing to the smiling salutes of her subjects did not deter the old lady in the least from carrying on a conversation. It only rendered it more difficult for her auditor, who would have half a sentence spoken across her, and the other half flung—so to speak—with a nod of the enormous bonnet over the farther side of the carriage.

'I'm an old fogram myself,' said the Great Duchess loudly towards Ottilie.

'Can't weed as I used'—words thrown over the carriage side.

'I think we must find a couple of bright young girls'—antiphon.

'So that you and I can weed'—response.

'By deputy!'—antiphon.

Ottilie, used as she was to this pattern of conversation, felt dizzied by it, especially after dinner. She gathered, however, that the Great Duchess had made up her mind to two extra ladies-in-waiting of less degree than herself and Augusta. If it meant weeding by deputy, then she could not bring herself to disapprove.

A week later, therefore, the beautiful Fräulein Sabania von Lausitz, with a complexion like strawberries and cream and eyes the dark blue of violets, made her appearance in the entourage of Highness.

Highness had decided that if violets and strawberries and cream did not do, she would add a symphony in forget-me-nots, milk and ripe corn.

But Sabania was an instant success. By unspoken understanding among all the elderly ladies and grizzled gentlemen she was metaphorically labelled 'Reserved', and by a wordless royal command all intruders were discreetly warned off. She was to be Christopher's playmate: and Christopher found her enchanting—a mixture of an Ossianic king's daughter and the more colourful ladies of Mr. Keats. He wrote poems about her in English and German.

She was not merely as lovely as his dreams, but—like all those ladies of that inner life—remote; that is, in fact, she did not say much.

Sometimes in those comfortable hours before supper he would have the chance of drawing his chair close to hers in the Green Gallery where the old ladies played cards and gossiped of an evening. There he would talk of Schiller and Goethe, or ask her opinion of the works of that rising young Jew, Herr Heinrich Heine.

Fräulein Sabania would listen most intelligently, although she made little comment, the violet-coloured eyes fixed on his face.

He found that she had read a translation of Sir Walter Scott's *Quentin Durward*.

'So *gemüthlich!*' she said.

It had not been quite his own idea, but he was prepared to agree. She warmed to the theme.

'A delicious book!' she declared. 'I assure you, Herr Harnish, that my mouth actually watered when I read that description of the pie King Louis gave the young Durwardt for breakfast! . . . What a pie! What a breakfast!'

Christopher was conscious of a first faint chill—of the first slight shadow on the rosiness of perfection.

Charlotte paid a flying visit: Setoun passed through on some fantastical journey to the Tsar. He was given his cornetcy. The Misses Case wrote long rambling letters, and told of Arabella's marriage to an officer in the Honourable East India Company's Service—Arabella married!—and threatened a visit.

At the end of his second year, shortly after Sabania's arrival, he celebrated his twenty-first birthday. It was all very disappointing, for two days before the celebration he received a letter from Charlotte telling him how Setoun had broken a leg in a carriage accident at Bath and could not make the journey to Neipperg. She, of course, must stay and look after Hurbles. The Great Duchess herself would give him Setoun's gift—wrote Charlotte—and meanwhile she sent him her everlasting love, and a banker's draft, and a dressing-case with silver and crystal fittings, and a new saddle by Wilton, and more love.

He had barely returned from early morning stables, on the momentous day, when he received the summons to Highness.

The old lady was in *négligé* lying on a sofa at the foot of her bed—a vast affair, with crimson hangings suspended from an enormous golden crown near the ceiling. She had a wide-frilled cap which hid her smooth grey hair, and a bright puce-coloured shawl over her shoulders. The curtains were pulled back from the tremendous windows, and in the cold morning light the huge room with its colossal furniture looked like a Cyclopean mausoleum full of mahogany sarcophagi.

'Well, Mr. Harnish,' said the Great Duchess, 'if there's one thing I cordially detest it is morning calls. I can barely be civil. So it says a lot that I send for you at this time of day. Still you can only be twenty-one once!'

She extended her hand, and Christopher kissed it with respectful affection.

'You ought to have someone of your own to greet you on such an occasion. . . . Come here and sit down in this chair where the light is good, and let me look at you—nephew!'

He was about to take the chair, but her words and the sudden change in her tone stiffened him into immobility. He looked questioningly at the jolly red face in the scalloped frame of her cap.

'Sit down!' said the Great Duchess, and for a time she remained silent.

He dropped his eyes uneasily under the regard which studied him intently—took in the broad high forehead with the sweep of waving yellow hair low over the lightly tanned skin: the long straight eyebrows and the straight nose and the rather full chin.

'You are very, very like!' said the Great Duchess at last.

Looking up quickly Christopher saw that her eyes were full of tears.

'Like whom, Ma'am?' he asked uneasily.

The Great Duchess dabbed her eyes with her handkerchief. She must have her smelling-salts. They were on the table by the great folding doors. They weren't? Then on the chest between the middle two windows. No? Good gracious! Ring for Schultz!

'Like whom, Ma'am?' he repeated when Schultz had produced the smelling-salts from a crevice in the sofa, and retired.

The Great Duchess did not reply directly.

'You see the old lady has not forgotten your birthday, Mr. Christopher! Look on the table at the head of the bed. No, the other side!'

He had risen, and, from an inlaid table with gilded ornamentation, picked up the only object lying on its surface—a small miniature in an ebony frame.

'This, Ma'am?'

She nodded.

He looked at it closely.

The portrait was of a young girl dressed in the fashion of twenty years before. She had a pale mournful face with dreaming eyes. Little curls escaped in front from under the brim of her small soft hat. She wore a short-waisted spencer of dark green tied with three bows in front, with a high wide collar. She resembled some-one that he knew.

'Who is it, Ma'am?' he asked, although he realized what the answer would be before she could tell him.

'It is your mother, Christopher,' said the Great Duchess. 'Your mother—and my sister! . . . That is my birthday present to you!'

He could find nothing to say, but stammered his thanks and stood before her staring at the portrait in his hand.

At last. . . .

'My mother! Your sister! But . . .'

'There are no "buts", child. It is so!'

'But, Ma'am . . . then she was a princess?'

'A princess of England.'

He looked from the portrait to the elderly red-faced lady with the slight grey down upon her upper lip. There seemed something strange to him in the idea that this slim, mournful, charming creature—his mother, just as he had always fancied her!—should be sister to a jolly fat old lady, who ate so heartily and got so purple in the face after tea. He tried to find the likeness between the sisters.

The princess read his thoughts.

'You won't find much in my funny old face, nephew, to remind you of her! . . . She was the beauty of the family. I was many, many years older. She was our poor old father's darling! She died young. She was often ill. She was always pale and slim and beauti-ful—dear angel!'

He was utterly at sea.

For a moment hideous doubts assailed him; he had to quell them by staring fixedly at the proud sad face. She could never have done anything disgraceful.

'But why, Ma'am—all so secret? . . . Only now . . .' he tailed off into silence.

'Your mother, Christopher, married your father secretly. You were born even more secretly, for in law the marriage could not be recognized. The King's assent is necessary for a royal marriage. I suppose one would call it a morganatic marriage, nowadays!'

'Then my father, Ma'am?'

'Your father was a monster,' said the Great Duchess vehemently. 'Although he was your father, he was a vile, horrid wretch. I will be savage about him. He was an infamous person. He broke the dear angel's heart. We will not speak of him. . . . Never mention him to me.'

Turning the miniature over and over between his fingers, Christopher had one more question:

'But my name is still Harnish, Ma'am, I suppose?'

It did not shock him that his father was an infamous person. He had never given him much thought. Whereas Setoun had again and again drawn pictures for him of his pretty young mother in the long ago—battling with the wind at Weymouth; bathing at Brighton from a hooded bathing-wagon; lying dying in her lamplit room with the covered canary-cage on the table near her; writing little pathetic verses, one of which he knew by heart; it began—

> 'Unthinking, idle, wild, and young
> I laughed, and danced, and talked, and sung.'

Poor pretty mother. Tears filled his eyes, and he lowered his head so that the Great Duchess should not see them.

'When the dear angel found out how evil a man your father was'—the Great Duchess seemed hardly able to bring herself to pronounce the word 'father'—'she arranged that you should be given the name of Harnish. It was the name of one of the Austrian estates of Lord Setoun. She . . . had been very fond of him.'

'I know, Ma'am,' said Christopher slowly.

'Now, Christopher,' said the old lady, 'you shall kiss your aunt for once in your life like a nephew should. And we shall never more talk about this. And you will never more talk about it—to anyone at all. That is understood, is it not? . . . The dear, kind, good Setoun has your baptismal certificate, and the wedding certificate, and the deed changing your name all locked away for you at his London bankers . . . and here is his birthday gift to you.'

She presented a cheek to be kissed as he stooped—a cheek still wet with tears; and pressed him to her for a moment.

Then with a brisk change of manner, she rummaged among the folds of shawls and wraps for her spectacles, for a comfit because her throat was hoarse from talking; and, finally, and fruitlessly, for a folded paper about so long and so wide—no! perhaps not *quite* so wide, but certainly so long!

It was eventually discovered after Ottilie had been sent for, and Augusta had been sent for, and Schultz had been sent for, in a portfolio of views of Windsor Castle and Windsor Great Park. It turned out to be a transfer of the estate of Harnisch in the Province of Salzburg, with a rent-roll of thirty-thousand florins, by the Right Honourable the Viscount Setoun, Prince of the Holy Roman Empire, etc. etc., to one, Christopher Harnish, a volunteer in the service of His Highness, etc. etc.

With it was a note from Setoun, and a patent with five seals signed with the imperial scrawl 'Francis' at the bottom, transferring also to the said Christopher Harnish, and his heirs and descendants for ever, the titles of Graf von Tollendhal and Freiherr von Harnisch.

'Your uncle—King William,'—his uncle, the King of England! —'and I arranged it with the Austrian Emperor,' explained the princess rather proudly. 'We did not think it suitable that our favourite sister's only son should go through life without some honourable distinction. We thought it would be nice, and a proper thing to do! But I shouldn't use the titles till you go back to England and settle down.'

Words stood out in the papers in his hand—words without meaning—written in very angular writing in very black ink on extremely crackly parchment which had a curiously greasy feeling to the hand. In that large cold room he felt as if he were in a museum examining some historical document which had no relation to himself. He didn't really understand it all: and when he had backed out of the presence and crossed to the Wall House in a daze, the only thing that stood out in his mind was that he was of the Blood Royal of England.

That was what the Great Duke had meant when he spoke about 'near-princes' months ago.

The personal aspect of the revelation principally concerned him. The parents he had never seen had, by reason of that very fact, meant little or nothing to him. They had just been but names: the names of two ghosts were altered—that was all. The unknown mother had always been a plaintive figure of romance; the romance was accentuated: the unknown father had been very vague and dim; he became still more so, now.

It was far more exciting that he himself was very nearly a prince; as nearly a prince as you could be; in fact he really was one! What a shame he could not tell Eckie all about it. You just signed your Christian name when you were a prince—and nothing else. He sat at the desk in his room covering sheets of paper with the signature of 'Christopher' and then 'Christopher P.' because the name by itself conveyed nothing of the dignity attaching to it.

He fixed the picture of his mother to the wall over his bed, and remained before it in rapt contemplation for a long time. Like the princess in the fairy story she had married the squire of low degree: but after that it had become tragedy. He wondered vaguely what his father had done amiss.

Perhaps if he had behaved himself the old King would have recognized the marriage, and then Mr. Harnish would really have been able to sign himself 'Christopher P.'!—or was it plain 'Christopher'?

Christopher P. joined the royal party at tea in the little pavilion in the glade. He sat next the exquisite Sabania on cushions on the low stone balustrade of the temple.

It was a really English tea in honour of the English birthday— said the Great Duchess condescendingly. There was a seed cake, and any amount of buttered toast in Sheffield-plated muffin dishes with hot-water containers, which had been specially and most acceptably presented to the Great Duchess by Setoun on a recent visit.

A lackey set one of the covered dishes conveniently between Fräulein Sabania and himself. The toast was quite English—golden brown, crustless, hot, and dripping with butter. The dish was full.

Christopher talked Schiller.

He talked Heine.

He talked Goethe.

And the beautiful Sabania listened intelligently, and looked at him sweetly out of her violet-blue eyes, and interjected an occasional 'So!' and—ate toast.

Christopher raised the lid to help himself to a first slice.

There was not any! It had all gone—to the last crumb. Sabania had eaten at least eight pieces!

Astounded, he looked at the exquisite creature. He thought he perceived a buttery mark round the exquisite lips.

After that he became more or less immune to women. Except for Eckie he preferred to talk to the older men, and in some ways still he found the unreal world of book and picture and distant landscape and dreams the more satisfactory.

Chapter 21

Life Becomes More Difficult

L IFE IN THE WALL HOUSE RAN EVENLY ENOUGH—OR SO IT seemed. The plump Sophie von Osterode, dewy, luscious, smiled at him and on him, and on von Metzsch—and any man in sight. She always seemed to squeeze his hand in her moist palm when they said 'Good night'; and, sometimes, he thought she pressed her rounded thigh against his when they sat at cards or supper by candle-light. He would see her face, too, peeping out of the darkness of her doorway when he came in at night, and she would appear rustling in the corridors at odd times in the dark on queer purposeless errands.

And Luise, her stepdaughter, remained silent and secret, unsmiling except when her great-uncle spoke to her. She seemed to lead a life remote from outer contacts, although once or twice he had found that she was looking at him in her mysterious way as if gauging him; but she always lowered her regard when caught and withdrew into the isolation that emanated from her.

It was not until his fourth summer in Neipperg was opening that he saw how strong and fierce were the currents that ran beneath the surface of her life.

One night on his return from rounds he stood in the deserted dining-room at the buffet, drinking a glass of wine and water, on his way to bed. From the passage without he heard the sound of boards creaking under a stealthy foot. He put the glass down and waited, and then went out into the long tunnel of a passage which was lighted at one end by the moon. It appeared to be empty, but a moment later he caught the gentle latching of a door.

He went to the round-topped window and looked out into the

moonlit alley. A cloaked man was hurrying to the gate, keeping well in the shadow of the giant yew hedge.

The curtain beside him slightly moved, and he saw hidden by its folds, the grey figure of Luise von Osterode.

'Ssh!' she said in a low whisper, and put a finger to her lips. 'Do you see?'

'What?'

'Him! Conrad!'

'I don't think it is von Metzsch,' said Christopher without conviction.

'It is! It is! He has been upstairs with *her* for two hours. I have waited here to see. She *sleeps* with him. I have thought it for a long time. Now I *know!*'

Although she spoke below her breath it was the first time he had ever heard any emphasis in her speech. She stood watching the dark figure slink into the darkness of the gate.

'It isn't possible,' stammered Christopher. 'Why, it is horrible! Your stepmother!'

'It's unclean,' she said quietly. 'But she is unclean. She is always hungry for men. She gets them. And she sits afterwards smiling and licking her lips like a cat that's eaten a mouse; and will be ready for another one soon. . . . I should not mind if he were not to be my husband!'

'Husband?' said Christopher. 'But you cannot marry him now. It would be infamous.'

She raised her colourless eyes to his. She was, indeed, entirely colourless: the indeterminate hair parted smoothly at her brow and coming to knots at either ear: the pale face with shadows under the eyes and the faint grey lines that curved with the curve of the wings of her nostrils.

'I shall have to,' she said. 'It was arranged before my father died. Our estates . . .'

'Damn your estates!' He forgot in his vehemence to lower his voice. She hushed him—'It's indecent.'

'There's no way out. I shall have to marry him. I am betrothed. It is arranged.'

She spoke with such utter resignation that he knew protests were hopeless.

'Betrothal means nothing!' he answered her.

'In Germany?' she replied with faint scorn. 'You should know I have no choice, now. It's too late.'

'Tell your great-uncle!' he said.

'You know it is true about them. I know it is true. But how could I ever prove it or persuade him? He can conceive of nothing but honour in his family. He would never believe.'

They still stood in the window, Christopher looking down upon her, and at the hands that clasped and unclasped against the grey folds of her dress.

'I have got to marry that—that monster, in a month! To bear his children! I who shall never forget for any single moment of my life! . . . I hate him! . . . I loathe him! . . . If I were brave I should kill myself.'

'I wish I could do something for you,' he said uneasily. 'Shall I tell him—your uncle?'

She remained a minute staring into the empty alley.

'There is—something.' She faltered a little before his questioning glance. 'You will not be angry?'

He shook his head. It was absurd to think he could be angry at anything this poor lady asked of him.

She caught him timidly by the sleeve.

'I mean to have a child of my own,' she said. 'I have thought about it for so very long. A child of which he will not be the father, though he will not know it. . . . A child of mine—untainted by him; something I can love . . . without thinking of him, or her.' She paused the duration of a breath. 'Will you be . . . the father?'

Although he had sensed what was about to come, he recoiled. His startled gaze was caught and held by hers.

'Oh, I am not asking you to love me. . . . Men don't want that. . . . You have always been thoughtful and kind. . . . There are so few people that I should care to ask. . . . It would be . . .' Her voice trailed away.

"How could I, Luise?' he asked, and took one of her chilly hands in his. 'I see your side—honestly I do—but I should never be able to respect myself again.'

'And me?'

'There is no shame for you in what you mean to do. . . . For m

to be consciously the agent of your—your vengeance, would . . .'
He broke off, not finding words to express his thoughts: but knowing that in his sympathy for this pale girl had been evoked a cold danger that beat against his inner world, almost as insistently as the strange power which had surged through him at Arabella's caress.

If perhaps she had softened and wept a little, and pleaded, and clung to him, he would have forgotten, and the outer world would have pushed past the portals of his secret life.

As it was she reasoned with him in her low insistent voice, while he stood looking out on to the moonlit path, his sword-hilt and a bunch of its scarlet sash gathered up in his folded arms.

'If I were to conceive a child now, so soon before my marriage, he would never know that it was not his. But I should. It would be mine! Mine alone! And no one else would know—but you!'

An owl swerved through the night and plunged into the twelve-foot hedge abruptly with a noise like a diver meeting water.

'You are very tired, Luise,' he said at length. 'Let's go to bed, and talk of it again. You have still four weeks!'

'Four weeks! What are four weeks?' she said, but turned and preceded him quietly to the stairs.

Her room was at the stairhead; and there she paused with her hand upon the latch while he wished her good night.

'Good night!' she answered; and then, as she opened the door, drew him forward by the sleeve, as though to whisper something to him.

Before he knew what had happened she had pulled him within and closed the door and stood with her back to it, shimmering before him like a grey moth in the dusk.

'Will you do what I ask you?'

'Luise, please!'

'It is a very little thing—for you.'

'I can't, Luise! Luise, don't ask me!'

'Do you know the story of Potiphar's wife, Christopher?' As she spoke she tore deliberately the broad lace collar from her dress, and dropped it on the floor.

'Do you, Christopher?'

He moistened his dry lips, but found no word.

She put her hands up to the neck of her grey dress, and tore it with a fierce jerk to the waist.

'I shall call aloud, and cry out, and cling to you—like this,' she said evenly and placed her hands upon his arms, and held them in a quiet grip. 'I shall cry—like Potiphar's wife, unless . . .'

'Luise,' he protested, endeavouring to withdraw. 'I've never done you any harm. . . . You don't love me. Why should you do this? Don't be a fool!'

'You know I'm not a wanton,' she said quietly. 'This is so different a thing. . . . I am making sure that there shall be something in my life to come that shall not be his—be theirs—besmirched by their trail! . . . Once again, Christopher! . . .'

Her clasp tightened. He stood rigid, with pinioned arms, looking into the face upturned like a white flower upon the stalk of the white rent in her dress.

'You couldn't do it, Luise!'

'I could! . . . I shall! . . .'

A lock had fallen on his forehead: his brows were anxiously knitted. He looked little more than a child.

'I might—but I shan't'—she flung her hands from off his arms.

She bowed her head against him and burst into a passion of dry sobs, while he comforted as best he might, a confusion of thoughts passing through his mind. Amid them all one faint idea crept to the front, and grew: and grew until it became monstrously dominant.

'Luise!' he said at length. 'Luise!' And so repeated her name until she ceased her hushed weeping, and looked up.

'What—is—it?' she asked.

'It did not need to . . . be . . . me?'

She shook her head.

'There are lots of other people who . . .' He paused for a long while, for he felt that he meditated a dreadful treason. 'There are many others,' he said, and tightened his clasp on her as if to tell her to hold her denials till he had done. 'Many others! . . .'

She shook her head again.

'What chance have I here?' she asked. 'I'm plain—you know it! —and dull. They just don't think of me.'

He nerved himself to the treason.

'There's . . . there's . . . Eckie!'

The sudden stiffening of her body told him that her attention was all alert.

'Eckie,' he said deliberately, 'takes what is sent to him. . . . He—asks no questions.'

'But . . .'

'Eckie, is a dear, good-hearted chap. He's a romantic, and—and —and he's not too innocent.'

She was silent for so long that he thought that she had become obdurate again. She lifted her face to his, and he felt rather than saw her eyes searching his.

'Christopher,' she said. 'I do not know what you think of me. But if you were I, and you were to face a lifetime of loathing and impotent hatred, I think that you would do what I am doing with calculation and without passion. To endeavour to have something of my own, unmarked by that foulness, to cling to by and by.'

'Eckie!' he repeated, and felt like Judas.

'Unless I die, I shall be married within the month. . . . And God will not let me die!'

It seemed inevitable—himself or Eckie.

'Eckie,' he said again.

'He will not be like you?' she murmured. 'Will he have pity on me?'

From some profound depth the knowledge came to him.

'Don't ask him for pity. . . . Don't explain.' He stammered a little. 'He will . . . be . . . v-very content.'

He knew that she smiled although he could not perceive it in the dark.

'You see, Christopher, I know so little that even you must tell me how to manage things like this—which every woman is supposed to know!'

'Think again, Luise—dear Luise!' He urged once more. 'Think before you take such a step. It will be so . . . irrevocable!'

'Think!' she said bitterly. 'Have I not thought enough—and thought—and thought until my head seemed about to burst? And all the time sitting with downcast face listening to *them*, and watching *them*, and hating *them*!'

She opened her door wide and stood back against it, leaving the passage clear. She held her tattered bodice with her left hand at the throat.

He made to go—paused by her a moment.

'Christopher! Again, don't think of me as wanton! . . . I wish, perhaps, it—had—been—you. . . . Eckie's door is never locked? Don't wait! You must not see me go.'

As he passed out he took her right hand and raised it to his lips.

'That is my answer,' said Christopher.

He lay awake all night. He prayed. He found his face wet with tears, and buried it in the pillows. He felt that a chill bleak wind had swept in through the gateway of his inner life, that an earthy fog was drifting about the bright tapestries of his dreams. He wondered whether he would not rather that their precincts should be invaded by the surging forces that Arabella had evoked.

And while he lay and thought and prayed, he listened for rustlings in the moonlit corridor, the creak of a board, or soft footfalls.

But the next morning when he sat heavy-eyed at the midday meal, barely daring to look on her who was opposite, he could with difficulty bring himself to believe that the night had not been a dream. Luise was unchanged and colourless, although the blood had risen to his own cheeks when he saw her come in. She was silent, unmoved; she did not seem to watch von Metzsch and her stepmother, although he knew she did. There were no deeper shadows on her face.

It was when he studied Eckie that he knew all that had happened—Eckie who sat uneasily through the meal, and looked at Luise and away again; and was falsely hearty, and greeted von Metzsch with an unusual restraint.

He did not, however, have much time to speculate, for his days just then were fully occupied. The Court was blazoning into an unaccustomed gaiety. There were to be royal visitors and State concerts and balls and banquets, a pyrotechnic display, performances at the Opera; and a review and many guard and police duties had to be prepared for.

He himself was detailed on the next morning to ride in full panoply to the borders of the duchy with an escort to accompany the Duke of Cumberland and Duke Charles of Brunswick to the palace.

He rode with Eckie a little to the rear of the column.

The horses splashed through roads that shone with recent rain: a sudden gust of wind would shake the wet branches, and the drops fringing the leaves like mercury would fall in a quick pattering shower. Wet leather squeaked against the saddles: the horses' legs were masked in mud. It was time for the midday feed, and the beasts knew it; above the squelch of hoofs and the faint jingle of steel, he sensed their restlessness, and some of them squealed in protest.

'Stables and harness will be a fine job to-night!' said Eckie in disgust, breaking a long silence. 'Lord God, it would be my turn! . . . and the old man is sure to come round himself!'

'I'll take it for you,' offered Christopher. He felt that he owed much to his friend. 'Judas that I am!' he thought.

'Would you really? That would be frightfully nice of you. There are one or two things I'd like to do.' Eckie always hated stable duty and rarely lacked an excuse for missing it.

'Going to meet Marianne?' asked Christopher, hoping, and yet not hoping, that the answer would be 'Yes'. . . . Judas! Judas!

'As a matter of fact . . .' said Eckie, and stopped.

'Another girl, again?' pressed the Christopher who had been Judas.

Eckie cocked a foot out of the stirrup and rode with the knee resting upon his horse's withers.

'Not exactly,' he said; and then with a burst of confidence: 'As a matter of fact, old fellow, it's serious, very serious—this time. . . . Frightfully serious. . . . I'm going to give up—knocking about. It is time I did, anyhow. I'm more than twenty now, you know. I don't want to become like old von Brahe. Besides, this girl . . .'

He rode on in silence, his freckled face puckered in thought.

'I can't tell you now,' he continued. 'Lord God, it would surprise you, though! . . . I may want your help, by and by. . . . You shall know first, of course. . . . But keep mum about it at present.'

Christopher swore secrecy as they halted at a rambling inn and stone guard-post in the dusk of the forest depths. The fat Court

Chamberlain and the lank figure of Michaeloff—who was Master of the Horse as well as Commander of the Garde du Corps—emerged from the carriage which the party had accompanied.

The chamberlain looked longingly at the open door of the inn, but before he could make a move there was a sound of distant hoofs and the rumble of carriage wheels. A black Brunswicker swung round a corner of the road between the trees, and reined up dramatically. Four carriages with an escort of hussars followed at a fast trot. They stopped, and the representatives of the Great Duke went bowing to the side of the closed landau that led the way.

A high-pitched voice complaining of the badness of the road, of the weather, and of the carriage springs, came from the depths.

'Here is an inn, Charles! Have a drink and cheer up!' said someone else gruffly.

'I don't want a drink,' said Charles peevishly. 'They'll probably poison us here. . . . I have had plenty.'

'Another won't do any harm. . . . There's bound to be a pretty girl at a frontier inn, I'll take my oath.'

'Oh, well, perhaps we might,' said Charles, and emerged from the depths, an unwholesome, white-faced young man with a blue coat ablaze with orders, and a great diamond on his finger. He was bareheaded and his light brown hair reeked of pomatum. Eckie—rigidly at attention beside Christopher—sniffed very gently his realization of the fact.

The other was a tall and powerful man in a black uniform laced with gold. He had a great hooked nose with the nostrils distended as though they scented prey. His eyes were deep-set, and a tufted eyebrow drooped over one which was turned out of place and glared with the glassy stare of the blind. He would have looked wholly the Devil—thought Christopher—had not he worn a thick coiling moustache like rams'-horns to hide his lips. He reminded Christopher of someone he once had seen, long ago.

He stalked across the pine-strewn sand to the inn, without appearing to listen to the deferential talk of Michaeloff at his side. His intent and unattending face was full of power, and his ungloved hands were clenched so tightly that the knuckles shone.

'He looks as if he hated God,' said Eckie when the dark figure had passed.

The halt at the inn became protracted. When they appeared at length Cumberland was ostentatiously walking by Brunswick's side, a hand under his elbow. The young man's face glistened with damp, and he was talking loudly and confusedly for the benefit of the bystanders. Cumberland did nothing to restrain him: Christopher thought, indeed, that he took a secret pleasure in listening to the folly—and perhaps, in encouraging it. For there was a thin crease to the Englishman's bluish lips as if to indicate the smile he would not permit himself in public.

Where had he seen that ogreish man before? Dark recollections mingled with chill forebodings in his mind.

'Shouldn't care to meet him on a dark night,' commented Eckie swinging himself into the saddle.

Baron Michaeloff remarked on the incident upon their return. He stood before the mirror in his slip of a dressing-room stropping his razor. His braces hung behind him, and his long mild face was covered with lather. He was about to undergo a second shave in honour of a State banquet, to be held that night at the unaccustomed hour of eight. Christopher stood respectfully within the door.

'I am afraid,' said the old man slapping the razor to and fro upon an old and favourite strop, 'that the Duke of Cumberland is inclined to lead his nephew astray.'

'Not a very difficult thing to do, I should think,' remarked Christopher.

'A very dangerous thing for Brunswick, though.' He held up a grey lock that curled forward by his ear, and scraped the keen edge through the lather. 'I have heard it whispered that his eccentricities have already caused considerable comment. . . . Of course you won't say anything about it. . . . There's some gossip . . .' He suddenly shut his mouth like a trap. 'I have no business to babble gossip; you have no business to listen to it. The honour of a great family, of any family, should not be at the mercy of a chatterer. . . . Honour is all that counts.'

He spoke with German sententiousness combined with a sudden spurt of Russian vehemence; and even stopped shaving while he talked, as if it were an indecent operation to perform while treating of so high a matter.

'You sent for me, sir?' asked Christopher.

God! The old man prated of honour while his niece slept with her stepdaughter's betrothed. While his great-niece became a plaything for Eckie!

'Ah, yes. You must take the late rounds to-night. With one thing and another the others have all that they can do. Take it at midnight—the function won't be over before—and three o'clock and six. . . . Keep a strict eye. There are too many half-empty bottles in circulation. See that the man on the postern by the kitchen is one that you can trust.'

Christopher always appreciated guard duty. He liked to sit with his sword on the table before him, in the small room in the Court of the Guard, beneath the oblique shadow of the Chapel, and think of what lay under his care. He liked to think of the vast building in his charge; of princes and princesses sleeping behind their guarded double doors; of the great galleries in which Rubens jostled Rembrandt, and Frans Hals was next Correggio; of rooms hung with priceless tapestries and littered with cabinets of gems. He was responsible for their safety: he, the Christopher who had trembled in a kitchen before Miss Severn only a few years ago, and had been threatened with the birch!

He liked, too, to walk silently with a sergeant at his elbow along a battlemented wall above the sleeping garden, and pass through winding passages and curling stairs to a turret that overhung the railed forecourt. From there the town lay dark beneath, fretted with towers and a few twinkling lights. It might be some other and fairy city rather than that in which Captain von Brahe got the pox and Eckie had love passages with innkeepers' daughters.

To-night there was no fantasy abroad for him. He sat gloomily in the shadowy room, a prey to misgiving. He felt an unclean thing —a traitor to his friend. Like Peter when he betrayed the Saviour!

There rose ever in his mind, too, the stony face of Cumberland —his mother's brother. He remembered that other brother—Kent. The pompous foolish face, congested with angry blood till it was as red as the wattles of a turkey. The spate of hideous threats that had poured from the angry mouth.

Nevertheless, he went his rounds most scrupulously, and came at length to the folding doors that gave on the State apartments where the Duke of Brunswick lay. One leaf of the door was flung back, and a small lamp burning in the inner lobby cast forward into the gallery the long shadow of the guard on duty outside. The sentry, bringing his sword to the salute, whispered most earnestly, 'Excellency!' as Christopher was about to turn on his heel.

'What is it, Möller?' he asked.

The man was a soldier of the old school, with a square, clean-shaven face under his shako, and with all the tough virtues of his class as well as the vices. Christopher liked him.

'He wanted me to take his boots off!' said Möller in disgust, and jerked his head in the direction of the open door.

'Take his boots off,' said Christopher, 'but! . . .'

'I told him, Excellency, that I could not leave my post. He ordered me to. I said I could take orders from my officers alone.'

'Very good,' muttered the sergeant beneath his moustache.

'And so . . . ?'

'So he cursed me. Very free with his oaths!' said Möller, and permitted himself to add something under his breath.

A door in the lobby crashed open, and a dishevelled figure appeared in the bright oblong it disclosed.

'Hi! You!' it called.

Christopher froze at the discourtesy of the summons.

'Wait for me,' he said to the sergeant and passed in, closing the door after him.

'Highness?'

'Come in, and don't stand gaping there,' said the duke thickly, leading the way into a large anteroom.

Crimson curtains fell in heavy folds from golden baldachins about the windows. Crimson and gilt settees were against walls hung with great battle scenes, and on a buhl table in a corner stood a three-quarters-full decanter and some glasses.

Christopher recognized immediately the dark man who lounged so much at ease in one of the chairs, with a glass beside him and a cigar in his mouth. He knew the pale languid features and the studied dark looks of Charlotte's husband although he hadn't seen him for many years. But Dunscore did not seem to recognize him

—or to care enough, perhaps, to rouse himself sufficiently to do so.

'There are no servants then, in this accursed place?' said Brunswick and gave so fierce a tug at a crimson cord that it fell upon the parquet, coiling like a snake.

'It is like a country ale-house,' he declared. 'I ring, and no one comes. Where are my people? Where are the servants? I might be dead for all they know. . . .'

'I regret, Highness . . .'

'Regrets? Pah! I'll guarantee there's better service at the inn you're staying at, Dunscore?'

The duke's red coat was undone, and an incredible number of stars and orders flapped loosely on it as he stamped up and down. There were yellow diamonds on the tassels of the epaulettes that gave his narrow shoulders a fictitious width; they rattled against one another like dried peas. The trousers buttons that showed in the opening of his coat were enormous emeralds. His flat pasty face was greasy with sweat and his prominent eyes red-rimmed. He was plainly three-parts drunk.

He pointed to the perfect lacquered boots he wore.

'There is not a soul in this infernal mausoleum even to take off my boots. . . . Do you know that your man outside refused to touch them?'

'His orders, sir,' said Christopher respectfully, 'are not to leave his post.'

'And my orders were—that he should take my boots off!'

'He may take no orders except from his own officers, sir.'

Brunswick swore foolishly.

Dunscore stretched out a lazy hand, and poured himself full measure into his glass. He appeared entirely indifferent to the proceedings.

'St-steady!' said Brunswick. 'Remember me! There'll be no more to be found in this lousy house. . . . Well?'

'I will send, sir, to summon your people.'

'Send? Send! Am I to be treated worse than a bag-man at a hedge tavern? . . . Here, you seem to have no post to quit . . . Take off my boots yourself!'

He flung himself into a settee, and stretched out a booted leg.

'I will send . . .' said Christopher, and hesitated before the hectoring air. He frankly did not know what he should do. It was not for a subaltern to quarrel with a sovereign.

'Is this the way you treat princes, God blast it?' asked Brunswick offensively. 'I say, take—my—boots—off!'

Dunscore lifted an indolent, insolent face. A thin smile curved his too perfect mouth.

'I am no . . .' began Christopher, and saw no hope for it. He flushed red—and felt that Dunscore had sardonically appreciated the fact. Still, after all, the fellow was drunk; he bent suddenly forward and took the boot between his hands. It came so easily that he knew Brunswick could have pulled it off unassisted—without even a jack. The duke gave a malicious thrust as he jerked at the second boot, and the thing shot from his hands and smeared a green-black polish across the creamy whiteness of his breeches.

'Here's to your boots!' said Dunscore in surprisingly good German, tossing off his tumbler in one breath.

The duke rose to his stockinged feet and filled his glass.

'I ne-never-d-drink to-my-boots,' he declared with drunken gaiety. 'Here's to my . . . here you, sir, take a glass! You won't, won't you? Well, wait till I see what more I want! Here's to my little girl!'

'What little girl?' asked Dunscore, lying back with his glass at a perilous angle in his hand.

'My little girl—the only one! My d-dear, d-darling little girl!'

'Who?' insisted Dunscore.

'Margaretha! You know, of course.' He stumbled lamentably over the name.

'She is not yours yet!' said Dunscore swinging his glass about, so that the liquid splashed upon the polished floor.

The duke supported himself against the marble mantelpiece under a great dim picture in a great dim frame. He swayed to and fro.

'How d-do you know?' he said thickly.

'Because,' drawled Charlotte's husband, lazily, 'she's going to be mine first.'

Brunswick was staggered for a moment. He fixed an owlish stare on the other. Christopher, watching him swing forward and back, wondered when he would fall.

'I t-tell you, she's mine. All of her!' . . . He went into gross details before which Christopher flinched.

'You can have her, Charles,' remarked Dunscore rising, 'when I have done.'

'Go to hell!' said the duke thickly. 'I say she's mine, you b-bastard! . . . I shee through you now. . . Turn up in N-neipperg' (he was shaken by a great hiccup) 'to shee ole fren' Brunswick, did you? . . . Liar! . . . Thought she'd be here, 'smarrer o' fact. . . . Well, she isn't!'

'. . . Yet!' amended Dunscore.

Brunswick hiccuped again so violently that his entire frame shook, and he lurched the length of his arm from the anchorage he held to the red marble slab above the black mouth of the empty hearth.

' 'N' if she does—come, it won't be any of your b-blasted business! Shee? Jus' keep out!'

'Go to bed, Charles, you're bottled. Utterly bottled.'

'I'm not. If you try t-to g-get my g-girl, I'll—I'll—I'll . . .'

'Get your boot-boy to take you to bed, Charles!' said Dunscore easily: and Christopher did not know which of the two men he would rather kill.

Just for one moment Brunswick held himself in control.

'If I find you trying for her, George,' he said with clenched teeth, 'God save you!'

He helped himself from the decanter again, and drank off the spirit neat. He fell over his words:

'I'll chreat you—like zhat.'

He swept decanter and glasses from the table to the floor. They splintered amid a reek of spirits.

'Not a zhentl'man! . . . You're a zhentl'm'n, boot-boy! We'll go! Zhall we, ole fren'?'

He put a scarlet arm round Christopher's neck, and stumbled to the door of his bedroom. A State bed with a canopy of purple that seemed as high as a mountain peak, loomed within.

'Lovely!' he said, halting in his lurch. 'Ver' lovely! Mosht sholitary for a p-prince. Look, ole fren'! Be a zhentl'm'n! Find me a nice fat—nice . . . nice . . .' He trailed hopelessly among his words. 'You kn-know what I m-mean!'

'I am not your Highness's pander,' said Christopher, and closed the door on him, and went without a word.

He returned to the guard-house in a cold rage—a greater hate of Dunscore in his heart, perhaps, than of the man who had put the first insult on him.

In the inner room the baron stood examining the report-book by the light of a solitary candle. His long thin face was so stooped down upon his high stiff collar that two curling lines ran from below his chin to his cheek bones.

'You have been a long time on your rounds, Christopher,' he said mildly, and smiling at the young man who stood before him with his plumed shako under his arm.

'His Highness . . .' began Christopher, and choked with anger.

'The Great Duke?'

'The Duke of Brunswick, sir!'

'What about him?' asked the baron looking at him keenly, taking a trifle of snuff from his box which lay on the table, and halting with it in mid-air—'Have you been up a chimney, Mr. Harnish? The state of your breeches would lead one to suppose so.'

Christopher looked down at the stain which was visible even in the subdued light.

'The Duke made me—insisted with oaths on my pulling his boots off. He would not let me send for a servant.'

'Take his boots off?' said the baron loudly, dropping the snuff-box with a clatter. 'Great God! I hope you did not do so!'

'What was I to do, sir?'

The old man rapped on the table with his knuckles.

'Refuse. And point-blank! . . . It is infamous that my officers should be treated as lackeys. You should have refused, Mr. Harnish.' The old man's mild face was distorted by a snarl that showed his yellowed teeth. The veins on his parchment-coloured temples stood out in faint blue lines. Christopher realized then that underneath the mild exterior undreamed-of fires might smoulder.

'Your honour!' said the baron.

How insistent the old man was on the matter of honour. Even at that moment Christopher was aware of the irony in a lecture on honour by one whose roof was doubly dishonoured—no, triply, for he himself partook of the shame that had come to it.

As rapidly as the fury had risen within Michaeloff, so rapidly it died away.

'No! I don't know, perhaps, that I can blame you so greatly. But honour, Mr. Harnish, is a very delicate thing. A whisper may tarnish it. The duke must apologize. I will not permit this sort of thing. One would think the man was a Turkish bashaw. The best that can be said is that he was drunk. I shall tell the Great Duke. He must protect his young officers, in a case such as this. The honour of his Garde du Corps is at stake!'

An appalling thought occurred to him. He looked at the mark upon Christopher's breeches.

'You took them off—with your hands?' he asked. 'Not like a lackey between the knees?'

'Good God, sir, no!' said Christopher, although he saw little of the fine shadings in the quality of the disgrace that had befallen him.

'I'm glad of that—glad of that,' commented Michaeloff, raising the long-delayed pinch of snuff to his nostrils. 'Don't worry about it, I shall arrange. You will not mention it, of course.'

'Is it likely, sir?' asked Christopher.

A roll of drums in the fore-court announced the approach of supper-time. Five games of whist were in progress in the Green Gallery, and at the farther end knots of non-players clustered round albums or engaged in talk. On non-ceremonial nights it often amused the Great Duchess to play with Christopher as partner. 'English against German,' she said. They played to-night against Ottilie and the silver-haired Marshal of the Court, whose long white wand of office and cocked hat were disposed of on the floor at his side.

The old lady had a favourite spot—by the farthest of the six tall windows that opened on the terrace; with her back to a life-size reclining statue by Canova of the Great Duke's first wife in a very considerable *négligé*, and a gargantuan and highly varnished portrait of the same lady in robes of state by Joseph Koch. She sat in her voluminous gown of puffed black satin, with a jolly red face on top, like a heap of shining coals, against the whiteness of the marble.

She dealt the cards; and Christopher noticed traces of the afternoon's weeding in the scratched surface of her finger nails.

'I suspect that you will trump my trick this hand, Mr. Harnish,' said she cheerfully.

'Ma'am!' protested Christopher, guiltily conscious of a certain abstraction.

'If you could throw away a perfectly good spade in one game, you will undoubtedly trump your partner in the next.' She counted the cards she had dealt. 'Now, I declare you have made me misdeal. . . . Yes . . . No, it's all right, after all.'

'But, Ma'am,' said Christopher, 'my King was twice guarded.'

A gold-braided aide bowed deferentially at her side and said something in a low voice. She cast a glance at Christopher and then to the curtains that marked a deep recess where sometimes the ducal throne was placed.

'He may go now. We'll wait, and tear his character as card-player to pieces while we do. Shan't we, Ottilie? It's the only scandal he has furnished us with, so far. . . .'

'His Highness, the Great Duke, commands your presence, Mr. Harnish,' said the aide, coming to his chair.

Christopher rose with a bow and apology, and, crossing the gallery, passed through the curtain archway to an anteroom where the Great Duke stood, flanked by his cousins. Cumberland towered over both, his face bent a little forward so that his dim hooded eyes should see the fun, and the dark lines on its bleakness accentuated by an enigmatic smile. Brunswick's mouth was opened vacantly, as if in uncompleted protest.

The Great Duke extinguished the cigar he had been finishing against the elbow of a gilded chair. He said abruptly:

'Mr. Harnish, I hear that you behaved extremely correctly last night in difficult circumstances.'

Christopher, having no comment to make, bowed.

'I hear that you reported the matter—I need go into no details —to your commanding officer. That also was very correct.'

As he paused Christopher bowed again.

'Your commanding officer then reported to me. Extremely correct.'

As Baron Michaeloff was not there, Christopher bowed on his behalf.

'I mentioned certain aspects of the matter to the Duke of Brunswick. His Highness desires to apologize for the misunderstanding—very correctly, too.'

The Duke of Brunswick showing no signs of acknowledging the correctness of all this, Christopher bowed twice—for himself, and for the duke.

'But . . .' bleated Brunswick.

'I think you understand now, Charles. My officers are not to be treated as men-servants?' rumbled the Great Duke, obviously annoyed by the other's hesitation to apologize.

'I can only say I'm sorry, if this gentleman took a silly prank amiss,' said Brunswick stiffly, and with lame dignity.

'Silly prank!' said the Great Duke. 'Silly pranks, Charles, are out of place with a gentleman of Mr. Harnish's antecedents! His family is . . . at any rate as good as yours. As good as yours!'

Brunswick looked at Christopher resentfully. He sniffed incredulity. Cumberland, who had been listening with indifference, swung his peering blind-man's gaze upon the lad.

'Really?' said Brunswick offensively doubtful.

'Would it be indiscreet to inquire *what* family?' observed Cumberland. 'His name is not familiar to me!'

'It is *yours!*' blurted out the Great Duke, in his jerky, rapid speech.

'It is yours?' repeated he with a note of interrogation, as if trying to recall whether he had really used the phrase or not, and hoping that he had not. His faded eyes caught Christopher's and read the answer.

'I don't seem to recognize him,' said Cumberland.

'No reason why you should,' said the Great Duke in a great flurry. 'No reason at all. . . . All right! All right! Matter's over. . . . Mr. Harnish . . .'

'Should he say "Papa" and fall into my arms?' inquired Cumberland. 'Touching meeting between father and son, and all that?' He sketched a gesture of opening his arms, and chuckled.

Christopher stood stiffly at attention. His face was scarlet.

'Let us leave the matter,' said the Great Duke in a hurry. 'Thank you, Mr. Harnish! You may withdraw.'

'It's like that,' said Cumberland, 'is it?'

The Great Duke trod on his cigar butt. He was purple with annoyance, and obviously taken aback by Cumberland's tone. He drove on to disaster.

'Your sister's son, Ernest!' he said, and snapped the sentence off, as if he were a sewing-woman biting a thread.

'Sister's son!' repeated Cumberland slowly. 'S-i-s-t-e-r's son! Amelia's?' His voice rose to a bellow as he pronounced the name, and he burst into a sudden roar of laughter. A roar of laughter which was horrifying because it appeared to be reasonless.

Christopher's eyes were fixed on the dark figure with a single star sparkling on his breast. Instinct told him that there was some cause—of which he did not know—for that laughter, in which there was no honest humour but only mirthless appreciation of misfortune. He took a step forward. Hot words trembled within his mouth.

'Mr. Harnish,' commanded the Great Duke, speaking rapidly, 'you may withdraw. You have behaved most correctly. You have earned promotion. You have it from to-day. . . . You may withdraw. . . . Very correctly!'

Christopher backed through the heavy curtains conscious that all three men were staring after him.

He returned to the card table, but played, however, a very distracted game.

The drums rolled for the second time.

The Court Marshal at the finish of the hand, collected his white wand and hat from beneath his chair. He besought the Great Duchess's permission to withdraw, levered himself to his feet with knobbly rheumatical hands upon the table-edge, proceeded to the door, turned on his heel, returned to the table, and bowed low to the great lady who was expostulating quite amiably about a nine of diamonds that had been seriously maltreated.

'Your Highness, I must announce that supper waits on your pleasure.'

He withdrew a pace or two and stood at stately attention, no longer the cautious and captious partner or opponent of a game of whist, but the Excellent Great Ducal Court High Functionary.

To Christopher at her chair-back the Great Duchess turned a red face and interrogative eyes as she rose.

'My little friend,' she said in a low voice, 'you look so serious that I suspect the Great Duke of whispering secrets to you. . . . Has he?'

'No, Highness,' he replied. The Great Duke had indeed evolved secrets, but not disclosed them. 'He has been good enough to promote me.'

'I am very glad,' she said—and Christopher thought how nice even fat old ladies could look when they smiled—and added, as though to herself, 'It is strange . . . keeping a secret usually hurts him. . . . Quite hurts him.'

Chapter 22

Footlight Adventure

CHRISTOPHER WROTE TO SETOUN.

'. . . Can't I come home now? Couldn't we set off on our Grand Tour together? They are very agreeable and kind to me here, but I am honestly tired of Germany. Let me hear from you at once. You cannot think how much I want to get away.'

He underscored the sentence so heavily that he splayed the quill, and had to pause and trim it with his pen-knife.

'To get away'; from what?—he asked himself as he sliced the crisp feather with the blade. From everything that reminded him of the Iscariot self that had betrayed Eckie. From the sight of the pink warm woman who took her pleasure with her stepdaughter's betrothed: whose lips were always almost as moist and red as if her kisses drained her lover of blood. And then Cumberland; head thrown back; staring blind eye in its pit under the shaggy brows; laughing! Laughing about what?

'I have been promoted lieutenant,' wrote Christopher. 'The G.D. said I had behaved very correctly in a small matter. So Williams went off to the tailor in a tearing hurry this morning, with the result that this evening my collar is stiff with gold embroidery, and my scarlet cuffs have two twirls of gold braid instead of being plain.

'We must all be painted in full regalia by Chalons one of these days, with Charlotte and her little spaniel, and a rose lying on the floor.'

He added a little more to no purpose, signed the letter, and hesitated with his pen in the air, watching the gay crowds pass to and fro under the lime trees beneath his window. A man with a

357

rod was perched on a white wall on the farther bank fishing in the troubled river. He wrote a postscript:

'You've not been saving up anything to tell me on your death-bed, have you? As they do in romances? I can't help mentioning it because the Great Duke seems always to be on the brink of some disclosure. Cumberland . . .'

The shaven face of Williams with a faint curve of whisker on each cheekbone appeared at the door. He was in a sleeved striped waistcoat as gay as the body of a wasp, and held a pair of admirably polished riding-boots in his hand.

'Word's just been sent you're wanted at the palace, sir.'

'What for?' asked Christopher.

'As iggerant as a babby, sir,' said Williams. 'Was told you was to go to Her Highness's boodoor.'

Christopher dashed off a final line or two to his letter, instructed Williams about its dispatch, and hurried through the gardens to the palace.

The Duke of Brunswick was sitting with the Great Duchess, in a small room so cluttered with miniatures in round black frames that the walls resembled a section of honeycomb, with the cells all outlined in lamp-black. They were unattended. Through the windows the terraced garden shone in the sunset with dramatic unreality, in purple shadow and golden glow.

'Very nice, indeed!' said the Great Duchess, acknowledging Christopher's salute, and highly approving the additions to his uniform. 'You look very well indeed. Now I can't have you turning the heads of any more young ladies! I could wish the Great Duke would have silver lace instead of gold. More to the modern taste, I think, don't you, Charles? Yes! Very like the picture!'

She did not, however, specify what picture; and Brunswick having thrown a swift scrutiny over the youthful study in cream and scarlet, regarded his own dark outfit with diminished satisfaction. He remarked at length:

'I have been trying to persuade Her Highness to visit the Opera with me this evening. The "Rose Garden", an entirely new work. The music very tuneful, I am told. Only been performed in Paris!'

'Paris! . . . Ah, Paris! Music! . . . H'm!' commented the Great

Duchess, shaking her head disapprovingly over one or the other—
or both.

'I am an enthusiast myself,' said Brunswick with an attempt at
brightness. 'Adore music. Runs in the family, I suppose. Can't keep
me away from opera. Anything new!—and, presto! there I am!'

'Music!' re-echoed the Great Duchess. 'So uncomfortable—so
upsetting!'

'I have asked Her Highness to excuse me to-night. Should never
forgive myself if I missed an opportunity of attending a first night!
Confirmed opera-goer! Confirmed first-nighter!'

He hummed a stave or two of some unrecognizable air as if to
show what a musical enthusiast he was; crossed and uncrossed his
black-pantalooned legs uneasily; cast a glance at the old lady to see
how impressed she was by the performance, and turned his flat,
silly face to Christopher.

'I thought, perhaps . . .' he addressed Christopher directly—'to
show that our—er—little misunderstanding was forgotten, that—
er—that is to say, you might care to come with me—as my equerry
to-night. . . . Henkel is ill—ate too much, I suppose, or drank too
much. He's given that way. The Great Duke has given his permission.'

Christopher bowed.

The Great Duchess sighed.

'You mustn't permit yourself to become too fond of music,
Charles,' she said earnestly. 'It's most dangerous for persons of high
rank.'

'Music?' inquired the duke, flushing.

The old lady drew her orange-coloured shawl closer about her
shoulders, either because of the sunset chill, or because the mention of the word 'music' had an adverse effect on her bodily warmth.

'Music makes people so enthusiastic that it is quite unpleasant,'
she said. 'Oh, I know it is a great accomplishment, but it can draw
you into such very unpleasant society.'

Brunswick became a darker red.

'Your poor aunt!' went on the old lady, observing him narrowly,
and again shook her head. 'No! Music is very nice in its place;
in church; and patriotic songs, and a military band! But otherwise
I really prefer to have nothing to do with it.'

Despite the Great Duchess's opinion of music, they set off very shortly in a closed carriage with two powdered and cockaded lackeys behind, and four running footmen with links to light their way home.

'If—I—am—delayed afterwards,' said Brunswick in an embarrassed manner, lighting a cheroot as they turned out of the forecourt, 'you may have to go home by yourself. If so, you—er—understand that there is no need to mention it.'

Christopher quite understood.

The stucco front and Doric columns of the Opera House commanded a steep little square of tall crowded houses with a railed garden in the centre. Its colonnade was ineffably dreary in the dusk, with a few oil lamps twinkling over bills announcing THE ROSE GARDEN, and—in fat letters below—MARGARETHA ACISLO. There was only a sprinkling of bystanders to witness their arrival, which appeared to disappoint the duke. He cheered up, however, at the sight of the crimson carpet laid up the shallow steps, and the deferential group in much-befrilled shirts, tights and silk stockings that awaited them.

The manager, a voluble little Italian with the round, thin-lidded eyes of a monkey, led them to their box chattering all the time.

Such new stage effects—His Highness would be ravished! Such dresses—from Paris! The Acislo— Ah, superb! He kissed his hand with the grimace of an intoxicated ape. When did she arrive? From Paris that very afternoon—in less than a week! Two carriages! One luggage coach! Three maids! Less than a week! Dressing-case full of tortoise-shell and gold! A hundred thousand florins' worth of diamonds! Superb! Ravishing! What a figure! What a voice! Had brought with her four tubs of sea-water and one of asses' milk for her bath! Champagne—she had said—could be got anywhere! Champagne—she declared—opened the pores of the skin! Had His Highness experimented?

In this flurry of conversation they attained their seats, not in the Royal Box in the middle of the theatre, but one in the lower of the two tiers of boxes and actually overhanging the stage.

His Highness would notice the new curtain. Story of Cupid and Psyche! Delicious! A little immoral? Ah, no! And a new Italian invention. Lever and counterpoise. Up it went like—like a twinkling! But, talking of champagne . . .

And, talking of champagne, there were three or four bottles in the small anteroom to the box, on a table lighted by a four-branched candlestick and mostly occupied by a bouquet of flowers as large as a hip-bath. Vintage 1822, explained the manager wrestling with the gold foil. And a bottle of 1776 cognac! Two or three indeterminate persons leaped forward to deal with the bottle. His Highness had a stiff peg of brandy, topped up to the brim of a tumbler with bubbling wine! He declared he felt better for it.

Christopher pretended to follow suit; the manager deferentially ventured to fill up the glasses—and his own. And the meek indeterminate persons appeared to deal very faithfully with what remained.

It was a small, crowded, astonishingly lofty little anteroom; and everybody's shadow ran all the way up the wall to the ceiling, so that the improper doings of the plump ladies who languished in fat nudity on the panels were charitably hidden.

The orchestra started a discordant scraping; the manager hurriedly withdrew, promising further supplies; the duke and Christopher seated themselves in their gilded and crimson box and examined the theatre. It was full from one-florin pit to fifty-groschen gallery. Both rows of boxes were crowded.

A vast sea of faces was turned in their direction—all, in the lamp-light, rather yellow-white with great staring eyes. Here a hand was raised to point royalty to a less observant companion. Here a black smudge where some indifferent Radical—must be a Radical!—pored over a playbill and declined to pay the homage of interest. There, exactly opposite, was the bored yawn of the Earl of Dunscore in a box with the Hanoverian envoy and his party.

'That fellow!' snorted Brunswick, ignoring the bow. Otherwise he gathered the meed of interest and flattery by hanging over the edge of the box, conspicuous with the enormous star on the breast of his plum-coloured coat, until the orchestra struck up the overture and the theatre was darkened.

Christopher was able to give little attention to the performance, although it opened with the death of an old gentleman in a rose garden between a water mill and a ruined tower. For no sooner had a young lady appeared on the stage, in white satin with a chip hat swinging by its ribbons in her hand, and cast herself down by the old gentleman's side, than the Duke of Brunswick appeared to be seized by delirium.

He leaned forward out of the box until Christopher expected him every minute to fall into the orchestra. He coughed in an affected and stentorian manner in the midst of a duet, and then slowly and ostentatiously would bring up a hand glistening with rings to his hair, and run it through the scented locks. He also loudly applauded every solo by the young lady with arms stretched out to their fullest extent over the stage, and continued so clapping after the rest of the applause had died away. It would have seemed impossible that the pretty actress, at whom all this demonstration was aimed, should not have had her attention attracted by it; but remarkably enough she never once looked up, although the audience showed signs of appreciative notice.

When the act closed with the lady in white satin straining most dramatically in the grip of the wicked knight, with the violins surging up and surging down in a perfect ecstasy of passion, and with the audience howling with enthusiasm, two lackeys appeared in front of the orchestra. They propelled beyond the footlights, with the aid of the conductor, one of the leading violins, and an unimportant member of the chorus in tin armour, the selfsame enormous bouquet that Christopher had noticed in the anteroom.

The young lady in white satin looked at the blossoming mass with considerable uncertainty, bowed again generally to the audience, and withdrew—without a glance to the still-applauding duke.

'Isn't she . . . ?' said he, unable to find sufficient encomium, turning to Christopher.

'She seems very charming,' replied the temporary aide-de-camp cautiously.

' "Charming"!' said Brunswick in great disdain. 'Why, you poor fish, she is superb! She is marvellous. Did you ever see such arms?'

Christopher quite truly never had.

'Did you ever see such large eyes—such black hair? . . . Now they are eyes, and it is hair!'

Christopher agreed that they were and it was.

'Such a face! Such a figure! Such lips! . . . And I don't mind telling you that—well, you know!'

Christopher did not know, but he agreed very heartily.

'Lovely creature! Lovely creature! . . . We shall . . . er . . . arrive at an understanding—in time! . . . That, of course, is not to be repeated at the present!'

Christopher thought that the lovely creature showed little sign of being ready for an 'understanding', but did not say so.

During the second act Christopher studied the lovely creature more closely. Her natural beauty shone through its stage overlay of powder and paint. She had grey eyes under level brows, and a gay face accentuated by a mass of impertinent black ringlets. She sang the meretricious stuff with an effortless grace, and fell into the arms of her lover with such a gleam of white arms and clinging abandon at the end of the second act, that there was not a man in the audience who would not have wished to be in his shoes.

'I shall go to the green-room,' said Brunswick abruptly as the curtain fell. 'There will be a fifteen-minute interval. Ring for the box-keeper!'

Under the guidance of the old hag who answered the summons, they passed through a narrow door outside the entrance to the box; trod cautiously a gloomy passage with dusty scenery propped against a bare brick wall; mounted a corkscrew staircase; and emerged into a room like a barn inhabited by plush benches, a fly-blown mirror or two, a table with decanters, a couple of large chandeliers, and a number of people in the most fantastical costumes.

Everything that was not dusty was greasy. The gay dresses on closer inspection appeared to be the cheapest of calico, and the shining complexions a compound of perspiration and paint. Everybody was talking at once. In a corner Christopher saw Dunscore condescending to the monkey-faced manager, who broke away and came leaping toward the duke.

'Your Highness,' he chattered, and bowed so low it was a marvel he ever recovered. 'Great honour! The cast—permit me to present.'

There was a moment or two of embarrassed affability to a dozen people on the part of the duke. Then he eventually broke through a monologue by a gentleman in a cocked hat and high boots to remark to the manager in a loud whisper:

'But where is Signorina Acislo?'

The little man clapped his hands together.

'But where, indeed, is our Acislo? Where is she, children?'

A half dozen voices answered with varying directions.

'Run you, my little one,' said he to a pretty *contadina*, 'and find the Acislo. She is wanted, ah, *pronto!* Royal Highness desires presentation. Run! Run!'

The contadina, who had been exchanging mischievous smiles with Christopher, vanished with a flash of long legs in soiled white cotton stockings, and a swirl of a very short skirt. She returned almost as soon as she went, and pulled the little man's sleeve and whispered to him earnestly. Whereat his round eyes seemed to become rounder and more anxious than ever.

' "Indisposed"?' he muttered. 'Impossible! . . . Where? . . . Ah, yes! . . . The little lady is occupied! Ah, so busy. You know these *prime donne!* If Your Highness forgives, will we seek her?'

Highness was prepared to forgive anything in such a cause.

'Await me in the box,' he commanded Christopher. 'I will find a guide back.'

The contadina ran her arm through Christopher's.

'Come on, pretty boy,' she said as royalty vanished through a door escorted by manager and deputy and *chef d'orchestre.* 'I'll take you back to mother!'

But it was a long way round they went, with a peep between two flat shaky pieces of canvas on to the stage. There was a pasteboard fountain in the centre and a slim white satin figure curtsying to the plum-coated duke. From behind the curtain came the continuous rumble and hum of the audience: high up through the flies darkness enveloped the roof.

'Just the two figures—like a little play!' whispered the contadina, and twitched him away. They passed Dunscore as they emerged from the wings—Dunscore exquisitely cold, exquisitely formal from gauze stockings to white stock and frilled shirt, talking to two men as if he did not see them, ignoring Christopher as if he did not exist.

'He looks as cold as a wet tree,' she said, as she guided Christopher through the half darkness beneath the stage, 'yet they say he is mad for Margaretha! I wonder what kissing a wet tree is like?'

Christopher had no experience.

'You know,' she said as they stopped under the lamp by the door of his box, 'you really are a pretty boy! I just love your uniform!'

Christopher flushed to the roots of his yellow hair.

'I shouldn't be safe with you for a moment. Not a moment.'

Christopher with a hand on the door latch protested his innocence.

'I—shouldn't—be—safe—with—you—for—a moment,' repeated the contadina: and with each word she rose a little higher on tiptoe and approached more nearly her very smiling lips to Christopher's face.

He, greatly daring, leaned forward and most gravely kissed her on the mouth.

'There, I knew it!' she declared, greatly elated, threw her arms about his neck, and kissed him very heartily in return.

'Oh, your face!' she exclaimed when that was done. 'It's all over paint. . . . Where's my handkerchief! . . . See, I'll wet it—that's kissing by deputy! . . . There, that's better!'

She subjected him to a close scrutiny, passed him as being fit for duty, squeezed his hand in a most loving way, told him to come and see her next night—Fanni, third in the front row on the prompt side—and vanished like an elfin through the little doorway.

Few of the audience had left their seats: the gallery, full of noisy students from the university, was entertaining itself by ribald choruses; and pit and boxes by a bubble of conversation.

Suddenly, without any warning whatever the curtain shot up. The audience instantly hushed.

Margaretha Acislo, laughing, angry, resistant, was revealed in the clumsy embrace of a plum-coloured figure in the centre of a setting intended to represent a medieval market-place.

The man's back was to the audience who, for the moment, imagined that a new scene had begun.

The next instant, however, Margaretha had given her assailant a resounding slap on the face, torn herself from his grasp and fled from the stage.

Plum-coat turned round, hand to cheek. The audience took in the dropped jaw of horrified astonishment and the great diamond star, with a howl of recognition and laughter. Their roar echoed to the roof like the sea in a cavern: the gallery screamed ribaldries; sober burghers clapped and stamped while they bellowed. From somewhere a large piece of sausage whizzed over the footlights.

For a brief appalled second the Duke of Brunswick stood in the centre of the stage by the ridiculous pasteboard fountain, facing the uproar. The look of amazement on his face gave way to one of blind fury. He clapped his hand to his sword. He swung round obviously mouthing curses and threats . . . and the merciful curtain descended on him.

Christopher drew into the shelter of the crimson hangings of the box. Opposite him the Hanoverian envoy was hiding his mirth in his hat, but the statuesque and weary face of Dunscore was missing. The theatre echoed with cries of 'Bravo!' shouts for an encore and loud catcalls.

The pandemonium showed no signs of abating, until, immediately beneath him, before the curtain, the gay figure of Margaretha Acislo appeared from the wings.

She swept into a deep curtsy in impertinent acknowledgment of the applause, and cast a roguish look upwards into the darkness of the stage box, while the theatre howled its appreciation. Christopher knew that somewhere in the course of his life he had seen that smiling heart-shaped face before.

Dunscore reappeared suddenly in the opposite box: he bent his head in faint mocking comment to the envoy. His long white fingers beat a languid tattoo of applause on the gilded ledge of the box.

Chapter 23

The Tale of a Great Duke

THE GREAT DUKE SENT FOR CHRISTOPHER SHORTLY AFTER his return from the theatre. He lay on an ottoman in his dressing-room in a flowered silk bedgown, his moustache waxed and greased against the morrow in a sort of gauze container which hooked behind his ears. He was a little bemused by drink, and mournfully angry.

He had heard the outline of the story almost before even Christopher had succeeded in extracting the screaming, furious Brunswick from a group that included a grovelling manager and a stage-hand with a battered face and a bloody mouth.

The news had come with the speed of the wind. Stage-door had whispered it to waiting lackeys: box-keeper had passed it to attendants in the front: a galleryite had slipped out to gather friends from beer-cellar and inn for a riotous reception to the royal lover: a court official in the audience had considered it his duty to leave his seat and arrive with urgent warning for Graf von Hompesch, the Court Chamberlain.

At first the Great Duke had just lain back on his ottoman and cursed the pimple-faced fool with round Germanic oaths. Serve him right if the King of England thought he was better off the throne of Brunswick and made him abdicate. A poor fish, who liked French kickshaws better than honest German dishes, made snivelling love and got his ears boxed, hung himself with diamonds like a woman, and painted his dirty face to get a pink complexion! A filthy, puling, violent, disordered creature! He even preferred to travel in a closed carriage—like a girl!

Closed carriages were not meant for young men! They made a

decent man sick! Stroking the cat that he always enticed to his dressing-room despite his wife's displeasure, he remembered his honeymoon journey to the Regent's Cottage at Windsor. How he had been sick in the stuffy chariot and ridden in the dickey, and been forced to put his equerry inside with his bride.

His bride! That nice fat comfortable woman, who did not mind tobacco smoke or beer or sauerkraut, and adored pork in every shape! She was a cousin of this little reptile—one of this appalling family, whose curse seemed to be hatred, perpetual disorder, and scandal. One of the blood of George the Treacherous, and Ernest of Cumberland the Violent, and Frederick the Corrupt, and Caroline the Persecuted and Foolish—the blood of wretched princesses and abominable princes.

She had escaped the taint: but how many of the line would do so? That boy, for instance, her unrecognized nephew—what would happen to him?

He sipped with appreciation his cold milk punch: wetted his finger and tried to seduce to alcohol the cat.

He was a nice lad, a nice, frank, pleasant boy! . . . It was a foul shame that he should so fatally represent the weakness and the misery of the princesses, and the disgrace and dishonour of the princes.

Someone should tell him! . . . He ought not to be left in ignorance of the taint that he must fight. . . . Tell him, so that he should strengthen himself to fight against it!

He sipped his punch again; then seized his bell cord and pulled violently; and, while he waited, fell to watching the contemptuous and offended cat as she washed from off her whiskered face the dab of punch with which he had surprised her.

Upon the summons Christopher left Brunswick pacing his sitting-room like a demented beast, spitting out oaths and threats, crashing emphasis to them with his sword against the table, soaking up brandy. In the darkest corner sat Cumberland quietly listening, his lips just twisted from his teeth in a snarl of a smile, the wide nostrils of his hooked nose twitched in a sneer. Christopher thought he looked like a Goya picture of Satan. Once and again the older man had let drop a barbed word that seared Brunswick's raw anger and vanity like vitriol. Without a word that could be called incitement he seemed to promote within the younger man the spirit of violence and revenge.

Christopher was glad to leave the raving fool and the grim man who spurred him on.

He told the Great Duke the story in the small candle-lit dressing-room which swirled in cigar smoke.

'Signor Cignani was good enough to lend me a private carriage,' he concluded. 'We came back in it. I do not know how the news got out, but our coach was surrounded by a noisy mob. I thought it best not to run any risk of further incident.'

'Herr Je!' said the Great Duke with a groan. 'I should think so. You did very wisely.'

'His Highness,' continued Christopher, 'would have killed the man, I think, if I had not arrived in time. He had him on the boards and was striking him about the head and face with the flat of his sword.'

'Thunder of Jesus!' commented the Great Duke, swinging himself to a sitting posture. With his black-haired legs revealed through the folds of his bedgown and the crescent-shaped bandage across his face, he looked like a wounded goblin. 'What a business! . . . And in my city! . . . He must go—and to-morrow! First a public scandal, and then attempted murder!'

'I think there can be no qustion, Your Highness, but that the Earl of Dunscore had bribed the fellow to raise the curtain.'

'Charles, anyhow, had no business to be there. When I was his age I didn't chase actresses on to the stage! Preposterous! If he wants to go wenching, let him do it in his own duchy—not mine! When I wanted a girl, it was done privately and decently. My amours were carried through with propriety—perfect propriety! My dear father once said to me, "Have all the little actresses you want, my boy. But remember: don't spend more than five thousand florins a year on them: don't get the pox, and don't let me know about them!" And I never did. . . . Never did! . . . While this dirty cub! . . .'

He picked up an extremely long nightcap and put it on very violently. The tassel hung over his ear. The tumbler containing the cold milk punch was on the floor at his feet and he drank in a worried manner—many quick short sips.

'I suspect . . .' began Christopher, and then wondered if he dared to say aloud his suspicions.

'What?'

'I hardly like to mention it to Your Highness. I may not be justified.'

'Out with it!' said the Great Duke. 'We have had enough trouble. If there's any more to come I should like to know of it in advance. . . . I order you!'

'Well, sir,' Christopher replied, 'it is my impression—only an impression, mind—that His Royal Highness the Duke of Cumberland is urging the Duke of Brunswick on . . .'

'Urging him on to what?' growled the Great Duke planting his large square-nailed hands on his knees.

'It seemed to me—it was my impression—that the Duke of Cumberland was making him much worse—making him angrier—leading him on to a wild talk of revenge. Laughing at him, and so making him more furious. I should not like to think of what he will not be capable if . . .'

Christopher came to a stop, uncertain how to proceed, and anxious lest he had overstepped the bounds of propriety.

But the Great Duke appeared to accept his reaction to the scene he had witnessed without question. He flung himself back on his ottoman in a paroxysm of rage.

'The dirty hound!' he roared, and struck out with his clenched fists as if he were fighting with ghosts—a goblin fighting with ghosts! 'God blast his soul to eternity! You are right! Of course you are right! And do you know why? . . . Because Charles is getting so outrageously lunatic that there has been talk of making him abdicate. It only needed one scandal like this! And who'll profit? Why, Ernest! He'll have Hanover after William, Victoria, or no Victoria!—Salic Law, you know!—Get rid of Charles, and Ernest will soon find means of swallowing up his duchy! Nice little addition to Hanover—very nice!'

'But . . .' began Christopher.

'There are no "buts",' said the Great Duke. 'If Ernest wants a thing he lets nothing stand in his way. He thought he'd get the English Regency by spreading abroad the story that William the

Fourth is mad—by encouraging him in imbecile outbreaks! He's been plotting to oust Victoria from the succession for years. Common knowledge! If he can work Charles up to some further folly —why, that will be just splendid—for him! Oh, God! I won't have him here! I won't have Brunswick here!' He took a great swig of his punch and swallowed it with a loud gulp. 'I won't have them! They are both mad—as mad as hatters!'

'Mad?' repeated Christopher.

The Great Duke set the tumbler down so clumsily that he upset it. He cursed loudly.

'Brunswick's plain mad,' he said, when Christopher had rescued the glass. 'But Cumberland's mad, and possessed by the devil. So mad that he is more homicidal than the other damned thug; and so much possessed that he can hide the madness.'

'You want to exorcise him, sir!' said Christopher.

'Exorcism!' He sat up again, entirely sobered betwixt consternation and anger. 'There is no priest or spell that can ever exorcise the devil that is within the Duke of Cumberland! I am not imaginative, my boy. You wouldn't call me imaginative?'

He spoke in an apologetic and pleading tone, and Christopher hastened to reassure him.

'Yes. I am not given to fancying things. But sometimes he makes me think of that monster—what was the name?'

'Frankenstein?'

'Frankenstein! That was it. I think he might drink human blood like Gilles de Retz, and strangle children in the dark.'

'My God! Sir!' protested Christopher. 'He's my . . .'

'Your uncle! Yes. . . . I'd forget it. There is not much to be proud of in that—or in any of the men of your family!'

Even in the subdued light in that small room of shadows he could see the angry flush that surged into the young man's face.

He took up a large china pipe with a silver cover to its bowl, found that it was partly charged with tobacco, rammed the load home with his forefinger, wiped his finger on his bedgown, and lighted up at the candle. Ash and specks of tobacco fell into the clear cup of melted wax about the candle-wick.

'I suppose you are rather proud of your family!' he said in a not unkindly tone between puffs. 'The Royal Family of England! Rulers of the greatest empire of the world! Romance! Glamour! . . . Well—I shouldn't be!'

He laid down the pipe beside him on the ottoman.

Ill-bred old devil!—thought Christopher, and clicked his heels together so that he stood at a sort of reproachful attention before impertinent Royalty.

The Great Duke, regardless of wordless protest, continued, 'You know, young man, the farther one keeps away from the Brunswick-Hanover families, the better for one—the happier one is! There have been one or two with honour and decency; but not many. I except my wife. We are naturally not speaking of the Great Duchess. Bless her! Or of your mother—of course!'

He rocked to and fro meditatively, took an absent-minded sip from his empty glass, examined the bare foot thrust into the loose morocco slipper, studied intently the young man standing before him in the dim room; assumed a pair of glasses in ebony frames inlaid with gold, and inspected him again; attempted to take another sip of punch, remembered as he reached for the tumbler, and looked up sharply.

'I am half inclined, Mr. Harnish . . .' he began, and then changed his mind. 'No, later will do. Have you ever thought of the family that rule England? Or their history?'

Until Cumberland had burst into his reasonless laughter the night before, Christopher had not given them much consideration. Vaguely the Duke of Kent was a figure in a nightmare; and Caroline an unheroic heroine; he still could hear her snoring, tortured breath as she lay dying in the windy house upon the Thames. They had been tangled in the hideous drama of his boyhood—of which he did not care to remind himself—but sometimes dreamed in uneasy slumber.

'It is as well you, particularly, should know,' said the Great Duke and launched into the horrific story in short broken sentences, pauses, bitter comments and asides.

He told how the princess of the House of Brunswick who wedded George the First had had an infamous lover, and expiated her crime by an imprisonment of more than thirty years;

how that lover had been murdered and his bleeding mouth stamped upon by a discarded mistress.

He told how from then every king had loathed his father and been loathed by his son, how the Second George had torn up his predecessor's will, and the Third never mentioned Frederick, his infamous father; how brother had fought brother, and mothers had unnaturally hated their sons. How the Third George's sister was said to have betrayed her young husband, King of Denmark, and had ended her days in captivity. He told of the old King's madness and the marriage of his brothers—one to a bastard, and the other to a woman whose sister was convicted of picking pockets and condemned to clean the streets of Augsburg.

He told of other unhappy Brunswick princesses—of Charlotte, wife of the Tsarevitch Alexis, brutalized by her husband; of Elizabeth, Princess Royal of Prussia, divorced and a prisoner within four years of marriage; and of Charlotte—Caroline of England's sister—Princess of Württemberg, who vanished from her husband's knowledge in Russia and died mysteriously in a castle prison. He told of the miserable Caroline's wedding with the 'First Gentleman in Europe'—how she had been given as bridal attendant his favourite concubine: how the bridegroom had lain drunk in the grate on his bridal night.

He left little unsaid, sitting there, tasselled nightcap nodding over spectacles and moustache-container, the solitary candle on a high chest casting goblin shadows upon him. There grew on Christopher the belief that there must be some purpose behind the recital as sinister in its way as the tale itself.

The old man rumbled on.

He told how great princes intrigued with one another, and one against another, and slandered each other in public places. He told of the sons of mad, blind George, of their fat harlots and their innocent victims. Of Caroline's husband—his debauchery and crazed treachery; his ignoble shifts to obtain money; the murder— that was the word he used—of a dozen debtors who had trusted to his honour; the purchase of daughters from their mothers for corruption; his pride and damnation; his hatred for his father, for his mother, for his wife; his vile jealousy of his daughter and, later, of Victoria the little princess who should eventually succeed him.

He told of the other brothers: of York, whose mistress, with his knowledge and participation, trafficked in honours and army promotion; of whining Kent with his twelve bastards; of half-crazed Clarence who spoke violently against adultery in the House of Lords, although he had a play-actress from whom he borrowed money, and whose bastards breakfasted with him and his Queen now that he ruled England. It was strange, was it not, that when Princess Charlotte died, to all the family of George III—twelve princes and princesses, none younger than forty years of age—there was not one single legal child that could be heir to England!

He paused for a moment.

Christopher listening to the tale imagined some shapeless thing of shadows, instinct with hate, forming itself in the farther corner of the room; some monster in which was materialized the curse that had overwhelmed five generations of princes; some monster which was not merely the fate of a great family, but the very family itself—a monster which, called up from the spirits of the living and dead, menaced those not yet born.

Cumberland—went on the Great Duke—was violent and crazed and evil. He had betrayed his brother, betrayed his sister, betrayed his niece. Set every friend and relation against every other. An apostle of Hate and Dishonour. Morally guilty of murder, if not actually so—and of a dozen nameless crimes as well.

He told of the death of Sellis, and the suicide of Lord Graves, of the affair of the girls at Richmond, and of Lady Lyndhurst. He lowered his breath when he told the hideous story of Princess Sophia. He spoke without comment on the death of Princess Charlotte in childbed, of the disappearance of the midwife and the suicide of the surgeon: he told how a small boy had nearly killed the Princess Victoria as an infant. He was said to be sparrow-shooting, but a plot . . .

'Sparrow-shooting?' said Christopher. 'Sparrow-shooting!'

The monster in the corner became now a vast and overwhelming thing. Its evil influence surged forward into innocent lives. White hand with pistol—man-trap snapping its jaws amid the brambles—jolting wagon with its bitter reek—dead lad hanging from the gallows outside Carmarthen jail—a thin arm held over a candle till it singed in the small flame—a woman screaming in a crowded courthouse—Deb saying, 'They'm a-goin' to hang we!'

'Oh, God, sir! What a story!' he stammered.

He felt that in some way the foul thing, in whose grip he had been long ago, was reaching out once more; that the security of his later life was on the verge of shattering—its pleasant scene lifting like a mirage and disclosing he knew not what horror behind it.

'A foul story!' said the Great Duke, getting to his feet. 'You are right. . . . It's devilish chilly! . . . I must go to bed. . . . So must you. . . . Yes, a foul story! I should remember it—if I were you. . . . Your father . . .'

'My father?'

It had been again on the tip of the older man's tongue to blurt out the truth. He quailed before the sudden harshness of the voice that had addressed him so respectfully until then; the paling of the face before him, and the tensing of its expression. He was afraid. His wife should tell anything further, if it must be told. It was a woman's job! The lad was her kin! He fumbled to hide his indiscretion.

'Your father? . . . What am I talking about? . . . Your mother, I mean. Still, your father, too, of course, was remotely connected with the family. Not a nice man'—and 'remotely' was quite correct; after all, the connection was unacknowledged. 'Oh, very remotely! Very remotely.' Quite true; if the connection wasn't legal, then it was necessarily remote, very remote. 'You mustn't think about it too much. . . . But a word to the wise. It is an ugly strain. You don't want it to come out. . . . It missed your mother and my wife, but it is there, in the blood.'

'But . . .'

The Great Duke did not like contact with the more violent manifestations of human conduct: affection he could stand, but not passion; sentiment, but not emotion; dislike, but not hatred. 'Very remote!' he said. 'But you want to remember it all the same. . . . Thought you knew. . . . No one, of course, knows all the branchings of the family tree. . . . Never knew mine. . . . Very remote. . . . Must go to bed. . . . At once. Very late. . . . Very remote.'

With that he bustled to his bedroom door.

Christopher forgot the profound respect due to a sovereign; he took two strides after the old gentleman, and seized him by a fold of his silken robe.

'How remote?' he insisted. 'How remote?'

For a moment Highness strained to break away from the grip that held him, in a sort of wild parody of a nymph escaping from the clutches of a satyr: then, conscious of the lack of dignity in the scene, he gave up the attempt, and came back rather sulkily.

'Why have I never been told before of the connection—even if it is remote?' asked Christopher, still maintaining his hold on the Grand-Ducal garment. 'Is there something else I have never guessed? . . . What is it?'

'S-sh!' said the Great Duke, greatly perturbed. 'You will wake my wife!'

'What is it?' asked Christopher again.

'Go to bed, boy!' said the other who was no longer—even to himself—a Great Duke, but an elderly and rather flurried gentleman. 'You have had a worrying evening. Extremely worrying! Don't blame you in the least if you are disturbed. Go to bed!'

'You have said too much, sir—or too little! The Great Duchess spoke of my father very strangely. And now—you!'

The Great Duke, grumbling, seated himself once more upon the ottoman. His slow intelligence sought for a means to tell the tale at its best. He prayed that the door would not open, and the nightcapped head of the Great Duchess suddenly appear in the midst of the forbidden story.

'It was a mistake,' he mumbled. 'I should have said nothing. I was just trying to warn you—warn you—er—warn you!'

'How remote?' repeated Christopher, and stood squarely before him with folded arms.

'This comes of trying to give a little advice!' said the Great Duke half to himself. If his wife got to hear about it there would be hell to pay. If he refused to answer, the lad was quite capable of going to the Great Duchess. If he told, on the other hand, then he could always insist on secrecy.

He made up his mind.

'If I tell you, Christopher'—he used the Christian name advisedly, feeling that by it he appealed to the faint relationship between them—'if I tell you, it is understood that you will never speak of it again. To anyone. To the Great Duchess least of all!'

Oh, God! thought Christopher—what is coming now?

'Your father was a natural son—of the late King!'

Christopher looked puzzled.

'I didn't know that. But he married my mother all the same. The wedding was legal—even if it wasn't recognized!'

'You don't understand . . . the *late* King!'

'The late King—of England?'

'King George the Fourth.'

'But,' said Christopher looking at the old goblin with bright astonished eyes, 'that's absurd. There must be some mistake. King George the Fourth was my mother's brother!'

The old man stirred uneasily. He wished to heaven that he had let the thing alone. The clock upon the wall was ticking unevenly. Someone had shifted it when dusting. Too annoying!

'No mistake!' he said at length.

'You mean—mean that my mother married—her brother's natural son? . . . But that is . . .'

Christopher could not bring himself to say the word, and became so white that for an instant the other thought the lad was about to faint. Curse! He would never get him out of the room, if he did so, without disturbing the Great Duchess! He wasn't really afraid of her, of course, but she could be most infernally unpleasant, if she liked! Oh, God!—prayed the Great Duke—I will never meddle in this sort of damned thing again! Let me get rid of him now, and I'll always let sleeping scandals lie!

'Of course, he wasn't legally George's son, so it wasn't quite so bad as all that!' He bustled to his feet once more. 'So now you know! Naturally your mother didn't know at the time. Although it is probable *he* did. He was a dirty swine! Now you must be off! . . . And remember, mum's the word!'

He took the dazed lad by the arm, and led him to the door.

'You must get some sleep!'

'Sleep!' said Christopher.

He went back to the Wall House to face the ruin of all his worlds, to sit brooding in horror on his birth, on the shame upon his mother's memory and the infamy of his father. He in his dishonour—she in her unhappiness, typified the tragedy that seemed to hang over their family.

Who was he to have dreams and ideals with that history behind him?

It was not as if he were merely linked with the House of Brunswick by the disgrace of his blood; there was, too, some other negus. Fate had decreed that as a child he should be the weapon—in sort—of their violence; as he had now this very night been brought in again to witness their plottings and their dishonour. Whatever they did among themselves involved him, in a measure, in horror or shame.

He laughed out loud (and heard Eckie stir in the adjoining room when he had done so) as he thought that, barely two years ago, he had sat at the selfsame table in the selfsame window writing 'Christopher P.' upon a sheet of paper, and feeling very royal and high and mighty and princely. A prince? He was worse than a bastard; he was a child born of what was practically incest—no matter how innocent his mother had been.

Every father in the line had hated his son—the Great Duke had said—and every son had repaid that hate. His father!—How that dim figure had grown into one huge and dark, and instinct with abomination and horror—into something to be loathed and abhorred and hated! So that was why Cumberland had laughed!

He sat till sunrise, seeing no fairy pageants, no fantasies from his secret life, but the memories of old terror and a darkness full of uncertain forms and half-seen crimes. He became a prey to foreboding and the certainty of spiritual disaster.

As he watched the golden flush rise in a dappled sky beyond the pleasant hills, he of a sudden recollected the roguish smile of the white satin singer, a marionette in this last sinister drama, like himself. In a flash it came to him where he had seen before that heart-shaped face, broad at the brow and pointed at the chin, the grey eyes fringed with long lashes, and the shapely nostrils curved like a dove's wing. Within his mind consciousness had noted an incident of the night—had reported it to memory: had seen a great bangle slip to the wrist as she had stood beneath the box, within touching distance, opening her arms with theatrical gesture to the audience. As the bangle had slipped it had revealed upon the rounded arm a large cicatrice—a burn harshly white upon its pearly whiteness. It was Deb! . . . Deb! . . . He would swear it was Deb; and started out of his chair as if to make certain on the spot of his discovery.

He recalled a hundred incidents of the deadly journey in the past: they built themselves into a picture that was but a frame for the one figure. Thinking of her he fell asleep at his table. . . .

He was very late for morning stable duty. The horses were filing back from watering through the barracks gate, as he arrived to find Eckie watching them with an assumption of keen-eyed inspection.

'Ha!' said Eckie. 'Good morning, sir!' and saluted his new senior with ridiculous precision. 'I wish I'd been at the Opera last night! . . . Lord God, it must have been a joke!'

'More nearly tragedy!' said Christopher, clanking across the Stable Court.

'They say that fellow had seven teeth knocked out! You were a lucky dog to see it all!'

Christopher was not so sure.

'At any rate they've gone!'

'Gone?'

'Cumberland and Brunswick left at day-break! They went in plain carriages. I suppose they'd have been hooted or stoned if they'd been recognized. Good thing, too!'

Eckie paused to examine the fetlock of a passing horse.

'Make him step out, Fabricius!' he commanded. 'No, he seems all right. Vratz was on duty at the Stable Gate,' he continued. 'He said they were in plain clothes, and that Brunswick looked like a lunatic snake. Every man-jack of 'em gone except that enormous nigger servant of Brunswick—left to bring on any dispatches that may arrive to-day or to-morrow. That black fellow who looks like Polyphemus!'

They walked back from the stables together to the Wall House, talking at random, as if to disguise their thoughts.

Eckie broke through to realities.

'Do you realize that there's barely three weeks left?' he asked.

'Three weeks?' questioned Christopher. He was thinking of Deb and himself again as marionettes in a grim show, moved at the whim of a brooding puppet master. For a brief second long ago he himself had held the stage in a drama of attempted murder, —attempted murder on whose behalf? Now the rôles were reversed, and she, who had been but a nameless supernumerary, was cast to shake a ducal throne, and he was the 'walker on'.

'Three weeks?' he echoed.

Eckie stuttered a trifle in reply.

'Luise, I m-m-mean! . . . Her marriage—you can't have forgotten!'

Good God! He had forgotten!

'I think,' said Eckie in an embarrassed way, 'it's a beastly shame! . . . She is an astonishingly nice girl—when you get to know her. . . . Takes some time, of course . . . I—I—I have rather studied her lately. . . . She grows on one! . . . Of course, I have known her longer than you! . . . And that fellow von Metzsch is one of the dirtiest pieces of work the Lord God ever made!'

He shot a quick, suspicious glance at his friend.

Christopher gravely nodded. He was wishing he could go away at once—escape from the pale downcast face of Luise and the knowledge of her tragedy; from this steep-roofed palace through whose high corridors and stately gardens the menace of chill evil swept. He must—must go away.

He paid but little attention to Eckie when, pausing as they entered the sunlit cloister of the Wall House, he said in a subdued tone:

'I suppose after this training one could always get a job in the Hanoverian army! After all I am a Hanoverian!'

'Who in the name of Heaven wants to join the Hanoverian army?' he asked indifferently.

'Oh, I don't know,' said Eckie. 'I was just wondering, you know. Just wondering!'

He went doubtfully up the steps.

Christopher went straight to the baron who was sitting up in bed, dipping a roll into a large basin of hot chocolate. Baldly he asked for leave.

The old man was kind but firm.

Impossible at the moment. Too much to do. Shorthanded, and more royal visitors arriving. Perhaps in a month, if he was getting a little stale, he should have ten days for himself.

'Take as few things as you can and ride into the Harz Mountains, or the Black Forest, keeping off the beaten track,' the baron added, and changed the subject.

'Thank Heaven Brunswick's gone! Pfui! it smells fresher already with the departure of that pestilential fellow!'

'You heard about last night?'

The old man added a chocolate stain to the yellow snuff smears on the front of his night-shirt. He clucked in regret.

'I was sent for at daybreak to see Brunswick off. What the Great Duke said to him I do not know, but Cumberland went with him —to keep him in order. I conceived it my duty to reprimand him for the language he used about His Highness. . . . And he swore at me, like a dog!'

'Dirty hound!' said Christopher.

'There may be a small outside duty for you to-day.' The baron smiled almost to himself; and he looked knowingly up at the lad. 'A curious little duty! A lot of young men would like it! You can take your leave in three weeks' time! . . . Go just after Luise's wedding. She would be disappointed if you were not there. . . . A fine match!'

He nodded retrospective approval.

Christopher went up to his room protesting to his soul. Oh, God, if only he could go away, just for a little! The idea of escape was so ever-present that for the time being he forgot Luise, forgot Deb. All that he desired was to evade the shadow out of the past that stretched its hands from English inn, from creaking wagon and Welsh jail, across Europe to the gold-tipped pinnacles and steep roofs and yew walks of the German palace: the shadow that blotted out all the fairy world within him.

An orderly appeared at the door as he finished changing his

uniform. He bore an order with the Colonel's initials still wet in ink upon it.

It ran:

'Colonel Baron Alexis Michaeloff, Commandant of the Garde du Corps.

'You will detail an officer to proceed to Domstrasse No. 17 in civilian dress with a mounted orderly in plain clothes for the purpose of escorting the opera-singer Fräulein Margaretha Acislo beyond the frontier of the Grand Duchy. He will treat that lady with the most distinguished consideration. Her departure must take place not later than midday. She has been already warned. He will report to you on his return.

'Von Hompesch
'Court Chamberlain to His Serene Highness, the Great Duke.'

and underneath,

'Lieutenant Harnish.
'You are hereby detailed for this duty.

'A. M.'

Chapter 24

A Meeting Is Arranged

MARGARETHA ACISLO WAS EXTRAORDINARILY ANGRY. Her two carriages with the imperials strapped to the roofs, her maid, her dresser, her companion, her footman, a sweating porter with a heavy trunk—these formed the nucleus of a small confused crowd that filled the narrow street under the windows of her sitting-room.

She had written letters to Brunswick and Dunscore which she fondly hoped they would never forget: she had left Signor Cignani reeling under the displeasure of the most popular light opera soprano in Europe: she had brought blushes to the cheek of the deferential agent of the Great Duke who had called her from her bed as dawn broke; she had rent to shreds a feathery fan that had cost thirty-five pistoles in Rome that winter.

She had burst into a brand-new costume of bronze-coloured barège with voluminous shoulders and billowy skirt that just showed her toes: she had clapped on a new Paris bonnet with a flaring brim and a curling feather: she had thrown round her neck a narrow mist-coloured wrap. She had examined herself in the mirror . . . with approval. She felt better.

Nevertheless when the fat maidservant tapped at the door to announce the arrival of 'Herr Leutnant Harnisch', she snapped in rapid indifferent German, 'He can wait in the street! Tell Signora Menzini to get into the carriage and to be ready to go at once.'

The maid's wide grin at her clumsy speech revived her anger momentarily. She turned so furious a face upon her that the girl blenched and vanished, stammering 'Jawohl! Jawohl!' and clumped into the passage and shut the door still muttering 'Jawohl', as if in apology.

She did not descend until she had kept the Great Duke's emissary waiting for the last stroke of the cathedral clock. She approached her carriage humming a little gay tune, and all but ignored the young gentleman in dark riding kit who attended her pleasure and bowed at her coming.

'Ah, Herr Polizei! . . . My lackey has the directions.' She threw the words at him over her shoulder with a swift disdainful look, and swept past before he could utter a single word. She joined her companion in the carriage, slamming the door so hard that a large chip of dark green paint flaked off at its edge.

'That gesture'll cost her ten florins in repairs,' thought Christopher with a surge of amusement ripping the flood of his gloom.

It was the signal for the cavalcade to move off. By the time his horse had been brought up and he had mounted, the carriages had swung into a wider street and were being drawn at a fast trot towards the River Gate.

It was impossible to talk to her so. He drew alongside as they passed through the leafy outskirts of the town, but she was invisible within her coach, and there was too much traffic to maintain the position. Not thus had he fancied meeting Deb again when he thought of her last night. He had visualized a recognition and a rapture: he had seen the years shredded away from between them at a word, a glance.

When they stopped to change horses at a posting house with peeling plastered walls in a little town two hours later, he dismounted and strode to the carriage door with determination. He opened it.

'Forgive, madam, but are you not . . . ?' he began.

The door was plucked from his grasp by a window strap and brought to with a crash.

He became a little angry—and uncertain of his memory. Was it Deb, after all? He wanted to talk to her; wanted to tell her so much, to hear so much—to make common cause with her, that other stray of fortune, against Fate.

They drove without halt in the afternoon sunshine, through a silver birchwood, by ripening fields of rye and wheat, orchards and little clustered hamlets, and farmhouses smelling of the byre. They came to a hilltop and a road that slanted down through an arcade of trees to a broad meadowy valley—became an avenue of cherry trees, and led to a bridge crossing a wide smooth stream a bare half-mile away. There was a guard house on the near side, and on the other a rambling inn with vast roofs, with poplars about it and gardens that ran to the water's edge. It was the frontier.

Christopher had ridden to the rear of the little column, his orderly behind him. It was now or never. He pressed his knees into his horse and came up at a gentle canter.

As he did so the leading carriage swerved a little on the road. There was a sharp crack, heard above the noise of hoofs, and the near hind wheel collapsed. The vehicle at once heeled over to a perilous angle, was dragged a yard or two amid shrieks and the splintering of glass; and came at last to a standstill with one side resting at an angle of forty-five degrees upon a low bank by a tree.

He leaped from his horse, ran to the carriage door and opened it with a wrench. He leaned over the edge into the confusion within.

'No one is hurt,' said an utterly composed voice. 'Menzini's squealing, so she isn't damaged. Thank God, she's fat—I'm sitting on her.' There was a gurgle of mirth in the voice. 'Give me your hands.'

Slim hands and wrists were in his grip. He saw the bronze dress and wide bonnet take shape from the huddle within. He was nearly pulled by a quick jerk into the carriage himself; and then suddenly Margaretha Acislo appeared poised above him on the edge of the doorway, laughing, a trifle dishevelled.

'Jump, Deb!' he said in English, his head cocked back to smile up at her. 'The "Herr Polizei" will catch you!'

His hat had fallen off. She looked down on the dishevelled yellow hair and tanned face; and though her lips were still parted to smile, it was as if they had become frozen in their curves.

'Deb?' she said. 'Deb! . . . Why, who are you?' and made no effort to move. Her fingers became slack within his clasp.

'I have helped you from—from a wagon before.'

Still poised to spring, with her hands resting within his as he strained upwards at full stretch of his arms, she stared down at him, and her face grew pale.

'Wagon! . . . Deb! . . . How do you know? . . . I don't know what you mean?'

She looked at him now with eyes that were frightened and remembering; as if beyond him she saw into the horrors of the past, and as if the crying of the yet imprisoned Menzini were transmuted into the wailing of the doomed children.

Something of this he realized, and in turn was chilled.

'Tops! I'm Tops!' he stammered. 'The—the wagon—you must remember me. . . . You remember me, really!'

'I think you had better help me down!'

In her speech, and in the clear note of her voice he caught a lilt that had been Deb's; and underlying its precise English, the faintest intonation of the West Country—so faint that it would have been imperceptible to anyone who had not strained, as he had done, for recognition of her in every vocable.

Without a word he clasped her with one arm about the knees, steadied her at the elbow with the other hand, and set her down.

The postilions, who had released the horses from their traces, went to the rescue of Menzini.

'How did you know me?' she asked, drawing away from the confusion about the wrecked carriage, and still without welcome.

'Deb!' he said, 'say you know me! Say you know me now. . . . I recognized you last night—even on the stage. I knew your face. Your bangle slipped. I knew the—the burn upon your arm!'

It was almost automatically that her eyes dropped to her close-fitting sleeve.

'Won't you know me now? . . . I can tell you where that burn was made—and why.'

With sudden violence . . .

'Stop! . . . Don't tell me! . . . I don't want to remember . . .' and then confessed, 'So you are Tops!'

'Tops. . . . Yes, Christopher!'

She turned to look at the road ahead, the river and the inn beside the poplars.

'It is only half a mile to the inn. Let us walk there. The carriages can follow. One of the men can ride ahead for help.'

He gave the necessary orders, and turned and walked with her under the cherry trees.

She went some way in silence.

'I thought that I had made myself forget,' she said at last. 'That —that it was just a nightmare all those years ago. That it was not me, but somebody I had dreamed of—some poor child from a brothel in a slum. Not me!'

She was so richly dressed and proud, and beautiful, that Christopher too, wondered if it had not been an evil dream through which she, as well as he, had passed. If by some queer jest of Fate they might not have dreamed together—or their consciousness been imprisoned for a little within the bodies and souls of two other children who had seen and endured hate and murder and iniquity.

'Your dream was mine then, too . . .' and found himself not knowing how to address her.

She regarded him gravely as they walked.

'Can you think,' she asked, 'that you—as you are now—or I— as I am now—could ever in our real selves have seen or done what we have dreamed that we saw and did?'

'Was it only a dream then, that we walked together as we are doing now—with the wagon lurching and rumbling on the road ahead!'

'No!' she cried. 'No!'

'Or that Gibbie—and Simmie—and Vergil . . .'

He remembered the names; and so did she, for she cried very loud again.

'No! . . . No! . . . I don't remember! . . . I won't!'

As they came to the door of the inn—a black mouth in a high bare wall—they passed a small forge in a mere shed. Before the entry a white cur lay eating the parings of a horse's hoof.

'Do you remember in our dream,' he insisted, 'how we once came to a blacksmith's shop, and a dog was curled like this one at the door—eating a hoof paring like this one; and you said . . .'

'Christopher!' she said in an agonized voice. 'Must I remember?'

'I shall have to go soon. There will be no one else to tell you of our dream. . . . At any rate let us have a glass of wine together and drink to your new days.'

She mutely consented, and they went through the low-browed entrance of the inn into darkness, and then into a bare white-washed room, with wooden benches under the windows that pierced the thick walls and looked on to the gaiety of a garden.

A blonde tanned maid, with hair strained back from her fore-head, brought them a bottle of Moselle, and set pale green twisted glasses upon the heavy oak table.

He poured out the wine.

'Deb!' he said, and saw she quivered at the name. 'I somehow felt that once we'd met again we should be together in a way like the old days—you and I against the world. . . . I don't know why I did. . . . There were such strange and hideous things then. There are such strange and hideous things now. They are linked together, and we—we seem to be in the pattern of them both. But perhaps you have escaped, while I am left in their web.'

She pushed from her the glass in which the sun was caught and imprisoned in yellow-green wine.

'It is strange,' she agreed, 'that we should find ourselves jour-neying together in reality, as once we did—in our common dream.'

'In that dream,' he returned, still standing, 'you made things as easy as you could for a small unhappy boy. You were the one loving thing—the only thing, he ever let himself remember out of a welter of hate. . . . You are escaping from another horror. I am enmeshed in it: for some reason I cannot tell. Selfishly, I suppose, I somehow felt that from you, as before, I should get strength and succour. You were weak and helpless then, but you always made me less afraid.'

She rose from her place and stood before him. They looked into one another's eyes: and, as he regarded her—the clear flushed pearliness of her face; the wide grey eyes under the arched brows; that straight short nose with one faintest freckle at the side—he saw before him the child of years before, the child that was like a lost fairy, against whose shoulder he had slept, whose thin hand had been clutched in his through all a night. She too saw in him the small boy that had been—in the dark shadows of the yellow hair, in the pointed chin and level eyes as grey as the sea.

'Why, Tops!' she said; and her expression changed. She looked at him now like a mother scrutinizing a long absent son.

'Why, Tops!' and put her hands upon his shoulders. 'It's true. . . . In that—that dream, I was very fond of you. . . . We *did* like one another, didn't we?'

She stood on tiptoe, and kissed him as a mother might have done.

At that first touch of her lips Christopher caught her by the arms. He beamed in a new sunshine.

'You *do* know me, Deb, really, don't you? And if you forget everything else, you still remember me?'

Somehow he found that they were holding one another in a close embrace, and that she was kissing him again—like a sister, like a sweetheart, like a grandmother.

'At first,' she said, when they faced across the table again, 'at first I was very frightened. It seemed as if a ghost had come— out of a ghost past. I did not want to remember. I don't now. . . . But you are different. We'll pretend we met in a dream, and have come out of the dream, and found that we alone are real.'

Said Christopher: 'I wish that everything now were only a dream, but you and me. . . . I can remember crying, after I woke up, for you—crying like anything.'

'How did you—wake up?' she asked. 'You went away, and never came back, so I never knew. I woke up soon afterwards and found myself a little maid. To an old couple at Bristol.' She paused, and studied her wineglass intently. . . . 'Oh, well! Their daughter was an actress. . . . She took me away with her, and I went on the stage. . . . Then, in Paris, Rossini heard me sing a little song. . . . He was Director of the Italian Opera. . . . Queer man, our Gioacchino! . . . Very angry when I wouldn't let him make love to me! . . . Used to stick out his lips at me—like this!' She imitated him ridiculously. 'But he made me learn to sing! So I became a singer!' and for a moment she smiled with consciousness of vast victory. 'A famous singer. They say I can make *anything* a success! I sing in Paris, and in Rome, and in Florence and in London. It's all true, like a fairy story! . . . Tell me about yourself!'

He was still telling her when within the silent dark recesses of the house a clock chimed out the hour.

'Oh, Deb!' groaned Christopher, recalled to reality. 'I've got to go in half an hour.'

It had not occurred to her that anyone must be the slave of time. She put down her glass and looked at him in consternation. 'But, Tops! . . .'

'It seems hard we should meet and part like this,' said Christopher. 'When first I realized it was you, I fancied that Fate had meant us to be together. I have been facing such hideous things that it seemed compensation that they should lead me, in a sense, to you.'

He told her all he knew and surmised—of the pistol-hand aimed at a baby princess; and of the dark tall man who drove a weak vain lad to folly and violence: even of his birth.

'But, Tops dear, why must you go back?' asked Deb. 'I am going now to Paris. If you come with me you will break away from all this. It will become an obsession with you, if you remain. We can travel together quietly, and talk, and forget about it. . . . I am going to forget again.'

She set her glass down on the bare table and rested her chin on her clasped hands.

'Be my escort, Tops! It would be romantic and lovely! My escort—to Paris!'

Christopher leaned his arms on the table. He looked at her in appealing fashion.

'Don't try and persuade me, Deb! Because I might come, you know. And that would be a bad business—to break my duty! I can't! How I wish I could! It is an echo of our dream that we should be torn from one another—just as we were—in that nightmare.'

She took one of his hands across the table and stroked it very gently.

'I am sorry, too, Tops. I hate to leave you behind—as you left me, in our dream. . . . I should not say such a thing, I think, to anyone but you. . . . Those others'—she included the rest of mankind in a disdainful smile—'I can laugh with, and perhaps love a little, and send away and forget without regret! But you and I

have something in common—something more than just memories
of horrors and evil. . . . Why not come now? I'll look after you—
as I did before; just like an aunt! . . . Come, Tops!'

The distant clock chimed again.

Christopher rose slowly to his feet, full of bitter regret.

'I can't! I must go back,' he said. 'Deb, write to me—often!
Write to me very often!'

She came before him, and put her hands to his face and brought
it down to hers, and kissed him on the lips.

'Dear Tops!' she said. 'So short a time after so long! I will write
to you, and you shall write to me. Often and long. And some
time when you are free again, you shall come and see me. Won't
you, Tops?'

He saw that there were tears in her eyes; so he turned and went,
lest he, too, should show his sorrow—unmanfully.

He had his foot in the stirrup ready to mount when she came
rustling to the dark entry of the inn.

'My address, Tops. . . . And a letter I had forgotten. I would
ask you to have it delivered. . . . Kiss me good-bye again!'

He rode gloomily back to Neipperg, and only recalled the letter
after he had entered the streets and dismissed his orderly. He
took the sealed and folded paper out of his pocket. It was addressed to Dunscore at the 'Englischer Hof'—a large inn built
about a cobbled courtyard not a hundred paces away. The name
was freshly painted in Gothic characters across the front.

On the spur of the moment he decided to deliver the missive
himself; he rode under the arch into the yard, and flung his reins
to an ostler.

Milord was at dinner. There!

The man pointed to a long window beside a door with orange
trees in tubs on either side.

He entered a room where the cloth was still laid upon a table
littered with napkins and glasses and bottles. An unknown man
was sitting with his feet upon the windowsill at one end of the
table. Von Metzsch, with a flushed face and unsteady hand, endeavoured to light a long cheroot at one of the two candles which
burned although it was not yet dark. Dunscore himself was negligently sprawled back in his chair, opposite his guest, burning

round holes with his red cigar end in the hanging folds of the table cloth.

He barely turned his head as Christopher announced himself, and said no word.

'I have brought a very personal letter to Your Lordship,' said Christopher, coming to his side and producing the epistle.

Dunscore reached out languidly for it.

"The boot-boy has now become ticket-porter!' he remarked indolently, in English.

The impertinence was so unprovoked that Christopher was too surprised for immediate reply. He stammered—the blood mounting to his forehead—a tumble of 'I's' and 'You's'.

'Why should you speak to me like that?' he said at length—in English also. 'I have done you no harm.'

Dunscore shrugged his shoulders.

'Just a little—what shall we say?—cousinly badinage? It amuses me sometimes to wecall our—er—connection!'

He glanced down at the folded sheet and uttered an exclamation as he recognized the writing.

'How did you get this?' he demanded.

'I was asked,' replied Christopher with the utmost formality, 'to give it to Your Lordship—by the writer.'

Dunscore cut round the seal with a small penknife; he cast an eye over the contents; but whatever they were he showed not a sign in the rigid control of his disdainful face. He crumpled the letter into his pocket, and grated his chair farther back. He slightly turned his head so that Christopher came within the range of his vision.

'How does your dear Duke feel to-day, after he's been diddled out of his girl? . . . Vewy like dear Hurbles after he was diddled out of his, I dare say?'

'With Your Lordship's permission I will withdraw,' said Lieutenant Harnish in his most freezing manner, and rather flattering himself upon it. He took up his hat from a chair feeling, despite his achievement, extremely young and immature before the mocking man.

'That would be a pity,' said the Earl of Dunscore. 'I had hoped to have had news from you of my wemarkable wife and her vewy wemarkable cousin.'

'I would suggest that you approach them by letter yourself!' said Christopher, and was rather pleased with the sentence.

'You do, do you?' remarked Dunscore, tilting the chair back as far as it would go, and planting his feet on the table. 'You think they would tell me whether they are living together yet? I have always been a twifle cuwious to know.'

'You—you hound!' stammered Christopher, and found himself shivering between hate and embarrassment and fear of what he had said.

'No!' Dunscore took no offence. He was mildly amused. 'Just a man of the world! . . . Man of the world enough—help yourself to some wine, and take a chair, Cousin—to diddle a poor bwain-less duke by bwibing a stage-hand.' The other two men, although, not comprehending what was said, yet listened intently. The hungry black eyes of von Metzsch travelled from Dunscore's face to Christopher's, as if they would read by expression of what the two Englishmen spoke; they showed no sentiment except that of cold curiosity. He picked his teeth with a savage thoughtfulness. 'Two hundwed flowins (a twifle out of Charlotte's money-bags), and I sweep the poor fool away! . . . Just like the other!'

' "Just like the other"?' repeated Christopher slowly. He flicked his long riding cloak back with his elbows, and looked into the lining of his silk beaver hat whilst he recovered his poise.

'Oh! Didn't you know? The pwettiest joke. Evwybody in town laughed till they cwied.'

' "Joke"!'

'Oh, yes,' said Dunscore easily. 'Charlotte, you know, said she'd mawwy me if I took my four votes to the Queen, and the old woman won. Well, I did take my four votes to the Queen, and the old woman did win. But the Government had decided to dwop the Penalties Bill, whatever the voting was at the Third Weading. They only let it go to division to please the King: it wouldn't have affected their decision.'

'I still don't follow,' said Christopher.

Dusk was falling. There were but the two candles on the table.

Von Metzsch was leaning across his place, a wine-glass at his nose, avidly regarding them both in much the same way that he regarded Sophie von Osterode. His eyes never blinked. The other man, sideways to the table, a foot on the windowsill, was endeavouring to balance a fork, a spoon and a crust of bread on the top of a bottle.

Dunscore drew at his cigar, and a thin wisp of smoke trickled from the corner of his smiling lips.

'Let me finish, my dear fellow,' he protested. 'The cweam of the joke was that Charlotte thought it was touch-and-go for the old lady. She bought my four votes and the Queen's victowy—as she thought, dear cweature!—when I had known a week before what the Government would do. I knew a week before that the Queen was to get off! Pwime Minister had told me so himself. It would have been just the same whether I'd voted or not! . . . But Charlotte didn't know—then.'

He laughed a quiet chuckling laugh in which there was little mirth: that is to say, he made the necessary sounds and movements for a laugh, as an actor might.

'So you see I diddled Charlotte and her fat boy fwiend—just as I have diddled Bwunswick. I like the first slice of a cake—anyone can have the west!'

Said Christopher, stammering:

'S-s-so that's the truth?'

'I'm a good jester, aren't I, Cousin Harnish?'

Cousin Harnish raised his hat. He took one step forward, and brought it down upon the smiling face so hard that it drummed upon it and crumpled into wreckage over it. And when the ruin fell away there was a cut on the marble cheek and cigar-ash smeared over the chill features.

'K-K-Kuppler!' he cried in German, with a voice that broke. 'Pimp!'

There was instant confusion. Dunscore's guests sprang to their feet, von Metzsch eagerly, like a crow to carrion; the other swaying a little and muttering, 'A hat! . . . M-most ungen'lmanly. . . . Ver' irregular. . . . Hat!'

Dunscore was the least discomposed. He brought his chair back to normal, swept the wreckage of the hat from off his lap, produced a handkerchief and wiped his face with delicate pats and dabs.

'Wather amateuwish!' he said collectedly. 'Not what I should have done myself! . . . I suppose I shall have to shoot you now. . . . Any little messages you would like to send Charlotte or Hurbles? . . . Perhaps, though, it would be incowwect for me to take them for you!' and then in German across the table to von Metzsch: 'You will act for me? . . . Thanks. The sooner the better.'

'The Freiherr von Eckstein will answer for me,' remarked Christopher at large, and found himself trembling as he left the room.

Chapter 25

Surprise for a Father

'OF COURSE I WILL!' SAID ECKIE. 'I'M NOT MUCH GOOD AT it, though. . . . No experience! . . . And I'm the world's worst shot, however much I practise.'

'You won't have to do the shooting!' remarked Christopher, flinging his cloak down and staring into space across von Eckstein's room.

'Of course not! I was forgetting. Tell you what, Tops! I'll run along to von Brahe—he won't have left quarters yet—and get some tips from him. He might act with me, don't you think? . . . But I'll be the principal second, of course!'

'Of course.'

'Well, I'll run round now. . . . If anyone comes from *him*, he can wait a bit. I won't be ten minutes.'

Christopher went to his room. He sat down in dazed sobriety at his window and looked out into the darkness. There was nothing distinguishable, except the little glittering lights on the far bank of the river.

He knew that this was the end. Rather a dramatic end, he felt, to die at sunrise for a very dear and beautiful lady who was much older than oneself!

'What's it all about?' had asked Eckie rather diffidently. 'Of course, old fellow, don't say anything if you'd rather not!'

And he had answered, with every high memory of chivalrous romance, tersely and tensely . . .

'It was a lady, Eckie!' Long pause. 'A lady!'

And particularized no more. One didn't in such cases!

396

And Eckie had looked at him in a rather—rather worshipping way.

Here's my friend going to fight, and to die for a lady . . . a great lady! said the soul of Eckie through the silence: the humble soul of the Eckie who loved innkeepers' daughters, and peasant girls, and was fobbed off with Luise!

'Is the lord a good shot?' asked he after a while.

'He's killed his man—twice!'

'Oh!'

'Twice!'

'Third time's lucky!' said Eckie, and then tried to puzzle out what he meant. Gave it up. Added, 'Mind you stand full face to him. Much less dangerous than sideways!'

'Why?'

'Sideways is a smaller target. But if you are hit, it'll be something vital. Bound to be! And old von Brahe told me that a man always takes much more careful aim when the other fellow is standing side on.'

So even Eckie reckoned it was the end!

He wondered how those two men had died—where they had been hit.

Did one just die, with the bang and finality with which a book was shut? It depended whether one was hit in the heart, or the brain, or the lungs, or the throat . . . or the throat! His overwrought imagination pictured himself lying on the grass sucking in blood, like wine—like wine of death!—through a shattered gullet.

He had put a hand up to his throat, and felt its crisp outline, and gone to the silence and loneliness of his own room.

He felt certain that he was about to die.

He could not follow the chain of reasoning, but he knew that there were links of some sort between the duel in which he was to perish and all that had gone before. He sat in his chair in the window, looking out on the lights across the river, and telling himself over and over again the infamous story of the family into which he had been born.

The seed of his death—he told himself—was sown when Queen Caroline went to trial, when she was married, when George the

Fourth was born and bred in hate, when all the Georges were born—even when Sophia of Brunswick-Celle passed under the gateway of the prison she should never leave in life. Fate for some unknown reason had decreed that he should be tangled in the tragedy of a great line.

He drew paper to him and wrote: wrote while a dignified Eckie dealt with von Metzsch at the prompting of von Brahe; while Williams came and went and returned, and stammered in the doorway with tears in his eyes; while Eckie whispered to him plans for what should happen after dawn; while Luise lay sleepless and staring into the shadows of her room; while the master of the house slumbered peacefully, his head high on the pillows, his mouth open, and his chin—released from the fence of high collar—dropped thankfully upon his chest.

He wrote to Setoun, and to Charlotte; he wrote—for some obscure reason he could not explain—to Severn; to Luise, and to Eckie a long memorandum that enclosed a bunch of bank notes —with his love. And last of all he wrote to Deb; and because he was a dying man and so it did not matter, it was passionate and a little stilted and rather proud.

The darkness lightened with the cold thrust of a sullen dawn, as he rose from his table . . .

. . . And as Dunscore woke—he knew not why—and looked with sleepy eyes about the chilly greyness of his room.

A dawn wind fluttered the thin chintz curtains before the low windows so that they rustled. The furniture had outline and a smoky solidity in the misty light, and cast fog-like shadows on the wide bareness of the floor. The pale curtains at the bed-head were half transparent, like ice upon a pond. That nearest Dunscore quivered a little, and a shapeless dark blur showed upon its screen.

He lay back against the pillows watching it for some moments, in the half-amused puzzlement with which the waking mind endeavours to sort reality from the dusk about it. He set fingers to a fold to twitch the curtain back, and, as he did so, knew suddenly within his heart that the blurred shadow was that of Death.

Before he could cry or even raise his head from the pillows that it pressed, Death had him in its grip. Enormous hands were at his throat; a vast weight was on his groin; great shoulders topped by a huge black face blotted out his view—a huge face which flickering consciousness recognised as that of the Duke of Brunswick's negro servant.

His head was forced back and back until he could not see the hands against which he beat, or the vast face slashed with a grin of white teeth and pink gums. All that his failing vision grasped was the thin cloth canopy of his bed, and the darkness in a corner of it where the dust had drifted against the frame.

He had meant to die with a disdainful smile—a bored twitch of indifferent lips: so he had always fancied. He died with a purple face and glazed bloodshot eyes and protruding tongue, and feeble shudders of the body, and saliva and blood trickling in a foam on to his cheeks.

He lay a dead and ugly thing upon his bed, while a negro ransacked his drawers; while, later, people looked on him and whispered, and while Christopher Harnish accompanied by two men walked through the early sunshine from the main road to a small meadow in a dingle between the wooded hills.

Christopher stood apart from the others. He was plainly dressed in black with a white frill on his pleated shirt. He held himself very upright, with his thumbs in the pockets of his waistcoat of black moiré silk. Williams had been very insistent that he should wear that splendid suit, which had travelled to and fro between Neipperg and Savile Row with long letters of instructions until it fitted to perfection. Williams obviously thought one should meet death dressed in one's best. The man was somewhere among the birch trees now, watching: he had taken his hand and gripped it for a second in a clasp of iron, and then turned and quickly gone away, dragging a vast red handkerchief from his tail.

How would they get him back to the road when he was dead? He wondered. There was no gate or door to carry him on. Would they wait for such to be brought, or drag him—bleeding—by legs and arms to the waiting carriage?

Said Eckie:

'Tops! They're coming through the wood-path now. . . . I can

see them. . . . Aim straight! I wish I could myself! You'll be as
right as right can be. . . . We'll be having breakfast, with cherries,
in half an hour. . . . God bless you, old fellow!'

Von Brahe grunted in annoyance.

'There are only two of them! He can have but one second! It is
not as was arranged. And where's the surgeon?'

Christopher did not turn. He heard Eckie utter an exclamation, echoed by the elder man. They went to meet the pair, while
Christopher filled his mind with a last vision of the wonder of the
earth—the slender silver shafts of birch trees; the delicate net of
quivering leaf they spread between the green of fern and grass
and the deepening blue of morning sky; the line marked by an
unseen bubbling stream along which a small bird flew swiftly and
dipped quickly. He began to work out an epitaph. He would like
it put on a tablet, on the south wall, in Southwell Minster. In
Latin, with all his titles, perhaps . . .

HIC JACET

CHRISTOPHERUS HARNISH

COMES DE TOLLENDHAL

ET BARO DE HARNISCH

ANNO AETATIS SUI

XXIII

MORS ACERBA

Von Metzsch's staccato voice struck on his ears.

'There can be no duel. I apologize. The Graf is dead.'

A babble of inquiry broke out, but Christopher did not turn.
So Dunscore was dead, and not he! It was Dunscore who would
have to be carried about like a sack of old clothes or a piece of
furniture; for whom the grave-digger would drive his mattock into
the earth, and throw up piles of soil and pebble and sodden root
and twisting livid worms!

'He was murdered last night,' said von Metzsch, the eager narrator. 'Or early this morning. He was still warm. Someone had
ransacked the room and taken all his jewellery and money.'

'Murdered!' cried Christopher swinging round. 'Murdered! Oh,
God!'

He knew that the great shadow of his fancies had taken shape and was reality; that it hunted in a far more subtle pursuit than would have been satisfied by his death upon the field of honour; that this murder by a hand unknown was yet another manifestation of the power which had stooped over him in his childhood, and now brooded over him again, as though determined that he should not escape its range. . . .

He found himself entering the postern by the Wall House beside a silent Eckie, saluting the long grey form of his colonel at the stair-foot.

The old man glanced at his civilian dress and the tell-tale pistol case that Eckie carried.

'If I had known of this,' and he nodded at the weapons, 'or if I had known that what has happened would, Dunscore would have been given less than his forty-eight hours to cross the frontier.'

'You know then he's murdered, sir?' asked Eckie, as Christopher stood silent.

'I also know why,' said the baron, and shut his mouth like a trap, turning to the stairs.

'I must ask for leave at once, said Christopher without prelude, putting out a hand to arrest his progress.

'We talked that over yesterday!' There was final decision in the baron's voice. 'You shall be relieved of duty for to-day, but long leave cannot be arranged so speedily as this. In three weeks' time you may go, as we agreed. . . Come, you need breakfast after your early morning outing.'

Coffee and Luise awaited them in the much-curtained dining-room. The younger girl always presided at *erste Frühstuck* since her stepmother rarely appeared before midday. He noticed that, though she kept her secretive eyes lowered, yet the faint twitch and tightening of the muscles about the lids showed her to be following Eckie's every movement. Amid all his confused emotions, realization of that fact gave him another stab of pain.

He had barely sipped his coffee when an orderly from the palace was announced.

Would His Excellency be so good as to spare Herr Leutnant

Harnish for special and confidential duty? He was wanted urgently and immediately.

A little jealously the baron sent Christopher off.

The Great Duke bade him enter. He was seated, as if settled for the day, upon the night-commode, his purple silk bedrobe spread decently round him in the sunshine. A curved pipe with a china bowl was pendent on his chest, and a pot of coffee stood on the low table under the window at his side. He wore the same long tasselled night-cap; the same cat curled about his legs: only the moustache-container had gone. He sat there with smoke-rings curling up before him, a whiskered priest of Cloacina on a night-commode altar, as if he had come to roost there two nights before and so remained cogitating on the sins of the Houses of Brunswick and Hanover.

Highness's first words, even, were:

'Now, you have not spoken of that—that matter we discussed, Mr. Harnish?'

Mr. Harnish had not.

The old gentleman supped his coffee rather noisily, dampening the lower fringe of his moustache when he did so. As he set the cup down, drips ran on to the dressing-gown and the table-cloth. He was already covered with tobacco ash, and his pipe bubbled and gulped like an angry turkey: Highness, indeed, was one of those unfortunate men who are constitutionally incapable of drinking, eating, or smoking without making a mess or a noise.

'You know about this . . . business in the town?' inquired Highness, at length.

'Only what I have been told, sir!'

'. . . And what you guess!'

'. . . And guess, sir!'

The Great Duke made no comment. He rammed down the ash in his pipe, and afterwards wiped the grubby forefinger upon his gown. He dealt with other small and personal matters, removed himself from the commode shut the lid, and settled down upon the ottoman.

'You are some sort of connection of the Earl?'

'His wife, sir, is Lord Setoun's cousin!'

Did one say 'is' of a wife of a dead husband? or 'was'?

'Sort of connection. Certainly. I know! I know! More or less,' said the Great Duke. 'Well, I want you to go to Dunscore's rooms and run through his correspondence for me!'

Said Christopher in shocked surprise:

'But I should have fought him this morning, and if . . .'

'I am aware of it,' said the Great Duke, as if preening himself on his early knowledge of social movements and so forth in his capital. 'I don't know what it was all about. I don't ask. The Great Duchess thinks it was about Charlotte. If it was, quite right! Charlotte is a great friend of hers. But I don't ask. Nothing to do with me. I don't ask.'

'It was Charlotte, Your Highness,' confessed Christopher in a low voice. 'He put a foul insult on her.'

'I wish you had killed him,' said the Great Duke vehemently. 'Anything rather than what has happened. He was a scoundrel and a blackguard and a cursed pest alive. He is a still more cursed pest now he's dead.'

He took so long and strenuous a pull at the protesting pipe that his face grew purple. The obstruction in the stem succumbed to the effort, and a sup of nicotine juice swam into the royal mouth. For a moment Christopher thought the Great Duke was going to be sick as he lay back with pursed lips, frantically gesticulating with the hand in which he held the pipe, and spluttering.

Highness pointed to the washstand urgently.

Christopher brought an empty basin and presented it to the royal face.

Highness disburdened himself, and sat up spitting, and grumbling, and sipping coffee.

When all was satisfactorily arranged:

'It might be a little incorrect for me, in the circumstances . . .' began Christopher in protest.

'Not at all! Reasons of State! There is no one who will know about it. And you will go as my agent! None of the police can understand a word of English. Someone has got to go over his letters. Somebody confidential. Someone I can trust. There may be some other explanation of this business than the one I fear. . . . There may be . . .'

His voice trailed off before the incredulity in Christopher's eyes.

'I wish, Mr. Harnish, you wouldn't think quite so visibly. Tact —diplomacy demands you should never show what you think. I never do!' he complained, and jerked his knees up to his chin and clasped them, and so sat for a while with his long pipe resting on them, in meditative dudgeon.

'It is true,' he admitted at last, 'that I do not think there is likely to be any other explanation. But for all Dunscore's follies he had brains of a kind. He was a High Tory, too. Ernest of Cumberland, it is said, found him very useful. That I know. We think —that is, I think—there might be documents I should care to see. There have been strange stories about Ernest and his agents lately. There may be something. The police have had instructions to touch no papers. . . . Report to me on your return.'

The door of the room where Dunscore had died was unlocked for him. As he went in he looked half-expectantly at the bed, but the body had been removed—even the bedding; and the light curtains fluttered about a naked frame and the bare grid of webbing that had supported the mattress.

A confusion of luxury was strewn over the bleakness of the inn room. Every chair was piled with clothes of all sorts; every table and chest-top with toilet articles of silver and crystal, writing-desks, or leather dispatch boxes. A pile of imperials in one corner was partly hidden by rugs, and crowned by an enormous brass-bound travelling book-case which would have weighed a hundredweight when full. A folding bed was covered with cushions in various shades of plain silk, and a canteen open on the floor showed a multiplicity of decanters with cut-glass stoppers as big as diamonds in an Ali Baba cave.

'I was packin' last night when his lordship went to bed,' said the dead man's valet, looking apologetically at the chaos. 'That there murderer ransacked everything; and the police this mornin' didn't do no good. Tho' I will say it for 'em, as they didn't take nothin'. Very respectful, too, as one might say, sir!'

The man was unfeignedly glad to find someone who spoke English and would relieve him of responsibility. He gave up the keys without demur.

'There was a gentleman came 'arf-an-hour ago that wanted to see 'is lordship's things! But the room was locked, and the gendarme what was at the door till you came wouldn't let 'em in. Spoke English, sir! As good as you or me!'

'Spoke English, did he?' said Christopher without interest, and wondered vaguely who it might have been. 'Are there any of his things in the sitting-room? All brought here for packing! . . . I see! . . . I will give you the keys back when I come downstairs. You had better wait there in case I have instructions to give you.'

When the man had gone he took the first dispatch box that came to hand, and seated himself with it before a mahogany travelling washstand that had been placed in the window. A silver basin in it was full of yellow water on whose surface floated a thin grey scum of soap. Dunscore might be shaven by obsequious servants; his romantic locks be scented and pomatumed by deferential dressers; he might be sponged and powdered delicately and softly by gentle-handed body-servants; but the raw fact that he washed and soaped and scrubbed himself and left the evidence in dirty water seemed to deprive him of that serene and mocking aloofness which had characterized him.

On the flaps on either side of the basin were scent bottles and soaps, and a jar of pomatum with one or two hairs stuck in a fleck of yellow jelly on its lip. The lid of the washstand was propped upright at the back on its hinges, and Christopher found that he was regarding himself from a silvered mirror set between two folding candlestick-arms. Last night Dunscore had sat on that chair before that mirror and regarded himself in it, and—like Narcissus—had admired his dark locks and the languid perfection of his features. Perhaps the picture was registered within its clear depths for ever!

Christopher swung the flaps over, regardless of the jars that toppled off to the floor, and shut the lid. It formed a convenient table-top on which he put the mass of letters from the dispatch box.

He searched in every other desk and box and article of luggage, and made a neat pile of all the documents he found upon his table.

He seated himself again, and took up the first paper.

The ghost of the dead man—it seemed to him—must stand behind him, looking over his shoulder, with bored deprecation of so ungentlemanly an intrusion upon privacies.

'Vewy incowwect!' he thought to hear the tired voice say, as the paper crackled in his hand.

'Thring and Pike: Savile Row' were owed a matter of eleven hundred pounds for clothes. He wondered whether it represented one or two years' expenditure. Three hundred pounds for two dressing-cases—a receipt. A note beginning 'Carissimo': he turned it over—did not the ghost rustle in its dry throat words like 'Dishonouwable! . . . Caddish!' The signature was Gio- something or other. There were dozens of bills, and dozens of notes, gilt-edged, with brightly coloured wax still adhering and faint perfumes still lingering.

Dunscore threw none of his correspondence away. It rose in a great mass from which a chronicler could have drawn him full-length—in his amours, extravagances, travels, scandals, vanities, foibles and friendships.

The pettiness of the man became so evident that Christopher felt that even if he were to stand behind him suddenly and drawl annoyance, he would merely have shaken his head before so pitiable a ghost and paid him no attention.

There was actually a note from Brunswick asking 'My dear Friend' to take pity on his ennui and loneliness, and signed, 'Your affectionate Charles'.

Christopher swept what he had dealt with into the gaping mouth of an empty bag, but put the last missive on one side.

He drew another pile toward him.

The topmost in a crabbed hand appealed mysteriously for funds. 'Londonderry in the last two years,' it said, 'has spent £7000 upon our cause. We must have more money if we are to make more headway.' There was an obscure reference to some 'Lodge' and the signature was illegible—all but the initials D.G.M. after the name.

He was about to drop it into the heap in the bag, when once again the obscurity of the language employed by the writer impressed him. He placed it with Brunswick's note at his elbow.

On through the rubbish heap! Love letters—invitations—bills—

jerky notes—drunken notes—hurried notes—notes in flowing Italian hand—all addressed to the nobleman who had choked to death under a strangler's hand, just as any poor wayfarer might have done in a common lodging-house; who had kicked a little, and writhed a little, and clutched a little, and then become a sense-less breathless lump, with nothing left of his hopes and fears and loves but what was reflected in the junk-heap of his cor-respondence.

It was a wearisome business until:

'Strictly Secret and Confidential. Destroy when read.'

'Dear Dunscore,' (the letter ran)

'The position is that the G.M. declines to take any active steps during the present reign, except such as are necessary to prepare the way for the change we have in contemplation. Set your mind at rest about that. Brotherly affection—ill-requited as it is—would forbid him to contemplate any more vigorous action unless a crisis of first-class magnitude arose.

'The G.M. and myself cannot agree that Revolution would have infallibly followed a refusal by Parliament to pass the "Reform Bill" this year. The abominable tergiversation and unpardonable procrastination of authority was responsible for the shameful sur-render to the mob. For instance one hundred and ten lives were lost in the Bristol riots: and untold damage done to private and public property. Yet a charge by dragoons and a whiff of grape-shot on the first day would have resulted in fewer lives being lost, infinitesimal damage to property and the proper subjection of turbulent scoundrels to duly constituted authority. A strong hand was needed then; it is needed now: it will be needed more than ever in the future if the Constitution is to be preserved.

'Only a man—and a strong one, at that—is capable of dealing with the crises that impend. One shudders to think of the fate of England should it rest in the hands of a woman.

'Since the G.M. took office our membership has swollen vastly —and they are all determined fellows who do not mean to let old England remain at the mercy of Whig politicians, Republicans, and mob orators.

'I am authorized specifically to give you the assurance that . . .'

A hand suddenly appeared over his shoulder and spread across the letter, wrenching it from his grasp and crumpling the paper within its palm.

For a heart-beat Christopher thought of the dead man. He rose slowly, as if forcing himself to the action, and turned as he rose.

He stood face to face with the man he knew as Heywood.

Even though many years had passed since he had last set eyes upon that figure, he knew it well.

There was little altered, from pale still face with the stray black lock upon the forehead, to white plump hands that twisted the letter quietly before rending it, to the fawn pantaloons that vanished into the tops of perfect and spotless riding boots.

'What—what are you doing here?' asked Christopher in a stammer.

There was no recognition in Heywood's eyes.

'Ah, English, I see!' he said composedly.

'I asked,' said Christopher—still quailing in his soul before the remembered face, the soft voice—'I asked—What are you doing here?'

'And I answer: What are you doing?'

'I represent the Great Duke. Give me that letter.'

'This private correspondence was not intended for any eyes but those of Lord Dunscore. I was a personal friend of his lordship—I will take the responsibility!'

Quietly he tore the letter across and across again, his cold eyes on the younger man, daring him to prevent the destruction.

'So Cumberland guessed what would happen,' Christopher said slowly. 'And hurried you here to look after his interests. I must ask you to go, and to give me the pieces of the letter you have destroyed.'

Said Heywood thoughtfully:

'You seem to be an imaginative person, sir! . . . I suppose you have read the letter?'

'I have. It was my duty.'

'And may I ask'—very confidentially spoken—'what you think of it?'

'I do not think of it. It is nothing to do with me. . . . I must ask you to go—and to give me the letter back.'

'It was a mistake on your part, my dear fellow, to read that epistle. A great mistake! A cardinal error! Unless, of course, you agree with the sentiments!'

Heywood spoke in a low conversational tone. He stood barely a foot away, with his hands behind his back under the tails of his coat of darkest blue. The expressionless eyes in his slightly bowed head studied the tanned face of the young man as if, on the instant, memory had started work.

Said Christopher:

'Captain Heywood. . . .' At that moment he saw recognition dawn in the pallid face, and—curiously—a sort of horror; at the same moment he saw the right hand start on its journey from the flank of the fawn pantaloons.

The memory of past terrors and hates, immediate suspicion and fear, and renewed loathing for the man and his masters, were in the quick, hard blow that Christopher struck without warning. His fist jarred against the firm smooth chin.

He heard Heywood's teeth crack together as the buffet sent him crashing back to the floor. His head struck a dispatch box in his fall, and he lay where he fell without word or movement. A small pistol dropped on the floor beside him, and glittered like water.

'You dirty murderer!' said Christopher, after he had stood for thirty seconds dumbfounded by the swift collapse of the ogre of his childish dreams. He—himself—had struck Heywood! Arabella had spat on him; and now he, Christopher, had knocked him down—perhaps killed him. Heywood was only fragile humanity after all!

He knelt down, satisfied himself that the senseless man was not dead, secured the letter and the pistol, and inexpertly tied the plump strong hands together with a piece of rope from a package in the room.

His loathsome family—he thought—collected about them loathsome instruments! The debauched Dunscore, the murderous Heywood—fair samples of the men they used in their conspiracies and dishonour!

He pushed the prostrate body where he could see it, and went back to his letters after seeing that the door-key was turned in the lock.

There were further jewels in the garbage heap of dead amours and unpaid bills—one, a sort of official document addressed to 'Our trusty, well-beloved, and right worshipful brother', signed 'Ernest, G.M.' and given under the said Ernest's seal 'at St. James's, this 13th day of August, 1831'. There was a great deal more.

When Heywood recovered consciousness, Christopher was in the chair, looking vaguely and unseeing at the pile of correspondence before him—correspondence that was further evidence of the truth of what the Great Duke had said about that damnable family of his.

Heywood rolled his head to one side to bring the young man into view. He spoke quite unconcernedly.

'You are a little quicker, Christopher, than you used to be. A little more the man of action. I congratulate you!'

Christopher said nothing.

The presence of Heywood in the room of the dead Dunscore linked the present with the past—linked murder to murder; conspiracy to conspiracy; memory of horror and hate to a present that seemed full of them.

'What do you think of our dear Dunscore's little correspondence?' said Heywood. 'Chatty letters, I think! Informative letters!'

'They appear to show,' replied Christopher bitterly, 'that my more-or-less uncle, Cumberland, is at the head of some sort of conspiracy against the Constitution, against Reform, against his niece Victoria. To establish reaction and absolutism in England. That he's been plotting for ten or fifteen years to that effect. . . . I haven't gathered exactly what coup he proposes, but I imagine a little pressure on one or two of the gentlemen mentioned would bring details bubbling out. Never happy unless he's plotting, my dear Uncle Cumberland! . . . I suppose that once upon a time I was involuntarily engaged in one of his exploits—at your instigation! I was, so to speak, your stalking-horse for murder!'

'Have you only just realized it?' asked Heywood lightly. He made no effort to rise, and spoke with as languid an accent as if he were lying upon a sofa in a cigar-divan, instead of upon the floor, with bound hands. He had rolled over on to his right side, and propped himself up on an elbow.

'You were the nightmare of my childhood,' said Christopher, rising and standing over him. 'You are a murderer in everything except fact. Someone ought to have killed you long ago. I can't think why no one has.'

'Tut-tut!' said Captain Heywood, chiding.

'Why was I dragged into your filthy plots? Why was I made the scapegoat? A child of nine!'

'Between ourselves, my dear Christopher!' said Heywood, yawning. 'Between ourselves, of course, if that little notion had succeeded, no one would have inquired too closely into what had happened. Because of the scandal they would have raked up—you being who you were! If it did not succeed—as it did not—the same thing applied. Everybody did their best to minimize the occurrence. You were quite a good card to play!'

Christopher tore himself away from the prostrate man, as though he were afraid he might kick him to death. He flung himself into a chair.

He spoke almost to himself.

'I inherit it on both sides! The blood of Cumberland, murderer and traitor; Kent, an ogre who frightened a small boy; the mad Brunswick; the loathsome George and his imbecile father; all the Georges; all the rotten, posturing, plotting lot; all the gang of nasty and debauched old men. Oh, Christ! Christ . . . I can't escape from them! . . . I can't escape!'

He had forgotten Heywood.

He was unclean! A leper! In a moment of hysteria he suddenly loosened his sword and flung it violently from him. It struck a small table nearly oversetting it, and clanked to the floor. There was silence.

'This murder was just another manifestation of the spirit that possesses them!' said Christopher, and again fell silent.

'So what now?' inquired Heywood after a long pause.

'I have been thinking,' said Christopher.

'A good exercise!' agreed Heywood cordially.

'I have been thinking what I should do. There is no reason why I should not tell you—or even show you. . . . I propose . . .' said Christopher with clenched teeth and thrumming temples—'I propose to let my bloody family look after itself! My hideous, loathsome family! I propose to let them hate and fight and betray one another, how and when and where they will! If they want to murder one another they may! If they want to disinherit one another, they may! They can carry on the family tradition of hating one another—hating their fathers, nieces, sons and brothers as much as they like! I only hope to God that they may destroy one another—as completely as I am going to destroy these letters! I am going to be done with them for good. I am going to escape!'

Under Heywood's watchful eyes he took up the armful of deadly letters, and dumped them in the great stove of white and green and black earthenware. He struck flint to tinder. A spark flew out among the papers. There was a quick yellow flare, and in one roar they vanished and were just a mass of brittle black ashes with faint red and gold lines dying at the edges.

'I shall report that I found nothing.'

He recovered his sword, stooped over Heywood, and released him from his bonds. The other rose to his feet, by some strange means without loss of dignity or loss of composure. Again they stood face to face as they had done twenty minutes before. For an appreciable space of time they studied one another in silence.

Then Christopher went to the door and opened it.

'You may go, Captain Heywood. . . .'

'. . . Colonel Fitzroy,' corrected the other placidly. ' "Heywood" was a nom de guerre for a little expedition I undertook to the West Country—as you may remember!'

'You may report, Colonel Fitzroy, to the Duke of Cumberland, that his nephew has saved his plot for him. He will enjoy it. He would hate to give up a scheme of hate. I hope he brings his whole house toppling about his ears!'

'I wonder . . .' said Fitzroy slowly, turning in the doorway.

'Don't wonder!' said Christopher. 'Go!'

Fitzroy bowed.

'You carry on the family tradition of hate pretty thoroughly—as you seem to know all about it—Mr. Harnish!'

'Hate!' echoed Christopher. 'I have heard nothing except madness and hate about them. Fathers—sons—mothers—husbands—wives: all hating!'

'Too, too unfortunate for me!' said Fitzroy.

'What do you mean?' asked Christopher quickly, and started to close the door as if to shut out the answer.

'As your father, Christopher!' said Colonel Fitzroy, and yawned a trifle as if weary of the conversation.

'My father! You! . . . Oh, God! Not you?'

He stood on the threshold of the room, his fingers crooked round the door-handle. For an instant he hoped that he might not have heard aright: saw in the other's face a sardonic appreciation of his horror, and knew the truth.

'Come back! Come back and tell me,' he said fiercely.

He seized Fitzroy by the arm as, with an assumption of courteous indifference, the other was turning to the stairs. He drew him within the room, and slammed and locked the door, and leaned his back against it.

'Tell me,' he insisted. 'Is it true?'

'True? . . . That I'm your father?' asked Fitzroy in chill tones. He crossed to the chair before Dunscore's dressing-chest, regarded the little fallen jars and bottles for a moment, soused himself down, and examined his nails.

'I think there can be no doubt, my dear sir, that I am your papa!' he remarked as if discussing a matter of no importance with an entire stranger.

'Yes. But were you—were you . . . Was it true, what the Great Duke said?' Christopher found himself stammering again. 'Is it . . . is it t-t-true that you were her nephew?'

'Technically, of course, there was no relationship,' said Fitzroy, still examining his nails. 'My birth, you know! . . . Unrecognized! . . . A slight error on the part of my mamma! But I am afraid that in a sense you might have called me my wife's nephew!'

Said Christopher:

'For God's sake, t-t-tell me more! When did you know? Did *she* know? . . . I feel sick when I think of it.'

He sat down, resting his head in his hands, running his fingers through his dishevelled yellow hair.

'Did *she* know?' he asked again.

'She learned soon enough!' said Fitzroy.

Christopher unbuckled his sword belt, and let the weapon fall to the floor with a crash. He set his foot on it.

'I want to know . . .' he began. 'To . . .' he found he could not pronounce the word, and stuttered helplessly for some moments: looked up; kicked angrily at the black and gilt scabbard, 'know everything!'

'Like myself,' said his father, 'you begin nowhere—legally! An investigation into nothingness is unlikely to be profitable. So why go into the matter?'

'Tell me!'

'You take an almost childish view of things, if I may venture to say so,' remarked Fitzroy continuing to inspect his nails. 'I can conceive no reason for your interest. You never knew your mother; and our acquaintanceship has really been of the slightest.'

Said Christopher:

'I think—I—I think I could strangle you, with my own hands . . . and be glad. . . . Tell me! Tell me. . . . T-T-Tell me!'

'Our relationship has been marked sufficiently by displays of violence,' said Colonel Fitzroy. 'Parricide never sounds well. I should deprecate the attempt myself. But, if you must really know . . .'

Christopher dropped his head, and clasped his hands above it, resting his elbows upon his knees. He drew his feet together. One of his spurs scratched the admirable gloss of a boot, and left a grey weal upon it.

'It's a long story,' remarked his father, in a tone of polite apology. 'I will keep it crisp.'

He stopped. Rose. Walked up and down the room amid the chaos of the dead man's baggage, picking his teeth with a small elephant-headed toothpick of ivory.

'My father,' he said, 'for various reasons which we need not go into at the present, was glad to help my career. I had one or two minor and decorative posts about the court. Eventually, I was sent to Weymouth when your mother was there—convalescing.

'Your mother was always convalescing.

'I made a highly ornamental equerry in those days. She was a romantic and sex-starved young woman. Like her sisters. When she was away from the chilling influence of the Queen it was surprising how approachable she was—like her sisters, particularly Sophia!'

'My mother!' said Christopher.

'It's your father who is telling you,' said Fitzroy; paused; looked with some distaste at the jar of pomatum with the hair or two stuck to its lip, and continued.

'Your mother had been wintering at Weymouth—furnished house—small suite. She decided to pay an incognito visit to some old friends at Wareham. She didn't. We got married—with considerable secrecy. She came on a honeymoon with me to a small cottage I rented in the country.

'On the third morning your mother was still in bed, watching me shave—all very connubial and domesticated. She had a pale blue wrap, I remember. Fancy me remembering after all these years!' He paused in a self-gratulatory manner. 'She was a pretty woman in her pale washed-out way! Well, she was sitting up in bed, watching the operation with childish interest, when in rushes . . .'

He stopped for so long that Christopher urged him on in a harsh voice.

'Well? . . . Well?'

'I won't go into matters that are not germane to the subject under discussion,' said Colonel Fitzroy, halting opposite the bowed figure of his son. 'If I say that there was a woman who had an overwhelming grievance against the House of Hanover, it is enough. An overwhelming hate which embraced every member! Which stuck at nothing! A hate for which she lived.

'Knowing everything she watched the progress of the romance. With interest. And, when the time was ripe, she struck.

'She broke in on our honeymoon—as I have said. She burst into our room, swept a great curtsy, and looked like the image of Britannia with a bad smell under her nose.

' "Oh, ma'am! Too late! Too late!" cries she.' Into his measured tones came a note of cynical appreciation of the drama. 'Your mother had never seen her before. She resented the intrusion. She was newly enough married to feel awkward at being found in a bedroom with a man. She pulled her wrap round her shoulders, and looked at . . . at the lady I have mentioned, in her most royal manner.

' "What is the meaning of this, madam?" she asked.

' "Meaning!" cries she, sweeping another curtsy. "Do you know, ma'am, that you have been to bed with your brother's son? Incest, ma'am! Incest with your own nephew!" I give you my word, I was sorry for the girl. She was an amiable creature, if nothing else. It was really rather a trying moment for me! Quite trying!'

He reflected a moment as if anticipating comment. There was none.

'The lady I have mentioned got great pleasure from witnessing the considerable distress your mother displayed. Even greater pleasure from telling my papa—the Prince Regent. He had some sort of seizure on the spot. I have forgotten how many ounces of blood they took off him. Quite a considerable quantity. And grandpapa, King George the Third, went out of his mind when he heard about it! Very ill-balanced intellect! Easily upset! . . . Yes, the lady I was telling you of took vengeance in good measure then! Very good!'

He chuckled drily.

'And d-d-did you know of the—the relationship, yourself?' asked Christopher, licking his lips.

'I cannot say that it worried me,' said his father. 'After all an illegitimate son has no legal relationship to his papa!'

Christopher rose. He took up the sword from the floor, and started to draw the blade from its scabbard.

'I think . . .' he began.

'I don't,' said Fitzroy, and suddenly struck him with the pistol butt on the temple, as his head was bowed over the slowly emerging blade. Struck so hard that the younger man fell to the floor as if he had been pole-axed; and the blood streamed on to his forehead, and matted his yellow hair, and trickled on to the polished boards.

His father looked down on him thoughtfully for a few minutes; dropped the pistol back in the skirts of his coat; dusted his hands, as if he were washing them of any blood-guiltiness; quietly withdrew.

It was more than an hour later when Christopher came back to the Wall House, with a rough bandage about his head.

He reported to no one; went to his room, sent for Williams, and made hurried arrangements with him.

Like a man in a daze he wrote a direction to Penhuys, the banker, for drafts and cash: a swift letter to Setoun; and a formal note in stilted language resigning his commission, which he propped against his glass. He sought for Eckie, and not finding him, threw on his bed the farewell he had written a few hours ago, with its enclosure of notes and a scrawled line upon the cover.

He slipped out of the house without a good-bye word or look. At his footfall Sophie von Osterode opened her bedroom door—as she often seemed to when she heard it—and hesitated on the threshold, as though about to undertake one of her meaningless errands.

Her provocative shoulders showed their bareness under a thin wrap, and her lips were as luscious a red as nectarines. He did not even bow to her, but quietly went downstairs and out of the house to the river promenade, where Williams awaited him beside a four-horse berline with a hooded rumble at the back.

He was entering it when Eckie appeared, walking under the lime trees with downcast head, holding his sword in the crook of his arm like an old man promenading with his walking stick.

'I say, what . . . ?' Eckie began.

'Good-bye, Eckie,' said Christopher taking him by the hand. 'God knows when we shall meet again. I am going. I must go. I can't stay. I think I shall go mad. . . . Remember me to Luise. . . . Good-bye!'

'But, Lord God! . . .'

He tore himself away. As they rattled over the stones he could see quite clearly in his mind's eye Eckie standing there, his sword under his arm, his mouth wide open in astonishment. He wondered if he would ever see Eckie again.

Chapter 26

The 'Infernal Defiance' Brings News to a Widow

CHARLOTTE, DROWSING OVER HER MORNING CHOCOLATE in the big front bedroom at an aunt's house in Weymouth Street, became increasingly conscious of turmoil in the street under her windows. There was a noise she could not recognize, underlying an excited babble of voices—a noise such as an angry beehive or a gargantuan kettle might make; a bubbling, sizzling noise; a humming, grumbling noise.

She raised herself upon an elbow among her pillows and listened. She almost fancied that she could distinguish Setoun's voice; but he had gone—she answered herself—to Dover only the previous night on one of his mysterious errands. The utterances—whoever made them—were in any event immediately overwhelmed by a renewed outbreak of buzzing, and by a noise such as might be made by someone shovelling gravel.

Then, without warning, there blew in through her open windows a sudden gust of dense black smoke, which dissipated itself in the room into fat smuts, settling upon her bedspread and the lace cloth of the silver tray.

She slipped out of bed, thrust her feet into slippers, threw a wrap round herself, and cautiously peered out of the window.

Against the curb was drawn up a black and yellow object which appeared to be a compound of closed travelling carriage and fac-tory: for at the back, between the dickey and its body, were three tall thin chimneys sprouting from something like an oven. A man in a white hat sat on the coachman's box, his hands grimly clasp-

418

ing a sort of ship's tiller, and another man shovelled coal into a container under the rumble. Guarded by two tall lackeys from the crowd, a pair of legs protruded on to the pavement, from the roadway beneath the monstrous hybrid.

Charlotte knew those legs. She looked down on them with affection, with laughter, and with a motherly consideration for eccentricity.

She drew her wrap more tightly about her shoulders and went downstairs to the breakfast room, where a round-eyed housemaid turned quickly from the window at her entry, and made feeble pretence at busy dusting.

'Lord Setoun is outside,' said Charlotte. 'He is underneath the— the kettle thing. Tell one of the men I want to see my Lord at once.'

From the window she saw him extricate himself as soon as the message was brought, and submit to violent brushing by one of his men. He looked at his hands regretfully, dusted them one against the other, shook his head over them, and entered the house, apparently unaware of the black oil marks on the bridge of his arrogant nose, his leathery cheek and his jutting chin.

Charlotte turned laughing to greet him as he entered the room.

'Eight hours from Dover!' exclaimed Setoun from the doorway. 'Eight hours instead of twelve! . . . Went like the wind. . . . Stormed along! . . . Can't touch you, Carlotta, my dear . . . covered with coal!'

'You'd better not examine me too closely, either,' said Charlotte. 'I'm barely decent. I've got nothing on except my nightrobe —practically. . . . Now, what's this all about? Hurbles, tell Mother! —Bad Hurbles with a thousand-pound transportable tea-kettle!'

The laughter left Setoun's face.

He gesticulated with an elbow.

'In my left tail-pocket, Carlotta. . . . Too dirty myself. . . . Editor of the paper came to see the packet arrive with the steam carriage. Gave me a paper just off the press. . . . So here I am. . . . Thought I'd better see you at once, if you didn't know.'

'Didn't know what?' said Charlotte, wrestling with a folded newspaper in the tail-pocket of his ill-used dark blue coat.

'Didn't know what?' she repeated.

He made no direct reply, but nodded to the paper. 'Third page . . . second column . . . half-way down.'

It was a copy of the *Dover Telegraph* dated that morning.

' "ROYAL AFFABILITY—A pleasing instance of condescension",' read Charlotte, casting her eye along the column.

'Farther down,' said Setoun gravely.

Two items below was set out in close-packed print with no headlines but a shoulder-head in small capitals:

DREADFUL MURDER.—The *Frankfort Zeitung* received last night reports from Neipperg that at an early hour on the morning of July 15th instant, the Right Honourable the Earl of Dunscore was discovered by one of his attendants dead in bed at his inn, having been most barbarously and inhumanly murdered by robbers. . . .

For a moment she swayed as though she might fall. Then she read on, till she came to the last sentences:

. . . A vast quantity of jewellery and gold fittings as well as a pocket book containing a large sum in bank notes is said to be missing. A negro who was seen behaving in a suspicious manner is sought by the police agents of the city. The deceased nobleman had figured, according to common report, in an incident which resulted in the departure of the half-mad Duke of Brunswick a few days previously. He was also engaged to meet an officer of the Grand-Ducal bodyguard in a *rencontre* with pistols on the very morning on which he was so shockingly assassinated.

She set the smudgy paper upon the table, and stood in silence tapping her fingers on the polished rosewood.

'I could have wished it had not happened quite like that,' she said at last. 'But that is all. I cannot regret that he is dead—only the manner of his death. . . . He has never meant anything to me. . . . I have seen him twice, for a minute, in the eleven years since our wedding. . . . He was an utter stranger to me. I cannot even recall the colour of his eyes. . . . His death can only fill me with

one emotion—the sense of freedom. I'm not going to be a hypo-
crite, Hurbles. I'm glad—glad—glad to be free!'

'He was a treacherous hound,' said Setoun, bluntly.

'I can't be sorry that he's dead,' said Charlotte, folding the paper
and unfolding it again. 'If only his death could make me free,
then I'm thankful that he is dead.'

Setoun produced a large red handkerchief from an inner pocket.
'He was a cold-hearted devil—a gamester, a rook, a cheat and a
duellist. Without your money he would have sunk to the level of
a common adventurer. He had no respect for a woman and no
honour among men. He has had eleven good years upon your
money. More than he deserved. He has publicly shamed you—
ever since he won you by a scandalous trick. . . .'

'Which he boasted of in the vestry as he signed his name,' said
Charlotte. 'Is it any wonder I thank God I'm free?'

There was a long minute's silence between them, while she
stood with downcast eyes, looking into the empty hearth.

'I tore off my wedding ring ten years ago,' she said. 'I have never
worn it since. It is really off now; that is all.'

His glance went automatically to the bare slim fingers with
which she held the thin wrap about her.

She was silent again, and then suddenly spoke, looking up directly at him:

'I'm going to pretend now that he never was—that those eleven
years have never been. . . . That I've just read a paragraph about
someone we knew casually long ago—someone who meant nothing
to us. Which is true.'

'But . . .'

Charlotte silenced him with a quick gesture.

'I have just said: "Dear Hurbles, I think perhaps you're right in
taking Tops away from Brandenburgh House. Dear Hurbles, of
course, you're right! You always are"!'

'But . . .'

'I have just said: "Dear Hurbles, I think I'll come back myself.
Perhaps . . ."'

'But Carlotta . . . !' protested Setoun stumbling behind the swift
movement of her fancy. He was conscious of the smear upon his

nose and, absurdly like a vast schoolboy, was spreading it across his face as he rubbed at it with the red handkerchief.

Charlotte watched his efforts, at first vacantly, and then with awakening interest.

'You can't possibly do it like that, Hurbles, you absurd creature!' she remarked. 'Give it to me!'

She wetted the handkerchief at her lips.

'I have just said: "So I think I shall come back to you and Cousin Jane," ' she said, scrubbing at the high-bridged nose. ' "The atmosphere is possibly . . ." ' she paused to remember the exact word—' "contaminating." '

She stepped back to study her handiwork.

'I think, perhaps, after all, you'd better go upstairs and wash yourself properly.'

'I'd rather you washed me,' said Setoun meekly.

'You've got such a very large face, if I'm to treat you like a cat does her kitten,' grumbled Charlotte . . . 'Hurbles, do you know you've got quite a lot of white in your hair—white, not grey!'

'My dear,' replied Setoun, bringing his face within easier reach of her attentions. 'I'm not getting any younger. You can forget eleven years. Make no difference to you. But to me! . . . Getting old!'

'You're not. You're not,' denied Charlotte, dealing with the smeared chin vigorously. 'And if you are, it is my fault. My fault.'

She looked at the clock upon the mantelpiece. The hands showed the time to be eight minutes before eight o'clock. She returned him the handkerchief.

'Eleven years, Hurbles! And eight minutes in which to catch up! We've got to get all those years into those few minutes.'

She smiled at his blank regard.

What little change eleven years had brought to her, in outward view, thought Setoun. Line, contour, and delicate colouring seemed to him the same; and out of the wide eyes looked a mischievous, benevolent, surprising Charlotte who was still the same.

'Do you know you've got brown flecks in the grey of your eyes, Hurbles?' the surprising woman asked.

Hurbles did not know.

'Stay quite still, Hurbles. . . . I'm going to look into your eyes. . . . I'm going to be psychic. . . . I'm going to "come over queer" and read the future in your eyes. . . . In the left hand one . . . I can see a respectable middle-aged couple travelling comfortably across Europe, as respectable middle-aged couples should. . . . I can see a young man with them. . . . Who is he? . . . He is their adopted nephew. . . . Who can that couple be, Hurbles? Now who?'

The tanned and brick-red face of Setoun became crimson.

He stammered.

'Who can they be, Hurbles?' she asked again. And then with sudden violence said, 'I'm a widow, Hurbles! I'm a widow woman. A lone, lorn widow woman! . . . Forget that man! . . . Forget all about him! . . . Just remember I'm a widow woman. . . . Eleven years into eight minutes! . . . No, five minutes now. . . . They've got to get in. . . . Hurbles, have I got to propose, myself?'

She had not. And the steam-kettle sizzled and boiled away in the street, and the breakfast-room door opened noisily and closed silently, and the little tortoise-shell clock struck the hour, and the dust on his clothes came off all over her wrap—without any attention being paid them.

'We might go in the "Defiance",' pondered Setoun much later.

'Do you mean the transportable kettle?' asked Charlotte, leaning back in his clasp.

'Full name "Infernal Defiance". Christened her by emptying a bottle of port into the boiler. . . . Power of fifteen horses. . . . Twelve miles an hour. . . . Whizz!—and you are anywhere you want.'

'Whizz!' said Charlotte, removing herself from the embrace, 'and a female in silks and muslins is in no condition she wants! Look!'

The once fresh and filmy wrap about her was grievously marked where large and dirty hands had held her firmly. A bare arm bore grimy fingerprints upon its rounded rosiness.

Setoun's face fell.

So it was in privacy and with great decorum that the Viscount and Viscountess Setoun fared forth, by more normal means of transport, two days later, to astound their adopted nephew.

But they did not find him to astound: they found only a rather incoherent Eckie, and a Great Duke reduced to meek apology by an angry wife.

Von Brahe's brother had seen that nephew enter an inn, while his horses were baiting fifteen miles out of Frankfort. The agent of Setoun's Paris bankers in that town had cashed a large draft for Christopher the same day; afterwards the young man had vanished utterly and entirely. No one could tell whether he had gone thence to Nuremberg and toward Vienna, or along the valley of the Rhine to Switzerland, or crossed through the Palatinate into Lorraine—or made his way to any one of a thousand places in a dozen countries.

Christopher had gone to seek his fellow waif, had pressed on across Europe on her trail, but failed to catch her up. She had had more than a day's start of him; twice his horses went lame; once a tree had been blown down across the highway, and, again, he was detained for twenty-four hours when one of the rear springs of the carriage broke on the vile roads near Cologne.

When he reached Paris she had already flown.

'Madame est en villégiature, monsieur,' said the fat concierge, looking out of his dark nesting-box in the echoing stone hall-way. She had been gone more than a day. He was desolated that he did not know her destination. He was more than desolated when the haggard young man produced a five-franc piece. He was spurred to endeavour by the sight of a gold louis. They would go and see, *Coquin de sort!*—for he came from Provence—whether Madame had left any address by chance in her apartment.

They climbed a noble stairway in the dark well of the house, and halted before one of a pair of double doors, which confronted each other from beneath elaborate architraves across a tessellated landing.

The fat man found the right key after many efforts, and they went into a wide and lofty hall hung with fine tapestry and softly carpeted. A Sèvres vase stood on a buhl table. A grandfather clock with a silver face still ticked. A glove lay on a carved and gilded chair—but no paper with direction or address.

'Madame should have sung at the Italian Opera next week,' said the concierge. 'She sent a note to Monsieur Rossini and said she could not. That she would be back in a month. And then was gone.'

They looked into a grey-hung dining-room filled with mahogany in the Chinese manner: into a drawing-room full of painted chairs and high mirrors and porcelain vases from which rose leaves spilled on to inlaid chests. Chandeliers with a hundred lustres hung like stalactites of ice from the ceiling, dimmed in a rose-coloured gloom.

They looked into a huge bedroom with a bed of green lacquer upon a dais, lacquer chests across which golden dragons sprawled, and soft-toned rugs of rose and apple-green spread over a silvered floor. They looked into rooms that gave in their costly and impersonal magnificence no clue at all to their owner save that they told of a taste for luxurious beauty. No portrait hung upon their silken walls—not even a miniature; an open bureau showed no letters.

Nowhere, either, was any hint of the destination whither the mistress of the household had hurried.

'Madame had a country retreat,' said the concierge. 'That is all I know. She has never told me where it is. And her servants!'—he shook his shiny close-cropped head—'they are silent ones! . . . No gossip. Never a word.'

'I have travelled across Europe to find Madame,' Christopher told him. 'I have journeyed for ten days as fast as horses will bring me. . . . I must see her. . . . I will see her. . . . There's fifty louis if you can find out her address.'

'Fifty louis, h'm!'

The man scratched his grey stubble reflectively.

'The lackey comes once a week to fetch her letters. Fifty louis! Something perhaps might be done. One will see. . . . And if one should have to make outlay? . . .'

He rubbed his left palm with his right fingers suggestively.

'What you will,' said Christopher. 'So long as I know—and know quickly.'

Chapter 27

The Rise of the House of Atchill

TOWARDS NIGHTFALL CHRISTOPHER RODE DOWN INTO A shallow valley narrowing in from grey and distant marshes. Dusky wooded hills bordered the level of its pasture-land, as if they were the coastline of a vanished bay.

A low causeway transversed the fading brightness of the meadows. It was hummocked by a bridge across a river that dawdled between sharp-cut banks.

Where the road at the farther side started steeply upwards again, a narrow lane turned off along the foot of the hills, between unfenced fields and a hedgerow which set the limit to climbing woods and orchards. A brown-red roof was visible amidst the darkening greenery.

Christopher had landed at Dover from the packet on the previous evening: he had set forth at dawn to ride along the coast and through the marsh to Rye. There had obtained his bearings, and set out alone on the last ten miles of his journey.

He dismounted and walked along the lane, followed by his jaded horse. The hedgerow was full of wild roses, pale in the dying day: in the darker patches of the wide pasturage faint-hued marsh flowers became yet fainter: the stillness was disturbed by no human sound, but fluttered only by the distant tinkle of a sheep bell and the tired bed-time twitter of birds.

A small red house looked on to the lane from many little windows across a strip of grass and a low box-hedge. Hollyhocks—their colour drenched in twilight—were on guard at the squat door; the gaiety of the long garden that ran betwixt slanting orchards and grey roadway was as subdued as a remote memory.

The ground floor windows glimmered with a candle-light as faint as if it had been reflected in still water.

He opened the little wicket gate and walked quietly up the path.

'Deb—at last!' he said to himself, and with such emphasis that for a moment he thought he had spoken aloud, breaking the twilight stillness.

Deb, at last!—and this little friendly house, whose homeliness and dim illumination ringed it about against the dusk, and the memory of horror and the presage of evil!

As he came up between the conch-shell borders of the path he could see, through one of the windows which flanked the door, that somebody sat within.

He stepped on to the close-cut grass and looked inside.

Deb was at a table in a low room. There were two candles in plain brass candlesticks on the green cloth, and a number of open books were strewn before her. With her dark head bent, she was writing slowly and intently on a fly-leaf, pausing every moment to compare—it seemed—each stroke of what she wrote with the inscription in another volume.

Presently she turned her head as if to listen to someone who spoke from the further invisibility of the room. Her cheek glowed with the faint tint of a blush rose petal and was curved with its curve. She looked back, and then sharply up to the window—as if in response to a warning—and gazed directly at him.

Even in the feeble light within he could see her face change, and that consternation and fear were in her expression.

With a sudden chilling of the heart he stepped back from the grass: reminded himself that he would have been unrecognized— a man's face against the dusk, peering upon her privacy: and so greeted her with smiles as the door swung open.

She stood in grey upon the threshold, the door held in her hand. There was no light of welcome in her pale face, only a set look of deep-seated alarm.

'Why have you come here?' she asked in a low voice. 'Oh, why have you come? You must not. . . . You can't!'

He stepped back as if he had been struck.

'But, Deb!' he said, and then again, 'But, Deb!'

He had been so sure of welcome; and of shelter from the monstrous things that had come back from the past and pressed into his mind; and of renewal of the strength and sympathy which had upheld him long ago!

'You can't come here! You can't come!' she repeated, and stood athwart the doorway in her wide dress, one white hand upon the panels and the other on the lintel as though to keep him out. She did not even say his name, but stopped short in her broken sentences as if it might not be mentioned in that place.

'But, Deb,' he began once more in confusion.

'Don't say that name! . . . Not here!' she said, and clasped her hands before her and almost wrung them.

'You said . . . in Paris. . . . You said you would be glad. . . . You . . .'

'Paris? . . . Yes, Paris—but not here. You may not come! . . . Oh, go away! . . . Please, go away!'

She stepped down to the pathway where he stood, as if she would hasten his departure by leading him to the gate.

He almost shrank from her, and stared uncomprehending from her strained face to open door and lighted windows; and held the little house under his regard as though to penetrate whatever secret it enfolded. . . .

He found himself at the gate, and addressing her coherently.

'I thought from what you said a few weeks ago,' he said with tired wistfulness, not seeking to solve the mystery of her displeasure, 'that you would be glad to see me again. A hideous thing has happened, and I thought you might help me to forget. I thought . . .'

He turned away, and gathered up the trailing reins of his grazing horse.

She came into the road, and as the little wicket shut behind her a change came over her, as if she had stepped from off the stage into the wings—from one pattern of drama to another. She even used his name.

'Tops,' she said. 'Don't ask me to explain. I should have been glad to see you in Paris. To have had your company on that long weary journey. If I had thought you were to come I should have waited. But here you may not come. . . . You may not. . . . Forgive me! . . . Really, Tops, you mayn't. . . . I can't explain.'

She even put a hand upon his arm.

'Come to me in Paris in a little. I shall be there so soon.'

'Deb,' he began, and seeing her shudder at the name, corrected himself . . . 'Margaretha! I'm sorry if I should not have come. I was not to know. I could not tell. I am very sorry. I will go away. At once.'

He mounted his horse, and looked down at her.

'I will go back to what I know I can't escape. I built up a sort of inner life—a fairy story—against it, but it has come pressing through. Everywhere I found reality too harsh for the fabric of my dreams. And now I know that in my blood is something which of itself would not permit me to keep my dreams in peace. Something which will not rest until I am not merely entangled innocently in horrors, but am myself an actor in them.'

He gave a short laugh.

'So I'm sorry, Margaretha. . . . And good-bye.'

The jaded beast flinched to his spur, looked round reproachfully, would not believe that the journey was unended, and hung its great head again to the juicy grass.

He jerked at the reins.

For a moment she was minded to let him go without a word of explanation. It surprised her, indeed, when she found that she had put a hand upon the horse's withers. She hesitated, and then spoke.

'Before you go,' she said. She was like a ghost in a ghost world as the dusk grew to darkness. 'Before you go. Do you not think that I have, too, those dreadful things to forget—and far, far worse? Worse, perhaps, than yours! And I cannot make fairy fancies as you were always able. This is the only place in all the world where I can forget. Where I must forget. . . . Good-bye!'

She stood rigid and silent till horse and man had almost vanished in the gloom, merged indistinguishably with falling night and hedgerow. She turned then to go back to the little lighted house, paused, turned again. She could not see them now, but could only hear the weary drag of hoofs upon the road.

A sudden new decision came upon her. A sequence of thoughts followed swiftly through her brain. She seemed to gather up hidden forces within herself that spurred her on to call in a high clear voice:

'Tony! . . . To-ny!'

The hoof beats ceased, as if the rider had reined in and listened for a repetition of the name.

'Come back a moment!' she cried. 'Come back!' and in a little he waited before her again. She could not see the questioning look in Christopher's eyes, but only the raising of his level brows as he regarded her wordlessly.

'Where are you going to-night?' she asked, knowing it was not what she had to say.

'There is an inn about three miles away, at Northiam,' he answered.

'Get off your horse, and listen to me!'

He obeyed her, and she walked beside him up the lane, away from the little house, the horse clip-clopping in their wake. He shot one glance at her—at the pale face, the night-black hair, and the long throat, curved with the curve of water, that rose from the pallor of her rustling dress.

'Tony,' she said.

'Tony?'

'Tony! . . .' she reiterated. 'Tony, do you remember that far away, and—it seems—long ago, we said that we had dreamed a dream, together?'

She paused for him to answer.

He nodded assent.

'Yes? A dream that was a nightmare! A dream we said that we'd forget! Here in this lane, Tony, you must even now dream again. That those who dreamed the dream were dreams themselves! Do you understand . . . Tony?'

'A dream within a dream!'

She was but a blur beside him now, as the lane wound upwards under the rustling archway of the trees.

'Here, Tony,' she said, 'is reality alone—for me. It must be so for you, if you're to stay. Those other things we have thought of were but dreams—the things you thought of were dreams: the things *I* thought of were dreams'—and she struck her hands together—'only dreams. And the You and I that thought them were just waking fancies as we drowsed this morning.'

'If here alone is reality for you . . .' he would have said her name, but, not knowing what she would be called, paused and went on— 'then here shall be the only reality for me, whether I go or stay. And I shall never think of you as other than here—in your little house with the hollyhocks at the door. And the long narrow garden beside the lane. And the big flagstone over the ditch before the wicket. And the woods. And the mist coming up from the river.'

They came to a grassy junction of two lanes with elms shaking in the night wind.

'Here the little house can't see or hear!' she said. 'No whisper can reach it. . . . Now swear to me by God that here I am not— not—not the child whose name you knew—not Deb; not the poorhouse waif from a Plymouth brothel; not even Margaretha Acislo. Swear that you are not Christopher Harnish, either child or man! . . . Swear it!'

He took her hand.

'I do not know who you are—or who I am! I swear it! And that we are who you wish we should be.'

He picked two stones from out a rut and held them in his palm.

'See,' he said. 'The You and I we dreamed! They're gone. Like that!'—and flung them over a high hedge with all the strength of his arm.

'You will ask no questions?'

'None at all. Not even who I am.'

She turned, and together they retraced their steps, the patient horse with faintly jingling stirrups plodding uneasily behind them. They walked without speaking down the grass-grown track, her dress rustling as she went like a flower garden in the wind.

At the wicket she paused and gave him both her hands.

'Cousin Tony,' she said, and her lips parted in a smile. 'Margaret Atchill welcomes you home! . . . Supper will soon be ready. . . . You must be very tired!'

A trim little country maid awaited them in the lamp-lit hall.

'Daphilda, tell Barbara that my cousin, Mr. Tony, has come to stay. Lay another place for supper. And send Silas out to look after the horse and bring the saddlebags upstairs. . . . He will have Mr. Tom's room.'

She opened a door on which the white paint had been rubbed almost to the wood by constant polishing.

'Before you go upstairs, you must meet Miss Comfort who keeps me company. . . . Miss Comfort, here is Cousin Tony Atchill, of whom you often hear me speak.'

In a low, snug, crowded room, an old gentlewoman sat before the fire in a large shabby armchair. She had a white shawl about her shoulders, and bright red knitting streamed from her lap.

While she murmured a pleasant greeting, looking over her steel-rimmed spectacles at him with faded incurious eyes; and while he spoke, in reply to her, of his journey, Christopher took in the scene.

There were big old-fashioned mirrors in wide white frames that made the room look larger, and repeated the ormolu candlesticks under glass shades beside a cheerfully ticking gilded clock. There were book-cases full of books in worn leather bindings, and por-traits—dark and indistinguishable in the lamplight—upon the walls. A sofa was set at the other side of the fireplace with a bright shabby footstool by it. A spinet opened with yellowed music on its stand: small tables with stray books and lustre vases full of flowers and silver snuffers and trinkets on them: a cabinet with a few pieces of old china; a tabby cat upon the worn hearthrug worshipping the fire.

The small maid appeared in the doorway.

'If you please, ma'am, there's hot water in Mr. Tom's room, and I've lighted the fire. And Silas wants to know should he go over to Farmer Timmins for some oats. He says there's barely one feed now! And Barbara would like . . .' What Barbara wanted was told in whispers.

'And now, Cousin Tony,' said Margaret, 'I'll show you to your room.'

She took a flat silver candlestick from a row upon the table with-out the door, and led the way up steep stairs and along a dark pas-sage.

The fire burnt briskly in the small grate in Mr. Tom's room. Cheerful flowered curtains had been drawn across the windows.

The handle of a warming pan lay on the pillows of a narrow bed, and towels were neatly folded over the hot-water can on the washstand in the corner.

'I think you have everything, Cousin Tony,' said Margaret looking round. 'I'll bring some flowers in the morning. We'll have supper whenever you are ready. But don't hurry!'

Without coherent thought Christopher undid the saddlebags which had been placed on the faded chintz of an ottoman in the window. From a post over the fireplace, between two high brass candlesticks, the portrait in chalks of a young man in uniform watched him as he washed and brushed. He became conscious of the regard.

' "Mr. Tom", I suppose,' said Christopher in a murmur to himself. It was an amateur's picture of a youngster in the scarlet coat and shako of an infantry officer of twenty years before—more than a trifle faded, and with damp spots showing brown on the cartridge paper. Above its frame hung a heavy cavalry sabre.

Why a cavalry sabre? thought Christopher.

There were other traces of 'Mr. Tom' about the room. A narrow shelf of books that included treatises on horsemastership and the Peninsular campaign, a commentary on Cæsar, Tristram Shandy, and Quentin Durward. On the high chest of drawers lay a shabby razor case and a patent strop, as though they had been left behind by an owner suddenly called away: a wooden uniform case, studded with brass nails stood at the bedfoot.

He picked up the copy of Quentin Durward and looked inside. 'THOMAS ATCHILL. 1814' was written upon the flyleaf in flowing script, and on the bottom of the inside of the cover was gummed the label of a Parisian bookseller.

He went downstairs very thoughtfully, his candlestick in his hand.

The dining-room was the counterpart of the drawing-room. They supped at a table covered with a cloth of fine and ancient linen very neatly mended. The dishes were of Swansea china, some of them slightly chipped and others beautifully repaired. The silver spoons and forks were old and worn with polishing until the initials on them were barely visible. A bird cage hung under its cover before the faded green velvet curtains.

They were benevolently regarded as they ate by large portraits in slightly tarnished frames—of a simpering woman with high powdered hair; an old man with a bluff red face; and a high-waisted girl with long bright eyes and a tress of hair drifting over a shoulder.

The talk was of garden. Miss Comfort lamented the ravages of birds among the currant bushes; and Margaret wondered whether Silas was giving them all the new potatoes that he might.

'I'm sure,' said Miss Comfort, 'that the mice are getting at the peaches in the greenhouse.'

'We shall have to put Tibbie there on watch to-night,' said Margaret Atchill gravely.

'Poor Tibbie!' sighed Miss Comfort. 'She won't like it. Do you not think that the close air may be bad for her, Margaret? I heard her coughing this morning.'

'It was only a fish-bone, ma'am,' said Daphilda removing a dish of trifle.

Miss Comfort looked unconvinced.

'You shall give her the old horse rug, Daphilda,' said Margaret, 'to make her comfortable. Silas always leaves one of the top lights open so that the air will still be fresh.'

After she had set the fruit upon the table, Daphilda looked at her mistress questioningly; Margaret nodded.

The little maid left the room. They heard a door unlocked and the sound of feet descending stone stairs. She presently reappeared beaming with smiles and carrying a dusty bottle wrapped carefully in a white napkin.

'We must drink your health on your arrival, Cousin Tony,' said Margaret. 'In one of our few bottles of old port.'

'That will be a treat!' commented Miss Comfort, watching anxiously Daphilda's effort to withdraw the cork. 'I don't know anything about wine, you know, my dear: but I think it is quite the nicest I have ever tasted.'

The cork emerged successfully, and she looked over her glasses at Christopher, as Daphilda poured out the wine with reverent attention.

'I am sure you will like this wine, Mr. Tony. It is one of the few bottles left which Margaret's dear father laid down. When you were born, was it not, my dear?'

Christopher's expression as he replied to Miss Comfort was one only of polite interest and anticipation. He knew that Margaret was watching him intently, that she hesitated to answer; and he took upon himself the immediate burden.

'Nearly a quarter of a century ago! It should be good.'

He was conscious that her face had lightened; and she shook her head in a quickly summoned gesture of laughing dismay.

'A quarter of a century! How ungallant to make me seem so old!'

Margaret Atchill raised the glass to her lips.

'Here's to your health and prosperity, Cousin Anthony Atchill!' she said.

They sat at the table when the cloth had been removed and talked about the weather, and the respective merits of the shops in Robertsbridge and Tenterden, and the legends of the marsh. Miss Comfort at a corner, with the lamp drawn a little closer to her, played a complicated patience in which she systematically cheated and got as angry as she might about a King of Spades that blocked her game.

Later, in response to the bell, Daphilda came in with Barbara, the cook. She put something enveloped in a chamois leather cover beside Margaret, and a well-worn book with embroidered marker at Miss Comfort's elbow. The little maids then sat themselves bolt upright on shabby padded chairs against the wall, while Miss Comfort put the cards away into a leather box.

Christopher found himself on his knees staring at the buttons in the claret-coloured leather of an armchair, while a soft old voice read fervently:

'O merciful Father in whose hands . . . this family. . . . Protect us this night from all dangers both of the body and the soul. . . . We humbly beseech Thee to remember . . .'

' "This family—protect us this night from all dangers both of the body and the soul"!'

In that quiet house lapped about in silence it seemed to him as if the mantle of God might be spread abroad. It seemed as if, in the darkness without, great wings might be stooped over its low roof.

He could not see the buttons on the upholstery of the chair, for his vision became blurred with tears of gratitude.

The little maids bobbed curtsies, and whispered 'good-nights'. The candlesticks were set upon the cloth, and Miss Comfort lighted hers from the fire with a paper spill and took it up. She kissed Margaret, placing thin veined hands quietly upon her shoulders as if to give a blessing by the touch.

'Amid all this excitement you must not forget to take the caddy upstairs with you, my dear! It would never do for anything to happen to it, after it's been in the family for so many years!'

And so to bed: but before he slipped in between warm linen sheets, he drew back the curtains and looked out.

A mist had crept from out the hidden river, and lay low and flat over the valley's width. It broke into a thin line of foam at the foot of the farther hills, and washed against the bank of the lane below like the ghost of a sea returned to its ancient coasts. There was no light upon its dark shore, and the grey flood lay becalmed under the stars.

He stood a long while at the window entranced by the scene and his imaginings. Almost he waited for fairy folk to come through the dark woods to the launching of an elfin craft upon the magic sea: or for the ghost of a Norse long-ship to float by, unstirring the ghost of the great vanished river up which it had swum with muffled oars more than a thousand years before.

As he went down to breakfast in the morning, he caught, through a half-open door along the passage, a glimpse of a low room with smooth unruffled bed. A vase of country flowers and two large volumes, one upon the other, were placed on the bare white toilet cover of a high chest of drawers. The pleasant chamber gave out the atmosphere of detachment that an unused room will gather through the years.

On the staircase wall there were one or two water-colours of old houses among trees, depicted in faint greys and greens and sepias by an unpractised hand.

Margaret at breakfast raised a cheerful face in greeting, and the canary sang in the sunshine. Miss Comfort, presiding at the teapot, dipped the foot of each narrow cup into a basin of hot water before she filled it, so that it would not slip on the ridgeless saucer.

'What shall we do with Cousin Tony to-day?' asked Margaret.

It was Margaret: not Margaretha: not Deb. The impertinence of the black ringlets about her face was now restrained: the dark blue dress was one the Acislo never would have worn: the slim fingers were ringless: there was another kind of laughter in her eyes. It needed the one small freckle on the clear skin at the side of the short straight nose to reassure him . . . or was it to bring back a disturbing memory—to make uncertainty of present reality?

'And now that **you** have contemplated the problem?' said Margaret.

'If I may stay,' said Christopher. 'If I may really stay.'

'You may take that for granted,' remarked Margaret, and Miss Comfort hummed and buzzed like a tea-kettle in protest and assurance.

'If I may stay, then I must ride over to Rye. I left my kit there. At the George. I have practically nothing but what I stand up in, here.'

'I had meant to spend the day weeding in the kitchen garden. Silas!' She shook her head over his deficiencies. 'But if you go to Rye we'll have the gig out, and you shall drive me in. It is market day and I can shop while you do your business. And then we'll dine on goose pie and porter at the George.'

'My dear!' protested Miss Comfort, horrified. 'Will you get for me some more Berlin wool of the same colour as before? And half a yard of gros de Naples to match my bonnet? And some pearl buttons? I'll show you which. And I'm certain the second volume of The Disinherited must be in by now. Even although the young lady at the circulating library told me there were always complaints about the time Mrs. Langley kept the books.'

So they drove to Rye along a winding road through a countryside green with spinneys and orchards and hazel thickets, and dotted with hamlets whose every other king-beam sagged under the weight of the dark red roof.

While Margaret shopped in the narrow busy street, Christopher ordered a private room and dinner at the George. He found a worried Williams in the tap-room, and gave him explicit instructions.

'Take lodgings in the town,' he told the man, 'and call here every day, for I will send word to you from time to time. There can be no

letters for me. No one knows where I am. I shall write to his lordship and say that I am well. I do not know how long I shall be
away.'

'If you'll forgive me, sir,' said Williams, twisting his gold-banded
hat in an embarrassed manner. 'If you'll forgive me, sir, but I hope
as nothing's wrong?'

Dark suspicions of designing women filled his honest mind.

'It's far from being wrong,' said Christopher with so quiet an air
of assurance that it brought immediate conviction to the manservant. The anxious look left his eyes. He raised his tanned face.

'But I wish I could be with you, sir! You're a perfect babby
when it comes to lookin' after yourself. To speak the truth, sir!'

Christopher made a quick explanation that was near the truth.

'I'm staying with friends, Williams. Friends I knew long before
you ever heard of me. One of them an old lady. It's a small house
with little room. I have been very worried, and I don't want to see
—or hear of—anyone else I know. I will arrange that someone shall
call here regularly or send a message by the carrier if I should need
you.' He shook his man by the hand warmly. 'Be sure that everything is as right as rain! . . . Now! About money . . .'

He wrote brief loving notes to Setoun and to Charlotte, having
bought some sheets of paper in the town. He did not say where he
was, but told them not to be anxious, and that he would be with
them in a month's time; and addressed it to the house in London.

He gave Williams the notes and told him to dispatch them, and
watched the reluctant man depart, with a smile in his heart, for
there—he felt—with man and letter walked out the wraith of Christopher Harnish.

'Anthony Atchill! Anthony Atchill! Anthony Atchill!' he repeated to himself again and again.

He looked down on the street crowded with market-day visitors.

Somewhere amid the throng was Margaret Atchill! Mar-ga-ret
Atchill! And Margaretha Acislo and Deb were just phantoms, uncertain shapes blown for a space out of such a mist as that which
lay across the lost river last night, and now was taken back into it.
Down there among the crowd of ruddy, booted farmers in broadcloth, buxom flushed women in bonnets brought from Tonbridge,
labourers in smocks of Russia duck or drabbet, shawled servant

girls and prim escorted ladies—down there was Margaret Atchill beautiful, smiling, in flesh and blood.

He went out to seek her.

It was no easy matter. He peeped diffidently into two haberdashers, meditated a raid upon the bonnet shop; apologized to a bookseller and stayed among the shelves awhile, to emerge with an English translation of Chamisso's *Peter Schlemihl*; thought he saw her figure in the steep lane leading to the church; found it was not she, and halted puzzled outside the bow window of a miscellaneous shop. A mandarin's silk coat—the colour of delphiniums at twilight —hung on a rod within, and before it stood a woman's work-box shaped like a coffer made of ebony and ivory squares. The thing was lined with worn and faded silk of pale rose, and there were little compartments in it with turned ivory knobs. If one foot had not been broken and clumsily repaired, he would have bought it as a gift for Miss Comfort.

He found Margaret at last in an apothecary's shop full of large canisters labelled 'Opium Pills—a sovran remedy against marsh damp'. She greeted him cheerfully.

'I shall not be more than ten minutes now. There are no parcels. They are being sent to wait us at the inn. We will put them into the gig after dinner. . . . Go back and drink a glass of beer until I'm ready.'

Although he protested she shooed him off, and he went back disconsolate to await her coming.

After dinner they walked in the town and drove back talking eager nothings in the bright afternoon.

And later, until dusk and supper came, they weeded in the kitchen garden, where a surge of groundsel had arisen between the currant bushes, great thistles had dug themselves in among the artichokes, and bindweed strangled elder bushes and climbed up pleached cherry trees against a wall.

'Silas! Ah, Silas!' grieved Margaret.

'Perhaps he hates to kill growing things,' suggested Cousin Tony.

'There is no love of nature about Silas,' she said. 'Only an all-pervading laziness.'

He examined the great bunch of greenery in his hand with its small plaintive yellow flowers doomed to destruction.

'Weeding makes one feel like God!' he remarked.

'Like God?'

'Well, God's vice-regent—in a garden. One walks along, and here one pulls up and slays, and there one waters and cherishes and makes to grow. Here I am, and I have said that all these little flowers shall die. I have pulled them up. They will be wilted in an hour, and to-morrow they'll be dead. I have left that one, you see. I decided he should live.'

Margaret looked at the small green weed that hid itself under the prickly spread of a gooseberry bush.

'But it'll flower, and seed itself, and spread—and where'll my garden be then?'

'Utter destruction is a dreadful thought,' he said. 'The complete extinction of anything is like damnation—remorseless.'

'Some things,' said Margaret pulling up the weed thoughtfully, 'are better utterly extinguished—are better remorselessly destroyed. . . . You are too imaginative, Tony!'

'I think the happiest portion of my life, almost, has been that in which I dreamt.' He dropped the mass of weeds into the wheel-barrow. 'Cloud fancies in which I have escaped the dust of reality. Fairy stories—sort of—some times: and at others fantastic imaginings.'

'I cannot follow you into those flights,' she said, her eyes lost on the long sunset flush over the opposing hills. Here and there a solitary tree raised itself above the smooth curves of the hazel wood and was outlined in black in every detail against a sky which held its colours and reflected them no more than does a dying rainbow.

'My imagination,' she went on, 'is rooted in realities. It does not float like yours as coloured bubbles in the air. It grows on facts—a hundred little facts. It builds itself twig by twig and leaf by leaf from facts. It may became a tree: and it may be blasted or be withered or cut down, like a tree.'

After supper that night they all played spillikins with ivory pieces yellowed with age. And then Miss Comfort settled to her patience at one little round table, while Margaret and Christopher rattled the dice over a backgammon board at another, till ten o'clock was struck from the hall by the grandfather clock which had daisies painted on its ancient dial.

'Good-night, dear Margaret!' he said at the stair-foot, taking her hand. 'It is kind of you to keep me. I won't be any trouble to you.'

'Dear Tony, I'm glad you're here,' she said, and returned his clasp. In the soft light of the lamp-lit hall there was a faint gold flush over her pale skin, and as she turned away—to see that the door was bolted, that the kitchen shutter had been closed—he realized the strength and pride in the exquisite profile. She was more beautiful than—than any woman he had ever seen, he thought; and more aloof, and yet more near.

She realized that his eyes were still upon her, and accepted the admiration by a last smiling look in which he fancied to read a knowledge of his thoughts.

The next morning as he started down to breakfast, he met Miss Comfort near the stairhead.

'We shall begin breakfast alone this morning,' said the old lady after they had exchanged greetings and while he waited to give her passage. 'Margaret has gone to church. She will be a little late. She said not to wait.'

'I thought she must be up,' said Christopher. 'I saw that her door was open.' He had noted that the door which he had remarked before was again ajar.

Miss Comfort followed the direction of his glance.

'That is not Margaret's room,' she answered, turning to it. 'I forgot that you have never been here before. . . . It was her dear Mother's. It is never used—of course!'

She opened the door more widely, and mutely invited him to look in and admire. It was a large low room with two windows, looking toward the hidden river and the hills, made smaller by a four-post bed with hangings of gay old chintz. The carpet was bright but worn. A shield-shaped mirror, so old that its reflections were like dull silver, sat on a serpentine-fronted chest. There were little drawings of children and places on the walls: a row of sombre books in an oak trough on a small table. A wing armchair was set before the duck's-nest grate, and over the mantel was the portrait of a man in a high white padded stock.

'Your uncle, of course, Mr. Tony,' said Miss Comfort. 'Such a handsome man, I think. I always fancy he has a mournful face—

as if he almost knew he was not long for this world. He looks so very sad. Such a tragedy it was, was it not?'

Nephew Tony agreed.

He dared not press for details of the 'tragedy', and followed her downstairs, bewildered. He had so easily forgotten his dreams of terror, and abandoned Christopher Harnish as a mere shell in the world without; yet, as in a dozen ways Margaret Atchill became more real, so he found himself now asking how she had absorbed in her reality the ghosts that had been the woman Margaretha Acislo and the child Deb. Or were they but projections of her mind, like the mist rising from the river?

The canary sang: the geraniums in the window were scarlet in the sun: Daphilda bobbed her 'good morning'.

'A cheerful little person,' said Cousin Tony as the door closed on her.

'A good servant,' agreed Miss Comfort, making sure that the teapot had been warmed. 'Not perfect, of course, but then none are these days! . . . Such an outlandish name, my dear Mr. Tony! Why, do you know the child's baptismal name is Treandaphilda! . . . What can her parents have been thinking about? . . . And from the poor-house, too—like Barbara. I suppose poor people give their children long names because it is all they have to give them. . . . I like plain names myself. I was called Charlotte after the late dear Queen. . . . And then Margaret, of course! That is a nice plain name! . . . There always have been Margarets in the Atchill family.'

She looked up at the picture of the long-eyed girl over the low bureau.

'And she was a Margaret, too, of course! Poor Mrs. Atchill! . . . You wouldn't remember her, naturally. She must have died soon after you were born.'

Said Christopher, feeling a traitor, and yet incapable of rejecting the question that rose to his lips:

'I suppose you knew Mrs.—my aunt Atchill?'

Miss Comfort spread quince jelly on a thin slice of toast.

'Oh, no!' she answered. 'I have only been here—let me see! It will be two years in September. September the fifteenth, to be exact. But I have got to know all the family now. I feel as though they were mine. I almost expect to see them coming in and out of the room, or hear them talking in the hall. . . . The house is full of things that belonged to one or other of them. Pictures and books and furniture. Each with its little story, you know. It makes them so very interesting. And dear Margaret won't replace anything, even when they are very shabby. She loves them so. . . . No, Mr. Tony, I was a governess—in very nice families—but I was getting old.' She hesitated. 'And when dear Margaret found me and brought me here . . . Well—it is a taste of paradise, I often say! . . . So happy. . . . So peaceful!'

She was lost in reflection for a moment—to look brightly up at a quick light step along the path.

'There is dear Margaret!' she said beaming. 'Would you please to ring the bell, Mr. Tony! We must have fresh tea made for her. And perhaps—just perhaps—we might squeeze a cup of it for each of us out of her pot.'

Chapter 28

The Fall of the House of Atchill

THE LONG SUMMER DAYS SWAM BY LIKE LEAVES UPON a stream.

They gardened, and went for drives and walks; had tea under apple trees at the edge of the lawn; watched top-hatted Northiam cricketers beat top-hatted Benenden at a match upon the green; Christopher borrowed Mr. Tom's old Purdey gun, and, with a fat spaniel, looked for rabbits in the few acres of pasturage and woodland that Margaret owned. They played quiet games at night or talked about books, and Miss Comfort began a marvellous shawl of cherry red and yellow which was to be a present for Margaret on her birthday.

'When *is* your birthday, Margaret?' he asked. 'I'm ashamed that I've forgotten.'

'Oh, New Year's Day!' she answered after a slight hesitation. Her head was averted, and she busied herself among the trifles on her writing-desk.

As the days passed, however, he found that she would speak now and again more freely of her family. Once Miss Comfort asked for some detail of the death of Mr. Tom at Waterloo, while they sat at tea near beds of larkspur and stock and snapdragons. And Margaret told how he had given chase to Napoleon's carriage as the Emperor fled, and had been pistolled by Marshal Soult as he drew abreast.

'He was in the cavalry, then?' said Christopher.

'The Hussars,' replied Margaret.

After that she vouchsafed information at various times. One Sunday night, looking at the clean white damask tablecloth with a shimmering pattern of peacocks and flowery urns, she remarked, 'Why, we've got Great-Aunt Sabrina's tablecloth to-night.'

Great-Aunt Sabrina—Christopher knew—regarded the sheen of her tablecloth from under a curling mass of powdered hair in a miniature beside the fire.

'It's a very beautiful cloth,' said Miss Comfort almost possessively. 'Too good to use except when there are guests. . . . I did not know it belonged to your great-aunt, my dear.'

'Great-Aunt Sabrina,' said Margaret firmly, holding a fold of the cloth and looking at the hem. 'Her wedding-breakfast was spread on this very cloth, and many of the guests were waiting, and, of course, she never came!'

'Never came?' repeated Miss Comfort in much mystification. 'I remember you telling me that she died young. I don't think you ever told me how.'

Margaret studied her glass of deep red port.

'She was taken—with a haemorrhage at the church door, and died before she could be taken home.'

'Oh, dear, dear!' said Miss Comfort. 'How very tragic! So young, too!'

She pressed for further particulars. Margaret gave them.

'I rather fancy we have something else of hers locked away upstairs,' she added. 'I will look, after we have finished supper.'

So afterwards she went away, and came back in a while to the drawing-room.

Under the lamp on the little round table at Miss Comfort's side, she placed an old-fashioned work-box inlaid with ebony and ivory squares. It was lined with rose-pink silk, and one foot was badly repaired.

Christopher, at the book-case in the shadows, quickly turned his back and rummaged among the volumes, each with its 'Atchill' signature and date.

He had been there a fortnight. The Atchills had become more real than any of the figures in his life beyond the horizon. He, too, had begun to accept them for his own, to think of them when all the house was still, as fingering affectionately trinkets that once were theirs, feeling the smooth paste of the treasured porcelain, fluttering the leaves of books that were beloved, lingering beside a favourite chair, or looking from timelessness on to the dim faces of old friendly clocks.

He knew that time was growing short—that she must go back to Paris, and he would have to return to some other world.

As they were coming back from a walk along a lane in whose banks wild strawberries were hidden, he said suddenly:

'I shall soon have to go, Margaret.'

'Why?' she asked pausing to pull a red berry from its nest, and contemplating it as it lay within her pink palm.

'Well, you'll be going soon, I suppose.'

Her bright face clouded. She was very still. Even the two long ringlets at either side of her wide bonnet hung unquivering.

'Yes. I must go—back, quite soon.'

'Must you really go back? Can't you stay here for ever?' he asked.

'Not yet,' she said. 'The day will come within a little while. In such a short space of time I can return—and never go away again. In such a little time! I pray for it to come.'

'Oh, Margaret! Why don't you stay now? Could you not arrange it? Go for a short time and settle things, and then come back at once! You would be so very happy here! For ever!'

She was walking quickly now, and he had to lengthen his pace to keep up.

'Don't you understand, Tony dear, that small as my home is, yet I still must earn the money to keep it?'

He had not thought of that, and fell silent at her side.

'There is no reason for you to go, even if I am not here. Stay, my dear, and go on staying as long as you will care to.'

He protested:

'But Margaret! Without you? It would not be the same.'

'My body may not be here—my hateful body—but the real Me stays. I am always here. And when my body dies I shall have it buried far away. So that it shan't creep out, and surprise Me in my home.'

He pondered a while.

'Margaret,' he said. 'I have got so much money. Couldn't I help? Then there would be no need for you to go away. . . . Couldn't I really help?'

She shot a grave and serious glance at him. He was carrying his hat in his hand and he turned to her an earnest face with a brow anxiously knitted.

She put her strawberry-stained fingers into his.

'Dear Tony,' she said. 'I could not do that. The little house and all that's in it is mine—is mine utterly, and alone. No one can share it with me. It is me! But you may stay here, Tony dear, for as long as it contents you. And I shall be glad—very glad.'

He held her fingers tighter and looked straight before him.

'I should like to stay . . . for ever. I . . .'

She came to a standstill, and turned him by the gentle pressure of her hand so that he stood before her with downcast head.

'Dear, dear Tony!' And at the infinite kindness in her voice he jerked up, to see her wistfully regarding him, her eyes smiling but sad; he dropped his gaze again to the end of the long silk lavender scarf that fluttered against a dress of silvery green.

'Dear, dear Tony!' she said again. 'I had half a fear last night that—that—you might . . .' and halted. Then she went on resolutely. 'Margaret Atchill exists, and is real, and is here for everything but love. She can give the love of a mother and a sister and a dear dear friend, but that is all.'

'I only—I only want to—worship you,' said Christopher shakily.

'And that,' the quiet voice went on, 'you must never do!'

After a moment she took him by the arm as though to show him that they were back again upon the footing of old friends, close relations enjoying a country walk.

He came down to breakfast a few days later to find commotion. There were trunks and plaid shawls lying in the hall, and Margaret sat at the table, bonneted and in a travelling dress.

'It's very sad dear Margaret should have to go,' said Miss Comfort furtively wiping her eyes behind her spectacles—a difficult process which made the glasses travel along her old bony nose and need readjustment at each dab. She forgot to put down the slop-basin for Tibbie, and could not find the tea-cosy, although it was where she always placed it, at the side of the chair.

'It's very sad, dear Margaret! Must you go?'

'Must you go?' echoed Christopher reproachfully. 'You never said a word about it last night—to me!'

She shook her head, and, breakfast over, stood at the open house-door, looking her 'good-byes' along the sunlit valley to the marshes and a red barn roof that glowed like a hot coal among the willows at a bend of the river.

Christopher took her by the shoulders, and, before she could resist, had run her before him down the path, until she was brought up breathless and laughing by the wicket.

'So anxious to get rid of me?' she asked. 'The post-chaise won't be here for half an hour!'

'Margaret,' said Christopher hoarsely. 'I must talk to you. . . . I must. . . . I am going to!'

She took in his set face, and the laughter died from hers.

'Don't, Tony!' she said very low. 'Don't, Tony! I can't bear it.'

'Margaret, I must! I will!'

Without another word, but with a sigh she began walking slowly up the lane, away from the house; and he said no more until they came to the junction of the two lanes at the hill-top under the elms. He drew her to the recess before a gate in a high blackthorn hedge.

'Margaret! Dear Margaret Atchill, you cannot go like this. . . . I love you very much indeed. . . . Let us stay always here . . . and forget for ever all our bad dreams.'

'I told you,' she answered, 'that Margaret Atchill . . . Look!—Margaret Atchill in a little while will have never been! There will be Margaretha Acislo, as there was once Deborah Hunt! So why . . . ?'

'They can be forgotten, as Christopher Harnish is.'

'They can't, indeed. . . . Tony, let me go! . . . I must go now, before the other world breaks in even here—my only refuge from it.'

He stood before her so that she might not pass.

'But, Margaret,' he stammered, baffled but determined. 'If you—if you were to marry me, Margaret Atchill would remain for ever. The others would be lost—swallowed up, gone!'

She raised her head and looked on him with a wise and pitying smile.

'Never!' she said, and 'Never! Never! Never!'

'But if you stay here and I stay here,' he pressed, 'then we are safe. Safe for ever! Safe from memories and nightmares, and for the future!'

'Are we? Should we be? . . . Cannot you understand? . . . Tony, let me go! Please let me go!'

'Margaret,' he said, and clenched his fists till the knuckles were white, and looked at all he could see of her averted face—the contour of a cheek, lowered dark lashes, and long swaying ringlets. 'Margaret, I swear that I shall follow you wherever you may go until you come back here with me!'

She did not move her head.

'Tony, won't you understand?'

He said obstinately:

'I can only understand that here you can be happy—as I can: and nowhere else.'

'Must I kill Margaret Atchill? Must I show you that she can only be reality for me and no one else? Must I try and tell you that Margaret Atchill is like—is like that woman in the fairy tales who vanished if she were touched in love or anger? The reality of Margaret Atchill cannot survive that touch. Tony, my fancies are more real than yours; they do not blow away at dawn; but even they cannot outlive a storm!'

'. . . Cannot survive a touch—my touch?'

'Yours least of all!'

'Oh, Margaret! . . . Margaret Atchill,' he repeated the name as if it were a spell to imprison her within that identity—'I love you so. I love you so!'

He babbled broken words of love to her averted ear.

'Christopher!' she said, and he started at the unwonted name. 'It is impossible. . . . Turn away! . . . Don't look at me! . . . Four years ago I saw that little house, and bought it for a trifle. It was nearly derelict. From what I earned—and I am well paid—I put it right. I made it a little house such as the Atchills might have had. And in it I have assembled such treasures, too, as the Atchills might have had. I made of it a shrine for such a family as I had read about. I found a picture, a chair, a clock or bed, and for them I wove a story. And, as the story grew, it drew to it other trifles that I found. Silver and china. A worn bright carpet to be degraded —as they might have degraded it—to a bedroom. Books to be given owners. Sketches of places they might have known—of children they might have been. A tablecloth. A sword. A work-box. A locket with hair in it. Such small things—but pebbles that built me a wall against the world.'

'I guessed it. But . . .'

'Christopher, listen! . . . I could make an Atchill family, and fill the house with their presence. I have watched so carefully through all my life and read, and read. I could make the Atchills—Father and Mother, Tom and Great-Aunt Sabrina, and Grandmamma— and the others. . . . But, Christopher, I could not make a Margaret Atchill! There is still this outer covering that is Margaretha—and Deb.'

'I love you whether you are Margaret or Deb,' he swore, and tried to take her hand.

'I wonder,' she said.

'Do you doubt me?' he asked.

She turned her head yet farther from him.

'Deborah Hunt,' she said, 'was the daughter of a prostitute by an unknown father . . .' and paused a long while.

'She was born in a Plymouth brothel among harlots and thieves and vice and dirt. She would have been a harlot herself, had not the woman who called herself her mother died. She went to the poor-house and was found to be . . . diseased—the legacy of her parents. . . . She was cured. She was apprenticed out, as you know. She, more than any other, was responsible for murder—if it was murder!'

'And I—and I!' cried Christopher.

She paid no heed to him, but went on.

'She was released from prison. She went into service with an old clergyman and his wife, and learned to read, and love pictures and china and silver and the quiet ways of life. There was a year or two of that . . .'

She halted for a long, long time before she continued.

'. . . The old man's grandson came home. When Deb was fourteen years and—and seven months, she had a baby.'

He seized the top bar of the gate in his hand. She could hear him breathe like a man who has been running for his life.

'Deb!' he said; and she knew that Margaret Atchill was dead.

'Deb!'

'She had a baby. She ran away. It died. She had no money. There were many things that might have happened to her, if a man who saw her in the street had not taken pity—of a sort—upon her. He took her to his lodgings. She lived with him.'

He had dropped her hand, and she could feel that his frozen stare upon her cheek was unseeing: that all he saw and knew were the pictures that she drew.

'He was an actor,' she said. 'He got the child—she was not yet sixteen—a part. She made a success. He passed her on to an old rich man who taught her once again to love books and lovely things and made her learn to sing. She was barely seventeen. Till he died three years afterwards when she had already made a name . . . she was his mistress—his kept woman.'

At each pause in her later story—and there were many—he had cast an agonized look at her. He was beyond analysis of his emotions: only he knew that a horror such as he had never dreamed of had possessed his soul. He dropped his bare head upon his arms on the top rail of the gate so that he should not see the lovely face, the slim proud figure that had been held so close by other men. He believed that now he never more would dream again—that the last wind had blown away the airy fabric of his fantasies, and that their tattered mists had dissipated into a greater nothingness than even had crumbled the house of Atchill.

'Poor Tony! Dear Tony!' she said, and knew that he was afraid lest she should touch him with her soiled hands.

She made no sound; but looked at his bowed yellow head and the wine-red coat of which he had been so proud, with understanding and with love.

'Tony!' she said at length. 'You see that, to you, either Margaret Atchill or Deb must die. And it is Margaret Atchill—although she is the Me within myself—who has died, to you.' She paused just a heart-beat; and in her level brows and in her eyes and in the faint catch in her voice there spoke the echo of a note of questioning, as if there were a chance—one drop of water to all an ocean—that her knowledge might be wrong. 'Isn't it so?'

But he did not stir.

She did not touch him—he could not have borne it—or even say good-bye; but she looked down on him as she left and gave him her blessing without words.

Chapter 29

The Fall of Christopher Harnish

WHEN HE EVENTUALLY RETURNED TO THE HOUSE Margaret Atchill had already gone, for he had purposely delayed until there should be no chance of meeting her. He said a muddled good-bye to Miss Comfort under the supercilious and contemptuous regard of all the painted Atchills, and took horse for London. Although he knew that nothing could bring him consolation, and that there were no questions he could answer, he was aware of the need for some presence to sustain him. He felt that sitting near a silent Setoun—in the green glimmer of the study wherein the fleet from Lilliput lay enchanted in glass cases round the wall—he might try to piece his shattered thoughts into a new shape. He did not want to see Charlotte, for she was a woman, too; he wanted no more of women.

At the top of the hill he turned and looked back upon the valley. He saw it as a gutter of marshy meadows, which lay cold and colourless below him. The enchantment had left it—dispersed like a mirage. It was an empty unlighted stage from which the scenery had been taken, and the characters had departed. He had been one of those actors, but now he had doffed his fantastic attire and become again the Christopher Harnish he had striven to forget.

He reached Sevenoaks by nightfall, and London the next afternoon. Outside the Bricklayers' Arms two drabs were fighting: at the Paragon one of the new police in blue tailed coat and top-hat stood guard between a crowd and the shattered window of a pawnbroker's shop: on Westminster Bridge a cur had been crushed by a dray, and lay mangled and bloody in the roadway: torn paper

453

and garbage twisted and twirled in the streets under a rising wind.

A pregnant woman stood in the doorway of a house in a mean street. She was very young. Christopher found something horrible in the contrast between her childish face and monstrous belly. Had Margaret Atchill once looked like that?

A fine drizzle began to fall as he turned into Church Lane, and when he reached home it seemed in tune with things that he should find the house desolate, with blinds pulled down—like something unconscious behind closed eyelids.

The entrance to the stable-yard was shut, and it was a long time before his summons was answered and someone grumbling undid the high green doors and pushed a tousled head through the aperture.

'Where's everybody? Where's his lordship?' asked Christopher.

''Is lordship 'as gone to Germany, your honour,' said the startled man taking the reins.

'Germany?' he questioned in astonishment.

'To where your honour was. I don't rightly remember the name. D'rec'ly after the weddin'!'

Christopher, idly flicking his crop against his riding-boots, let fall the stick.

'Wedding?' he repeated. 'What wedding?'

The man became garrulous on the subject. 'The wedding had been at St. Mary's, privit-like. They said the special licence 'ad cost a matter of fifty pun's. The women all said as 'er ladyship. . . .'

Charlotte! Married to Hurbles—as Margaret might have been married to him! For a few seconds he was so lost in retrospect that he heard nothing that the man said.

'Is there no one in the house, then, Thompson?' he asked at last.

'There's me in the stables, but I sleeps in the 'ouse at night. An' old Mrs. Chisholm wot answers the door bell—when she 'ears it, which isn't often as your honour knows. Wot horses and servints didn't go abroad furrin wiv 'is lordship 'ave gone to Nottinghamshire wiv Lady Jane.'

He could not bear the thought of sleeping in that deserted house, alone with his thoughts and memory. He could not bear to think of even entering that house where the unfriendly silence would be accented by the slow shuffle of the caretaker and the ticking of the clocks. But neither could he bear to face solitariness, and nights in the frowzy magnificence of the best bedroom at an inn where little bunches of combings from women's hair would linger in the dust under the dressing-table mirror, or in the grate behind a paper fan; or the fly-blown splendour of coffee-room or sitting-room, and the sideboard where sat the ruins of a meal upon a stained mahogany gritty with yesterday's toast-crumbs.

He felt utterly friendless; London a desolate waste before him— but better yet than the haunted place which he had left.

It was then that he thought of Alabama Lodge. Arabella would be away in the East Indies with her husband; and even he could deal with the simple questionings of the Miz' Case. They were too old for one to think of them as women.

There he would be welcome and could stay awhile until he should have decided on a plan. The memory of Arabella, and that minute in the bay-window opening on the moon-drenched garden, shaped itself before him like a picture in a cloudy sky. It was very faint. He almost laughed to think of the devastation which he once had found in it.

He left word for Williams, and within ten minutes Isaac, with gold shoulder knots upon his green velvet coat, was greeting him with an enormous smile on the threshold of Alabama Lodge.

'Bless yo' soul, Mas'r Christopher, ef dis ain't a sight fer sore eyes, yess—suh!' said Isaac, and extended respectfully a large cotton-gloved hand in welcome. 'It'll be like de good ole days. Miz' Anne ain't none too spry dese yer days, but I spects Miz' Elizabeth kin come down right now.'

He conducted Christopher to the dim, warm drawing-room, aromatic of strange woods, with the Chinese jars glowing against the sombre panels of cedar, and a cherry log fire crackling on the hearth as it always had within his memory.

Through the glass doors the strange plants still flourished tall and green and sharp-cut in the conservatory.

He looked through the colonnade, and thought how here the two old ladies had raised a house in such a pattern, and filled it with such treasures, as had been that other home of theirs five thousand miles and more away, where the Alabama River rolled its yellow flood through swamp forests to the sea. They had conjured up America for themselves, and surrounded themselves with America; it was always about them: as—as Margaret Atchill had conjured up the Atchill home and filled it with ghosts and memories of people who never were.

Margaret Atchill—he shuddered.

And as he shuddered his eyes were suddenly blinded by soft hands, and a remembered voice said:

'I suppose you think it's Wordie!'

'Arabella!' he exclaimed in astonishment.

She dropped her hands, and he turned round. She was unchanged, while he knew that he had grown old, grown very old. Her skin had still the glow of pale honey, her dark gold ringlets the darker shadows, her eyes the sea-green lights that he remembered.

She laughed at his amazement.

'Well, do we kiss or just shake hands?' she asked, and solved the problem for him by kissing him on the cheek.

'I thought you had gone to the Indies, Arabella,' he said.

'Oh, Henry has gone,' she answered. 'But it didn't appeal to me, in the end. So I stayed behind. But it's a queer welcome after all these years to be in consternation at me being here!'

He did not want Arabella to be here—only old soft voices and easily satisfied minds. He had wanted to be by himself and work out some new pattern for his life; but he was able to produce some acceptable formulae.

She studied him very narrowly in the hazy light.

'You look older, Tops!' she announced. 'You look wiser—or is it perhaps less wise? You look thin, too! . . . I don't believe that you are really glad to see me.'

Politeness demanded that he should make an effort, and he did. He sat under the sea-green watchfulness of her eyes and heard how Wordie had gone to soothe a dying sister, and Miz' Elizabeth with all the female household was occupied with Miz' Anne.

'She has bronchitis,' said Arabella. 'It isn't really very bad. But she likes facts so much that she has read every word of the *Household Physician* and imagines she has every ailment in the world. The doctor says the trouble is only slight. But she is preparing to meet her God! God won't be ready for her! Guests that arrive too soon are not welcome even in Heaven. Great-Aunt Elizabeth is supervising the steam-kettle now. She will be down later. We shall have dinner together alone—quite grown-up! Won't that be fun?'

He hardly responded as she could have wished. She challenged him with being a grump. He was forced to explain that he had ridden—from Dover, he said, erasing the Atchill episode in any shape from his story, as he could never from his mind.

She was all sympathy and loving-kindness.

He should—he must have—sherry now, and a biscuit: dinner should be early—as soon as he liked.

She poured him out a brimming glass of wine.

'We'll make a loving cup of it, Tops! . . . In memory of old days!' and touched the rim with her lips, and laughed at him across the glass.

He didn't want to remember old days, or anything; and presently was allowed to withdraw and make what toilet he could.

How easily she forgot, he thought as he stood staring about a room he did not know. You could not read in her mysterious eyes, or her voice, or in any gesture or expression, any remembrance or shame for those moments of four years ago. Perhaps with her, too, there was a Margaret Atchill who walked apart and lived apart from the self that had pulsated beneath his arm and clung for kisses.

Miz' Elizabeth fluttered round him for a moment in the drawing-room when he went down, brought all her sister's love, and tore herself away to the sick-bed when Aaron with a beaming smile announced that dinner was served.

He followed Arabella across the hall, where the candles glowed in their high hurricane shades like giant hour-glasses, into the dining-room where curtains shut out the day and the shining table was as a drift of snow in the midst of a warm dimness spangled by candle-light.

He felt marooned in the intimacy of those two close chairs and narrow-seeming cloth. Arabella strove to break through his gloom, pressed him to wine, talked gaily of life, wisely asked no questions, ordered a very precious bottle of ancient port—so had done Margaret Atchill!—and said she would not go, but sit with him while he drank, and even have half a glass herself.

'Men sit over their wine too long after dinner by themselves,' she said. 'Henry always did. He used to sit as long as there was a bottle in sight. I died of boredom in the drawing-room—I hate women! And when he came in the tea was cold and he was not fit to talk to. . . . Not that he ever was a conversationalist.'

'You were in Geneva, I think,' remarked Christopher, 'when I came home on leave, two years ago. And I was abroad, of course, when you got married. Miz' Anne wrote to me about it. Where did you go for your honeymoon?'

'And what a honeymoon! I yawned my head off. We went to Henry's uncle's place in Wales. It rained. It rained. Henry spent all his time in the stables when he wasn't hunting. The people are perfect savages. The trees dripped. We went out to dinner with the Dunands. They gave us mutton and onion sauce. They always give it you there to live down the story that they gave it to the Prince Regent once in mistake for venison. The people all snivelled prayers, talked about funerals and committed adultery. Henry said there are more bastards in Merionethshire than any other county. I don't know whether he had anything to do with it!'

'My God,' thought Christopher. 'This is Arabella!'

'You know, I like riding, Tops; but I hate it in the wet with surly men chasing a little fox. And they ride like sacks of coals in Wales! There was nothing else to do. There was not even a book in the house, and the nearest booksellers eighteen miles away. The local big-wigs had two generations of big-wiggery: on one side descended from a cattle-thief, on the other from a pig-drover! At the end of a fortnight I said to Henry, "I'm going home". So we went home.'

'Home?'

'We came back here. Henry hasn't a penny. But, of course, I've got plenty.'

'It was an unfortunate start, my dear Arabella,' he said, meditating upon the honeymoon.

'Only in a way. When we got home I found that it hadn't been Wales after all that had got on my nerves, but Henry himself.'

She talked like that of the man whose heart had beaten against her own, with whom she must have caught such a glamour as came, to his knowledge, from a moonlit garden! Something of this must have shown in his eyes.

'You always were a strange old-fashioned fogram, Tops,' she said lightly.

She set her bare elbows on the table and cupped her chin within her hands. Her scarlet silken dress was cut so low and straight across the front that it was a marvel that it did not slip from off her shoulders of golden brown, and reveal the curved bosom at which it more than hinted. In the subdued light the golden flecks danced in her tawny hair like sparks of sunlight. Her golden face was framed by two careful-careless clusters of curls, and from each almost-hidden ear a ruby hung. She was lovely—but in the darkness beyond her he saw the proud face of Margaret Atchill coloured like a rose petal and her long jetty ringlets. Margaret Atchill—Deb! and he actually shook his shoulders as if he could physically shake the memory away.

'Well?' said Arabella, having waited.

'I am sorry,' he lied, playing with his wineglass foot. 'I was trying to think out seriously if I really were old-fashioned.'

Silence again.

'You haven't said "Well?" to me yet,' she complained.

He raised his eyebrows, anxious to comprehend and be polite. She explained.

'I said "Well!" to make you carry on the conversation. You should have said "Well?" inquiringly to make me finish my story. . . . For heaven's sake, Tops, don't get like Henry!'

'Well?' he repeated dutifully and hurriedly.

'Say it again, as if you were interested!'

'Well?' he said once more with new emphasis, and was forced to smile.

'Well, the upshot was I found Henry such a bore that I sent him off!'

'"Sent him off"?' He felt he did nothing but echo what she said; but this time he spoke with sufficient genuine astonishment to meet her exacting taste, and she lifted her eyes from the cloth to amused contemplation of his face.

'I got tired within a month of his clumsiness, and his dullness and the smell of wine and stables, and—and the sort of soap he used to shave with. So we packed him off two months ago, back to his regiment in India. We bought him his majority and gave him a nice allowance. And there we are.'

'It's a tragedy that your married life should end like that,' said Christopher chilled. 'But what did your great-aunts say?'

Arabella tasted her wine.

'You funny old antiquity! They say what I say, always—in the end. I just love being married—now. I'm married—and free! Henry is married—and free: that I am sure of! Very free!'

He studied her face to see if she were in earnest: she unquestionably was; for she burst into a peal of infectious laughter in which there were no regrets.

'From your expression, dear Tops, we might be living in 1732, not 1832,' she said, and filled up his glass afresh with wine, and renewed her own. 'So now you shall drink to my health and liberty. And no heel-taps—as Henry would say!'

He wished she would not vaunt her freedom and talk of Henry in the same breath. . . . Only thirty-six hours ago he had been facing Margaret Atchill across a table, like this—the Margaret Atchill who was so horribly to become Deb and Margaretha Acislo, who was to go a million miles farther than the brief span between London and Paris; who in five minutes was to become as remote as if she had lived thirty-six thousand years ago.

'No heel-taps, Arabella!' he said, and drained the glass.

'I'll allow you another glass, Tops!' she said. 'I think you need it. You look very tired and strained to me.'

She rose from her place this time, and brought the bottle round in its cradle, and leaned over him to pour out the wine, so that her bosom touched his shoulder, lightly as a bird's wing, and the perfume that she used drifted to his nostrils.

He was flushed with the wine, a trifle unsteady on his legs when he rose to go to bed, pleading to be excused on the score of fatigue from long journeying.

She saw him up the stairs, playing the hostess. So Margaret Atchill had done!

They went along the lofty gallery to his door; but, no! . . .

'I'm afraid I've got the room you used to have, Tops,' she said. 'It is larger than mine was, and I've settled in past all eviction.'

They turned a corner.

'I've given you my old room, it is more comfortable than the one you were put in when you got here.'

They turned the other corner.

He saw on his left the great bay window before the door; its curtains partly closed and a moonbeam slanting through the gap and giving a radiance to an Eastern god upon a scarlet lacquer chest. As once before.

He stopped dead for a space barely to be measured on the arbitrary scale of time, but long enough for her to know it.

'So you remember . . . too?'

He did remember; and he hated to remember. He wanted to remember nothing, to be by himself. He turned a pleading look on her as she halted by the heavy folds, but she was not looking at him. She took his cold hand into her warm one, and drew him within the recess by so gentle and inexorable a clasp.

The lawn lay before them silver and black.

'Look, Tops! Just like . . . that other night!'

She turned to him and came the half-step closer which brought her body against his, so that he could feel the soft movement of her breathing.

He looked desperately without.

'If you had been Henry, I do not think I should have let you go to India without me, Tops!'

'You would have been just as tired of me, just as soon!' he managed to say.

'Do you think so—really think so? . . . Look me in the eyes, and answer!'

Unwillingly in that fatal moment, still slightly hazed by wine, he looked at her. In the next instant—how he never knew—she was in his arms, clinging to him and stopping his lips from speech with a kiss that never ceased. Within him was panic for a moment; an immense chaos as if a whirlwind had blown across the ruins of his inner world; a sudden craving for the momentary forgetfulness which some instinct told him she would bring.

At dawn she slipped from his bed, a silken thing glimmering in the twilight like a moonstone in deep water.

He caught her hand, and she came back and leaned over him.

'Arabella!' he began diffidently, and hesitated.

'What is it, darling? . . . You must call me "darling" too—or I shan't answer.'

He shaped his lips to the word.

'Darling,'—he said it still with difficulty—'what . . . ?' and came again to a halt.

She threw herself upon the coverlet and held his head between her hands, and looked closely at him, smiled and kissed him.

'Put your arm round me!'

He did as he was bid, and she lay for a while with her head against his, her face pressed down upon the pillows.

'I wish I hadn't got to go,' she sighed.

He was glad she could not see him. He put his lips near her ear.

'Arabella,' he said, '. . . darling. . . . What about . . . I mean . . . supposing . . . a . . . baby?'

She shot upright, sitting on the bed. She looked at him and laughter rippled from her.

'Honey! . . . Honey! . . . Honey! . . . Trust me for that. . . . I told you before it is not 1732. . . . And anyhow, we could blame Henry!'

As soon as she had stolen away, he rose and dressed in violent haste. His thoughts were full of shame and horror: shame for himself and horror of Arabella.

She could speak lightly of her husband upon the bed of another man—of the husband he had dishonoured and whom she had thus doubly dishonoured. It came to him in a sudden flash that perhaps Margaretha Acislo had spoken like light words when she had risen first from the arms of the 'old rich man'.

His mind eddied with memories of vampire and succubus—ghost women who came to dreamers at night from hell and lay with them. He found no pardon for himself, but a double guilt—the guilt of having sinned, and the guilt that such sin had been with such a woman!

He could not bear to look on her again, such was his sense of shame and hate. The pale honey-coloured arms held death in their embrace. . . . 'We could blame Henry.'

He did not even write a note to leave behind. He stole away from the sleeping house into the early morning chill. He walked along soggy footpaths through the fields to Porto Bello Farm, crossed the canal, and wandered on through the shabby pastures till he saw before him the dapper ornate villas at Pineapple Place in Maida Vale.

He thought only of the woman behind the mask of Margaret Atchill, and of the devil who was Arabella. He must find Setoun although it might mean going back to Neipperg. Setoun had been the one fixed certain thing in life even when Charlotte had failed them. There was so massive a security about him: the big soul and the mighty frame were strongholds against disaster spiritual as well as physical.

He turned and walked back rather wearily—so wearily that when he was near his empty home he stopped at a corner where stood a low white-washed tavern, with red blinds and the windows shining as if they had been buffed up like silver. A tremendous representation of a white bull snorting fire and smoke was on the signboard over the door.

He stepped down into a sanded bar where rows of extremely cheerful bottles glowed behind the scrubbed counter, and a small door opened on to a gravelled garden with an arbour at the end.

A large and cheerful woman poured him out some brandy as a restorative.

As he was sipping his drink a man appeared in the garden from some other door, and walked with a book held in his hand to the clematis-covered arbour.

There was something familiar in the grey and ruffled hair and the stooped shoulders. Christopher stepped nearer the doorway with vague curiosity, and at the sound of his foot the other turned.

He saw the mild lined face and anxious-seeming eyes of Mr. Severn; he was not as hollow-cheeked as before and bore a look of contemplative pleasure.

His old tutor recognized him simultaneously, and beamed on him and came towards him with outstretched hand.

'It's little Harnish!' said he. 'Well, well! Little Harnish grown a man! Little Harnish nearly six-foot tall! *Eheu fugaces!* . . . "*O mihi praeteritos referat si Jupiter annos!*" '

They shook hands most cordially, Christopher still bearing with him his glass of brandy and water.

'This is an uncommonly early hour to be drinking brandy and

water, little Harnish!' said Mr. Severn twitching the end of his long sad nose in a sniff. 'Uncommonly early!'

'I am extremely fatigued,' pleaded Christopher in extenuation. 'I had a long journey yesterday. This morning, foolishly, I walked too far without any breakfast.'

'Good gracious me!' said Mr. Severn. 'This must be corrected at once.'

He led him to the arbour, calling 'Mary! . . . Mary!'

He need not have called; for the sound of their voices had already set her first a-peeping from a small doorway, and then brought her out into the sunlight-dappled garden, which, with its bright gravel and small arbour, reminded Christopher of nothing so much as a nicely sanded birdcage.

'Well, I never!' said Mary. 'If it isn't Mr. Harnish come to see you, sir!'

'Little Harnish!' said Mr. Severn explanatorily.

'Well,' said Mary, 'that is nice!' And her smiling face looked exactly as if she meant it. She greeted him like an old friend.

'Mr. Harnish has had no breakfast, Mary. He'll join me—in the arbour.'

So immediately a tremendous bustle broke out, as the result of which Christopher found himself eventually confronting toast and tea and eggs and bacon at a small table in the green nest in the corner of the birdcage-garden, under the immediate supervision of Mary herself. The crockery had a deep violet lustre border, and highly edifying apophthegms inscribed on the white portions. By eating a couple of rashers Christopher disclosed to himself the pious ejaculation, 'Thou, God, seest me!' His tea-cup announced, 'I will lift up mine eyes unto the Lord!'

'I think,' said Mr. Severn, discovering his interest, 'that breakfast services with quotations from the better-known Greek authors should have a success at the universities. Homer! Anacreon! Thucydides! Sophocles! Plato! Aristophanes! Learning while feasting! I think there should be money in it! Don't you, my dear Harnish?'

'Why not Lucian?' inquired Christopher, flogging up polite interest. 'How's the Lucian translation going?'

'Lucian!' said Mr. Severn, his eyes kindling. 'Mary, my dear! Bring me my schema if you would be so very kind!' For Mary was hovering round to press more eggs, more tea, more toast upon them whenever appetites showed signs of flagging. 'For the moment— for the moment only—I have given up the translation. I have an idea. I think it may, indeed, prove profitable. I hope so. I am proposing to break away from all pedagogic convention. I am planning a course of classical instruction upon a new method. Setoun thoroughly agrees. He was most interested. In fact he has commissioned me to carry out my scheme. Very financially agreeable, my dear fellow, I can assure you! It is the essence of my theory that difficulty of language should be rated second in importance to continuity and vividness of interest for the young. I am planning a classical reader that shall include Lucian, Petronius, Apuleius—ah, here's the schema! Thank you, Mary! Thank you very much!'

She was on her way back to the house with some of the breakfast things, her ringlets and apron a-flutter in the little breeze for which the garden was a playground.

'I don't know what I should do without Mary, I really don't,' said Mr. Severn. 'I am very fond of her!'

'She is an exceptionally nice girl,' agreed Christopher.

'You know,' said Mr. Severn, watching her with much affection, 'she found me this very comfortable little home with her mother. She makes life a very pleasant thing, compared with . . .' He paused. 'And it is surprising, to be quite frank, how inexpensive I find it. For you know my resources are not great. Not great! But I can say with Terence now "Pecuniam in loco negligere, maximum interdum est lucrum"! Of course, here, in her mother's house, one can no longer regard her as a servant. We have most interesting talks! She has a really great intelligence.'

'What will you do when she marries?' asked Christopher.

'Marries?' repeated Mr. Severn, and his jaw dropped. 'Marries? Why should she marry?'

'Well, she's young and vigorous. You'd expect her to want husband and children!'

Mr. Severn's face clouded over. He fluttered the leaves of the schema and entered into an exposition of his plans. His mind, however, was obviously elsewhere.

'As a matter of fact, I believe, between ourselves, Harnish, that

Mary has a child,' said he, suddenly interrupting himself. His face cleared. 'About four years old! I have only just thought about it. It may be hers. In fact there's nobody else's it could be. A very nice child. Very nice! Very like, now I come to think about it! So I don't see why she should want another!'

So Mary, too, had felt that urge which had driven Arabella into his arms! Mary had had a child—like Margaret Atchill—but had the shelter and protection of a mother in her shame. It was all like a farm-yard!

'She certainly may not want another,' said Christopher. 'But the existence of one may be a very good reason for her to want a husband!'

He heard again the ripple of Arabella's laughter. Only a few hours ago, it was. 'Anyhow, we could blame Henry!'

'Good gracious me!'

Mr. Severn fell silent. He stirred his tea without stopping for nearly five minutes, in deep reverie.

'Do you think? . . .' he began at last, and then halted in some embarrassment. He coughed nervously, and fluttered the pages of the schema. 'I am afraid, my dear Harnish, that I have been very inconsiderate. I deserve your implied reprobation. I ought to have thought of it at the time. My excuse must be that I really failed to realize the situation at all. I am very fond of Mary, indeed. . . . An extremely nice girl, of whom anyone should be proud! . . . I certainly ought to have made the offer, at any rate! . . . I am a queer-looking old fellow, but you remember what Horace says, "Sic visum Veneri; cui placet impares formas——" . . . Perhaps it's not too late, even now?'

'Good God!' said Christopher, shattered.

Mr. Severn looked mildly, inquiringly at him: chided himself again, reached out to the small handbell upon the rustic table, rang it with an air of great decision, and relapsed into a fresh reverie.

Christopher watched Mary come across the little shady pleasure-garden. Such a desirable, pretty, comfortable Mary! Yet she had had a baby to which she had no right, for all that she looked smiling and care-free! Like Margaret Atchill! She had once looked like that girl on a Southwark doorstep! She had been big with child!

Big! He saw again that curved enormous belly. Margaret Atchill, too, had looked like that! So might Arabella, if . . . He felt physically sick.

He went to Dover as if the devil drove behind him, and started across the Channel in a steam-packet, in a squall of blinding rain and a rising wind.

He leaned over the side of the little ship as she rolled in a sea that at one moment lay like a pit beneath her and at the next rose as a wall into the heavens above. Traversing those narrow waters between coast and coast, it came to him how, in such a small floating hamlet on wider seas, one might escape from everything but oneself or death.

The gale rose in the hour to a screeching fury. Under its buffets the vessel made no headway; nor could she turn, and the great paddlewheels, lifted alternately from the water as she lurched, clanked dolorously amid the creaking of every timber and the whine of the wind as it gnawed at every rope.

The immensely tall funnel with a serrated top like the teeth of a crocodile suddenly crashed on the deck, and smoke and cinders were belched from out the gaping aperture as if by a volcano.

He spent the afternoon and night in the crowded after-cabin with a sea-sick crowd. The ship lay helpless for seven hours, rolling, and swept by great seas that cleared the deck of all its hamper and washed away two large travelling carriages as morning broke. Through the streaming port-hole he watched the vehicles floating absurdly alongside for a little while before they sank.

He went on deck. The engine fires had been quenched: the tangle of tattered mast and rigging cut away.

Williams, the ex-seaman, very much in his element, his gold-laced hat jammed on his head, and stripped to the waist, was supervising the erection of a jury-mast.

He touched his hat as Christopher appeared.

'I was cap'n of the fore-top in the old *Wasp*,' he said in explanation, and balanced on the restless deck imperturbably. 'We'll be in Calais in three or four hours from now. Mark my words, sir. Perfect moral agin' goin' to sea in these 'ere floating stoves. No reelibility, sir! No reelibility!'

He shook his head over the foolishness of tempting Providence, and turned to the task in hand.

Surely enough in four hours' time Christopher was sitting in yellow-washed Dessein's Hotel arranging to go post to Neipperg.

Nine days later, from the bend in the road, he was looking once more down on the crooked alleys and huddled red roofs of the capital of the Grand Duchy he had wished never to see again. The grey-blue smoke from its countless chimneys drifted about it in the early morning sun. High over all glittered the weathercock on the cathedral spire. It had been newly gilded, he recognized. The thin sweet jangle of Sunday bells rose to him from the plain. Near by a dog at a hillside farm barked violently.

'You want to go to the Palace, as I suppose, sir?' asked Williams.

The Palace where Cumberland had plotted the downfall of his cousin and spun dark conspiracies and fomented murder?—No!

'While you find out where his lordship is staying I will take rooms at . . .' he had nearly said the Englischer Hof, where Dunscore had choked out his life— '. . . at the Weisses Rössel!'

Eckie liked the Weisses Rössel. He would be glad to see Eckie again. . . . Would he—on second thoughts?

Chapter 30

In the Manner of Ezekiel

CHRISTOPHER WAS GIVEN A SITTING-ROOM ON THE ground floor. Its windows opened on to a walled garden full of green tables placed under the shade of young lindens.

The sun, through the canopy of leaves, made a tessellation of black and grey upon the gravel. In one corner was an attempted rockery in which the rocks rose bleakly in a mound of soil like miniature tombstones. At the far end three fiddlers tuned their violins, and the flautists started wonderfully sweet notes that ended in bronchial gurgles and violent shakings.

Already the garden was filling up with townspeople in their Sunday best, a sprinkling of officers and their ladies, and students with scarred faces and tasselled caps.

The fat old Grand-Ducal-Court-Upper-Forester in a tight bottle-green coat contentedly smoked his china pipe in company with his fat old wife and two flaxen-haired daughters. The young ladies were deliciously aware of the admiring glances they secured from a half-dozen subalterns very gay in scarlet and white and gold at the next table.

There was a constant procession of hurrying waiters in white aprons and grey woollen stockings.

Christopher, at the open window, halted one of the men as he passed.

'Fritzi!' he called.

Fritzi paused in his journey, turned his head, saw the slim figure —in dark blue coat and high black stock—of an honoured patron. He came a step nearer. heavy beer-mugs foaming in each hand.

'The Gracious Gentleman desires? . . .' he inquired, and smiled a respectful greeting.

'Tell the Freiherr von Eckstein that I am here—Mr. Harnish—when he comes.'

The waiter cocked his streaming face a little to one side like an inquiring sparrow. A curious look came into his eyes.

'If the Gracious Gentleman will have the goodness to wait one moment,' he suggested, and vanished with his burden.

He came back mopping the perspiration from his brow with a corner of his apron, and approached the window more nearly.

'The Freiherr von Eckstein will not be coming here, Excellency,' he said mysteriously in a low voice.

'He has gone away, then?' asked Christopher in sudden surprise.

'The Freiherr von Eckstein is in his grave,' said the waiter in a still lower tone.

Christopher became very white. He stared incredulously at the man.

'Plunk-plunk,' said the drums of the orchestra; 'tweedle-eedle-eedle,' said the violins; 'too-la-oola-roola,' said the flutes; 'life is so amusing and elegant,' said the whole orchestra a-dance. Life is no more important than the pointing of a toe, and the flaunting of a scarf, and the setting to partners. Then the cymbals clashed like the keys of great ladies' apartments clashing in the hands of venal eunuchs.

Clash! The Freiherr von Eckstein—Clash!—is in his grave. Clash-clash! He's dead because of you. Clash-clash!

'Why?' said Christopher. 'What do you mean?'

'He was shot dead, Your Excellency, a month ago. He was shot by Herr von Metzsch. It was a duel. Herr von Metzsch went after him into Hanover. He had run away with Herr von Metzsch's bride. Herr von Metzsch said he would shoot him, and he did. He —he . . .' and the waiter stammered into silence.

It seemed to him for just an instant that the youthful tanned face, with the yellow hair swept across the brow, had become a skull. So quick and violent had been the change that he backed away, as if from death, and turned with relief, and went whispering to his mates.

Eckie was dead! Laughing Eckie, who could never use a pistol straight, had been shot dead! He remembered a hundred traits of the dead man—a dozen adventures—his mournful mother with the drip at the end of a melancholy nose. She had something to be mournful about now!

He had killed Eckie, as certainly as if with his own hand he had raised the pistol and put a bullet into his brain. He had sent Luise to Eckie—selfishly to preserve his dreams. He had sent Luise and Death to Eckie.

He still stood in the window, unconscious of the whispers and sideways glances of the waiters as they passed.

He stepped across the sill into the crowded garden. The waiters stopped to watch him as he made his way through the tables, each with its placid gossiping group.

He came to the table that was gay like a cottage garden with bright uniforms. Many of the men were his friends. Their swords trailed the gravel.

He stood over the table, ignoring the greetings as they looked up to see him. He struck his fingers on the painted wooden boards.

'Is there one among you here who will take a message from me to Herr von Metzsch?' he asked.

Von Metzsch was not popular: they guessed what the message was: a stillness fell on them which spread to the adjacent tables. At last one rose, an officer in von Metzsch's own regiment, and bowed formally.

'As a fellow officer of Herr von Metzsch,' he said, 'I will take the responsibility upon myself—but,' he lowered his voice and looked anxiously and kindly at Christopher, 'you are tired, and . . .'

'I am not too tired,' said Christopher, 'to send a message. It is this . . .'

The man nearest him placed a restraining hand upon his arm.

'Everyone is looking this way! Everyone is listening! Mr. Harnish, for God's sake, speak lower!'

He shook off the hand, and would have broken out in a voice that could have been heard throughout the garden in the ominous hush that had fallen. Someone spoke quietly at his elbow.

'Mr. Harnish is overwrought! He will say what he has to say to you, Herr von Lyding, within doors. . . . You will come inside with me, Christopher!'

The tall figure of Captain von Brahe was at his side. His rugged face above the high scarlet collar was composed, but his solitary eye gleamed warningly. Even in that confused minute Christopher wondered for the first time since he knew him what was under the black patch over his right eye. Was it a hollow with the lids lying in it like lips sucked into a toothless mouth? Or a white sightless orb? Or . . .

Von Lyding extricated himself from his place, and the others rose. They bowed, with swords that clinked against chair and table, and in silence watched the three men go back to the inn through the hushed company.

Within the room von Brahe flung himself grumbling on to a clumsy sofa. He scrubbed at his bristling moustache of badger-grey, while von Lyding held himself stiff and erect by the door.

Christopher was about to speak when the captain turned his battered face on him.

'If I did my duty as your company officer, Mr. Harnish,' he said, 'I should put you under arrest!'

'Why?'

'Failure to report on return to duty!'

'Must we discuss this before a third party? In any case, I am no longer an officer of the Corps du Garde.'

'So you think!' said von Brahe. 'Your resignation was refused by the Great Duke. Herr von Lyding will not repeat what I say to anyone,' he interjected, and the other gravely bowed. 'There was the devil of a row. The Great Duchess gave the old man hell about you—I don't understand why. That's neither here nor there. You probably do. Anyway, the old man informed Baron Michaeloff that you were to be put in orders as being granted indefinite leave. . . . So you are one of my young men, still!'

'That,' said Christopher, with dazed composure, 'need not prevent me from saying what I will about Herr von Metzsch. I do not accept the position, anyhow. I have resigned once and for all.'

The other two exchanged quick glances.

Von Brahe shrugged his shoulders.

'I am going to say to you, in front of Herr von Lyding as witness for von Metzsch'—now he spoke rapidly for fear of interruption—'that von Metzsch is an incestuous murderer: that he is dishonoured: that if he will not fight me I will publicly insult him: that I will kill him—as he murdered my friend!'

Again the two other men exchanged glances.

Von Lyding bowed as if in formal acknowledgment. He was about to reply, when von Brahe rose briskly to his feet.

'Now that you have given your message to von Metzsch, I will have a word with Herr von Lyding about preliminary arrangements,' he said, and before Christopher could say a word he had hurried the other from the door.

When he returned Christopher was still standing at the window looking out on to the gaiety of the garden—seeing Eckie laughing under the trees with a high pot of foaming beer before him; twisting his head round to get a better view of a pretty girl; or massaging the down upon his upper lip because he thought thus to make the hair grow.

'I think you're mad, Christopher!' said von Brahe to the back, throwing his sword upon the table and himself upon the sofa. 'You are just asking for murder!'

'Murder!' replied Christopher without turning.

'Von Metzsch is the best pistol shot between here and Frankfort—and you know it.'

'I am not afraid of that. I shall kill him. Eckie must be revenged. Wasn't he murdered—for it came to murder? Everyone knows he could never hold a pistol straight. It was a byword. Shouldn't he be avenged?'

'I was very fond of Eckie, too,' said von Brahe, cocking his spurred feet upon the sofa and resting the back of his head upon folded arms. 'But you cannot get away from the fact that he did a bolt with Luise!'

'And had Luise no right of choice? No right when her betrothed betrayed her with her stepmother?'

'I've heard that gossip, young fellow,' said von Brahe. 'You can't believe all you hear.'

'I know it is true. . . . Eckie knew it was true. . . . Luise knows it. . . . I have seen von Metzsch creep out of the house at three in the morning—seen him myself only a few weeks before the marriage should have taken place!'

'Pfui! The dirty beast!' Von Brahe spat out the words as if he had rinsed his mouth and spat out the water.

'It is not Eckie's death only,' said Christopher, 'but the dishonour to Luise, the girl he loved!'

'Herr Je!' said von Brahe. 'It may all be extremely true, but it won't alter the fact that by this time to-morrow you'll be a dead man.' He paused as if an idea had come to him—'Unless I arrest you as a madman!'

'I am not going to die,' said Christopher turning round at length. 'I am going to live and live—and go on living and hating myself—and everything!'

Von Brahe shot off the sofa.

'Christopher,' he exploded, 'you talk like the Wandering Jew, or Job or the so-sorrowful Werther! You will now drink with me one bottle only of Piesporter. After that I shall put you to bed myself. You will sponge your face, and keep your wrists immersed in cold water for half an hour. And when I let you get up, you will do the same again. You must have a steady hand for our little appointment . . .' He broke off, and continued after a moment, 'For just these few hours, you are in my charge!'

He fussed about the overwrought lad like a rather whiskery and vinous aunt in fancy dress, and Christopher in a daze submitted. He pulled the blinds down in the bed-chamber, helped him off with boots, and tip-toed out.

At the door Christopher suddenly remembered—

'My uncle, Lord Setoun—is he here still?'

Von Brahe shook a blunt finger in warning.

'You are not to talk! . . . He and his wife left a fortnight ago. They found—and God knows how!—that you had gone to Paris, and followed you there.'

'And Luise?'

'A prisoner in her room—until they send her to a convent.'

He lay on the soft bed, his head on the wedge-shaped bolster, staring at the black beams against the white-washed ceiling. He fancied that he heard Eckie whispering arrangements in his ear. But he had murdered Eckie, who had been so proud to be the second in a duel with an English lord; who would never more sit in the guard room expatiating on his latest love, or invent wonderful excuses for non-attendance at early morning stable duty! He, the murderer, was going to take vengeance for Eckie upon his fellow-murderer.

While Christopher dozed and dreamed, Captain von Brahe, his uniform coat unbuttoned, sat after dinner at ease in his lodgings. He lounged by a latticed window from which—if he had so desired—he could have shaken hands across the narrow alley with his opposite neighbour. On the ledge, amid the pots of scarlet English geraniums which Christopher had had sent to him two years ago, was a tremendous earthenware mug of beer. His grizzled hair was ruffled, and with his black patch, his battered face, and fleshy nose, he looked like a brigand chief taking his leisure.

A stretch of stiff canvas lay upon his knees, and he was rug-making with a crochet hook and wool of black and red. The youngest daughter of the landlady, two flaxen plaits lying on her little plump chest, sat bolt upright with a book spread on the table before her, reading aloud in a treble voice emotional passages from a highly sentimental novel.

As he deftly pulled each length of wool through the mesh and knotted it, his mind was busy on the problems before him. Von Lyding had arranged to be called away before he could repeat the ominous message to von Metzsch, which must therefore wait till morning.

Von Lyding was a good fellow—excellent fellow—would like to get him transferred to the Corps—had behaved very well. At any rate gave him a few hours in which to compose the matter, although he saw no honourable way out.

His rigid code would not allow him to warn the superior authorities even if, for some reason unknown to him, they seemed particularly interested in Christopher: even if more young blood was to be spilled by a worthless man. He grumbled to himself about Court favour; drew a loop through the canvas, failed to make his knot, and cursed a good round military oath.

Flaxen-Plaits, intent on a gush of sentiment, broke off and regarded him with pained surprise in her large light-blue eyes.

'Na! Na! Eulalia.' It was a standing rule that Kätti should always be called by the name of the current heroine. 'It is not thou! Go on, child!'

'Eulalia' gave him a look that implied that she would brook no further interruption of the sort during the present crisis in the affairs of her namesake. She read on in an aggrieved tone which gradually faded away before the interest of what she read.

As the story approached its crisis von Brahe dropped his work and leaned forward, listening with the greatest attention, wagging his head at each high-toned sentiment, and watching the child's lips shape each word as if he would wrest the meaning in advance.

Over the housetops the cathedral clock chimed out the hour of four.

'Eulalia' shot from her chair in great alarm and closed the book.

'Ach!' she said, 'I am a quarter of an hour late. The little Mother will be very angry. It is a great shame we cannot finish! Only twelve more pages to the end!'

'This is terrible!' said von Brahe. 'But we can't leave them like this, with Ferdinand facing the Count's pistol.'

'I dare not stay!' said 'Eulalia' unhappily, and looked longingly at the book. Indeed at that moment from somewhere below came the echo of her real life name—'Kätti! Kätti! Where art thou?'

'Look at the end quickly, little one,' said von Brahe. 'Look at the end quickly, and see if all ends well.'

Kätti, poised for flight, ruffled the leaves. Her eyes scanned the lines.

'Ferdinand kills his jailer and escapes with Eulalia,' she summarized.

'Very good!' said von Brahe, highly satisfied.

'Eulalia falls from the pillion as they ride away. She is hurt. Ferdinand has to stop. . . . The Count catches them up.'

Von Brahe shook his head in grave concern.

'Oh, it is a shame!' announced Kätti, turning to the final pages. 'That poor Eulalia is shot! . . . Ferdinand dies on her bleeding body! . . . They are buried together! . . . And the Count laughs

"Ha! Ha!" . . . It is a shame, is it not, Herr Hauptmann?' Her sentimental blue eyes misted with tears.

'We like our stories to end happily, don't we, Kätti?' said the captain looking fixedly out of the window.

'They must end happily! . . . And the bad man should always be killed! . . . Always,' said Kätti decidedly. 'We will read no more that end like this. I will ask Fräulein Kühler to see that we have only happy endings in future.'

'Quite right! Quite right!' said von Brahe a trifle abstractedly. He remembered, however, Kätti's customary reward of a handful of violently coloured sweetmeats.

The child clattered downstairs.

We only want happy endings! thought von Brahe. We want the bad man killed! And to-morrow under his supervision would be presented to the world another single-volume story with a tragic finish, and a bad man left alive! He wondered if the code was worth while!

So Eulalia had been killed, and Ferdinand had died on her bleeding corpse, and the Count had laughed! He had laughed, had he?

What would happen were he to inform Michaeloff of the coming duel? For a second thus to ask for interference might well lead to social ostracism. He supposed it didn't matter; he could always listen to Kätti reading, and the Great Duchess would probably see him through with the people who counted. It wouldn't be a pretty business, all the same.

Michaeloff would doubtless want to learn a great deal more. He knew how the baron would worry through to the roots of things. It gave him the cold shudders to think of what might happen then. He could see himself stammering, before eyes grown very cold, on the verge of appalling revelations. Now and again there showed beneath the old man's gentleness strange complexes and inhibitions and moods that betrayed his Tartar blood. At the best Michaeloff would never forgive him for merely knowing of the dishonour; he saw the prospects of promotion fading into the far distance.

Above an armoire, presiding over a huddle of pipes, tobacco jars, cravats, cigar-boxes, and other oddments, was a small portrait of a singularly rigid young woman with a large fat face seen in silhouette. He looked sentimentally at it.

What do you think, Heart-Beloved?' he addressed the portrait. 'One story's ended badly already. Is the next to do so? . . . Is more good young blood to be shed, and is the bad man to laugh, "Ha! Ha!"?'

Heart-Beloved, who had mouldered in her grave twenty years before, made no comment. The solitary eye that was visible perhaps urged the need for a happy ending.

'The poor old Max. His chance of a happy ending went with you!' said von Brahe, not altogether truthfully. 'His career is nearly at an end. If he does get overlooked and superseded—what does it matter?'

His mind conjured up for a moment a melancholy picture of a blasted career and social ostracism—of a white-haired old man with no solace but the portrait of the Well-Beloved (whom he actually forgot for three hundred and sixty days out of the year) and the reading of sentimental novels by Kätti.

He looked at Heart-Beloved again. Her eye suddenly moved: its regard was no longer at the distance, but turned on him as if pronouncing definitely in favour of a happy ending.

He leaped to his feet with an oath; and then dropped back resentfully. A fly wandered from the portrait's eye on a voyage of exploration down the nose. . . . Perhaps, though, it was the instrument of the expression of a divine command! There was no reason why a fly should not be—he meditated.

A minute or so later he rose with sudden decision, swept the crumbs of wool from his lap, helped himself to a very large glass of schnapps, and proceeded to button up his uniform coat. He knew the risks and the code. Be damned to them both.

The Grand Ducal supper was always earlier on a Sunday than on a week-day. As card-playing was frowned on, the Great Duke withdrew, by invariable custom after the meal, to his small cabinet where he sat late with Baron Michaeloff and one or two cronies discussing the campaign of Suvarov over pipes and beer.

This night Michaeloff excused himself.

He went quietly on the rounds, acknowledging the salutes of

sentries with his customary gentle smile, debating a minor point with the duty officer with an opinion inflexibly based on the principle of adhesion to the uttermost letter of regulation.

He returned to the Wall House rather wearily, with his head a little bent so that it seemed to be wilting over the scarlet wall of his collar. He had gathered up his sword, and walked with the gilded hilt pressed against him above his folded arms.

The light was dying: a young moon, chasing the sunset, glimmered through the trees: the lawns were as lifeless and as lightless as green velvet.

He went very quietly in the hush of the evening from the small door of the palace library, past the pleached cherry trees against the outer wall to the cloister beneath his house.

One of his maids, hurrying to snatch a surreptitious five minutes with her lover, dropped a frightened curtsy to him: and he smiled as he touched his shako in reply.

He stopped the girl.

'Trüdchen,' he asked, 'has Hans'—his soldier servant—'left the house yet?'

She bobbed another curtsy and squeaked a nervous 'Yes!'

'And I suppose then, Trüdchen, that though Maria has not come back yet Anna said you might go out for half an hour to meet him—at the Fountain Gate?'

He turned his long ivory-pale face on her with the faint white eyebrows raised in inquiry.

Trüdchen, conscious of guilt, blushed deeply and curtsied, but made no reply.

He drew out his watch from between the gold buttons of his coat.

'You need not come back for an hour,' he said, and watched her vanish with something of a smile.

He paused before he went up the staircase in the cloister, and thought how the yew hedge in the closing dusk had lost its shape and substance and become a rampart of unidentifiable blackness that loomed up into the darkening shield of the sky.

He entered the house silently enough in his thin lacquered boots; paused a moment and walked quiet-footed down the long tunnel to the kitchen quarters. Anna, the cook-maid, sat over the stove knitting by candle-light.

'Put on your shawl at once, Anna,' he said, 'and go to Herr Hof-Apotheke Crespel in the Parade-strasse. Get him to make me up another bottle of my rheumatism cure. Wait for it, and bring it back with you.'

He did not go to his room until he saw the girl leave the house.

He knelt by the side of his narrow bed in prayer for a while, and then rose heavily to his feet. He took a box from a shelf in the cupboard where his winter uniforms hung amid a smell of camphor, and placed it beside a book upon a table at the bed-head.

From another cupboard he brought out two bottles, one full of a brown fluid and the other squat and dark. He held the second up to the light, and saw through the seaweed-green glass that it held about a tumblerful of a liquid, in which floated a multitude of little flecks.

He uncorked the first bottle and tilted some of its contents into the other. A sickly sweet smell escaped as he did so.

With the vessel in his hand, and box and book under his arm, he walked to the salon, treading very lightly.

He flung the door open wide.

Sophie von Osterode shifted swiftly from the embraces of von Metzsch who was sitting on the sofa by her.

The heavy curtains had been drawn. A pair of candles were on the marble-topped commode between the windows, and a lamp stood with a decanter and some glasses on the heavily draped table a few feet from them.

In the subdued light her arms, and the rosy shoulders and bosom that emerged from her dishevelled dress, glowed as if with an inner warmth, and her lips were moistly red.

The old man made no comment. He drew up a clumsy copy of an Empire chair to the table, and seated himself sideways to it and facing them. Still in silence he placed bottle and box and book close to the lamp at his elbow. Still in silence he opened the box and opened the book, and then with long thin fingers rearranged them; shifted them again, and finally propped the volume against the mahogany casket.

'Conrad and I,' began Sophie von Osterode, endeavouring to compose herself, 'were talking . . .'

Her uncle paid no attention and she broke off lamely.

Von Metzsch, sitting stiffly in his corner, gathered as far away from her as possible, watched the old man as though hypnotized. The woman, too, began to follow with strained eyes the fingers fumbling with the leaves—began to stare at the stooped forehead with the grey receding hair, as if she would penetrate its ivory whiteness and read how much he knew and guessed. Her hands clenched themselves on the folds of the wide rose-pink dress spread about her on the sofa.

Baron Michaeloff found the place he sought. He looked up.

'It appears, Herr von Metzsch, that you keep your amours very much in one family—stepmother and stepdaughter are all one to you! . . . You do me too much—honour!'

Von Metzsch's eager nostrils widened a trifle; his lips parted as if they would say something; his Adam's apple rose against the stiff embroidered collar of his uniform. His bright black eyes restlessly ranged the room as though seeking a way of escape.

Sophie von Osterode became very pale.

'What is this—this nonsense that you say?' she said at last, and stared at her uncle.

He ignored her.

'I have heard it called incest. . . . Sit down! . . . I call it incest, myself! . . . Looking at it dispassionately, Sophie—sit down!—one might call it incest, don't you think?'

'You are mad—mad!' she stammered.

'If I were mad, Sophie,' he corrected very quietly, although the gaze turned on her was stony—'If I were mad, I should do something very different from what I am going to do. . . . Sit down, Herr von Metzsch!'

'These are shameful things to say,' said von Metzsch breathlessly. 'You cannot . . .'

'They were more shameful things that were done. . . . Sit down, Sophie!'

'You—you have no proof. This is madness!'

'I have enough proof. And a dozen things I never gave a moment's thought to at the time, have come to my mind since I learned . . .'

'From whom?'

They were the only words von Metzsch could find to say; and after them he sagged back against the sofa with drooping shoulders, and desperately studied the pattern of the carpet.

'From whom?' demanded Sophie. She had drawn herself together. Pale and discomposed as she was, she still endeavoured to beat down her uncle.

He ignored her question. He pulled the book a little nearer to him and began to read out loud to them.

There was no sound but of his quiet voice. He sat with his grey head bowed over the volume in the radiance of the lamp that illumined the pleasant room. A peaceful Sunday evening scene!

He read from Ezekiel the denunciation beginning:

' "Wherefore, O harlot, hear the word of the Lord: Thus saith the Lord God; Because thy filthiness was poured out, and thy nakedness discovered through thy whoredoms . . ." '

'Must I listen to this abomination?' asked Sophie. She rose with rustling dress. Von Metzsch did not stir: neither did her uncle.

'Sit down!' he commanded without raising his head or altering his tone, and continued:

' "Behold, therefore . . . and will discover thy nakedness unto them, that they may see all thy nakedness. . . . they shall strip thee also of thy clothes, and shall take thy fair jewels, and leave thee naked and bare".'

'This is appalling!' said Sophie. 'It is not to be borne. . . How dare you read such filth? . . . Conrad—tell the old fool! . . .'

She rose once more to her feet, magnificent in anger and fear; and as her lover made no move, disdain was added to her other emotions.

But von Metzsch merely brought up his gaze from the floor and stared without stirring at the old man.

'Sit down, Sophie,' said her uncle. 'There must be no scenes. We must arrange this matter without further scandal. There has been dishonour enough—dishonour enough!'

'I will go to my room!'

But she could not keep her voice steady; and in the end she was afraid to move, and stood at bay; for she caught sight of that which lay in the mahogany box propping the Bible.

The old man's hands went to the case. He lifted out the pistols one at a time, delicately as if they were fragile things, and placed them so that they rested each upon a page of the open book.

The woman's face had no loveliness in it now. The mouth was open and the eyes staring, the skin lustreless; and perspiration dampened the curls upon her brow.

'I had thought,' said Baron Michaeloff, 'to kill you both for the dishonour you have put upon my family. I have changed my mind.'

Neither of them moved, although a sort of groan came from between the man's parted lips.

'It is not fitting that by your deaths you should confirm the scandal you have already made. . . . It is for that reason that I recommend Herr von Metzsch to do as he is bidden. I do not suppose either of you wish to die with your sins still on you.'

Said Sophie, speaking with the harsh, dry voice of an old woman:

'What are you going to do?'

Her uncle held one of the pistols loosely in his hand. It was a double-barrelled weapon, long and silvered. The hammers were at full cock, like snake heads about to strike. He pointed it directly at von Metzsch.

'Herr von Metzsch,' he said formally. 'I am not going to kill you—or this wanton. I give you my word. But before I let you go there is a little comedy in the Russian manner that I would have you play. If you do not do as I desire, I shall kill you. Make no mistake! If you do not—I shall kill you. . . . I think, perhaps, you need some stimulant.' He filled a large glass from the dark green bottle with his disengaged hand. It was full of little flecks of gold. He pushed it across the table. 'I have a great fancy to see you both drink from a loving cup. . . . Sophie, take up that glass and taste of it! And present it to your lover afterwards! It will be sweeter where your lips have pressed the rim.'

She looked at him with horror widening her eyes.

'You—you—?'

'It is not poison. I have sworn it. I am not going to kill you. Take up the glass, foolish one—and taste. It is Danzig Goldwater, good for the nerves on occasions such as this! . . . Take it up, I tell you! . . . I will not wait. Do you wish to force me to shoot you both?'

She came to the table with uncertain steps and raised the glass.

'Drink!' he said. 'Drink to your lover! . . . It is not poison. . . . Have I ever broken my word?'

Even in that moment his vehemence brought assurance to her stunned mind.

She set her lips to the glass.

'Again!'

Obediently she drank of the fiery stuff once more, conscious only of its hot sweetness, and of the faded eyes and pistol that watched her.

'Give it to him!'

Again obedient, she stooped to von Metzsch with the glass. The man took the goblet from her in both hands, and sat motionless, looking at the flecks of gold that danced within it.

'Would you ignore your loving cup?' said the baron, and his finger tightened on the trigger. Sophie saw the imperceptible flattening of the crease in the second joint.

'Conrad, drink! For God's sake, drink! And let us get this over!'

He raised the glass like a blind man to his mouth and drained it clumsily to the end; sat back, and raised eyes in which speculation and memory struggled with fear. He licked his dry lips: his throat made motions as of swallowing—as if he would recapture the taste that lingered in his saliva and recall its name.

'Herr von Metzsch,' said Baron Michaeloff. 'You will now arise and salute—your last embrace!—Frau von Osterode! You will kiss her on the lips—your last kiss!'

'No!' she cried, and 'No!' and clutched her mouth with her hand.

'It is that—or death for both!' said the baron quietly. 'I am a good shot—better even than yourself, Herr von Metzsch. . . . Come, Herr von Metzsch, do not deprive the lady of that last pleasure! None will witness the shame of it, except myself!'

'No!' cried Sophie again.

She put out her hands to keep him off, as he rose and took uncertain steps towards her, like an automaton that became unwound.

'Sophie,' said the baron. 'This modesty is too late! I shall certainly kill your lover if he does not give you the last token of his affection—and more than that . . . !'

Her mouth was opened to scream.

The long white face turned towards her with a grave regard. The yellow lids drooped over faded eyes.

'There is no one to hear you. The house is empty—except for the girl upstairs, whom you betrayed. . . . Herr von Metzsch!'

The man approached her with downcast eyes. He stood opposite her. She caught his arms.

'Conrad! Don't! Don't!'

But he seemed stupefied and unaware of anything but the even voice that said, 'Herr von Metzsch, you will do as you are bid!'

He leaned over her, while she strained away her head from side to side, whimpering.

'You do not appear to understand, Sophie,' said the baron, 'that you have no alternative. You will submit to his caresses—his so ardent caresses! Or I shall kill you both. . . . Is it clear? Is it quite clear?'

He rapped the butt of the pistol in his right hand gently against the table.

'Put a hand upon each of her shoulders, Herr von Metzsch, and kiss the wanton as you were used!'

Von Metzsch, like a thing without a will—like an automaton made to obey his master's voice, put his hands upon the cold bare shoulders. He bent his lips obediently against the mouth which she strained back and away until her long white throat was stiff and upright as a column from breast to chin. Her mouth was open, so that his dry lips kissed her teeth.

' "I will even gather them round about against thee, and will discover thy nakedness unto them, that they may see all thy nakedness. . . ." '

The baron read on as if to himself. Von Metzsch heard nothing. He swayed a little: he knew that his senses were leaving him, that he was incapable of anything but obedience.

'No!' said Sophie, moaning. 'No!'

Michaeloff read the sentence again more loudly, and with a deadly emphasis—

' ". . . Discover thy nakedness unto them, that they may see all thy nakedness".'

Into the dulled mind of von Metzsch the idea came slowly. He remained stooped over the woman, his hands still clutching her shoulders, his eyes turned—as a puppet's might—upon his master.

'You understood?'

'No! No!' moaned Sophie. Her body curved farther back from her lover: her hands beat frantically at his arms.

Von Metzsch's black dazed eyes never left the figure beside the shaded lamp. On his crossed knees the baron supported one pistol in his hand: the other weapon he swayed slowly to and fro, resting an elbow on the table. Below the second joint of his middle finger was a ring with a great stone in it as red as blood.

'You have looked on the dishonour of my family, Herr von Metzsch, many times, as I gather. You shall look once again—and for the last time. . . . Do you understand me?'

'No!' said Sophie. 'Oh, no! . . . Let me be. . . . No!'

She tried to scream, but only a harsh croaking came from her dry throat.

As a marionette obeys the strings pulled by a puppet master, so von Metzsch obeyed the strings pulled by Death. His hands closed more tightly on her shoulders, gathered in their grip the satin of her sleeves, shut more tightly on the material and the ribbons that lay below. He looked down on her distorted face with the chin thrown up, into the open mouth with the bared upper teeth, into the widened nostrils, into the eyes of which the whiteness alone showed.

He mumbled something beneath his breath, and inexorably strained at the rending stuff in his hands. It tore like the peeling rind from an orange. It fell about her.

Naked to the waist she swayed before them for an instant, tottered two steps, and then crumpled on the sofa.

'Look as much as you like—for the last time!' said Michaeloff with a chill ferocity. 'It is a pretty sight, is it not? Well worth the price, you think, Herr von Metzsch? Now look at me!'

Von Metzsch turned from the bare huddle. It seemed as if his feet could no longer support him. He rested a hand upon the gilded frame of the brocaded settee. His eyes were glazed.

'Remember this all your life! Remember her rosiness and her whiteness—and me! . . . You will not talk of it, I think!'

The old man's words beat on his distracted ears. He made half a step towards the lamplight and the wavering pistols. The hands that bore the weapons stiffened. The jetty eyes of their muzzles stared up into his black eyes.

Then his knees gave way under him, and it was all he could do to drag his trailing limbs back to the sofa by his grip upon its elbow. He opened his mouth as if to speak, but no words came.

'I would remind you of the words of Leviticus, Herr von Metzsch,' said the baron: ' "Thou shalt not uncover the nakedness of a woman and her daughter . . . it is wickedness".'

But von Metzsch did not hear him. He sprawled on the sofa by the other huddle, his eyes closed, his mouth open to stertorous breathing.

The baron placed the pistols back in their case, and closed the book. He rose and settled the woman as if more comfortably in her corner. Her head lolled back over the gilded frame of the sofa, her arms limp at her side, her bare bosom rising above the ruins of her dress.

He took the unconscious von Metzsch by the long black hair and pulled him like a sack across the rich cushions and let his head fall on her nudity.

Barely had he completed the arrangement when there was a quick footfall without: the door opened, and Christopher entered.

For a moment the younger man saw only the baron standing by the table.

'You are a little late, Mr. Harnish,' he said.

Christopher was angry and young, and a little afraid.

'You interfered with my arrangements, sir,' he replied. 'Your guard has only just left me. I saw no reason why . . .'

Suddenly he saw the couple on the sofa. His jaw dropped.

'Shut the door, Mr. Harnish.'

He closed it automatically and waited against it.

The baron stood looking down upon his niece and her lover. He spoke in a quiet everyday tone. His face was unchanged.

'I have very little to say to you, Mr. Harnish, but something to show you. . . . No! They are not dead! They have merely had three hundred drops or so of laudanum in Danzig Gold-water—to soothe the nerves! . . . It appears that as the best friend of von Eckstein you thought it your duty to avenge an insult to the woman he loved. That was laudable. It might have cost you your life. It would have added to a scandal already great. My dishonour would have been patent. In Russia when I was young, we avenged such sort of dishonour in a different way!

'As your dead friend's champion I wish you to be here now to see how we dealt with those who looked on our shame and gloried in it.'

Christopher stared into the curve of radiance in the dark room—at the huddled man near him, dark head buried and snoring upon white flesh; at the tall figure of the old man paring his nails with a little knife.

'You see them,' said the baron, 'presented symbolically of their crime. They look like hogs wallowing in their iniquity—do they not, Mr. Harnish?'

There was, indeed, something so indecent in the spectacle that it filled him with as much disgust as fear.

'I wish you to see,' said the baron, 'that in Russia we knew how to deal with those who uncovered and regarded a forbidden nakedness.'

By the hair he lifted up the sagging head of von Metzsch from its resting place, and twisted it round so that Christopher could see. The hungry eyes were shut; the eager mouth open and uttering little sighs and gasps.

With his right hand he drew the pen-knife across each eyelid, pressing the blade lightly into the eyeball. It was done—as if a thing of no account, almost with indifference—before Christopher could move a finger or utter a word. Christopher was yet as still as any stone when von Metzsch rose screaming to his feet, with eyesockets that were blank hollows filling with blood; when he fell on to his paramour and the blood from what had been his eyes streamed on her naked flesh.

Michaeloff watched as a dispassionate god might survey agony.

'I think that Herr von Metzsch will no more look and lust after forbidden things.'

'Oh, God!' said Christopher. 'Oh, God! . . . He's blind!'

The agonized man was on his feet again. The meaning of the words, and who their speaker was, dawned on his tortured mind at the same moment. In the unreasoning of the sudden madness that seized him he blamed Christopher for what had befallen him. For an instant he confronted Christopher with sightless eyes; and then flung himself at him—tore at his coat, sought with eager hands for his throat—slavering and bleeding.

'You did this! You did this!' he cried.

Under the impact Christopher reeled against the panels of the door. He endeavoured to wrench himself away, to push the other off, to keep the ruined bleeding face from his.

Von Metzsch had him by the throat and was clawing at his face.

Christopher brought his left fist up with all his force, and struck the blind man on the chin, so that he fell back upon the table and went crashing with it, and the lamp, to the floor.

The oil ran out from the shattered glass in a dark rivulet along the carpet. A ripple of flame ran with it, gathered its blue into a yellow flare and flickered at the bleeding head, singed the black locks and died away.

The baron leant over the unconscious body, placed a long thin hand over its heart; then straightened himself, satisfied.

'You may go, Mr. Harnish!' he said. 'This matter arranges itself. There will be no dishonour. I shall wait here a little till the maids come back. On my return I shall have discovered an over-set lamp and a fainting niece. This—this person undoubtedly lost his sight in saving her life. . . . Good night, Mr. Harnish. You know better than to speak of this!'

Christopher stood in the darkness of the stairs. He had brought Eckie to destruction: and because of that he had, too, brought about this other horror. Shame had come long ago to Arabella and Miss Severn because he had tried to keep his dreams: shame and death had come again because he had tried to keep them, because he had driven Luise into Eckie's arms.

For a moment or so he felt physically sick: but there was one thing still to be done. He trod softly up the stairs to the floor above.

The key of Luise's door was in the lock. He turned it and entered without knocking.

Luise sat in a high-backed chair facing the door, her hands folded in her lap. A solitary candle burned on a low table at her side. Her eyelids were lowered; her breathing imperceptible; she did not stir at his coming or raise her eyes.

'Luise!' he said harshly.

She looked up in that slow, secret and remembered way; and the unfathomable expression on her face did not change. Her lips moved but said nothing, and she rose and stood before him in her grey dress with head that drooped afresh.

'Luise!' he said once more. 'Eckie has been avenged!'

At that she looked up again. Across the pale face there flashed and passed in one instant—like the shadow of a swift-moving cloud on water—the shadow of a great pleasure.

'That is very good,' she said: her voice held no emotion.

'Luise,' he went on, 'I want you to marry me!'

Her eyes widened at that, but she did not move except her fingers which twisted and untwisted before her.

'But why, Christopher?' she asked.

'Eckie's child must—shall have a name,' he replied. 'I am going now, and you must come with me.'

Eckie's child which might have been his! Eckie's child which would be fatherless because of him!

She made no reply, but went to a chest. She drew out a heavy grey silk shawl and threw it across her shoulders. From a cupboard she brought out a grey bonnet trimmed beneath the brim with a little spray of silk lilies of the valley: from a drawer a packet of papers.

Then she came back across the room to where he stood watching her dully.

'Christopher,' she said, her lips barely moving, 'I have been a prisoner here for more than three weeks. You will take me away although I cannot marry you!'

'You shall marry me!' said Christopher. 'You owe it to Eckie. I say that Eckie's child shall have a name!'

'Your name?—Least of all!'

He drew back a step.

'My name!'

'I shall not marry you for many reasons,' said Luise. 'I shall always feel that, after myself, you were to blame for Eckie's death. You sent me to him because—because you were afraid! So I went to Eckie—and so Eckie died.'

'Afraid?' he echoed in stunned amazement. 'Afraid of what?'

She shrugged her shoulders so lightly that the movement was barely to be seen.

'Afraid of Conrad, I suppose. . . . Of the death that came to Eckie!'

'It is not true, Luise! It is not true. I did not give it a thought! I was not afraid of that!'

'Don't explain now,' she said wearily. 'What does it matter? It is over . . . and done with . . . and dead.'

'It was not fear,' he insisted. 'I—I sent you to him because I would not abate one tittle of my pride, and my ideals, and my dreams!'

'That is your story! . . .' She hesitated and raised her eyes to him, as if assessing his sincerity. 'It may have been so. . . .

But whatever was the reason, we killed him—you and I.'

He stood before her and groaned.

'It is true, Luise! It is true! I murdered Eckie, too! I murdered Eckie!'

'You murdered him,' said Luise, 'because of your selfishness in idealism. I murdered him, too, because of my selfishness in despair. It was he who was the true romantic, who made the despairing effort for an ideal—an ideal that was me. You used him! I used him! And we killed him—you and I.'

'Oh, God, Luise! Must you say this again? This—which I've told myself a hundred times to-day. Luise—I can't bear it! I know it all so well! There is a curse on me, Luise. I've lost my ideals, and my honour, and, I think, everything I love! For weeks, Luise, I've dreamed awake and asleep of the taint in my blood. Of the family I come from. Without honour. Without faith. Without love. Without unselfishness.'

He put his arms upon a high chest, and bent his head on them and wept. She said no word.

After a little he spoke again.

'I was born in shame. As a child I was made a tool for murder, by the infamy of my own kin. I watched the torment of a queen by one who was infamously of my own blood. I watched another kinsman drive on a fool to murder and madness; I have seen his plots against his own kith. I heard another tell me, with horror, the shame and dishonour of my lineage. Needlessly I thrust death upon Eckie. I ran away when he most needed me. In my meanness and pride I deserted a woman that I loved. I went—and sinned her sin: without her excuse. Without her need. With no hope of forgiveness. And came back here to bring more dishonour. . . . That man downstairs! His eyes! Oh, God, they weren't eyes! They were . . .'

Said Luise:

'Christopher, I was more to blame than you. I was more to blame. There are other reasons why I shall not marry you.'

He half lifted his head to hear.

'I shall not marry you,' she said, 'because I came to love Eckie—because Eckie's child *shall* have a name—because *I* have a name!'

She held the papers out to him.

'We were married when we crossed the frontier. He had arranged. I have not spoken because I wished that *she* and *he* should suffer agonies of shame. . . . I want you to take me to his mother. . . . If I should have a child it will be a help to her—too! . . . Let us go!'

They descended the dark stairs.

Outside the salon door she paused. Faint whimperings came from within and groans.

She looked at Christopher, drew her shawl more closely about her, and went unmoved down the stairs to where the carriage waited under the limes.

Chapter 31

Bricks for Dreams

'CHRISTOPHER IS COMMUNICATIVE WITHOUT BEING explicit,' said Setoun to his wife.

He filled to overflowing a chaise-longue on the balcony outside her bedroom window. Charlotte was sitting up in her large bed, rose-pink shawl over shoulders, hair in two thick plaits on either side of her, bowl of chocolate and morning correspondence on a silver tray awaiting attention. Christopher had arrived in Paris in the small hours of the morning, and had been immediately tucked up in bed with a strong opiate and a glass of old armagnac neat, by the hurriedly aroused Setoun.

'I make out from what he says that not merely did the Great Duke blow the gaff—which we knew—but his infernal father has turned up from somewhere. They tried to murder one another. That's what it sounds like at least. Don't understand why . . . thought the swine was dead long ago.

'He's torn up all the evidence of some plot of Cumberland's. Again, don't understand why. He's tried to fight another duel. He's fallen in love with a girl who seems to have had a baby by somebody else. That shook him, so he was immediately seduced by Arabella. Von Eckstein's been killed and someone else blinded —all because he wouldn't be seduced by yet another girl. Lot's been happening, but can't get the hang of it. . . . He was dropping tired, anyhow.'

'Who was the girl?' asked Charlotte, ignoring every other point.

'Which girl, Carlotta? There are three.'

'The one he fell in love with, stupid!'

'Very confused! Very confusing! She seems to have been a sort

494

of trinity. Talked of her as Deb—talked of her as Margaret—talked of her as the Acislo!'

'Acislo!' said Charlotte. 'She's the girl Dunscore ran after without success. And Brunswick! Lady Blessington got worried about D'Orsay because of her. She'd have nothing to do with any of them, or anyone else. Lady Granville told me she was once mistress of the Duc de Chastellux. She's been a succès pyramidal in light opera.'

'Well, she wouldn't marry our Tops, all the same!' said Setoun. . . . 'Just listen to those bees in the limes, Carlotta. They hum in the leaves like harp chords thrumming. I wonder . . .'

'Wouldn't marry him,' interrupted Charlotte, her eyes widening in astonishment, and setting the chocolate bowl down with a clatter. 'In fortune's name, why not? You've given him a big enough settlement to make him very eligible—even for an opera singer!'

'Dunno!' said Setoun. 'The girl said that Margaret could marry him. But Margaretha Acislo wasn't good enough. Sounds all a little mad to me. . . . Think his damned family has got on top of him. Could have handled one or the other problem by itself and come out best. Both together have done him in.'

Charlotte pushed a bare ankle from between the sheets.

'I'll guarantee he told you he couldn't dream any more,' she said. 'That something had barred the exit from this world which he used to have in his mind?'

'Witch!' replied Setoun.

'Intimate contact of any kind with the material world is inclined to have that effect,' said Charlotte sarcastically. 'Marriage has definitely removed you, Hurbles, from the list of the world's more prominent day-dreamers. I've already noticed it.'

She pulled a flowered bedgown about her.

'I'm going to sit on the bed of my first love, Hurbles dear, à grande scandale! And I'm going to stroke his hair and coo to him. And I'm going to hear about everything—even Arabella! I always said that girl was cut in brass. I'm so glad he's been seduced. Every man ought to be. It gives the finishing touch—the patina of sex-experience!'

'Dear Heart!' said Setoun, pityingly. 'It's all right talking like that to me. But it would be thought old-fashioned by most people—quite Regency, in fact! We've become respectable in England in the last ten years. We've only forgiven ladies being Royal Mistresses latterly because they have invariably been grandmothers. We like bloom of virginity on youth—not patina of sex-experience!'

'Don't care a damn about fashion,' said Charlotte, half out of bed. 'I'm *not* old-fashioned. You can't get away from promiscuity any more than you can from eternity. They are both with us. You can think of both with horror, if you like. I don't. I face facts—like Miz' Anne. I'm not worried by virginity or the lack of it. It's an astonishingly small matter, really.'

'You . . .' began Setoun.

Charlotte put foot to carpet. She wrapped her flowered robe about her.

'We will not be personal,' said she. . . . 'I'm going to hear *everything*. And especially about this actress girl! He won't be so *bouché* with me! . . . You, my pretty, will set off at once to your agents and find out what nice ships they know of that are sailing —anywhere; anywhere far away!'

In the result, when the full-rigged ship *Camden*, a thousand tons register, stood out of the West India Dock into Blackwall Reach, and slowly floated with the tide past the Artichoke Tavern, the Plough, and the King's Arms, Christopher stood on the poop waving in reply to the fluttering handkerchiefs at the top of Blackwall Stairs.

In his remarkable apartment below—more like a room in chambers in the Temple than a cabin, only a great deal less dusty— four small oblong windows aslant looked over the ship's wake in the muddy flood to the reed-fringed shore of the Isle of Dogs, and the plantation of masts in dock. Setoun had provided a mahogany medicine chest for all emergencies: he had sent him to sea with the works of Jane Austen and Thomas Love Peacock; a patent collapsible life-saving chair, a microscope, a telescope, and a pistol with four barrels. It was Charlotte who had prescribed a half bottle of champagne a day as a tonic, and sent a dozen cases, as well as many other additions for his commissariat, to the care of the purser.

They were not to touch land until they reached the broad Mississippi and the fabulous city of New Orleans. For weeks they would swim as remote from their fellows, and from the making of human history, as any new planet, torn from its parent star and speeding through the firmament. They would be in the world, but not of it.

Christopher went down to the cabin which was not a cabin, but a room in the Temple, a private foothold in this timber planet travelling through liquid space.

Williams was battling with trunks and bags and books; spreading Paisley shawls over the brown blankets on the wide bunk which had lockers beneath it; arranging a dish of plums on the small buffet against the forward bulkhead, and begonias on the ledges beneath the little windows.

'Quite homelike. All shipshape and Bristol fashion, sir!' said he looking proudly round the snug attic. 'When the crew got to hear that her ladyship 'ad sent this 'ere green carpet for the cabin —w-w-whew!' he indicated their reactions by an expressive whistle. 'I 'ad to show one or two of 'em pretty quick that a cap'n o' the foretop of the *Wasp* warn't no lady's maid!'

Christopher sat down upon the bunk. There was something very important he must say before any fresh relationships were established in this new world, which every minute drew away from the old to the music of the singing waters about its sides and the creaking of shrouds and timbers.

'Did you know, Williams,' he started as nonchalantly as he might, 'that besides the name I use I am also a baron and a count?'

'Good gracious, sir!' said Williams. 'You kep' it very dark!'

'I saw no reason to use the titles. Now we are going away—from everything; starting afresh, so to speak—I think I shall call myself by one of them in future.'

'I hope it runs well, sir,' said Williams, rubbing his clean-shaven chin with his hand, and looking up at him with singularly bright eyes under heavy eyebrows. 'Christopher Harnish, I allus thought, ran very well. Like poetry. Mis-ter Chris-toph-er Har-nish! Said slow it makes one think of wine coming slowly out of a full bottle!'

'I don't know whether it's so poetical, Williams: but I shall use it all the same. It is that of Graf von Tollendhal. Count Tollendhal, you can call me among English people. Between you and me I have had enough of Christopher Harnish to last me the remainder of my life!'

'Count Tollendale! . . . Count Tollendale!' Williams shook his head. He could find no music to the name. He was divided between regret at lost poetry and pleasure at the noble appellation. 'Do I say "My Lord", my Lord?'

'Just "sir" will be accurate in English. . . . But . . . er . . . Williams, I should like—that is to say it would be doing me a great favour if you would change your name, too!'

'Change my name? My name?' said Williams in great astonishment. 'But I ain't got any other to take. If you take my surname away, there's nothing left . . . except plain William! Not like your Lordship with a whole basketful to choose from. Williams isn't much of a name, but it's my own, and wot would my old father say? . . . I don't know as I could do that. Besides 'arf the crew already knows me!'

'You see, Williams,' said Christopher earnestly, opening a dispatch box, 'I want to lose every link with the Me of the past. I don't want to be reminded that Christopher Harnish ever existed. I needn't go into details, but I want to come back in a year or two someone else; not merely with new ideas and thoughts but with a new name. In this time in which I have got to make a new man, you will be the only link with the past: in your mere name you will remind me of it. I want you, but not your name. I don't mind what you call yourself!'

He unfolded a crackling banknote.

'Supposing . . . I make it worth your while to change your name? That would be only fair. Say twenty pounds, for the inconvenience!'

Williams protested.

He didn't want to change his name! He didn't want to be paid!

Well, perhaps he didn't really mind, after all! But he didn't want payment!

Well, if Mister—Count—and he fumbled over the name—really insisted! But not twenty pun'! He wouldn't take it! . . . Say, ten pun', if it must be!

So the ten-pound note was folded, put in one of the deep pockets of the sailor-like white trousers that he considered suitable for voyaging, and acknowledged with a sailor-like touch of the forelock. Christopher was watching the red sun set over the marshes when his man returned.

'Bosun 'n' Chips 'n' the "Doctor" 'n' I have been talking it over, sir,' he said respectfully. 'Chips's a reg'lar sea-lawyer! Says it wouldn't be legal without a receipt in proper form.'

He placed a narrow strip of paper, torn from the bottom of a bill of lading, on the table before his master. It ran:

'August 20th 1832.

'Recd. from Count Tollendall Esquire the sum of Ten Pounds for sole leggal right and use to and off my Name as from this present date.

signed William X.

witnesses: Jno. Clark, Bo's'n.
    Wm. Hopkins, Carpt'r.
    Saml. Yeo, Cook.
The Ship Camden
At Sea.'

'I couldn't put my name to it very well, sir, because when I'd sold it, I hadn't, so to speak, got one. So I put a cross agin my baptism name,' explained the late Williams.

The choice of a new surname kept him mentally stimulated for a great part of the voyage. The entire crew was called into consultation on the matter, their suggestions ranging from Montmorency to Whoggins—tentatively put forward by one of the apprentices on the score that it would be a novelty.

They were some hundred miles west of Brest when, presumably at the instigation of the ship's carpenter, who was something of a literary man—he decided to assume thenceforward the name of Camden in honour of the craft.

So known as Camden he was, until they were well into the 'roaring forties', and driving southwest through grey seas topped with foam like dirty snow. The activities of the crew in the rigging reminded him of older days when his nimbleness among the shrouds had won him the nickname of 'Spider'. It seemed a good name for a former captain of the foretop of the Wasp: another document was accordingly prepared, dated, and signed, recording that in longitude 19° 30′ W., latitude 40° 40′ North, 'William—formerly Williams—assumed the tittle and name of Spider for himself and his forbears in the presence of . . .'

Christopher gravely signed as a belated god-parent for Mr. William Spider.

Although the ship was large, there was only one other saloon passenger—an American, a little old man with white hair whose face was concentrated into an enormous wrinkle from which tributary furrows ran in every direction. His cabin being small he sat all day in the saloon, playing solitaire, smoking an unending succession of untidy cheroots and expectorating into the spittoon beside him. Three or four black hairs grew half-way up the bridge of his nose, the end of which twitched every twenty seconds or so with the regularity of the beat of a pendulum. He had one topic of conversation alone—the search of vanished cities and submerged continents, with particular reference to the possibility of finding the lost Seven Cities of Cibola somewhere in the wild mountains along the Rio Grande in Texas-Coahuila. When he embarked on the subject, which he did at least twice a week, the rate of nose-twitching and expectoration was greatly increased.

The captain was a prim Presbyterian who always wore a top-hat and double-breasted blue tail-coat: the first mate a soured Aberdonian with overwhelming grievances. The other officers may have been talkative among themselves, but a few words a day constituted the sum total of the conversation they exchanged with their passengers.

Christopher was thus thrown entirely upon his own resources; and found it no hardship.

Each morning that he awoke to see the sunlight—reflected from the restless waters—dancing on the deck above him, he found that the memories of the past had grown more dim. The days passed by, eventless but for the changing wonders of the sea; the appearance of some strange ship, a distant tossing thing across the molten silver of the Atlantic; the swooping of a bird from God knew where, with a flash of white on its under-wings as it wheeled about the masts against the wind; a whale bobbing like wet india-rubber out of a sea hummocked to the horizon by billows, which were crested with foam as brilliantly white as snow lying on ridges of grass after the wind.

He became a man without a past, unthinking of the future, treasuring only the present sensations in sight and sound.

They had been thirty days out when they ran into calm on the fringe of the Sargasso Sea, and lay motionless with unstirring sails on the vast sparkling plain.

Against the middle distance great reefs of orange-brown seaweed lay, with the ocean beyond rising—it seemed—to the horizon in a thin dark line, as if a coast high over the dusky sands of a distant seashore.

'It looks exactly like land,' said Christopher to the American who joined him at the poop-rail, wearing a round flat hat with the widest imaginable brim.

'Near enough, I figger,' answered Mr. Samuel P. Glasscock, 'to explain some of the legends of floating islands. Seaweed's probably the explanation of the story of St. Brandan's Isle. It's said to swim off the Irish coast in 'tarnal mist.' He spat thoughtfully into the glassy water. 'None of these stories and myths are jest pure fancy. They air built up on a foundation of some sort, yessir! The foundation mayn't be what you calc'late it oughta be, but it'll be thar jest the same, as solid as that thar bank of seaweed. It'll be a rock, a stone, an ole-time murder, a bunch of bones under a Celtic barrow. On'y the Awmighty can make suthin' outa nuthin'. Humanity can git no comfort outa its fancies and put no faith in them unless they air anchored good and sure to fact.'

'But when you harness your imagination to the earth, it is bound to become earthy. And it seems to me that the principal use for one's imagination should be to get away from earth,' said Christopher.

Mr. Glasscock spat over the ship's side once more.

'I've just spat into the Atlantic,' he remarked, and wagged a demonstrative finger at Christopher. 'If you think about that with all your imagination, you air stimulatin' your brain or takin' your mind off your troubles far more than by buildin' up baloney castles-in-the-air second-hand from po'try books. I've dropped such and such a fraction of an ounce of saliva tinctured with terbacca juice and full of mi-nute air bubbles into the sea. Thet may spell life or death to some small organism: it may give a flyin'-fish the belly-ache or becalm a nautilus. Perhaps that spittle may drift unbroken to the bank of seaweed and strand thar. And the little air bubbles be imprisoned under the fronds and lashes. Thet's an extreme instance, but if you follow up even such a thought as thet, it'll do you more durn good than blowin' castles in the air from bubbles. Make a castle on a fine hill-top that you see, or a city along a bayou where it winds jest out of sight! But if you build yourself a city of refuge out of other people's thoughts, then you'll put your foot through the floor when you come to tread in it in earnest.'

Christopher objected.

Mr. Glasscock spat over the side again. The eyes of both men followed the white blob into the water.

'I don' mind layin' two bits to a picayune,' said Mr. Glasscock, 'thet all your ideas and fancies and ideals—I sez it without disrespect—are second-hand. If I jedge your per-spective rightly. All based on books! Pretty imaginin's from books air no real comfort to a real man. And they give such a false idea of life that they may do him more harm 'n good. My kind of imaginin's air good man-made Montgolfier balloons thet'll lift you right off the earth if you want to—not airy bubbles thet'll blow away from you when you want to go aboard. A man kin git better ideals and ideas, too, from rubbin' up agin his fellers than from any amount of book learnin'.'

'But books are the greatest stand-by,' said Christopher in the most orthodox manner. 'They are friends who are always there, no matter where or how you are . . .'

'I like to chew over my thought myself,' replied Mr. Glasscock. 'Yessir! I don' like havin' my food chewed over fer me, whether it's fer my belly or my mind. I wuz out with Magee's expedition down to Texas in '12 and '13. I guess I wuz the on'y survivor after the force got cut up by Arredondo at the battle of Medina. They shoved me into jail in San Antonio de Bexar, 'n' thar I stayed two livelong years. Did I read? Nossir! I got me a Bible—for the looks of it! But I got me, too, a yard-wide plank of S'uthern red oak and yanked out a picture of the Flood. I had castles 'n' cities goin' down under the waves, 'n' the animiles from armadillo to zebra enterin' the Ark. Ef I couldn't git all I wanted outa that thar plank 'n' my old knife 'n' my brains, I'll be doggoned! I got so I knew the family history of the feller that made the last grab as the Ark floated off! I coulda told you the accommodation of ev'ry homestead thet went a-tumblin' under the flood. I warn't in the calobozo at San Antonio—I wuz back in the days of the Deluge!'

He spat once more into the water.

'I bin all over the world, lookin' fer lost cities,' said he. 'Thet plank gave me a taste for vanished things. I bin to the Ay-zores a-lookin' fer Atlantis—into the Indian jungles fer buried temples. I dug about in Tehualpec lookin' fer forgotten palaces of the Maya. I spec'lated in Newport, Wales, England, about Arthur's Camelot; and now I'm goin' up the Rio Grande—ole Arredondo's bin dead these many years—to find the Seven Cities of Cibola. I don' mind ef I don't find 'em: one brick—one stone'll do. I kin think 'em all out then! I kin see 'em!'

He turned to the companionway with one final expectoration:

'But I must have my brick.'

A breeze rustled: a wind loitered up, warm and wet as though from a laundry: a studding sail quivered like a boxer recovering from a knock-out: dry shrouds creaked under an almost forgotten strain: the ship—which for days had had the rigidity of an island—stirred slightly, and promised movement in the multitude of its whisperings in rigging and timbers.

Mr. Glasscock must have his brick!

So Margaret, two thousand miles away, had said that her imagination, too, must be rooted in realities before its magic tree could spring up and flower. With her realities—a picture, a chair, a tea-caddy—she had raised a protective fantasy such as he had been unable to do.

And Setoun! His models, his maps, his velocimanipedes and perambulating steam-kettles, provided him with escape into a world of enchantment! You had to have some solid scenery to make your fairyland, even if it were only two or three chairs and a rug—not just thoughts and fancies of a book, but something that was three-dimensional!

He refused to let himself think of his father, of the bleeding eyelessness of von Metzsch, of the goblin Great Duke unfolding his shameful history. Every night he read himself to sleep so that he might not lie awake thinking in the dark. But as they drew nearer to the forest-covered shores of the New World through the blue waters of the Gulf of Mexico, he found his mind harking back to Margaret—the Margaret he had played with during the long summer days; not the Margaret who had been Deb. He found that the fantasy she had created round herself was more real to him than the actualities of which he knew, and of which she had told him in a low voice, under the whispering elms. He could picture Margaret, but not the other unhappy child. He found his reason and his imagination refusing to admit that they could be one and the same person. He found himself prepared to forgive Margaret for having evoked a nightmare . . . and, at last, wondering if she were prepared to forgive *him* for having destroyed a dream.

When at length they came to anchor, and he set foot ashore in New Orleans after two months at sea, he would see her among the pretty women who thronged the narrow streets, or smiled from the galleried houses—in the turn of a head, or a fleeting expression, or the structure of a face.

In the window of a small shop beside a dark archway in Bourbon Street he found a gift for her. It was a French trinket box, in silver filigree, with a domed lid. Within there were compartments lined with faded velvet, some of them holding tiny vials with gold threads and flowers in their glass. The marvel of it was that the letters 'M. A.' were engraved on the shield it bore in front. So he bought it, and packed it very scrupulously, and sent it back to England in the care of the captain of the *Camden*. He wrote no letter with it, and two days later booked a passage in a schooner bound for Havana and the Caribbean.

Before he was due to sail, however, he had dinner with Glasscock in a French restaurant in the paved courtyard of a large house with green-painted balconies in Royal Street.

The old gentleman had ordered the meal with care—baked pompano with a salad large enough for a family; filets of beef ('Bull-beef', said he explanatorily; 'bin in Mexico long enough to git them dago idees thet cow-beef's on'y good fer wimmin') with roast yams and sweet corn; and every other local delicacy he could find. There was even a thin tart wine pressed from the wild mustang grape.

They smoked black cheroots and drank black, sweet coffee afterwards, under the rustling leaves of a palmetto, to the tinkle of a fountain. Then Mr. Glasscock fumbled in the tails of his coat for a moment, and produced something wrapped in a red handkerchief, which he placed on the table.

The vast wrinkle into which his face was concentrated, furrowed itself more deeply in what passed for a smile.

'Thet thar's my brick!' said he, and folded his lower lip over the upper in a gesture that implied conviction and satisfaction.

'I bought it,' he continued, undoing the wrapping, 'from a Cajun from Natchitoches, up the Red River. He got it from a Wichita Injun.'

It was an elaborate necklace of rough turquoises, some of them carved into grotesque masks.

'Can I build on thet?—Yessir, yessirree! Am I goin' to look fer the Seven Cities of Cibola?—Yessirree!'

So Mr. Glasscock had got his brick!

Christopher sat with the heavy thing coiled in his cupped hands. An almond-eyed mask glared up at him out of the mass of blue stones veined with brown.

'I wonder what city that came from?' he said. 'What king wore it? Or was it a high priest's ephod? Or the dowry of a princess?'

'Aha!' chuckled Mr. Glasscock. 'Now you're tryin' to pinch my bricks. I tell ya, I'm gwine up the old Mississippi, an' up the ole Red River, fifteen hunderd miles 'n' more, to fin' the place whar thet thar Wichita foun' it. I'm gwinter risk cypress swamps, 'n' Injuns, 'n' alligators, 'n' moccasins, 'n' rattlers—fifteen hunderd miles on 'em—ter fin' my cities! 'N' ef I don'—well, I got this, 'n' I'll still know they're thar!'

He took the bauble back: the bright eyes amid the wrinkles under the bushy brows and wide black hat glanced swiftly from necklace to young and interested face.

'King's? Priest's? Princess's?' He folded his lips up and remained silent for a while, but for the spirt of his expectoration.

'Thet Wichita sez to the Cajun thet in the big plains, up the Red River country, thar wuz a ruin with three hunderd rooms! . . . Comin' too?'

He shot the invitation out so suddenly and folded up his lips so firmly afterwards—as if he blamed them for a sad error—that Christopher gave him a close scrutiny to gauge the sincerity of the offer.

'Dunno why you air gwine lookin' fer happiness outa dreams, boy! Et ain't none o' my business. But *I* gotta fin' 'em! *I* gotta fin' bricks to build 'em on.'

To Christopher's astonishment Mr. Glasscock became extremely emotional. He blinked the vast pits in which his eyes were set, and corrugated his face into a relief map of the world. His explanation was given in a husky shaking voice.

'I warn't no chicken w'en I got me a young lady,' said he. 'Et wuz after my dad died in '15. I wuz a matter of forty. She wuz the purtiest thing between Charleston and Portland, Maine. She . . . Wal, she 'n' her ole momma bin stayin' up with an a'nt at Richmond, Virginia. How should they come back? "Why," sez porc 'Titia to her a'nt, "we'll take one o' Samuel's ships. One o' the ships he's allus fussin' over." So back they set out fer Charleston in my schooner *Eagle*. . . .' He stopped for so long that Christopher thought the story was going to be left at that crisis.

'The *Eagle* wuz rotten,' said Mr. Glasscock. 'Her timbers were rotten: her cordage wuz rotten: her bolts were rotten: a man coulda put his foot through her planks. I knew it! 'N' the *Eagle* never came to port! She went down like a sieve in a screamin' storm off the North Car'lina coast! . . . I'm a rich man, so now I look fer buried cities, 'n' lost cities—jesta fergit!'

Faintly above the hum and manifold noises of the city, from somewhere near at hand, came through the dusk rhythmic bumping and snatches of a strange high chant.

'Them niggers dancin' a voodoo dance in some cellar, 'roun' an obeah man with a fetish of bone 'n' a hank of hair! . . . They gotta have their brick, too!'

Said Christopher, shamefacedly affected by the contagion of emotion:

'Bricks for dreams! . . . I believe I'd like a brick, Sam! . . . I'll come with you, if I may.'

Chapter 32

Mr. Glasscock's Second Brick

SIX MONTHS LATER THE EXPEDITION REAPPEARED, DRAG-
ging its way slowly through the mesquite and huisache scrub;
across bright green rivers in gorges overhung with giant willows
and pecan; across prairies, gay with blue-bonnets and wine-cups,
where distant long-horn cattle grazed; along trails where fire-flies
threaded their dance; through swamps where the trunks of cypress rose, from the black water that moccasins loved, to the
black night of their boughs all hung with Spanish moss.

In the rolling hills above San Antonio de Bexar they struck
the river and followed it toward the sea. Mr. Samuel P. Glasscock had not found the Seven Cities of Cibola.

Way up in the Palo Duro country, Glasscock and Christopher
had ridden out alone, from their camp in the early morning, pros-
pecting across a prairie as interminable as the sea, studded with
islets of scrub and stunted oaks.

They rode silently northwest, jack-rabbits skipping from their
path. Once a breakfast-party of turkey-buzzards heaved themselves
regretfully into the air from a feast on something very dead: an
armadillo slid into the long grass; and, in the distance, a herd of
mustangs galloped away in a cloud of dust.

Glasscock reined up his 'paint' horse with its melancholy white
face.

He pointed an arm to the far horizon where a dark rim told
of a coast of tall timber.

There was a stiff breeze blowing, but, from a patch of scrub
between them and the woodland, a tall column of grey smoke

rose against the sky and remained vertical, unaffected by the wind,
its head spreading out umbrella-wise.

'Injuns!' said he. 'Them thar Comanches! Bad folk! Signal-
smoke! . . . Look!'

The grey column suddenly vanished, as if it had been extinguished, like a candle-flame, by a single puff. Then, a moment
later, it was answered, many miles north, by another pillar that
rose to an immense height, spread its top like the monstrous
sunshade of a toadstool, and disappeared.

'Injuns! Don't like them signals! For what air they signallin'?'
reflected Mr. Glasscock, folding his lower lip over the upper in
a thoughtful manner. He made up his mind. 'I reckon we don't
wait ter see. Right here's whar wise men git—'n' git quick! Let's
git!'

He turned his horse's head and set off at a lope toward the
greater security of their camp.

An antelope careered past them—a biscuit-toss away. Then
another.

Then a whole herd—at no easy gallop, but in a panic flight,
the dust scuttering under their small hoofs, and so blindly that
one went neck-and-crop over a tussock.

Glasscock reined in. He cast one quick look over his shoulder.

'Christ-Awmighty!' he said. 'They've fired the prairie!'

They had.

Miles behind them, like a tidal wave, a low grey billow had
sprung up and surged over the landscape. The horns of the crescent formed by the smoke were fifteen miles apart, and rose in a
sort of spray into the air.

'We gotta git goin'!' said Mr. Glasscock. 'An' git goin' good!
Thisyere's death, young feller!'

He crammed his wide hat firmly on to his head, took a reef
in his reins, and set spurs to his horse.

They went thudding across the grasslands, where the last sea-
son's growth—eighteen inches high and as dry as tinder—was
mingled with the greenery. Vultures and hawks followed their
flight, and swooped at intervals on small squeaking fugitives whom
panic had driven from their lairs.

A bitter-sweet reek was swept along on the wind, and, looking back for one fleeting instant, Christopher saw that the wall of fire and smoke was quickly gaining on them. Tongues of flame flashed up at intervals: and, in the stiff breeze, blazing tufts of grass—like gouts of foam—were torn from the edge of the wave and tossed a hundred yards ahead. There was a dull continuous roar, as of an angry tide beating against a low shore.

It was then that Mr. Glasscock's 'paint' chose to stumble, throw his rider heavily over his head, rise, and streak like a mad thing with red distended nostrils for the horizon.

Christopher reined in with difficulty.

Samuel P. lay motionless on the sandy trail. His hat had fallen off: a little blood stained his thin lips: he looked no longer a live man, but a caricature by Rowlandson of Dr. Syntax, or a Punchinello hurled from the stage of a puppet theatre. An astonished horny-frog, with antlers projecting from his head like a palaeozoic monster, sat by a limp hand and speculated.

Christopher dismounted, looped his reins over his arm, clutched savagely at the bit of his plunging horse, and struck it yet more savagely on the poll with his pistol butt, as it reared in frantic fear.

While the beast was still half-stunned he bent over Glasscock, and scooped under the thin body with his free arm.

God knew if the horse could bear him alone to safety! God would certainly guarantee nothing for two of them!

He realized that a stream of blasphemy was pouring from his mouth, and that he was shivering with fright.

Glasscock sagged over his supporting arm like a broken doll. The horse reared again.

Suddenly he found that fear had left him, as he clung to the demented horse with one arm through reins and cheek-strap, and the other holding a limp body with loosely swinging limbs.

Would Margaret ever know—he wondered—that he had met with death horribly while rescuing his friend? In the flash of one second he heard the voice of a priest booming up into the vaulted roof of Southwell Minster four thousand miles away; saw a fat thrush outlined on a cedar bough on the lawn at Kensington Park Place; and knew that at that moment his ghost was walking through the front-door of Margaret's house, and climbing the steep stair, and merging for ever into the portrait of Tom Atchill, into the dark corner at the half-landing, into the spinet within the shabby drawing-room, so that in some strange way the fantasy of her home became still more real with the accession of his disembodied spirit and will. When he was dead he would no longer be Christopher Harnish or Count Tollendhal, but Anthony Atchill—'dear Mr. Tony', who had sent strange gifts from Louisiana and been killed by Red Indians in Texas: he would undo the evil he had wrought to the fabric of Margaret's life. He would not go to heaven when his bones lay calcined among the funeral crape of burned grass, but to that more lovely paradise that Margaret had built of shabby furniture and old-fashioned pictures and battered silver. His spirit would talk with the beautiful spirit that was Margaret Atchill, free of the encumbrance of the flesh and ancestry they hated. He realized then with sudden clarity of vision how little the body mattered—that poor mechanism which did not always answer the direction of the pilot-soul.

Man and beast swung in narrow circles, as the horse gyrated with flattened ears, and foam like fat soap-suds dripping over the bridle.

The wall of fire leaped on in a galloping tide: it was barely two miles away, and as it neared so it seemed to increase its speed. The grass was alive with fugitive creatures; birds wheeled and screamed overhead: a snake slid up the trail faster than a running man: little puffs of smoke rose in advance of the rolling fire like range-finding shots by hidden artillery.

Glasscock suddenly stiffened, slid from Christopher's arm, and slipped to a sitting position on the tuft where he had originally fallen. His eyes became wide open, and the furrows in his face creased in a smile.

'Guess sump'n's bruck!' said he. 'Git your tinder. 'S our only chance!'

'Tinder?' echoed Christopher, fumbling with his free hand in a side-pocket, and extracting it in the wrapping of greased cloth that kept it dry.

'Frontier rule. Fire agin fire,' said Glasscock.

He rose to his feet with infinite difficulty, one hand pressed against his side, and his face screwed up with pain until it looked like a baked apple.

'Guess sump'n's vurry bruck!' said he.

He took flint and steel from his pocket, struck a spark, and ignited the tinder which he had placed in a handful of dry grass.

The stuff blazed at once with a flame that was white in the sunlight. Glasscock, with the action of a man sowing, one hand still pressed against his side, swung the torch to and fro amid the dry grass beside the trail.

While Christopher hung to his horse's head, the old man lit a fresh torch, and sprayed fire anew fan-wise from where they stood. He staggered by tremendous effort for a hundred yards or so along a line parallel to the advancing death, setting light to the dry grass as he went. The wind seized his offering, drove thin white flame and dense white smoke in a long slant before them. The fire fizzed; it crackled; it rose to a roar; it sprang onward, and away from them, as if it were the herald of the tornado of smoke and flame that came behind—as if it were greedy to destroy what it might before greater destruction should overtake its puny efforts.

It spread sideways: it raced on: it was yards away, leaving a blackened waste behind it which blew in powder and small intense sparks after it.

'Fire agin fire!' said Mr. Glasscock, laughing and coughing, and doubled with pain so that his body, in its baggy clothes, looked as furrowed and wrinkled as his extraordinary face.

'Guess sump'n's 'stonishingly bruck!' said he, and supported himself against the saddle of the sweating horse.

They walked slowly along the narrow trail of sand through the desolation of their making, in the wake of the fire of their making.

The moving wall behind them was eighty feet high, and of dense black and grey solidity with a flickering red line of fire at its base. Its summit was rounded and hollowed as are the peaks of clouds or the roof of a great forest; and above it hung a thin shapeless fog, into which stray tatters of darker smoke would whirl.

The heat was that of a furnace; Christopher found the sweat

pouring off his face until the red handkerchief knotted round his neck was a sopping rag.

The sky above was now so grey with smoke that the sun was hidden, and the air was full of hot dust.

'What about the others?' said Christopher.

'Other side of gulch,' said Mr. Glasscock. 'They're all right!'— and slipped to his knees, clinging with one hand to a stirrup leather.

But by then they were several hundred yards from where they had started their fire; and the conflagration behind them, had come to the edge of the waste, had found no prey, had parted, and was passing in a paroxysm of furious crackling and thunder to the right and left at some distance.

They made the passage to safety, like the hosts of Israel, through a Red Sea—of flame.

Glasscock made nought of his injuries when they reached camp; but it soon became obvious that they could not push on towards the misty lands where lay his fabulous cities. It was apparent that he had suffered internal injuries, besides the more obvious hurts of broken ribs; so they turned and travelled south to make their way to one of the Missions near the coast.

Soon, however, he could not ride at all, and the former-Williams devised a horse-litter for him, with the aid of a blanket and two young fir saplings. Even then they could not proceed at more than walking pace, and it was seven days before they found a practicable crossing of the Colorado River.

Each day the journey that the wounded man could support became shorter. He spat blood when he coughed: there were no wrinkles on his face now, for all the flesh had wasted until it lay like a fine dried paste over the bones of his skull.

He would not stop at San Antonio. He must see the sea—although one of the Mission fathers who examined his injuries shook his head and protested. They hired, however, more horses from the Indians, and pressed onward along the trail across the rolling prairies.

At night they would make a little bower of branches under a mesquite or scrub oak. There he would lie quietly with blood on his lips and shallow breath, looking up into the dark interlacement above him, his bony fingers playing with the necklace of turquoises.

'Say, brother!' said he one night, as Christopher sat silently beside him, watching the yellow and red of the camp fire with the Indians squatted about it, and the grey smoke rising in a thin line against the star-lit night. 'Say, brother! I calc'late thisyere brick ain't goin' ter be much use ter me. I guess I passed the stage o' lookin' fer vanished cities.'

He pushed the necklace along the hairy brown blanket with a tiny feeble gesture, as if renouncing it for ever.

Christopher watched uncomprehending.

'I reckon you'd better have it. Mout be mortar fer bricks o' yours.'

' "King's? Priest's? Princess's?" ' quoted Christopher taking it up, and letting the great dull stones slip slowly through his fingers. 'You'll want it again. The Cities of Cibola wait you still, Sam!'

'The Cities of Cibola don' spect me now,' said Mr. Glasscock. 'Et's another city thet waits fer me!'

His eyes in their hollows—like water shining at the bottom of deep wells—watched the pale glint of the stones in the firelight.

'I want another brick!' he said; and his breath seemed to bubble between each syllable. 'Another brick! . . . Fer another city!'

There was a long silence.

'I've got a Bible,' said Christopher at last. 'I'll fetch it!'

Very feebly the other shook his head and lay staring upwards.

'I—can't see thet other city,' he said. 'I've allus gone lookin' fer secret cities. . . . But fust I've allus had to have a brick— sump'n to touch and feel. Doubtin' Thomas, p'raps! . . . But I've allus asked the Lawd fer a brick fust—one little brick!'

Christopher rose quietly. He went out into the scrub with his knife.

When he came back he pushed into the almost nerveless clasp a rough cross fashioned of two huisache twigs bound together with long grass.

Glasscock said nothing; but he raised his heavy head and so held it, regarding the emblem which quivered between his fingers.

Christopher folded up an old coat and placed it under his

head, and wiped the sweat from off his brow with a handkerchief. He sat down cross-legged, and, holding the book between his knees slanting downward toward the fire-light, read from Revelations the description of 'that great city, the holy Jerusalem, descending out of Heaven from God'.

' "And had a wall great and high, and had twelve gates, and at the gates twelve angels, and names written thereon . . .
' "And the building of the wall of it was of jasper: and the city was pure gold, like unto clear glass." '

In the cool, a little before dawn, they were on their way again across the downlands, so that, coming from the northwest along the trail, they saw far away over the thickets the sunrise gilding the cross upon the grey bell-tower of La Bahía Mission.

Christopher, walking beside the litter, told of it to the dying man.

There was the faintest convulsion among the myriad lines on Glasscock's face, as though he would smile; and he made a feeble effort to lift himself to look across the scrub—a mere shudder of his frame.

'I'm a good Methody,' he said in a whisper at length, 'but—but I allus—liked—a brick.' And died.

They buried him outside the settlement of Goliad, above the tree-clad gully through which the river ran. There was a tussock of lantana at his head and purple-red wine-cups starred the pale grass about his grave.

'He was a good man, sir!' said the former-Williams laying his machete down, and going on his knees and pressing the grass tufts back into place upon the mound. 'I never thought to like a Yankee. Difficult to tell, sir, as who's a gen'elman! But Mr. Glasscock was—for all his spittin'! . . . It's a pity we ain't got no tombstone for him!'

They pressed on to the coast, and then along the shore trail to Corpus Christi, winding for long miles under wooded bluffs broken by bright green lawns and shadowy pools in which egrets and ibis fished.

A cardinal flew across their path, a flash of red.

'It's a pity,' said the ex-Williams to his master for the third time that day, 'that we couldn't give Mr. Glasscock a proper tombstone!'

It seemed to worry him to think of Glasscock, lying friendless and far away, without any label to his bones against the Resurrection.

'We'll put up a tablet to his memory in Southwell Minster,' said Christopher. 'Nottinghamshire is a few thousand miles off, but Mr. Glasscock will know where to find it.'

The man cleared his throat as if he would speak, rode a mile or so in silence behind his master; cleared his throat again, and spoke in an embarrassed manner to the back before him.

'I've bin a-thinking, sir,' he said, 'that it don't seem right Mr. Glasscock shouldn't have a tombstone. . . . Not right, at all! . . . He's got a name, an' I ain't got one! Leastways, I'm not that taken with Spider after all! I've bin thinking it 'ud be a nice sort of memorial in a manner o' speaking, if I was to take his name. Quite respectful-like, you know, sir. Jest in memory of him—wot was a real gen'elman, albeit he was a Yankee!'

'I'm sure Mr. Glasscock would be very touched,' said Christopher, smiling to himself, and without turning his head. 'But I should settle down to something definite pretty soon. Or you'll get confused—yourself!'

'I shouldn't dream of changin' arterwards, sir,' protested the ex-Williams reproachfully to the back. 'It would be disrespekful to alter it, once it had been used. Of course I shouldn't arst you to call me by it, sir! Orkard for you to call a servant by a gen'elman's name! P'raps you could speak to me as William— my baptism name? It would be a great comfort to me to think I'd given Mr. Glasscock a memorial, in a manner of speakin'!'

And so it was all arranged before they reached the settlement at Corpus, where Christopher found a Mexican fisherman to take them to Galveston Island. Thence, after ten days' wait, an American schooner carried them back to New Orleans.

At the agent's a budget of letters awaited him from England, including one addressed to 'Anthony Atchill Esquire, by the favour of Chris. Harnish Esquire'. He dared not open the folded and sealed sheet there before an inquisitive clerk, but walked back to his hotel, clapping his hand at intervals against the pocket where it lay to assure himself of its existence.

He flung himself into a rocking-chair on the immensely wide balcony of the hotel, and stared across the canyon of the street, which was full of shadow and noise and the smell of ripe fruit and newly watered pavement.

There was only one other occupant—a long gentleman in a wide straw hat and white suit, sitting with his feet upon the rail of the elaborate blue-green ironwork of the *galerie*, and muttering to himself.

Christopher drew out his letter and stared at it. That fold of stiffish paper, four inches long by three inches wide, with ink already becoming rusty, had traversed the Atlantic and the Gulf of Mexico, linked New Orleans with a Kentish village, linked Margaret Atchill with a personage she had conjured up into reality. He stamped out his cheroot.

'Clam chowder!' said the long gentleman in white sharply, staring up at his feet and at the two Creole ladies on the *galerie* of the house opposite.

Christopher cut round the seal.

As he did so he felt that he was releasing a spell; that in the mirror of his mind, if he could only look within it, there were reflected the rose-tinted face of Margaret, and the little house where the low hills curved from the valley of the lost river.

He unfolded the sheet contained in the wrapper; and the lines of writing across it, and the single word 'Margaret' at the end made it a paper of enchantment. For he stood once more against the window of the little house. He looked within. He saw her dark head bowed over the writing-table between two candles—the smooth gleam of the silver inkstand that had been given by the Fellows of his College to Thomas Atchill—a friendly fire-light and shadows in the low room behind her. He saw her put the feathery tip of her quill between her teeth. She raised her head and saw his soul standing outside and smiled, although he was four thousand miles away. So would she have seen him too, and smiled, even if he had stood and watched her all life and death away.

He shaped the word 'Margaret!' with his lips.

'S'rimp gumbo!' said the long gentleman thoughtfully rocking himself. His sallow puffy face was stippled with enlarged pores, and yet riven with deep lines, as if years of shrimp gumbo and corn whisky had not been able to efface the trail of annoyances sustained a quarter of a century before.

Christopher schooled himself to read his letter word by word, so that the initial pleasure should be protracted.

'It was very kind of you, my dear'—she wrote, without preamble —'to send me your gift from New Orleans. I have placed it on a table in my room, by itself, and filled it with all my treasures, and look at it, and think of the thousands of miles it has travelled, and wonder where you bought it. I fancy it is a box that has magic in it, or dreams: or perhaps you put a thought in one of the little compartments that are lined with velvet.

'You see I know where to write to. Lady Setoun came a few days after you sailed, and had tea with Miss Comfort under the apple trees and won the old lady's heart. She came again when I had come back'—she had struck out the words 'from abroad'—'and ate toasted muffins with us, and admired the view, and won my heart, too.

'I am making a little summer house in the corner where we weeded so busily, because from it you can see the red roof of a distant tithe barn across the grey of the marsh—so red that it is like a glowing coal.

'We think and talk of you very often—Miss Comfort and I. The old lady is so worried lest you get scalped by Indians, and lose all your yellow hair and come back bald.

'If you can buy gifts, then you can write letters. So write and assure us that you are so far safe.'

He read it again; and then once more, and weighed the sentences sitting back in his chair with his chin on his chest, and a half smile of sheer ecstasy on his lips.

So Charlotte had been to see her! Charlotte had said nothing about it. He wondered if they had just exchanged the chatter of strangers, or . . .

He knew now that he loved Margaret with something much

deeper than passion: knew that Margaret Atchill was a reality—more than a reality, immortality itself; for the soul that had called her into being, and had wrested her from disaster, must endure for eternity.

Bitter scorn and hatred of himself welled up. So vivid was the recollection of the shame he had put upon her that he said loudly, 'Fool!' and rapped the fist of one hand against the open palm of the other.

The long gentleman looked sharply round, and revolved the cheroot in his mouth rapidly from right to left, as if revolving similarly a desire to interrogate.

'S'rimp gumbo!' said he at length, continuing his meditations on the dinner he proposed to enjoy; and out loud, for he intended to allow no stranger to infringe his monopoly of soliloquy.

'S'rimp gumbo!—Baked pompano!—Tenderloin!—Candied yams!'

Christopher, however, had passed on in thought.

Margaret had risen unaided, unguided, from misery and despair; she had emerged, smiling, strong in herself, and still strong enough to give out strength—and forgiveness. While he . . .

Now, deliberately opening his mind to remembrance, he was surprised how faint the terrors had become. He thought of his father almost without bitterness, and of all the others of his blood with a dispassionate contempt. Even the tragedy of Eckie seemed to have been inevitable.

How faint the terrors! . . . But how strong the shame!

There came to his mind that other betrayal, the shameful thing he had done—the wilful destruction of the evidence of Cumberland's plot.

He saw himself once again piling the letters from Dunscore's dispatch boxes into the stove, and watching them vanish in a great gout of yellow flame. He had avenged himself upon his family! Upon his ogre uncles? Yes, and upon an innocent child! A child who, like himself, might well desire to break away from all the old traditions of hate and dishonour; might well set up a new and prouder line if ever she came to the throne.

The anger of a boy might have altered the history of England; have wrecked a dynasty-to-be; have let loose a civil war.

He was a traitor—not to the past and its traditions, but to the future, and the traditions that were to be.

Once again he hit his fist against his hand.

'Say, brother!' said the long gentleman in white, turning his head slightly. 'Ef you're gwine ter call anyone a fool agin, I'd be right glad to know that present company's excepted.'

'I was not aware, sir,' said Christopher flushing, 'that I had addressed any remark to you! . . . I will if you like!'

In his annoyance that he should have betrayed his anger with himself thus publicly, he looked so furious that the long gentleman subsided and rocked himself round in his rocking chair until his back was turned. The long gentleman had recollected that a little lady from Rampart Street was to help him eat his dinner, and that a visit to the Duelling Oaks might seriously affect his programme, which included bed for two but not coffin for one.

'Gumbo!' said the long gentleman in a subdued tone, calming himself with the thought.

'Gumbo!—Squab chicken!—Fried egg-plant!—Lima beans!'

Stray phrases in the correspondence he had found in Dunscore's dispatch boxes flashed through Christopher's mind. He remembered particularly the reference to work among the armed forces of the Crown, and the constitution of 'Lodges'—whatever they were—in North America and Bermuda. Or was it the Bahamas? Or —perhaps—the Barbados? All he could remember was that the place began with a 'B'.

He rose.

The long gentleman, at the scrape of the chair, cast a glance over his shoulder. He expectorated.

His voice rose in a triumphant chant:

'Stewed corn!—Berry pie!—Oyster brochette!—Bacon 'n' greens!'

Christopher went to his shuttered bedroom; among his baggage he found a small map-book, and lay with it under the mosquito net upon the bed, searching among the pages. The names dotted round the pear-drop shapes of India, Africa, and the Americas wakened no echoes in his mind: but amid the Mediterranean puddle, spotted with islands, the word 'Malta' stood out. Malta! He was certain there had been mention of a 'Lodge' among the garrison there.

Margaret had forgiven him: but he must deserve that forgiveness. . . . He could not face her until lost honour had been restored. If it took him across the world he must find that honour, before he could hope to enter into her magic world.

Hot on the decision he went down to the quays in the steamy afternoon.

Chapter 33

A Gentleman in Search of a Plot

$\mathscr{C}\!\!\!\mathscr{S}\!\!\!\mathscr{S}\!\!\!\mathscr{Q}$

IT WAS A SEARCH ON WHICH HE SPENT MANY MONTHS; that took him from Malta to Corfu, and thence to Alexandria, on his way to Gibraltar.

He played the High Tory aristocrat loitering across the world. His rank and obvious wealth made him a welcome guest at messes where Whiggism was tantamount to treason, an affected accent the patent of gentility, and snobbery the sauce in which to serve middle-class manners. By common consent his money was won from him at cards, and he was sponged on for loans and drinks; in return he had the doubtful pleasure of eating bad dinners, listening to bad jokes, and hearing an infinite amount of twaddle about women and horses.

He learned little, however, beyond the fact that Orange Lodges were in existence in the army. Of the real object beneath their ostensible policy of propaganda against Romanism his discreet inquiries could ascertain nothing—till he arrived in Alexandria in a Neapolitan schooner.

The ship put into port for urgent repairs, and Christopher went ashore and stayed at a small hotel owned by a Provençal from Arles, and built round a tiny colonnaded court. The only other English guest was a disgruntled major of the Sappers who had been sent to study the possibilities of the overland route to India, could get no reply to his letters to Authority, and was marooned, drinking himself to death.

Christopher took pity on the man. They went on expeditions together, through the cluttered ruins without the town, to the sandy wastes of Sidi Bishr; rode at night by the dark phosphorescent waters that broke in green fire and foam along the endless miles of beach beyond the forts, towards the wilds of Tripoli; investigated miserable villages where children with sore eyes made pies of camel dung, amid clouds of flies.

'Bloody country! Bloody country!' grumbled Major Hargreaves flicking his whip at an importunate beggar in tattered blue *galabeya*, whose eyes were filming over with cataract. 'And the bloody Government keeps me assing about here when I might be comfortably at home in Woolwich! Just like these bloody Whigs! Never make up their mind about anything—damn 'em! . . . Well, they'll find out! They'll find out!'

Christopher discovered a new interest in the man.

He insisted on Hargreaves dining with him that night—his birthday, he said—and paid a fabulous price for alleged steak with sweet potatoes and two large bottles of so-called Burgundy.

Afterwards they sat in his bare whitewashed room, with the lattices thrown open to the night and drank fiery Greek brandy by the light from two Provençal lamps shaped like oranges of glass set on top of high brass candlesticks.

It was not difficult to get Hargreaves to talk politics—generally. He did not become specific until Christopher cursed Catholic Emancipation and the Reform Act of two years before.

'D'you know, my dear major,' said Christopher, 'the Reform Act's cost me many a pretty penny. I'd a nice little pocket borough which was worth quite a bit, between you and me! Where's it now? Washed out! Vanished! And they've given the seat in Parliament to a lot of dirty mechanics!'

'Hard luck, old boy,' said Hargreaves a little thickly, helping himself to more brandy. 'Hard, hard luck! Very! Hard luck, indeed!'

He was a large man with a small screwed-up red face under a bulging bald forehead. Every time he repeated a phrase—which was very often—he screwed up his face still more, as if he were trying to get his features into the smallest compass possible.

'It's all very well saying "Hard luck!" ' grumbled Christopher, 'but what am I going to do about it? Nothing is safe nowadays! They take my property without compensation! They'll take more next time!'

'You wait! You wait and see!' said Major Hargreaves. 'P'raps they will, and p'raps they won't. More likely they won't. More likely!'

And again he screwed and unscrewed his face, and flashed a look, meant to be very cunning, from glazed blue eyes that seemed to be all whites.

'How do you mean?'

Christopher took off his light coat as he spoke, and flung it on the bed as though his remark were but the small change of conversation.

'You'll shee! You'll shee!' said Major Hargreaves throwing off his coat too, and sitting very upright and mysterious in a white shirt sodden with sweat. He unfurled his face so that he could take another swig of brandy, found it conformable to the palate, and slightly relented—'Not jus' yet, of course! Not jus' yet! Oath to old Silly-Billy, y'know!'

'Old Silly-Billy! Of course!' remarked Christopher nodding sagely, although entirely at a loss.

'Took oath to old Shilly—Silly-Billy! And his heirs and shuc-successors! But what I say is—Who's to be his heirs and shuccessors? Who's to be? Who's to be?'

'Ah!' said Christopher. 'Now if you were to ask me . . .'

But Major Hargreaves did not want to ask him—or anybody. Major Hargreaves was quite satisfied to ask himself rhetorically, and leave the question unanswered—for a while.

'I've been in the shervice shirty—thirty years,' he announced. 'I've been put upon and kept down—put upon! Put upon! Put upon! But zey'll shoon—soon know all about it! Or my name's not Tiger—old Tiger, they called me in Bengal!—Tiger Hargreaves. I'll show 'em! We'll show 'em!'

'After King William . . .'

'J'ew think a young woman ought to be at the head of the army and the navy? J'ew think a bit of a gal with her mind on ribbonsh —ribbonsh—ribbonsh—should be head-of-army, 'n' navy? . . . Becaush if you do—thenyourafool! Yeshir! You're a fool. You're a fool! You're a fool!'

Tiger Hargreaves made the candlesticks rattle with the blow he gave the table. He flung himself back in his wooden chair, crossed his white-trousered legs, and knocked the ash of his cigar off on to his lap.

Christopher hurried to disclaim any such preposterous belief.

'Yesh you do! Yesh you do!' persisted the Tiger. 'You're one of the prettiesh—pretties that'll like a young 'ooman tatting on the throne! Tatting! Tatting! Nysshe thought for a gemlem'n! School-girl sitting on the throne!'

Christopher determined to risk it.

'All wrong!' he said. 'Quite wrong! I think'—and he spoke very slowly so that the import of what he said should impinge on the dulled brain of the other—'We ought to have the Salic Law in England!'

For a moment he thought he had gone too far. The Tiger straightened his crumpled face. He shot a look, in which alarm was mingled with suspicion, at the younger man: and then a wave of alcoholic confidence overwhelmed him. He filled his tumbler to the brim:

'Goo' boy!' he mumbled. 'Ver' goo' boy! Here's to—youknow-who! . . . Shalic-ic Law . . . Ver' good!'

He made a cabalistical gesture with his right hand as he set his glass down; seemed dissatisfied with the effort, made it again: and so spent two or three minutes watching with screwed-up eyes and a puzzled expression, swollen-jointed fingers writhing in an effort to make some secret sign.

After a while he forgot what he was about, and would have fallen asleep upon the table, if Christopher had not shouted suddenly:

'So you're one of us!'

As the other furled his eyelids, Christopher flashed a movement of his right hand close to them—a mystic muddled movement of thumb and little finger. He hoped it would pass for the signal which the Tiger had been attempting.

Hargreaves drew himself up, and swayed to and fro over the table, a tremendous smile revealing long yellow teeth like a horse's.

'Goo' boy! Goo' boy!' said he. 'Ver' pleashed! I'm Dep-deputy Mashter—Master, Lodge 83. Woo-wool-wich Gran' Military! Dep-deputy Mashter. Ver' pleashed to meetabro'er! Ver' pleashed! Ver' pleashed!'

'Salic Law's just common sense!' suggested Christopher.

'Shallie Claw—Sallie Law!' said the Tiger, drawing himself up as if he had been a respectable spinster before whom the name of a young woman of ill-fame had been mentioned. 'Who's talking of Shallic Law?'

'You were,' said Christopher.

'Oh!' He meditated upon this new angle to the situation. 'That's different thing—very different thing! We'll shee about this Shalic—Sallie Claw! We'll shee—we'll shee—we'll shee! You'll shee, my boy! You'll shee! Ev'rybody'll shee!'

There was obviously nothing to be got from the man in his present condition! It was equally obvious that to a certain extent he was a repository of secrets. A repository that would have to be broached, even if it took three months of solid drinking of fiery brandy only remotely acquainted with the grape.

Hanging outside the window by a thong was a porous earthen jar full of water deliciously cold.

'You're a bit sleepy, old fellow,' said Christopher, fetching the vessel. 'Too early yet! I'll give you a real stinger that'll wake you up. New Orleans stinger!'

The other benevolently watched the preparation of a deadly mixture: absinthe strained through sugar into chill water that suddenly became opal, and brandy poured atop till the fluid looked like a draught of the Alabama River in flood.

'Not shleepy! Not shleepy at all!' protested the Tiger, whose dimmed intelligence was still capable of realizing the unusual appearance of the beverage. 'Looksh like something the dog brought up!'

'My God!' said Christopher in seeming indignation. 'I go to all the trouble of mixing this for you—and then you complain!'

Tears came to the Tiger's eyes.

'Shorry! Shorry! Un-ungra'ful hound! Shay you forgive me, ole boy!'

He polished off the glassful: looked in profound surprise at Christopher: hiccuped, meditated a moment on his internal and cerebral reactions with still profounder surprise, and toppled forward on to the table as if he had been pole-axed.

A moment later Christopher was quietly going through his coat pockets to find nothing except a little money, a letter to a banker's agent, and an epistle from his 'affectionate Clara'.

He cast a look at the stunned man, and went out into the corridor with one of the lamps.

Hargreaves's door was opposite, and open. He appeared to have only two valises, but with their contents he had been able to transform his stuffy bedroom into a close resemblance to the junkroom of a slop-dealer. Piles of half-clean clothes, with the sour smell of sweat in them, were on the chairs and tables, and were revealed by the feeble yellow flame in the yawning mouths of his baggage.

Christopher dived into the unsavoury jumble.

Tiger was obviously an Empire-builder of the old school. It was clear from the condition of his belongings that he would be quite happy to set off anywhere, at the traditional moment's notice, without even the traditional toothbrush, provided there was plenty of brandy in the offing.

Except for Clara he appeared to have no correspondents. There was, however, a manuscript book full of elaborate notes on the road from Alexandria to Suez, and a complete résumé of the tranship-ment facilities. From the back of the book dropped out two greasy and thumbed papers. One was a letter of instruction to him from the Horse Guards, the other a memorandum announcing 'to whom it might concern' that the Right Honourable the Lord Kenyon, Deputy Grand-Master of the Orange Society of the United King-dom of Great Britain and Ireland, commended to their brotherly love 'his trusty and worshipful Brother, Timotheus Hargreaves, Deputy Master of Lodge 83 of the Society'.

'First brick!' said Christopher. He folded the letter, and put it in his pocket.

Afterwards he made hay with the Tiger's belongings about the room, as if their owner had had a drunken frolic with them. Then he summoned William to his aid, and together they placed the un-conscious man upon the floor, decoratively athwart a pile of crum-pled shirts, a riding-boot and his best uniform coat.

The Tiger gave a little sigh, drew his knees up toward his chin, burrowed his cheek into a hummock of dirty socks, and gurgled and snorted on in his intoxicated sleep.

'Very nacheral and life-like, sir!' said William approvingly, as he opened the door and peered out. There was no one about. Christopher dropped a boot and the notebook on the floor outside, to complete the picture, and retreated with his man, leaving the door ajar.

It was not till long past dawn that one of the Berber housemen, starting work with his broom, discovered chaos.

Christopher lying guiltily awake heard him hissing over the stair-rail to attract the attention of his mate; heard the throaty whisper:

'Abdullah! ta'ala hinna! Ta'ala igarig!'

But neither they, nor Hargreaves himself, suspected anything but a drunken frenzy. Said the Tiger explanatorily when they met later in the day:

'Got very lit last night! Very lit, old boy!'

He projected his indiarubber mouth, retracted it, looked at Christopher anxiously. 'Didn't by any chance try to fight you, did I?— try to fight you, did I?'

'You were a bit unsteady on your feet, I thought, but that was all.'

The Tiger averted his bleared eyes from the fountain in the shadowed court, as if it pained him to see the movement and the thin light within its silver-grey jet.

'Must have fought with something!' he grumbled. 'Or else I thought I did! Looks as if an elephant had been loose—an elephant loose in my room! . . . Went to bed on a boot and a dirty sock— boot and dirty sock! . . . Thought I was a volcano, I suppose! Brandy? . . . Yes, my boy! . . . Brandy—brandy—brandy!'

Chapter 34

Journey with a Ghost

THEY SAT ROUND THE FIRE IN THE ROSE DRAWING-ROOM. The curtains were snugly drawn; and the bland gentlemen with high foreheads and lace cravats, and the blander ladies with powdered hair simpered out of the frames at their reflections in the long mirrors; the great silver tea-tray glittered with all its apparatus on the table beside the Lady Jane: everything twinkled and glowed in the fire-light and in the light of the tall candles scattered about the room, except the chill lady of marble who struggled eternally with her recalcitrant clothing on a porphyry pedestal by the door.

The Lady Jane, her shawl over her shoulders, her cap discreetly gay with purple ribbons, had mumbled her tea-time incantation, had poured out with shaking hand the amber fluid into the thin green cups of Worcester china.

'If it weren't for Henry Christopher, I could fancy I had never been away!' said Christopher. 'That and Charlotte's new style of doing her hair!' He glanced from the nutcracker face of Lady Jane to Setoun lounging by the fireplace.

Charlotte put up a hand to a great loop of smooth dark hair that lay close to her cheek before a small ear.

'And if it weren't for the original Christopher, too!' she said.

'Oh, come!' said Christopher. 'You haven't had much time to take in any changes in me! After all, I only arrived four hours ago! And we've talked of nothing serious.'

'You can tell death in a second!'

'Death?'

'My nice old-fashioned Tops is dead! . . . Quite dead! I remember years ago saying to Hurbles that you were grown up. I was wrong then. You are grown up now, though! . . . But somehow I am sorry about it.'

'You're quite right,' said Christopher smiling alternately at her and Setoun. 'The boy Christopher is dead—as dead as a doornail. He lived too long, I am afraid! The new Me has inherited some of his dreams and some of his ideals. He bequeathed to Me, too, all his memories of you and Hurbles. Christopher Harnish is gone; but Christopher von Tollendhal has inherited everything that was good to remember.'

'Seem to recognize true Christopher ring in those sentences, Count Tollendhal!' said Setoun crossing his silk-stockinged legs.

His leathery face creased in a smile as he lounged back, with his jutting chin thrust down into the frills of his shirt.

Christopher, Count von Tollendhal, realized the truth of the dig and flushed—to his annoyance—under the kindly irony. Charlotte rushed in to his rescue.

'I know I'm not changed at all, Tops! But do you find any difference in Hurbles? Do you think marriage has altered him?'

Christopher was remorseless in his vengeance.

'The first thing Hurbles said to me after he had slapped me on the shoulders and shaken me by the hand like a boa-constrictor, was: "Came by steam railway from Liverpool to Manchester, of course!" Then he said, "Got new 'Defiance'. Tubular boilers. Fifteen miles an hour! Come and see it. Burns coke and charcoal!" '

'Didn't he say anything about me—or Henry Christopher?' asked Charlotte in a voice of menace.

'Not a word! We watched my baggage being unloaded and discussed the advantage of—coupled driving wheels, was it?'

'Don't know that change has been for the better,' grumbled Setoun before his wife's onslaught. 'Christopher Harnish wouldn't have spoken of me with such disrespect!'

The slim gilt clock under a glass shade on the mantelpiece chimed the hour. From his fob pockets Setoun drew two watches, shook his head over them, pressed the knobs, watched goats and native warriors spring to their sudden frenzied life, counted their thin jangling strokes, and shook his head again.

'Ten o'clock!' said Charlotte. 'You'll be ready for early bed, Tops! You must be tired after your journey!'

'I'll turn in pretty soon, if you don't mind, as I shall have a long day to-morrow.'

'Why on earth to-morrow?' asked Setoun.

'I've got to go somewhere!'

'You're going to . . .' began Charlotte, and was brought to a halt by Setoun's warning glance.

'I've got to go into Wales. I must be there without fail by Christmas Eve, and I've got to do some nosing about before.'

Setoun held one of his watches up to a large red ear and listened to the ticking of the escapement wheel.

'Something to do with your mysterious epistle from Nova Scotia?' he asked, as if only casually interested.

Christopher nodded.

Charlotte looked at him narrowly. She leaned forward, cupping her chin in her hands, her elbows resting on her knees. Great sapphires in the heavy gold bangles on her arms repeated the blue of her spreading satin dress.

'Hurbles and I know only very vaguely what you have discovered, Tops. Still less what you mean to do. But if it is anything that will help the little Princess, then do it!'

'I told you,' said Christopher, and rose and stood looking down on them with his back to the fire, 'that once I—at least, the I who was—decided the whole of my—Christopher Harnish's—family could go to hell! That I hoped they would go to hell; that I did my best to make certain that they should.

'I did not tell you then, but I will tell you now. Christopher Harnish destroyed letters that showed that Cumberland was conducting some strange conspiracy. What was the purpose of the plot was not then clear. It was something reactionary; something against reform; something hare-brained. Why did the late Mr. Harnish destroy the evidence? Because he was perfectly certain that the inevitable end of such a coup would be revolution that would bring down all the family! King, Dukes, Princes, Princesses!'

Said Charlotte:

'Before you go on, Tops, I must say something. You went away in order to come back someone else. You went away a boy with shattered dreams—so you thought—and an overwhelming nightmare. You come back a man without a nightmare, but—I'm sure I'm right—still with dreams.'

'I've come back forgetting utterly the antecedents of Christopher Harnish. He was a foundling. He had no mother. He had no father. He has no relatives—but those who adopted him!'

She made no comment and went on:

'Lately I have seen something—a good deal—of the Duchess of Kent, and the child who will be Queen. I will tell you this. The Duchess is fat. She is red-faced with swimmy eyes. She's probably got a much less innocent amour with her major-domo, Conroy, than Caroline had with Bergami: but she has ideals of a sort. The Princess Victoria is fat; she is the white of cold mutton fat; she has rabbit teeth and weak ankles and a mouth that can't stay quite shut. But if the Duchess could isolate her completely from her family, she'd do it. If she could make her relationless, she would. To all practical purposes she does.

'If ever a child were brought up to think her family mad and bad and ogreish, that child has been. She has been made to think of herself as the foundress of a new line. She has been kept from the contamination of her family like a fairy princess—hidden behind walls of triple brass in a castle of iron! . . . She will be as new and relationless as you . . . So, Tops, do whatever you must do quickly, and before it is too late!'

Old Lady Jane with a clove orange on her puce lap was nodding in the dreamless slumber of the aged, protected from the roaring fire by the tapestry fire-shield on the spindly mahogany rod. Setoun, with a watch held between finger and thumb on the straining knees of his black pantaloons, stared at the crackling logs.

'Quite right that curse that began with a woman should end with a woman!' he said.

Christopher flung himself into a chair.

'What do you mean, Hurbles?' he asked.

'Mary betrayed her father, James the Second. Took his throne for herself and Dutch William, her husband. Hasn't there been a curse on those who succeeded her ever since? Wasn't there a curse on her! Mary herself barren! Anne, her sister, without heir! Faithless husbands: faithless wives: faithless children! There's no family in the meanest slum can equal the royal record of scandal and shame! Victoria's got the chance to break the spell. . . . Twaddle? But may be something in it!'

'Victoria's chances of getting the throne are pretty thin!' said Christopher, rather proud of his position as informant with inside knowledge.

"Be a bit more explicit, young feller!' said Setoun, making his watches repeat the hour.

'Well, I've found out what it's all about: and most of the "how" and "when". There's a gap here and there. That's why I must be off to-morrow,' said Christopher. 'Victoria shall have her chance to start a new line. And I who am starting my new line have got to give it her! The new I must undo what the old I did before I can be reborn.'

'Go on!' said Setoun, smiling a little to himself.

'I know I didn't tell you much. I didn't want to risk anything to the posts. . . . I stole in Alexandria a document by which I masqueraded as the Deputy-Master of an Orange Lodge . . .'

'Orange!' said Setoun. 'So that's the clue!'

'With that I went to Gibraltar and found more evidence. Then I went to Bermuda, and last of all to Nova Scotia. At all those places there are army lodges—army, mind you! It was far less dangerous than doing it at home. Far less risk of being recognized as an impostor. But I chanced it at York after I landed, and learned by sheer bluff a great deal. Actually I did not find it difficult anywhere to pick up the threads—carefully, of course—with my credentials! They fell for me in the most child-like way!'

'How much have you found out?' asked Setoun.

'I have found out that there is a definite plot to oust Victoria and proclaim Ernest as King immediately William dies . . .'

'Which he may do any day!'

'Yes. Which he may do any day. The idea has been simmering more or less for thirteen years. Since 1828 there has been definite propaganda on behalf of Cumberland among the Orange Lodges and Brunswick Clubs. He himself is Grand Master. There are over three hundred thousand members in Great Britain.'

Setoun whistled.

'There are forty thousand members in London alone. I don't say that they all know the ultimate aims of the society, but many of them are pretty well ripe for anything. The real danger is that the army is largely tainted. There are nearly four hundred lodges in England and thirty exclusively for the army. They're everywhere. Lord Londonderry, Lord Kenyon, the Bishop of Salisbury, Lord Langford, Lord Cole, Lord Wynford and others I have forgotten for the moment are in it. A fellow called Fairman, who's been a sort of wandering commissioner for Cumberland, told me they are going to seize the Tower and Bank, and surround Whitehall the minute the breath's out of William!

'Money has been poured out like water. Kenyon has spent twenty thousand pounds on propaganda alone in the last two years. And there's buckets of cash coming from somewhere else—from somebody else. Who, I am going to find out. There's to be a secret meeting of some sort at a house in Carmarthenshire in a few days. To get their plans cut and dried. Cumberland's going himself to meet some mysterious supporter. So am I!'

' "Ernest the Assassin",' said Setoun thoughtfully, quoting from Henry Brougham. 'Know enough, Tops! Shouldn't go if I were you! You can blow the thing sky-high now!'

'I want to blow it sky-higher!' said Christopher looking very important. 'You see, I know enough to pass as one of them. Visiting Master of the Halifax Lodge, for instance. Knew of meeting. Came to report. Something of that sort. Haven't worked details out.'

'It's a desperate venture!' declared Setoun; and Charlotte broke out:

'Tops, it's ludicrous! You can't go! You must have got ample evidence already! . . . If they find you out they'll kill you!'

Said Christopher:

'If I go—nobody can do it except myself—I may find out who stands behind them with the purse. I may find, too, the exact pattern of their plans. It's a chance, and worth while!'

They could not dissuade him. There were new elements of resistance in the long young man with the tanned face, and the fair hair that had been bleached almost white in places by the fierce Texan sun.

They could not dissuade him—though they sat arguing and talking—while the Lady Jane nid-nodded over her pomander by the dying fire—until the clock upon the mantelpiece had struck twelve and was answered by Setoun's repeaters—over which again he shook his ruffled grey head.

The next morning Christopher set out from Piccadilly by the Gloucester Mail, dressed like a cross between an army officer on a sporting holiday and a country squire with military proclivities. He wore a long drab overcoat of military cut over a green shooting jacket with a tartan neckerchief wound round his shirt collar, and long buttoned gaiters that came past the knee. It seemed to him a useful costume for all eventualities including exploration. A passenger by coach, he felt, would also be less liable to remark and possible suspicion than one who travelled by post chaise or private carriage.

To Charlotte's horror he took no baggage; but carried razor and toothbrush in his pocket with a small pistol.

'What'll you sleep in, my dear?' she asked as he kissed her good-bye in the dim sea-green depths of the shrubbery-shadowed break-fast room.

'My skin!' said Christopher.

'The old Christopher *is* dead,' she asserted. 'The old Christopher would never have said that!' And threw a look demanding con-firmation from Setoun, who had risen to accompany Christopher to the door.

'The old Christopher *did* it, all the same,' said the new owner of the old name. 'He *did* sleep in his skin because you made him—as you well know! Good-bye, Charlotte dearest!'

Setoun watched the phaeton rattle out of the drive with slow speculation. Meditatively he walked through the damp shrubberies to the coach-house, and stood for a long time confronting that strange abortion between coach and locomotive which had the words 'Infernal Defiance' painted on its canary-yellow door panels. He sighed heavily.

William had been sent ahead with one of Setoun's light trav-elling carriages. He was to await a summons at a posting inn on the main road some five miles across the mountains—as far as could be judged—from the house where Cumberland's meeting was to take place.

It was long past nightfall with snow threatening in the bitter wind, when Christopher reached Gloucester and the thin welcome ordinarily extended to an outside passenger without baggage. He cursed accordingly boots, waiter, and chambermaid with the new certainty that was in him; ordered a private room and a roaring fire, the purchase of a nightrobe; and supped amidst the most deferential attention.

He bought woollen gloves and scarf in the town the next morning, before setting out early on the penultimate stage of his journey; for the clouds were heavy with snow, and the rim of the Cotswolds behind was sugar-white against the leaden sky.

He shared a seat behind the coachman on the Carmarthen stage-coach with a small schoolboy returning home for the holidays. 'Shared a seat' is the correct term, for the third occupant was a large and spreading lady who occupied fully two places to herself, and even overflowed little parcels and reticules and a large and precious basket (covered with a white cloth) which perpetually nudged the coachman between his green broadcloth shoulders. The small boy and Christopher divided what space there was left; and devilish unpleasant Christopher found it, between a small bony elbow and the low guard rail at the end of the seat, which just caught his thigh bone sufficiently to be uncomfortable and insufficiently—he was certain—to prevent his being thrown off if the coach were to lurch going round a corner. He was careful not to look downwards from his overhanging precipice to the grey-fawn road so far below, with jagged loose flints like a torture-bed of the Inquisition.

A well-corded load of Christmassy packages creaked above them.

He was reminded of that journey of long ago down the selfsame highway—he imagined—toward the Welsh hills. As they went briskly along the hard road, still sparkling with frost, he could almost see again that cavern under the tilt of the hooded wagon—which had been so like a barge on land—smell the sour reek of it—hear the jingle of the little bells upon the leading horse, and the clanking and the clattering of pots and pans against its lofty sides

—see the bright eyes and heart-shaped face of Deb, and listen to her voice raised in mocking imitation of Lewis.

With memory still filling his mind he turned to the small person next him, who was rubbing his small gloved hands, stamping his small feet, and rubbing his small red nose in a fruitless effort to keep warm.

'You are very young, sir,' said Christopher, 'to be taking so long a journey by yourself!'

'I've travelled alone for years—and years!' replied the small person in a high treble, flashing an indignant look at him, and then whistling in a most nonchalant way to show how unstirred he was by the thrill of travel and speed.

'I went to school all by myself four years ago!' continued the small person, tilting his high tasselled hat over his nose to look more the man of the world. 'I was quite small then—about six. . . . Didn't I, Jenkins?'

'Yess, yess, inteet, Master Howell!' said Jenkins flicking the off-leader most scientifically and dispassionately with the tip of the whip, and turning a purple face over his shoulder for an instant. 'The marvel iss to me that you were never kidnapped!'

'Kidnapped! Oh, I say, Jenkins!' said Mr. Howell drumming his heels on the coach-top. 'I'd like to see anyone try that on with me! . . . I'd punch 'em on the nose! I'd half kill them!'

Christopher wondered why it had never occurred to the child-that-he-had-been to do some desperate break-away instead of resigning himself to fate. He looked at Mr. Howell with new respect. Mr. Howell would be quite capable of looking after himself even now, at the age of ten: in another ten years he would be ready to cope with any situation, without having to travel to Germany and to Texas and half round the world to find himself.

By the time they reached Monmouth Mr. Howell had become silent—after a spell of hard chatter—and positively blue in the face.

Christopher helped the child down that he might stretch his legs and stamp to and fro; and turned under the arch into the passage to the bar of the Beaufort Arms. Brandy, hot water, a slice of lemon, two lumps of sugar, and the clink of a spoon in a large and steaming tumbler represented to him the quintessence of warmth and comfort and loveliness.

As he mounted the single step to the door, out of the tail of his eye he saw, however, the disconsolate small figure of Mr. Howell sheltering from the bitter wind in the draughty archway. Propped against a half-door down the long yard, lounged an ostler in sleeved waistcoat and half-boots, chewing a straw. The memory came back to him, across the years, of another disconsolate small boy on the bitter eve of night, shivering at an inn-door, of another ostler, and of rum and tea, and of broken meats in a chamber pot.

'Mr. Howell! Hi! Mr. Howell!' he called.

Mr. Howell turned sharply.

"Come and have a hot drink with me, Mr. Howell! Rum and hot tea! Make you as warm as an engine boiler! Come on!'

Would Mr. Howell come on? He would!

Would Mr. Howell gasp and splutter and dip his nose into the wide-mouthed goblet, and scrape up the aromatic sugar crystals afterwards with his spoon? He would and did! And cheek the fat and admiring barmaid into the bargain!

'I sa-a-ay!' said Mr. Howell trotting back to the coach at Christopher's side. 'Do you know, that was a bit of all right. And I'm not in the least tiddley. . . . Am I, sir? . . . I think I'll be a three-bottle man when I'm older.'

Whatever Mr. Howell's capacity might be in the future as a consumer of alcohol, his present abilities as a trencherman were superb, as was discovered when he gladly accepted, a little later, an invitation to dinner instead of feasting on dry sandwiches done up in a brown paper parcel.

When they arrived at the town of Llandeilo Fawr, Christopher was sorry to part from the small person, who, he felt sure, would have handled the problems of the late Christopher Harnish so much more adequately than that gentleman himself had done. They shook hands very cordially on the wide steps before the hospitable door of the Cawdor Arms, and Mr. Howell staggered off with his immense carpet-bag down the narrow street to the churchyard wall that flanked the steeply sloping market-place.

'The gig'll be waiting there for me! Good-bye, sir!'

Christopher ordered a room, supper; and in a corner of the crowded smoky bar found William enjoying a pipe over a pint of dog's-nose. He sat down beside him, and entered into what might well have seemed the casual conversation of a stranger.

'I shall stay here to-night, William,' he said in a low voice, 'and explore the country to-morrow. I must get the lie of the land before I do anything. Especially as I don't think I shall be able to carry out any imposture. They'll be too careful. My old idea was absurd. I shall just have to try and get into the house as best I can.'

'Nothing despirit to-morrow, then, sir?' said William pulling at his pipe. 'You promise to do nothing despirit without me being somewhere near at hand!'

He spoke in a most conspiratorial manner out of the side of his mouth, gazing steadfastly at the wall opposite.

'Honour bright, you old ruffian!' said Christopher. 'Be about here to-morrow in the early afternoon so that I can talk to you when I get back. The place can't be more than five miles away.'

After a casual good night, as though to a tavern acquaintance, he walked out to the wide flagged hall.

Supper, said the affable waiter, would be ready in half an hour.

It was still early. He went into the street and down towards the market-place where, he was told, a shop might be open. Anyhow, Mr. Jones next Red House would sell a nightgown, even if the shop was shut. Only too glad to! Ring the bell at the door, and speak very slowly, because Mr. Jones spoke the English very slightly.

Christopher bought the only nightgown in his size that Mr. Jones stocked. He was fery pig—fery pig, indeed! Yess? But the gown! It was of fla-nell! Fery good fla-nell from Carmarthen, look-you! It was grey, and large, and incredibly hairy: but there was no choice. So he bought it, with misgivings, and issued out into the freezing cold moonlight night from the dark shop with its smell of greasy wool.

The market-place slanted steeply down a hillside, narrowing as it went, to the main road that precipitated itself to the river and thence to Carmarthen. On the farther side of the market, facing the line of low houses and little shops, a long grey wall fenced off a graveyard studded, under the moon, with ghost-like tombstones and a few funereal yews.

The moon was high, white and cold in a shining sky. There was a silver sheen on the house-tops that followed the road to the river, and the ground sparkled as if with powdered glass. A small cypress, in the angle of the churchyard by the highway, threw a dense shadow across narrow road and narrower footway. From the darkness under the tree it seemed to Christopher that a strange choking noise came. It sounded like a sob. Something appeared to stir.

He shifted his bundle under his arm, and prepared to cross and investigate. But before he ever set foot in the roadway he had recognized the small and forlorn figure in high tasselled cap and grey overcoat, and the stupendous carpet-bag which comprised the forlorn figure's luggage. It was the competent Mr. Howell.

He whistled to attract Forlornness's attention.

'Hi! Mr. Howell!' said he. 'Still waiting for the gig? Come over and have some supper with me. They'll find you all right!'

There was another choke, hurriedly suppressed, across the road. Mr. Howell, with head bent to hide a tear-stained face, staggered across the road with his carpet-bag.

'M-may I?' said he with frantic effort at self-control. 'I—I—think' —very long pause—'that they've forgotten me!'

'Too bad!' said Christopher briskly. 'Too bad! Let's have some supper and talk it over.'

Ah—ha!—said the spirit of the late Christopher Harnish—there's our self-reliant Mr. Howell far more flummoxed than I ever was over a much smaller catastrophe!

The three of them—Christopher, Mr. Howell, and the ghost of the small unhappy boy of fifteen years before—walked back together: two of them in silence, for above their ringing footfalls the little ghost was talking—of Deb, and Vergil, and Simmie, and pistols that burst into sudden flame, and man-traps (which clashed their teeth in wet and silent woods), and a man with a long face like a blanched almond sitting very far away and very high up in robes of red.

Mr. Howell w-w-would l-like s-supper very much! Yes! A wash would be a f-frightfully good idea!

When Mr. Howell, still hiding his face as best he could, had bolted upstairs, returned afterward to the snug sitting-room with tear stains washed away, heard a 'chay' ordered for an hour's time, confronted an enormous dish of cutlets, tackled a suet pudding with treacle, and a pony of table-ale and half a glass of port—then he looked confidingly at his host, shook his head slightly, and remarked once more:

'I really believe, sir, I'll be a three-bottle man when I'm a bit older!'

It appeared on investigation that Mr. Howell lived at a hamlet called Caerbannel, and that he might—just possibly—have said that he was arriving on Saturday, and not Friday, when he wrote to his uncles. 'You know what it's like, sir, at end of term!'

It was still early, and a fine night. Christopher had nothing to do. He undertook delivery of Mr. Howell himself.

So a little later, all very comfortable and satisfied, they bundled themselves into the mildew-smelling darkness of a closed chaise and jolted off, up the lane that climbed into the moonlit hills above the mists of the river.

It was a narrow rutted lane that curved under woods and above swift streams, and was terraced over steep small fields. It topped eventually a high hill, and slanted down between dark trees to a valley full of moonshine.

Mr. Howell had been very silent for most of the way. He appeared as wrapped in meditation as Christopher was in recollections. He said at length:

'I shall be a two-bottle man, anyhow! Don't you think so, sir?'

He rubbed his nose, and Christopher could feel that his eyes were anxiously turned toward him.

'You certainly should be!' he agreed.

'If anybody had tried to kidnap me, I should have given them what for! I should have punched them in the eye. Shouldn't I?'

'I'm sure you would have!'

Mr. Howell reflected a long time.

Then he said tentatively:

'It's curious how cold makes one's eyes water, isn't it?'

Christopher was very careful that even in the concealing darkness there should be no vestige of a smile upon his face.

'Very curious!' said Christopher. 'But it does! Just like it makes one's nose drip!'

'Just like one's nose! . . . of course!' said Mr. Howell in a tone of great relief and satisfaction. 'Just like one's nose! . . .' He perked up. 'I'd have biffed them on the conk if they'd tried to kidnap me. I'd have tapped their claret for 'em! . . . I've got a very knobby fist. . . . Woodford Major said so!'

They had arrived at the valley bottom, where a stream hurried between black fringes of trees to a narrow bridge; on the far side a group of small white buildings were clustered behind a creaking inn-sign under the lee of a steep-wooded hill.

The inn looked up the shallow furrow of the valley, across the patchwork of moonlit fields and slanting copses that was threaded by the stream. Half a mile away the valley was closed in to a narrow gorge by a great wooded crag that rose black against the sky, above the surrounding hills. One face of it fell sheer in precipice to the stream: grey walls and towers shone under the moon above the baldness of its summit.

'That's Caer Iglwys!' said Mr. Howell when his attention was called to the castle. He spoke casually and without interest, as of a very commonplace land-mark. Christopher, however, was still staring at it when the chaise drew up before the inn door.

He had never pictured the meeting-place of the inner ring of the Orange plot to be a castle perched upon a precipice, as if it had been arranged in the terms of a Gothic romance by Horace Walpole or Mrs. Radcliffe. He had thought it would be a large secluded country house, with parks and ha-ha and walled garden, where commonplace men would discuss commonplace conspiracy. It seemed a far more perilous adventure when it centred round a stronghold such as this: on the other hand some inner self felt satisfaction that the décor of his enterprise should carry all the elements of romance.

Mr. Howell and his carpet-bag appeared to fall out of the carriage simultaneously, and to bundle themselves in a struggling mob through the inn door.

'May at least have a drink before I go back,' thought Christopher, and followed him leisurely in.

There was a door on either side of the slate-flagged entrance: from one came a babble of Welsh, and from the other the excited treble of Mr. Howell. At the end of the passage a bow window, with raised sash, projected into a small deserted bar parlour, ornamented by a weary trio of sporting dogs.

At the window, flanked by casks of beer, and outlined by dim candle-light against rows of tankards and shelves of spirit bottles was the upper half of a fat and comfortable lady. A large pink good-natured face fell away into a triple chin, as if it had started to melt. An enormous bosom endeavoured to burst through her cherry-coloured merino dress, and, being defeated, flopped over her large arms.

'Good-evening, sir!' said she, with great affability.

'Good-evening, ma'am!' said Christopher. 'It's a bitter night to be sure. A brandy "with" would be a help to a cold gentleman!'

The lady gave a throaty chuckle, and was in the process of instructing a bright-cheeked maid to fetch a kettle of hot water from the kitchen, when someone came bellowing into the parlour.

'Most kind! Most devilish kind! Most infernally kind! My brother and I are teetotally obliged to you, sir. Allow me to shake your hand, sir, and assure you how accursedly grateful my brother and I are!'

A square fat man had rolled up, beamed at him, and seized his hand and shaken it up and down like a pump handle, talking rapidly all the time. A tremendous pair of spectacles sat on his brief nose; his grey hair had been cut so short that it stood erect like the stubble on a cornfield: a watch-chain as thick as a ship's cable crossed the expanse of a dark red waistcoat, and his cord breeches disappeared into a pair of riding boots that sagged almost half-way down his mighty calves.

'Abscrobiously polite of you!' said the fat gentleman. 'What's that, Annie? Gentleman ordered a drink? Certainly not! Drink it yourself, my girl, and put it to the account! Never known you refuse. Gentleman coming to drink a jorum over the fire with Mr. Charles and myself. No refusal! Abscrobiously no! Real excuse for a little festivity, my dear sir. Annie will get us to bed if necessary. She's done it dozens of times. Blister my liver!—dozens of times. . . . Haven't you, you old witch?'

Christopher found himself propelled down the passage, through a door which gave the fat gentleman only just enough clearance, into an extremely small room. A round table with bottles, jugs, glasses and all the materials for a punch had been pushed into a corner: two easy-chairs were drawn up before the fire, and from one of them rose another square fat gentleman with spectacles, cropped head, breeches and boots, in a most hospitable manner. He was a perfect replica of the first in appearance and attire.

Mr. Howell, looking extremely small, was accommodated on a little footstool against the fender.

'Moth-whew-t gla' dto th-whew-ee you,' said the second gentleman, and broke into a perfect cascade of whistling, spluttering and rumbling.

'Jesus Christ! Jesus Christ! My dear Charles!' said the first gentleman in a matter-of-fact manner; whereat the second fat gentleman's face became positively purple, and he seized from the mantelpiece a small bar of ivory which he proceeded to adjust across a wide gap in his top front teeth.

'Dear Charles,' said the other—drawing up to the fire the only other chair in the room for Christopher—'was a clergyman. He lost his front teeth out with the Duke's, when his horse tossed him over a hedge.'

'Not tothed! Not tothed!' said Charles indignantly, between a whistle and a lisp, in the midst of adjustment.

'Good thing in a way! Devilish good thing! He had to leave the Church. He was too much of a coward to have the holes left open and his teeth filed and put back. So he could never say "Jesus Christ"! Quite impossible, and most awkward for a parson, of course!' He gave an appalling reproduction of his brother endeavouring to pronounce the Holy Name, to the vast joy of Mr. Howell.

'Henry!' said Charles in a warning manner, and with slightly thick utterance, and shook hands with Christopher pump-handle fashion. 'You're a bad fellow, Henry!'

'You know it is true, Charles! . . . And,' added Henry with much pride, 'you will be saying next I didn't invent your conversation-piece. For talking with strangers! Ivory and whale-bone —most inventinious!'

'You'll bore Mr. . . .' Charles came to a pause.

'Tollendale,' proffered Christopher.

The old gentleman bowed.

'Gainer,' said Charles. 'Henry Gainer and Charles Gainer—by name. Henry Loser and Charles Loser—by nature! . . . Now sit down, do, my dear sir! There's enough punch here to see us through till the cows come home—and more where it came from! And Annie shall order us a devilled bone or two in an hour or so.'

So up they drew their chairs and toasted their toes, and sip-sipped their punch, and talked hunting, fishing, and shooting, and smoked till the room was so hazy that the whips and guns and spurs and fishing tackle that ornamented the walls were barely visible.

The chiming of the clock on the mantelpiece brought Christopher—slightly bemused by warmth, spirits and pleasant com-pany—back to earth.

'Good Lord!' he said getting to his feet, 'I've had that po'chay outside for nearly three hours. I hate going, but it is time I went back to my inn!'

'Now that,' said Henry, 'is what I call nonsense. Just as we are getting settled! Not friendly—in fact damned unfriendly! You must stay here the night.' He drew the window curtains aside for a moment. 'Specially as it is snowing. Small room but snug! Then we can finish the session properly. We'll send your 'chay back, and the driver can take word to have your things brought over to-morrow.'

'Well! . . .' began Christopher doubtfully.

'In fact,' said Brother Charles, 'why not a day or two here as our guest? You say you are a tourist. Time can be no object to you then. Now come, stay with us and do as you like—a bit of fishing, a bit of walking, a bit of shooting, a bit of riding—can find you a nag—and a bottle or two. Lend you a bedgown and razor myself! . . . Tell us some more about Texas!'

Under the aegis of the two kind old men Christopher felt that he could stay thus close to Caer Iglwys without arousing sus-picion: in fact it seemed a very good plan to have the base of his expedition so far advanced. He accepted the offer after very little persuasion, wrote a hurried line to William, and settled down to make an evening of it with his hosts.

Much later, Mr. Howell, asleep on the floor with his head on his carpet-bag, was routed out and sent protesting to bed: and eventually Charles and Henry squeezed their way up a narrow staircase and conducted Christopher to a room which was heavily overcrowded by a narrow bed, a chest of drawers, and a washstand with a willow pattern jug and basin approximately the size of a cream jug and soup-plate. There was a warming pan in the bed and Charles's ample nightgown had been brought up, as hot as the shirt of Nessus, from the kitchen fire.

He awoke as dawn was breaking, drew his curtains, and looked out on to the valley.

The sun lay just below the verge of the hills upon his right. Its presence was marked by a thin lemon-coloured rim to the pale blue sky, under which the frost-covered fields lay unshadowed by the grey hedges and colourless trees.

At the far end of the valley the castle rose in silhouette against the heaven, the sheer crag on its southern side a twisted black, its long northern slope a sheet of white.

The sun swam up. A rosy fire illumined the hill-tops. Long shadows and colour slid across the land. Fields that had been but white showed patches that were brown from fallen leaves, or faintly green: steel sheen came to the sunward of the beeches: warmth glowed along the edges of bare boughs: the sallow walls of cottages shone: and a hundred thousand blades of grass bore each their myriad spikes of frost that caught the sun and became jewels.

The greater hills beyond the valley were violet, were grey, were blue: and the thickets along the stream were no longer bare and black, but from a dark base broke into faint colour against the frosted fields, as if they were smouldering into wood-smoke without visible flame.

There was no sign of life about the inn except in the kitchen premises. Christopher bundled into his clothes and out into the open air, to take a preliminary survey of his problem.

A path ran through the fields along the stream as it curved between a line of bare willows and alder thickets. The water ran swiftly but not very deep, and glassy icicles hung from low boughs that dipped their tips into its dark flood like trailing fingers.

He followed the track into the gorge where, on his right, the woods rose steeply, and on his left the castle rock descended from the walls in sheer precipice into a short slope covered by a thicket. The grey walls shone a pale gold in the early sunlight, while the cleft below was still cold and dark in shadow.

A quarter of a mile beyond the castle he forded the stream, scrambled through undergrowth among woods of young ash and oak, and emerged on to a narrow road.

He walked back towards the inn under a high and ruinous wall, above which rose the bare boughs of a thin barrier of large trees. The towers and battlements of the castle loomed above them on a steep bare knoll, from the rock on which the snow was beginning to melt.

On three sides the castle was guarded by its precipice—obviously unscalable by the inexpert, and especially so at night. There seemed, however, to be no difficulty of approach through the park. He paused for a moment and stared up at the fortress. No smoke rose from the roofs hidden behind its ramparts: utter stillness wrapped it about: a large black bird rose heavily from one of the towers and beat against the wind across the valley. He slowly realized that the place was unkempt, forlorn, and that the merest sheep-track led to the gate set deep in the barbican. A multitude of little things forced themselves on his notice— a decaying buttress, a mass of stone at the foot of a tower; and then, as the sun rose higher, a beam of light shone through an unglazed loophole in one of the turrets. The castle was but a shell—perfect, but still an uninhabitable shell!

After he had recovered from the first shock he climbed a gate on the other side of the road, and walked up the sharp curve of a meadow cleft by a vociferous brook that babbled to overhanging oaks.

From the hedge at the top he was more nearly on a level with the building. Its desolation became obvious. It was highly improbable that there could be a dwelling place of any size within the walls. Something had gone very wrong with his plans!

'Hell!' said Christopher, and was about to set off for the inn and breakfast, in considerable consternation, when he heard a loud and artificial cough behind him.

A man in velveteen breeches and a battered hat was standing

in a gateway in the hedge examining him, with his thumbs in the pockets of a canary-coloured waistcoat. A gun was propped against the rails before him.

Christopher was anxious to arouse no suspicions, so he remained where he was for a moment or two, as though admiring the view, and for long enough to demonstrate the easiness of his conscience. Then he set off down the hillside whistling, with his hat cocked at a jaunty angle.

'Hi!' said the man at the gate.

Christopher went on. He was glad, though, that the road was barely a hundred yards away.

'Hi!' repeated the man at the gate in a loud shout.

Christopher continued on his way, with the uncomfortable feeling that there was not merely a man, but also a gun at his back.

There was a thud of heavy feet, and his interlocutor came running after him.

'Hi, you!' said the man. 'Don't you 'ear me?'

'If you were proposing to address me,' said Christopher in his coldest tone, coming to a halt, 'why did you not do so when I was near you—at the gate?'

The man had a leaden, cunning face, and a black lock strayed on to his forehead from under his hat.

'D'you know you're trespassin'?' he growled. 'Wot you doin' here?'

'If I was trespassing I am sorry,' declared Christopher. 'I can have done little harm in looking at the ruins. Your manners are not ingratiating, my man!'

'Ho! "My man" am I? . . . Trespassin'—that's wot you were a-doin', my spark, I'll have you know. Probably poachin'.'

'Don't be a damned fool!' said Christopher irritably. 'How can I be poaching without a gun? I haven't even got a stick, you fathead.' And he made as though to go on his way across the snow-powdered tussocks.

The man with a quick movement sprang before him.

'"Fat-'ead", sez you?' quoted he with a face distorted by anger. 'I'll show you 'oo's a fat-head. . . . You just turn your pockets out, my spark! Or I'll make you!'

'I'll be damned if you do,' said Christopher in a fury. 'Let me pass. I don't like your smell.'

He advanced so angrily that the other stepped back a pace, and started to bring up his gun.

Christopher, entirely ignoring him, set off as nonchalantly as he might toward the gate into the road. The man, uncertain how to proceed, watched him go for a few yards: then he raised his gun.

'You come 'ere,' he called. 'You come back, you bleedin' poacher! Or I'll bleedin' well shoot!'

Christopher paid no heed to the warning. The tarred gate and rutted grey road were barely a hundred feet away. He went on, conscious though he was, without turning to look, that the muzzle of the gun was following him.

A bellow suddenly came from the hedge before him.

'No, you don't!' it said; and there was a loud explosion; shot whistled past Christopher's ear and a plume of smoke rose through a gap in the tangle of twigs. For an instant he thought that a companion of his pursuer had cut off his retreat. Then in the gateway there appeared the cube-like figure of Mr. Charles Gainer in a coat that nearly swept the ground, his stubbly head crowned by a black flat hat. He held a smoking double-barrelled gun in his hand.

The man behind Christopher swore a startled oath, recovering from momentary panic.

'Just in time to prevent him shooting,' said Mr. Charles in tones of high self-gratulation as Christopher vaulted the rail to his side. He raised his voice to a bellow that echoed in the valley. 'Come here, you elephant-bottomed canary! Come here, you hybrid son of a Cardiff concubine! Come here, Smith!'

Smith came slowly toward them.

'If you think I am a parson and can't swear,' said Mr. Gainer, 'you are very mistaken, you misbegotten fish! What d'you mean by shootin' my friends? What d'you mean by insultin' my friends, you vomitorium? I'll see Miss Annie never sells you another tankard of beer again! I'll see Miss Price never gives your wife credit for three-penn'orth of tea again! What do you mean by it, you Cockney cow-dung?'

'Didn' know as ge'mman was a fren' of yours, Mister Charles!' said Smith in a half-surly, half-apologetic manner.

'If your mistress wants to keep her fields to herself like a bitch in a manger,' said Charles, 'the least she can do is to put notices up. This gentleman's a friend of mine. If he had known he wouldn't have set foot on an inch of your filthy land! I'd a very good mind to give you that barrel in earnest, you putrescence. It would have let some clean sunshine into your muck-heap innards!'

'There's no call . . .' said Smith sulkily.

' "No call"! . . . my friend . . .' and Charles in his apoplectic emotion let fall the conversation piece out of his mouth, and then dropped the spectacles off his short nose in the effort to retrieve it.

He rose panting in such a state of purple-faced ire that Smith vanished, leaving Mr. Gainer nothing to do but shake his fist at large and hurl a few round hearty oaths into the air after him.

'My dear fellow,' said Mr. Gainer recovering his temper, tucking his gun under an arm and offering the other to Christopher, 'how can I apologize? I heard you go downstairs for an early amble, and turned over for another forty winks. Then it suddenly dawned on me that you might take it into your head to wander on to Caer Iglwys land. The old harridan who owns it cuts up so rough that I bundled into my things and hurried after you.'

'Somebody still lives in Caer Iglwys then?' asked Christopher. 'I thought it looked just a ruin!'

'Ah! You're thinking of Caer Iglwys Castle! Been uninhabited for centuries. Caer Iglwys is also the name of the big house on the lip of the valley. Old harridan has owned it for years. Never moves outside. Nobody has ever seen her. She doesn't own much land—barely two hundred acres. But it's guarded night and day as if she were preserving great auks or moas!'

Mr. Gainer pointed up the slope at whose foot the road ran. Two or three steep fields, their hollows white with snow, mounted up to a long grey wall above whose coping showed a dense mass of trees—pine and fir and a clump of larch.

'I don't see a house,' said Christopher.

'It sits at the top, in the midst of the densest wood imaginable. There's an entrance, with lodge and locked gates, on the road to Llandeilo Fawr.'

'Who owns it?' he asked.

'An old Frenchwoman. I don't think I ever heard her name. Nobody ever sees her. Her steward does everything. She won't let hounds even go over her land. They're pretty tough poachers round here, but none of them'll go near it. A fellow from a farm went out one night and got into one of the fields by accident. They've been picking buckshot out of him ever since. . . . Now, if you want shooting, Brother Henry and I . . .'

The old man harangued on the subject of shooting and fishing and hunting all the way back to the inn, and through most of the enormous breakfast that awaited them.

It was a non-hunting day, so that afterwards they lent Christopher a gun, and the three of them—escorted by Mr. Howell, and a fat efficient manservant carrying provender—set off to the lonely moors overlooking the valley.

They had a good, companionable day, supported by cold pie, Caerphilly cheese and punch.

'Excellent, my dear sir,' said Brother Henry wiping his glasses and beaming benevolently upon Charles and Christopher and the massed 'bag' upon a low wall. 'Six brace of snipe: three of black game: brace and a half of wild duck: two of grouse: three hare! Ve-e-ery satisfactory! Abscrobiously so!'

The valley was spread at their feet: already the outlines of its folds and wrinkles were becoming hazy with long shadows as the sun sank in a frosty sky.

'Can one see Caer Iglwys from here?' said Christopher.

Charles extended an arm and pointed into the distance.

'This is about the only view you can get of it,' he said.

Topping the first of the ridges that surged up on the other side of the valley was a dense mass of dark green woodland. In the midst of it were the jumbled roofs of a large house round a courtyard. Seen from a distance its surrounding plantations seemed to lap its very walls, as though it were an island in a lake of greenery.

'Like a poached egg on spinach!' said Henry.

To-morrow night—thought Christopher—he must penetrate that forbidding wood and be within the walls. God knew how!

It could not be much more than a bare ten minutes uphill from the inn, which he could see beside the stream. Above it was an alder wood that in the sunlight took on the colour of the bloom upon a plum.

A larch wood below them was the pale reflection of a flame.

They turned homewards down lanes where the snow lay on the grass banks like crystallized sugar.

'A bottle of your best vino de pasto in ten minutes, and supper as early as you like, Annie, my dear!' said Henry stumping past the fat lady's bow window on his way to the stairs. 'That dish of baked tench, and the saddle of mutton we arranged, and devilled biscuits. . . . Blister my liver, I could eat a saddle myself!'

Chapter 35

Strange Eyes of a Strange Lady

TOWARDS MOONRISE CHRISTOPHER EMERGED ON HANDS and knees into the dark thickets about Caer Iglwys. He had evaded detection by crawling along a dark tunnel, through which a small torrent poured itself out of the forbidden territory under the main road and into a wooded gully.

The stream rustled and bubbled and hurried in a narrow cleft through a plantation of young pine trees. The ground was cushioned with pine-needles and scattered with dead twigs that crackled horrifically underfoot.

As the moon rose above the hills across the valley, the faint radiance trickling between the tree-trunks showed the depths of the wood like a solid wall of night. The darkness and the silence —broken by no sound from the outer world, but only by the faintest stirrings and rustlings within—gave the place something of the sinister expectation which he remembered to be instinct in the great cypress swamps of Louisiana.

He felt that the wood was waiting for something to happen— for somebody to come. The farther he penetrated the stronger the feeling became. He stopped after a while to hear what the wood was listening to: he looked over his shoulder at each pause to perceive—if he could—that of which the wood was aware.

His inner consciousness told him that the awareness was of Death: that within the wood, or beyond the wood, Death lay.

Just for a moment he hesitated and thought what life meant— the curve of a billow in the sun; the rushing noise in the air made by a flock of starlings springing to their flight; the pearl-grey of cities rising from the sea at dawn half a world away; the light in a winter larch wood; a pecan grove in Texas, pale green over grass studded with flowers of blue and red; the march of violins in unison in a great concerto; the sand ripples in the Sinai desert as the sun rose and gilded their waved edges and left the hollows as pools of shadow.

A knife, a pistol, a stick torn from a tree, could mean the end of the awareness of all that: could even mean the end of the memory of that quick glimpse he had once had of Margaret smiling at him with wet eyes. . . . Or would it not?

He went on.

The wood became a thicket. The tall trees diminished to small trees, closely huddled together in the dark. He stumbled into an ice-cold rivulet that ran along a wrinkle in the earth, and so was brought up against a solid wall of foliage—a plantation of young fir trees, none of them more than ten feet tall, whose lacy boughs intersected one another, leaving no gap from knee-height to head.

He pressed against the resistant barrier and forced his way within.

The trees fought him every inch of the way: their arms tore at his clothes, and their long wet fingers trailed across his face, smote his face, sent his hat flying. It was as if he were penetrating the hostile ranks of materializing ghosts. Great brambles had grown up the trees and struck at him as he struggled, flails of wire barbed with spear-points.

He had to turn and fight his way through backwards, after he had narrowly missed being blinded by the sweep of a long whip-lash of thorn.

Although it was snow-cold he dripped with sweat. Although the moon was high he could see nothing, except layers of flattish boughs interlocked and forming patterns of black and silver above him, below him, and all around him.

The gruesome fancy seized him that by and by the clutch of the trees would retain him: so that a generation after, foresters would find his skeleton in the wood, impaled upon bough and twig as they had closed deeper into his mouldering flesh.

He suddenly emerged on the bank of a wide moat. Across the thirty feet of black water, wherein the moon and its reflection lay like quicksilver, were the white blank walls of the house rising from a narrow grassy verge.

No light showed until he had worked his way, bent nearly double under over-hanging boughs, round an angle. From there he saw a single-arched bridge, the white of dirty snow, which crossed the moat to the gushing light of an open door. Beyond it were four tall windows, with lemon-yellow slits of light showing between the curtain folds.

A man stood very still for a moment, on the upper step, regarding the night.

Christopher heard him say: 'I do not think so. . . . The sky is quite . . .' He turned in as he spoke, and the shutting of the great door snapped off his sentence.

Not a sound came from within the house across the dark waters that shone like blank window panes at night. Guarded by walls and moat and thicket, it seemed to lie as remote from the outside world and the passage of years as the palace of the Sleeping Beauty.

Christopher crept in the secrecy of the bushes to the bridge, crossed it cat-wise on the shadowed side, and slipped along the bank under the windows. There was no cover and no alternative; if he were seen—well, he was seen, and he must take the consequences.

The lighted windows were fast shut.

He crawled on hands and knees along the narrow verge of grass between wall and water, and was rounding a corner beyond which high lavender bushes fringed the bank, when the thin splash of water and the dry rubbing of oars against rowlocks told of an approaching boat.

He fell flat in the shelter of the lavender, and, so lying, drew the pistol from his pocket and cocked it.

He was now on the shadow side of the house and invisible from the water.

The man in the boat approached with slow strokes, and passed without seeing him. A gun rested against the gunwale, and he was singing below his breath between the creaking of the oars.

As Christopher lay waiting till the sentry should be out of

earshot, he realized that a thin crack of light split a French window which was within reach of his left hand. He pressed against the edge and felt it give way a little.

The moment boat and man had passed out of sight he rose to his feet, opened the glass door, slid through a mere crack, and stood motionless behind the curtains.

Presently he peered through the folds—into a lofty room and on to a cream-coloured wall panelled with tapestry. Opposite him, in needlework mainly of rose and olive green, an exquisite shepherdess with hooped dress and powdered hair swung for ever in calm delight in a faded romantic world of statuary and high box-hedge. When he pressed one of the curtains aside and examined the wider field of vision, he brought into view a silver candle-sconce, and then another panel showing a naked lady poised coquettishly immodest on the edge of a pale green pool.

No sound disturbed the room—not even the tick of a clock.

He was encouraged to widen his gap. More tapestry panels; a chair and table in the fretted Chinese manner; a huge unlighted chandelier which caught stray gleams on the myriad facets of its cut-glass drops.

So far as he could see from where he stood, there was no living person within: the nymphs and courtly milkmaids of forgotten years displayed their faint elegance to none except himself.

He stepped quietly into a long gallery lighted softly from silver sconces, and found that he was wrong.

Far away, on a gilded and brocaded couch, beside a dying fire and near the door, lay a lady dressed in pearl-grey silk stippled with a faint small pattern in leaf green. She seemed to be asleep, her head resting on a cushion upon the arm of the divan.

Her hair was powdered and puffed in the fashion of half a century before, and a long ringlet fell on to the folds of lace that covered her bosom. Her gown, of a forgotten pattern, was shaped to the waist by a lavender sash and, thereafter, spread voluminous, billowing about her. A bracelet of enormous opals burned upon her arm.

Christopher watched her entranced, as she slept, easily as a child—easily as the dreaming princess in the enchanted castle behind the towering thickets of the fairy tale. In the dim pale-gold light, arched eyebrows, curved lips, slender hands resting folded on her lap, were of a remote and fragile elegance.

In that swift moment he felt that in her was the exquisiteness of the proud ladies who had once passed in the pageantries of his vanished dream-world: and thought of Margaret in the fantasy which she had made reality, with a longing and a love that became an ache.

He took one cat-footed step toward the distant door. Then another.

He had progressed to within ten paces of the couch when the lady stirred: one hand moved upward slightly, and then paused, and lay still on the lavender sash.

He halted, churning in his mind apologies, excuses, and explanations. He armed himself with a story in the fraction of time it took him to come to the belief that she had not awakened. A poor story; but something to proffer instantly—'Count Tollendhal—wandered into the wood—lost myself—saw lighted window—did not desire to disturb household.'

Still she did not move. He took three more quick paces, till he reached the wall opposite the windows, so that he should pass up along it toward the door, under the benign gaze of the Watteau shepherdesses, but out of her field of vision.

She stirred again when he was within twenty feet of her; for her hand started slowly to travel up to her bosom, fumbled amid the filmy lace above her gown, and paused, when it had surmounted that obstacle, at the spring of her throat. Watching, hypnotized by the slow movement, he saw that as the slim fingers continued to travel up the throat they left a grey wake in the whiteness—that they trailed through and not against a milky skin. It was the breaking of a spell. It was no enchanted girl that lay there, but an old woman, with dark hollows and harsh cords marring the once perfect curves of the throat.

Her lips parted; and, in their parting, shadows appeared in the contours of the cheek, and a network of fine lines revealed themselves about the mouth.

It was as if he watched the crumbling to dust of some exquisite princess who had lain undisturbed for long centuries in her alabaster sarcophagus beneath a pyramid.

He was too fascinated by horror to escape.

The fingers crept to the chin; passed infinitely wearily to the lips; the middle finger with a great diamond ring upon it caught for a moment in the corner of the upper lip, and dragged it upward a little in its passage. The fingers reached the cheek-bone, smearing paint and powder as they went, dipped into the eye-socket. Her hand spread across the forehead, and so remained spread, thumb and little finger resting on the closed lids of her eyes.

She suddenly addressed him without turning her head or moving at all.

'I imagine,' she said in a thin fluting voice, as—thought Christopher—a ghost might speak in a shadowy pinewood at twilight. . . . 'I imagine that our uninvited guest presents himself!'

He could not make up his mind to retreat, and stood uncertainly those few feet away from her, rather ashamedly drawing comfort from the pistol which his right hand clutched in the recesses of a pocket.

'Introduce yourself to me, guest!' she said, her fingers still pressing against the lids of her closed eyes.

There was some slight foreign intonation in her voice, and such lack of surprise that he knew his coming was not unexpected, and had been prepared against. He felt immediately convinced that the window had been left unlatched for him, and that already a sentinel was posted without.

He walked deliberately up to her couch. He bowed low before that masquerade of youth, that fading simulacrum of the loveliness of half a century before.

'I am Count von Tollendhal, madam,' he said formally. 'I wandered into your wood; lost myself for hours—utterly benighted. Then I saw your lighted windows, and made my way round. I did not wish to disturb your entire establishment.'

His story sounded, even to him, utterly false: and his voice was that of a stranger.

So, too, thought the ghost upon the settee, for she cackled with dry laughter.

Her fingers pressed deeper against her eyeballs. Then slowly she raised the eyelids with her finger by the lashless and mascaraed edges; and so held them open with hand and arm curved above, in the manner of one shielding her gaze from a glare. She was no longer even human, but something mechanical that was running down: a puppet with a vast wig of white ringlets, animated by some exterior and invisible force.

He suppressed a shudder and found himself looking into two green ice-cold eyes, youthful eyes—eyes in which no emotion of interest or curiosity or anger was displayed.

'Ah, Count von Tollendhal? . . . I am Madame de Boucher! . . . That conveys nothing to you? . . . No matter; it was all very long ago. Others may forget! . . . We are very glad to see you, Monsieur le Comte! We have been expecting you for a day or two! Ever since we heard that Colonel Fairman had been very indiscreet at York. Colonel Fairman is given to indiscretion. One of these days Colonel Fairman's indiscretions will be sadly awkward—for him. . . . As well as—for you!'

'I am at a loss, madam . . .' began Christopher.

'Yes,' she said; not interrogatively but in profound agreement. She did not turn her head to him as she spoke: its direction was toward the tips of her pointed satin shoes resting on the cushions, and the fire; but her eyes, as expressionless as those of a snake, were bent on him.

'I am an old woman,' she continued. 'I am partly paralysed, as you see. I have a great deal to do, and very little time in which to do it. So let us drop pretence. You have been interfering in my affairs. I do not know why. We heard from the drunken sot in Alexandria of a lost paper. We find that Colonel Fairman has been talking with his customary volubility to the bearer of that document. In view of what the colonel said we were certain you would honour us by a surreptitious visit. . . . Gustave! Jacques!'

She raised her voice very slightly.

From his place of concealment behind her couch rose a tall man in dark purple livery with a powdered club wig.

Christopher started back, and his right hand shot to his pocket; as it did so a strong grip closed on the wrist, and he swung a little round to see that another man, similarly dressed, had appeared behind him from God knew where.

He had no alternative to an attempt at escape.

He tried to jerk himself free from the clasp. At the same time, thrusting his right shoulder round into the man's chest, he struck fiercely with his left hand at the dark clean-shaven face.

The other's teeth clashed under the blow; but he did not let go, and flung his free arm round Christopher's throat. For a moment Christopher was thus helpless, whilst the second servant came quietly round the settee, walking with the gentle precision of a well-trained lackey about to fling wide a door.

Christopher bent his knees to a spring, and suddenly hurled himself backward. He fell with his captor violently to the floor; in the fall the servant released him; but before he could make use of the advantage, the second man was upon him.

The three of them rolled furiously along the parquet almost to the edge of Madame de Boucher's settee, striking and clutching at one another in a wild confusion.

Even as he struck at a snarling face beneath him, Christopher was conscious that Madame de Boucher spoke.

'Stay here,' said the flute-like voice, 'where I can see!'

He struck again at the face. The wig came off the man, and the shaven head cracked drily against the floor. Blood streamed from a great cut in the brow.

The other lackey flung himself squarely on top of Christopher. He pressed bony fingers into Christopher's throat, and tore at it, shaking his head from side to side with the violence and ferocity of a wild beast.

'Good!' said Madame de Boucher. 'Good!'

Christopher rose to his knees, by a great effort, upon the squirming body under him. He drove a fist home against the open mouth below, felt teeth breaking under the blow (in a split second's grim amusement wondered whether it was Gustave or Jacques he had thus disfigured) and wrenched himself round against his victim's mate. The man propelled himself forward against him. Christopher went over, and the two slid along the highly polished floor, against the malachite and bronze pedestal of a marble shepherdess in hoops and panniers, in a space between windows.

The second man's wig had fallen off as well. Christopher lying beneath him, tearing at the hands upon his throat, saw a red seam on his enemy's forehead running into the short dark stubble of his head.

At that minute the shepherdess toppled over. Her full weight crashed on to the lackey's unprotected skull, with a noise like the butt-end of a cue striking a billiard ball. A corner of her marble petticoat flicked Christopher on the temple and into unconsciousness.

He recovered his senses to find himself tied in an elbow-chair, facing Madame de Boucher across a fire-place where cupids in marble and gilt rioted amid cornucopias and lovers'-knots. There were no signs of disorder now amid the elegance of the gallery. In the amber light from innumerable sconces, the hooped ladies in swings, the exquisite hay-makers, the mock-modest bathers, simpered out of the tapestry panels in unperturbed amours. It was a little shocking to confront their delicacy with long drab gaiters that gaped at the thigh, where buttons had been reft away in conflict!

Madame de Boucher was regarding him, her eyelids still propped open by her fingers. She seemed to read his mind.

'Yes, Monsieur le Comte,' she said. 'You have lost a few gaiter buttons; and I have lost a very charming statue by Caffieri—and a lackey!'

With a brusque movement she took her hand away from her face, and the lids slid over her eyes like blinds being lowered suddenly and without a jerk, with the slick easy motion of the weighted eyeballs of an expensive doll.

A threatening silence reigned, broken only by the crumbling and settling of the logs in the grate.

'Madame,' he began—and, as he spoke, saw that the door behind her had swung open, and that the Duke of Cumberland, with a diamond star upon his coat, stood there peering at them. The distorted eyes in the famished face viewed them with the unwinking stare of a blind man. There was the white thread of a scar upon his forehead. He had not noticed it before.

'Ah, Mathilde, so you are entertaining—late though it is!' said the harsh voice. 'You must present your friend to me, before I leave. . . . The carriage, I am told, is ready.'

Madame de Boucher did not turn her head. A curious spasm convulsed her face, whereby every wrinkle, every line, and every hollow showed its chiselling. Innocent-seeming ice cracked over deep water. She did not even trouble to raise her hands, and go through the weary process of lifting her eyelids.

'Yes, monseigneur,' said she, 'I am entertaining, as you see. It is a visitor we have both desired to meet!' The duke approached, as she spoke, and sank into a chair set at some distance from them—'You permit me then to present to Your Royal Highness . . .'

'Ah, madame,' said Christopher, having no weapon left him but impertinence, 'would you present a nephew to his uncle?'

He bobbed his head forward in such ridiculous sketch of a bow as was permitted by the bonds that fastened his arms straitly behind the chair.

'Nephew!' said Madame de Boucher. 'Nephew!' And her hands began again the slow journey up to her eyes.

'My sight is not very good,' said the duke, turning his bleak face to Christopher. 'I thought, however, from the door that I knew that yellow head. We have been expecting you, nephew, for some little while!'

He clasped and unclasped his hands on the polished arm of the chair. A flush rose to his cheekbones, staining them to the colour of a bruised plum.

Christopher, despite his helplessness, flashed a half-look over his shoulder to the curtained windows.

A slow smile.

'We cannot let you go yet, nephew! Can we, madame? . . . We have counted so much on your coming—even though I did not know I should have the infinite pleasure of seeing my sister's son. . . . After all our little fun at Neipperg! I suppose, incidentally, you heard on your wanderings that it was thought best that poor Charles of Brunswick should abdicate?'

'Bit of a bad lad—Charles!' said Christopher.

Cumberland ignored the comment.

'Well, well!' said he indulgently. 'You would have found that we had left other windows open; but I imagine the mysterious influence of feminine elegance and charm guided you to these!'

He chuckled as he spoke. At least a sort of minor convulsion shook his mighty shoulders, although no sound accompanied the movement. He raised his great arms, and folded them, and hugged them against the barrel of his chest. There was such restrained violence in the action that Christopher called to mind how he was said to have emerged from battle at Minegueux, and returned to camp with an enemy captive crushed squirming to him. He held his head with its great beaked nose at a proud angle, like a falcon about to be unhooded and sent after the quarry from the wrist of a falconer.

'Well, nephew, those are odd clothes you are wearing to appear before a lady in! Even if the lady herself is dressed to look like her grandmother! A little unceremonious, my dear—er—Christopher!'

He chuckled again.

'This is your nephew then, monseigneur?' asked Madame de Boucher, utterly expressionless. She looked at Christopher once more, the forefinger of either hand pressed with her upper lids against the bony ridges of her eye-sockets. Moisture collected within the rim of her eyes, and oozed out and trickled down beside her painted nose.

'Nephew of sorts, Mathilde!' said the duke. 'Not the wrong side of the blanket exactly, but certainly born in the wrong bedroom. . . . Colonel Fitzroy has given me scraps of news about him since our last rencontre. Let me see; what was the name?—Christopher . . . Christopher Harnish! That was it.'

'Count von Tollendhal and Baron Harnisch—with a "c"—nowadays!' said Christopher.

'Christopher Harnish?' said Madame de Boucher: and let the blinds of her eyes fall, as if the windows of her soul had gone into mourning. 'Well, indeed! You always appear to be fighting when we meet! . . . The last time I saw you was when you were doing your best to kill your step-brother in a garden near the Kensington Gravel Pits! I suppose one would call him your step-brother! At any rate he was your father's son, by a second, and slightly more legal marriage. I remember quite well. You escaped next door. Colonel Fitzroy was very annoyed.'

'Papa has been annoyed with me on one or two occasions,

madame. On that particular occasion an acquaintance of mine spat on his nice new mourning suit—if I recollect rightly!'

'Tcha!' said the duke, crossing his legs clad in black stockingette pantaloons, and uncrossing them; and beating an irritable tattoo on the arms of the chair.

'Now, Mr. What's-your-name, what's the meaning of all this? Spying; and sneaking; and prying about into things that don't concern you in the least! I understand from Colonel Fitzroy that a short time ago you expressed your sympathy with a certain policy: that, in fact, you destroyed some letters which might have been difficult of explanation! Very right and wise! Letters which the damn-fool Dunscore—most unreliable man—saw fit to leave lying about. . . . Now I find you completely turned round, like a wigwam, or tee-totum, or whatever it may be, and nosing about like a damned secret agent. What's the meaning of it all?'

'It means, sir,' said Christopher, 'that I've had a change of heart since I burned Lord Dunscore's correspondence. There is no need for me to go into reasons. I am ashamed I did it—so ashamed that I've been trying to undo what I did.'

'Ashamed, by God!' said the duke. He produced a very small penknife, and set to paring his finger-nails with such ferocity that he drew blood. A thin red thread ran round the cuticle of his forefinger. 'Ashamed, were you? Well, the fact that you had a childish attack of conscience doesn't explain your intrusion here as a spy.'

Christopher remained silent.

The duke put away his little knife.

'It may amuse you to know, Mr. Bloody Harnish, that your visit here was planned for you!'

'Oh, was it?'

'It was, my young friend. Colonel Fairman may be a garrulous ass, but he's no fool. When he had already told you a great deal too much, his suspicions were aroused. He concocted a pretty little story that should bring you here. These headquarters, which Madame de Boucher has provided, are pleasantly private—pleasantly remote! Most convenient for all sorts of purposes.'

'Throat-cutting, for instance!' remarked Christopher.

'Throat-cutting?' repeated the duke slowly on a note of self interrogation. He ground his back teeth together, so that there came from them the little dry squeak of a pencil travelling over a slate. He rocked himself to and fro, with his hairy hands clasped between his knees. He turned his dark regard on the motionless woman in the grey silk sprigged with green. He brooded over her, as Belphegor might brood over one possessed.

'Throat-cutting?' said the duke again, and continued to brood. And then, as if he had realized the implications of the word, he raised his head and said in mild protest, 'Oh, come, come!'

Madame de Boucher's jaw quivered with faint quick vibrations. The invisible puppet-mistress was having difficulty with her eighteenth-century marionette!

Madame de Boucher's mouth suddenly came under control, was obedient, and shaped husky words:

'And why not throat-cutting! . . . One throat is a small and easily destructible'—she pronounced the word as if it were French —'thing to stand between Your Royal Highness and a throne! The cutting of a thousand throats would not deter *me*!'

'Yes, don't let considerations of family deter you, sir! Any more than they did from arranging target practice at Victoria! When she was a child in arms.'

The duke paid Christopher no attention.

'The point against throat-cutting, my dear Mathilde, is that in itself it would be believed to be evidence of the justice of the claims made by this young man. There is the same argument against keeping him prisoner until—until events occur. His disappearance might be held extremely suspicious in the circumstances —extremely suspicious.'

He crossed his legs—uncrossed them again; patted the great star on his chest; turned his dark twisted eyes on Christopher.

'You've been very foolish, my boy,' he said in a softened tone. Wasn't it the wolf in the legend who ate chalk to soften the harshness of his voice? Christopher felt there was something of the chalk-eating wolf in that dark sinister man. 'Very foolish!' he went on. 'Now let me see if I can't persuade you to let things alone, to give me your word to keep silence. And then you can go home, and we shall all be happy and comfortable. You must, of course, realize that we can't let you go otherwise!'

'I got caught rather badly, didn't I?' said Christopher thoughtfully. 'Fairman isn't such a fool as his long tongue would lead one to believe.'

'You will be doing nothing unpatriotic or anti-dynastic,' continued Cumberland persuasively. 'I'm not thinking of myself in this business—not at all. Only of England—our dear old England! Your England! My England!'

'Madame de Boucher's England?' inquired Christopher with a hint of insolence.

'Madame de Boucher is my old friend, and a very valued adviser,' said Cumberland shortly. 'Now I want you to think sensibly upon the position. Clear your mind of all this treason rubbish. When poor William goes—and he cannot last long—what happens? A girl in her teens inherits the Crown at the most crucial period in English history! It's ludicrous! It's criminal! It's madness! Things are bad enough now. They'll be infinitely worse then. We've got to have a strong hand.' His voice rose as he spoke, and he became furious with excitement. 'We've got to have no more truckling to Popery! No more pandering to the mob! No more proselytizing by these blackguard Republicans! No ignoring treason and sedition preached in the muck-heap newspapers! No failure to send dragoons after rick burners, or to puff grape-shot into threatening crowds!'

'Can you guarantee all this, sir?'

'Will you get it with a half-witted girl brought up in the worst possible way? Like a nun! By that fat Cat of Kensington—that bloody aboriginal from Coburg? No! She'll be in the hands of the Whigs, and Papists, and so-called Reformers from the moment she pulls the Crown down over her rabbit face! . . . No, the really patriotic thing for you to do, my boy, is either to forget what you were never intended to know, or, possibly, to join us yourself. That is my honest advice.'

Christopher appeared to meditate. He had no plans, and knew that he must play for time.

'Supposing things turn out as I expect, then there will be plenty of reward. We might ignore, for instance, certain aspects of your descent: remember only that your mother was a Princess of Great Britain. William made his eldest illegitimate son Earl of Munster. There's no reason why your status should not be recognized in the same manner.'

He paused with his head slightly tilted to one side; and a smile, supposed to be ingratiating, lifted his lips sideways like a snarling beast's.

Something about the offer—perhaps it was the bracketing of himself with William's casually begotten bastards—infuriated Christopher, and drove common sense from his head.

'Honours such as are given to the come-by-chance children of Uncle William mean very little to me,' said he. 'I am afraid, dear Uncle, that you and he are so frightfully out of date! You should have been born in the time of Charles the Second, when the normal means of recruiting the peerage was through the willing co-operation of royal concubines.'

'Tcha!' interjected the duke.

'To-day, it won't do! Whatever Uncle William may think!'

'There are other rewards,' suggested Cumberland.

'There are the gallows, the firing squad, and Tower Hill—for traitors!' said Christopher.

Something in the duke's expression told him that the older man had never thought of the penalties of failure. He had visualized only a shattering and successful coup that would leave him master of England—not the fatal barge journey from Whitehall Stairs to Traitor's Gate.

'Do you really count on success?' said Christopher, after a short period of silence.

'I can seize control of every garrison town when the time comes.' His nostrils dilated. He threw his great head back. 'I have enough men in London to deal with every eventuality. I can have an armed ring around Whitehall, seize the Mint and the Tower and the Government offices, and whisk niece Victoria and her mamma into—into security, within four hours of knowing that the time is ripe.'

'You are very certain, sir!'

'Certain? Of course I am! I have been a soldier for forty-six years and a politician for twenty.'

'This very theoretical discussion,' said the ice-cold voice of Madame de Boucher, 'really carries us no farther. The point at issue is whether our argumentative young friend will behave himself or not.'

'If by "behave" you mean act as a traitor; then I am not g-g-going to be-behave,' said Christopher, stammering with a fury which he was unable to analyse. 'I've b-b-been a traitor in the past. I'd rather die than be one again.'

'Fine words!' said Madame de Boucher, sarcastically. 'Fine-fine words!'

'Fine words, m-m-ma'am! But I mean them. I'm sick of my family. England's s-s-s-sick of it. I'd rather mildew here than join you. I want to start a new f-f-family that begins with me. Victoria's job is the same. I'm g-g-going to do nothing that shall spoil her chance!'

He found it impossible to feel heroic, shattered by his stammer whenever he spoke; strapped so tightly as he was to the chair; and in the face of the unmoved woman and the formidable menace of the duke. And since he could strike none of the accepted postures, he tinged his sentences with a little of the histrionic—knew it, and was a trifle ashamed.

Madame de Boucher realized it, and tittered. He felt himself blush.

The duke brooded, chin on fist, elbow on knee, equidistant between the painted mummy of a woman, and the young man with his arms tied behind him in his chair.

Madame de Boucher said nothing. The duke remained silent, but in that silence there seemed to be growing within him a great and terrible anger—too enormous for words, so enormous that his body appeared hardly able to contain it. An anger, like a demoniac possession, that shook his whole being; brought dark blood to his face; and lowered the brows over his eyes, as though to hide murder, should it peer out!

'My dear Ernest, we can stage a little shooting accident, a carriage mishap, even a duel!' said Madame de Boucher at last. 'It is all quite easy. My people can deal with most situations—and particularly with potential informers! It would not be the first time!'

She spoke very easily, without any visible movement to show that she was a living woman. The body in the sprigged gown lying on the carved and gilded couch, in the soft glow of the candles, might have been long dead—painted and dressed to lie in a silken shroud and coffin of cedar under a sarcophagus of white alabaster—and used but as a vehicle for speech by some remorseless spirit.

The duke remained silent, but he shook like a palsied man.

He rose presently. He stood over Madame de Boucher.

'It will be best to leave you to deal with the situation as you think fit,' he said, and looked down on her, keeping his face turned away from the captive.

'I suppose that I remind you too m-m-much of your sister,' hazarded Christopher in comment on the averted countenance. 'I imagine that Richard Crookback felt the same when he g-g-gave orders for the murder of the Princes in the Tower. Or K-King John when he arranged for little Arthur to be put away. You and I are joining a fine company, Uncle! Uncle! Uncle! Even poor old James the Second must have had something of the same qualms when he sent Monmouth to execution! . . . Uncle!'

He found a malicious joy in claiming his relationship again and again.

'Uncle! . . . Uncle! . . . Uncle!' repeated Madame de Boucher thoughtfully, in a soft-toned version of Christopher's crescendo— in a voice that seemed to come from far away. Her repetition of the word, unexpected as it was, struck the Duke of Cumberland as if it had been a physical blow. Christopher, watching the dark figure posed above the near-corpse, saw it quiver.

The big man turned abruptly, flung across the floor, and loomed over his nephew. There was a faint smell of lavender-water about him; his clasped hands, smooth and white, were but a little below the level of Christopher's eyes; his nails were white too, and well kept, but short as if they had been much bitten in childhood, and one of them was rimmed with the dull red of dried blood. He stood with head a little turned, so that it was his sightless eye that glared down at the young man through a mesh of shaggy grey eyebrows.

'You are wrong about two things, nephew,' he said. 'Firstly, if you think that the appeal to our relationship will affect me in the least. Secondly, if you still think that I am going into this matter for myself alone. God ordained the Church, Kingship and Property! He ordained classes, and set them in their order. He ordained the duties of Kingship. His enactments must be observed despite the bloody pratings of shoddy democracy. It would take you and a million like you to turn me from my course. . . . And my rights!'

Suddenly rage seemed to overmaster him. He stormed up and down the room, raving; with restless hands that clasped themselves, unclasped, pulled at his coat-collar, at his waistcoat, clenched into fists, and spread themselves into the talons of a strangler. He pushed forward his great head with its beak of a nose, so that he resembled a vulture contemplating carrion. His face had become the colour of dark wine.

Words bubbled to his lips, came tumbling out, so fast that but one in three was comprehensible. He cursed his brother William, Wellington, Brougham, Cobbett . . . a whole string of names: he threatened, railed, blasphemed. He pulled himself up with a sudden jerk, in front of the young man, and darted his head out toward him in the manner of a striking snake.

'So, nephew,' said he, with a deadly calm, 'on the whole it will be better to leave you to the care of Madame de Boucher. It is a pity, but your own fault! She was right. She usually is. . . . I *will* say that for you, Mathilde!'

A little bell sounded without the door. Both folds were on the instant flung open and two tall men in purple livery with powdered wigs appeared.

'Take this gentleman to the room that has been made ready for him,' said Madame de Boucher, in French. 'It would be as well, perhaps, were you to carry him in the chair. It would prevent any further needless destruction.'

The lackeys hoisted chair and man up together, so that Christopher rode between them like some Oriental prince, too high-born to soil his dangling feet upon the earth—or, perhaps, a Guy Fawkes on his way to the bonfire.

'I should think over things during the night, young man,' said the duke watching the operation with the dispassionate interest of a foreign military attaché at a review. 'I should reflect. I should weigh pros and cons. I should disencumber my mind of dangerous fantasies. Sanity, balance, and tact are the cardinal virtues! And to-morrow I should send word to Madame de Boucher that I had come to my senses. I fear it may be very unpleasant for you, otherwise!'

'Thank you for your advice,' said Christopher violently. 'I still would rather have my throat cut than live in an England ruled by you—and your lady friend!' . . . Felt he had been rather melodramatic, and, to his horror, found himself giggling.

perous fantasies. Swiftly I glanced at her and the cardinal declined. And to-morrow I must not speak to Madame de Boufflers that I had come to my senses. I felt it must be very unpleasant for you to—
'I had told her about the cardinal—'
would rather have the blood out of my face in an English role. be you—and your lady (how—?). The lady was rather more dramatic, and, to his horror, found himself laughing.

Chapter 36

Chit-Chat Between Father and Son

A SQUARE FOUR-POSTER BED WITH GREEN CURTAINS, itself as large as a small room, awaited Christopher in a fire-lit bedchamber hung with tapestries telling of the amours of Sappho and Bilitis. A candlestick, a decanter of light pink wine, and a plate of sandwiches were on a table at the bedhead. A chair covered in a brocade of faded rose and old ivory was drawn up before the fire: otherwise the room was bare of furniture.

A grave groom of the chambers in black livery presided at the bed-going ceremonial—with a brace of long pistols. Under the almost apologetic menace of their muzzles Christopher was courteously inducted into a bedgown and night-cap, was put to bed, was comforted with his wine and meat, and, finally was padlocked by a light steel bracelet and long chain to a bedpost. With low bows and all his clothing the party then withdrew, as if they had been attendant noblemen at the coucher of a Prince of the Blood: indeed, they all but backed out of the Presence—after one of them had indicated a small silver bell that had been hidden behind the decanter of vin rosé.

'S'il-y-a quelque chose que Monsieur le Comte desirerait!'

Monsieur le Comte desired nothing—nothing at least that he could get for the mere sounding of a little silver bell.

He lay awake watching the coals sift through the bars of the grate on to the white marble hearthstone, and the red glowing mass crumble into fawn and grey dust. He wondered if the house-keeper would guess that the long scratches on the delicate fluting of the bedpost were caused by the swinging, at his every movement, of the long chain by which he was padlocked to it. In sheer malice he swung his hand to and fro until the wine-coloured column was as scarred by the steel links as if an army of cats had climbed up and down during an entire night; reproved himself for his childishness; fell to deeper meditation.

Lying there, in the profound stillness of a house as silent as the sky, with death waiting for him as certainly as dusk waits upon day; with his very breath muffled by tapestries telling of forgotten lovers and woven by hands long since quiescent, folded, mouldered —lying there in the house of impending death, he thought of Margaret.

He knew, even more surely than he had known in Texas, that when he should be dead—and death, he conceived, must be very near—something within him would go faring out of his useless body, through the night, to the quiet home above the misty marsh, and would enter, and would be welcomed there. He was so certain of the glad recognition that would be given to his ghost that he became equally certain how unimportant a body was. It would make no change in the quality of Margaret's love whether he were in the spirit or the flesh—or in the quality of any love, if it were really love! What did it matter should anything happen to the vessel that contained the essence which was himself: whether anything had happened long ago to the vessel that contained the soul of Margaret?

A door opened and shut softly. Quiet feet trod the deep carpet. A figure stood at the foot of the bed, darkly silhouetted against the glow of the fire, framed between the tall carved posts that bore the tasselled canopy. Although he could not see the features, he knew who it was.

'Here's Papa come to comfort his little son!' said the cold mocking voice.

'Dear, dear Papa!' said Christopher ironically, levering himself against the pillows. 'Come to kiss me good-bye?'

'Yes, I think you might almost say that,' replied Fitzroy thoughtfully. 'I am rather afraid that I may have to steel myself to be the Roman father!'

He pulled the chair from the fireside, and established himself in it near the table at the bedhead. He sat in the light of the solitary candle, with crossed knees, and white hands pressed finger to finger together on his lap. He appeared to have changed not one whit through the years—face as full and smooth and white; a dark correct lock arranged upon the forehead; cold black eyes, heavy-lidded with faint blue stains under them.

'Quite a family gathering!' said Christopher conversationally. 'It has been nice having a heart-to-heart talk with Uncle Ernest. . . . And now Papa!'

'Don't omit your Grandmamma! To make the circle complete!'

'Grandmother!'

'The lady you broke in on . . .'

'Oh, Christ!' said Christopher. 'That!'

He shut his eyes, closing the lids hard; as if he could, by so doing, shut out the very memory of the woman who was so obscenely dead and yet alive.

'That! Yes!'

The two remained in silence. The candle flickered in its socket. A small wind got up, and rustled without the house among the trees that pressed against its walls. The glow of the fire diminished until the reflection of it in the dark hearth was as the cold after-light of a wintry sunset.

It took all his imagination to remind him that Christopher Harnish lay dead with Glasscock among the prairie flowers of Texas—under the surge of the Atlantic—in a cypress swamp of Louisiana: that Christopher von Tollendhal knew no more of these revolting people than Margaret Atchill did of the harlot who had spawned Deborah Hunt.

'Well! So that was Christopher's grandmother!' he said at last, and turned his regard from the dim canopy of the bed upon his father, and swung over on his side with a faint jingle of chains so that he could see him the better.

'Your mother?' he added with faint interrogation.

'My mother,' assented Fitzroy easily. 'Definitely my mother—although very few people know it.'

'Mistress of the Prince Regent!' continued Christopher, bringing the matter to its logical conclusion.

'That was her sister!'

'But George . . .'

'No, George was not my father,' said Fitzroy with sudden violence. 'Not my father!'

Christopher sat bolt upright in bed.

'Then it was untrue that my mother's marriage . . .'

'Contrary to belief, it was quite respectable. Against the Royal Marriage Act, of course, but quite in order otherwise! I was of no kin to her at all. Your grandmother has a deep sense of humour. Her little joke—which we have kept entirely to the family—cost old George the Third his reason, as I told you. It nearly sent my presumed papa out of his mind as well. How we laughed!'

Christopher wondered if he could leap from bed quickly enough to seize his father and squeeze the full throat until the pallid face became purple, and blood burst from the heavy-lidded eyes.

'It was a neat conception,' said Fitzroy, taking another candle which lay in the dish of the chamber candlestick, lighting it, and planting it in the hot grease of its predecessor; and talking while he did so.

'I am telling you this so that you shall thoroughly understand the real position—our position—that of your grandmother and myself! It may persuade you to be a little less recalcitrant and disobliging. Don't think I am impelled by any fatherly feeling. I am not. But neck-breaking of any sort is always a nuisance, and it will come to neck-breaking, I am afraid, if you are not sensible.'

'You dirty misbegotten bastard!' said Christopher.

Before his eyes—staring into the dimness of the room—there swam the likeness of his mother which he had long since thrown away in his passion of horror: the likeness of that pale princess with the long tragic face—the princess whom Setoun had loved. He rolled over on to his face to hide the tears that streamed down his cheeks at the thought of her needless agony.

'You poor, miserable whelp!' said Fitzroy rising to his feet. 'Do you realize that your mother's brothers murdered my father? Murdered him as surely as if they had strangled him with their own hands?'

Christopher lay silent upon his face.

Fitzroy stooped over the bed and shook him by the shoulder.

'Listen to me! You *shall* listen to me! I tell you, you shall. I *will* tell you.' He spoke with extraordinary violence. 'My father fled from France with my mother and with me when the Revotion broke out. He had invested money in a loan raised by George and his brothers, Clarence and York. When he asked for the agreed interest, it was contested. When he asked again he was deported. Sent back to France under the Aliens Act, without right of appeal! To death! To the guillotine! My father! My father! He was murdered by the swine! They knew what would happen.'

He paused, chided himself for his excitement with a mild 'Tut tut!' Seated himself again.

'Does the story interest you, Count von Tollendhal?' he asked politely.

'Go on!' said Christopher into the pillows.

'From that moment your grandmother lived for nothing but revenge. She bred me up for it. We *have* taken it. We are taking it. We *will* take it. Against that miserable family—against England.

'Your grandmother was a very good-looking young woman. She was immensely rich. It was not difficult for her to attract Cumberland—the mad wolf. She became his mistress. She urged him on in every conspiracy and madness to which his ambition led him. She lay in his arms and fondled him so that she might be better able to strike at his family, at his brothers, and at him. She had a child by him. Born on a winter night—down here. She rose herself in the darkness and placed it in the snow and watched it die. So that on the Hanoverian blood in it she should have her revenge!'

Christopher turned his head, so that, while he still lay face down, he could watch his father.

Fitzroy was sitting with one lavender-trousered leg cocked over the other. He was regarding the glint of a thin lacquered boot. He went on:

'I do not think there has been a single revolutionary plot in England to which she has not subscribed—from that piece of foolishness in Cato Street to the insurrection schemes which the Political Unions had prepared in case the Reform Bill did not get through.'

'Tell me,' said Christopher, 'more—more . . . about yourself!'

'It's really very simple,' said his father flashing him a glance. 'Your grandmother's sister was George's mistress when he was young. She died in giving birth to a still-born child—his—in France—at our place; before the Revolution. After mamma had collected up Cumberland it was as easy as winking to pass me off to George as that child. He'd been very fond of my aunt. Very fond! So I got my little places at Court. Naturally we didn't spread abroad the story of my supposed relationship—at the time. Your grandmother was a great tactician. She had all the influence in the world over Cumberland. And Cumberland used to bully poor George. . . . So there's your genesis. Literally, there you are!'

Fitzroy extracted a leather case from a pocket, produced a long cheroot, and lit it at the candle; drew appreciatively for a moment or two at the brown cylinder; flicked the ash off on to the floor; examined the tip to see that it was burning evenly.

'When you were born,' he said. 'Parenthetically, I hope I don't weary you.—When you were born you represented the highly successful fruition of the most subtle of your grandmother's schemes of revenge. Except for the little affair with Victoria, she has had no interest in you since. . . .' He chuckled. '. . . I don't think I have ever seen anyone more pleased than she was when she broke the news of the marriage to George. She came down here afterwards—her father bought this place when he bolted from France at the Revolution—and had bonfires lighted, gave village treats with free beer, and general high jinks.'

'Giddy old creature!' said Christopher rather childishly, picturing the dead-alive thing downstairs capering like a skeleton strung on wire about a balefire on a mountain top. 'Giddy old creature!' he said again.

The wind was rising; the susurration of the encircling woods surged upwards into a rush as of a great sea; the fire collapsed with a crash; the tapestries billowed a little in a stray draught that had crept into the room and could not escape.

Christopher, lying in bed, with the thin steel chain resting on the pillow an inch or so from his face, felt an entire detachment from the drama of which his father told. He was sorry for the poor pale princess. He was sorry for that wretched baby who had lain out in the snow. For the unknown grandfather who had been sent out of safety to death upon the scaffold. But he felt no more personal grief or interest than if the hideous story had been played out before the footlights in simulated emotions by hireling actors. They were remote from him. He had disowned the play and left the theatre.

'Of course,' said Fitzroy, negligently swinging a toe up and down, 'you may well imagine, my dear Christopher, that there was nothing more to be got out of my dear "papa", after that. However, your grandmother pulled a string or two, and lo and behold, I was very comfortably placed with Cumberland—your dear Uncle Ernest! If Ernest ever could do anything to annoy his brothers or sisters you could rely on him to do it. For the sheer pleasure of maddening the Regent he made me equerry, and his very special agent. So I've helped his funny plans—very funny plans! And I've helped your grandmother's funny plans—still funnier plans: and got a great deal of fun in doing it! Uncle Ernest would have a nasty shock if he knew how much enjoyment she and I get out of forwarding his schemes—so long as they agree with our own! And this time I think we are on the best thing we have ever struck.'

'Meaning to say,' interpreted Christopher, rolling over at last on to his back, 'that you are helping Cumberland because you are sure that revolution would immediately follow any coup by him? A revolution that would bring down the whole royal family? Probably end in a republic?'

'You sum it up quite succinctly,' said Fitzroy in a tone that suggested that he was anxious to encourage political-mindedness in a not unintelligent offspring. 'Uncle Ernest will pull the chestnuts out of the fire—the royal chestnuts—for your grandmother. And he will undoubtedly burn his paws! Burn them right off. We have waited a long time, my mother and I. My father's blood still cries for vengeance. It shall have it. In full measure. In brimming measure.'

There was a strange fierce light in his eye. He added:

'I adored my father. You—being a Hanoverian—don't, I fear, adore me! Too bad! You will hardly understand the emotion. I was a boy, but my mother made me swear to exact full vengeance. . . .'

He paused, and continued after a while in an utterly different tone—drily, speaking as one man of the world to another. 'Incidentally she is a remarkably rich woman. Perhaps the richest woman in England!'

Christopher said nothing.

'I am not going to ask you to come to any decision, now,' continued Fitzroy. 'But I ask you to meditate during the watches of the night on the folly of interference. Give your word to keep silence, and you'll go free. Otherwise—well, you can't think that the plans that have been maturing for something like ten years are going to be upset because of you, now can you? You really can't count on any sympathy from me. Our relationship is purely accidental, and incidental. Fatherhood often is. You probably know it yourself. I daresay you've got one or two stray brats knocking about the world—even in Kent!'

Even in Kent! So they knew about Margaret! If he had not been fettered like a wild animal he would, like that wild animal, have thrown himself at the other's throat.

'By Christ,' he said, 'I believe I would rather have had a roadsweeper for a father than you!'

A slight flush mounted to Fitzroy's white cheek. He flicked ash over on to the quilt, and rose.

'We'll continue our talk with your grandmother at a later date. I should recommend you to curb a tendency to impertinence in her presence. She appreciates it singularly little. And she is a dangerous woman to offend.

'I am afraid you must count as one of the Hanoverian family. She does not love them. Neither do I,' and he ground his teeth. 'They have been a curse for a long time to the nation. They have been a curse to themselves for almost as long. Your grandmother is making certain that the curse recoils in full upon their own heads. I should remain safely neutral, if I were you, rather than partake of their fate.'

'Good night!' said Christopher.

But he found it difficult to sleep, for, apart from his furious imaginings, the wind had risen to a rushing, roaring storm. It beat against the house—a clamorous sea; and all the woodlands round rustled and sighed with the perpetual song of an undertow along a pebbly shore, amid the booming of breakers.

Something fell with a crash and was shattered upon the roof, and avalanched in pieces across the slates: the noise of its final fall was drowned in a blast that made the house quiver.

Morning came; thin light slid into the room through a narrow line between the heavy window-curtains—grey light that grew white by slow degrees. Hours seemed to pass before the groom of the chambers eventually appeared with his bodyguard of two stalwart footmen, pulled back the curtains, and set a tray of coffee and rolls on a silver platter at the bedside.

Christopher propped himself up on his pillows, and ate his breakfast, watching the efforts of one of the men to light the fire.

William, and the Gainers, would be beginning to wonder what had become of him, he told himself. But he did not see how they would be able to conduct a relief expedition past padlocked lodge-gates, guards, and thicket and moat. Or, indeed, how they could guess where he had gone, as he had said nothing. The fire belched out a sudden cloud of smoke over the man who, on his knees, was lighting it.

For long afterwards he lay there, staring through the square panes of the window at the windy sky, the white-grey cloud mass that sped past as if it were the wake of the world through the seas of heaven.

The roaring of the wind seemed to him to sing the dirge of the dishonoured princes from whom he sprang: whose sins had raised up so monstrous a revenge.

No one came near him all day except the silent servants. They brought him a recherché lunch on a tray, and Voltaire's *Candide* and *Princesse de Babylon* for light entertainment. It was dusk before they again returned, with candles, his clothes neatly brushed and folded, and a light dinner which they set out for him on the bedside table.

He had felt all along that nothing would happen until nightfall. He had been certain that nothing ever could happen before material darkness had been joined to those shadows out of the past: then only would that strange house wake to violent life.

The great wind still stormed without; its violence battered on the walls and shook the window frames, and its uproar wearied the ears and brain.

'Monsieur le Comte will be so good as to dress himself after dinner,' said one of the cat-footed servants persuasively as he withdrew. 'Madame will wish to receive him.'

It was while he was eating his dinner—a sole beautifully cooked; the wing of a chicken; a cream cheese—that he remarked that the bedside table had a drawer with a little yellowed ivory knob amid the sherry-coloured sheen of its mahogany.

He had no expectation but to find it empty when he idly pulled it open: within, however, lay a copy of the indecent *Heptameron* of Marguerite of Navarre, beautifully bound in rosy leather with a ducal coronet and the initial letter 'C' stamped on the binding. There was also a pocket-pistol no longer than the palm of a hand, with chased silver butt and the same tokens of ownership. Obviously Cumberland had been the previous tenant, and left his bedside literature and defence behind him.

'Dear, dear Uncle Ernest!' said Christopher aloud, and laughed at the irony of such an involuntary bequest from one of his doomsmen. Uncle Ernest probably never felt safe of nights unless he slept with a pistol beside him. He examined the weapon. It was loaded. He had one shot! Well, even one shot was a very useful thing—if one could arrange to fire it.

His clothes had been tidily placed over the back of the brocade chair, which was drawn up close to the table to carry a tray with the surplus of his dinner—a decanter and a dish of fruit. There was no need to examine them: he could see even in the mild light of the candles that the pockets of the green shooting-jacket were empty. They had been obviously searched. They—had—been obviously—searched! And if they had been so searched once, they would probably not be looked at again. There was enough length of chain to permit him to get out of bed and drop the little pistol into one of the capacious side-pockets of the jackets.

He had leaped back into bed, and was quietly enjoying a glass of excellent claret when his decorous guards reappeared.

He was freed from his chain, allowed to bathe decently before the fire, and clothe himself under the supervision of the groom of the chambers, and with the respectful assistance of two man-servants. He shrugged himself into the coat held for him, whistling gaily. No one noticed the extra weight!

One shot! It might stave someone off sufficiently for him to make a breakaway. One shot!

He was taken downstairs again. To a great dim room, at the far end of which an enormous gilded bed stood upon a dais. The pillars of it, supported by fat cherubs, carried a high tented canopy, crowned by a shrubbery of ostrich feathers that mingled with the shadows of the ceiling. It sat in a golden radiance amid the gloom, as if it were a high altar in a darkened church.

In the centre of that radiance, propped up high by a snowy mountain range of pillows there faced him the powdered romantic wig, the delicately tinted mask, behind which moved restlessly the brain of Madame de Boucher. Her eyes were shut. Like the Sleeping Beauty—thought Christopher, and toyed with fantastic imaginings of the shock that any prince would sustain who should try to awaken her in the accepted manner.

A frozen Court stood about her—a grim woman in antique dress with iron-grey ringlets falling upon the white scarf covering her neck and shoulders; a tall red-headed young man fiddling all the time with his over-tight wrist-bands; the sallow major-domo whose long narrow eyes regarded him sideways like a cat's.

His father, nearer to him, was propped against a carved mantel-piece, his features just visible in the firelight, one violet-clad arm lying along the shelf and playing negligently with a double-bar-relled pistol that lay there. A vast indistinct man in the livery of an upper servant guarded the door, and another stood motion-less before the long curtains of one of the many windows.

Colonel Fitzroy beckoned Christopher to an isolated chair set in front of a window and opposite him; and signed to the escort that they might depart.

'You and I, my dear Christopher, are, I fear in *négligé*,' said

Fitzroy. 'But your grandmother will excuse us, I am sure, as we are necessarily not constant visitors at her little Court.'

Madame de Boucher's hands went up to her face, travelling slowly with spread fingers. Again she dragged back the lids from the green-glinting eyes. She murmured a word to the iron-grey woman at her side. The iron-grey woman bent over her, and with expert deftness pressed something delicately upon each eyelid—a white demi-lune of sticking-plaster, which gummed it in position.

The long hands dropped wearily upon the coverlet of rose and silver.

She looked—thought Christopher—like Marie Antoinette at her *petit lever*. No, she didn't. He knew the violence and the vengeance that lay behind that still figure, that pink-and-white mask. She looked like the wolf in the story of Red Riding Hood, masquerading as the Grandmother. In the second before she spoke, as he sat isolate in his chair, the cynosure of all eyes, he suddenly felt that she might spring at him from the unruffled bed in one bound, her thin robe revealing the shaggy haunches of a great beast. No bullet could stop her—save it were of silver, and marked with the sign of the Cross!

'Well, Grandson,' said Grandmother Wolf, 'so now you know a little more about things?'

'A little, ma'am.'

'You are not surprised at my somewhat marked dislike of the—of your family!'

'Not "my family", ma'am. I disown 'em. My connection is less voluntary than—for instance, than your association with the Duke of Cumberland.'

She apparently approved the remark, for the Cupid's bow painted about her lips altered its shape into the resemblance of a faint smile. Fitzroy shot him one quick look—of warning, was it, or just sardonic appreciation?

'Your birth and my "association" with the duke are both incidental to the theme,' said the remote high voice from the bed. 'Useful enough in their time and in their way. Let us leave the matter. . . . I judge from your statement that you do not particularly care for the family you have disowned.'

Christopher appeared to meditate, arm akimbo, with the palm of a hand resting upon a hip, and the fingers pressing against that small pistol which lay secretly and snugly within the pocket flapping over his thigh. A single candle burned upon the table beside him. In the accentuation of chin and nose and cheekbone by its light, his father caught the likeness to the dead Princess—that Princess who had wept and turned from him and guessed, by some too late instinct the part which he had played. Behind the smooth calm brow he cursed the ghost.

As if she had read his mind Madame de Boucher said suddenly: 'Yes, Grandson, you are certainly like your mother!'

There was no warmth in her voice: she stated only a rather unpleasant fact . . . diagnosed an irritation.

'My mother?' said Christopher, slowly. 'My mother! There was an unhappy girl who brought my outer husk into the world. But motherhood is something more than a physical accident. Within this body is the real Me! And it is no more a son of the Hanoverians than of—him!' He turned his head slightly in the direction of Fitzroy, and ended 'Thank God!' Hadn't Margaret said the same thing?

He wondered if the demi-lunes of plaster hurt the eyelids they hid. At the distance he was from Madame de Boucher, they lent to her face the appearance of a mask with empty eye-sockets, through which the whiteness of the pillows showed. The iron-grey woman bent over the mask, and delicately wiped the corners of the blankness, as if she were the guardian of a statue that had become a trifle stained.

'You apparently are no enthusiast for your mother's family,' said his grandmother, paying no more heed to the operation than if she had been that statue. 'They are foul, treacherous, murderous, lustful, lunatic, dishonoured . . .'

Her voice rose, grew thinner, became a high piping as though the wind were blowing through her teeth. Christopher knew that a storm was sweeping across the sea of restless anger that lay within her soul—knew that if she had been whole she would have raged about the room, that her wrath was battering against her immobile body—a wild thing in a cage.

Antoine!' she said with an extraordinary urgency. 'Antoine!'

The big man on duty by the door raised an arm as long as a gorilla's; the shadow of it for an instant lengthened up the wall to the high ceiling. Then with one quick jerk, the fellow swept a tall Chinese vase from a commode near him to the floor. It crashed with the noise of a bomb bursting, and the shards of it went skimming across the floor as if on ice.

The destruction fulfilled some spiritual need, for she went on more quietly.

'You have seen for yourself the filthiness of them! You have seen how a King can treat his wife! You know what Cumberland can do—without my assistance! You have seen the imbecile Brunswick —the fat idiot Caroline. You have heard a great deal more. They have the mercenary brains of little tradesmen in the lusty bodies of peasants. You know it. You know they are without honour. You know they nonchalantly sent my husband to the guillotine—and many others—to avoid paying their just debts. Do you still persist in your attitude?'

'Think before you answer,' said Fitzroy, idly weighing the long pistol in the palm of his white plump hand. The fire-light caught the muzzle of the weapon so that it shone like a hot coal. He spoke in the manner of a schoolmaster prompting a pupil.

Christopher was conscious of sympathy for this woman who had been so foully wronged. She had been robbed of love—and, therefore, of her life and youth—by that orgulous parade of bewigged and padded and hair-dyed gentlemen with high complexions and tight clothes and their fat unlovely mistresses.

It was without the defiant note in his voice that he replied:

'Believe me, ma'am, that I shouldn't stir a hand to help them. They can all quadrille their way to hell, for all I care. But . . .'

'But . . . ?'

'This girl, Victoria! She isn't tainted. She's been brought up away from them. She's been brought up to new ideas—and new ideals. She's new. She's 1835—and not 1735. She's a new line— the foundress of a new dynasty. She can mean something as important as Magna Charta—as the Flood. If there were no hope from her, I should say—and do—nothing!'

'You realize, you didactic fool,' said Fitzroy, 'that you are not being asked to join us, but to keep silence of your own accord.

Otherwise you will be silenced. Silenced—or silence! There's your choice.'

He repeated the last words with a slow gusto, as if he were savouring the emotions they should awaken. He turned his flattish head, with the dark horn-shaped lock stabbed across the low brow, to his son.

'You know, ma'am,' said Christopher, turning his long brown face from his father toward her, 'that little as I like my mother's people, I find myself liking Papa even less—if we must talk of relationships. Papa is not one of our prettier specimens of manhood! They say that children can be changelings. Why shouldn't fathers?'

There was silence. The frozen Court about the bed stirred not a finger: no voice came from out the mask: Fitzroy lounging against the marble of the fire-place had his dark regard bent on the pale green trousers that were strapped beneath his lacquered boots.

'A little recalcitrant, this young demagogue of ours, my dear Mother! I am afraid we shall have to—dispose of him—as we planned. It is a pity, of course, but still. There is an old castle near here, as you probably have remarked, my dear Christopher. Most ruinous! Very dangerous for the incautious sight-seer! It would be a pity to be found with a broken neck at the foot of a shattered stairway. By—say—a farmer looking for a strayed sheep!'

As the man—who was but incidentally his father—spoke, Christopher looked from face to face in the golden glow about the bed —from the white sockets in the mask propped high on the pillows, to the grimness of the iron-grey woman, the cat-like sideway regard of the major-domo, the vacant freckled face of the young man with frilled shirt and tight wrist-bands.

The man at the door was watching him from the outer dimness across the polished floor: he had twisted eyebrows and dark hollows in his cheeks, as if he had sucked them in and was biting them in an intense and murderous excitement. Perhaps it would be he who should carry out the neck-breaking! . . . Or, perhaps, the lackey who stood so close to him before the long curtains? . . . One shot would not carry him very far against five men—all of them probably armed.

Although he knew now that death was very near, he found himself unable to make any plan. If he were to die Margaret would never know how much he loved her: if he were to die the little Queen-to-be would never mount that throne under its heavy canopy. If he were to keep silence (and live) he would at least have Margaret—or would he not? Could he go to her, to start a new life begun with a blot across his personal honour?

'We are not joking now,' said Fitzroy. 'At least the jest will not be one you will appreciate. Let me put it again quite baldly. Are we to shut your mouth for ever, in the only way in which that can be assured? Or are you going to give us your word to keep silence? . . . There is no use thinking of escape. The house is surrounded by men—as a precaution. Your step-brother'—he waved his pistol-hand vaguely toward the lumpish man with the red head (step-brother! step-brother whom he had battered in the garden in Church Lane long ago, before he met Arabella!)—'is armed. So am I, as you see. And the servants! . . . Yes, or No! Say one or the other!'

'You forget,' said Christopher with sudden inspiration, 'that I have left behind me, neatly documented, all the evidence I have been able to gather about your very odd little conspiracy. Neatly documented, and tied up in pink ribbon. If I don't come back, people will begin to wonder—they'll undo the pink ribbon, and unfold my papers, and read what I have to say. And then the fat will be in the fire, won't it? Tower Hill for the Duke of Cumberland, and the gallows for you—gallows with a medical student neatly disjointing you afterwards! You wouldn't like that, I am sure!'

Those wonderfully curving lips of Madame de Boucher opened: from out of their voluptuous bow came her thin clear voice.

'After your remarks last night, my friend, we thought it better to search your rooms at the inn. Very easily arranged. Very fruitful. I do not think you can have any other papers than those you brought with you. The problem you suggest does not, therefore, arise.'

'But . . .'

Madame de Boucher said something in a low voice. The iron-grey woman wiped the horrible eyes again.

'I am tired of all this debate about a trifle,' she said in her expressionless voice. 'You all stand round me like mummies talking

—talking—talking. I'll talk—talk! It's all I can do except think. I want you to do—to move! I want violence! Violence! Violence! . . . Antoine!'

Again the man by the door shot out his arm. He lifted by its neck a tall porcelain jar—mate to the first; raised it high in the air and threw it with astonishing violence to the floor so that it smashed at his feet.

'Shoot him, George, if he doesn't agree. Shoot him now. Shoot him where I can see him.'

'You hear?' said the dark, cold man by the fire. 'You've got just one minute. That's all. You see, if we drop you on your head from the castle wall no one will know that your brains were blown out first. It's easier to stage a little tragedy like that with a dead body than a living actor. . . . It'll be quite easy! Like this!'

The double-barrelled pistol swung up—languidly, wearily. . . . So too had the pistol in the inn years and years ago swung up, while waiter and fat chambermaid mounted the stairs with brandy and candles to the porch-room in the Seven Stars! . . . It exploded with a stunning concussion. The bullet passed his head like a hornet, and the window behind tinkled with the sound of breaking ice. He heard that stammering titter of Madame de Boucher.

'Does that convince you?' asked Fitzroy.

Christopher rose to his feet: he dropped his hands into the deep pockets of his jacket, and stared at his father and the smoking pistol that was aimed so carelessly—oh, so carelessly!—in his direction. Within him something told him that what he was about to do might be as important to him as was her little house to Margaret— but that where she had been able to find a new self by construction, he could only do it by destruction.

'You are not my father,' he said in a high unnatural voice. 'I won't have you as a father! I dreamed you were, and woke up to find it wasn't true. My father was someone else—someone my mother loved—not you. You are a murderer, and a traitor! I just dreamed you were my father. I have dreamed all this—I am dreaming now. Dreaming that I am about to do what I shall! I shall wake up in a little and know that everything was a dream—even this!'

As he spoke his forefinger closed on the trigger of the little pistol within his pocket, and the burst of its explosion followed directly on his words.

The man by the fire-place staggered, like a tree struck by the full force of a gale. A great stain showed red on the whiteness of his cravat. His pistol hand fell to his side. His mouth opened in horrified surprise, but no word came from the orifice—only blood. He hurtled to the floor as though he had been thrown down from behind by a giant hand.

Simultaneously with the thud of his fall, a thin wail came from the bed and stopped as if a violin string had snapped on a high note; a pistol crashed; the nearest servant woke to life.

In one moment the scene was pictured indelibly, eternally in Christopher's mind: the dead man lying before the fire face downward; the group stirring into movement about the High Altar whereon reposed the masks with its white eye-sockets and open mouth; a hummocking of the body under the rose and silver coverlet, and then the sagging of the head on to a shoulder—as the head of the hanged boy outside Carmarthen jail had sagged years and years ago.

He felt no fear, no horror, no shame—only triumph.

Then, like a dream, the scene vanished as he leaped through the curtains behind him—through the splintering glass of the window into the roaring night, through the thick ice into the death-cold of the moat.

Chapter 37

'Infernal Defiance' to the Rescue

AS CHRISTOPHER GAINED THE FARTHER BANK OF THE moat, the main door of the house was flung wide open, gushing light on to the bridge and the dark water. Men came running out. One of them fired a gun, as he dived into the thicket; and the shot whistled and pattered among the tangle of branches on his right.

Once more he fought his way through the interlacement of the larches, but the noise of his passage was swallowed up in the storm, and in the groaning and rustling and crackling of trees. He knew the chase was up, but he could hear nothing of it—except once in a lull in the fury of the wind, when a whistle shrilled madly somewhere behind him, and was cut off in full blast by a renewal of the gale as if the sound had been cut off by a knife.

He paused—after hours, it seemed—to try to get his bearings, but the darkness of the wood walled and roofed him. In spite of the violence with which he had had to force his way through the barrier branches and the barbed brambles that lay over them like cordage, he was as cold as a stone. He felt that his sodden clothing was freezing upon him.

He pushed on blindly, and, to his surprise, found himself at last on the edge of the avenue that wound from high-gated lodge to the house. A double line of elms and beeches on either side fringed the thicket, and formed a loftly tunnel of black wind-tormented branches. He was staring out on to this shadowy road when two men rode by, silently because of the uproar of the wind, their horses leaning against the blast that met them. He realized that, beside searches in the woods, patrols were being sent out along little frequented roads and in the fields beyond the wall.

In the distance two or three lights glimmered vaguely where the lodge gates should be.

At any rate he knew now the direction in which to seek the streamlet that ran through the gully into the ivy-hidden tunnel under the highroad. He turned on his heel, and plunged afresh into the resistant brake, bearing always to his right the deeper he penetrated.

As the ground sloped downward the trees thinned out, and between the slender shafts he caught again the twinkle of lanterns. He dropped on hands and knees, and remained so, motionless, watching the watchers.

He felt the pistol in his pocket bump against his thigh as he slid to the ground: the pistol which had dissipated a nightmare; the pistol which had shattered the man who had called himself his father—in that dream; the pistol which had made him a parricide—in that dream.

The dream was just a dream, and the pistol was just a dream, to be dissipated too!

He put his hand into the pocket, withdrew the weapon, and sent it far away among the pine-needles with a twist of the wrist. He had no pistol! He had dreamed it, like everything else! Once he escaped from here he had escaped from the past, as far as Margaret Atchill had escaped from her past—as far as the past is ever escapable!

Above the tumult sounded a great crackling, as if some giant bonfire had burned up of a sudden; a groaning as of the timbers of twenty ships in a hurricane; a crash as if a roof had been lifted from its moorings. Somewhere a large tree had fallen; and Christopher saw the lantern-bearers, either from curiosity or anxiety lest their wall should have been damaged, make their way in the direction of the sound. They were invisible but for their dim lanterns which flickered between the trees, were hidden by the trunks, came level with him far down the slope, passed and finally vanished in the murk.

Christopher rose to his feet, and ran downhill swiftly, and into the gully—into the breast-high channel that the ice-cold stream had cut out for itself in the earth. He stumbled over the loose stones in the rivulet's bed, crouching as he went toward the culvert, which was hidden among boulders and mantled by a tangle of brush. Unscalable bank and wall, into which the water vanished, loomed black above him, like the ramparts of a great city.

He crawled into the impenetrable darkness of the tunnel.

A sudden blinding light flashed in his eyes. The treble voice of Mr. Howell said with the utmost satisfaction, 'Hallo! I betted you'd come this way if you ever came!'

'You've won,' said Christopher, and shielded his eyes.

'The others are watching from the woods along the road. But I was right. I knew I should be.' Mr. Howell clicked the shutter of his dark lantern with a chuckle.

Christopher caught one glimpse of him sitting hunched on a stone, with his feet in the stream, his head and back curved to follow the line of the arch above him, and a fowling-piece on his knee. Then darkness fell.

'Good lad!' said Christopher crawling like a large lizard along the torrent bed toward the boy. 'Can we get out safely the other end?'

'There are a couple of fellows with guns sitting on the wall above. We shall have to be very careful!'

'I can't stay here much longer,' said Christopher. 'I am wet through and freezing with cold.'

Indeed his hands were so numbed with the rush of water that he could barely support himself on them, and his wet clothes clung to him and stiffened about him. He felt encased in ice.

Mr. Howell chuckled again, gave a loud grunt, and apparently proceeded to wrestle with himself.

'Here you are!' he said at last. 'It was my idea!'

Christopher felt the cold metal of a flask pressed against his face. He eased himself sideways on to two stones in a reclining position; fumbled with the top of the vessel with hands that seemed half-paralysed, eventually unscrewed it, and drank the fiery brandy until he had swigged more than three-quarters of the contents.

'I think I should make a good scout against Indians, don't you, Mr. Tollendale?' suggested Mr. Howell.

'Good scout!' said Christopher, the liquor running like fire through his veins. 'Good scout! Why, you and I would scalp the

Mohicans themselves! And the Apaches! And the Seminoles! And the Karankawas! And the Comanches! No doubt about it!'

'Karankawas?' said Mr. Howell, greatly intrigued.

'Even the Cherokees,' said Christopher firmly. 'Now what are we going to do?'

'Lord Setoun . . .'

'Setoun?'

'He came late last night. That's how we found you had gone. Two in the morning he came! My eye, there's a oner! There's a snorter! I'll be like him when I grow up! He came into the yard puffing and snorting! They thought the devil was come!'

'Puffing?' inquired Christopher. He could not see why Setoun should enter any inn yard puffing and snorting.

'He swept away the horse-trough, and frightened old Annie into seven fits, and dropped red-hot coals all over the yard. I say, sir, do you think he'd let me drive it one of these days?'

Christopher visualized a grim-faced Setoun hard on his trail, careering across England to his aid, with that fantastic steam-carriage of his belching smoke and dropping cinders across the face of a dozen counties. Some deep suspicion of overmastering danger, for the son of the woman he had once so greatly loved, had sent him adventuring forth in the 'Infernal Defiance' from placid Kensington.

Setoun, it was, had been his father in everything but fact: not that foul nightmare which lay face downwards by the fire.

'He's a oner,' said Mr. Howell. 'Oh, he is a oner! Uncle Charles and he sat up all night. He saw Uncle Henry under the table. He swore he wouldn't go to bed until he'd found you. He said if you didn't appear by nine o'clock to-night, he'd bash the bloody gates in. "Bash the bloody gates in", was what he said. And Uncle Charles lost his mouthpiece and got down his gun, and said he'd come too. And Uncle Henry's sitting in a wet ditch under the hedge opposite the lodge. And Annie lent me her watch so I'd know when to be near the road. We've been watching ever since the afternoon. An hour ago a lot of men came out and have been doing sentry on the road. They nearly caught me when I looked out last time.'

The dark lantern flashed again.

'It's twenty to,' said the fascinated Mr. Howell. 'Let's get down toward the entrance. Oh, my eye, isn't it a lark! Isn't it, sir? Did you get any papers? Did you shoot anyone? How did you get out? I wonder if Lord Setoun has got enough coke. The inside of the thing is full of it—like a coal cellar. Come on!'

They set off down the tunnel to the mouth, where the water gushed out over a little cascade of slippery rocks between steep banks covered with dead leaves.

Mr. Howell, who, by dint of bending double, could just walk, peered out of the tangled curtain at the exit of the stream. With a whispered admonition he slipped out—to return in a few moments.

'They're still there,' he said, bringing his lips close to Christopher's ear, although the bustle of the rivulet and the turmoil of the wind would have blown his words away (even if he had shouted them) long before they could have reached the watchers. 'They've got a lantern, and one of them's leaning over the wall. We can't get out yet. They'd shoot us like rabbits. And there are two men on horseback by the inn. They don't know about the "Defiance". That'll give 'em fits! That'll give 'em the squitters!'

They waited in silence.

One of the men above them looking down the road toward the bridge and the grey huddle of the inn, saw something large and dark emerge from the stable-yard. It seemed to his astounded gaze to be as large as a herd of elephants, and from its hinder parts great clouds of smoke and sparks blew out banner-wise.

He was a hard-headed Ulsterman, but for a moment it shook him. It looked to him like the Beast of Revelations. With blasphemy on his lips he drew his companion's attention to the thing.

Hurrying clouds tore themselves from before the moon—seas revealing a shining flotsam—and, by the pale light, they saw the thing swerve violently before the inn, and come at the trundling pace of some great pachyderm toward the bridge and the steeply slanting road.

The disappearance of the black blob of the man's head from the wall above them was the moment for which Mr. Howell had been waiting. He popped back to their refuge.

'It's nine o'clock exactly. He said he'd start on the stroke. Isn't he a oner? They've gone. I'll bet they're standing pop-eyed in the middle of the road. Anyhow, they're not there. It must be that. Come on!'

As nimbly as a squirrel he danced down into the gully, and started to climb the precipitous bank that rose from the stream's bed up to the level of the road. Christopher, half frozen with cold, half drunken with brandy, scrambled in his wake. Dead bracken and fern were frosted till they were as slippery as ice, and the slope seemed as steep as the side of a house, for the level of the road was a good thirty feet above the narrow chasm that it crossed. They reached the summit at last, dived panting into a copse, and peered out on the road from the security of a hedge.

Fifty yards away on their left two figures stood in the middle of the road, with guns in the crooks of their arms. Even at that distance it was obvious that they were very uncertain figures, for one of them had pushed his hat back and was scratching his head.

A hundred yards below them, on the right, advancing slowly up the steepness of the hill, came the monster. Smoke and flame were blown forward from the high stacks at its hinderparts, so that it resembled a scorpion going into battle with its poisonous tail reared like a spear above its head. It marched onward—soundless in the noise of the wind—at a steady four miles an hour. It was fifty yards away—twenty yards away. One of the men stepped forward. He brought up his gun.

'Jeee-hoshaphat,' said Mr. Howell. 'What a do! What a go! What a buzz!'

He raised his musket to his shoulder, and let them have both barrels in a quick right-left, although the kick of the first explosion sent the muzzle and the second shot up towards the moon.

'Winged 'im!' said Mr. Howell in a perfect scream of delight. 'Come on, sir!'

The monster was on them. It towered over them, its body at least three feet from the ground, its belching chimney stacks between coach and lofty rumble giving it an insane resemblance in the night to a church organ that spouted smoke instead of music from its pipes.

'Hi, Tops! Daren't stop!' roared a great voice from a perch somewhere in the region where the coachman's box should be. Christopher caught a glimpse of the big nose and leathery face of Setoun, of jammed-down hat, of gauntleted hands clinging grimly to a tiller. Lying flat on the roof of the coach was a large bundle to which—the moonlight showed—were attached the large face and wide-brimmed hat of Mr. Charles Gainer. He peered over the edge at them, a gun in his hand.

'Ain't it fun, Uncle Charles? . . . Fun?' gasped Mr. Howell, trotting alongside.

'Blister my liver!' bellowed Mr. Charles. 'Good shot, Howell! Give you a guinea for it. . . . Give you two . . .'

William had leapt down from the post in the dickey under the fuming chimneys.

'Get on board, sir! For Christ's sake!' he panted. 'The place is lousy with men. Get on board!'

Someone thrust open the door of the coach. A step unfolded and nearly swept Mr. Howell's head off as he ran alongside. Someone leaned out, caught the young gentleman by the scruff of the neck, and hoisted him on board in the midst of a Niagara of coke.

'Coming up with you, Hurbles!' cried Christopher. 'Get back, William! I'm all right.'

He ran before juggernaut, turned into the path of the machine, seized the projecting front of the footboard of the driving seat, and endeavoured to lever himself up beside Setoun. The footboard was a good six feet from the ground, and as he hung with wrists and elbows over its lip, he heard a sudden warning bellow from Mr. Charles, and felt a violent clutch at his coat. Someone seized him by the waist, and clung like death itself to him.

The monster lumbered on, bearing the pair of them engaged in silent, violent struggle, as if it were some deadly thing that had pounced on two small creatures while they battled, and had pursued its way with them trailing from its jaws.

Christopher's assailant was sheltered from Charles's gun by the slant of the footboard: Setoun could not leave the kicking tiller.

For two breathless moments there was an intolerable strain upon Christopher's arms: he kicked frantically: then the weight upon him suddenly increased with a violent jerk. He realized that the man had lost his footing, was scrabbling with his feet, and hanging to him for dear life. With one despairing heave he brought

himself waist-high to the footboard, crushing the gripping hands
against its edge, and kicking violently behind.

The 'Infernal Defiance' lurched half across the road, and as it
did so the attacker was shaken from his hold, and fell screaming
under a wheel which rode over his thighs, lifting a little on one side
as it crushed them to pulp.

There was a cluster of men on the road ahead, and as Christopher eased himself on to the seat beside Setoun, a crash from
behind announced that Mr. Charles had gone into action.

'Hot spot, my lad,' said Setoun, clinging to the tiller with both
hands. 'Feel in my coat pocket. You'll find a pistol there.'

The machine picked up to five miles an hour as the gradient
became easier towards the curve at the lodge gates, but it swayed
sickeningly on the loose surface. It creaked. It jerked. It groaned.
It belched smoke and sparks that were swept back into the darkness of its carriage—a darkness filled with coke dust and the shouts
of Mr. Howell and the smell of oil and the mutterings of William
who had leaped in after him and was concerned for Christopher's
safety.

A fusillade of shots came from ahead: was replied to by Mr.
Charles with a cascade of curses and both barrels of his second
gun.

A man's face suddenly appeared grinning at the coach window
and was bashed with a large lump of coke from the mountain on
the floor, by Mr. Howell who screamed with delight.

A man on horseback galloped alongside and loosed his pistols
point-blank at Setoun before Christopher could reply to his fire.

'Not touched!' bellowed Setoun, and swerved the coach in on
the man toward the hedge at the moment that Christopher, leaning forward, shot him in the body so that he tossed backward over
his horse's rump.

A whistle blew, so shrilly that Setoun could hear it, even above
the uproar of the wind and the rumbling thunder of his juggernaut.
Before they reached the lodge the group awaiting them had vanished, running, through the gates.

'Dirty work afoot!' cried Setoun, but could not guess what.

It needed all his skill to hold the rutted road with the top-heavy vehicle. They took the bend at an appalling angle. Before them now were the first slopes of the long downhill road that led to Llandeilo Fawr and safety. The highway corkscrewed down for several miles between woodland and meadow: the moon was again obscured, and all he could see was a dim greyness dropping steeply downwards between hedge and trees.

'What were they up to?' Setoun asked himself again, but could find no answer: indeed had no time to, for the machine picked up speed and charged onward like a mad elephant with howdah and cooking range over its tail. Even his strong wrists could barely stand the lashing of the tiller with which he was supposed to control the small pair of steering wheels under his perch.

Christopher, clinging to the low rail of the seat, was aware of Henry Gainer scrambling up the side of the coach-body on to the roof—God knew how!—hatless, and with a pistol between his teeth, like a pirate boarding a merchant ship. He himself had nothing now to fight with except the butt-end of his weapon.

'Fhlot phewr!' said Brother Charles—who had again lost his conversation piece—lending Brother Henry a hand: but breathlessness and ecstatic excitement had put Brother Henry beyond power of speech. He lay, clutching the low iron rail along the roof, panting and grinning.

They crashed on for two or three miles: took another corner at twenty miles an hour, with a tail-skid that shot the furnace man out of the rumble into the hedge; careered a straight stretch of thirty yards crab-wise; took the next corner with a sickening lurch that rolled Brother Henry and Brother Charles into one large hummock of bellowing humanity, held them poised over the precipitous side for an instant, and then relented.

As the 'Infernal Defiance' paused for an infinitesimal space of time at the ridge before she sprang into the straight steep drop before her, Setoun saw why the attackers had so suddenly vanished from the lodge gates.

While he had been following the winding road among the hills, they had come across footpaths and field and blocked the way. Five hundred yards away in the moonlight he could see them—small black figures—easing a wagon into position across the highway, out of some farm buildings on the roadside. There was no room to pass.

The machine had already taken the plunge. She was driving downhill at a terrific pace, shaking, leaping, so that he could barely keep his seat. He jammed on the hand brake at his side in a frantic effort to moderate the speed. For a moment only did it hold, and then he heard the snapping of the rods.

As if the 'Infernal Defiance' had resented the effort at restraint, her velocity accelerated. Christopher dropped the pistol and clung for dear life to the rail beside him, with feet braced against the footboard.

The frenetic Mr. Howell was shot across the interior into a huddle with William and some unseen man.

'My eye! Ain't it a oner?' said Mr. Howell, bouncing to the roof. 'My eye! A hunderd miles an hour! Two hunderd miles an hour!' He landed on William's stomach. 'Don't you think so, William?'

'Both barrels and then jump for them,' roared Henry to Charles, assessing the danger ahead with a bellow of delight. 'In to . . .'

At that moment Setoun saw a narrow opening in the hedge upon his left, and the dark thread of what seemed to be a lane running in the same general direction as the road, at a not too sharply diverging angle.

It was his only chance, and he took it. He wrenched at the tiller: the machine lurched over, nosed the hedge, recovered, lurched a trifle less, recovered again, and swept into the precipitous track with undiminished speed, amid a shower of sparks and with a wake of red-hot ashes.

They went through a gate as if it were paper: they were in a graveyard—'Suitable, highly!' thought Christopher grimly—sailing along a wide path towards a squat building with lighted windows.

Setoun bellowed to the Gainers to jump for their lives, but they did not hear, for they were chorusing some wild ecstatic chant on the roof. He made one more effort to swing the machine, but she would not answer the helm. She made an elaborate skid, slapped her great tail violently against the porch of the chapel—so violently that the chimneys heeled over and the back wheels crumpled. That was the end.

With a noise like an earthquake the 'Infernal Defiance' shook herself—sweeping the Gainer brothers into a laurel bush—and quietly sat down to die, the near-side propped against the chapel wall.

The coach door flew open, bursting one of the Bethel's windows through which Mr. Howell flew like a rocket into an ample lap amid a petrified congregation.

For a moment Christopher clutched at tiller, at Setoun, at anything. Then he, too, went head-first through another window full of greenish glass—rather slowly, as if he were sinking for the third time through thin ice into a stiff sea—and landed on his skull amid a pew of screeching girls.

He lay with shut eyes for a while after he had recovered consciousness. He was warm. His head ached. He was lying on something soft. His head was on something soft. Against a background of twittering incomprehensible speech he heard Setoun suddenly say: 'Yes, five pounds of fuel'—buzz-buzz buzz-buzz . . .

'Abscrobiously, Charles!' . . . 'Psht phetw!' . . . 'Can't I go out, and have one shot at 'em?'

Somebody was tilting something between his lips, something that trickled very warming and enlivening down his gullet. He opened one eye cautiously, and saw a woman's large red face bent over him, and above it the murk of a lofty arched roof. He was covered with a rug. There appeared to be dozens of people all talking at once. He opened the other eye. Setoun was leaning over the back of the pew upon which he lay, with a bloody handkerchief staunching a cut on the chin. Five people at least were talking to him at once, and he was replying to them.

'Five pounds of coke. And charcoal, of course! . . . My dear sir, I regret . . . Build you a new chapel . . . They won't touch us now, William! . . . No, my dear sir—little accident—steering gear broke.'

'Best half-hour in my life!'—regretful bellow from Henry Gainer. 'All over now.'

'Is it?' said Mr. Howell's treble plaintively. To his view, obviously the day had only just begun.

All was well. Very well . . . Margaret. . . . He decided to shut his eyes again.

Chapter 38

The Royal Wizard

WILLIAM, BY THE GRACE OF GOD, OF GREAT BRITAIN, Ireland and Hanover, King, Defender of the Faith, nodded his old fir-cone-shaped head over the breakfast-room fire. He was still awake, though twice the narrator had paused in the story, thinking he had dozed, and he had said, 'Exactly so, my boy! Exactly so, my boy!' It was easier looking as if one dozed when one was old and weary, for people did not then expect immediate comment and decision. One had time to make up one's slow mind without interference. Sometimes, of course, it was also pleasant to take a short nap after breakfast, to help one's digestion, and to aid recovery from the annoyance of reading the blackguardly nonsense in *The Times*.

Opposite him, across the hearth, lounged his eldest illegitimate son, the black-whiskered Earl of Munster, slippered feet stretched toward the fender. He had been reading *Bell's Life in London*, but his attention had been caught at length by the low-told story, and he had set the paper down across his knees and listened intently to the young man whose chair was drawn up so closely to his father's side.

So, too, the thin ugly woman sitting between them, bolt upright in her chair, had laid down the green silk purse she had been netting upon her green satin lap. At her back a child rummaged to and fro with a ball under the canopy of the heavy red cloth that covered the breakfast table.

Out of earshot of Christopher's low voice a couple of pretty dark-eyed women—Munster's sisters—gossiped on a settee in the window. The sunlight streamed in; on to the coquettish portrait of

601

the poor actress who had borne them—as well as children to other fathers; on to the portraits of a dozen royal by-blows, or of the royal by-blows' own progeny; on to the queerly shaped silvering head of the father of the miscellaneous litter.

It was an intimate and domesticated scene. It might have been the breakfast-room of any large and respectable mansion in Tyburnia or the Portland Place region: Papa—rather a common bustling old person, in a dark blue coat with a tremendous collar—gathering up strength before leaving for the grave and ancient place of business, surrounded by his family; and stepmamma placidly tatting before interviewing the housekeeper, and starting the proper occupations of the day. But it was not. It was Windsor Castle. It was one of the private apartments of royalty. It was the King of England leading a home life among his bastards—and the Queen, with God knew what thoughts under that high, shiny forehead, had set her work down, and sat contemplating her long hands.

As Christopher paused, the voice of one of the younger women tinkled across the silence: 'Perhaps Papa will . . .'

At that moment in a thousand homes young women were saying that, hopefully, uncertainly, menacingly.

As if she had guessed his thoughts the Queen suddenly looked up, and held his regard. He realized the loveliness of the eyes in that long and sallow face, and the infinite kindness of expression. . . . All her married life had been spent amid this degradation of her wifehood and her queenhood! And yet she was not degraded! 'Perhaps Papa will . . . !'

'We'll have to see about this—have to see about this! Good boy! Very good boy!' burbled the old man by the fire, stirring into some semblance of life. 'But no scandal, mind! Vicky and that old mother of hers will have a nice job with Ernest. So did I . . .' His mind went back to disturbing history. His eyes rolled uneasily, and the hands on the chair-arms trembled a little. . . . 'Always trickling about like a snake with his stories and his whisperings. Tried to get me off the quarter-deck. Talked to his friends about a Council of Regency—didn't he, damn his eyes? And he thinks I don't know! Wonders why I took the command of the Household Troops away from him! . . . Mad! . . . I know which of the two of us is mad!'

His old head nodded with such vehemence, and his voice began to rise so loudly, that his wife came to the rescue. She soothed him as if he were a fractious child.

'Of course, dear!' Her voice was nasal, unlovely, with a foreign accent, and she coughed as she spoke. 'No one would give the idea a moment's thought. You are too sensitive. Much too sensitive.'

Christopher surprised a secret smile on Munster's dark face.

'Mad!' continued the old man in a lower tone, the memory of Cumberland's campaign still rankling. 'If anyone in this family has got his head screwed on tightly, it's myself.' He turned his long face—the colour of a boiled and peeled shrimp—to Christopher, sitting at his elbow. His dewlaps folded over his high, stiff collar and overhung it. 'My boy, I have weathered a lot of storms that Brother Ernest would have foundered in. A lot of storms. . . .' No. One was becoming too discursive. Unwise! One must withdraw again into one's shell, and meditate in safety. Adelaide was looking at one in a meaning way. That always implied that one was running the risk of being unwise.

'Poppet, give Grandfather his coffee!' said he.

The child carried carefully to him from the table the large cup of chilled coffee that had awaited Majesty's attention for nearly an hour: and stood at his side, a little sentinel in stiff glacé silk dress and starched petticoats, waiting for him to drink.

He stirred the muddy fluid slowly, reflectively, round and round, holding the spoon clutched in the whole of his great paw. Clink—clink—round and round and round. It became a maddening thing to watch. Clink—clink. The King of England stirring his coffee! Christopher thought of Nero fiddling while Rome burned. William stirring while—

'You must have stirred it enough, Grandfather!' said Poppet, becoming impatient.

The King drank, carrying the cup to his lips, not by the handle, but swallowed up in his hand.

'Put it down, Pussy, and give Grandfather the papers on the table.'

'The crinkly one, Grandfather?'

'The one next it,' said Christopher, seeing that the old man would look, at last, at the list of names and evidence he had collected.

The child brought from the table the long blue foolscap, studying the hieroglyphics on it as she approached.

'What's it mean, King-dear?' she asked, spelling a long name out. 'L-O-N-D-O-N-D-E-? . . .' She gave it up. 'What's that?'

'That's a list of naughty people who hate poor Cousin Vicky,' said the old man, taking the paper from her.

'Vicky!' said the child, pleating the front of her primrose-coloured dress. 'I don't like Cousin Vicky!'

'Ssh! Darling!' said the Queen.

'But I don't!'

The King dropped the paper. He took the chubby hands in his gouty hands, and brought her round to stand against his knees.

'And why don't you like Vicky, Poppet?' he asked.

'At Krisslemas Cousin Vicky was here,' said Poppet. 'And I said "How-d'you-do". And she said nothin'. . . . An' I said you'd given me two dolls, an' a doll's-house, an' a box that played "Ben Bowling", an' What'd she got? An' she said nothin', didn't say anythin'.'

The dark-eyed women in the window had fallen silent. The child's voice carried across the room.

'She didn't say anything?' said the King.

'No. An' a lady came to me and said I mustn't talk to her!'

'Mustn't talk to her!'

'The Duchess of Kent apparently thought,' said Munster in a bitter tone, 'that her pure little daughter would be contaminated by speech with the brats of your bastards, Sir! Victoria must have had her own doubts about the permissibility of such speech. So she waited in silence for her mamma to explain to Poppet—that a by-blow mayn't look at a queen-to-be! Even if a cat may!'

'Bloody sow!' said the King. He took up the blue foolscap with a hand that trembled with anger. 'Bloody old strumpet! Fornicates with . . .'

'Wil—liam!' said the Queen in deprecation.

'All right, my dear! All right! All right! . . . All right!'

He produced a pair of spectacles, adjusted them on his high bony nose, and peered at the document. So that damned woman thought Vicky too good and too pure to talk with his grandchildren! She did, did she! Well, he could teach her a lesson! Ernest would eat

her up like the wolf, supping off Red Riding Hood! . . . No! Better
keep cool. . . . *Must* keep cool. He concentrated on the list of
names. . . . The Bishop of Salisbury was in it, was he? . . . And
Londonderry! Predecessor had cut his throat. This fellow'd go the
same way! . . . And Kenyon! Father a stinge: died of eating pie-
crust at breakfast to save muffins! He spelt the names out with his
lips as he read down the roll—spelling them more slowly—spelling
them not at all—withdrawing once more into that interrupted semblance of a doze.

'My dear, I said it was much too expensive. . . . Of course the
woman was furious. . . . I said to De Lisle . . . Can't afford it. . . .'
Snatches of talk came across.

'Father's gone to sleep again,' remarked Munster watching the
fir-cone nodding. 'Better wake the old buffer up!'

'Exactly so, my boy! Exactly so!' said the old man automatically,
without stirring an eyelid.

Christopher timidly touched the arm of the dozing figure. Munster looked on with a sardonic smile.

'I don't think Father's very concerned about what happens to
Vicky!' he said maliciously.

Twitter-twitter! Whisper-whisper! went the women on the
settee.

Did they not realize that he had travelled thousands of miles,
risked his life again and again, to reveal conspiracy to this old
dotard? He had pictured excitement, thrill, galloping messengers,
thanks, gratitude. He had found the vastest palace he had ever
imagined, which contracted itself at last to a middle-class breakfast-room in which dozed a sleepy old man who said 'Exactly so,
my boy!' at regular intervals, as if by machinery; while the old
man's illegitimate daughters twittered about dressmaking and
parties in the background; and a fellow with black whiskers peered
over the top of his sporting paper at intervals and harkened as
if dispassionately interested. He had saved Victoria's throne: there
was something he must have in return—*must!* Or wasn't 'Father'
really 'concerned about what happens to Vicky'?

The Queen rose with a rustle of stiff skirts—he noticed as he
got up that the others did not stir.

'You know very little about your father, George,' she said, 'if you think that. You know very little about me if you think for one moment I should imagine him capable of that attitude.' With solicitude for Christopher's feelings she explained, turning directly to him, the charming tentative smile again flickering on her plain features: 'His Majesty slept very ill last night. He had State business until dinner-time; and for two hours afterwards he did nothing but sign documents. He had to dip his wrist every ten minutes in hot water. Otherwise he would have never got through. Although Princess Augusta and I did all we could to help. It wearies him so.'

She took up the papers and her half-finished silk purse from the table. From the resistless clasp of the old man by the fire she extracted gently the list of names. Christopher's eyes fixed themselves on the large red hand lying on a dark blue knee—a King's hand, to hold sceptre and orb and sword and marshal's baton; a hand that became puffed and swollen from signing silly papers; a sort of human stamping-machine for the one word 'William'!

Perhaps she saw what was in his mind, for she said—'Always, always, papers to sign! William—William—William—William— William! The late King left him forty-eight thousand papers to sign! Forty-eight thousand papers! Forty-eight thousand Williams!'

She looked down on her husband with the protective tenderness of a mother for her child, smiled at Christopher, and said:

'Come! You and I will go over this matter together. I know the points that will be raised: you will tell me the answers. It will save time. . . . George, tell His Majesty that Count Tollendhal has accompanied me to my—to the turret room, when he awakes.'

Munster lounged to his feet, as the Queen turned to the door, and the dark-eyed women rose gracefully. The child ran up to her, and caught at the green folds of her dress—such a beautiful dress, and so unbecoming to the long-nosed sallow face! 'Don't go, Queenie—dear Queenie! . . . Let me come too!' urged Poppet.

She disengaged herself from the little clutch with the gentlest of hands.

'Not now, dear. You must stay with mamma, and be a good girl. I shall come back soon.'

'Bu-u-ut I want to stay wiv you!'

'Dear little Heart, I shall come back so soon! Stay with mamma, now!'

The child's eyes filled with tears; but she obediently ran back to her mother with a flutter of stiff dress and petticoats.

And so—thought Christopher—could the Queen of England make herself beloved by the children of her husband's bastards!

Good bitch!—thought the old man—She knew I wasn't asleep: she knew that I was just lying doggo to think things out for my-self! She knew I'd hear when she said that she was going to her —no, the turret room. She knew that I would understand that she had gone with the lad—Amelia's boy! nice boy!—because she did not think that George and the FitzClarences should hear matters of State debated! The turret room, too! Why the turret room—her innermost sanctuary—the Holiest of her Holy Places?

Suddenly he understood. Clever slyboots! She was afraid I might let Ernest off too lightly, because I loathe the Whigs so much, and that damned woman at Kensington is a Whig— damned woman was a snob to Poppet! All the Whigs in the world are better than Ernest the True-blue Tory—Ernest, whom that pestilential fellow Brougham once termed an assassin! Clever slyboots!

The turret room!—his thoughts ran on. She would hear his footsteps in the passage without; and when he came in, she would be showing the lad that pathetic little alabaster effigy of Eliza-beth! Elizabeth who would have been about Victoria's age—if she had lived, and not made that lonely journey in a coach and six to the Royal Vault at Windsor one March morning long ago. Elizabeth, his daughter, who would have been Queen of England! Elizabeth of England! By God! He wouldn't have cared to have died and left his daughter unprotected against the wiles of Ernest. By God! if he had ever thought that Ernest would plot against a daughter of his in that way, he would—would have put Ernest away, would have had him murdered! Plenty of people only too glad to do it!

In the muddled old mind there swam the idea that perhaps

Vicky in some way had received within her soul something of the spirit of his daughter, when it left the tiny tortured body, all those years ago.

Clever, loving bitch—Adelaide! She was quite right. She was always right! Had been ever since that day he had first seen her —long-nosed and anxious, in the dreary apartments at Grillon's Hotel in Albemarle Street, which had been thought good enough for his unimportant bride. He had married a wife young enough to be his daughter, who had given him the love of a mother.

He rose to his feet.

'Ask Papa, now—before he goes!' He heard the urgent whisper. 'Papa! Could you . . . Would . . .'

He stamped out of the room. The FitzClarences could wait. He was King, as well as father of that brood.

He walked noisily to the turret room, and opened the door very slowly, for he did not wish to spoil what she had planned. He had been right! He heard that kind, ugly voice say:

'Just eighteen months and seventeen days younger than Vicky!'

By God! Vicky should have the same chance that he would have secured to Elizabeth! Damn her mother! No hankypanky this time! He would smash Ernest's plot to smithereens—and Ernest himself, if he did not knuckle under! They should have some of the bones of the conspiracy to mumble over in Parliament—nothing definite, but just enough to make them very suspicious. That would be the way to frighten Brother Ernest! And unless Brother Ernest gave surety for good behaviour, he would throw the whole carcass to the Commons, and that would mean the Tower for Brother Ernest! For a moment he visualized, with a gasp of excitement, Brother Ernest standing gaunt and bleak on a scaffold looming over a sea of heads. And a masked man with an axe. You could hardly hang the son of a King! Axe—definitely axe! . . . And then, 'This is the head of a traitor!'

'. . . Traitor!' In his growing excitement he let the word fall out loud.

'Traitor!'

They looked up, as if startled, from the pathetic effigy of Elizabeth, Queen-that-might-have-been: the effigy in which the little rounded face was frozen in a stone like clouded ice. There were tears in his wife's eyes.

The boy took her long hand—the long hand that still held the half-made purse of green silk—and kissed it. As he did so, Christopher remembered kissing, so long ago, the hand of another unhappy queen—far more unhappy: remembered suddenly the beringed plump hand of Caroline. What a lot of unhappy queens! A childless queen following a betrayed queen. And before that a queen whose elder children hated her! And before that a queen with a dozen ugly rivals in her husband's seraglio. And before that a queen who faded out of life within a fortress prison.

Something in that very respectful homage to his ugly Queen affected the old man.

'Good girl!' said he in a low voice. 'Good girl! Quite right. It might have been Elizabeth! . . . Good boy, too! Very good boy! Must see what we can do for you. . . . But we'll draw Ernest's teeth for him. We'll clip his claws. For good and all.'

The room was full of cold light from the flat curtain of cloud across the heaven: a light that showed up remorselessly the artistic poverty of the humble relics the Queen had gathered within her sanctuary—effigy of child; clumsy model of her dear home in Germany; water-colours, hideously executed and tastelessly framed, of all sorts of relatives; olive-wood boxes from the Holy Land; gloves in cases, fans in cases, albums full of cherished portraits, samplers, bits of china, bookcase with ill-bound books with German Gothic titling: tables covered with shapeless bric-à-brac.

Christopher looked from the woman's long face, more sallow than ever in the cruel glare, to the queerly shaped head of the old man who was King of England and Hanover, and Lord and Master of God knew what else besides. They—he suddenly thought—might have had a daughter who should have reigned after them in Britain; a daughter who would have had the brains of her mother, and the good nature of her father. Better, perhaps, than Victoria with a sadist of a father and a termagant of a mother!

'I could have wished, Ma'am,' he said without prelude, 'that it might have been the Princess Elizabeth for whom I was able to do this.'

Again she smiled at him. He was to remember the smile of the ugly Queen all his life. It was the beauty of sunrise in a dark place. It was the miracle that clothed the Cinderella in stuff of gold and woven glass. It was Charity in a slum.

'Good boy!' said the King, and suddenly added, 'Setoun's letter of introduction tells me you are Amelia's boy! . . . Good fellow—Setoun! See a lot of him. A gentleman. Very few nowadays.'

'Setoun!'

Christopher suddenly found himself telling the story of that frantic ride on the 'Infernal Defiance' to Llandeilo Fawr, of the running battle fought on the night-dark road outside the lodge gates, of Brother Charles, and Mr. Howell, of the woman with the gummed eyelids, and the death of Fitzroy.

'Fitzroy!' said the King, and fell silent, while he gathered up the loose threads of the story in his mind. 'Fitzroy! . . .' He ambled obliquely on. 'So you're Amelia's boy! Amelia! . . . You don't remember Amelia, my dear. She died long before we were married. Long time ago. Nice girl. Very—very fond of her!'

'You see,' said the Queen, 'what your brother is capable of!' She held the old man's regard, bent over the pathetic piece of marble, wiping the little marble face with her lace handkerchief. 'You see what he is prepared to do to cut a path to the throne.' She wiped the marble simulacra of the lips that had once been pressed to her bosom. White tiny lips of a queen-that-might-have-been.

The old man's mind went back—as she had meant it to do—to that day years before when the heralds and pursuivants had ridden out to proclaim him 'By the Grace of God, King'.

He found her looking up at him across the doll-like image of their child, her lovely eyes telling him how angry he must be— how the heralds and trumpeters might have gone forth one day for Elizabeth, and how Ernest might have torn the proclamations from their hands . . . and it should have been 'Ernest . . . By the Grace of God'. How the heralds and trumpeters would one day go forth to proclaim Victoria . . . and Ernest might wrench the roll from their hands.

His mind was back. He was full of wordy fury. He cursed Ernest and his fellow-traitors.

'I'll break him and his plots for good and all,' he swore; and as he swore he let his big blunt fingers rest on the effigy of his child. 'For good and all.'

He spoke calmly and collectedly.

'It shall be done without scandal or furore. Ernest shall hear from me to-day. I'll send for Peel at once. He'll know how to deal with the business. Good man, Peel! Very good man. . . . You've done good work, my boy! Very good work! . . . The Princess Victoria will owe you a lot. Lot. Hell of a lot! . . . Amelia's boy—you said?'

'Yes, Sir, I am,' said Christopher. It was easier to agree than to go into explanations that he proposed to be nobody's boy. That he was no longer Christopher Harnish, the nephew of kings— and grandson of Madame de Boucher; a relative of the Earl of Munster, and Poppet; of the Duke of Cumberland, and the pretty women gossiping on the sofa downstairs; but Christopher von Tollendhal who never had a father or mother, whose line began with him—exactly as if he were his own First Book of Genesis.

'Very fond of her,' said William. 'Very fond, indeed. . . . Must do something for you. What shall we do, my Queen? Very good —useful boy!'

He took his wife by the arm, and they stood thus together confronting his sister's son.

'Nothing for me, Sir!' said Christopher. 'Nothing at all. I have everything. I've got all the money, and all the rank I shall ever want. I want you to do something else—very easy. Very simple!'

'I shan't grudge you anything, my lad,' said the King, letting himself down into a chair of golden mahogany set at a table on which stood a folding writing-desk with a green baize slope. His mind was clear, now. Wonderful how mere contact with that funny ugly wife of his helped him think clearly, strengthened him!

'If you wanted to make me an earl, Sir,' said Christopher, 'I suppose you could do it just by the writing of your name. If you wanted to make me a baron, it would be just the same. No one dare question your signature!'

'An earl?' said the King. 'You want to . . .'

'Good God, Sir, I don't want to be an earl! If you look at those papers you'll see what I want!'

'Ho!' said Majesty, rather intrigued by the statement; even more intrigued by the documents which he unfolded with fumbling fingers. His wife peered over his shoulder at them.

'Hey!' said Majesty, as he grasped their purport. 'What's all this about? What's all this about?'

'That, Sir,' said Christopher firmly, 'is what I ask you to do for me. A king can make a duke: he can make an earl—or viscount—or baron. If I remember rightly, he can also make a bishop, declare war, or turn a village into a university!'

'You make kingship sound almost like a fairy story! Fairy story!' said the owner of these magical powers. So enchanted was he with the notion, that he turned a beaming face on the young man and Christopher fancied to see in him a retired admiral who had taken up necromancy as a hobby. 'I'll grant,' continued the Admiral-Wizard, 'that theoretically you are right. What then?'

'I'll ask you to use just a tithe of those wonderful powers of yours, Sir. Just straightforward forgery. Quite simple—for you!'

'And perjury!' said Majesty with a chuckle. 'And perjury! . . . Do we do this, my Queen? . . . You are a spark, my lad! Persuading an old man to take up crime in his declining years! . . . Crime! . . . Penalty—Death! . . . Do I ask you for explanations? Do I? . . . Should I?'

'They're unnecessary, Sir. On my honour! There's no hurt to living or dead in what I ask you to do.'

While the potential felon was holding the documents before him and meditating on the crimes that would be perpetrated in their completion—and still chuckling—the Queen had taken them in and their purport at one swift glance. She looked equally swiftly at that unacknowledged nephew and smiled.

The Admiral-Wizard-Forger chuckled more heartily still. He delved into his memory for strange rewards that had been bestowed on those deserving well of their Sovereign: ambled along a side-path into the affair of Admiral Cochrane, and finally tangled himself up in the matter of Persian politics.

'I think I understand—from what Lady Setoun has told me,'

said the Queen in a low voice. She placed her hand upon Christopher's arm, and so motioned him gently toward the door. 'A King has promised to commit forgery and perjury on your behalf. A Queen will be accessory before and after the fact.'

He knew it was her promise. He kissed the gouty old hand that was to perpetrate the crime: a convention! Over hers **he** bowed very low. Very, very low.

Chapter 39

Beyond the Mist

AT THE BROW OF THE HILL, WHERE THE ROAD PLUNGED down between steep banks to the valley and the marsh, Christopher stopped the carriage.

The mist of a late afternoon faintly clouded the farther hills, subdued the outline of the dark red roofs of the cottages clustered round inn and turnpike at their foot, rose in thin steam from the grey curves of the river that lay between. So still was the chill air that the vapour mounted straight upward from the surface of the water, and was thus divided at the bridge, leaving a clear passageway through its tenuous wall.

The horses stamped on the hard road. Their harness jingled with their restlessness. The postboy dropped with a clatter of iron-tipped boots to the ground. A dog barked at the gate of a cottage they had left behind them. A child cried shrilly to another, and a distant voice objurgated distant cattle. The postboy spat with sudden explosiveness.

Before him that quivering impalpable wall, guarding the low, dark hills, the cluster of roofs! Before him silence—magic—dreams! He had travelled across Europe, tossed across the uneasy wastes of the Atlantic, stood in the spike-guarded dock, traversed the wide Texan plains in search of the Seven Cities, watched a swinging pistol ride upwards to a burst of flame, waited for death in a dark house and on the duelling field—so that toward this nightfall he might find a gateway opening in the mist. A gateway that would close after him. A gateway not unlike that which gave on to the fairy-lands of his childish dreams.

He flung back his fur-lined cloak, and found a bank-note.

614

'Take my things to the Three Bells at Northiam. I will send for them. . . . I shall walk the rest of the way.'

'Farther than you think, your honour,' said the postboy, looking down into the valley and the mist. 'Thanking you very kindly, I'm sure!'

'Farther than you think!' said Christopher. 'Much farther than you think!'

He went down toward the river, and the bridge, and the swaying wall of magic. The postboy, chewing a straw, watched him go.

He was out of sight beyond a bend of young fir. He reappeared on the slope of the causeway leading to the bridge—a slope with white-painted railings. He was on the bridge.

As he crossed, the gates of the mist surged together and closed after him. The greying wall that had opened for him was shut. The haze beyond thickened; wavered in billows over low hills and snuggling roofs; and then withdrew them utterly from view.

Strange thoughts moved vaguely in the postboy's slow mind. He straightened the crumpled bank-note that he still held in his hand. It rustled drily, musically, in a reassuring manner.

Christopher walked up the narrow path between the grass plats to the door. On either side there was yellow glow in the windows; but the mist, that had accompanied him as he came, seemed to repel the radiance. The warmth and the light were within the little house, and not permitted to escape. The dark stuff of his cloak was misted with pin-point globules. It was silver-grey—unsubstantial. A wet shining film covered the panels of the door. Behind him the low hedge and garden gate were blotted out.

It was as if the magic thorn-thicket had drifted in the wake of the Prince to the Sleeping Castle, and closed in behind him, so that he should join the enchanted sleepers, and never go back to the world of reality.

He let himself into the hall, and closed the door behind him, bolted it quietly and chained it.

The heavy curtains fell into their place. It was warm and welcoming and silent within, and there was a faint fragrance as of lavender. A lighted lamp had been placed on a chest at the foot of the stairs, and the balusters cast their long thin shadows upon the wall behind. Out of a maple frame, above the chair on which he put his cloak and hat, the face of Tom Atchill smiled a solemn welcome—Tom who was so like him, and had fallen at Waterloo!

The only sound was the ticking of the grandfather clock with faded daisies painted on its dial. It seemed to him that, in some way, it ticked a different sort of time to that by which life outside the fast-shut door was arbitrarily divided into minutes and hours, and days and weeks. That it told the magical time of a dream, when a minute could be eternity and a year could pass in a breath. He had put off mechanical time and material reality, as he crossed the threshold: he had been taken into a dream—he hoped it would be for ever.

He walked to the drawing-room door and opened it.

The grey of the dusk pressed against the windows. The room was full of dancing shadows and fire-light.

Margaret sat sewing by the hearth, a china lamp supported by two rosy naked cherubs on the small work-table at her elbow. For a moment he saw only the silver scissors and needle-box on the table, and the white stuff over which her head was bent, and the swift movement of her fingers.

She was alone, but for the wraiths of her dream-world whose fulfilment was so near. Christopher fancied that they were crowding the shadows of the room in breathless anticipation.

She raised her eyes, and saw him standing—so little changed—by the door, regarding her wordlessly; in his hand a folded paper.

She rose. She came to him where he stood beyond the lamp-light, her dress rustling with the sound of fallen leaves in the wind. She stood at arm's length from him, and put her pale hands up to his shoulders—as if to reassure herself that it was man and not ghost.

'It is you!' she said. 'It is you!'

'It is I, Margaret,' he answered, and looked gravely down on her.

There was the faintest flush upon her clear pale cheeks: the eyebrows over the wide grey eyes were lifted a little as though in unspoken question: her lips were parted to speech that did not come. He, too, had much to say and yet found himself without a word. And so they confronted one another for a while in silence.

At last he lifted her hands away, and placed them one above the other, palm uppermost, on one of his own. He folded the slim fingers over the paper that he had carried. She stood before him, unresistant, half-smiling, half-wondering.

'Dear Margaret,' he said hurriedly, 'I broke a spell once. I broke an enchantment. . . . Margaret, I hate to think about it. . . . I—I— I . . . My dear, I have brought for you the strongest spell the outer world can brew . . . made by a King—by a Queen. . . . Is it a magic?'

She gave him a strange, puzzled, smiling look. She took the packet to the little table and unfolded it beneath the radiance of the lamp.

He felt that her fantasies now were clustered round her, look-ing down, with her, at what lay upon the rosewood surface. He felt an air of tense expectancy within the tangle of fire-light and shadow about the room. The Atchills that had read the calf-bound books within the glass-fronted case; that were portrayed upon the walls; that had dozed in the shabby chairs; played thin music on the tinkling spinet; sipped tea from the Swansea china in the corner cabinet; they should become memories instead of mere dreams. The child Deb was about to become a dream in-stead of a memory.

Margaret turned to him.

'What does it say? Read it for me!' she said. He saw that her eyes were blinded with unshed tears.

He took up the topmost document, and read it aloud as if it were an incantation, a most potent spell, holding her hand in his.

' "Windsor Castle,
' "December 30th
' "Sir, I have it in command from her Majesty the Queen to forward to you for Miss Margaret Atchill, of Newenden, in the County of Kent, the following documents. To wit—

' "An attested copy of the entry made in the register of the Chapel Royal, Windsor, recording the marriage of William Atchill, a personal secretary of his Royal Highness the Duke of

Clarence (now his Most Gracious Majesty the King), with Margaret Atchill, on March the Sixth, 1807, the witnesses being His Royal Highness, and H.R.H. Frederick, Duke of York.

' "An attested copy of an entry made in the register of the Chapel Royal, Windsor, of the baptism of an infant, Margaret, daughter of the above, on the First day of January 1808, His Royal Highness being godfather . . ." '

'Your spell, Tops!' said Margaret very slowly and softly. 'Listen!' Was that the light footfall of the other Margaret Atchill, on the threshold of her home—coming as bride from the pomp of a wedding under the high vaulting and the Garter banners at Windsor? Did they hear the faint jingle of Tom Atchill's spurs as he strode up from the garden gate? or Great-Aunt Sabrina's high heels tap upon the stairs as she went down to the carriage that was to carry her to church—and death? or the tread of William Atchill coming up from the wine-cellar with a bottle of old port with which to celebrate the birth of his only child?

'My spell!' said Christopher, listening to the rustle of the fantasies become ghosts.

'All your spell? All?'

He fell upon his knees before her. He put his lips to her hands. 'I have no more, Margaret. . . . Unless . . .'

The wall of mist closed about the house.

Carreg Cenneg, Wales.
Buckingham Street, London.
Goliad, Texas.

A TABLE SHOWING THE RELATIONSHIP OF SOME OF THE VARIOUS ROYAL PERSONAGES MENTIONED IN THIS BOOK

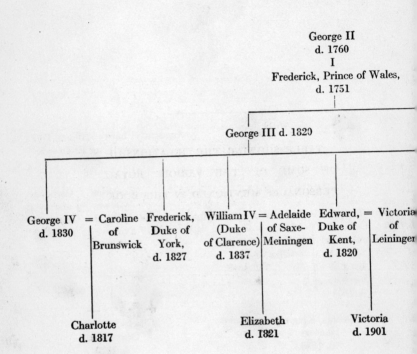

George II
d. 1760
I
Frederick, Prince of Wales,
d. 1751

George III d. 1820

George IV = Caroline   Frederick,   William IV = Adelaide   Edward, = Victoria
d. 1830   of   Duke of   (Duke   of Saxe-   Duke of   of
             Brunswick   York,   of Clarence) Meiningen Kent,   Leininger
                         d. 1827   d. 1837   d. 1820

Charlotte   Elizabeth   Victoria
d. 1817   d. 1821   d. 1901

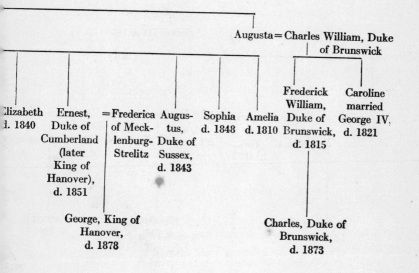

Augusta = Charles William, Duke
of Brunswick

Elizabeth
d. 1840

Ernest,
Duke of
Cumberland
(later
King of
Hanover),
d. 1851

= Frederica
of Meck-
lenburg-
Strelitz

Augus-
tus,
Duke of
Sussex,
d. 1843

Sophia
d. 1848

Amelia
d. 1810

Frederick
William,
Duke of
Brunswick,
d. 1815

Caroline
married
George IV,
d. 1821

George, King of
Hanover,
d. 1878

Charles, Duke of
Brunswick,
d. 1873